DAPHNIS & CHLOE

BY LONGUS

WITH THE ENGLISH TRANSLATION OF
GEORGE THORNLEY

REVISED AND AUGMENTED BY
J. M. EDMONDS
FELLOW OF JESUS COLLEGE, CAMBRIDGE

THE LOVE ROMANCES OF
PARTHENIUS
AND OTHER FRAGMENTS

WITH AN ENGLISH TRANSLATION BY
S. GASELEE
FELLOW OF MAGDALENE COLLEGE, CAMBRIDGE

CAMBRIDGE, MASSACHUSETTS
HARVARD UNIVERSITY PRESS

LONDON
WILLIAM HEINEMANN LTD

MCMLXXXIX

American ISBN 0-674-99076-5

British ISBN 0 434 99069 8

First printed 1916
Reprinted 1924, 1935, 1955, 1962, 1978, 1989

Printed in Great Britain by
St Edmundsbury Press Ltd, Bury St Edmunds, Suffolk

CONTENTS

PAGE

LONGUS (DAPHNIS AND CHLOE)—

INTRODUCTION vii
BIBLIOGRAPHY xxiii
PROEM 7
BOOK I 11
BOOK II 63
BOOK III 125
BOOK IV 185

PARTHENIUS—

INTRODUCTION 251
THE LOVE ROMANCES 257
FRAGMENTS 351

THE ALEXANDRIAN EROTIC FRAGMENT . . 374

THE NINUS ROMANCE 382

APPENDIX ON THE GREEK NOVEL 401

INDEX TO DAPHNIS AND CHLOE 417

INDEX TO PARTHENIUS, THE ALEXANDRIAN
    EROTIC FRAGMENT, THE NINUS ROMANCE,
    AND APPENDIX ON THE GREEK NOVEL . 419

Editorial Note (1978): Those passages of the translation which in previous impressions appeared in Latin have now been replaced by English renderings. *G.P.G.*

Tell me, O thou whom my soul loveth, where thou feedest, where thou makest thy flock to rest at noon.

Song of Solomon, 1. 7.

INTRODUCTION

I.—Longus

Nothing is known of the author of the *Pastoralia*. He describes Mytilene as if he knew it well, and he mentions the peculiarities of the Lesbian vine. He may have been a Lesbian, but such local colouring need not have been gathered on the spot, nor if so, by a native. His style and language are Graeco-Roman rather than Hellenistic; he probably knew Vergil's *Bucolics*[1]; like Strabo and Lucian he writes in Greek and yet bears a Roman name. Till the diggers discover a dated papyrus-fragment, we can say provisionally that he may have written as early as the beginning of the second century after Christ, probably not much later than the beginning of the third.

Two of Longus' characters connect him, indirectly at least, with the New Comedy, Gnatho the parasite, and Sophrone the nurse who exposed the infant Daphnis.[2] It is to be noted that he and Horace, some of whose names are found like his in the

---

[1] Cf. 2. 7 ἐπῄνουν τὴν Ἠχὼ τὸ Ἀμαρυλλίδος ὄνομα μετ᾽ ἐμὲ καλοῦσαν with *Buc.* i. 5.   [2] Cf. Terence *Eun.*, Menander *Epitr.*

INTRODUCTION

New Comedy, are the only literary users of the name Chloe.[1] He knows and loves his Sappho; witness the crushed but still beautiful flowers in the ravaged garden, and the lovely apple left by the gatherers upon the topmost bough.[2] To Theocritus he plainly owes more than the locust-cage and the name Clearista.[3] Not only has he numerous verbal imitations of Theocritus, but the whole atmosphere of the book is, in a sense, Theocritean. And there are passages reminiscent of the other Bucolic poets.[4] In one place Longus definitely connects his rustic characters with the herdsmen of Bucolic poetry. When Lamo tells the Story of the Pipe, we are told that he had it from a Sicilian goatherd. And it is hardly going too far, perhaps, to see a similar intention in the name he gives to the old herdsman Philetas, who is second only to Pan in playing the pipe, and who tells Daphnis and Chloe the nature of love. For Philetas or Philitas was the father of Hellenistic poetry, the great man who taught the elegiac love-poet Hermesianax and the pastoral, epic, and lyric love-poet Theocritus, and was himself, perhaps, the first writer of love-tales in elegiac verse.

[1] Except Longus' Byzantine imitators. [2] Cf. 4. 8, 3. 33 with Sapph. 94, 93 (Bgk.); and i. 17 χλωρότερον τὸ πρόσωπον ἦν πόας (ms. χλόας) with Sapph. 2. [3] Amaryllis, Chromis, Daphnis, Tityrus he *might* have got from Vergil. [4] Cf. 2. 5 with *Ep. Bion.* 16 (Wilam.), i. 18 with Mosch. *Runaway Love* 27, 2. 4 with Bion *Love and the Fowler* (and Theocr. 15. 121).

INTRODUCTION

This is the only Greek prose-romance we have which is purely pastoral, and the inclusion of this feature in its title may show that in this respect it was a new departure. It is by far the best of the extant romances. Rohde[1] saw the forerunners of the prose-romance in two kinds of literature. The first is the erotic tale of the elegiac writers of the Hellenistic age, dealing with the loves of mythical personages. These poems formed the material of such works as Ovid's *Metamorphoses*. Three of Longus' names, Astylus, Dryas, and Nape, are the names of mythical personages in Ovid. The second literary ancestor Rohde believed to be the traveller's tale, such as the *Indica* of Ctesias, a type parodied by Lucian in the *True History* and not unconnected with the Utopias of Aristophanes, Plato, and others. A trace of this ancestry survives perhaps in the title of this book " The *Lesbian* Pastorals of Daphnis and Chloe." [2]

It is now generally thought that Rohde's pedigree hardly accounts for all the facts.[3] In Chariton's *Story of Chaereas and Callirrhoe*, of which the date cannot be much later than 150 A.D. and may be a century earlier, the heroine is the daughter of Hermocrates, the Syracusan general of whom we read in Thucydides. The *Romance of Ninus*, of which

---

[1] *Der griechische Roman und seine Vorläufer.* [2] The word Λεσβιακῶν occurs in the colophon of A, but appears to have been neglected. [3] See particularly W. Schmid *Neue Jahrb. für das Klass. Altertum*, 1904, p. 465.

a few pages have been found in Egypt, and which
was probably written in the last century before
Christ, is in all probability the love-story of the
famous Semiramis and Ninus the founder of Nineveh.
The author of the Ninus-romance takes two
historical personages and weaves a story—not the
traditional story—around them ; Chariton, showing
perhaps a later stage of development, merely tells
us that his fictitious heroine was the daughter of an
historical personage. These are the only instances,
in the extant romances, of the consistent employ-
ment of historical matter. But they may well be
the evolutionary survival of a once essential feature.
If so, our second forerunner will not be merely
the traveller's tale, but what often, as in the case
of Herodotus, included it, history ; but history,
of course, in the Greek sense. For even in
Thucydides there is an element of what to us
is fiction, and the line between history and myth
was never firmly drawn.

The enormous preponderance, in the extant
romances, of invented, and sometimes confessedly
invented matter,[1] matter having no foundation either
in history or in mythology, and involving invented
persons as well as invented circumstances, points
again to elements outside of Rohde's list. There
may well be some connexion with the Mime, not only
as we have it in the pages of Theocritus and

---

[1] Cf. Longus' Proem.

INTRODUCTION

For the readings of A and B, I have used (1) Seiler's edition of 1843, which was based ultimately, through Sinner's of 1829, upon Courier's of 1810, (2) Cobet's corrections of Courier's account of A, made from an inspection of the MS. and published partly in *Variae Lectiones* and partly in the preface to Hirschig's edition of 1856 (Didot), and (3) a few corrections of Cobet made by Castiglioni in *Rivista di Filologia* 1906; for the readings of the three Paris MSS. I have used Villoison's edition of 1778; for the readings of the MS. of Alamannius and the three MSS. of Ursinus, I have used a copy of the *Editio Princeps* of 1598;[1] for the readings of Amyot's translation published in 1559, nearly forty years before the Greek text was printed, I have used the double French edition of 1757, which gives Amyot's rendering side by side with a modern one. The weak point in this *materia critica* is the record of the readings of B; for there is good reason to believe that Courier's scholarship was not always above suspicion. Still I believe it will be found that his account of B is substantially correct.

About the year 1595 Fulvius Ursinus (Fulvio Orsini), the great scholar and collector of MSS. who from 1559 to his death in 1600 was librarian to the Farnese cardinals at Rome, appears to have made a MS. of the *Pastoralia* with marginal variants. This is the MS. mentioned by the scribe of

---

[1] Seiler was unable to find a copy of this book, and was led into mistakes on this account.

Parisinus iii as having been collated by him in 1597,[1] and it was doubtless from this MS. that Ursinus answered Columbanius' request for variants on certain passages when he was preparing the Juntine edition of 1598. In compiling his MS. Ursinus used three MSS., known to editors as Ursiniani i, ii, and iii. These have not been identified, and their readings can only be gathered from the text and notes of the Juntine edition. Courier, however, speaks of the existence of other MSS. besides B in the Vatican Library; and since Ursinus is known to have bequeathed his collection to the Vatican, these may well prove to be the three Ursiniani.

The MSS. of the *Pastoralia* at present known either from Columbanius' edition or from the work of later editors, arrange themselves by means of the great lacuna comprising chapters 12 to 17 of the first book. This occurs in all the MSS. except A, which was discovered at Florence by P. L. Courier in 1809. The MSS. which have the lacuna arrange themselves further in two groups, one where it begins at § 13, which I call *p*, and the other where it begins in the middle of § 12, which I call *q*. The extension of the lacuna in the latter group was probably due to a clumsy piece of emendation; however it was caused, the former group, despite

[1] That this scribe was a Frenchman appears from the inadvertent use of the abbreviation *p* (*peut-être*) instead of *f* (*forte*) in a single passage.

INTRODUCTION

Courier's enthusiasm for B—an enthusiasm which
B often deserves—must be considered as representing the older tradition.

I have identified the three Ursiniani as follows,
the first two belonging to p and the third to q :—

Urs. i : a MS. used by Amyot ; this as well as
  Urs. iii was perhaps acquired by Ursinus on
  Amyot's death in 1593,

Urs. ii : a MS. from which Parisinus iii is partly
  derived,

Urs. iii : a MS. used by Amyot, ancestor of Parisini
  i and ii and (in common with Urs. ii) of
  Parisinus iii. It appears to have had one
  variant ($\overset{\omega\varsigma}{\delta\mu o\acute{\iota}o\upsilon\varsigma}$ 3. 34) derived from the common
  ancestor of itself and B, and four of its own,
  ($\overset{\mu\epsilon\tau\grave{\alpha}\ \ \kappa\rho\acute{\alpha}\tau o\upsilon\varsigma}{\kappa\alpha\tau\grave{\alpha}\ \kappa\rho\acute{\alpha}\tau o\varsigma}$ 1. 21, $\pi\rho\epsilon\sigma\beta\acute{\upsilon}\tau\alpha\tau\overset{\tau}{\acute{o}\varsigma}\ \gamma\epsilon$ 2. 15, $\kappa\alpha\tau\acute{\epsilon}\chi o\overset{\omega}{\nu}$
  2. 24, and $\nu\epsilon\mu\acute{\eta}\overset{o}{\sigma}\epsilon\tau\epsilon$ 2. 23), due to emendation
  or correction. It also seems to have contained
  several lacunae which it did not share with
  B ; some of these omissions, as appears from
  his translation, were regarded as correct by
  Amyot.

Columbanius, the editor of the Juntine edition,
the *Editio Princeps* of 1598, used, as he tells us,
(1) a MS. belonging to Aloisius Alamannius, which I
take to have been a conflation of Urss. i and iii, with
many but not all variations between these two MSS.

added in the margin; (2) the readings sent him by Ursinus from the MS. Ursinus had copied and equipped with variants from his three MSS. (Urss. i, ii, and iii). Ursinus does not appear to have made any note of correspondences between his MS. and the text of Columbanius, and it is important too to remember that the variants recorded as his in the Juntine edition are only those belonging to the passages on which he was consulted. In his note on page 82 he says : " Is [Ursinus] enim antequam nos hunc librum impressioni subijciendum traderemus, locos aliquot cum suis codicibus collatos, Roma ad nos remiserat." It is clear that Columbanius had but one MS. He refers to it in the singular in several places, notably in his preface. In the two passages where he speaks of *nostri libri*,[1] he means either the four "books" of the *Pastoralia*, or the MSS. from which both the text and the *marginalia* of his own MS. were derived. His note on p. 87 "τε] N. al. γε al. τότε " merely means that his MS. here had two marginal readings; and since all three readings were known to Ursinus, and he was asked only for variants, no note of Ursinus' readings is made by Columbanius. It is unfortunate that Columbanius' notes tell us neither which were the readings of Alamannius' text and which of the margin, nor make any distinction of name in recording the variants of the three Ursiniani.

[1] Both on p. 82.

INTRODUCTION

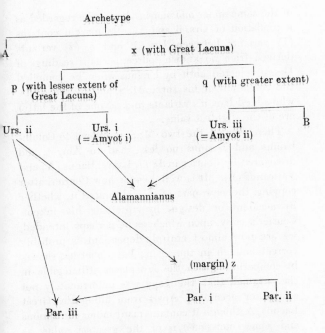

The Parisini are all of the sixteenth century.
i and ii belong to group *q*, and were derived from
a copy of Urs. iii which I call *z*. This contained
the few variants of its parent, as well as about thirty
derived from Urs. ii. The special minor omissions
of Urs. iii, as well as those it shared with B, appear
in Parr. i and ii. Par. iii, though, unlike them, it has
the lesser extent of the Great Lacuna, shows many

of the same minor omissions. It may be regarded as a conflation of Urs. ii and z. Its margin contains (1) variants between Urs. ii and z, (2) variants derived from no known source, perhaps readings of Urs. ii rejected both by Ursinus when he compiled the conflation of his three MSS. and by the scribe who added Urs. ii's variants to z. None of the latter are of the slightest value.

There remain the two MSS. unknown to Columbanius and Ursinus no less than to Amyot, and discovered by Courier in 1809, Laurentianus (A) and Vaticanus (B). It is well known how Courier, after copying the new part of A, obliterated it, whether by accident or design, by upsetting his inkpot. Courier's copy, upon which, as he perhaps intended, we are now almost entirely dependent, is probably correct enough in the main; but Cobet has shown, by comparing it with the few places still legible in the original, that the copy was unfortunately not altogether accurate. Apart from filling the Great Lacuna, A, though it contains many minor corruptions and some omissions, is of the greatest value as representing the oldest extant tradition. It is ascribed to the thirteenth century.

Of Courier's other discovery, B, I have found no description. His record of its readings is given by Seiler. It contains several special lacunae of minor importance aud shares others with Urs. iii, and, as belonging to q, does not represent so old a tradition as Urss. i and ii; but it nevertheless fully deserves the position assigned it by Courier of second in value to A.

The text of the present edition is the result of my investigations into the recorded readings of the manuscripts. When the variation among the manuscripts lies merely in the order of the words, I have often followed A without recording the variant readings. Otherwise, the critical notes contain all the variants of any importance for the history of the text. But it should be remembered that the ascription of variants to the individual MSS. of Ursinus, is conditional upon the acceptance of my *stemma* and the identifications it involves. Emendations of previous editors I hope I have acknowledged in every case. Emendations which I believe to be my own, I have marked *E*. Sometimes an emendation appears from his translation to have been anticipated by Amyot. In these cases I have added his name in brackets. I have done the same where his translation indicates that the reading in question was the reading of one of his MSS. In the notes on the passage included in the Great Lacuna, I have given both Furia's and Courier's readings of A. It should be borne in mind that Furia saw the text only after the spilling of the ink.

III.—THE TRANSLATION

There is nothing on Thornley's title-page to tell us that his book is a translation, and if his "most sweet and pleasant pastoral romance" ever came into the hands of the "young ladies" for whom he wrote it, they may well have supposed it to be his original work. For although his rendering is generally close enough to the Greek to satisfy the most fastidious modern scholar, it has all the graces of idiom, rhythm, and vocabulary characteristic of the best English prose of the day. Of most of his excellences I must leave the reader to judge, but I cannot forbear to remark upon one outstanding feature of his style. He always shows you that he has a complete grasp of the situation he is describing. He not only sees and hears, but he thinks and feels. He knows what it was like to be there.

In making his translation Thornley had before him the parallel Latin and Greek edition of Jungermann, published in 1605. His English is often suggested by Jungermann's Latin; in one or two places he has made mistakes through paying more attention to the Latin than to the Greek; and he sometimes prefers a reading only to be found in Jungermann's notes. That he was familiar with Amyot's French version of 1559 I have not been able to establish.

In my revision of Thornley's work, I set myself to alter only what was actually wrong; but right and wrong being so often a matter of opinion, I cannot hope to have pleased all my readers as well as myself and the editors of this series. I can only say that I have corrected as little as seemed in the circumstances possible, and tried to make the corrections

INTRODUCTION

consonant with my conception of Thornley's style. In the long passage where Thornley's translation was not available, I have imitated him as nearly as I could.

I have not discovered that any other work was. ever published by the maker of this delightful book; indeed, the following are the only facts I have been able to glean about him. George Thornley was born in 1614. He was the son of a certain Thomas Thornley described as "of Cheshire," and was at Repton School under Thomas Whitehead, the first master appointed on the re-founding of the school in 1621. Whitehead's usher at the time, John Lightfoot, was afterwards master of St. Catherine's, and was elected Vice-Chancellor of the University of Cambridge in 1655. Whitehead sent many of his scholars to his old college, Christ's, and it was here that Thornley was admitted sizar—sizarships were given to poor students—under Mr. King in 1631. This King is the Edward King who is the subject of Milton's *Lycidas*, and Milton resided at Christ's from 1625 to 1632. In 1635 Thornley proceeded Bachelor in Arts, and we hear no more of him save that in his forty-fourth year he is described upon the title-page of his *Daphnis and Chloe* as "Gentleman."

J. M. E.

CAMBRIDGE, 1913.

BIBLIOGRAPHY

Editio Princeps: Longus was first printed in the French translation of Amyot published in 1559. The Greek text was first published by Philip Junta at Florence in 1598.

The Best Commentary is that contained in Seiler's parallel Greek and Latin edition published in Latin at Leipzig in 1843.

The Earliest English Version is rather an adaptation than a translation ; the following is its title-page : *Daphnis and Chloe | excellently | describing the weight | of affection, the simplicitie of loue, the purport | of honest meaning, the resolution of men, and disposi- | tion of Fate, finished in a Pastorall, and interlaced with the praises | of a most peerlesse Princesse, wonderfull in Maiestie, | and rare in perfection, celebrated within | the same Pastorall, and therefore | termed by the name of | The Shepheards Holidaie. | By Angell Daye. | Altior fortuna virtus | At London | printed by Robert Waldegraue, and are | to be sold at his shop in Paules church-yard | at the signe of the Crane | 1587.* (Reprinted and edited by Joseph Jacobs, London, 1890.)

THE LESBIAN PASTORALS

OF

DAPHNIS AND CHLOE

ΛΟΓΓΟΥ ΠΟΙΜΕΝΙΚΩΝ ΤΩΝ ΠΕΡΙ
ΔΑΦΝΙΝ ΚΑΙ ΧΛΟΗΝ
ΛΕΣΒΙΑΚΩΝ

ΛΟΓΟΙ Δ΄

DAPHNIS AND CHLOE

A MOST SWEET AND PLEASANT PASTORAL ROMANCE FOR YOUNG LADIES

BY

GEO. THORNLEY, Gent.

Humili casâ nihil antiquius nihil nobilius. —Sen. Philos

LONDON :

PRINTED FOR JOHN GARFIELD, AT THE SIGN OF THE ROLLING,
PRESSE FOR PICTURES NEAR THE ROYAL-EXCHANGE IN
CORNHILL, OVER AGAINST POPES-HEAD-ALLEY.

1657.

A SUMMARY OF THE FIRST BOOK

THE *author sees a picture of curious interpretation in the island Lesbos. And he describes it in four books. The situation of Mytilene (the scene of the story) is drawn. Lamo a goatherd, following a goat that neglected her kid, finds an infant-boy exposed with fine accoutrements about him, takes him away, keeps him, and names him Daphnis. Two years after, Dryas a shepherd, looking for a sheep of his, found in a cave of the Nymphs a girl of the very same fortune, brings her up, and calls her Chloe. Dryas and Lamo, warned by dreams, send forth the exposed children together to keep their flocks. They are joyful, and play away their time. Daphnis, running after a he-goat, falls unawares together with him into a trap-ditch made for a wolf, but is drawn up alive and well. Chloe sees Daphnis at his washing and praises his beauty. Dorco the herdsman woos Chloe with gifts, and contends with Daphnis for her favour. Daphnis praises Chloe and she kisses him. Dorco asks of Dryas Chloe for his wife, but all in vain. Therefore, disguised in a wolf-skin, he thinks to seize her*

4

A SUMMARY OF THE FIRST BOOK

from a thicket and carry her away by force, but the flock-dogs fall upon him.

Daphnis and Chloe are variously affected. Daphnis tells the Tale of the Stock-Dove. The Tyrian pirates plunder the fields and carry away Daphnis. Chloe, not knowing what to do, runs up to Dorco whom she finds a dying of his wounds. He gives her a pipe of wonderful power. She plays on it, and the oxen and cows that were carried away turn over the vessel. They and Daphnis swim to the land while the armed pirates drown. Then they bury poor Dorco and return to their wonted game.

<ΠΡΟΟΙΜΙΟΝ>

1. Ἐν Λέσβῳ θηρῶν ἐν ἄλσει Νυμφῶν θέαμα εἶδον κάλλιστον ὧν εἶδον, εἰκόνα γραπτήν,[1] ἱστορίαν ἔρωτος. καλὸν μὲν καὶ τὸ ἄλσος, πολύδενδρον, ἀνθηρόν, κατάρρυτον, μία πηγὴ πάντα ἔτρεφε καὶ τὰ ἄνθη καὶ τὰ δένδρα, ἀλλ' ἡ γραφὴ τερπνοτέρα καὶ τέχνην ἔχουσα περιττὴν καὶ τύχην[2] ἐρωτικήν, ὥστε πολλοὶ καὶ τῶν ξένων κατὰ φήμην ᾔεσαν τῶν μὲν Νυμφῶν ἱκέται, τῆς δὲ εἰκόνος θεαταί. γυναῖκες ἐπ' αὐτῆς τίκτουσαι καὶ ἄλλαι σπαργάνοις κοσμοῦσαι, παιδία ἐκκείμενα, ποίμνια τρέφοντα, ποιμένες ἀναιρούμενοι, νέοι συντιθέμενοι, λῃστῶν καταδρομή, πολεμίων ἐμβολή.

2. Πολλὰ ἄλλα καὶ πάντα ἐρωτικὰ ἰδόντα με καὶ θαυμάσαντα πόθος ἔσχεν ἀντιγράψαι τῇ γραφῇ. καὶ ἀναζητησάμενος ἐξηγητὴν τῆς εἰκόνος τέτταρας βίβλους ἐξεπονησάμην ἀνάθημα μὲν

Title: A Λόγου : pq Λόγγου Σοφίστου   Λεσβ. only in colophon   [1] so Brunck : Ap εἰκόνα γραφήν : q εἰκόνος γραφήν
[2] so Heusinger : mss invert τέχνην and τύχην

PROEM

1. When I was hunting in Lesbos, I saw in the grove of the Nymphs a spectacle the most beauteous and pleasing of any that ever yet I cast my eyes upon. It was a painted picture, reporting a history of love. The grove indeed was very pleasant, thick set with trees and starred with flowers everywhere, and watered all from one fountain with divers meanders and rills. But that picture, as having in it not only an excellent and wonderful piece of art but also a tale of ancient love, was far more amiable. And therefore many, not only the people of the country but foreigners also, enchanted by the fame of it, came as much to see that, as in devotion to the Nymphs. There were figured in it young women, in the posture, some of teeming, others of swaddling, little children; babes exposed, and ewes giving them suck; shepherds taking up foundlings, young persons plighting their troth; an incursion of thieves, an inroad of armed men.

2. When I had seen with admiration these and many other things, but all belonging to the affairs of love, I had a mighty instigation to write something as to answer that picture. And therefore, when I had carefully sought and found an interpreter of the image, I drew up these four books, an oblation

7

DAPHNIS AND CHLOE

Ἔρωτι καὶ Νύμφαις καὶ Πανί, κτῆμα δὲ τερπνὸν πᾶσιν ἀνθρώποις, ὃ καὶ νοσοῦντα ἰάσεται καὶ λυπούμενον παραμυθήσεται, τὸν ἐρασθέντα ἀναμνήσει, τὸν οὐκ ἐρασθέντα παιδεύσει.[1] πάντως γὰρ οὐδεὶς Ἔρωτα ἔφυγεν ἢ φεύξεται, μέχρι ἂν κάλλος ᾖ καὶ ὀφθαλμοὶ βλέπωσιν. ἡμῖν δὲ ὁ θεὸς παράσχοι σωφρονοῦσι τὰ τῶν ἄλλων γράφειν.

[1] Parr προπαιδεύσει

to Love and to Pan and to the Nymphs, and a
delightful possession even for all men. For this will
cure him that is sick, and rouse him that is in
dumps; one that has loved, it will remember of it;
one that has not, it will instruct. For there was
never any yet that wholly could escape love, and
never shall there be any, never so long as beauty
shall be, never so long as eyes can see. But help
me that God to write the passions of others; and
while I write, keep me in my own right wits.

ΛΟΓΟΣ ΠΡΩΤΟΣ

1. Πόλις ἐστὶ τῆς Λέσβου Μυτιλήνη μεγάλη
καὶ καλή. διείληπται γὰρ εὐρίποις ἐπεισρεούσης[1]
τῆς θαλάττης καὶ κεκόσμηται γεφύραις ξεστοῦ
καὶ λευκοῦ λίθου· νομίσεις[2] οὐ πόλιν ὁρᾶν, ἀλλὰ
νῆσον. ἀλλὰ ἦν ταύτης[3] τῆς πόλεως τῆς Μυτι-
λήνης ὅσον ἀπὸ σταδίων διακοσίων[4] ἀγρὸς ἀνδρὸς
εὐδαίμονος, κτῆμα κάλλιστον, ὄρη θηροτρόφα,
πεδία πυροφόρα, γήλοφοι κλημάτων, νομαὶ
ποιμνίων· καὶ ἡ θάλαττα προσέβλυζεν[5] ἐπ' ἠιόνος
ἐκτεταμένης ψυχαγωγίαν μαλθακήν.[6]

2. Ἐν τῷδε τῷ ἀγρῷ νέμων αἰπόλος Λάμων
τοὔνομα, παιδίον εὗρεν ὑπὸ μιᾶς τῶν αἰγῶν[7]
τρεφόμενον. δρυμὸς ἦν καὶ λόχμη, ⟨ἧς⟩ κατω-
τάτω[8] καὶ κιττὸς ἐπιπλανώμενος καὶ πόα μαλ-

---

[1] p ἐπεισρεούσαις: q ὑπεισρεούσης   Ap τῇ θαλάσσῃ (A
without iota)   [2] Ap -αις   [3] ἦν ταύτης: pq ἐκ τ. (p ταύτης)
and ἦν after ἄγρος   [4] Uiii εἴκοσιν   [5] pq -έκλυζεν   q ἐν
ἠϊόνι (B lacuna)   [6] so E, prob. old variant: Ap ψάμμῳ
μαλθακῆς (p -κῇ): q ψυχαγωγίας μαλθακῆς   [7] μιᾶς τ. αἰγῶν
Ap (Amyot): q αἰγὸς   [8] so E, cf. μεσαίτατον 4: B κάτω:
Uiii κάτω βάτων: Ap βάτων old var. of corruption κάτω

THE FIRST BOOK

1. MYTILENE is a city in Lesbos, and by ancient titles of honour it is the great and fair Mytilene. For it is distinguished and divided (the sea flowing in) by a various euripus,[1] and is adorned with bridges built of white polished marble. You would not think you saw a city, but an island. From this Mytilene some two hundred furlongs there lay a manor of a certain rich lord, the most sweet and pleasant prospect under all the eyes of heaven. There were mountains stored with wild beasts for game; there were hills and banks that were spread with vines; the fields abounded with all sorts of corn; the valleys with orchards and gardens and purls from the hills; the pastures with sheep and goats and kine; the sea-billows, swelling and gushing upon a shore which lay extended along in an open horizon, made a soft magic and enchantment.

2. In this sweet country, the field and farm of Mytilene, a goatherd dwelling, by name Lamo, found one of his goats suckling an infant-boy, by such a chance, it seems, as this: There was a lawn,[2] and in it a dell, and in the nethermost part of the dell a place all lined with wandering ivy, the ground

---

[1] *i.e.* euripuses or canals.   [2] *i.e.* a glade, the Greek is "oakwood."

θακή, ἐφ᾽ ¹ ἧς ἔκειτο τὸ παιδίον. ἐνταῦθα ἡ αἲξ
θέουσα συνεχὲς ἀφανὴς ἐγίνετο πολλάκις, καὶ τὸν
ἔριφον ἀπολιποῦσα τῷ βρέφει παρέμενε. φυλάττει
τὰς διαδρομὰς ὁ Λάμων οἰκτείρας ἀμελούμενον
τὸν ἔριφον, καὶ μεσημβρίας ἀκμαζούσης κατ᾽
ἴχνος ἐλθών, ὁρᾷ τὴν μὲν αἶγα πεφυλαγμένως
περιβεβηκυῖαν, μὴ ταῖς χηλαῖς βλάπτοι πατοῦσα,
τὸ δὲ ὥσπερ ἐκ μητρῴας θηλῆς τὴν ἐπιρροὴν
ἕλκον τοῦ γάλακτος. θαυμάσας, ὥσπερ εἰκὸς ἦν,
πρόσεισιν ἐγγὺς καὶ εὑρίσκει παιδίον ἄρρεν, μέγα
καὶ καλὸν καὶ τῆς κατὰ τὴν ἔκθεσιν τύχης ἐν
σπαργάνοις κρείττοσι. χλανίδιόν ² τε γὰρ ἦν
ἁλουργὲς καὶ πόρπη χρυσῆ καὶ ξιφίδιον ἐλεφαν-
τόκωπον.

3. Τὸ μὲν οὖν πρῶτον ἐβουλεύσατο μόνα τὰ
γνωρίσματα βαστάσας ἀμελῆσαι τοῦ βρέφους·
ἔπειτα αἰδεσθεὶς εἰ μηδὲ αἰγὸς φιλανθρωπίαν
μιμήσεται, νύκτα φυλάξας κομίζει πάντα πρὸς
τὴν γυναῖκα Μυρτάλην, καὶ τὰ γνωρίσματα καὶ
τὸ παιδίον καὶ τὴν αἶγα αὐτήν. τῆς δὲ ἐκπλα-
γείσης εἰ παιδία τίκτουσιν αἶγες, ὅδε ³ πάντα
αὐτῇ διηγεῖται, πῶς εὗρεν ἐκκείμενον, πῶς εἶδε ⁴
τρεφόμενον, πῶς ᾐδέσθη καταλιπεῖν ἀποθανού-
μενον. δόξαν δὴ κἀκείνῃ, τὰ μὲν συνεκτεθέντα
κρύπτουσι, τὸ δὲ παιδίον αὑτῶν ἐπονομάζουσι, τῇ
δὲ αἰγὶ τὴν τροφὴν ἐπιτρέπουσιν. ὡς δ᾽ ἂν καὶ
τὸ ὄνομα τοῦ παιδίου ποιμενικὸν δοκοίη, Δάφνιν
αὐτὸν ἔγνωσαν καλεῖν.

¹ so E: mss καθ᾽ corruption of κάτω above from marg.
² p Uiii χλαμύδιον, cf. 4. 21   ³ so E: mss ὁ δὲ   ⁴ q εὗρεν

furred over with a finer sort of grass, and on that the infant lay. The goat coming often hither, disappeared very much, neglecting still her own kid to attend the wretched child. Lamo observes her frequent outs and discurations, and pitying that the kid should be so forsaken, follows her even at high noon. And anon he sees the goat bestriding the child carefully, lest she should chance to hurt it with her hooves, and the infant drawing milk as from the breast of a kind mother. And wondering at it, as well he might, he comes nearer and finds it a man-child, a lusty boy and beautiful, and wrapped in richer clothes then you should find upon a foundling. His mantle or little cloak was purple, fastened with a golden brooch, and by his side a little dagger, the handle polished ivory.

3. He thought at first to take away the tokens and take no thought about the child. But afterwards conceiving shame within himself if he should not imitate the kindness and philanthropy he had seen even in that goat, waiting till the night came on he brings all to Myrtale his wife, the boy, his precious trinkets, and the goat. But Myrtale, all amazed at this, " What ? " quoth she, " do goats cast boys ? " Then he fell to tell her all, namely how he had found him exposed, how suckled ; how overcome by mere shame he could not leave the sweet child to die in that forsaken thicket. And therefore, when he discerned Myrtale was of his mind, the things exposed together with him are laid up carefully and hid, they say the boy's their own child, and put him to the goat to nurse. And that his name might be indeed a shepherd's name, they agreed to call him Daphnis.

4. Ἤδη δὲ διετοῦς χρόνου διηνυσμένου,[1] ποιμὴν ἐξ ἀγρῶν ὁμόρων, Δρύας τὸ ὄνομα, νέμων[2] καὶ αὐτὸς ὁμοίοις ἐπιτυγχάνει καὶ εὑρήμασι καὶ θεάμασι. Νυμφῶν ἄντρον ἦν, πέτρα μεγάλη, τὰ ἔνδοθεν κοίλη, τὰ ἔξωθεν περιφερής. τὰ ἀγάλματα τῶν Νυμφῶν αὐτῶν λίθοις πεποίητο· πόδες ἀνυπόδητοι, χεῖρες εἰς ὤμους γυμναί, κόμαι μέχρι τῶν αὐχένων λελυμέναι,[3] ζῶμα περὶ τὴν ἰξύν, μειδίαμα περὶ τὴν ὀφρύν· τὸ πᾶν σχῆμα χορεία[4] ἦν ὀρχουμένων. ἡ ὤα τοῦ ἄντρου τῆς μεγάλης πέτρας ἦν τὸ μεσαίτατον. ἐκ δὲ ἀναβλύζον ὕδωρ ἀπῄει χεόμενον,[5] ὥστε καὶ λειμὼν πάνυ γλαφυρὸς ἐκτέτατο πρὸ τοῦ ἄντρου, πολλῆς καὶ μαλακῆς πόας ὑπὸ τῆς νοτίδος τρεφομένης. ἀνέκειντο δὲ καὶ γαυλοὶ καὶ αὐλοὶ πλάγιοι καὶ σύριγγες καὶ κάλαμοι πρεσβυτέρων ποιμένων ἀναθήματα.

5. Εἰς τοῦτο τὸ νυμφαῖον οἷς ἀρτιτόκος συχνὰ φοιτῶσα δόξαν πολλάκις ἀπωλείας παρεῖχε. κολάσαι δὲ βουλόμενος αὐτὴν καὶ εἰς τὴν προτέραν εὐνομίαν καταστῆσαι, δεσμὸν ῥάβδου χλωρᾶς λυγίσας ὅμοιον βρόχῳ τῇ πέτρᾳ προσῆλθεν, ὡς ἐκεῖ ληψόμενος[6] αὐτήν. ἐπιστὰς δὲ οὐδὲν εἶδεν ὧν ἤλπισεν, ἀλλὰ τὴν μὲν διδοῦσαν <παιδίῳ> πάνυ ἀνθρωπίνως τὴν θηλὴν εἰς ἄφθονον τοῦ γάλακτος ὁλκήν, τὸ δὲ παιδίον ἀκλαυστὶ[7] λάβρως εἰς ἀμφοτέρας τὰς θηλὰς μεταφέρον τὸ στόμα καθαρὸν καὶ φαιδρόν, οἷα τῆς οἰὸς τῇ γλώττῃ τὸ πρόσωπον ἀπολιχμωμένης μετὰ τὸν κόρον τῆς τροφῆς. θῆλυ

---

[1] so p, prob. old var : Aq διήκνουμ. [2] so E (Amyot by emendation): mss νέμων τὸ ὄν. [3] pq sing. [4] perh. χορὸς E. [5] so E, cf. 3. 16 ἐκ ... ἥρπασεν : A ἐκ δὲ πηγῆς ἀναβ. ὕδ. ἐπηεγχεόμενον : pq ἐκ δὲ τῆς πηγ. ὕδ. ἀναβ. ῥεῖθρον

4. And now, when two years' time was past, a shepherd of the neighbouring fields, Dryas by name, had the luck, watching his flock, to see such sights and find such rarities as Lamo did. There was a solitary sacred cave of the Nymphs, a huge rock, hollow and vaulted within, but round without. The statues or images of the Nymphs were cut out most curiously in stone; their feet unshod, their arms bare to the shoulder, their hair loose over their necks, their eyes sweetly smiling, their lawny petticoats tucked up at the waist. The whole presence made a figure as of a divine amusing dance or masque. The mouth of the cave was in the midst of that great rock; and from it gushed up a strong crystal fountain, and running off in a fair current or brook, made before the holy cave a fresh, green, and flowery mead. There were hanging up and consecrated there milking-pails, pipes, and hautboys, whistles, and reeds, the offerings of the ancient shepherds.

5. To this cave the often gadding of a sheep newly delivered of young, made the shepherd often think that she undoubtedly was lost. Desiring therefore to correct the straggler and reduce her to her rule, of a green with he made a snare, and looked to catch her in the cave. But when he came there he saw things he never dreamed of. For he saw her giving suck from her dugs in a very human manner to an infant, which, without crying, greedily did lay, first to one dug then the tother, a most neat and fair mouth; for when the child had sucked enough, the careful nurse licked it still and trimmed

ἐποίει χεόμ.   [6] Parr συλλήψ.   <παιδίῳ> E (Amyot by em.)   [7] q ἀκλαυτὶ : q ἀκλαγγὶ

ἦν τοῦτο τὸ παιδίον. καὶ παρέκειτο καὶ τούτῳ
γνωρίσματα,[1] μίτρα διάχρυσος, ὑποδήματα
ἐπίχρυσα καὶ περισκελίδες χρυσαῖ.

6. Θεῖον δή τι νομίσας τὸ εὕρημα καὶ διδασκό-
μενος παρὰ τῆς οἰὸς ἐλεεῖν τε τὸ παιδίον καὶ
φιλεῖν, ἀναιρεῖται μὲν τὸ βρέφος ἐπ᾿ ἀγκῶνος,
ἀποτίθεται δὲ τὰ γνωρίσματα κατὰ τῆς πήρας,
εὔχεται δὲ ταῖς Νύμφαις ἐπὶ χρηστῇ τύχῃ θρέψαι[2]
τὴν ἱκέτιν αὐτῶν. καὶ ἐπεὶ καιρὸς ἦν ἀπελαύνειν
τὴν ποίμνην, ἐλθὼν εἰς τὴν ἔπαυλιν τῇ γυναικὶ
διηγεῖται τὰ ὀφθέντα, δείκνυσι τὰ εὑρεθέντα,
παρακελεύεται θυγάτριον νομίζειν, καὶ λανθά-
νουσαν ὡς ἴδιον τρέφειν. ἡ μὲν δὴ Νάπη (τοῦτο
γὰρ ἐκαλεῖτο) μήτηρ εὐθὺς ἦν καὶ ἐφίλει τὸ
παιδίον, ἅτε[3] ὑπὸ τῆς οἰὸς παρευδοκιμηθῆναι
δεδοικυῖα, καὶ τίθεται καὶ αὐτὴ ποιμενικὸν ὄνομα
πρὸς πίστιν αὐτῷ, Χλόην.

7. Ταῦτα τὰ παιδία ταχὺ μάλα ηὔξησε καὶ
κάλλος αὐτοῖς ἐξεφαίνετο κρεῖττον ἀγροικίας.
ἤδη τε ἦν[4] ὁ μὲν πέντε καὶ δέκα ἐτῶν ἀπὸ γενεᾶς,
ἡ δὲ τοσούτων δυοῖν ἀποδεόντων, καὶ ὁ Δρύας καὶ
ὁ Λάμων ἐπὶ μιᾶς νυκτὸς ὁρῶσιν ὄναρ τοιόνδε τι.
τὰς[5] Νύμφας ἐδόκουν ἐκείνας, τὰς ἐν τῷ ἄντρῳ,
ἐν ᾧ ἡ πηγή, ἐν ᾧ τὸ παιδίον εὗρεν ὁ Δρύας, τὸν
Δάφνιν καὶ τὴν Χλόην παραδιδόναι παιδίῳ μάλα

---

[1] so Hercher : mss σπάργανα γνωρ.   incorporated gloss,
cf. 8   [2] cf. 14 : A τρέψαι   [3] so Hirschig : mss ὥστε
[4] p ἤδη ἦν or οὖν   [5] Ap εἶναι τὰς

it up. That infant was a girl, and in such manner as before, there lay tokens beside her; a girdle embroidered with gold, a pair of shoes gilded, and ankle-bands all of gold.

6. Wherefore Dryas, thinking with himself that this could not come about without the providence of the Gods, and learning mercy and love from the sheep, takes her up into his arms, puts her monuments into his scrip, and prays to the Nymphs they may have happily preserved and brought up their suppliant and votary. Now therefore, when it was time to drive home his flocks, he comes to his cottage and tells all that he had seen to his wife, shews her what he had found, bids her think she is her daughter, and, however, nurse her up, all unbeknown, as her child. Nape, that was her name, began presently [1] to be a mother, and with a kind of jealousy would appear to love the child lest that ewe should get more praise; and, like Myrtale before, gives her the pastoral name of Chloe to assure us it's their own.

7. These infants grew up apace, and still their beauty appeared too excellent to suit with rustics or derive at all from clowns. And Daphnis now is fifteen and Chloe younger two years, when upon one night Lamo and Dryas had their visions in their sleep. They thought they saw those Nymphs, the Goddesses of the cave out of which the fountain gushed out into a stream, and where Dryas found Chloe; that they delivered Daphnis and Chloe to a certain young boy, very disdainful, very fair, one

---

[1] immediately.

σοβαρῷ καὶ καλῷ, πτερὰ ἐκ τῶν ὤμων ἔχοντι,
βέλη σμικρὰ ἅμα τοξαρίῳ φέροντι· τὸ δὲ ἐφα-
ψάμενον ἀμφοτέρων ἑνὶ βέλει κελεῦσαι λοιπὸν
ποιμαίνειν,[1] τὸν μὲν τὸ αἰπόλιον, τὴν δὲ τὸ
ποίμνιον.

8. Τοῦτο τὸ ὄναρ ἰδόντες ἤχθοντο μέν, ποιμένες[2]
εἰ ἔσοιντο καὶ αἰπόλοι <οἳ> τύχην ἐκ γνωρισμά-
των[3] ἐπαγγελλόμενοι κρείττονα· διὸ[4] αὐτοὺς καὶ
τροφαῖς ἁβροτέραις ἔτρεφον καὶ γράμματα ἐπαί-
δευον καὶ πάντα ὅσα καλὰ ἦν ἐπ᾽ ἀγροικίας.[5]
ἐδόκει δὲ πείθεσθαι θεοῖς περὶ τῶν σωθέντων
προνοίᾳ θεῶν.

Καὶ κοινώσαντες ἀλλήλοις τὸ ὄναρ καὶ θύσαντες
τῷ τὰ πτερὰ ἔχοντι παιδίῳ παρὰ ταῖς Νύμφαις
(τὸ γὰρ ὄνομα λέγειν οὐκ εἶχον), ὡς ποιμένας ἐκ-
πέμπουσιν αὐτοὺς ἅμα ταῖς ἀγέλαις[6] ἐκδιδάξαντες
ἕκαστα, πῶς δεῖ νέμειν πρὸ μεσημβρίας, πῶς ἐπι-
νέμειν[7] κοπάσαντος τοῦ καύματος, πότε ἄγειν ἐπὶ
ποτόν, πότε ἀπάγειν ἐπὶ κοῖτον, ἐπὶ τίσι καλαύ-
ροπι χρηστέον, ἐπὶ τίσι φωνῇ μόνῃ. οἱ δὲ μάλα
χαίροντες ὡς ἀρχὴν μεγάλην παρελάμβανον καὶ
ἐφίλουν τὰς αἶγας καὶ τὰ πρόβατα μᾶλλον ἢ
ποιμέσιν ἔθος, ἡ μὲν ἐς ποίμνιον ἀναφέρουσα[8] τῆς
σωτηρίας τὴν αἰτίαν, ὁ δὲ μεμνημένος ὡς ἐκκεί-
μενον αὐτὸν αἶξ ἀνέθρεψεν.

---

[1] for λοιπ. ποιμ. A has νέμειν   [2] so Seiler: mss οἱ ποίμ.
αἰπόλοι A : p ἴσως οὗτοι αἰπ.: q οὗτοι αἰπ.   <οἳ> E   [3] so
E (Amyot by em.) : mss σπαργάνων   [4] so p prob. old var. :
Aq δι᾽ ἣν   [5] pq dat.   [6] Uiii omits ἅμα τ. ἀγ.   [7] so B,
prob. old var.: Ap ἐπιμένειν : Uiii δεῖ νέμειν   [8] q ἄγουσα

that had wings at his shoulders, wore a bow and little darts; and that this boy did touch them both with the very selfsame dart, and commanded it from thenceforth one should feed his flock of goats, the other keep her flock of sheep.

8. This dream being dreamed by both, they could not but conceive grief to think that those should be nothing but shepherds or goatherds to whom they had read better fortune from their monuments, and indeed for that cause had both allowed them a finer sort of meat, and bin at charge to teach them letters and whatsoever other things were passing brave among the rural swains and girls. Yet nevertheless it seemed fit that the mandates of the Gods concerning them who by their providence were saved, should be attended and obeyed.

And having told their dreams one to another and sacrificed in the cave of the Nymphs to that winged boy (for his name they knew not), they sent them out shepherds with their flocks, and to everything instructed: how to feed before high noon and drive them to fresh pasture when the scorching glare declined, when to lead them to water, when to bring them to the folds, what cattle was disciplined with the crook, what commanded by the voice alone. And now this pretty pair of shepherds are as jocund in themselves as if they had got some great empire while they sit looking over their goodly flocks, and with more then usual kindness treated both the sheep and goats. For Chloe thankfully referred her preservation to a sheep, and Daphnis had not forgot to acknowledge his to a goat.

DAPHNIS AND CHLOE

9. Ἦρος ἦν ἀρχὴ καὶ πάντα ἤκμαζεν ἄνθη, τὰ
ἐν δρυμοῖς, τὰ ἐν λειμῶσι, καὶ ὅσα ὄρεια. βόμβος
ἦν ἤδη μελιττῶν, ἦχος ὀρνίθων μουσικῶν, σκιρ-
τήματα ποιμνίων ἀρτιγεννήτων· ἄρνες ἐσκίρτων
ἐν τοῖς ὄρεσιν, ἐβόμβουν ἐν τοῖς λειμῶσιν αἱ
μέλιτται, τὰς[1] λόχμας κατῇδον ὄρνιθες. τοσαύ-
της δὴ πάντα κατεχούσης εὐωρίας,[2] οἱ ἁπαλοὶ
<οὗτοι> καὶ νέοι μιμηταὶ τῶν ἀκουομένων ἐγί-
νοντο καὶ βλεπομένων. ἀκούοντες μὲν τῶν ὀρνί-
θων ᾀδόντων ᾖδον, βλέποντες δὲ σκιρτῶντας τοὺς
ἄρνας ἥλλοντο κοῦφα, καὶ τὰς μελίττας δὲ
μιμούμενοι τὰ ἄνθη συνέλεγον, καὶ τὰ μὲν εἰς
τοὺς κόλπους ἔβαλλον, τὰ δὲ στεφανίσκους πλέ-
κοντες ταῖς Νύμφαις ἐπέφερον. 10. ἔπραττον δὲ
κοινῇ πάντα πλησίον ἀλλήλων νέμοντες. καὶ
πολλάκις μὲν ὁ Δάφνις τῶν προβάτων συνέ-
στελλε[3] τὰ ἀποπλανώμενα, πολλάκις δὲ ἡ Χλόη
τὰς θρασυτέρας τῶν αἰγῶν ἀπὸ τῶν κρημνῶν
κατήλαυνεν. ἤδη δέ τις καὶ τὰς ἀγέλας ἀμφοτέρας
ἐφρούρησε θατέρου προσλιπαρήσαντος ἀθύρματι.

Ἀθύρματα δὲ αὐτοῖς ἦν ποιμενικὰ καὶ παιδικά.
ἡ μὲν ἀνθερίκους ἀνελομένη ποθὲν ἐξελθοῦσα[4]
ἀκριδοθήκην ἔπλεκε καὶ περὶ τοῦτο πονουμένη
τῶν ποιμνίων ἠμέλησεν, ὁ δὲ καλάμους λεπτοὺς
ἐκτεμὼν καὶ τρήσας τὰς τῶν γονάτων διαφυὰς
ἀλλήλους τε κηρῷ μαλθακῷ συναρτήσας, μέχρι

---

[1] A εἰς τὰς   [2] so Uiii prob. old var. : ApB εὐωδίας
ἁπαλοὶ : p παλαιοὶ   <οὗτοι> E (Amyot by em.)   [3] A
συνέλεγε   [4] q omits   q ἀκριδοθήραν

9. It was the beginning of spring, and all the
flowers of the lawns, meadows, valleys and hills were
now blowing. All was fresh and green. Now was
there humming of bees, and chanting of melodious
birds, and skipping of newborn lambs; the bees
hummed in the meadows, the birds warbled in the
groves, the lambs skipt on the hills. And now,
when such a careless joy had filled those blest and
happy fields, Daphnis and Chloe, as delicate and
young folks will, would imitate the pleasant things
they heard and saw. Hearing how the birds did
chant it, they began to carol too, and seeing how the
lambs skipt, tript their light and nimble measures.
Then, to emulate the bees, they fall to cull the
fairest flowers; some of which in toysome sport they
cast in one another's bosoms, and of some platted
garlands for the Nymphs; 10. and always keeping
near together, had and did all things in common;
for Daphnis often gathered in the straggling sheep,
and Chloe often drove the bolder venturous goats
from the crags and precipices; and sometimes to one
of them the care of both the flocks was left while
the other did intend some pretty knack or toysome
play.

For all their sports were sports of children and of
shepherds. Chloe, scudding up and down and here
and there picking up the windlestraws, would make
in plats a cage for a grasshopper, and be so wholly
bent on that, that she was careless of her flocks.
Daphnis on the other side, having cut the slender
reeds and bored the quills or intervals between the
joints, and with his soft wax joined and fitted one to
another, took no care but to practise or devise some

νυκτὸς συρίζειν ἐμελέτα. καί ποτε δὲ ἐκοινώ-
νουν γάλακτος καὶ οἴνου, καὶ τροφὰς ἃς οἴκοθεν
ἔφερον εἰς κοινὸν ἔνεμον.[1] θᾶττον ἄν τις εἶδε τὰ
ποίμνια καὶ τὰς αἶγας[2] ἀπ᾽ ἀλλήλων μεμερισμένας
ἢ Χλόην καὶ Δάφνιν.

11. Τοιαῦτα δὲ αὐτῶν παιζόντων τοιάνδε σπου-
δὴν Ἔρως ἐνέκαυσε.[3] λύκαινα τρέφουσα σκύμνους
νέους ἐκ τῶν πλησίον ἀγρῶν ἐξ ἄλλων[4] ποιμνίων
πολλὰ ἥρπαζε, πολλῆς τροφῆς ἐς ἀνατροφὴν τῶν
σκύμνων δεομένη. συνελθόντες οὖν οἱ κωμῆται
νύκτωρ σιροὺς ὀρύττουσι τὸ εὖρος ὀργυιᾶς, τὸ
βάθος τεττάρων. τὸ μὲν δὴ χῶμα τὸ πολὺ σπείρουσι
κομίσαντες μακράν, ξύλα δὲ ξηρὰ μακρὰ τείναντες
ὑπὲρ τοῦ χάσματος τὸ περιττὸν τοῦ χώματος κατέ-
πασαν τῆς πρότερον γῆς εἰκόνα· ὥστε, κἂν λαγὼς
ἐπιδράμῃ, κατακλᾷ τὰ ξύλα κάρφων ἀσθενέστερα
τυγχάνοντα,[5] καὶ τότε παρέχει μαθεῖν, ὅτι γῆ οὐκ
ἦν, ἀλλὰ μεμίμητο γῆν. τοιαῦτα πολλὰ ὀρύγ-
ματα κἂν τοῖς ὄρεσι κἂν τοῖς πεδίοις ὀρύξαντες
τὴν μὲν λύκαιναν οὐκ εὐτύχησαν λαβεῖν· ᾐσθά-
νετο[6] γάρ, ὡς γῆς σεσοφισμένης· πολλὰς δὲ αἶγας
καὶ ποίμνια διέφθειραν καὶ Δάφνιν παρ᾽ ὀλίγον
ὧδε·

12. Τράγοι παροξυνθέντες ἐς μάχην συνέπεσον.

---

[1] so *E*: mss ἔφερον   [2] so Schaefer: mss ἀγέλας, cf. 13
[3] q ἀνέπλασε   [4] Haupt ἄλλων ἄλλοτε   [5] pq ὄντα   [6] so
E: mss αἰσθάνεται   ὡς *E*, cf. 16: mss καὶ

22

tune even from morning to the twilight. Their wine
and their milk and whatsoever was brought from
home to the fields, they had still in common. And
a man might sooner see all the cattle[1] separate from
one another then he should Chloe and Daphnis
asunder.

11. But while they are thus playing away their
time to sweeten pleasure, afterwards Love in good
earnest kindled up this fire. A wolf that had a kennel
of whelps was come often ravenous upon the neigh-
bouring fields, and had borne away from other flocks
many cattle, because she needed much prey to keep
herself and those cubs. The villagers therefore
meet together, and in the night they dig ditches a
fathom wide and four fathom deep; of the earth
flung up they scatter the more part all abroad at a
good distance, and laying over-cross the chasm long,
dry, and rotten sticks, they strow them over with the
earth that did remain, to make the ground like it
was before; that if a hare do but offer to run there,
she cannot choose but break those rods that were as
brittle as the stubble, and then does easily make it
known that that indeed was not true, but only
counterfeited soil. Many such trap-ditches were
now digged in the mountains and the fields; yet
they could not take this wolf (for she could perceive
them because of the sophistic and commentitious
ground), but many of their sheep and goats were
there destroyed, and there wanted but a little that
Daphnis too was not slain. And it was on this
chance:

12. Two he-goats were exasperated to fight, and

---

[1] here sheep and goats.

τῷ οὖν ἑτέρῳ τὸ ἕτερον κέρας βιαιοτέρας γενομένης
<τῆς> συμβολῆς θραύεται, καὶ ἀλγήσας, φριμα-
ξάμενος ἐς φυγὴν ἐτρέπετο.[1] ὁ δὲ νικῶν ἑπόμενος
κατ᾽ ἴχνος ἄπαυστον ἐποίει τὴν φυγήν. ἀλγεῖ
Δάφνις περὶ τῷ κέρατι καὶ τῇ θρασύτητι ἀχθε-
σθεὶς ξύλῳ[2] ἐδίωκε τὸν διώκοντα. οἷα δὲ τοῦ μὲν
ὑπεκφεύγοντος, τοῦ δὲ ὀργῇ διώκοντος, οὐκ ἀκρι-
βὴς ἦν τῶν ἐν ποσὶν ἡ πρόσοψις, ἀλλὰ κατὰ
<τοῦ> χάσματος ἄμφω πίπτουσιν, ὁ τράγος
πρότερος, ὁ Δάφνις δεύτερος. τοῦτο καὶ ἔσωσε
Δάφνιν χρήσασθαι τῆς καταφορᾶς ὀχήματι τῷ
τράγῳ. ὁ μὲν δὴ τὸν ἀνιμησόμενον, εἴ τις ἄρα
γένοιτο, δακρύων ἀνέμενεν· ἡ δὲ Χλόη θεασαμένη
τὸ συμβὰν δρόμῳ παραγίνεται εἰς τὸν σιρόν, καὶ
μαθοῦσα ὅτι ζῇ, καλεῖ τινα βουκόλον ἐκ τῶν
ἀγρῶν τῶν πλησίον πρὸς ἐπικουρίαν. ὁ δὲ ἐλθὼν
σχοῖνον ἐζήτει μακράν, ἧς ἐχόμενος, ἀνιμώμενος
ἐκβήσεται. καὶ σχοῖνος μὲν οὐκ ἦν· ἡ δὲ Χλόη
λυσαμένη <τὴν> ταινίαν δίδωσι καθεῖναι τῷ
βουκόλῳ. καὶ οὕτως οἱ μὲν ἐπὶ τοῦ χείλους
ἑστῶτες εἷλκον, ὁ δὲ ἀνέβη[3] ταῖς τῆς ταινίας
ὁλκαῖς[4] ταῖς χερσὶν ἀκολουθῶν. ἀνιμήσαντο[5] δὲ
καὶ τὸν ἄθλιον τράγον συντεθραυσμένον ἄμφω τὰ
κέρατα· τοσοῦτον ἄρα ἡ δίκη μετῆλθε τοῦ νικη-
θέντος τράγου. τοῦτον μὲν δὴ τυθησόμενον[6]
χαρίζονται σῶστρα τῷ βουκόλῳ, καὶ ἔμελλον
ψεύδεσθαι πρὸς τοὺς οἴκοι λύκων ἐπιδρομήν,[7] εἴ

<τῆς> E   [1] pq ἐτράπετο   [2] A ξύλῳ τὴν καλαύροπα λαβὼν :
pq ξύλον καὶ τὴν καλ. λαβ. (incorp. gloss)   <τοῦ> Herch.
<τὴν> E   [3] ἀνέβη is the first word of the Great Lacuna
in q : B marg. λείπει φύλλα ε´   [4] so Uii : A τῆς ὅλης
ταινίας : Ui ταῖς τῆς ὅλκῆς ταινίαις : Amyot omits   [5] Ui -τες
[6] Ui -οι : Uii τεθυσόμενοι   [7] A corr. to -ᾱς

the shock was furious. One of them, by the violence
of the very first butt, had one of his horns broke.
Upon the pain and grief of that, all in a fret and
mighty chafe he betakes himself to flight, but the
victor, pursuing him close, would not let him take
breath. Daphnis was vexed to see the horn broke
and that kind of malapertness of the goat. Up he
catches a cudgel, and pursues the pursuer. But as
it frequently happens when one hastes away as fast
as possibly he can and the other with ardency pur-
sues, there was no certain prospect of the things
before them, but into the trap-ditch both fall, first the
goat, then Daphnis. And indeed it was only this
that served to save poor Daphnis, that he flundered
down to the bottom a-cockhorse on the rough goat.
There in a lamentable case he lay, waiting if per-
chance it might be somebody to draw him out.
Chloe seeing the accident, away she flies to the ditch,
and finding he was alive, calls for help to a herdsman
of the adjoining fields. When he was come, he
bustled about for a long cord, which holding, Daphnis
might be drawn up; but finding none, Chloe in a
tearing haste pulls off her stomacher or breastband,
gives him it to let down, and standing on the pit-
brim, they both began to draw and hale; and Daph-
nis, holding fast by it, nimbly followed Chloe's line,
and so ascended to the top. They drew up too the
wretched goat, which now had both his horns broke
(so fiercely did the revenge of the vanquished pursue
him); and they gave him to the herdsman to sacri-
fice, as a reward of the rescue and redemption of
their lives. And if anybody missed him at home,

τις αὐτὸν ποθήσειεν.[1]   αὐτοὶ δὲ ἐπανελθόντες
ἐπεσκοποῦντο τὴν ποίμνην καὶ τὸ αἰπόλιον.

Καὶ ἐπεὶ κατέμαθον ἐν κόσμῳ νομῆς καὶ τὰς
αἶγας καὶ τὰ πρόβατα, καθίσαντες ἐπὶ στελέχει
δρυὸς ἐσκόπουν μή τι μέρος τοῦ σώματος ὁ Δάφνις
ἥμαξε καταπεσών.   τέτρωτο μὲν οὖν οὐδέν,
ἥμακτο οὐδέν, χώματος δὲ καὶ πηλοῦ πέπαστο
καὶ τὰς κόμας καὶ τὸ ἄλλο σῶμα. ἐδόκει δὲ
λούσασθαι πρὶν αἴσθησιν γενέσθαι τοῦ συμβάν-
τος Λάμωνι καὶ Μυρτάλῃ.

13. Καὶ ἐλθὼν ἅμα τῇ Χλόῃ πρὸς τὸ νυμφαῖον,[2]
τῇ μὲν ἔδωκε καὶ τὸν χιτωνίσκον[3] καὶ τὴν πήραν
φυλάττειν,[4] αὐτὸς δὲ τῇ πηγῇ προστὰς τήν τε
κόμην καὶ τὸ σῶμα πᾶν ἀπελούετο. ἦν δὲ ἡ μὲν
κόμη μέλαινα καὶ πολλή, τὸ δὲ σῶμα ἐπίκαυτον
ἡλίῳ· εἴκασεν ἄν τις αὐτὸ χρώζεσθαι τῇ σκιᾷ
τῆς κόμης. ἐδόκει δὲ τῇ Χλόῃ θεωμένῃ καλὸς ὁ
Δάφνις, ὅτι <δὲ οὐ> πρότερον αὐτῇ καλὸς ἐδόκει,
τὸ λουτρὸν ἐνόμιζε τοῦ κάλλους αἴτιον. καὶ τὰ
νῶτα δὲ ἀπολουούσης ἡ σὰρξ καθυπέπιπτε[5] μαλ-
θακή· ὥστε λαθοῦσα ἑαυτῆς ἥψατο πολλάκις, εἰ
τρυφερωτέρα εἴη πειρωμένη. καί, τότε μὲν γὰρ ἐν
δυσμαῖς ἦν ὁ ἥλιος, ἀπήλασαν τὰς ἀγέλας οἴκαδε,
καὶ ἐπεπόνθει Χλόη περιττὸν οὐδέν, ὅτι μὴ Δάφνιν
ἐπεθύμει λουόμενον ἰδέσθαι πάλιν.

Τῆς δὲ ἐπιούσης[6] ὡς ἧκον εἰς τὴν νομήν, ὁ μὲν
Δάφνις ὑπὸ τῇ δρυῒ τῇ συνήθει καθεζόμενος

---

[1] so Schaefer : mss ἐπόθησεν   [2] Ui ἄντρον τῶν Νυμφῶν : Uii
ἀντ. τ. Ν. ἐν ᾧ ἡ πηγή   [3] Ui and ii χιτῶνα   [4] φυλάττειν is
the first word of the Great Lacuna in p : A is the only ms
till the last line of 17   <δὲ οὐ> : Seil. <δὲ μὴ>   [5] so
A (Furia): A (Courier) ὑπέρ.   [6] so A (Fur.): A (Cour.)
ὑστεραίας

they would say it was an invasion of wolves. And
so returned to see after their sheep and goats.

And when they had found that all were feeding
orderly, both goats and sheep, sitting down upon the
trunk of an oak they began curiously to search
whether he had hurt any limb in that terrible fall.
But nothing was hurt, nothing bloodied; only his
hair and the rest of his body were dirtied by mud
and the soil which covered over and hid the trap.
And therefore they thought it best before the
accident was made known to Lamo and Myrtale,
that he should wash himself in the cave of the
Nymphs.

13. And coming there together with Chloe, he
gave her his scrip and his shirt to hold, and standing
by the spring fell to washing himself from top to toe.
Now his hair was long and black, and his body all
brown and sunburnt, insomuch that the one seemed
to have taken colour from the shadow of the tother;
and to Chloe's eye he seemed of a sweet and beauti-
ful aspect, and when she wondered that she had not
deemed him such before, she thought it must be the
washing that was the cause of it. And when she
washed his back and shoulders the flesh yielded so
softly and gently to her hand, that again and again
she privily touched herself to see if hers were more
delicate than his. Sunset now coming on, they drove
home their flocks, and that night there was but one
thing in Chloe's mind, and that the wish she might
see Daphnis at his washing again.

When they came out to pasture in the morning,
and Daphnis, sitting down under the oak where

ἐσύριττε καὶ ἅμα τὰς αἶγας[1] ἐπεσκόπει κατακει-
μένας καὶ ὥσπερ τῶν μελῶν ἀκροωμένας, ἡ δὲ Χλόη
πλησίον καθημένη, τὴν ἀγέλην μὲν τῶν προβά-
των ἐπέβλεπε, τὸ δὲ πλέον εἰς Δάφνιν ἑώρα. καὶ
ἐδόκει καλὸς αὐτῇ συρίττων πάλιν, καὶ αὖθις
αἰτίαν ἐνόμιζε τὴν μουσικὴν τοῦ κάλλους, ὥστε
μετ' ἐκεῖνον καὶ αὐτὴ τὴν σύριγγα ἔλαβεν, εἴ πως
γένοιτο καὶ αὐτὴ καλή. ἔπεισε δὲ αὐτὸν καὶ
λούσασθαι πάλιν καὶ λουόμενον εἶδε καὶ ἰδοῦσα
ἥψατο, καὶ ἀπῆλθε πάλιν ἐπαινέσασα, καὶ ὁ
ἔπαινος ἦν ἔρωτος ἀρχή.

Ὅ τι μὲν οὖν ἔπασχεν οὐκ ᾔδει νέα κόρη καὶ ἐν
ἀγροικίᾳ τεθραμμένη καὶ οὐδὲ ἄλλου λέγοντος
ἀκούσασα τὸ τοῦ ἔρωτος ὄνομα. ἄση[2] δὲ αὐτῆς
εἶχε τὴν ψυχήν, καὶ τῶν ὀφθαλμῶν οὐκ ἐκράτει
καὶ πολλὰ ἐλάλει Δάφνιν· τροφῆς ἠμέλει, νύκτωρ
ἠγρύπνει, τῆς ἀγέλης κατεφρόνει· νῦν ἐγέλα, νῦν
ἔκλαεν· εἶτα ἐκάθευδεν, εἶτα ἀνεπήδα· ὠχρία τὸ
πρόσωπον, ἐρυθήματι αὖθις ἐφλέγετο· οὐδὲ βοὸς
οἴστρῳ πληγείσης τοσαῦτα ἔργα.

Ἐπῆλθόν ποτε αὐτῇ καὶ τοιοίδε λόγοι μόνῃ
γενομένῃ· 14. "Νῦν ἐγὼ νοσῶ μέν, τί δὲ ἡ νόσος
ἀγνοῶ· ἀλγῶ, καὶ ἕλκος οὐκ ἔστι μοι. λυποῦμαι,
καὶ οὐδὲν τῶν προβάτων ἀπόλωλέ μοι· κάομαι,

---

[1] so Cour.: A ἀγέλας cf. 10   [2] A ἄσση

they were wont, played his pipe and watched the
flocks that lay around as if to listen to the music
of it, Chloe, sitting close by, although she looked
well after her sheep, looked better after Daphnis.
And piping there, he seemed again to her goodly
and beautiful to look to, and wondering again,
she thought the cause must be the music; and so,
when he was done, took the pipe from him and
played, if haply she herself might be as beautiful.
Then she asked him if he would come again to
the bath, and when she persuaded him, watched
him at it; and as she watched, put out her hand
and touched him; and before she went home had
praised his beauty, and that praise was the beginning
of love.

What her passion was she knew not, for she
was but a young girl and bred up among clowns,
and as for love, had never so much as heard the
name of it. But her heart was vexed within her,
her eyes, whether she would or no, wandered
hither and thither, and her speaking was ever
Daphnis this and Daphnis that. She could neither
eat nor take her rest; she neglected her flock;
now she would laugh and now would weep, now
would be sleeping and then again up and doing; and
if her cheek was pale, in a twink it was flaming
red. In sum, no heifer stung with a breese [1] was
so resty and changeable as the poor Chloe.

And one day when she was alone she made
such lamentation as this: 14. "I am sick now, but
of what disease? I know not, save that I feel pain
and there is no wound. I mourn, though none
of my sheep is dead. I burn, and here I sit in

[1] gadfly.

καὶ ἐν σκιᾷ τοσαύτῃ κάθημαι. πόσοι βάτοι
με πολλάκις ἤμυξαν, καὶ οὐκ ἔκλαυσα· πόσαι
μέλιτται κέντρα ἐνῆκαν, ἀλλ᾽ οὐκ ἔκραγον.¹ τουτὶ
δὲ τὸ νύττον μου τὴν καρδίαν πάντων ἐκεί-
νων πικρότερον. καλὸς ὁ Δάφνις, καὶ γὰρ τὰ
ἄνθη· καλὸν ἡ σύριγξ αὐτοῦ φθέγγεται, καὶ γὰρ
αἱ ἀηδόνες· ἀλλ᾽ ἐκείνων οὐδείς μοι λόγος. εἴθε
αὐτοῦ σύριγξ ἐγενόμην, ἵν᾽ ἐμπνέῃ μοι· εἴθε αἴξ,
ἵν᾽ ὑπ᾽ ἐκείνου νέμωμαι. ὦ πονηρὸν ὕδωρ, μόνον
Δάφνιν καλὸν ἐποίησας, ἐγὼ δὲ μάτην ἀπελουσά-
μην. οἴχομαι, Νύμφαι, καὶ οὐδὲ ὑμεῖς σώζετε
τὴν παρθένον τὴν ἐν ὑμῖν τραφεῖσαν. τίς ὑμᾶς
στεφανώσει μετ᾽ ἐμέ; τίς τοὺς ἀθλίους ἄρνας
ἀναθρέψει; τίς τὴν λάλον ἀκρίδα θεραπεύσει; ἣν
πολλὰ καμοῦσα ἐθήρασα, ἵνα με κατακοιμίζῃ
φθεγγομένη πρὸ τοῦ ἄντρου, νῦν δὲ ἐγὼ μὲν
ἀγρυπνῶ διὰ Δάφνιν, ἡ δὲ μάτην λαλεῖ."

15. Τοιαῦτα ἔπασχε, τοιαῦτα ἔλεγεν, ἐπιζη-
τοῦσα τὸ ἔρωτος ὄνομα. Δόρκων δὲ ὁ βουκόλος,
ὁ τὸν Δάφνιν ἐκ τοῦ σιροῦ καὶ τὸν τράγον ἀνιμη-
σάμενος, ἀρτιγένειος μειρακίσκος καὶ εἰδὼς ἔρωτος
τὰ ἔργα² καὶ τὸ ὄνομα,³ εὐθὺς μὲν ἐπ᾽ ἐκείνης τῆς
ἡμέρας ἐρωτικῶς τῆς Χλόης διετέθη, πλειόνων δὲ
διαγενομένων μᾶλλον τὴν ψυχὴν ἐξεπυρσεύθη,
καὶ τοῦ Δάφνιδος ὡς παιδὸς καταφρονήσας ἔγνω
κατεργάσασθαι δώροις ἢ βίᾳ.

Τὸ μὲν δὴ πρῶτον⁴ δῶρα αὐτοῖς ἐκόμισε, τῷ
μὲν σύριγγα βουκολικὴν καλάμους ἐννέα χαλκῷ⁵

---

¹ ἀλλ᾽ οὐκ ἔκραγον E : A ἀλλὰ ἔφαγον emendation of ἀλλο
υκραγον (haplogr.)   ² τὰ ἔργα A (Fur.) : A (Cour.) καὶ τὰ
ἔργα   ³ so Hirsch : A plur.   ⁴ so E : A plur.   ⁵ so
A (Cour.) : A (Fur.) χρυσῷ

the deepest shade. How many the briers have torn me, and I have not wept! How many the bees have stung me, and I have not squeaked! But this that pricks my heart is worse to bear than any of those. Daphnis is fair, but so are the flowers; and fair the sound of his pipe, but so is the voice of the nightingales: and yet I care nothing for those. Would to God I might have been his pipe that his mouth might inspirit me, or a goat that he might be my keeper! Thou cruel water! thou hast made Daphnis beautiful, but I for all my washing am still the same. Alas! sweet Nymphs, I am undone, and you will not lift a hand to save your fosterling. Whence shall you get garlands when I am gone? or who shall bring up my poor lambs, and tend the prattling locust I was at such pains to catch? I used to set him before the cave to lull me to sleep with his pretty song, but now long of Daphnis I am fain to watch, and my locust prattles on in vain.''

15. In such case was Chloe, and with such words she spoke, in her seeking after the name of love. But the oxherd Dorco (he that had drawn Daphnis and the he-goat out of the pit), a stripling of the first down, acquainted alike with the name and the works of love, not only on that day was straightway struck with love of Chloe, but every day that followed it he was the more inflamed, till at last, despising Daphnis for a child, he determined either by gifts or force to have his way.

For a beginning he brought them gifts, to Daphnis a pastoral pipe of nine quills bound with brass for

δεδεμένους ἀντὶ κηροῦ, τῇ δὲ νεβρίδα βακχικήν, καὶ αὐτῇ τὸ χρῶμα ἦν ὥσπερ γεγραμμένον χρώμασιν. ἐντεῦθεν δὲ φίλος νομιζόμενος τοῦ μὲν Δάφνιδος ἠμέλει κατ᾽ ὀλίγον, τῇ Χλόῃ δὲ ἀνὰ πᾶσαν ἡμέραν[1] ἐπέφερεν ἢ τυρὸν ἁπαλὸν ἢ στέφανον ἀνθηρὸν ἢ μῆλα ὀπωρινά·[2] ἐκόμισε δέ ποτε αὐτῇ καὶ μόσχον ἀρτιγέννητον[3] καὶ κισσύβιον διάχρυσον καὶ ὀρνίθων ὀρείων νεοττούς. ἡ δὲ ἄπειρος οὖσα τέχνης ἐραστοῦ, λαμβάνουσα μὲν τὰ δῶρα ἔχαιρεν ὅτι Δάφνιδι εἶχεν αὐτὴ χαρίζεσθαι.

Καί, ἔδει γὰρ ἤδη καὶ Δάφνιν γνῶναι τὰ ἔρωτος ἔργα, γίνεταί ποτε τῷ Δόρκωνι πρὸς αὐτὸν[4] ὑπὲρ κάλλους ἔρις, καὶ ἐδίκαζε μὲν Χλόη, ἔκειτο δὲ ἆθλον τῷ νικήσαντι φιλῆσαι Χλόην. Δόρκων δὲ πρότερος ὧδε ἔλεγεν· 16. "Ἐγώ, παρθένε, μείζων εἰμὶ Δάφνιδος, καὶ ἐγὼ μὲν βουκόλος, ὁ δὲ αἰπόλος· τοσοῦτον <οὖν ἐγὼ> κρείττων ὅσον αἰγῶν βόες· καὶ λευκός εἰμι ὡς γάλα καὶ πυρρὸς ὡς θέρος μέλλον ἀμᾶσθαι, καὶ ἔθρεψέ <με> μήτηρ, οὐ θηρίον. οὗτος δέ ἐστι μικρός, καὶ ἀγένειος ὡς γυνή, καὶ μέλας ὡς λύκος. νέμει δὲ τράγους, ὀδωδὼς ἀπ᾽ αὐτῶν[5] δεινόν. καὶ ἔστι πένης ὡς μηδὲ κύνα τρέφειν. εἰ δ᾽, ὡς λέγουσι, καὶ αἲξ αὐτῷ γάλα δέδωκεν, οὐδὲν ἐρίφων διαφέρει."

Ταῦτα καὶ τοιαῦτα ὁ Δόρκων, καὶ μετὰ ταῦτα

---

[1] so Hirsch : A (Cour.) ἀνὰ πάσας ἡμέρας : A (Fur.) ἐν ἀπάσαις ἡμέραις   [2] so A (Fur.) : A (Cour.) μῆλον ὡραῖον ἐκόμισε Cour.: A ἐκόσμησε   [3] so A (Fur.) : A (Cour.) ὀρειγεν.   [4] A αὐτὴν   <οὖν ἐγὼ> Cobet : A has lac. of 6 or 7 letters   <με> Hirsch.   [5] ὀδ. ἀπ᾽ αὐτῶν Cob : A ὀδω and lac.

wax, and to Chloe a fawnskin of the sort that
Bacchae use, the colour of it like the colours of
a painted picture. Soon they believed him their
friend, and he by little and little neglecting Daphnis
came to bring Chloe every day either a dainty
cheese or a garland of flowers or two or three
early apples. And one day he brought her a
young calf, a gilded tankard, and a nest of moun-
tain birds. The simple girl, that knew nothing of
lovers' tricks and wiles, accepts the gifts with
joy; for now she herself had something to give
Daphnis.

And thus (for Daphnis too must then know the
works of love) one day there arises between him and
Dorco a strife and contention of beauty, and the
judge was Chloe, and the prize to kiss Chloe. Dorco
spoke first: 16. "I, sweet girl, am taller then Daphnis,
and an oxherd. He is but a goatherd, and therefore,
as goats are of less account then oxen, so much
the worser man. I am as white as milk, and my
hair as ruddy as the fields before harvest, and what
is more, I had a mother, not a beast, to my nurse.
But this fellow is of little stature ; he has no more
beard then a woman, and is as black as a wolf.
Moreover he tends he-goats, as any may know by
his rankness. And he's so poor that he could not
keep a dog. And if what they say is true, that
he was suckled and nursed up by a she-goat,
he is every whit as much a kid as any in these
fields."

This and the like said Dorco, when Daphnis

DAPHNIS AND CHLOE

ὁ Δάφνις· "'Εμὲ αἲξ ἀνέθρεψεν ὥσπερ τὸν Δία.
νέμω δὲ τράγους τῶν τούτου βοῶν μείζονας· ὄζω
δὲ οὐδὲν ἀπ' αὐτῶν, ὅτι μηδὲ[1] ὁ Πάν, καίτοι γε
ὢν τὸ πλέον τράγος. ἀρκεῖ δέ μοι ὁ τυρὸς καὶ
ἄρτος ὀβελίας καὶ οἶνος λευκός, ὅσα ἀγροίκων
πλουσίων κτήματα. ἀγένειός εἰμι, καὶ γὰρ ὁ
Διόνυσος· μέλας, καὶ γὰρ ὁ ὑάκινθος· ἀλλὰ
κρείττων καὶ ὁ Διόνυσος Σατύρων, ὁ ὑάκινθος
κρίνων. οὗτος δὲ καὶ πυρρὸς ὡς ἀλώπηξ καὶ
προγένειος ὡς τράγος καὶ λευκὸς ὡς ἐξ ἄστεος
γυνή. κἂν δέῃ σε φιλεῖν, ἐμοῦ μὲν φιλεῖς τὸ
στόμα, τούτου δὲ τὰς ἐπὶ τοῦ γενείου τρίχας.
μέμνησο δέ, ὦ παρθένε, ὅτι καὶ σὲ ποίμνιον
ἔθρεψεν, ἀλλὰ καὶ ὡς[2] εἶ καλή."

17. Οὐκέθ' ἡ Χλόη περιέμεινεν, ἀλλὰ τὰ μὲν
ἡσθεῖσα τῷ ἐγκωμίῳ, τὰ δὲ πάλαι ποθοῦσα
φιλῆσαι Δάφνιν, ἀναπηδήσασα αὐτὸν ἐφίλησεν,
ἀδίδακτον μὲν καὶ ἄτεχνον, πάνυ δὲ ψυχὴν θερ-
μᾶναι δυναμένην. Δόρκων μὲν οὖν ἀλγήσας ἀπέ-
δραμε ζητῶν ἄλλην ὁδὸν ἔρωτος· Δάφνις δὲ ὥσπερ
οὐ φιληθεὶς ἀλλὰ δηχθείς, σκυθρωπός τις εὐθὺς ἦν,
καὶ πολλάκις ἐψύχετο, καὶ τὴν καρδίαν παλλο-
μένην κατεῖχε, καὶ βλέπειν μὲν ἤθελε τὴν Χλόην,
βλέπων δὲ ἐρυθήματος[3] ἐπίμπλατο· τότε πρῶτον
καὶ τὴν κόμην αὐτῆς ἐθαύμασεν[4] ὅτι ξανθὴ <ὥσπερ
πῦρ>, καὶ τοὺς ὀφθαλμοὺς ὅτι μεγάλοι[5] καθάπερ
βοός, καὶ τὸ πρόσωπον ὅτι λευκότερον ἀληθῶς
καὶ τοῦ τῶν αἰγῶν γάλακτος, ὥσπερ τότε πρῶτον

---

[1] for οὐδὲ, cf. 19 [2] καὶ ὡς Seil. cf. 11 : Α καὶ [3] so
Cob : Α -τι   [4] so Cour : Α ἔθραυσεν   <ὥσπερ πῦρ>
Naber, cf. 2. 4   [5] so Cour : Α -λη

began thus : "As for me, my foster-mother was a goat, and so was Jove's ; and if I tend he-goats, yet are they finer than this fellow's cows ; and I carry no taint of them neither, for even Pan himself, for all he is more goat then man, is as sweet company as can be.   And as for my living, I have plenty cheese and rye-bread [1] to eat, and good store of white wine to drink, and indeed all that makes a rustic rich is ready to my hand.   If I have no beard to my chin, neither has Bacchus; if I am black,[2] so is the hyacinth ; and yet Bacchus is better then a Satyr and the hyacinth then a lily.   But this man, look you, is red as a fox, bearded as a goat, and white and pale as a city wench.   And if kissing is toward, you may come at my lips, but his kiss is a thing of hairs and bristles.   And lastly, sweet girl, I pray you remember that you too had a mother of the flock, and yet you are of sweet and beautiful aspect."

17. This said, Chloe tarried no longer, but what with his praise of her beauty and her long desiring to kiss him, she started up and gave him a kiss; and though it were the kiss of a novice, 'twas enough to heat and inflame a lover's heart.   With that, Dorco in an agony betakes himself off to seek other means to win his end.   But Daphnis, more like one that is bitten than kissed, was suddenly downcast and sad. He went often cold, and laid hand to his panting heart.   He was fain to look upon Chloe, and yet looking was all on a blush.   Then too for the first time he marvelled at her hair golden as fire, and her eyes great and gentle like the kine's, and bethought him that her face was truly as white as the milk of his

---

[1] the Greek has ' bread baked on the spit,' a cheaper sort.
[2] i.e. dark.

ὀφθαλμοὺς κτησάμενος, τὸν δὲ πρότερον χρόνον
πεπηρωμένος. οὔτε οὖν τροφὴν προσεφέρετο πλὴν
ὅσον ἀπογεύσασθαι, καὶ ποτόν, εἴ ποτε ἐβιάσθη,
μέχρι τοῦ διαβρέξαι[1] τὸ στόμα προσεφέρετο.
σιωπηλὸς ἦν ὁ πρότερον τῶν ἀκρίδων λαλίστερος,
ἀργὸς ὁ περιττότερα τῶν αἰγῶν κινούμενος·
ἠμέλητο[2] ἡ ἀγέλη· ἔρριπτο καὶ ἡ σύριγξ· χλωρό-
τερον τὸ πρόσωπον ἦν πόας[3] καιρίμης. εἰς μόνην
Χλόην ἐγίγνετο λάλος.

Καὶ εἴποτε μόνος ἀπ᾽[4] αὐτῆς ἐγένετο, τοιαῦτα
πρὸς αὑτὸν ἀπελήρει· 18. "Τί ποτέ με Χλόης
ἐργάζεται[5] φίλημα; χείλη μὲν ῥόδων ἁπαλώτερα
καὶ στόμα κηρίων γλυκύτερον, τὸ δὲ φίλημα
κέντρου μελίττης πικρότερον. πολλάκις ἐφίλησα
ἐρίφους, πολλάκις ἐφίλησα σκύλακας ἀρτιγεν-
νήτους καὶ τὸν μόσχον ὃν ὁ Δόρκων ἐδωρήσατο·[6]
ἀλλὰ τοῦτο φίλημα καινόν. ἐκπηδᾷ μου τὸ
πνεῦμα, ἐξάλλεται ἡ καρδία, τήκεται ἡ ψυχή, καὶ
ὅμως πάλιν φιλῆσαι θέλω. ὦ νίκης κακῆς· ὦ
νόσου καινῆς, ἧς οὐδὲ εἰπεῖν οἶδα τὸ ὄνομα· ἆρα
φαρμάκων ἐγεύσατο ἡ Χλόη μέλλουσά με φι-
λεῖν; πῶς οὖν οὐκ ἀπέθανεν; οἷον ᾄδουσιν αἱ
ἀηδόνες, ἡ δὲ ἐμὴ σύριγξ σιωπᾷ· οἷον σκιρτῶσιν
οἱ ἔριφοι, κἀγὼ κάθημαι· οἷον ἀκμάζει τὰ ἄνθη,
κἀγὼ στεφάνους οὐ πλέκω. ἀλλὰ τὰ μὲν ἴα καὶ
ὁ ὑάκινθος ἀνθεῖ, Δάφνις δὲ μαραίνεται. ἆρά μου
καὶ Δόρκων εὐμορφότερος ὀφθήσεται;"

19. Τοιαῦτα ὁ βέλτιστος Δάφνις ἔπασχε καὶ

---

[1] Α ἂν διαβ.   [2] Α ἠμελῆτο   [3] so Cour: Α χλόης corr.
to χλόας   καιρίμης Ε 'at its best': Cour. ἐαρινῆς: Α
καιρινῆς corr. to θερινῆς   [4] so Cour.: Α ἐπ'   αὐτῆς is
the last word of the Great Lacuna in pq   [5] Uiii fut.
[6] pq ἐχαρίσατο

36

goats. Indeed 'twas as if hitherto he had no eyes. And he would none of his meat but a taste in the mouth, nor yet of his drink, if drink he must, save so much as to wet his lips. He that prattled aforetime like a locust, opened not his mouth, he that used to be as resty and gadabout as a goat, sate ever still. His flock was neglected, his pipe flung aside, his cheeks grew paler then grass in season. For Chloe only he found his tongue.

And if ever she left him alone, he fell to mutter with himself such fancies as these : 18. "Whither in the name of the Nymphs will that kiss of Chloe drive me? Her lips are softer then roses, and her mouth sweeter then the honeycombs, but her kiss stings sharper then a bee. I have often kissed the young kids, I have kissed a pretty whippet and that calf which Dorco gave me, but this kiss is a new thing. My heart leaps up to my lips, my spirit sparkles and my soul melts, and yet I am mad to kiss her again. Oh what a mischievous victory is this! Oh what a strange disease, whose very name I know not! Did Chloe take poison before she kissed me? How then is she not dead? How sweetly sing the nightingales, while my pipe is silent! How wantonly the kids skip, and I lie still upon the ground! How sweetly do the flowers grow, and I neglect to make garlands! So it is, the violet and the hyacinth flourish, but alas! Daphnis, Daphnis withers. And will it come at length to this, that Dorco shall appear hereafter handsomer then I?"

19. These passions and complaints the good Daphnis

ἔλεγεν, οἷα πρῶτον γευόμενος τῶν ἔρωτος καὶ
ἔργων καὶ λόγων. ὁ δὲ Δόρκων, ὁ βουκόλος, ὁ
τῆς Χλόης ἐραστής, φυλάξας τὸν Δρύαντα φυτὸν
κατορύττοντα πλησίον κλήματος, πρόσεισιν αὐτῷ
μετὰ τυρίσκων τινῶν γεννικῶν.[1] καὶ τοὺς μὲν
δῶρον[2] εἶναι δίδωσι, πάλαι φίλος ὢν ἡνίκα αὐτὸς
ἔνεμεν, ἐντεῦθεν δὲ ἀρξάμενος ἐνέβαλε λόγον περὶ
τοῦ τῆς Χλόης γάμου. καὶ εἰ λαμβάνοι γυναῖκα,
δῶρα πολλὰ καὶ μεγάλα, ὡς βουκόλος, ἐπηγγέλ-
λετο, ζεῦγος βοῶν ἀροτήρων, σμήνη τέτταρα
μελιττῶν, φυτὰ μηλεῶν πεντήκοντα, δέρμα ταύρου
τεμεῖν ὑποδήματα, μόσχον ἀνὰ πᾶν ἔτος μηκέτι
γάλακτος δεόμενον· ὥστε μικροῦ δεῖν ὁ Δρύας
θελχθεὶς τοῖς δώροις ἐπένευσε τὸν γάμον. ἐννοήσας
δέ, ὡς κρείττονος ἡ παρθένος ἀξία νυμφίου, καὶ
δείσας, φωραθεὶς μήποτε[3] κακοῖς ἀνηκέστοις περι-
πέσῃ,[4] τόν τε γάμον ἀνένευσε καὶ συγγνώμην
ἔχειν ᾐτήσατο καὶ τὰ ὀνομασθέντα δῶρα παρῃ-
τήσατο.

20. Δευτέρας δὴ διαμαρτὼν ἐλπίδος ὁ Δόρκων
καὶ μάτην τυροὺς ἀγαθοὺς ἀπολέσας, ἔγνω διὰ
χειρῶν ἐπιθέσθαι τῇ Χλόῃ μόνῃ γενομένῃ, καὶ
παραφυλάξας ὅτι παρ᾽ ἡμέραν ἐπὶ[5] ποτὸν ἄγουσι
τὰς ἀγέλας ποτὲ μὲν ὁ Δάφνις ποτὲ δὲ ἡ παῖς,
ἐπιτεχνᾶται τέχνην ποιμένι πρέπουσαν· λύκου
δέρμα μεγάλου λαβών, ὃν ταῦρός ποτε πρὸ τῶν
βοῶν μαχόμενος τοῖς κέρασι διέφθειρε, περιέ-
τεινε τῷ σώματι ποδήρες κατανωτισάμενος,

---

[1] Uiii τυρῶν καὶ (from below) συρίγγων (corruption of
τυρίσκων) τινῶν γαμικῶν (emendation following the corrup-
tion) [2] Uiii τυροὺς δῶρον (from gloss on τοὺς) [3] A καὶ
φωρ. μήποτε : pq μὴ φωρ. ποτε [4] p opt. [5] pq ἐπὶ τὸν

felt and murmured to himself, as now first beginning to taste of the works and language of love. But Dorco, the herdsman that loved Chloe, waiting till Dryas was planting the scions of his vines near by, came to him with certain fine cheeses and presented him withal, as one who had long been his acquaintance and friend when he himself tended cattle. And taking his rise from thence, he cast in words about the marrying of Chloe, and, if he might have her to his wife, promised many and great gifts according to the estate of herdsmen: a yoke of oxen for the plough, four hives of bees, fifty choice young apple-trees, a good bull-hide to make shoes, every year a weaned calf. So that it wanted but a little that allured by these gifts Dryas did not promise Chloe. But when he had recollected himself and found the maid deserved a better husband, and likewise that he had reason to fear, lest at any time, being deprehended to have given her to a clown, he should fall into a mischief from which he could no way then escape, he desires to be excused, denies the marriage, rejects the gifts.

20. But Dorco, falling again from his hope and losing his good cheeses, resolves with himself to lay his clutches upon Chloe if ever he could catch her alone. And having observed that by turns one day Daphnis, the next the girl, drove the flocks to watering, he practised a trick not unbecoming one that tended a herd of cattle. He took the skin of a huge wolf, which formerly a bull fighting for the herd had killed with his horns, and flung it o'er his back, and it dangled down to his feet; so that the

ὡς τούς τ᾽ ἐμπροσθίους πόδας ἐφηπλῶσθαι ταῖς
χερσὶ καὶ τοὺς κατόπιν τοῖς σκέλεσιν ἄχρι
πτέρνης, καὶ τοῦ στόματος τὸ χάσμα σκέπειν τὴν
κεφαλὴν ὥσπερ ἀνδρὸς ὁπλίτου κράνος. ἐκ-
θηριώσας δὲ αὑτὸν ὡς ἔνι μάλιστα παραγίνεται
πρὸς τὴν πηγήν, ἧς ἔπινον αἱ αἶγες καὶ τὰ πρό-
βατα μετὰ τὴν νομήν. ἐν κοίλῃ δὲ πάνυ γῇ ἦν ἡ
πηγὴ καὶ περὶ αὐτὴν πᾶς ὁ τόπος ἀκάνθαις,
βάτοις καὶ ἀρκεύθῳ ταπεινῇ καὶ σκολύμοις
ἠγρίωτο· ῥᾳδίως ἂν ἐκεῖ καὶ λύκος ἀληθινὸς ἔλαθε
λοχῶν.[1]

Ἐνταῦθα κρύψας ἑαυτὸν ἐπετήρει τοῦ ποτοῦ τὴν
ὥραν ὁ Δόρκων καὶ πολλὴν εἶχε τὴν[2] ἐλπίδα τῷ
σχήματι φοβήσας λαβεῖν ταῖς χερσὶ τὴν Χλόην.
21. χρόνος ὀλίγος διαγίνεται, καὶ Χλόη κατή-
λαυνε τὰς ἀγέλας εἰς τὴν πηγὴν καταλιποῦσα τὸν
Δάφνιν φυλλάδα χλωρὰν κόπτοντα τοῖς ἐρίφοις
τροφὴν μετὰ τὴν νομήν. καὶ οἱ κύνες, οἱ τῶν
προβάτων ἐπιφύλακες καὶ τῶν αἰγῶν ἑπόμενοι,
οἷα[3] δὴ κυνῶν ἐν ῥινηλασίαις περιεργία, κινού-
μενον τὸν Δόρκωνα[4] πρὸς τὴν ἐπίθεσιν τῆς κόρης
φωράσαντες, πικρὸν μάλα ὑλακτήσαντες ὥρμησαν
ὡς ἐπὶ λύκον, καὶ περισχόντες πρὶν ὅλως ἀνα-
στῆναι[5] δι᾽ ἔκπληξιν, ἔδακνον κατὰ τοῦ δέρματος.[6]
τέως μὲν οὖν τὸν ἔλεγχον αἰδούμενος καὶ ὑπὸ[7] τοῦ
δέρματος ἐπισκέποντος φρουρούμενος ἔκειτο σιω-
πῶν ἐν τῇ λόχμῃ. ἐπεὶ δὲ ἥ τε Χλόη πρὸς τὴν
πρώτην θέαν διαταραχθεῖσα τὸν Δάφνιν ἐκάλει

[1] ApUiii λόχῳ   [2] p ταύτην εἶχε τὴν: q πολλὴν εἶχεν
[3] so Passow: mss οἷα   p ῥινηλασίας and περιεργίᾳ
[4] Uiii omits τὸν Δ.—μάλα   [5] A omits   [6] Uiii μετὰ
κράτους and κατὰ κράτος: B κατὰ κράτος   [7] A ἐπὶ

fore-feet were drawn on his hands, the hinder over his thighs to his heels, and the gaping of the mouth covered his head like the helmet of an armed man. When he was got into this lycanthropy [1] as well as possibly he could, he makes to the fountain where the flocks after their feeding used to drink. But that fountain lay in a bottom, and about it all the place was rough with bushes, thorns, brakes, thistles, and the brush juniper, so that indeed a true wolf might very well lie lurking there.

Therefore, when he had hid himself, he waited the time when the cattle were driven thither to drink, and conceived no small hope that in that habit he should affray and so snap the poor Chloe. 21. After a while she left Daphnis shaking down green leaves for the kids, and drove the flocks down to the fountain. But the flockdogs of the sheep and the goats, following Chloe and (so busy upon the scent are dogs wont to be) catching Dorco in the act to go to set upon the girl, barked furiously and made at him as at a wolf, and before he could wholly rise from the lurk because of the sudden consternation, were all about the wolf-Dorco and biting at his skin. However, fearing lest he should be manifestly discovered, blamed, and shamed, guarding himself as he could with the skin he lay close and still in the thicket. But when Chloe was feared at the first sight and cried out to Daphnis for help, the dogs soon tore

---

[1] made himself a werewolf.

βοηθόν, οἵ τε κύνες περισπῶντες τὸ δέρμα τοῦ σώματος ἥπτοντο αὐτοῦ, μέγα οἰμώξας ἱκέτευε βοηθεῖν τὴν κόρην καὶ τὸν Δάφνιν ἤδη παρόντα. τοὺς μὲν δὴ κύνας ἀνακαλέσαντες συνήθως[1] ταχέως ἡμέρωσαν, τὸν δὲ Δόρκωνα κατά τε μηρῶν καὶ ὤμων δεδηγμένον ἀγαγόντες ἐπὶ τὴν πηγήν, ἀπένιψαν τὰ δήγματα ἵνα ἦσαν τῶν ὀδόντων αἱ ἐμβολαί, καὶ διαμασσησάμενοι φλοιὸν χλωρὸν πτελέας ἐπέπασαν.

Ὑπό τε ἀπειρίας ἐρωτικῶν τολμημάτων ποιμενικὴν παιδιὰν νομίζοντες τὴν ἐπιβολὴν τοῦ δέρματος,[2] οὐδὲν ὀργισθέντες ἀλλὰ καὶ παραμυθησάμενοι καὶ μέχρι τινὸς χειραγωγήσαντες ἀπέπεμψαν. 22. καὶ ὁ μὲν κινδύνου παρὰ τοσοῦτον ἐλθὼν καὶ σωθεὶς ἐκ κυνός, οὐ λύκου, φασίν,[3] στόματος, ἐθεράπευε τὸ σῶμα. ὁ δὲ Δάφνις καὶ ἡ Χλόη κάματον πολὺν ἔσχον μέχρι νυκτὸς τὰς αἶγας καὶ τὰς ὄις συλλέγοντες. ὑπὸ γὰρ τοῦ δέρματος πτοηθεῖσαι καὶ ὑπὸ τῶν κυνῶν ὑλακτησάντων ταραχθεῖσαι, αἱ μὲν εἰς πέτρας ἀνέδραμον, αἱ δὲ μέχρι καὶ τῆς θαλάττης αὐτῆς κατέδραμον. καίτοιγε ἐπεπαίδευντο καὶ φωνῇ πείθεσθαι καὶ σύριγγι θέλγεσθαι καὶ χειροπλαταγῇ[4] συλλέγεσθαι· ἀλλὰ τότε πάντων αὐταῖς ὁ φόβος λήθην ἐνέβαλε. καὶ μόλις ὥσπερ λαγὼς ἐκ τῶν ἰχνῶν εὑρίσκοντες εἰς τὰς ἐπαύλεις ἤγαγον.

---

[1] q ἀνακλήσει συνήθει   [2] p ἐπιβουλὴν τοῦ Δόρκωνος   [3] οὐ λύκου, φασίν so Brunck : mss φασίν, οὐ λύκου   [4] for ill-formed compound cf. 2. 22 λιπεργάτης : pq χειρὸς παταγῇ

his vizard off, tattered the skin, and bit him soundly. Then he roared and cried out amain, and begged for help of Chloe and of Daphnis who was now come up. They rated off the dogs with their usual known recalls, and quickly made them quiet, and they led Dorco, who was torn in the shoulder and the thigh, to the fountain; and where they found the dogs had left the print of their teeth, there they gently washed, and chawing in their mouths the green rine of the elm, applied it softly to his wounds.

Now because of their unskilfulness in amorous adventures, they thought Dorco's disguising and hiding of himself was nothing else but a pastoral prank, and were not at all moved at it. But endeavouring rather to cheer him, and leading him by the hand some part of his way, they bid him farewell and dismissed him. 22. Thus came Dorco out of great danger, and he that was saved from the jaws, not of the wolf in the adage, but of the dog, went home and dressed his wounds. But Daphnis and Chloe had much ado to get together, before it was late in the evening, their scattered straggling sheep and goats. For they were terrified with the wolfskin and the fierce barking and baying of the dogs, and some ran up the steep crags, some ran on rucks [1] and hurried down to the seashore, although they were taught not only to obey the voice and be quieted by the pipe, but to be driven up together even by the clapping of the hands. But fear had cast in an oblivion of all, so that at length with much stir, following their steps like hares by the foot, they drave them home to their own folds.

---

[1] stampeded.

DAPHNIS AND CHLOE

Ἐκείνης μόνης τῆς νυκτὸς ἐκοιμήθησαν βαθὺν
ὕπνον καὶ τῆς ἐρωτικῆς λύπης φάρμακον τὸν
κάματον ἔσχον. αὖθις δὲ ἡμέρας ἐπελθούσης
πάλιν ἔπασχον παραπλήσια. ἔχαιρον ἰδόντες,
ἀπαλλαγέντες[1] ἤλγουν· ἤθελόν τι, ἠγνόουν ὅ τι
θέλουσι. τοῦτο μόνον ᾔδεσαν, ὅτι τὸν μὲν φί-
λημα, τὴν δὲ λουτρὸν ἀπώλεσεν.

Ἐξέκαε δὲ αὐτοὺς καὶ ἡ ὥρα τοῦ ἔτους. 23.
ἦρος ἦν ἤδη τέλος[2] καὶ θέρους ἀρχὴ καὶ πάντα
ἐν ἀκμῇ, δένδρα ἐν καρποῖς, πεδία ἐν ληΐοις·
ἡδεῖα μὲν τεττίγων ἠχή, γλυκεῖα δὲ[3] ὀπώρας
ὀδμή, τερπνὴ[4] δὲ ποιμνίων βληχή. εἴκασεν ἄν
τις καὶ τοὺς ποταμοὺς ᾄδειν ἠρέμα ῥέοντας, καὶ
τοὺς ἀνέμους συρίττειν ταῖς πίτυσιν ἐμπνέοντας,
καὶ τὰ μῆλα ἐρῶντα πίπτειν χαμαί, καὶ τὸν ἥλιον
φιλόκαλον ὄντα πάντας ἀποδύειν. ὁ μὲν δὴ
Δάφνις θαλπόμενος τούτοις ἅπασιν[5] εἰς τοὺς
ποταμοὺς ἐνέβαινε,[6] καὶ ποτὲ μὲν ἐλούετο, ποτὲ
δὲ καὶ τῶν ἰχθύων τοὺς ἐνδινεύοντας ἐθήρα,
πολλάκις δὲ καὶ ἔπινεν, ὡς τὸ ἔνδοθεν καῦμα
σβέσων.

Ἡ δὲ Χλόη, μετὰ τὸ ἀμέλξαι τὰς οἶς καὶ τῶν
αἰγῶν τὰς πολλάς, ἐπὶ πολὺν μὲν χρόνον <πολὺν
πόνον> εἶχε πηγνῦσα τὸ γάλα· δειναὶ γὰρ αἱ
μυῖαι λυπῆσαι καὶ δακεῖν εἰ διώκοιντο· τὸ δὲ

---

[1] so Hirsch: mss ἐλυποῦντο ἀπαλλ.   [2] so Hirsch: mss ἦρ.
οὖν ἤδ. τέλη   [3] pUiii καὶ ἡ τῆς : B lac.   [4] τερπνή—βληχή
and ᾄδειν—ῥέοντας : q has lacunae   [5] Uiii ὑφ᾽ ἅπ.
[6] ἐνέβ.: A ποτ᾽ ἀνέβαινε   <πολὺν πόνον> E

44

That night alone Daphnis and Chloe slept soundly, and found that weariness was some kind of remedy for the passion of love. But as soon as the day appeared they fell again to these fits. When they saw one another they were passing joyful, and sad if it chanced that they were parted. They desired, and yet they knew not what they would have. Only this one thing they knew, that kissing had destroyed Daphnis and bathing had undone Chloe.

Now besides this, the season of the year inflamed and burnt them. 23. For now the cooler spring was ended and the summer was come on, and all things were got to their highest flourishing, the trees with their fruits, the fields with standing corn. Sweet then was the singing of the grasshoppers, sweet was the odour of the fruits, and not unpleasant the very blating of the sheep. A man would have thought that the very rivers, by their gentle gliding away, did sing; and that the softer gales of wind did play and whistle on the pines;[1] that the apples, as languishing with love, fell down upon the ground; and that the Sun, as a lover of beauty unveiled, did strive to undress and turn the rurals all naked. By all these was Daphnis inflamed, and therefore often he goes to the rivers and brooks, there to bathe and cool himself, or to chase the fish that went to and fro in the water. And often he drinks of the clear purls, as thinking by that to quench his inward caum and scorching.

When Chloe had milked the sheep and most of the goats and had spent much time and labour (because the flies were importune and vexatious, and would sting if one chased them) to curdle and

---

[1] there is a play (as above in § 14) upon the word ἐμπνεῖν, which was used of a lover *inspiring* his beloved.

ἐντεῦθεν ἀπολουσαμένη τὸ πρόσωπον πίτυος
ἐστεφανοῦτο κλάδοις καὶ τῇ νεβρίδι ἐζώννυτο, καὶ
τὸν γαυλὸν ἀναπλήσασα οἴνου καὶ γάλακτος
κοινὸν μετὰ τοῦ Δάφνιδος ποτὸν εἶχε.

24. Τῆς δὲ μεσημβρίας ἐπελθούσης ἐγίνετο ἤδη
τῶν ὀφθαλμῶν ἅλωσις αὐτοῖς. ἡ μὲν γὰρ γυμνὸν
ὁρῶσα τὸν Δάφνιν ἐπ᾽ ἄθρουν[1] ἐνέπιπτε τὸ κάλλος
καὶ ἐτήκετο μηδὲν αὐτοῦ μέρος μέμψασθαι δυνα-
μένη, ὁ δὲ ἰδὼν ἐν νεβρίδι καὶ στεφάνῳ πίτυος
ὀρέγουσαν τὸν γαυλόν, μίαν ᾤετο τῶν ἐκ τοῦ
ἄντρου[2] Νυμφῶν ὁρᾶν. ὁ μὲν οὖν τὴν πίτυν ἀπὸ
τῆς κεφαλῆς ἁρπάζων αὐτὸς ἐστεφανοῦτο πρότερον
φιλήσας τὸν στέφανον, ἡ δὲ τὴν ἐσθῆτα αὐτοῦ
λουομένου καὶ γυμνωθέντος ἐνεδύετο πρότερον καὶ
αὐτὴ φιλήσασα. ἤδη ποτὲ καὶ μήλοις ἔβαλον
ἀλλήλους καὶ τὰς κεφαλὰς ἀλλήλων ἐκόσμησαν
διακρίνοντες τὰς κόμας. καὶ ἡ μὲν εἴκασεν αὐτοῦ
τὴν κόμην, ὅτι μέλαινα, μύρτοις, ὁ δὲ μήλῳ τὸ
πρόσωπον αὐτῆς, ὅτι λευκὸν καὶ ἐνερευθὲς ἦν.
ἐδίδασκεν αὐτὴν καὶ συρίττειν, καὶ ἀρξαμένης
ἐμπνεῖν ἁρπάζων τὴν σύριγγα τοῖς χείλεσιν αὐτὸς
τοὺς καλάμους ἐπέτρεχεν·[3] καὶ ἐδόκει μὲν διδά-
σκειν ἁμαρτάνουσαν, εὐπρεπῶς δὲ διὰ τῆς σύριγγος
Χλόην κατεφίλει.[4]

25. Συρίττοντος δὲ αὐτοῦ[5] κατὰ τὸ μεσημβρι-
νὸν καὶ τῶν ποιμνίων σκιαζομένων, ἔλαθεν ἡ
Χλόη κατανυστάξασα. φωράσας τοῦτο ὁ Δάφνις
καὶ καταθέμενος τὴν σύριγγα, πᾶσαν αὐτὴν

---

[1] so Coraes: A ἐπαθροῦν: pq ἐπανθοῦν   [2] pq ἐν τῷ ἄντρῳ
[3] Ap ἐπέλειχεν old var.   [4] p ἐφίλει: q ἐξεφίλει (B lac.)
[5] pq omit (B lac. betw. συρίττον and μεσημ.)

press the milk into cheeses, she would wash herself and crown her head with pine-twigs, and when she had girt her fawnskin about her, take her piggin and with wine and milk make a sillibub for her dear Daphnis and herself.

24. When it grew towards noon they would fall to their catching of one another by their eyes. For Chloe, seeing Daphnis naked, was all eyes for his beauty to view it every whit; and therefore could not choose but melt, as being not able to find in him the least moment to dislike or blame. Daphnis again, if he saw Chloe, in her fawnskin and her pine coronet, give him the sillibub to drink, thought he saw one of the Nymphs of the holy cave. Therefore taking off her pine and kissing it o'er and o'er, he would put it on his own head; and Chloe, when he was naked and bathing, would in her turn take up his vest, and when she kissed it, put it on upon herself. Sometimes now they flung apples at one another, and dressed and distinguished one another's hair into curious trammels and locks. And Chloe likened Daphnis his hair to the myrtle because it was black; Daphnis, again, because her face was white and ruddy, compared it to the fairest apple. He taught her too to play on the pipe, and always when she began to blow would catch the pipe away from her lips and run it presently o'er with his. He seemed to teach her when she was out, but with that specious pretext, by the pipe, he kissed Chloe.

25. But it happened, when he played on his pipe at noon and the cattle took shade, that Chloe fell unawares asleep. Daphnis observed it and laid down his pipe, and without any shame or fear was

DAPHNIS AND CHLOE

ἔβλεπεν ἀπλήστως οἷα μηδὲν αἰδούμενος, καὶ ἅμα
κρύφα¹ ἠρέμα ὑπεφθέγγετο· "Οἷοι καθεύδουσιν
ὀφθαλμοί. οἷον δὲ ἀποπνεῖ στόμα.² οὐδὲ τὰ
μῆλα τοιοῦτον, οὐδὲ αἱ λόχμαι.³ ἀλλὰ φιλῆσαι⁴
δέδοικα· δάκνει τὸ φίλημα τὴν καρδίαν καὶ ὥσπερ
τὸ νέον μέλι μαίνεσθαι ποιεῖ· ὀκνῶ δὲ⁵ καὶ μὴ
φιλήσας αὐτὴν ἀφυπνίσω. ὢ λάλων τεττίγων·
οὐκ ἐάσουσιν αὐτὴν καθεύδειν μέγα ἠχοῦντες.
ἀλλὰ καὶ οἱ τράγοι τοῖς κέρασι παταγοῦσι⁶
μαχόμενοι· ὢ λύκων ἀλωπέκων δειλοτέρων, οἳ
τούτους οὐχ ἥρπασαν."

26. Ἐν τοιούτοις ὄντος αὐτοῦ λόγοις, τέττιξ
φεύγων χελιδόνα θηρᾶσαι θέλουσαν κατέπεσεν εἰς
τὸν κόλπον τῆς Χλόης, καὶ ἡ χελιδὼν ἑπομένη τὸν
μὲν οὐκ ἠδυνήθη λαβεῖν, ταῖς δὲ πτέρυξιν ἐγγὺς
διὰ τὴν δίωξιν γενομένη τῶν παρειῶν αὐτῆς ἥψατο.
ἡ δὲ οὐκ εἰδυῖα τὸ πραχθέν, μέγα βοήσασα τῶν
ὕπνων ἐξέθορεν, ἰδοῦσα δὲ καὶ τὴν χελιδόνα ἔτι
πλησίον πετομένην καὶ τὸν Δάφνιν ἐπὶ τῷ δέει
γελῶντα, τοῦ φόβου μὲν ἐπαύσατο, τοὺς δὲ
ὀφθαλμοὺς ἀπέματτεν ἔτι καθεύδειν θέλοντας.
καὶ ὁ τέττιξ ἐκ τῶν κόλπων ἐπήχησεν ὅμοιον ἱκέτῃ
χάριν ὁμολογοῦντι τῆς σωτηρίας. πάλιν οὖν ἡ
Χλόη μέγα ἀνεβόησεν· ὁ δὲ Δάφνις ἐγέλασε, καὶ
προφάσεως λαβόμενος καθῆκεν αὐτῆς εἰς τὰ
στέρνα τὰς χεῖρας καὶ ἐξάγει τὸν βέλτιστον τέτ-
τιγα μηδὲ ἐν τῇ δεξιᾷ σιωπῶντα. ἡ δὲ ἥδετο
ἰδοῦσα καὶ ἐφίλησε καὶ λαβοῦσα ἐνέβαλεν⁷ αὖθις
τῷ κόλπῳ λαλοῦντα.

---

¹ p ἅμα καὶ αὐτῇ   ² pq τὸ στόμα   ³ Wyttenbach ὄχναι
⁴ Uiii φιλεῖν μὲν : B φιλ and lac.   ⁵ Uiii omits καὶ μὴ :
pq μὴ καὶ   ⁶ so Hirsch : mss παιοῦσι   ⁷ A ἔβαλεν

bold to view her, all over and every limb, insatiably ; and withal spoke softly thus : " What sweet eyes are those that sleep ! How sweetly breathes that rosy mouth ! The apples smell not like to it, nor the flowery lawns and thickets. But I am afraid to kiss her. For her kiss stings to my heart and makes me mad like new honey. Besides, I fear lest a kiss should chance to wake her. Oh the prating grasshoppers ! they make a noise to break her sleep. And the goats beside are fighting, and they clatter with their horns. Oh the wolves, worse dastards then the foxes, that they have not ravished them away ! "

26. While he was muttering this passion, a grasshopper that fled from a swallow took sanctuary in Chloe's bosom. And the pursuer could not take her, but her wing by reason of her close pursuit slapped the girl upon the cheek. And she not knowing what was done cried out, and started from her sleep. But when she saw the swallow flying near by and Daphnis laughing at her fear, she began to give it over and rub her eyes that yet would be sleeping. The grasshopper sang out of her bosom, as if her suppliant were now giving thanks for the protection. Therefore Chloe again squeaked out ; but Daphnis could not hold laughing, nor pass the opportunity to put his hand into her bosom and draw forth friend Grasshopper, which still did sing even in his hand. When Chloe saw it she was pleased and kissed it, and took and put it in her bosom again, and it prattled all the way.

27. Ἔτερψεν αὐτούς ποτε[1] φάττα βουκολικὸν ἐκ τῆς ὕλης φθεγξαμένη. καὶ τῆς Χλόης ζητούσης μαθεῖν ὅ τι λέγει, διδάσκει αὐτὴν ὁ Δάφνις μυθολογῶν[2] τὰ θρυλούμενα· "Ἦν οὕτω, παρθένε, παρθένος[3] καλή, καὶ ἔνεμε βοῦς πολλὰς οὕτως ἐν ὕλῃ.[4] ἦν δὲ ἄρα καὶ ᾠδική, καὶ ἐτέρποντο αἱ βόες ἐπ' αὐτῆς τῇ μουσικῇ, καὶ ἔνεμεν οὔτε καλαύροπος πληγῇ οὔτε κέντρου προσβολῇ, ἀλλὰ καθίσασα ὑπὸ πίτυν καὶ στεφανωσαμένη πίτυϊ ᾖδε Πᾶνα καὶ τὴν Πίτυν, καὶ αἱ βόες τῇ φωνῇ παρέμενον. παῖς οὐ μακρὰν νέμων βοῦς καὶ αὐτὸς καλὸς καὶ ᾠδικὸς[5] φιλονεικήσας πρὸς τὴν μελῳδίαν, μείζονα ὡς ἀνήρ, ἡδεῖαν ὡς παῖς, φωνὴν ἀντεπεδείξατο, καὶ τῶν βοῶν ὀκτὼ τὰς ἀρίστας ἐς τὴν ἰδίαν ἀγέλην θέλξας ἀπεβουκόλησεν. ἄχθεται ἡ παρθένος τῇ βλάβῃ τῆς ἀγέλης, τῇ ἥττῃ τῆς ᾠδῆς, καὶ εὔχεται τοῖς θεοῖς ὄρνις γενέσθαι πρὶν οἴκαδε ἀφικέσθαι. πείθονται οἱ θεοὶ καὶ ποιοῦσι τήνδε τὴν[6] ὄρνιν ὄρειον καὶ μουσικὴν[7] ὡς ἐκείνην. καὶ ἔτι νῦν ᾄδουσα μηνύει τὴν συμφοράν, ὅτι βοῦς ζητεῖ πεπλανημένας."

28. Τοιάσδε τέρψεις αὐτοῖς τὸ θέρος παρεῖχε. μετοπώρου δὲ ἀκμάζοντος καὶ τοῦ βότρυος, Τύριοι λῃσταὶ Καρικὴν ἔχοντες ἡμιολίαν ὡς μὴ[8] δοκοῖεν βάρβαροι, προσέσχον τοῖς ἀγροῖς, καὶ ἐκβάντες

---

[1] q τότε and βουκολικὴ   [2] mss -εῖν   [3] p παρθένος παρθένε οὕτω : q παρθένος παρθένε ὡς σὺ οὕτω: cf. Plat. *Phaedr.* 237 B
[4] q ἡλικίᾳ   [5] καὶ ᾠδ. A : pq ᾠδ.: mss add ὡς ἡ παρθένος incorp. gloss on καὶ αὐτὸς   [6] p omits τὴν ; but supply αὐτὴν with ποιοῦσι   [7] A ὄρειον ἡ παρθένος μουσ.(ἡ παρθ. gloss on ἐκείνην): pq ὄρ. ὡς παρθένον μουσ. (correction of ἡ παρθ.)
[8] so Uiii and prob. B : A ἂν : p ἴσως μὴ (ἴσως shows the corrector)

27. But besides these the stock-dove did delight them too, and sang from the woods her country song. But Chloe, desiring to know, asked Daphnis what that complaint of the stock-dove meant. And he told her the tradition of the ancient shepherds: "There was once, maiden, a very fair maid who kept many cattle in the woods. She was skilful in music, and her herds were so taken with her voice and pipe, that they needed not the discipline of the staff or goad, but sitting under a pine and wearing a coronet of the same she would sing of Pan and the Pine, and her cows would never wander out of her voice. There was a youth that kept his herd not far off, and he also was fair and musical, but as he tried with all his skill to emulate her notes and tones, he played a louder strain as a male, and yet sweet as being young, and so allured from the maid's herd eight of her best cows to his own. She took it ill that her herd was so diminished and in very deep disdain that she was his inferior at the art, and presently prayed to the Gods that she might be transformed to a bird before she did return home. The Gods consent, and turned her thus into a mountain bird, because the maid did haunt there, and musical, as she had been. And singing still to this day she publishes her heavy chance and demands her truant cows again."

28. Such delights and pleasures as these the summer-time entertained them withal. But when autumn was coming in and the grapes were ripening, some Tyrian pirates, in a Carian vessel lest perchance they should seem to be barbarians, sailed up to the

σὺν μαχαίραις καὶ ἡμιθωρακίοις κατέσυρον πάντα
τὰ εἰς χεῖρας ἐλθόντα, οἶνον ἀνθοσμίαν, πυρὸν
ἄφθονον, μέλι ἐν κηρίοις· ἤλασάν τινας καὶ
βοῦς ἐκ τῆς Δόρκωνος ἀγέλης. λαμβάνουσι
καὶ τὸν Δάφνιν ἀλύοντα παρὰ¹ τὴν θάλατταν· ἡ
γὰρ Χλόη βραδύτερον ὡς κόρη² τὰ πρόβατα
ἐξῆγε τοῦ Δρύαντος φόβῳ τῶν ἀγερώχων ποιμέ-
νων. ἰδόντες δὲ μειράκιον μέγα καὶ καλὸν καὶ
κρεῖττον τῆς ἐξ ἀγρῶν ἁρπαγῆς, μηκέτι μηδὲν
μηδὲ εἰς τὰς αἶγας μηδὲ εἰς τοὺς ἄλλους ἀγροὺς
περιεργασάμενοι, κατῆγον αὐτὸν ἐπὶ τὴν ναῦν
κλάοντα καὶ ἠπορημένον καὶ μέγα Χλόην κα-
λοῦντα. καὶ οἱ μὲν ἄρτι τὸ πεῖσμα ἀπολύσαντες
καὶ τὰς κώπας ἐμβαλόντες³ ἀπέπλεον εἰς τὸ
πέλαγος.

Χλόη δὲ κατήλαυνε τὸ ποίμνιον σύριγγα καινὴν
τῷ Δάφνιδι δῶρον κομίζουσα. ἰδοῦσα δὲ τὰς
αἶγας τεταραγμένας καὶ ἀκούσασα τοῦ Δάφνιδος
ἀεὶ μεῖζον αὐτὴν βοῶντος, προβάτων μὲν ἀμελεῖ
καὶ τὴν σύριγγα ῥίπτει, δρόμῳ δὲ πρὸς τὸν
Δόρκωνα παραγίνεται δεησομένη βοηθεῖν. 29. ὁ
δὲ ἔκειτο πληγαῖς νεανικαῖς συγκεκομμένος ὑπὸ
τῶν λῃστῶν καὶ ὀλίγον ἐμπνέων, αἵματος πολλοῦ
χεομένου.⁴ ἰδὼν δὲ τὴν Χλόην καὶ ὀλίγον ἐκ
τοῦ πρότερον ἔρωτος ἐμπύρευμα λαβών, "Ἐγὼ
μέν," εἶπε, "Χλόη, τεθνήξομαι μετ' ὀλίγον· οἱ
γάρ με ἀσεβεῖς λῃσταὶ πρὸ τῶν βοῶν μαχόμενον
κατέκοψαν ὡς βοῦν. σὺ δὲ καὶ σοὶ⁵ Δάφνιν
σῶσον κἀμοὶ τιμώρησον κἀκείνους ἀπόλεσον.

---

¹ so Cob : mss περὶ   ² p γυνὴ   ³ pq ταῖς χερσὶν ἐμβ.
⁴ q φερομένου   A ἰδὼν τὴν : pq ἰδ. δὲ καὶ τὴν   ⁵ A σὺ δὲ
σοὶ καὶ : p σοὶ δέ μοι καὶ : q σὺ δέ μοι καὶ

fields, and coming ashore armed with swords and half-corslets, fell to rifle, plunder, and carry away all that came to hand, the fragrant wines, great store of grain, honey in the comb. Some oxen too they drove away from Dorco's herd, and took Daphnis as he wandered by the sea. For Chloe, as a maid, was fearful of the fierce and surly shepherds, and therefore, till it was somewhat later, drove not out the flocks of Dryas. And when they saw the young man was proper and handsome and of a higher price then any of their other prey, they thought it not worth their staying longer about the goats or other fields, and hauled him aboard lamenting and not knowing what to do, and calling loud and often on the name of Chloe. And so, waiting only till they had loosed from the shore and cast in their oars, they made in haste away to sea.

Meanwhile Chloe had brought out her sheep, and with her a new pipe that was to be a gift to Daphnis. When Chloe saw the goats in a hurry,[1] and heard Daphnis louder and louder call "Chloe," she presently casts off all care of her flocks, flings the pipe on the ground, and runs amain for help to Dorco. 29. But he, being cruelly wounded by the thieves and breathing yet a little, his blood gushing out, was laid along upon the ground. Yet seeing Chloe, and a little spark of his former love being awakened in him, "Chloe," said he, "I shall now presently die, for alas! those cursed thieves, as I fought for my herd, have killed me like an ox. But do thou preserve Daphnis for thyself, and in their sudden destruction take vengeance on the rogues for me. I

---

[1] commotion.

ἐπαίδευσα τὰς βοῦς ἤχῳ σύριγγος ἀκολουθεῖν
καὶ διώκειν τὸ μέλος αὐτῆς, κἂν νέμωνταί ποι[1]
μακράν. ἴθι δή, λαβοῦσα τὴν σύριγγα ταύτην
ἔμπνευσον αὐτῇ μέλος ἐκεῖνο, ὃ Δάφνιν μὲν
ἐγώ ποτε ἐδιδαξάμην, σὲ δὲ Δάφνις.[2] τὸ δὲ
ἐντεῦθεν τῇ σύριγγι μελήσει καὶ τῶν βοῶν ταῖς
ἐκεῖ. χαρίζομαι δέ σοι[3] καὶ τὴν σύριγγα αὐτήν,
ᾗ πολλοὺς ἐρίζων καὶ βουκόλους ἐνίκησα καὶ
αἰπόλους. σὺ δὲ ἀντὶ τῶνδε καὶ ζῶντα ἔτι
φίλησον καὶ ἀποθανόντα κλαῦσον, κἂν ἴδῃς
ἄλλον νέμοντα τὰς βοῦς, ἐμοῦ μνημόνευσον."
30. Δόρκων μὲν τοσαῦτα εἰπὼν καὶ φίλημα
φιλήσας ὕστατον ἀφῆκεν ἅμα τῷ φιλήματι καὶ
τῇ φωνῇ τὴν ψυχήν.

Ἡ δὲ Χλόη λαβοῦσα τὴν σύριγγα καὶ ἐνθεῖσα
τοῖς χείλεσιν ἐσύριττε μέγιστον ὡς ἐδύνατο. καὶ
αἱ βόες ἀκούουσι καὶ τὸ μέλος γνωρίζουσι, καὶ
ὁρμῇ μιᾷ μυκησάμεναι πηδῶσιν εἰς τὴν θάλατταν.
βιαίου δὲ πηδήματος εἰς ἕνα τοῖχον τῆς νεὼς
γενομένου καὶ ἐκ τῆς ἐμπτώσεως[4] τῶν βοῶν
κοίλης τῆς θαλάττης διαστάσης, στρέφεται μὲν
ἡ ναῦς καὶ τοῦ κλύδωνος συνιόντος ἀπόλλυται.
οἱ δὲ ἐκπίπτουσιν οὐχ ὁμοίαν ἔχοντες ἐλπίδα
σωτηρίας. οἱ μὲν γὰρ λῃσταὶ τὰς μαχαίρας
παρήρτηντο καὶ τὰ ἡμιθωράκια λεπιδωτὰ ἐνεδέ-
δυντο καὶ κνημῖδας εἰς μέσην κνήμην ὑπεδέδεντο·
ὁ δὲ Δάφνις ἀνυπόδητος ὡς ἐν πεδίῳ νέμων,
καὶ ἡμίγυμνος ὡς ἔτι τῆς ὥρας οὔσης καυμα-
τώδους. ἐκείνους μὲν οὖν ἐπ' ὀλίγον νηξαμένους
κατήνεγκε τὰ ὅπλα εἰς βυθόν, ὁ δὲ Δάφνις τὴν
μὲν ἐσθῆτα ῥᾳδίως ἀπεδύσατο,[5] περὶ δὲ τὴν

[1] q μοι [2] A Δαφ. δὲ σέ [3] Uiii omits [4] A ἐκπτώσεως [5] pq impf.

have accustomed my herd to follow the sound of a pipe, and to obey the charm of it although they feed a good way off me. Come hither then and take this pipe, and blow that tune which I heretofore taught Daphnis and Daphnis thee. Leave the care of what shall follow to the pipe and to the cows which are yonder. And to thee, Chloe, I give the pipe, this pipe by which I have often conquered many herdsmen, many goatherds. But, for this, come and kiss me, sweet Chloe, while I am yet awhile alive ; and when I am dead, weep a tear or two o'er me, and if thou seest some other tending my herd upon these hills, I pray thee then remember Dorco." 30. Thus spake Dorco and received his last kiss ; and together with the kiss and his voice, breathed out his soul.

But Chloe, taking the pipe and putting it to her lips, began to play and whistle as loud as possibly she could. The cows aboard the pirates presently hear and acknowledge[1] the music, and with one bounce and a huge bellowing shoot themselves impetuously into the sea. By that violent bounding on one of her sides the pinnace toppled, and the sea gaping from the bottom by the fall of the cows in, the surges on a sudden return and sink her down and all that were in her, but with unequal hope of escape. For the thieves had their swords on with their scaled and nailed corslets, and greaves up to the middle of their shins. But Daphnis was barefoot because he was tending his flocks in the plain, and half-naked, it being yet the heat of summer. Wherefore they, when they had swom a little while, were carried by their arms to the bottom. Daphnis on the other side, easily got off his clothes, and yet was much

---

[1] recognise.

νῆξιν ἔκαμνεν[1] οἷα πρότερον νηχόμενος ἐν ποτα-
μοῖς μόνοις. ὕστερον δὲ παρὰ τῆς ἀνάγκης τὸ
πρακτέον διδαχθεὶς εἰς μέσας ὥρμησε τὰς βοῦς,
καὶ βοῶν δύο[2] κεράτων ταῖς δύο χερσὶ λαβόμενος
ἐκομίζετο μέσος ἀλύπως καὶ ἀπόνως, ὥσπερ
ἐλαύνων ἅμαξαν. νήχεται δὲ ἄρα βοῦς, ὅσον
οὐδὲ ἄνθρωπος· μόνον λείπεται τῶν ἐνύδρων
ὀρνίθων[3] καὶ αὐτῶν ἰχθύων. οὐδ' ἂν ἀπόλοιτο
βοῦς νηχόμενος, εἰ μὴ τῶν χηλῶν οἱ ὄνυχες
περιπέσοιεν[4] διάβροχοι γενόμενοι. μαρτυροῦσι
τῷ λόγῳ μέχρι νῦν πολλοὶ τόποι τῆς θαλάττης,
Βοὸς πόροι λεγόμενοι.

31. Καὶ σώζεται μὲν δὴ τοῦτον τὸν τρόπον
ὁ Δάφνις δύο κινδύνους παρ' ἐλπίδα πᾶσαν
διαφυγών, λῃστηρίου καὶ ναυαγίου. ἐξελθὼν δὲ
καὶ τὴν Χλόην ἐπὶ τῆς γῆς γελῶσαν ἅμα καὶ
δακρύουσαν εὑρών, ἐμπίπτει τε αὐτῆς τοῖς κόλ-
ποις καὶ ἐπυνθάνετο τί βουλομένη συρίσειεν.
ἡ δὲ αὐτῷ διηγεῖται πάντα, τὸν δρόμον τὸν ἐπὶ
τὸν Δόρκωνα, τὸ παίδευμα τῶν βοῶν, πῶς
κελευσθείη συρίσαι, καὶ ὅτι τέθνηκε Δόρκων·
μόνον αἰδεσθεῖσα τὸ φίλημα οὐκ εἶπεν.

Ἔδοξε δὲ τιμῆσαι τὸν εὐεργέτην, καὶ ἐλθόντες
μετὰ τῶν προσηκόντων Δόρκωνα θάπτουσι τὸν
ἄθλιον. γῆν μὲν οὖν πολλὴν ἐπέθεσαν, φυτὰ
δὲ ἥμερα πολλὰ ἐφύτευσαν, καὶ ἐξήρτησαν αὐτῷ
τῶν ἔργων ἀπαρχάς. ἀλλὰ καὶ γάλα κατέ-
σπεισαν καὶ βότρυς κατέθλιψαν καὶ σύριγγας

---

[1] A aor.   [2] p δύο βοῶν δύο : q δύο βοῶν   [3] q omits
[4] Naber περισαπεῖεν

56

puzzled to swim because he had been used before only to the brooks and rivers. But at length, being taught by necessity what was best for him to do, he rushes into the midst of the cows and on his right and left laid hold on two of their horns, and so without trouble or pain was carried between them to the land as if he had driven a chariot. Now an ox or cow swim so well that no man can do the like, and they are exceeded only by water-fowl and fish; nor do they ever drown and perish unless the nails upon their hooves be thorough drenched with wet and fall. Witness to this those several places of the sea to this day called *Bospori*, the trajects or the narrow seas swom over by oxen.

31. And thus poor Daphnis was preserved, escaping beyond hope two dangers at once, shipwrack and latrociny. When he was out, he found Chloe on the shore laughing and crying; and casting himself into her arms asked her what she meant when she piped and whistled so loud. Then she told him all that had happened, how she scuttled up to Dorco, how the cows had been accustomed, how she was bidden to play on the pipe, and that their friend Dorco was dead; only for shame she told him not of that kiss.

They thought then it was their duty to honour their great benefactor, and therefore they went with his kinsfolk to bury the unfortunate Dorco. They laid good store of earth upon the corse, and on his grave they set abundance of the most fragrant lasting sative[1] plants and flowers, and made a suspension to him of some of the first-fruits of their labour. Besides they poured on the ground a libation of milk, and pressed with their hands the fairest bunches of the

---

[1] cultivated.

πολλὰς κατέκλασαν. ἠκούσθη καὶ τῶν βοῶν
ἐλεεινὰ μυκήματα καὶ δρόμοι τινὲς ὤφθησαν
ἅμα τοῖς μυκήμασιν ἄτακτοι· καί, ὡς ἐν ποιμέσιν
εἰκάζετο καὶ αἰπόλοις, ταῦτα θρῆνος ἦν τῶν
βοῶν ἐπὶ βουκόλῳ τετελευτηκότι.

32. Μετὰ δὲ τὸν Δόρκωνος τάφον λούει τὸν
Δάφνιν ἡ Χλόη πρὸς τὰς Νύμφας ἀγαγοῦσα εἰς
τὸ ἄντρον.[1] καὶ αὐτὴ τότε πρῶτον Δάφνιδος
ὁρῶντος ἐλούσατο τὸ σῶμα λευκὸν καὶ καθαρὸν
ὑπὸ κάλλους καὶ οὐδὲν[2] λουτρῶν ἐς κάλλος
δεόμενον. καὶ ἄνθη δὲ[3] συλλέξαντες, ὅσα ἄνθη[4]
τῆς ὥρας ἐκείνης, ἐστεφάνωσαν τὰ ἀγάλματα
καὶ τὴν τοῦ Δόρκωνος σύριγγα τῆς πέτρας
ἐξήρτησαν ἀνάθημα. καὶ μετὰ τοῦτο ἐλθόντες
ἐπεσκοποῦντο[5] τὰς αἶγας καὶ τὰ πρόβατα.
τὰ δὲ πάντα κατέκειτο μήτε νεμόμενα μήτε
βληχώμενα, ἀλλ᾽, οἶμαι, τὸν Δάφνιν καὶ τὴν
Χλόην ἀφανεῖς ὄντας ποθοῦντα. ἐπεὶ[6] γοῦν
ὀφθέντες καὶ ἐβόησαν τὸ σύνηθες καὶ ἐσύρισαν,
τὰ μὲν <ποίμνια> ἀναστάντα ἐνέμετο, αἱ δὲ
αἶγες ἐσκίρτων φριμασσόμεναι, καθάπερ ἡδόμεναι
σωτηρίᾳ συνήθους αἰπόλου.

Οὐ μὴν ὁ Δάφνις χαίρειν ἔπειθε τὴν ψυχὴν
ἰδὼν τὴν Χλόην γυμνὴν καὶ τὸ πρότερον λανθάνον
κάλλος ἐκκεκαλυμμένον. ἤλγει τὴν καρδίαν ὡς
ἐσθιομένην ὑπὸ φαρμάκων. καὶ αὐτὸ τὸ πνεῦμα
ποτὲ μὲν λάβρον ἐξέπνει καθάπερ τινὸς διώ-

[1] p λούτρον : mss add εἰσαγαγοῦσα   [2] so Cob : mss οὐδὲ
[3] so E : mss τε   [4] Erfurdt ἀνθεῖ   [5] so E, cf. 12 : A
ἐσκόπουν : pq ἐπεσκόπουν   [6] pq ἐπειδὴ : cf. 2. 2   <ποίμνια>
Herch.

grapes, and then broke many shepherd's-pipes o'er him. There were heard miserable groans and bellowings of the cows and oxen, and together with them certain incomposed cursations and freaks were seen. The cattle amongst themselves (so the goatherds and the shepherds thought) had a kind of lamentation for the death and loss of their keeper.

32. When the funeral of Dorco was done, Chloe brought Daphnis to the cave of the Nymphs and washed him with her own hands. And she herself, Daphnis then first of all looking and gazing on her, washed her naked limbs before him, her limbs which for their perfect and most excellent beauty needed neither wash nor dress. And when they had done, they gathered of all the flowers of the season to crown the statues of the Nymphs, and hanged up Dorco's charming pipe for an offering in the fane. Then coming away they looked what became of their sheep and goats, and found that they neither fed nor blated, but were all laid upon the ground, peradventure as wanting Daphnis and Chloe that had been so long out of their sight. Certainly when they appeared and had called and whistled as they were wont, the sheep rose up presently and fell to feed, and the mantling[1] goats skipped and leapt as rejoicing at the safety of their familiar goatherd.

But Daphnis for his life could not be merry, because he had seen Chloe naked, and that beauty which before was not unveiled. His heart ached as though it were gnawed with a secret poison, insomuch that sometimes he puffed and blowed thick and short as if somebody had been in a close pursuit of him,

---

[1] eagerly desiring.

κοντος αὐτόν, ποτὲ δὲ ἐπέλειπε[1] καθάπερ ἐκδα-
πανηθὲν ἐν ταῖς προτέραις ἐπιδρομαῖς. ἐδόκει
τὸ λουτρὸν εἶναι τῆς θαλάττης φοβερώτερον.
ἐνόμιζε τὴν ψυχὴν ἔτι παρὰ τοῖς λῃσταῖς μένειν,
οἷα νέος καὶ[2] ἄγροικος καὶ ἔτι ἀγνοῶν τὸ Ἔρωτος
λῃστήριον.

[1] so p, prob. old var. : Aq ἐπέλιπε   [2] pq omit

sometimes again he breathed so faintly as if his breath had bin quite spent in the late incursions. That washing seemed to him more dangerous and formidable then the sea, and he thought his life was still in the hands and at the dispose of the Tyrian pirates, as being a young rustic and yet unskilled in the assassinations and robberies of Love.

THE END OF THE FIRST BOOK

THE SECOND BOOK

A SUMMARY OF THE SECOND BOOK

THE *Vintage is kept and solemnized.*

*After that, Daphnis and Chloe return to the fields.
Philetas the herdsman entertains them with a discourse of
Cupid and love. Love increases betwixt them. In the
mean time the young men of Methymna come into the
fields of Mytilene to hawk and hunt. Their pinnace
having lost her cable, they fasten her to the shore with a
with. A goat gnaws the with in pieces. The ship with
her money and other riches is blown off to sea. The
Methymnaeans, madded at it, look about for him that did
it. They light upon Daphnis and pay him soundly.
The country lads come in to help him. Philetas is
constituted judge. A Methymnaean is plaintiff, Daphnis
defendant. Daphnis carries the day. The Methymnaeans
fall to force, but are beaten off with clubs. Getting home
they complain of injury and loss by the Mytilenians.
The Methymnaeans presently command Bryaxis their
general to move with 10 ships against the Mytilenians
knowing nothing. They land at the fields, plunder all
they can lay their hands on, and carry away Chloe.*

A SUMMARY OF THE SECOND BOOK

Daphnis, knowing it, would die, but the Nymphs comfort him. Pan sends a terror (which is rarely described) upon the Methymnaeans, and warns their captain in his sleep to bring back Chloe. The captain obeys, and she returns joyful to Daphnis. They keep holy-days to Pan, and Philetas is there. Lamo tells the Story of the Pipe. Philetas gives Daphnis his most artificial pipe. Daphnis and Chloe proceed to the binding of one another by amorous oaths.

ΛΟΓΟΣ ΔΕΥΤΕΡΟΣ

1. Ἤδη δὲ τῆς ὀπώρας ἀκμαζούσης καὶ ἐπεί-
γοντος τοῦ τρυγητοῦ, πᾶς ἦν κατὰ τοὺς ἀγροὺς
ἐν ἔργῳ. ὁ μὲν ληνοὺς ἐπεσκεύαζεν, ὁ δὲ πίθους
ἐξεκάθαιρεν, ὁ δὲ ἀρρίχους ἔπλεκεν· [1] ἔμελέ τινι
δρεπάνης μικρᾶς ἐς βότρυος τομήν, καὶ ἑτέρῳ
λίθου θλῖψαι τὰ ἔνοινα τῶν βοτρύων δυναμένου,
καὶ ἄλλῳ λύγου ξηρᾶς πληγαῖς κατεξασμένης,
ὡς ἂν ὑπὸ φωτὶ νύκτωρ τὸ γλεῦκος φέροιτο.
ἀμελήσαντες οὖν καὶ ὁ Δάφνις καὶ ἡ Χλόη τῶν
αἰγῶν καὶ τῶν προβάτων χειρὸς ὠφέλειαν ἄλλην
ἄλλοις [2] μετεδίδοσαν. ὁ μὲν ἐβάσταζεν ἐν ἀρ-
ρίχοις βότρυς, καὶ ἐπάτει ταῖς ληνοῖς ἐμβάλλων,
καὶ εἰς τοὺς πίθους ἔφερε τὸν οἶνον, ἡ δὲ τροφὴν
παρεσκεύαζε τοῖς τρυγῶσι, καὶ ἐνέχει ποτὸν
αὐτοῖς πρεσβύτερον οἶνον, καὶ τῶν ἀμπέλων δὲ
τὰς ταπεινοτέρας ἀπετρύγα. πᾶσα γὰρ κατὰ
τὴν Λέσβον ἄμπελος [3] ταπεινή, οὐ μετέωρος
οὐδὲ ἀναδενδράς, ἀλλὰ κάτω τὰ κλήματα ἀπο-
τείνουσα καὶ ὥσπερ κιττὸς νεμομένη· καὶ παῖς
ἂν ἐφίκοιτο [4] βότρυος ἄρτι τὰς χεῖρας ἐκ σπαρ-
γάνων λελυμένος.

---

[1] Uiii ἐπελέκιζεν   [2] ἄλλην ἄλλοις E : mss ἀλλήλοις
   A ἐβάπτιζεν   [3] so Herch : mss ἦν ἄμπ.   [4] A ἀφίκ.

THE SECOND BOOK

1. The autumn now being grown to its height and the vintage at hand, every rural began to stir and be busy in the fields, some to repair the wine presses, some to scour the tuns and hogsheads; others were making baskets, skeps, and panniers, and others providing little hooks to catch and cut the bunches of the grapes. Here one was looking busily about to find a stone that would serve him to bruise the stones of grapes, there another furnishing himself with dry willow-wood [1] brayed in a mortar, to carry away [2] the must in the night with light before him. Wherefore Daphnis and Chloe for this time laid aside the care of the flocks, and put their helping hands to the work. Daphnis in his basket carried grapes, cast them into the press and trod them there, and then anon tunned the wine into the butts. Chloe dressed meat for the vintagers and served them with drink of the old wine, or gathered grapes of the lower vines. For all the vines about Lesbos, being neither high-grown nor propped with trees, incline themselves and protend their palmits towards the ground, and creep like the ivy; so that indeed a very infant, if that his hands be loose from his swathes, may easily reach and pull a bunch.

---

[1] *i.e.* to make some sort of torch or lamp. [2] draw off.

DAPHNIS AND CHLOE

2. Οἷον οὖν εἰκὸς ἐν ἑορτῇ Διονύσου καὶ
οἴνου γενέσει, αἱ μὲν γυναῖκες ἐκ τῶν πλησίον
ἀγρῶν εἰς ἐπικουρίαν οἴνου [1] κεκλημέναι τῷ
Δάφνιδι τοὺς ὀφθαλμοὺς ἐπέβαλλον,[2] καὶ ἐπῄνουν
ὡς ὅμοιον τῷ Διονύσῳ τὸ κάλλος. καί τις τῶν
θρασυτέρων καὶ ἐφίλησε, καὶ τὸν Δάφνιν παρώ-
ξυνε, τὴν δὲ Χλόην ἐλύπησεν.

Οἱ δὲ ἐν ταῖς ληνοῖς ποικίλας φωνὰς ἔρριπτον
ἐπὶ τὴν Χλόην, καὶ ὥσπερ ἐπί [3] τινα Βάκχην
Σάτυροι μανικώτερον ἐπήδων, καὶ ηὔχοντο γε-
νέσθαι ποίμνια καὶ ὑπ' ἐκείνης νέμεσθαι· ὥστε
αὖ πάλιν ἡ μὲν ᾔδετο, Δάφνις δὲ ἐλυπεῖτο.
εὔχοντο δὲ [4] δὴ ταχέως παύσασθαι τοῦ τρυγητοῦ [5]
καὶ λαβέσθαι τῶν συνήθων χωρίων, καὶ ἀντὶ
τῆς ἀμούσου βοῆς ἀκούειν σύριγγος ἢ τῶν
ποιμνίων αὐτῶν βληχωμένων.

Καὶ ἐπεὶ διαγενομένων ὀλίγων ἡμερῶν αἱ μὲν
ἄμπελοι τετρύγηντο, πίθοι δὲ τὸ γλεῦκος [6] εἶχον,
ἔδει δὲ οὐκέτ' οὐδὲν πολυχειρίας, κατήλαυνον τὰς
ἀγέλας εἰς τὸ πεδίον. καὶ μάλα χαίροντες τὰς
Νύμφας προσεκύνουν, βότρυς αὐταῖς κομίζοντες
ἐπὶ κλημάτων ἀπαρχὰς τοῦ τρυγητοῦ. οὐδὲ τὸν
πρότερον χρόνον ἀμελῶς ποτὲ παρῆλθον, ἀλλ'
ἀεί τε ἀρχόμενοι [7] νομῆς προσήδρευον καὶ ἐκ
νομῆς ἀνιόντες προσεκύνουν, καὶ πάντως τι

---

[1] Uiii omits   [2] A ἀδελφοὺς ἐμβάλει (corr. to ἐπάτει)
[3] A omits   Uiii Βάκχον (Amyot)   [4] A omits   [5] so
Hirsch : mss acc.   [6] Parr τεῖχος   [7] A ἐρχ.

2. Now as they were wont in the feast of Bacchus and the solemnisation of the birth of wine, the women that came from the neighbouring fields to help, cast their eyes all upon Daphnis, gave him prick and praise for beauty, and said he was like to Bacchus himself. And now and then one of the bolder strapping girls would catch him in her arms and kiss him. Those wanton praises and expressions did animate the modest youth, but vexed and grieved the poor Chloe.

But the men that were treading in the press cast out various voices upon Chloe, and leapt wildly before her like so many Satyrs before a young Bacchant, and wished that they themselves were sheep, that such a shepherdess might tend them. And thus the girl in her turn was pleased, and Daphnis stung with pain. But they wished the vintage might soon be done that they might return to their haunts in the fields, that instead of that wild untuned noise of the clowns they might hear again the sweet pipe or the blating of the cattle.

And when after a few days the grapes were gathered and the must tunned into the vessels, and there needed no longer many hands to help, they drove again their flocks to the plain, and with great joy and exultation worshipped and adored the Nymphs, offering to them the firstfruits of the vintage, clusters hanging on their branches. Nor did they in former time with negligence ever pass by the Nymphs, but always when they came forth to feed would sit them down reverentially in the cave, and when they went home would first adore and beg their grace, and brought to them always something,

DAPHNIS AND CHLOE

ἐπέφερον, ἢ ἄνθος ἢ ὀπώραν ἢ φυλλάδα χλωρὰν
ἢ γάλακτος σπονδήν. καὶ τούτου μὲν ὕστερον
ἀμοιβὰς ἐκομίσαντο παρὰ τῶν θεῶν. τότε δὲ
κύνες, φασίν, ἐκ δεσμῶν λυθέντες ἐσκίρτων,
ἐσύριττον, ᾖδον, τοῖς τράγοις καὶ τοῖς προβάτοις
συνεπάλαιον.

3. Τερπομένοις δὲ αὐτοῖς ἐφίσταται πρεσβύτης
σισύραν ἐνδεδυμένος, καρβατίνας ὑποδεδεμένος,
πήραν ἐξηρτημένος καὶ τὴν πήραν[1] παλαιάν.
οὗτος πλησίον καθίσας αὐτῶν ὧδε εἶπε· "Φιλητᾶς,
ὦ παῖδες, ὁ πρεσβύτης ἐγώ, ὃς πολλὰ μὲν
ταῖσδε ταῖς Νύμφαις ᾖσα, πολλὰ δὲ τῷ Πανὶ
ἐκείνῳ ἐσύρισα, βοῶν δὲ πολλῆς ἀγέλης ἡγη-
σάμην μόνῃ μουσικῇ. ἥκω δὲ ὑμῖν ὅσα εἶδον
μηνύσων, ὅσα ἤκουσα ἀπαγγελῶν. κῆπός ἐστί
μοι τῶν ἐμῶν χειρῶν <ἔργον>, ὅν, ἐξ οὗ νέμειν
διὰ γῆρας ἐπαυσάμην, ἐξεπονησάμην, ὅσα ὧραι
φέρουσι[2] πάντα ἔχων ἐν αὐτῷ καθ' ὥραν ἑκάστην·
ἦρος ῥόδα, κρίνα καὶ ὑάκινθος[3] καὶ ἴα ἀμφότερα,
θέρους μήκωνες καὶ ἀχράδες καὶ μῆλα πάντα,
νῦν ἄμπελοι καὶ συκαῖ καὶ ῥοιαὶ καὶ μύρτα
χλωρά. εἰς τοῦτον τὸν κῆπον ὀρνίθων ἀγέλαι
συνέρχονται τὸ ἑωθινόν, τῶν μὲν ἐς τροφήν, τῶν
δὲ ἐς ᾠδήν. συνηρεφὴς γὰρ καὶ κατάσκιος καὶ
πηγαῖς τρισὶ κατάρρυτος· ἂν περιέλῃ τις τὴν
αἱμασιάν, ἄλσος ὁρᾶν οἰήσεται.

4. "Εἰσελθόντι δέ μοι τήμερον ἀμφὶ μέσην
ἡμέραν ὑπὸ ταῖς ῥοιαῖς καὶ ταῖς μυρρίναις
βλέπεται παῖς μύρτα καὶ ῥοιὰς ἔχων, λευκὸς

---

[1] τὴν π. : Headlam ταύτην   <ἔργον> Hirsch.
[2] omission of αἱ is strange ; perh. ὀσῶραι and delete φερ. as
gloss E   [3] Ap -θον

either a flower or an apple or an apronful of green leaves or a sacrifice of milk. And for this they afterwards received no small rewards and favours from the Goddesses. And now, like dogs let slip, as the saying is, they skip and dance and sing and pipe, and wrestle playfully with their flocks.

3. While they thus delight themselves, there comes up to them an old man, clad in his rug and mantle of skins, his carbatins or clouted shoes, his scrip hanging at his back, and that indeed a very old one. When he was sate down by them, thus he spoke and told his story : " I, my children, am that old Philetas who have often sung to these Nymphs and often piped to yonder Pan, and have led many a herd by the art of music alone. And I come to shew you what I have seen and to tell you what I have heard. I have a garden which my own hands and labour planted, and ever since by my old age I gave over fields and herds, to dress and trim it has been my care and entertainment. What flowers or fruits the season of the year teems, there they are at every season. In the spring there are roses and lilies, the hyacinths and both the forms of violets ; in the summer, poppies, pears, and all sorts of apples. And now in the autumn, vines and figtrees, pomegranates, and the green myrtles. Into this garden flocks of birds come every morning, some to feed, some to sing. For it is thick, opacous, and shady, and watered all by three fountains ; and if you took the wall away you would think you saw a wood.

4. " As I went in there to-day about noon, a boy appeared in the pomegranate and myrtle grove, with myrtles and pomegranates in his hand ; white as milk, and his hair shining with the glance of fire ; clean

ὥσπερ γάλα καὶ ξανθὸς ὥσπερ[1] πῦρ, στιλπνὸς
ὡς ἄρτι λελουμένος. γυμνὸς ἦν, μόνος ἦν· ἔπαι-
ζεν ὡς ἴδιον κῆπον τρυγῶν. ἐγὼ μὲν οὖν ὥρμησα
ἐπ᾽[2] αὐτὸν ὡς συλληψόμενος, δείσας μὴ ὑπ᾽ ἀγε-
ρωχίας τὰς μυρρίνας καὶ τὰς ῥοιὰς κατακλάσῃ·
ὁ δέ με κούφως καὶ ῥαδίως ὑπέφευγε, ποτὲ μὲν
ταῖς ῥοδωνιαῖς ὑποτρέχων, ποτὲ δὲ ταῖς μήκωσιν
ὑποκρυπτόμενος, ὥσπερ πέρδικος νεοττός. καίτοι
πολλάκις μὲν πρᾶγμα[3] ἔσχον ἐρίφους γαλαθηνοὺς
διώκων, πολλάκις δὲ ἔκαμον μεταθέων μόσχους
ἀρτιγεννήτους· ἀλλὰ τοῦτο ποικίλον τι χρῆμα
ἦν καὶ ἀθήρατον.

"Καμὼν οὖν ὡς γέρων καὶ ἐπερεισάμενος τῇ
βακτηρίᾳ καὶ ἅμα φυλάττων μὴ φύγῃ, ἐπυνθα-
νόμην τίνος ἐστὶ τῶν γειτόνων καὶ τί βουλόμενος
ἀλλότριον κῆπον τρυγᾷ. ὁ δὲ ἀπεκρίνατο μὲν
οὐδέν, στὰς δὲ πλησίον ἐγέλα πάνυ ἁπαλὸν καὶ
ἔβαλλέ με τοῖς μύρτοις καὶ οὐκ οἶδ᾽ ὅπως ἔθελγε
μηκέτι θυμοῦσθαι. ἐδεόμην οὖν εἰς χεῖρας ἐλθεῖν
μηδὲν φοβούμενον ἔτι, καὶ ὤμνυον κατὰ τῶν
μύρτων ἀφήσειν[4] ἐπιδοὺς μήλων καὶ ῥοιῶν
παρέξειν τε ἀεὶ τρυγᾶν τὰ φυτὰ καὶ δρέπειν
τὰ ἄνθη, τυχὼν παρ᾽ αὐτοῦ φιλήματος ἑνός.

5. "'Ενταῦθα πάνυ καπυρὸν γελάσας ἀφίησι
φωνήν, οἵαν οὔτε ἀηδὼν οὔτε χελιδὼν οὔτε κύκνος

---

[1] pq ὡς   [2] A εἰς   [3] p πράγματα   [4] A ἀφεῖναι

and bright as if he had newly washed himself.
Naked he was, alone he was; he played and wan-
toned it about, and culled and pulled, as if it had bin
his own garden. Therefore I ran at him as fast as
I could, thinking to get him in my clutches. For
indeed I was afraid lest by that wanton, untoward,
malapert ramping and hoity-toity which he kept in
the grove, he would at length break my pomegranates
and myrtles. But he, with a soft and easy sleight, as
he listed, gave me the slip, sometimes running under
roses, sometimes hiding himself in the poppies, like a
cunning, huddling chick of a partridge. I have often
had enough to do to run after the sucking kids, and
often tired myself off my legs to catch a giddy young
calf; but this was a cunning piece and a thing that
could not be catched.

" Being then wearied, as an old man, and leaning
upon my staff, and withal looking to him lest he
should escape away, I asked what neighbour's child
he was, and what he meant to rob another man's
orchard so. But he answered me not a word, but
coming nearer, laughed most sweetly and flung
the myrtle-berries at me, and pleased me so, I know
not how, that all my anger vanished quite. I asked
him therefore that he would give himself without
fear into my hands, and swore to him by the myrtles
that I would not only send him away with apples and
pomegranates to boot, but give him leave whensoever
he pleased to pull the finest fruits and flowers, if he
would but give me one kiss.

5. "With that, setting up a loud laughter, he sent
forth a voice such as neither the swallow nor the
nightingale has, nor yet the swan when he is grown

DAPHNIS AND CHLOE

ὁμοίως¹ ἐμοὶ γέρων γενόμενος· ʿἘμοὶ μὲν, ὦ
Φιλητᾶ, φιλῆσαί σε φθόνος² οὐδείς· βούλομαι γὰρ
φιλεῖσθαι μᾶλλον ἢ σὺ γενέσθαι νέος· ὅρα δέ, εἴ
σοι καθ' ἡλικίαν τὸ δῶρον. οὐδὲν γάρ σε ὠφελήσει
τὸ γῆρας πρὸς τὸ μὴ διώκειν ἐμὲ μετὰ τὸ ἓν
φίλημα. δυσθήρατός εἰμι³ καὶ ἱέρακι καὶ ἀετῷ
καὶ εἴ τις ἄλλος τούτων ὠκύτερος ὄρνις. οὔτοι
παῖς ἐγὼ καὶ εἰ δοκῶ παῖς, ἀλλὰ καὶ τοῦ Κρόνου
πρεσβύτερος καὶ αὐτοῦ τοῦ παντός.⁴ καί σε οἶδα
νέμοντα πρωθήβην ἐν ἐκείνῳ τῷ ἔλει⁵ τὸ πλατὺ
βουκόλιον, καὶ παρήμην σοι συρίττοντι πρὸς ταῖς
φηγοῖς ἐκείναις, ἡνίκα ἤρας Ἀμαρυλλίδος· ἀλλά
με οὐχ ἑώρας καίτοι πλησίον μάλα τῇ κόρῃ
παρεστῶτα. σοὶ μὲν οὖν ἐκείνην ἔδωκα, καὶ ἤδη
σοι παῖδες ἀγαθοὶ βουκόλοι καὶ γεωργοί. νῦν δὲ
Δάφνιν ποιμαίνω καὶ Χλόην· καὶ ἡνίκα ἂν αὐτοὺς
εἰς ἓν συναγάγω τὸ ἑωθινόν, εἰς τὸν σὸν ἔρχομαι
κῆπον καὶ τέρπομαι τοῖς ἄνθεσι καὶ τοῖς φυτοῖς
κἂν ταῖς πηγαῖς ταύταις καὶ λούομαι. διὰ τοῦτο
καλὰ καὶ τὰ ἄνθη καὶ τὰ φυτὰ τοῖς ἐμοῖς λουτροῖς
ἀρδόμενα. ὅρα δὲ μή τί σοι τῶν φυτῶν κατακέ-
κλασται, μή τις ὀπώρα τετρύγηται, μή τις ἄνθους
ρίζα πεπάτηται, μή τις πηγὴ τετάρακται. καὶ
χαῖρε μόνος ἀνθρώπων ἐν γήρᾳ θεασάμενος⁶ τοῦτο
τὸ παιδίον.'

6. ʿΤαῦτα εἰπὼν ἀνήλατο καθάπερ ἀηδόνος

¹ so Brunck : mss ὅμοιος   γενόμ. ; A φαινόμ.   ² so
Wytt : mss πόνος   ³ pq ἐγὼ   ⁴ so Herch : mss παντὸς
χρόνου (gloss on Κρόνου)   ⁵ A ὄρει : but cf. Theocr. 25. 16
⁶ Uiii omits

74

old like to me : ' Philetas,' said he, ' I grudge not
at all to give thee a kiss; for it is more pleasure for
me to be kissed then for thee to be young again. But
consider with thyself whether such a gift as that be of
use to thy age. For thy old age cannot help thee that
thou shalt not follow me, after that one kiss. But I
cannot be taken, though a hawk or an eagle or any
other swifter bird were flown at me. I am not a
boy though I seem to be so, but am older then
Saturn and all this universe. I know that when
thou wast yet a boy thou didst keep a great herd on
yonder water-meadow; and I was present to thee
when under those oak-trees thou didst sing and play
on the pipe for the dear love of Amaryllis. But thou
didst not see me although I stood close by the maid.
It was I that gave her thee in marriage, and thou
hast had sons by her, jolly herdsmen and husband-
men. And now I take care of Daphnis and Chloe ;
and when I have brought them together in the
morning, I come hither to thy garden and take
my pleasure among these groves and flowers of thine,
and wash myself also in these fountains. And this is
the cause why thy roses, violets, lilies, hyacinths, and
poppies, all thy flowers and thy plants, are still so
fair and beautiful, because they are watered with my
wash. Cast thy eyes round about, and look whether
there be any one stem of a flower, any twig of a
tree, broken, whether any of thy fruits be pulled or
any flower trodden down, whether any fountain be
troubled and mudded ; and rejoice, Philetas, that
thou alone of all mortals hast seen this boy in thy
old age.'

6. "This said, the sweet boy sprang into the

νεοττὸς ἐπὶ τὰς μυρρίνας, καὶ κλάδον ἀμείβων ἐκ
κλάδου διὰ τῶν φύλλων ἀνεῖρπεν[1] εἰς ἄκρον. εἶδον
αὐτοῦ καὶ πτέρυγας ἐκ τῶν ὤμων καὶ τοξάρια
μεταξὺ τῶν πτερύγων καὶ τῶν ὤμων, καὶ οὐκέτι
εἶδον[2] οὔτε ταῦτα οὔτε αὐτόν. εἰ δὲ μὴ μάτην
ταύτας τὰς πολιὰς ἔφυσα, μηδὲ γηράσας ματαιοτέ-
ρας τὰς φρένας ἐκτησάμην, Ἔρωτι, ὦ παῖδες,
κατέσπεισθε, καὶ Ἔρωτι ὑμῶν μέλει."

7. Πάνυ ἐτέρφθησαν ὥσπερ μῦθον οὐ λόγον
ἀκούοντες, καὶ ἐπυνθάνοντο τί ἐστί ποτε ὁ Ἔρως,
πότερα παῖς ἢ ὄρνις, καὶ τί δύναται. πάλιν οὖν
ὁ Φιλητᾶς ἔφη· "Θεός ἐστιν, ὦ παῖδες, ὁ Ἔρως,[3]
νέος καὶ καλὸς καὶ πετόμενος. διὰ τοῦτο καὶ
νεότητι χαίρει καὶ κάλλος διώκει καὶ τὰς ψυχὰς
ἀναπτεροῖ, δύναται δὲ τοσοῦτον ὅσον οὐδὲ ὁ
Ζεύς. κρατεῖ μὲν στοιχείων, κρατεῖ δὲ ἄστρων,
κρατεῖ δὲ τῶν ὁμοίων θεῶν· οὐδὲ ὑμεῖς τοσοῦτον
τῶν. αἰγῶν καὶ τῶν προβάτων. τὰ ἄνθη πάντα
Ἔρωτος ἔργα· τὰ φυτὰ ταῦτα τούτου ποιήματα.
διὰ τοῦτον καὶ ποταμοὶ ῥέουσι καὶ ἄνεμοι πνέου-
σιν. ἔγνων δὲ ἐγὼ καὶ ταῦρον ἐρασθέντα, καὶ ὡς
οἴστρῳ πληγεὶς ἐμυκᾶτο· καὶ τράγον φιλήσαντα
αἶγα, καὶ ἠκολούθει πανταχοῦ.

"Αὐτὸς μὲν γὰρ ἤμην[4] νέος, καὶ ἠράσθην Ἀμα-
ρυλλίδος· καὶ οὔτε τροφῆς ἐμεμνήμην, οὔτε ποτὸν

---

[1] Α ἀνῆλθεν [2] Parr omit [3] ὁ Ἔρως : Α Ἔρως,
Christian emendation? cf. ἐβάπτιζεν 2. 1 [4] Α ἦν, but cf.
παρήμην 2. 5

myrtle grove, and like a young nightingale, from bough to bough under the green leaves, skipped to the top of the myrtles. Then I saw his wings hanging at his shoulders, and at his back between his wings a little bow with darts; and since that moment never saw either them or him any more. If therefore I wear not now these gray hairs of mine in vain, and by my age have not got a trivial mind, you two, O Daphnis and Chloe, are destined [1] to Love, and Love himself takes care of you."

7. With this they were both hugely delighted; and thought they heard a tale, not a true discourse, and therefore they would ask him questions: "And what is Love? is he a boy or is he a bird? and what can he do I pray you, gaffer?" Therefore again thus Philetas: "Love, my children, is a God, a young youth and very fair, and winged to fly. And therefore he delights in youth, follows beauty, and gives our fantasy her wings. His power's so vast that that of Jove is not so great. He governs in the elements, rules in the stars, and domineers even o'er the Gods that are his peers. Nay, you have not such dominion o'er your sheep and goats. All flowers are the work of Love. Those plants are his creations and poems. [2] By him it is that the rivers flow, and by him the winds blow. I have known a bull that has been in love and run bellowing through the meadows as if he had been stung by a breese, a he-goat too so in love with a virgin-she that he has followed her up and down through the woods, through the lawns.

"And I myself once was young, and fell in love with Amaryllis, and forgot to eat my meat and drink

---

[1] consecrated.   [2] things made.

προσεφερόμην, οὔτε ὕπνον[1] ᾑρούμην. ἤλγουν τὴν
ψυχήν, τὴν καρδίαν ἐπαλλόμην, τὸ σῶμα ἐψυχό-
μην· ἐβόων ὡς παιόμενος, ἐσιώπων ὡς νεκρού-
μενος, εἰς ποταμοὺς ἐνέβαινον ὡς καόμενος. ἐκά-
λουν τὸν Πᾶνα βοηθὸν ὡς καὶ[2] αὐτὸν τῆς Πίτυος
ἐρασθέντα. ἐπήνουν τὴν Ἠχὼ τὸ Ἀμαρυλλίδος
ὄνομα μετ' ἐμὲ καλοῦσαν· κατέκλων τὰς σύριγγας,
ὅτι μοι τὰς μὲν βοῦς ἔθελγον, Ἀμαρυλλίδα δὲ οὐκ
ἦγον. Ἔρωτος γὰρ οὐδὲν φάρμακον, οὐ πινόμενον,
οὐκ ἐσθιόμενον, οὐκ[3] ἐν ᾠδαῖς λεγόμενον, ὅτι μὴ
φίλημα καὶ περιβολὴ καὶ συγκατακλιθῆναι γυμ-
νοῖς σώμασι."

8. Φιλητᾶς μὲν τοσαῦτα[4] παιδεύσας αὐτοὺς
ἀπαλλάττεται, τυρούς τινας παρ' αὐτῶν καὶ
ἔριφον ἤδη κεράστην λαβών. οἱ δὲ μόνοι κατα-
λειφθέντες καὶ τότε πρῶτον ἀκούσαντες τὸ Ἔρω-
τος ὄνομα, τάς τε ψυχὰς συνεστάλησαν ὑπὸ
λύττης καὶ ἐπανελθόντες νύκτωρ εἰς τὰς ἐπαύλεις
παρέβαλλον οἷς ἤκουσαν τὰ αὐτῶν· "Ἀλγοῦσιν
οἱ ἐρῶντες, καὶ ἡμεῖς· ἀμελοῦσιν, ἵν' ἠμελήκαμεν·[5]
καθεύδειν οὐ δύνανται, τοῦτο μὲν καὶ νῦν πάσχο-
μεν καὶ ἡμεῖς· κάεσθαι δοκοῦσι, καὶ παρ' ἡμῖν τὸ
πῦρ· ἐπιθυμοῦσιν ἀλλήλους ὁρᾶν, διὰ τοῦτο
θᾶττον εὐχόμεθα γενέσθαι τὴν ἡμέραν. σχεδὸν
τοῦτό ἐστιν ὁ ἔρως· καὶ ἐρῶμεν ἀλλήλων οὐκ

---

[1] A πνοὴν   [2] A omits, cf 2. 16   [3] A omits   pq λαλού-
μενον   [4] Uiii μέντοι ταῦτα   [5] Uiii ἀμελοῦσιν ἴσως· καὶ
ἡμεῖς ἠμελήκαμεν (incorp. gloss following loss of ἵν' by
haplogr.) : B ἀμελοῦσιν ἵν' ἠμελήκαμεν, ἠμελήκαμεν ὁμοίως
(incorp. gloss on ἵν' ἠμελήκ.) : p doubtful

my drink, and never could compose to sleep. My panting heart was very sad and anxious, and my body shook with cold. I cried out oft, as if I had bin thwacked and basted back and sides; and then again was still and mute, as if I had layen among the dead. I cast myself into the-rivers as if I had bin all on a fire. I called on Pan that he would help me, as having sometimes bin himself catched with the love of peevish Pitys. I praised Echo that with kindness she restored and trebled to me the dear name of Amaryllis. I broke my pipes because they could delight the kine, but could not draw me Amaryllis. For there is no medicine for love, neither meat, nor drink, nor any charm, but only kissing and embracing and lying side by side."

8. Philetas, when he had thus instructed the unskilful lovers, and was presented with certain cheeses and a young goat of the first horns, went his way. But when they were alone, having then first heard of the name of Love, their minds were struck with a kind of madness, and returning home with the fall of night, they began each to compare those things which they had suffered in themselves with the doctrine of Philetas concerning lovers and love: "The lover has his grief and sadness, and we have had our share of that. They are languishing and careless in just such things as we. They cannot sleep, and we still watch for the early day. They think they are burnt, and we too are afire. They desire nothing more then to see one another, and for that cause we pray the day to come quickly. This undoubtedly is love, and we, it seems, are in love without knowing whether or

εἰδότες εἰ τοῦτο μέν ἐστιν ὁ ἔρως ἐγὼ δὲ ὁ ἐρώ-
μενος. τί οὖν ταῦτα ἀλγοῦμεν; τί δὲ ἀλλήλους
ζητοῦμεν; ἀληθῆ πάντα εἶπεν ὁ Φιλητᾶς. τὸ ἐκ
τοῦ κήπου παιδίον ὤφθη καὶ τοῖς πατράσιν ἡμῶν
ὄναρ ἐκεῖνο καὶ νέμειν ἡμᾶς τὰς ἀγέλας ἐκέλευσε.
πῶς ἄν τις αὐτὸ λάβοι; μικρόν ἐστι, καὶ φεύ-
ξεται. καὶ πῶς ἄν τις αὐτὸ φύγοι; πτερὰ ἔχει, καὶ
καταλήψεται. ἐπὶ τὰς Νύμφας δεῖ βοηθοὺς κατα-
φεύγειν.[1] ἀλλ᾽ οὐδὲ Φιλητᾶν ὁ Πὰν ὠφέλησεν
Ἀμαρυλλίδος ἐρῶντα. ὅσα εἶπεν ἄρα φάρμακα,
ταῦτα ζητητέον,[2] φίλημα καὶ περιβολὴν καὶ κεῖ-
σθαι γυμνοὺς χαμαί· κρύος μέν, ἀλλὰ καρτερήσο-
μεν[3] δεύτεροι μετὰ Φιλητᾶν."

9. Τοῦτο αὐτοῖς γίνεται[4] νυκτερινὸν παιδευτή-
ριον. καὶ ἀγαγόντες τῆς ἐπιούσης ἡμέρας[5] τὰς
ἀγέλας εἰς νομήν, ἐφίλησαν μὲν ἀλλήλους ἰδόντες,
ὃ μήπω πρότερον ἐποίησαν, καὶ περιέβαλον τὰς
χεῖρας ἐπαλλάξαντες· τὸ δὲ τρίτον ὤκνουν φάρ-
μακον, ἀποδυθέντες κατακλιθῆναι· θρασύτερον
γὰρ οὐ μόνον παρθένων ἀλλὰ καὶ νέων αἰπόλων.
πάλιν οὖν νὺξ ἀγρυπνίαν[6] ἔχουσα καὶ ἔννοιαν
τῶν γεγενημένων καὶ κατάμεμψιν τῶν παραλελειμ-
μένων· " Ἐφιλήσαμεν, καὶ οὐδὲν ὄφελος· περιε-
βάλομεν, καὶ οὐδὲν πλέον. σχεδὸν τὸ συγκατα-
κλιθῆναι[7] μόνον φάρμακον ἔρωτος. πειρατέον καὶ

---

[1] pq aor.   [2] p -τέα : A omits ταῦτα   [3] so Heinsius
(Amyot) : mss μαρτυρήσομεν   p δεύτερον   [4] Uii γίγνεται
[5] A dat.   [6] νὺξ ἀγρυπνίαν : A ἐξαγρυπνίαν (ν lost after οὖν) :
p ἀγρυπνία : q ἀγρυπνίαν (B marg. νὺξ)   p ἔννοια   B omits
τῶν γεγεν.   κατάμεμψιν Jungermann : mss -ις : Uiii omits
καὶ   [7] so E, cf. 8 and 11 : mss σχεδόν. τὸ οὖν κατακλ.

no this be love or ourself a lover. And so if we ask why we have this grief and why this seeking each after the other, the answer is clear : Philetas did not lie a tittle. That boy in the garden was seen too by our fathers Lamo and Dryas in that dream, and 'twas he that commanded us to the field. How is it possible for one to catch him ? He 's small and slim, and so will slip and steal away. And how should one escape and get away from him by flight ? He has wings to overtake us. We must fly to the Nymphs our patronesses ; but Pan, alas ! did not help his servant Philetas when he was mad on Amaryllis. Therefore those remedies which he taught us are before all things to be tried, kissing, embracing, and lying together on the ground. It 's cold indeed, but after Philetas we 'll endure it."

9. Of this sort then was their nocturnal schooling. When it was day and their flocks were driven to the field, they ran, as soon as they saw one another, to kiss and embrace, which before they never did. Yet of that third remedy which the old Philetas taught, they durst not make experiment ; for that was not only an enterprise too bold for maids, but too high for young goatherds. Therefore still, as before, came night without sleep, and with remembrance of what was done and with complaint of what was not : "We have kissed one another and are never the better ; we have clipped and embraced, and that 's as good as nothing too. Therefore to lie together is certainly the only remaining remedy of love. That must be tried by all means.

τούτου. ἐν αὑτῷ πάντως τι κρεῖττον ἔσται[1] φιλήματος."

10. Ἐπὶ τούτοις τοῖς λογισμοῖς, οἷον εἰκός, καὶ ὀνείρατα ἑώρων ἐρωτικά, τὰ φιλήματα, τὰς περιβολάς· καὶ ὅσα δὲ μεθ' ἡμέραν οὐκ ἔπραξαν, ταῦτα ὄναρ ἔπραξαν· γυμνοὶ μετ' ἀλλήλων ἔκειντο. ἐνθεώτεροι δὲ κατὰ τὴν ἐπιοῦσαν ἡμέραν ἀνέστησαν, καὶ ῥοίζῳ τὰς ἀγέλας κατήλαυνον ἐπειγόμενοι πρὸς[2] τὰ φιλήματα. καὶ ἰδόντες ἀλλήλους ἅμα μειδιάματι προσέδραμον.[3] τὰ μὲν οὖν φιλήματα ἐγένετο καὶ ἡ περιβολὴ τῶν χειρῶν ἠκολούθησε· τὸ δὲ τρίτον φάρμακον ἐβράδυνε, μήτε τοῦ Δάφνιδος τολμῶντος εἰπεῖν μήτε τῆς Χλόης βουλομένης κατάρχεσθαι, ἔστε τύχῃ[4] καὶ τοῦτο ἔπραξαν·

11. Καθεζόμενοι ἐπὶ στελέχους δρυὸς πλησίον ἀλλήλων καὶ γευσάμενοι τῆς ἐν φιλήματι τέρψεως, ἀπλήστως ἐνεφοροῦντο τῆς ἡδονῆς. ἦσαν δὲ καὶ χειρῶν περιβολαὶ θλῖψιν τοῖς στόμασι παρέχουσαι. καὶ κατὰ[5] τὴν τῶν χειρῶν περιβολὴν[6] βιαιότερον δὴ τοῦ Δάφνιδος ἐπισπασαμένου, κλίνεται[7] πως ἐπὶ πλευρὰν ἡ Χλόη· κἀκεῖνος δὲ συγκατακλίνεται τῷ φιλήματι ἀκολουθῶν. καὶ γνωρίσαντες τῶν ὀνείρων τὴν εἰκόνα, κατέκειντο πολὺν χρόνον ὥσπερ συνδεδεμένοι. εἰδότες[8] δὲ τῶν ἐντεῦθεν οὐδέν, καὶ νομίσαντες τοῦτο εἶναι πέρας ἐρωτικῆς ἀπολαύσεως, μάτην τὸ πλεῖστον τῆς ἡμέρας δαπανήσαντες διελύθησαν, καὶ τὰς ἀγέλας ἀπήλαυνον τὴν νύκτα μισοῦντες.

---

[1] A ἐστι   [2] q κατὰ   [3] pq κατέδ.   [4] ἔστε τύχῃ : A lac.
[5] καὶ κατὰ so É : Aq κατὰ: p καὶ   [6] A προσβολαὶ (from περιβολαὶ above): p προσβολὴν   [7] A δὲ συγκλ. from below
[8] p ἰδόντες

There's something in it, without doubt, more efficacious then in a kiss."

10. While they indulged these kind of thoughts, they had, as it was like, their amorous dreams, kissing and clipping; and what they did not in the day, that they acted in the night, and lay together. But the next day they rose up still the more possessed, and drive their flocks with a whistling to the fields, hasting to their kisses again, and when they saw one another, smiling sweetly ran together. Kisses passed, embraces passed, but that third remedy was slow to come; for Daphnis durst not mention it, and Chloe too would not begin, till at length even by chance they made this essay of it:

11. They sate both close together upon the trunk of an old oak, and having tasted the sweetness of kisses they were ingulfed insatiably in pleasure, and there arose a mutual contention and striving with their clasping arms which made a close compression of their lips. And when Daphnis hugged her to him with a more violent desire, it came about that Chloe inclined a little on her side, and Daphnis, following his kiss, fell beside her. And remembering that they had an image of this in their dreams the night before, they lay a long while clinging together. But being ignorant as yet, and thinking that this was the end of love, they parted, most part of the day spent in vain, and drove their flocks home from the fields with a kind of hate to the oppression of the night.

ἴσως δὲ κἂν τῶν ἀληθῶν τι ἔπραξαν,[1] εἰ μὴ
θόρυβος τοιόσδε τὴν ἀγροικίαν ἐκείνην ὅλην[2]
κατέλαβε·

12. Νέοι Μηθυμναῖοι πλούσιοι διαθέσθαι τὸν
τρυγητὸν ἐν ξενικῇ τέρψει θελήσαντες, ναῦν
μικρὰν καθελκύσαντες καὶ οἰκέτας προσκώπους
καθίσαντες, τοὺς Μυτιληναίων ἀγροὺς παρέ-
πλεον,[3] ὅσοι θαλάσσης πλησίον. εὐλίμενός τε
γὰρ ἡ παραλία[4] καὶ οἰκήσεσιν ἠσκημένη πολυ-
τελῶς. καὶ λουτρὰ συνεχῆ παράδεισοί τε καὶ
ἄλση,[5] τὰ μὲν φύσεως ἔργα, τὰ δὲ ἀνθρώπων
τέχναι· πάντα ἐνηβῆσαι[6] καλά.

Παραπλέοντες[7] δὲ καὶ ἐνορμιζόμενοι κακὸν μὲν
ἐποίουν οὐδέν, τέρψεις δὲ ποικίλας ἐτέρποντο,
ποτὲ μὲν ἀγκίστροις καλάμων ἀπηρτημένοις ἐκ
λίνου λεπτοῦ πετραίους ἰχθῦς ἁλιεύοντες ἐκ
πέτρας ἁλιτενοῦς, ποτὲ δὲ κυσὶ καὶ δικτύοις λαγὼς
φεύγοντας τὸν ἐν ταῖς ἀμπέλοις θόρυβον λαμ-
βάνοντες. ἤδη δὲ καὶ ὀρνίθων ἄγρας ἐμέλησεν
αὐτοῖς, καὶ ἔλαβον[8] βρόχοις χῆνας ἀγρίους καὶ
νήττας καὶ ὠτίδας. ὥστε καὶ ἡ τέρψις αὐτοῖς
καὶ τραπέζης ὠφέλειαν παρεῖχεν. εἰ δέ τινος
προσέδει, παρὰ τῶν ἐν τοῖς ἀγροῖς ἐλάμβανον
περιττοτέρους τῆς ἀξίας ὀβολοὺς καταβάλλοντες.
ἔδει δὲ μόνον ἄρτου καὶ οἴνου καὶ στέγης· οὐ γὰρ
ἀσφαλὲς ἐδόκει μετοπωρινῆς ὥρας ἐνεστώσης
ἐνθαλαττεύειν· ὥστε καὶ τὴν ναῦν ἀνεῖλκον ἐπὶ
τὴν γῆν νύκτα χειμέριον δεδοικότες.

[1] A ἴσως ἄν τι καὶ τ. ἀληθῶν ἔπρ. : κἂν for καὶ Schaef.
[2] pq πᾶσαν (before τὴν)   [3] so Herch. (Amyot) : mss
περιέπλ.   [4] A παραθαλασσία and omits πολυτελῶς   [5] Uiii
ἀλωή   [6] so Valckenaer : A ἐνβῆσαι (corr. to ἐμ.): pB
ἐνικῆσαι : Uiii ἐνοικ.   [7] p καταπλ.   [8] A ἔβαλον

And perchance something that was real had then
bin done, but that this tumult and noise filled all
that rural tract:

12. Some young gallants of Methymna, thinking
to keep the vintage holy-days and choosing to take
the pleasure abroad, drew a small vessel into the
water, and putting in their own domestic servants to
row, sailed about those pleasant farms of Mytilene that
were near by the seashore. For the maritim coast
has many good and safe harbours, and all along
is adorned with many stately buildings. There are
besides many baths, gardens, and groves, these by
art, those by nature, all brave for a man to take
his pastime there.

The ship therefore passing along and from time
to time putting in at the bays, they did no harm
or injury to any, but recreated themselves with
divers pleasures, sometimes with angles, rods, and
lines taking fish from this or the other prominent
rock, sometimes with dogs or toils[1] hunting the
hares that fled from the noise of the vineyards;
then anon they would go a fowling, and take the
wild-goose, duck, and mallard, and the bustard of
the field; and so by their pleasure furnished them-
selves with a plenteous table. If they needed any-
thing else they paid the villagers above the price.
But there was nothing else wanting but only bread
and wine and house-room. For they thought it
unsafe, the autumn now in its declination, to quit
the land and lie all night aboard at sea; and there-
fore drew the vessel ashore for fear of a tempestuous
night.

---

[1] nets.

DAPHNIS AND CHLOE

13. Τῶν δή τις ἀγροίκων ἐς ἀνολκὴν λίθου
<τοῦ> θλίβοντος τὰ πατηθέντα βοτρύδια[1] χρῄζων
σχοίνου, τῆς πρότερον[2] ῥαγείσης, κρύφα ἐπὶ τὴν
θάλατταν ἐλθών, ἀφρουρήτῳ τῇ νηὶ προσελθών,
τὸ πεῖσμα ἐκλύσας, οἴκαδε κομίσας, ἐς ὅ τι
ἔχρῃζεν ἐχρήσατο. ἕωθεν οὖν οἱ Μηθυμναῖοι
νεανίσκοι ζήτησιν ἐποιοῦντο τοῦ πείσματος, καὶ
(ὡμολόγει γὰρ οὐδεὶς τὴν κλοπὴν) ὀλίγα μεμ-
ψάμενοι τοὺς ξενοδόκους παρέπλεον. καὶ στα-
δίους[3] τριάκοντα παρελάσαντες προσορμίζονται
τοῖς ἀγροῖς ἐν οἷς ᾤκουν ὁ Δάφνις καὶ ἡ Χλόη·
ἐδόκει γὰρ αὐτοῖς καλὸν εἶναι τὸ πεδίον ἐς θήραν
λαγῶν. σχοίνινον[4] μὲν οὖν οὐκ[5] εἶχον ὥστε
ἐκδήσασθαι πεῖσμα· λύγον δὲ χλωρὰν μακρὰν
στρέψαντες ὡς[6] σχοῖνον ταύτῃ τὴν ναῦν ἐκ τῆς
πρύμνης ἄκρας εἰς τὴν γῆν ἔδησαν. ἔπειτα τοὺς
κύνας ἀφέντες ῥινηλατεῖν, ἐν ταῖς εὐκαίροις
φαινομέναις[7] τῶν ὁδῶν ἐλινοστάτουν.

Οἱ μὲν δὴ κύνες ἅμα ὑλακῇ διαθέοντες ἐφό-
βησαν τὰς αἶγας, αἱ δὲ τὰ ὀρεινὰ καταλιποῦσαι
μᾶλλόν τι πρὸς τὴν θάλατταν ὥρμησαν, ἔχουσαι
δὲ οὐδὲν ἐν ψάμμῳ τρώξιμον, ἐλθοῦσαι πρὸς τὴν
ναῦν αἱ θρασύτεραι αὐτῶν τὴν λύγον τὴν χλωράν,
ᾗ δέδετο ἡ ναῦς, ἀπέφαγον.[8] 14. ἦν δέ τι καὶ
κλυδώνιον ἐν τῇ θαλάττῃ, κινηθέντος[9] ἀπὸ τῶν
ὀρῶν τοῦ πνεύματος. ταχὺ δὴ μάλα λυθεῖσαν
αὐτὴν ὑπήνεγκεν ἡ παλίρροια τοῦ κύματος καὶ
ἐς τὸ πέλαγος μετέωρον ἔφερεν.

Αἰσθήσεως δὴ τοῖς Μηθυμναίοις γενομένης, οἱ

<τοῦ> E   [1] grape-stones=ἔνοινα 2. 1   [2] A -ας
[3] Parr στάδια   [4] so E: mss σχοῖνον   [5] A οὐδὲν   [6] A
στέψαντες εἰς   [7] A φαννουμένων   [8] A ἐπ.   [9] A κινηθὲν

13. Now it happened that a country fellow wanting a rope, his own being broke, to haul up the stone wherewith he was grinding grape-stones, sneaked down to the sea, and finding the ship with nobody in her, loosed the cable that held her and brought it away to serve his business. In the morning the young men of Methymna began to enquire after the rope, and (nobody owning the thievery) when they had a little blamed the unkindness and injury of their hosts, they loosed from thence, and sailing on thirty furlongs arrived at the fields of Daphnis and Chloe, those fields seeming the likeliest for hunting the hare. Therefore being destitute of a rope to use for their cable, they made a with of green and long sallow-twigs, and with that tied her by her stern to the shore. Then slipping their dogs to hunt, they cast their toils in those paths that seemed fittest for game.

The deep-mouthed dogs opened loud, and running about with much barking, scared the goats, that all hurried down from the mountains towards the sea; and finding nothing there in the sand to eat, coming up to that ship some of the bolder mischievous goats gnawed in pieces the green sallow-with that made her fast. 14. At the same moment there began to be a bluster at sea, the wind blowing from the mountains. On a sudden therefore the backwash of the waves set the loose pinnace adrift and carried her off to the main.

As soon as the Methymnaeans heard the news,

μὲν ἐπὶ τὴν θάλατταν ἔθεον, οἱ δὲ τοὺς κύνας
συνέλεγον, ἐβόων δὲ πάντες, ὡς πάντας τοὺς ἐκ
τῶν πλησίον ἀγρῶν ἀκούσαντας συνελθεῖν. ἀλλ᾿
ἦν οὐδὲν ὄφελος· τοῦ γὰρ πνεύματος ἀκμάζοντος,
ἀσχέτῳ τάχει κατὰ ῥοῦν ἡ ναῦς ἐφέρετο. οἱ δ᾿
οὖν οὐκ ὀλίγων κτημάτων[1] στερόμενοι ἐζήτουν
τὸν νέμοντα τὰς αἶγας, καὶ εὑρόντες τὸν Δάφνιν
ἔπαιον, ἀπέδυον· εἷς δέ τις καὶ κυνόδεσμον ἀρά-
μενος περιῆγε τὰς χεῖρας ὡς δήσων. ὁ δὲ ἐβόα
τε παιόμενος καὶ ἱκέτευε τοὺς ἀγροίκους, καὶ
πρώτους γε[2] τὸν Λάμωνα καὶ τὸν Δρύαντα
βοηθοὺς ἐπεκαλεῖτο. οἱ δὲ ἀντείχοντο σκιρροὶ[3]
γέροντες καὶ χεῖρας ἐκ γεωργικῶν ἔργων ἰσχυρὰς
ἔχοντες, καὶ ἠξίουν δικαιολογήσασθαι περὶ τῶν
γεγενημένων. 15. ταῦτα δὲ καὶ τῶν ἄλλων
ἀξιούντων, δικαστὴν καθίζουσι Φιλητᾶν τὸν βου-
κόλον· πρεσβύτατός τε[4] γὰρ ἦν τῶν παρόντων
καὶ κλέος εἶχεν ἐν τοῖς κωμήταις δικαιοσύνης
περιττῆς.

Πρῶτοι δὲ κατηγόρουν οἱ Μηθυμναῖοι σαφῆ
καὶ σύντομα, βουκόλον ἔχοντες δικαστήν· "᾿Ήλ-
θομεν εἰς τούτους τοὺς ἀγροὺς θηρᾶσαι θέλοντες.
τὴν μὲν οὖν ναῦν λύγῳ χλωρᾷ δήσαντες ἐπὶ τῆς
ἀκτῆς κατελίπομεν,[5] αὐτοὶ δὲ διὰ τῶν κυνῶν
ζήτησιν ἐποιούμεθα θηρίων. ἐν τούτῳ πρὸς τὴν
θάλατταν αἱ αἶγες τούτου κατελθοῦσαι τήν τε
λύγον κατεσθίουσι καὶ τὴν ναῦν ἀπολύουσιν.

---

[1] after κτημ. p Μηθυμναῖοι: Aq οἱ M.   [2] so Hirsch:
mss τε   [3] Α σκληροὶ prob. old var: q σκηροὶ   [4] Uiii
πρ. τε and πρ. γε : ᾿p πρ. τότε : Α πρεσβυτα (corr. to -την)
τότε   [5] Α impf.

some of them posted to the sea, some stayed to take
up the dogs, all made a hubbub through the fields,
and brought the neighbouring rurals in. But all
was to no purpose ; all was lost, all was gone. For
the wind freshening, the ship with an irrevocable
pernicity and swiftness was carried away.

Therefore the Methymnaeans, having a great loss
by this, looked for the goatherd, and lighting on
Daphnis, fell to cuff him, and tore off his clothes, and
one offered to bind his hands behind him with a
dog-slip. But Daphnis, when he was miserably
beaten, cried out and implored the help of the
country lads, and chiefly of all called for rescue to
Lamo and Dryas. They presently came in, and
opposed themselves, brawny old fellows and such as
by their country labour had hands of steel, and re-
quired of the furious youths concerning those things
that had happened a fair legal debate and decision.
15. And the others desiring the same thing, they made
Philetas the herdsman judge. For he was oldest of
all that were there present, and famous for upright-
ness among the villagers.

The Methymnaeans therefore began first, and
laid their accusation against Daphnis, in very short
and perspicuous words as before a herdsman-judge :
" We came into these fields to hunt. Wherefore
with a green sallow-with we left our ship tied
to the shore while our dogs were hunting the
grounds. Meanwhile his goats strayed from the
mountains down to the sea, gnawed the green cable
in pieces, set her at liberty, and let her fly. You
saw her tossing in the sea, but with what choice and
rich good laden ! what fine clothes are lost ! what

εἶδες αὐτὴν ἐν [1] τῇ θαλάττῃ φερομένην, πόσων
οἴει μεστὴν ἀγαθῶν; οἵα μὲν ἐσθὴς [2] ἀπόλωλεν·
οἷος δὲ κόσμος κυνῶν. ὅσον δὲ ἀργύριον· τοὺς
ἀγροὺς ἄν τις τούτους ἐκεῖνα ἔχων ὠνήσαιτο.
ἀνθ' ὧν ἀξιοῦμεν ἄγειν τοῦτον πονηρὸν ὄντα
αἰπόλον, ὃς ἐπὶ τῶν αἰγῶν τὰς [3] αἶγας νέμει."

16. Τοιαῦτα οἱ Μηθυμναῖοι κατηγόρησαν. ὁ
δὲ Δάφνις διέκειτο μὲν κακῶς ὑπὸ τῶν πληγῶν,
Χλόην δὲ ὁρῶν παροῦσαν πάντων κατεφρόνει
καὶ ὧδε εἶπεν· "Ἐγὼ νέμω τὰς αἶγας καλῶς.
οὐδέποτε ᾐτιάσατο κωμήτης οὐδὲ εἷς, ὡς ἢ κῆπόν
τινος αἲξ ἐμὴ κατεβοσκήσατο ἢ ἄμπελον βλαστά-
νουσαν κατέκλασεν. οὗτοι δέ εἰσι κυνηγέται
πονηροὶ καὶ κύνας ἔχουσι κακῶς πεπαιδευμένους,
οἵτινες τρέχοντες [4] πολλὰ καὶ ὑλακτοῦντες σκληρὰ
κατεδίωξαν αὐτὰς ἐκ τῶν ὀρῶν καὶ τῶν πεδίων
ἐπὶ τὴν θάλατταν ὥσπερ λύκοι. ἀλλὰ ἀπέφαγον
τὴν λύγον. οὐ γὰρ εἶχον ἐν ψάμμῳ πόαν [5] ἢ
κόμαρον ἢ θύμον. ἀλλ' ἀπώλετο ἡ ναῦς ὑπὸ
τοῦ [6] πνεύματος καὶ τῆς θαλάττης· ταῦτα χει-
μῶνος, οὐκ αἰγῶν ἐστιν ἔργα. ἀλλ' ἐσθὴς
ἐνέκειτο καὶ ἄργυρος· καὶ τίς πιστεύσει νοῦν
ἔχων, ὅτι τοσαῦτα φέρουσα ναῦς πεῖσμα εἶχε
λύγον;" [7]

17. Τούτοις ἐπεδάκρυσεν ὁ Δάφνις καὶ εἰς
οἶκτον ὑπηγάγετο [8] τοὺς ἀγροίκους πολύν· ὥστε
ὁ Φιλητᾶς ὁ δικαστὴς ὤμνυε Πᾶνα καὶ Νύμφας,

[1] A ἐπὶ   [2] Uiii εὐθὺς   [3] so Bonner-E : mss ἐπὶ τῆς
θαλάσσης ἰδὼν τὰς (pq omit ἰδὼν and read νέμει before τὰς)
and at end ὡς ναύτης (a gloss)   [4] Uiii τρύχ.   [5] prob.
old var : A λύγην : p λύγον   [6] A omits, and following
καὶ   [7] perh. λύγινον E   [8] A προσ.

rare harness and ornaments[1] for dogs are there!
what a treasury of precious silver! He that had all
might easily purchase these fields. For this damage
we think it but right and reason to carry him away
our captive, him that is such a mischievous goatherd
to feed his goats upon those other goats,[2] to wit, the
waves of the sea."

16. This was the accusation of the Methymnaeans.
Daphnis on the other side, although his bones were
sore with basting, yet seeing his dear Chloe there,
set it at naught and spoke thus in his own defence :
" I, in keeping my goats, have done my office well.
For never so much as one of all the neighbours of
the vale has blamed me yet, that any kid or goat
of mine has broke into and eaten up his garden or
browzed a young or sprouting vine. But those are
wicked cursed hunters, and have dogs that have no
manners, such as with their furious coursing and
most vehement barking have, like wolves, scared my
goats and tossed them down from the mountains
through the valleys to the sea. But they have
eaten the green with. For they could find nothing
else upon the sand, neither arbute, wilding, shrub,
nor thyme. But the ship's lost by wind and wave.
That's not my goats, but the fault of seas and
tempests. But there were rich clothes and silver
aboard her. And who that has any wit can believe
that a ship that is so richly laden should have
nothing for her cable but a with ? "

17. With that Daphnis began to weep, and made
the rustics commiserate him and his cause, so that
Philetas the judge called Pan and the Nymphs to

---

[1] gear.   [2] the word for 'goats' also means 'waves.'

μηδὲν ἀδικεῖν Δάφνιν, ἀλλὰ μηδὲ τὰς αἶγας, τὴν
δὲ θάλατταν καὶ τὸν ἄνεμον, ὧν ἄλλους εἶναι
δικαστάς. οὐκ ἔπειθε ταῦτα Φιλητᾶς Μηθυ-
μναίους [1] λέγων, ἀλλ' ὑπ' ὀργῆς ὁρμήσαντες ἦγον
πάλιν τὸν Δάφνιν καὶ συνδεῖν ἤθελον. ἐνταῦθα
οἱ κωμῆται ταραχθέντες ἐπιπηδῶσιν αὐτοῖς ὡσεὶ
ψᾶρες ἢ κολοιοί, καὶ ταχὺ μὲν ἀφαιροῦνται
τὸν Δάφνιν ἤδη καὶ αὐτὸν μαχόμενον, ταχὺ
δὲ ξύλοις παίοντες ἐκείνους εἰς φυγὴν ἔτρεψαν.
ἀπέστησαν [2] δὲ οὐ πρότερον, ἔστε τῶν ὅρων [3]
αὐτοὺς ἐξήλασαν εἰς ἄλλους ἀγρούς.

18. Διωκόντων δὴ τούτων [4] ἡ Χλόη κατὰ
πολλὴν ἡσυχίαν ἄγει πρὸς τὰς Νύμφας τὸν
Δάφνιν, καὶ ἀπονίπτει τε τὸ πρόσωπον ἡμαγμένον
ἐκ τῶν ῥινῶν ῥαγεισῶν ὑπὸ πληγῆς τινος, κἀκ [5]
τῆς πήρας προκομίσασα [6] ζυμίτου μέρος καὶ
τυροῦ τμῆμά τι δίδωσι φαγεῖν. τό τε [7] μάλιστα
ἀνακτησάμενον [8] αὐτόν, φίλημα ἐφίλησε μελιτῶδες
ἁπαλοῖς τοῖς χείλεσι. 19. τότε μὲν δὴ παρὰ
τοσοῦτον Δάφνις ἦλθε κακοῦ.

Τὸ δὲ πρᾶγμα οὐ πάντῃ [9] πέπαυτο, ἀλλ'
ἐλθόντες οἱ Μηθυμναῖοι μόλις εἰς τὴν ἑαυτῶν,[10]
ὁδοιπόροι μὲν ἀντὶ ναυτῶν, τραυματίαι δὲ ἀντὶ
τρυφώντων,[11] ἐκκλησίαν τε συνήγαγον τῶν πολι-
τῶν, καὶ ἱκετηρίας θέντες ἱκέτευον τιμωρίας
ἀξιωθῆναι, τῶν μὲν ἀληθῶν λέγοντες οὐδὲ ἕν,

[1] mss dat.   [2] A ἀπέστρεψαν   [3] U iii ὁρῶν   [4] τούτων:
pq τοὺς Μηθυμναίους ἐκείνων   [5] so Hirsch : mss καὶ   [6] A
pres.   [7] mss τότε   [8] so Seil : mss -η   [9] pq ταύτῃ
[10] A ἑαυτ. πόλιν and omits by homoiotel. ὁδοιπ.—ναυτῶν
[11] A τραυμ. τῶν ἐγχωρίων τρυφ. by em.   after τρυφ. ApB
καὶ ἐν ἡσυχίᾳ ὄντων τούτους εἰς βοήθειαν ἥξειν ἱκέτευον (two
incorp. glosses and τούτους by em.)

witness that neither Daphnis nor his goats had done any wrong, but that it was the wind and sea, and that of those there were other judges. Yet by this sentence Philetas could not persuade and bind the Methymnaeans, but again in a fury they fell to towse Daphnis, and offered to bind him. With which the villagers being moved, fell upon them like flocks of starlings or jackdaws, and carried him away as he was bustling amongst them, never ceasing till with their clubs they had driven them the ground, and beaten them from their coasts into other fields.

18. While thus they pursued the Methymnaeans, Chloe had time without disturbance to bring Daphnis to the fountain of the Nymphs, and there to wash his bloody face,[1] and entertain him with bread and cheese out of her own scrip, and (what served to restore him most of all) give him with her soft lips a kiss sweet as honey. 19. For it wanted but a little that then her dear Daphnis had bin slain.

But these commotions could not thus be laid and at an end. For those gallants of Methymna, having been softly and delicately bred, and every man his wounds about him, travelling now by land, with miserable labour and pain got into their own country; and procuring a council to be called, humbly petitioned that their cause might be revenged, without reporting a word of those things which indeed had happened, lest perchance over

Thornley omits 'nose' as suggesting the comic.

μὴ καὶ πρὸς καταγέλαστοι[1] γένοιντο τοιαῦτα
καὶ τοσαῦτα παθόντες ὑπὸ ποιμένων, κατηγο-
ροῦντες δὲ Μυτιληναίων, ὡς τὴν ναῦν ἀφελομένων
καὶ τὰ χρήματα διαρπασάντων πολέμου νόμῳ.

Οἱ δὲ πιστεύοντες διὰ τὰ τραύματα, καὶ
νεανίσκοις τῶν πρώτων οἰκιῶν παρ᾽ αὐτοῖς τιμω-
ρῆσαι δίκαιον νομίζοντες, Μυτιληναίοις μὲν πό-
λεμον ἀκήρυκτον ἐψηφίσαντο, τὸν δὲ στρατηγὸν[2]
ἐκέλευσαν δέκα ναῦς καθελκύσαντα κακουργεῖν
αὐτῶν τὴν παραλίαν· πλησίον γὰρ χειμῶνος
ὄντος οὐκ ἦν[3] ἀσφαλὲς μείζονα στόλον πιστεύειν
τῇ θαλάττῃ.

20. Ὁ δὲ εὐθὺς τῆς ἐπιούσης[4] ἀναγόμενος
αὐτερέταις[5] στρατιώταις ἐπέπλει τοῖς παραθαλατ-
τίοις τῶν Μυτιληναίων ἀγροῖς· καὶ πολλὰ μὲν
ἥρπαζε ποίμνια, πολὺν δὲ σῖτον καὶ οἶνον, ἄρτι
πεπαυμένου τοῦ τρυγητοῦ, καὶ ἀνθρώπους δὲ οὐκ
ὀλίγους ὅσοι τούτων ἐργάται. ἐπέπλευσε καὶ τοῖς
τῆς Χλόης ἀγροῖς καὶ τοῦ Δάφνιδος· καὶ ἀπό-
βασιν ὀξεῖαν θέμενος λείαν ἤλαυνε τὰ ἐν ποσίν.

Ὁ μὲν Δάφνις οὐκ ἔνεμε τὰς αἶγας, ἀλλ᾽ ἐς τὴν
ὕλην ἀνελθὼν φυλλάδα χλωρὰν ἔκοπτεν, ὡς ἔχοι
τοῦ χειμῶνος παρέχειν τοῖς ἐρίφοις τροφήν· ὥστε[6]
ἄνωθεν θεασάμενος τὴν καταδρομὴν ἐνέκρυψεν
ἑαυτὸν στελέχει ξηρᾶς[7] ὀξύης· ἡ δὲ Χλόη παρῆν
ταῖς ἀγέλαις, καὶ διωκομένη καταφεύγει[8] πρὸς τὰς
Νύμφας ἱκέτις καὶ ἐδεῖτο φείσασθαι καὶ ὧν ἔνεμε
καὶ αὐτῆς διὰ τὰς θεάς. ἀλλ᾽ ἦν οὐδὲν ὄφελος· οἱ

---

[1] mss προσκαταγ.　　[2] A dat.　　[3] Uiii omits　　[4] A dat.
[5] p ἀντερ.　　[6] p καὶ ὥστε　　[7] mss στελ. ξύλῳ ξηρ.
[8] p φεύγει : Uii καὶ φεύγ.

and above their wounds they should be laughed at for what they had suffered at the hands of clowns; but accused the Mytilenaeans that they had taken their ship and goods in open warfare.

The citizens easily believed their story because they saw they were all wounded, and knowing them to be of the best of their families, thought it just to revenge the injury. And therefore they decreed a war against the Mytilenaeans without denouncing it by any herald, and commanded Bryaxis their general with ten sail to infest the maritim coast of Mytilene. For the winter now approaching, they thought it dangerous to trust a greater squadron at sea.

20. At dawn of the next day the general sets sail with his soldiers at the oars, and putting to the main comes up to the maritims of Mytilene, and hostilely invades them, plundering and raping away their flocks, their corn, their wines (the vintage now but lately over), with many of those that were employed in such business. They sailed up, too, to the fields of Daphnis and Chloe, and coming suddenly down upon them, preyed upon all that they could light on.

It happened that Daphnis was not then with his goats, but was gone to the wood, and there was cutting green leaves to give them for fodder in the winter. Therefore, this incursation being seen from the higher ground, he hid himself in an hollow beech-tree. But his Chloe was with their flocks, and the enemies invading her and them, she fled away to the cave of the Nymphs, and begged of the enemies that they would spare her and her flocks for those holy Goddesses' sakes. But that did not help

γὰρ Μηθυμναῖοι πολλὰ τῶν ἀγαλμάτων κατακερ
τομήσαντες καὶ τὰς ἀγέλας ἤλασαν κἀκείνην
ἤγαγον ὥσπερ αἶγα ἢ πρόβατον, παίοντες λύγοις.
21. ἔχοντες δὲ ἤδη τὰς ναῦς μεστὰς παντοδαπῆς
ἁρπαγῆς οὐκέτ᾽ ἐγίνωσκον περαιτέρω πλεῖν, ἀλλὰ
τὸν οἴκαδε πλοῦν ἐποιοῦντο καὶ τὸν χειμῶνα καὶ
τοὺς πολεμίους δεδιότες. οἱ μὲν οὖν ἀπέπλεον
εἰρεσίᾳ προσταλαιπωροῦντες, ἄνεμος γὰρ οὐκ ἦν.

Ὁ δὲ Δάφνις, ἡσυχίας γενομένης, ἐλθὼν εἰς τὸ
πεδίον ἔνθα ἔνεμον, καὶ μήτε τὰς αἶγας ἰδὼν [1] μήτε
τὰ πρόβατα καταλαβὼν μήτε Χλόην εὑρών, ἀλλὰ
ἐρημίαν πολλὴν καὶ τὴν σύριγγα ἐρριμμένην ᾗ
συνήθως ἐτέρπετο ἡ Χλόη, μέγα βοῶν καὶ ἐλεεινὸν
κωκύων ποτὲ μὲν πρὸς τὴν φηγὸν ἔτρεχεν ἔνθα
ἐκαθέζοντο,[2] ποτὲ δὲ ἐπὶ τὴν θάλατταν ὡς [3]
ὀψόμενος αὐτήν, ποτὲ δὲ ἐπὶ τὰς Νύμφας, ἐφ᾽ ἃς
ἑλκομένη κατέφυγεν. ἐνταῦθα καὶ [4] ἔρριψεν ἑαυτὸν
χαμαὶ καὶ ταῖς Νύμφαις ὡς προδούσαις κατεμέμ
φετο·

22. "Ἀφ᾽ ὑμῶν ἡρπάσθη Χλόη καὶ τοῦτο
ὑμεῖς ἰδεῖν ὑπεμείνατε; ἡ τοὺς στεφάνους ὑμῖν
πλέκουσα, ἡ σπένδουσα τοῦ πρώτου γάλακτος, ἧς
καὶ ἡ σύριγξ ἥδε ἀνάθημα; αἶγα μὲν οὐδὲ μίαν μοι
λύκος ἥρπασε, πολέμιοι δὲ τὴν ἀγέλην καὶ τὴν
συννέμουσαν. καὶ τὰς μὲν αἶγας ἀποδεροῦσι [5] καὶ
τὰ πρόβατα καταθύσουσι·[5] Χλόη δὲ λοιπὸν πόλιν
οἰκήσει. ποίοις ποσὶν ἄπειμι παρὰ τὸν πατέρα

---

[1] A εὑρὼν [2] A ἐκάθηντο [3] A omits [4] A ἐντ.
κατέφυγε καὶ [5] so Cob : mss pres.

her at all. For the Methymnaeans did not only mock
at and rail upon the statues of the Nymphs but drove
away her flocks and her before them, thumping her
along with their battons as if she had bin a sheep
or a goat. 21. But now their ships being laden
with all manner of prey, they thought it not con-
venient to sail any further but rather to make home,
for fear of the winter no less then of their enemies.
Therefore they sailed back again, and were hard put
to it to row because there wanted wind to drive
them.

The tumults and hubbubs ceasing, Daphnis came
out of the wood into the field they used to feed in,
and when he could find neither the goats, the sheep,
nor Chloe, but only a deep silence and solitude and
the pipe flung away wherewith she entertained her-
self, setting up a piteous cry and lamenting miserably,
sometimes he ran to the oak where they sate, some-
times to the sea to try if there he could set his eyes
on her, then to the Nymphs whither she fled when
she was taken, and there flinging himself upon the
ground began to accuse the Nymphs as her betrayers :

22. "It was from your statues that Chloe was drawn
and ravished away ! and how could you endure to
see it ? she that made the garlands for you, she
that every morning poured out before you and
sacrificed her first milk, and she whose pipe hangs
up there a sweet offering and donary ! The wolf in-
deed has taken from me never a goat, but the enemy
has my whole flock together with my sweet companion
of the field ; and they will kill and slay the sheep
and goats, and Chloe now must live in a city. With
what face can I now come into the sight of my

97

καὶ τὴν μητέρα, ἄνευ τῶν αἰγῶν, ἄνευ Χλόης
λιπεργάτης ἐσόμενος; ἔχω γὰρ καὶ νέμειν ἔτι
οὐδέν. ἐνταῦθα περιμενῶ[1] κείμενος ἢ θάνατον ἢ
πόλεμον δεύτερον. ἆρα καὶ σύ, Χλόη, τοιαῦτα
πάσχεις; ἆρα μέμνησαι τοῦ πεδίου τοῦδε καὶ
τῶν Νυμφῶν τῶνδε κἀμοῦ; ἢ παραμυθοῦνταί
σε τὰ πρόβατα καὶ αἱ αἶγες αἰχμάλωτοι μετὰ
σοῦ γενόμεναι;"

23. Τοιαῦτα λέγοντα αὐτὸν ἐκ τῶν δακρύων
καὶ τῆς λύπης ὕπνος βαθὺς καταλαμβάνει.[2] καὶ
αὐτῷ αἱ τρεῖς ἐφίστανται Νύμφαι, μεγάλαι γυ-
ναῖκες καὶ καλαί, ἡμίγυμνοι καὶ ἀνυπόδητοι, τὰς
κόμας λελυμέναι καὶ τοῖς ἀγάλμασιν ὅμοιαι. καὶ
τὸ μὲν πρῶτον ἐῴκεσαν ἐλεούσαις[3] τὸν Δάφνιν,
ἔπειτα ἡ πρεσβυτάτη λέγει ἐπιρρωννύουσα· "Μη-
δὲν ἡμᾶς μέμφου, Δάφνι· Χλόης γὰρ ἡμῖν μᾶλλον
μέλει ἢ σοί. ἡμεῖς τοι καὶ παιδίον οὖσαν αὐτὴν
ἠλεήσαμεν καὶ ἐν τῷδε τῷ ἄντρῳ κειμένην αὐτὴν
ἀνεθρέψαμεν. ἐκείνη πεδίοις[4] κοινὸν οὐδὲν καὶ
τοῖς προβατίοις τοῦ Δρύαντος.[5] καὶ νῦν δὲ ἡμῖν
πεφρόντισται τὸ κατ' ἐκείνην, ὡς μήτε εἰς τὴν
Μήθυμναν κομισθεῖσα δουλεύοι μήτε μέρος γένοιτο
λείας πολεμικῆς. καὶ τὸν Πᾶνα ἐκεῖνον τὸν ὑπὸ
τῇ πίτυϊ ἱδρυμένον, ὃν ὑμεῖς οὐδέποτε οὐδὲ ἄνθεσιν
ἐτιμήσατε, τούτου ἐδεήθημεν ἐπίκουρον γενέσθαι
Χλόης· συνήθης γὰρ στρατοπέδοις μᾶλλον ἡμῶν,
καὶ πολλοὺς ἤδη πολέμους ἐπολέμησε τὴν ἀγροι-

---

[1] mss pres.   [2] after καταλαμ. A has καὶ ὁρᾷ ἡμιγύμνους
τινας γυναῖκας καὶ ἀνυποδέτους τὰς κόμας λελυμένας ἐχούσας
καὶ τοῖς ἀγάλμασιν ὁμοίας by em. after loss of 45-letter line

father and my mother, without my goats, without
Chloe, there to stand a quit-work and runaway? For
now I have nothing left to feed, and Daphnis is no
more a goatherd. Here I'll fling myself on the
ground, and here I'll lie expecting my death or else
a second war to help me. And dost thou, sweet
Chloe, suffer now in thyself heavy things as these?
Dost thou remember and think of this field, the
Nymphs, and me? Or takest thou some comfort
from thy sheep and those goats of mine which are
carried away with thee into captivity?"

23. While he was thus lamenting his condition, by
his weeping so much and the heaviness of his grief
he fell into a deep sleep, and those three Nymphs
appeared to him, ladies of a tall stature, very fair,
half-naked, and bare-footed, their hair dishevelled,
and in all things like their statues. At first they
appeared very much to pity his cause, and then the
eldest, to erect him, spoke thus: "Blame not us at
all, Daphnis; we have greater care of Chloe then
thou thyself hast. We took pity on her when she
was yet but an infant, and when she lay in this cave
took her ourselves and saw her nursed. She does
not at all belong to the fields, nor to the flocks
of Dryas. And even now we have provided, as to her,
that she shall not be carried a slave to Methymna,
nor be any part of the enemies' prey. We have
begged of Pan, Pan that stands under yonder pine,
whom you have never honoured so much as with
flowers, that he would bring back thy Chloe and
our votary. For Pan is more accustomed to camps
then we are, and leaving the countryside has made

καὶ αὐτῷ ... γυναῖκες   3 so Wytt: mss nom.   4 A ἐκεῖ
παιδίοις   5 so Huet (Amyot): mss Λάμωνος

κίαν καταλιπών. καὶ ἄπεισι τοῖς Μηθυμναίοις
οὐκ ἀγαθὸς πολέμιος. κάμνε δὲ μηδέν, ἀλλ᾽
ἀναστὰς ὄφθητι Λάμωνι καὶ Μυρτάλῃ, οἳ καὶ
αὐτοὶ κεῖνται χαμαὶ νομίζοντες καὶ σὲ μέρος γεγο-
νέναι τῆς ἁρπαγῆς· Χλόη γάρ σοι τῆς ἐπιούσης[1]
ἀφίξεται μετὰ τῶν αἰγῶν, μετὰ τῶν προβάτων,
καὶ νεμήσετε[2] κοινῇ καὶ συρίσετε κοινῇ· τὰ δὲ
ἄλλα μελήσει περὶ ὑμῶν Ἔρωτι."

24. Τοιαῦτα ἰδὼν καὶ ἀκούσας Δάφνις ἀνα-
πηδήσας τῶν ὕπνων καὶ κοινῶν[3] μεστὸς ἡδονῆς καὶ
λύπης δακρύων τὰ ἀγάλματα τῶν Νυμφῶν προσ-
εκύνει, καὶ ἐπηγγέλλετο σωθείσης Χλόης θύσειν
τῶν αἰγῶν τὴν ἀρίστην. δραμὼν δὲ καὶ ἐπὶ τὴν
πίτυν, ἔνθα τὸ τοῦ Πανὸς ἄγαλμα ἵδρυτο, κερασ-
φόρον, τραγοσκελές, τῇ μὲν σύριγγα, τῇ δὲ τράγον
πηδῶντα κατέχον,[4] κἀκεῖνον προσεκύνει καὶ ηὔ-
χετο ὑπὲρ τῆς Χλόης καὶ τράγον θύσειν ἐπηγγέλ-
λετο.

Καὶ μόλις ποτὲ περὶ ἡλίου καταφορὰς[5] παυ-
σάμενος δακρύων καὶ εὐχῶν, ἀράμενος τὰς
φυλλάδας ἃς[6] ἔκοψεν, ἐπανῆλθεν εἰς τὴν ἔπαυλιν,
καὶ τοὺς[7] ἀμφὶ τὸν Λάμωνα πένθους ἀπαλλάξας,
εὐφροσύνης ἐμπλήσας, τροφῆς τε ἐγεύσατο καὶ ἐς
ὕπνον τρέπεται,[8] οὐδὲ τοῦτον ἄδακρυν, ἀλλ᾽
εὐχόμενος μὲν αὖθις τὰς Νύμφας ὄναρ ἰδεῖν,
εὐχόμενος δὲ τὴν ἡμέραν γενέσθαι ταχέως, ἐν ᾗ
Χλόην ἐπηγγείλαντο αὐτῷ.

---

[1] A dat.   [2] Ap νεμήσεσθε prob. old var. : Uiii νεμήσετε
and νομήσετε   [3] Å κινῶν : pq κοινῇ   p ἡδ. κ. λύπ. μεστὸς
δακ. (Uii ὑφ᾽ ἡδ.) : q ὑφ᾽ ἡδ. κ. λύπ. δακ.   [4] Uiii κατέχον

many wars; and the Methymnaeans shall find him
an infesting enemy. Trouble not thyself any longer,
but get thee up and shew thyself to Myrtale and
Lamo, who now themselves lie cast on the ground
thinking thee too to be part of the rapine. For
Chloe shall certainly come to thee to-morrow, ac-
companied with the sheep and the goats. You shall
feed together as before and play together on the
pipe. For other things concerning you, Love himself
will take the care."

24. Now when Daphnis had seen and heard these
things, he started up out of his sleep, and with tears
in his eyes both of pleasure and of grief, adored
the statues of the Nymphs, and vowed to sacrifice
to them the best of all his she-goats if Chloe should
return safe. And running to the pine where the
statue of Pan was placed, the head horned, the
legs a goat's, one hand holding a pipe, the other a
he-goat leaping, that too he adored, and made a vow
for the safety of Chloe and promised Pan a he-goat.

Scarce now with the setting of the sun he made
a pause of his weeping, his wailing, and his prayers,
and taking up the boughs he had cut in the wood,
returned to the cottage, comforted Lamo and his
household and made them merry, refreshed himself
with meat and wine, and fell into a deep sleep; yet
not that without tears, praying to see the Nymphs
again and calling for an early day, the day that they
had promised Chloe.

and -ων : p κατέσχε   5 A -βολὰς   6 A ἀράμενοι ἐκ τῶν
φυλλάδων ὧν   7 Uiii τοῦ : Parr τῶν by em.   8 pq ὥρμησεν

DAPHNIS AND CHLOE

Νυκτῶν πασῶν ἐκείνη ἔδοξε μακροτάτη γεγονέναι. ἐπράχθη δὲ ἐπ' αὐτῆς¹ τάδε· 25. ὁ στρατηγὸς ὁ τῶν Μηθυμναίων ὅσον δέκα σταδίους ἀπελάσας ἠθέλησε τῇ καταδρομῇ τοὺς στρατιώτας κεκμηκότας ἀναλαβεῖν. ἄκρας οὖν ἐπεμβαινούσης τῷ πελάγει λαβόμενος ἐπεκτεινομένης μηνοειδῶς, ἧς ἐντὸς θάλαττα γαληνότερον τῶν λιμένων ὅρμον εἰργάζετο, ἐνταῦθα τὰς ναῦς ἐπ' ἀγκυρῶν μετεώρους διορμίσας, ὡς μηδὲ μίαν ἐκ τῆς γῆς τῶν ἀγροίκων τινὰ λυπῆσαι, ἀνῆκεν τοὺς Μηθυμναίους εἰς τέρψιν εἰρηνικήν. οἱ δὲ ἔχοντες πάντων ἀφθονίαν ἐκ τῆς ἁρπαγῆς ἔπινον, ἔπαιζον, ἐπινίκιον ἑορτὴν ἐμιμοῦντο.

Ἄρτι δὲ παυομένης ἡμέρας καὶ τῆς τέρψεως ἐς νύκτα ληγούσης, αἰφνίδιον μὲν ἡ γῆ πᾶσα ἐδόκει λάμπεσθαι πυρί, κτύπος δὲ ἠκούετο ῥόθιος κωπῶν ὡς ἐπιπλέοντος μεγάλου στόλου. ἐβόα τις ὁπλίζεσθαι τὸν στρατηγόν, ἄλλος ἄλλο² ἐκάλει, καὶ τετρῶσθαί τις ἐδόκει καὶ σχήματι³ ἔκειτο νεκροῦ. εἴκασεν ἄν τις ὁρᾶν νυκτομαχίαν οὐ παρόντων πολεμίων.

26. Τῆς δὲ νυκτὸς αὐτοῖς τοιαύτης γενομένης ἐπῆλθεν ἡ ἡμέρα πολὺ τῆς νυκτὸς φοβερωτέρα. οἱ τράγοι μὲν οἱ τοῦ Δάφνιδος καὶ αἱ αἶγες κιττὸν ἐν τοῖς κέρασι κορυμβοφόρον εἶχον, οἱ δὲ κριοὶ καὶ αἱ οἷς τῆς Χλόης λύκων ὠρυγμὸν ὠρύοντο. ὤφθη δὲ καὶ αὐτὴ πίτυος ἐστεφανωμένη. ἐγίνετο καὶ περὶ τὴν θάλατταν αὐτὴν πολλὰ παράδοξα· αἵ τε γὰρ ἄγκυραι κατὰ βυθοῦ πειρωμένων ἀναφέρειν

---

¹ A dat.   ² mss omit   ³ "like" : pUiii σχῆμά τι : B σχῆμά τις : perh. σχήματί τις E   pq νεκροῦ μιμούμενον by em.

That night seemed the longest of nights, but in it these wonders were done. 25. The general of the Methymnaeans, when he had borne off to sea about ten furlongs, would refresh his wearied soldiers after the incursion and plunder. Coming up therefore to a promontore which ran into the sea, winding itself into a half-moon within which the sea made a calmer station then in a port—in this place when he had cast anchor (lest the rustics should mischieve him from the land), he permitted them securely to rant and be jovial as in peace. The Methymnaeans, because by this direption they abounded with all things, feasted, caroused, and danced, and celebrated victorials.

But the day being now spent and their mirth protracted to the night, on a sudden all the land seemed to be on a light fire; then anon their ears were struck with an impetuous clattering of oars as if a great navy were a coming. Some cried out the general must arm; some called this and others that; here some thought they were wounded, there others lay like dead men. A man would have thought he had seen a kind of nocturnal battle, when yet there was no enemy there.

26. The night thus past in these spectres, the day arose far more terrible than the night. For on the horns of all Daphnis his goats there grew up on a sudden the berried ivy, and Chloe's sheep were heard to howl like wolves in the woods. Chloe herself in the midst of her flocks appeared crowned with a most fresh and shady pine. In the sea itself too there happened many wonders, paradoxes, and prodigies. For when they laboured to weigh their

DAPHNIS AND CHLOE

ἔμενον, αἵ τε κῶπαι καθιέντων εἰς εἰρεσίαν ἐθραύ-
οντο, καὶ δελφῖνες πηδῶντες ἐξ ἁλὸς[1] ταῖς οὐραῖς
παίοντες τὰς ναῦς ἔλυον τὰ γομφώματα. ἠκούετό
τις καὶ ἀπὸ[2] τῆς ὀρθίου πέτρας τῆς ὑπὲρ[3] τὴν
ἄκραν σύριγγος ἦχος· ἀλλὰ οὐκ ἔτερπεν ὡς σύριγξ,
ἐφόβει δὲ τοὺς ἀκούοντας ὡς σάλπιγξ. ἐταράτ-
τοντο οὖν καὶ ἐπὶ τὰ ὅπλα ἔθεον καὶ πολεμίους
ἐκάλουν τοὺς οὐ βλεπομένους·[4] ὥστε πάλιν
ηὔχοντο νύκτα ἐπελθεῖν ὡς τευξόμενοι σπονδῶν ἐν
αὐτῇ.

Συνετὰ μὲν οὖν πᾶσιν ἦν τὰ γινόμενα τοῖς
φρονοῦσιν ὀρθῶς, ὅτι ἐκ Πανὸς ἦν τὰ φαντάσματα
καὶ ἀκούσματα μηνίοντός τι τοῖς ναύταις. οὐκ
εἶχον δὲ τὴν αἰτίαν συμβαλεῖν (οὐδὲν[5] γὰρ ἱερὸν
σεσύλητο Πανός), ἔστε[6] ἀμφὶ μέσην ἡμέραν εἰς
ὕπνον οὐκ ἀθεεὶ τοῦ στρατηγοῦ καταπεσόντος
αὐτὸς ὁ Πὰν ὤφθη τοιάδε λέγων· 27. "Ὦ πάντων
ἀνοσιώτατοι καὶ ἀσεβέστατοι, τί ταῦτα μαινο-
μέναις φρεσὶν ἐτολμήσατε; πολέμου μὲν τὴν
ἀγροικίαν ἐνεπλήσατε τὴν ἐμοὶ φίλην, ἀγέλας δὲ
βοῶν καὶ αἰγῶν καὶ ποιμνίων[7] ἀπηλάσατε τὰς
ἐμοὶ μελομένας, ἀπεσπάσατε δὲ βωμῶν παρθένον
ἐξ ἧς Ἔρως μῦθον ποιῆσαι θέλει, καὶ οὔτε τὰς
Νύμφας ᾐδέσθητε βλεπούσας οὔτε τὸν Πᾶνα ἐμέ.
οὔτ' οὖν Μήθυμναν ὄψεσθε μετὰ τοιούτων λαφύ-
ρων πλέοντες οὔτε τήνδε φεύξεσθε τὴν σύριγγα
τὴν ὑμᾶς ταράξασαν,[8] ἀλλὰ ὑμᾶς βορὰν ἰχθύων

---

[1] mss ἐξ ἁλ. after ναῦς   [2] so Cour: mss ὑπὲρ   [3] pq ὑπὸ
ἄκραν: A πέτραν   [4] οὐ βλεπ.: A δεομ.   [5] A οὐδὲ
[6] A omits   [7] Uiii omits: A ἀγέλας δὲ ποιμ. καὶ βοῶν
ἀπηλ.   [8] A pres.

anchors and be gone, their anchors stuck as fast as
the earth; and when they cast their oars to row,
they snapped and broke; leaping dolphins with the
thumping of their tails loosened the planks of the
barges. From that crag which lifted up itself over
the promontore, was heard a strange sound of a pipe;
yet it was not pleasing as a pipe, but like a trumpet
or a terrible cornet, which made them run to their
arms and call those enemies whom they saw not at
all. Insomuch that they wished it night again, as if
they should have a truce by that.

Yet those things which then happened might very
well be understood by such as were wise, namely
that those spectres, phantasms, and sounds proceeded
from Pan, shewing himself angry at the voyagers.
Yet the cause they could not conjecture (for nothing
sacred to Pan was robbed), until about high noon,
their grand captain not without the impulse of some
deity fallen into a sleep, Pan himself appeared to
him and rated him thus: 27. " O ye most unholy
and wickedest of mortals! What made you so bold
as madly to attempt and do such outrages as these?
You have not only filled with war these fields that
are so dear to me, but also you have driven away
herds of cattle, flocks of sheep and goats that were
my care. Besides, you have taken sacrilegiously
from the altars of the Nymphs a maid of whom
Love himself will write a story. Nor did you at all
revere the Nymphs that looked upon you when you
did it, nor yet me whom very well you knew to be
Pan. Therefore you shall never see Methymna,
sailing away with those spoils, nor shall you escape
that terrible pipe from the promontore, but I will

θήσω καταδύσας, εἰ μὴ τὴν ταχίστην καὶ Χλόην
ταῖς Νύμφαις ἀποδώσεις καὶ τὰς ἀγέλας Χλόης
καὶ τὰς αἶγας καὶ τὰ πρόβατα. ἀνάστα[1] δὴ καὶ
ἐκβίβαζε τὴν κόρην μεθ᾽ ὧν εἶπον· ἡγήσομαι[2] δὲ
ἐγὼ καὶ σοὶ τοῦ πλοῦ κἀκείνῃ τῆς ὁδοῦ."

28. Πάνυ οὖν τεθορυβημένος ὁ Βρύαξις (οὕτω[3]
γὰρ ἐκαλεῖτο ὁ στρατηγὸς) ἀναπηδᾷ, καὶ τῶν νεῶν
καλέσας τοὺς ἡγεμόνας ἐκέλευσε τὴν ταχίστην ἐν
τοῖς αἰχμαλώτοις ἀναζητεῖσθαι Χλόην. οἱ δὲ
ταχέως καὶ ἀνεῦρον καὶ εἰς ὀφθαλμοὺς ἐκόμισαν·[4]
ἐκαθέζετο γὰρ τῆς πίτυος ἐστεφανωμένη. σύμ-
βολον δὴ καὶ τοῦτο τῆς ἐν τοῖς ὀνείροις ὄψεως
ποιούμενος, ἐπ᾽ αὐτῆς τῆς ναυαρχίδος εἰς τὴν
γῆν αὐτὴν κομίζει. κἀκείνη δὲ ἄρτι ἀποβεβήκει
καὶ σύριγγος ἦχος ἀκούεται πάλιν ἐκ τῆς πέτρας,
οὐκέτι φοβερὸς καὶ πολεμικός, ἀλλὰ ποιμενικὸς
καὶ οἷος εἰς νομὴν ἡγεῖται ποιμνίων. καὶ τά τε
πρόβατα κατὰ τῆς ἀποβάθρας ἐξέτρεχεν ἐξολι-
σθάνοντα[5] τοῖς κέρασι τῶν χηλῶν, καὶ αἱ αἶγες
πολὺ θρασύτερον, οἷα καὶ κρημνοβατεῖν εἰθισμέ-
ναι. 29. καὶ ταῦτα μὲν περιίστατι κύκλῳ τὴν
Χλόην ὥσπερ χορός, σκιρτῶντα καὶ βληχώμενα
καὶ ὅμοια χαίρουσιν· αἱ δὲ τῶν ἄλλων αἰπόλων
αἶγες καὶ τὰ πρόβατα καὶ τὰ βουκόλια κατὰ
χώραν ἔμενεν ἐν κοίλῃ νηΐ, καθάπερ αὐτὰ τοῦ
μέλους μὴ καλοῦντος.[6]

Θαύματι δὲ πάντων ἐχομένων[7] καὶ τὸν Πᾶνα

[1] pq ἀνίστω   [2] A omits ἡγήσ. . . . ὁδοῦ   [3] pq τοῦτο
[4] A ἤγαγον   ἐκαθές. . . . ἐστεφ. : A καθεζομένῃ ἐπὶ τῆς πίτυος
ἐστεφανωμένῃ   [5] pq οὐκ ἐξολισθ.   [6] Uiii ἐκκαλοῦντος
[7] Uiii ἔνεχ.

drown you every man and make you food for the
fish, unless thou speedily restore to the Nymphs
as well Chloe as Chloe's herds and flocks. Rise there-
fore and send the maid ashore, send her with all that
I command thee; and I shall be as well to thee a
convey[1] in thy voyage home as to her a conduct on
her way to the fields.''

28. Bryaxis, being astonished at this, started up,
and calling together the captains of the ships, com-
manded that Chloe should be quickly sought for
among the captives. They found her presently and
brought her before him; for she sate crowned with
the pine. The general, remembering that the pine
was the mark and signal distinction which he had in
his dream, carried the maid ashore in the admiral[2]
with no small observance and ceremonious fear. Now
as soon as Chloe was set on shore, the sound of the
pipe from the promontore began to be heard again,
not martial and terrible as before, but perfectly pas-
toral such as is used to lead the cattle to feed in the
fields. The sheep ran down the scale[3] of the ship,
slipping and sliding on their horny hooves; the
goats more boldly, for they were used to climb
the crags and steeps of the hills. 29. The whole
flock encircled Chloe, moving as in a dance about
her, and with their skipping and their blating
shewed a kind of joyfulness and exultation. But
the goats of other goatherds, as also the sheep
and the herds, stirred not a foot, but remained still
in the holds of the ships as if the music of that pipe
did not at all call for them.

When therefore they were all struck with admira-

---

[1] so Thornley. [2] the flagship. [3] ladder.

DAPHNIS AND CHLOE

ἀνευφημούντων, ὤφθη τούτων ἐν τοῖς στοιχείοις
ἀμφοτέροις θαυμασιώτερα. τῶν μὲν Μηθυμναίων
πρὶν ἀνασπάσαι τὰς ἀγκύρας ἔπλεον αἱ νῆες,
καὶ τῆς ναυαρχίδος ἡγεῖτο δελφὶς πηδῶν ἐξ ἁλός.
τῶν δὲ αἰγῶν καὶ τῶν προβάτων ἡγεῖτο σύριγγος
ἦχος ἥδιστος, καὶ τὸν συρίττοντα ἔβλεπεν οὐδείς·
ὥστε τὰ ποίμνια καὶ αἱ αἶγες προῄεσαν ἅμα καὶ
ἐνέμοντο τερπόμεναι τῷ μέλει.

30. Δευτέρας που νομῆς καιρὸς ἦν καὶ ὁ
Δάφνις ἀπὸ σκοπῆς τινος μετεώρου θεασάμενος
τὰς ἀγέλας καὶ τὴν Χλόην, μέγα βοήσας "ὦ
Νύμφαι καὶ Πὰν" κατέδραμεν εἰς τὸ πεδίον,
καὶ περιπλακεὶς τῇ Χλόῃ καὶ λιποθυμήσας[1]
κατέπεσε. μόλις δὲ ἔμβιος ὑπὸ τῆς Χλόης
φιλούσης καὶ ταῖς περιβολαῖς θαλπούσης γε-
νόμενος, ὑπὸ[2] τὴν συνήθη φηγὸν ἔρχεται, καὶ
ἐπὶ[3] τῷ στελέχει καθίσας ἐπυνθάνετο πῶς ἀπέδρα
τοσούτους πολεμίους. ἡ δὲ αὐτῷ κατέλεξε πάντα,
τὸν τῶν αἰγῶν κιττόν, τὸν τῶν προβάτων ὠρυ-
γμόν, τὴν ἐπανθήσασαν τῇ κεφαλῇ πίτυν, τὸ
ἐν τῇ γῇ πῦρ, τὸν ἐν τῇ θαλάττῃ κτύπον, τὰ
συρίσματα ἀμφότερα τὸ πολεμικὸν καὶ τὸ εἰρη-
νικόν, τὴν νύκτα τὴν φοβεράν, ὅπως αὐτῇ τὴν
ὁδὸν ἀγνοούσῃ καθηγήσατο τῆς ὁδοῦ μουσική.

Γνωρίσας οὖν ὁ Δάφνις τὰ τῶν Νυμφῶν

[1] mss λειπ.   [2] pq ἐπὶ   [3] so Brunck : mss ὑπὸ

108

tion at these things and celebrated the praises
of Pan, there were yet seen in both the elements
things more wonderful then those before. For
the ships of the Methymnaeans before they had
weighed their anchors ran amain, and a huge dolphin
bouncing still out of the sea went before and led
their admiral. On the land a most sweet melodious
pipe led the goats and the sheep, and yet nobody
saw the piper; only all the cattle went along
together and fed rejoicing at his music.

30. It was now the time of the second pasturing,
when Daphnis having spied from a high stand Chloe
coming with the flocks, crying out mainly " O ye
Nymphs, O blessed Pan!" made down to the plain,
and rushing into the embraces of Chloe, in a swoon
fell to the ground. With much ado when he was
come to himself with Chloe's kisses and embraces in
her close and warm arms, he got to the oak where
they were wont, and when he was sate down on
the trunk he asked her how she had escaped such a
dangerous captivity as that. Then she told him
everything one after another; how the fresh and
berried ivy appeared on the horns of all the goats,
how her sheep howled like wolves, how a pine
sprung up upon her head, how all the land seemed
on a fire, what horrible fragors and clashings were
heard from the sea; with the two tones of that
pipe from the crag of the promontore, the one to
war, the other to peace, the terrible spectres of
the night, how she not knowing her way had
for her companion and guide the sweet music of
that strange invisible pipe.

Daphnis then acknowledged [1] the vision of the

---

[1] recognised.

ὀνείρατα καὶ τὰ τοῦ Πανὸς ἔργα, διηγεῖται καὶ αὐτὸς ὅσα εἶδεν, ὅσα ἤκουσεν, ὅτι μέλλων ἀποθνήσκειν διὰ τὰς Νύμφας ἔζησε. καὶ τὴν μὲν ἀποπέμπει κομίσουσαν[1] τοὺς ἀμφὶ τὸν Δρύαντα καὶ Λάμωνα καὶ ὅσα πρέπει[2] θυσίᾳ, αὐτὸς δὲ ἐν τούτῳ τῶν αἰγῶν τὴν ἀρίστην συλλαβών, καὶ κιττῷ στεφανώσας ὥσπερ ὤφθησαν τοῖς πολεμίοις καὶ γάλα τῶν κεράτων κατασπείσας, ἔθυσέ τε ταῖς Νύμφαις καὶ κρεμάσας ἀπέδειρε καὶ τὸ δέρμα ἀνέθηκεν.

31. Ἤδη δὲ παρόντων τῶν ἀμφὶ τὴν Χλόην, πῦρ ἀνακαύσας καὶ τὰ μὲν ἐψήσας τῶν κρεῶν τὰ δὲ ὀπτήσας, ἀπήρξατό τε ταῖς Νύμφαις καὶ κρατῆρα γλεύκους ἐπέσπεισε μεστόν. καὶ ἐκ φυλλάδος στιβάδας ὑποσωρεύσας[3] <πᾶς> ἐντεῦθεν ἐν τροφῇ ἦν καὶ ποτῷ[4] καὶ παιδιᾷ. καὶ ἅμα τὰς ἀγέλας ἐπεσκοποῦντο[5] μὴ λύκος ἐμπεσὼν ἔργα ποιήσῃ πολεμίων. ἦσάν τινας καὶ ᾠδὰς εἰς τὰς Νύμφας, παλαιῶν ποιμένων ποιήματα. νυκτὸς δὲ ἐπελθούσης αὐτοῦ κοιμηθέντες[6] ἐν τῷ ἀγρῷ, τῆς ἐπιούσης τοῦ Πανὸς ἐμνημόνευσαν,[7] καὶ τῶν τράγων τὸν ἀγελάρχην στεφανώσαντες πίτυος προσήγαγον τῇ πίτυϊ, καὶ ἐπισπείσαντες οἴνου καὶ εὐφημοῦντες τὸν θεόν, ἔθυσαν, ἐκρέ-

---

[1] p pres. [2] pB πρέπον : Parr πρέποντα [3] Uiii ἀποσωρεύσας prob. old var. : A ὑποστορεύσας : pB ὑποστορέσας <πᾶς> E [4] ἐν τροφῇ ἦν καὶ ποτῷ : A τρυφὴ ἦν and lac. [5] so E cf. i. 32 : mss -ει (sing. following loss of πᾶς above) [6] Uiii -τος [7] pq impf.

Nymphs and the works of Pan, and storied to her
what he himself had seen, and what he had heard,
and how when he was ready to die for grief his life
was saved by the providence and kindness of the holy
Nymphs. And then presently he sent her away to
bring Dryas and Lamo and their wives to the sacri-
fice, and all things necessary for such a devotion to
Pan and the Nymphs. In the meantime he catched
the fairest of all his she-goats, and when he had
crowned it with ivy in that manner as the whole
flock had appeared to the enemy, and had poured
milk on the horns, in the name of the Nymphs
he struck and killed it, and sacrificed it to them.
He hanged it up, took off the skin, consecrated that,
and made it an offering.

31. When Chloe with her company was come,
he made a fire, and some of the flesh being boiled
and some roasted, he offered the first and chiefest
parts of both to the Nymphs, and filling a bowl
with new wine, made a libation; then, having made
several beds of green leaves, every man gave himself
wholly to eating, drinking, and playing; only they
looked out now and then lest the irruption of a
wolf upon the flocks should chance to do something
like an enemy. They sung too certain songs in
the praise of the Nymphs, the solemn carmens
of the ancient shepherds. All that night they lay
in the fields; and the next day they were not
unmindful of the wonder-working Pan, but took
the he-goat that was captain and leader of the
flock, and when they had crowned him with pine-
garlands they brought him to the pine, and pouring
wine upon his head, with benedictions and thankful

μασαν, ἀπέδειραν. καὶ τὰ μὲν κρέα ὀπτήσαντες
καὶ ἐψήσαντες πλησίον ἔθηκαν ἐν τῷ λειμῶνι
ἐν τοῖς φύλλοις, τὸ δὲ δέρμα κέρασιν αὐτοῖς
ἐνέπηξαν τῇ πίτυϊ πρὸς τῷ ἀγάλματι, ποιμενικὸν
ἀνάθημα ποιμενικῷ θεῷ. ἀπήρξαντο καὶ τῶν
κρεῶν, ἀπέσπεισαν καὶ κρατῆρος μείζονος. ᾖσεν
ἡ Χλόη, Δάφνις ἐσύρισεν.

32. Ἐπὶ τούτοις κατακλιθέντες ἤσθιον καὶ
αὐτοῖς ἐφίσταται ὁ βουκόλος Φιλητᾶς, κατὰ
τύχην στεφανίσκους τινὰς τῷ Πανὶ κομίζων
καὶ βότρυς ἔτι ἐν φύλλοις καὶ κλήμασι. καὶ
αὐτῷ τῶν παίδων ὁ νεώτατος εἵπετο Τίτυρος,
πυρρὸν παιδίον καὶ γλαυκόν, λευκὸν παιδίον
καὶ[1] ἀγέρωχον· καὶ ἥλλετο κοῦφα βαδίζων
ὥσπερ ἔριφος. ἀναπηδήσαντες οὖν συνεστεφά-
νουν τὸν Πᾶνα καὶ τὰ κλήματα τῆς κόμης τῆς
πίτυος συνεξήρτων,[2] καὶ κατακλίναντες πλησίον
αὐτῶν συμπότην ἐποιοῦντο. καὶ οἷα δὴ γέροντες
ὑποβεβρεγμένοι πρὸς ἀλλήλους πολλὰ ἔλεγον,
ὡς ἔνεμον ἡνίκα ἦσαν νέοι, ὡς πολλὰς λῃστῶν
καταδρομὰς διέφυγον. ἐσεμνύνετό τις ὡς λύκον
ἀποκτείνας· ἄλλος ὡς μόνου τοῦ Πανὸς δεύτερα

---

[1] Β λευκ. δὲ καὶ : Uiii omits betw. γλαυκ. and ἔριφος
[2] so E : mss ἐξήρτων

praise they sacrificed him to Pan the preserver. Then hanging him up they flayed him, and the flesh, part roasted, part boiled, they set upon banks of green leaves hard by in the meadow. The skin, horns and all, they pegged to the pine close to the statue, to a pastoral God a pastoral offering. They offered too the first carvings of the flesh, and made him a libation with a greater bowl then to the Nymphs.[1] Chloe sang and Daphnis played upon the pipe.

32. These rites performed, they sate down and fell to feast. And it happened that Philetas the herdsman came up to them bringing with him certain garlands to honour Pan, together with grapes hanging still among the leaves and branches. His youngest son Tityrus came along with him, a ruddy lad, greyeyed and fair-skinned, stout and fierce, and of a nimble bounding pace like a kid. When they saw what the intention of the good old Philetas was, they started up, and all together crowned the statue of Pan with garlands, and hanged the palmits with their grapes upon the leaves of the pine; and then they make Philetas sit down to the feast and be their guest, to eat and drink and celebrate. Then, as old men use to do when they are a little whittled with wine, they had various discourses and chats amongst them; how bravely in their youth they had administered the pasturing of their flocks and herds, how in their time they had escaped very many invasions and inroads of pirates and thieves. Here one bragged that he had killed a wolf, here another that he had bin second to Pan alone in the skill

---

[1] the Greek is simply 'greater': perhaps 'a good large bowl.'

συρίσας. τοῦτο τοῦ Φιλητᾶ τὸ σεμνολόγημα ἦν·
33. ὁ οὖν Δάφνις καὶ ἡ Χλόη πάσας δεήσεις
προσέφερον μεταδοῦναι καὶ αὐτοῖς τῆς τέχνης
συρίσαι τε ἐν ἑορτῇ θεοῦ σύριγγι χαίροντος.

Ἐπαγγέλλεται Φιλητᾶς, καίτοι τὸ γῆρας ὡς
ἄπνουν μεμψάμενος, καὶ ἔλαβε σύριγγα τὴν τοῦ
Δάφνιδος. ἡ δὲ ἦν μικρὰ πρὸς μεγάλην τέχνην,
οἷα ἐν στόματι παιδὸς ἐμπνεομένη. πέμπει οὖν
Τίτυρον ἐπὶ τὴν ἑαυτοῦ σύριγγα, τῆς ἐπαύλεως
ἀπεχούσης σταδίους δέκα. ὁ μὲν ῥίψας τὸ ἐγκόμ-
βωμα γυμνὸς ὥρμησε τρέχειν ὥσπερ νεβρός· ὁ δὲ
Λάμων ἐπηγγείλατο αὐτοῖς τὸν περὶ τῆς σύριγγος
ἀφηγήσασθαι μῦθον, ὃν αὐτῷ Σικελὸς αἰπόλος
ᾖσεν ἐπὶ μισθῷ τράγῳ καὶ σύριγγι·

34. "Αὕτη ἡ σύριγξ τὸ ἀρχαῖον[1] οὐκ ἦν ὄργανον,
ἀλλὰ παρθένος καλὴ καὶ τὴν φωνὴν μουσική.
αἶγας ἔνεμεν, Νύμφαις συνέπαιζεν, ᾖδεν οἷον νῦν.
Πάν, ταύτης νεμούσης, παιζούσης, ᾀδούσης, προσ-
ελθὼν ἔπειθεν ἐς ὅ τι ἔχρῃζε καὶ ἐπηγγέλλετο
τὰς αἶγας πάσας θήσειν διδυματόκους. ἡ δὲ ἐγέλα
τὸν ἔρωτα αὐτοῦ, οὐδὲ ἐραστὴν ἔφη δέξασθαι μήτε
τράγον μήτε ἄνθρωπον ὁλόκληρον. ὁρμᾷ διώκειν
ὁ Πὰν ἐς βίαν· ἡ Σύριγξ ἔφευγε καὶ τὸν Πᾶνα
καὶ τὴν βίαν.[2] φεύγουσα, κάμνουσα ἐς δόνακας
κρύπτεται, εἰς ἕλος ἀφανίζεται. Πὰν τοὺς δόνακας
ὀργῇ τεμών, τὴν κόρην οὐχ εὑρών, τὸ πάθος μαθὼν

---

[1] so Koen (Amyot by em.): mss ὄργανον   [2] p omits ἡ
Σ. . . . βίαι

and art of piping. And this was the crack[1] of Philetas; 33. and therefore Daphnis and Chloe used all manner of supplications to him, that he would communicate with them that art of piping, and play upon the pipe at the feast of that God whom he knew to delight so much in the pipe.

Philetas promised to do it, although he blamed old age for his short breath; and so took Daphnis his pipe. But that being too little for so great an art, as being made to be inspirited by the mouth of a boy, he sent his son Tityrus for his own, the cottage lying distant from thence but ten furlongs. Tityrus, flinging off his jacket, ran swift as a hind. But Lamo promised to tell them that tale of the pipe which a Sicilian goatherd, hired by him for a goat and a pipe, had sung to him:

34. " This pipe was heretofore no organ, but a very fair maid, who had a sweet and musical voice. She fed goats, played together with the Nymphs, and sang as now. Pan, while she in this manner was tending her goats, playing and singing, came to her and endeavoured to persuade her to what he desired, and promised her that he would make all her goats bring forth twins every year. But she disdained and derided his love, and denied to take him to be her sweetheart who was neither perfect man nor perfect goat. Pan follows her with violence and thinks to force her. Syrinx fled Pan and his force. Being now aweary with her flight, she shot herself into a grove of reeds, sunk in the fen, and disappeared. Pan for anger cut up the reeds, and finding not the maid there, and then reflecting

1 boast.

καὶ τοὺς καλάμους κηρῷ συνδήσας ἀνίσους, καθ'
ὅτι καὶ ὁ ἔρως ἄνισος αὐτοῖς, τὸ ὄργανον νοεῖ,[1] καὶ
ἡ τότε παρθένος καλὴ νῦν ἐστι σύριγξ μουσική."

35. Ἄρτι πέπαυτο τοῦ μυθολογήματος ὁ Λάμων
καὶ ἐπῄνει Φιλητᾶς αὐτὸν ὡς εἰπόντα μῦθον ᾠδῆς
γλυκύτερον, καὶ ὁ Τίτυρος ἐφίσταται τὴν σύριγγα
τῷ πατρὶ κομίζων, μέγα ὄργανον καὶ καλάμων[2]
μεγάλων, καὶ ἵνα[3] κεκήρωτο χαλκῷ πεποίκιλτο·
εἴκασεν ἄν τις εἶναι ταύτην ἐκείνην ἣν ὁ Πὰν
πρώτην[4] ἐπήξατο. διεγερθεὶς οὖν ὁ Φιλητᾶς καὶ
καθίσας ἐν καθέδρᾳ ὄρθιον, πρῶτον μὲν ἀπεπειράθη
τῶν καλάμων εἰ εὔπνοοι· ἔπειτα μαθὼν ὡς ἀκώ-
λυτον διατρέχει τὸ πνεῦμα, ἐνέπνει τὸ ἐντεῦθεν
πολὺ καὶ νεανικόν· αὐλῶν τις ἂν ᾠήθη συναυλούν-
των ἀκούειν, τοσοῦτον ἤχει τὸ σύριγμα. κατ'
ὀλίγον δὲ τῆς βίας ἀφαιρῶν εἰς τὸ τερπνότερον
μετέβαλλε τὸ μέλος. καὶ πᾶσαν τέχνην ἐπιδεικνύ-
μενος εὐνομίας μουσικῆς ἐσύριττεν, οἷον[5] βοῶν
ἀγέλῃ πρέπον, οἷον αἰπολίῳ[6] πρόσφορον, οἷον[7]
ποίμναις φίλον. τερπνὸν ἦν τὸ ποιμνίων,[8] μέγα
τὸ βοῶν, ὀξὺ τὸ αἰγῶν. ὅλως πάσας σύριγγας μία
σύριγξ ἐμιμήσατο.

36. Οἱ μὲν οὖν ἄλλοι σιωπῇ κατέκειντο τερπό-
μενοι· Δρύας δὲ ἀναστὰς καὶ κελεύσας συρίττειν
Διονυσιακὸν μέλος, ἐπιλήνιον αὐτοῖς ὄρχησιν

---

[1] τὸ ὄργ. νοεῖ here *E*, in mss after μαθὼν, the emendator
thinking P. must have thought of it before making it, but
the putting together of the reeds *is* the invention of the
pipe   [2] so Villoison : mss αὐλῶν   [3] prob. old var. : Ap
ὅτι   pq τῷ χαλ.   A and perh. p omit πεποικ.   [4] so

upon what had happened, joined together unequal quills, because their love was so unequal, and thus invented this organ. So she who then was a fair maid is now become a musical pipe.''

35. Lamo had now done his tale and Philetas praised him for it as one that had told them a story far sweeter then any song, when Tityrus came in and brought his father's pipe, a large organ and made of great quills, and where it was joined together with wax there too it was set and varied with brass. Insomuch that one would have thought that this had bin that very pipe which Pan the inventor made first. When therefore Philetas was got up and had set himself upright on a bench, first he tried the quills whether they sounded clear and sweet; then, finding never a cane was stopped, he played a loud and lusty tune. One would not have thought that he had heard but one pipe, the sound was so high, the consort so full. But by little and little remitting that vehemence, he changed it to a soft and sweeter tone, and displaying all the art of pastoral music, he shewed upon the pipe what notes were fit for the herds of cows and oxen, what agreed with the flocks of goats, what were pleasing to the sheep. The tones for the sheep were soft and sweet, those of the herds were vehement, and for the goats were sharp and shrill. In sum, that single pipe of his expressed even all the shepherd's-pipes.

36. Therefore the rest in deep silence sate still, delighted and charmed with that music. But Dryas, rising and bidding him strike up a Dionysiac tune, fell to dance before them the dance of the wine-

Hirsch. (Amyot): mss πρῶτον   [5] mss ὅσον from μέγα below   [6] A and perh. p αἰπόλῳ (Amyot)   [7] A omits

[8] p ποιμενικὸν

ὠρχήσατο. καὶ ἐῴκει ποτὲ μὲν τρυγῶντι, ποτὲ δὲ
φέροντι ἀρρίχους, εἶτα πατοῦντι τοὺς βότρυς, εἶτα
πληροῦντι τοὺς πίθους, εἶτα πίνοντι τοῦ γλεύκους.
ταῦτα πάντα οὕτως εὐσχημόνως ὠρχήσατο ὁ
Δρύας καὶ ἐναργῶς, ὥστε ἐδόκουν βλέπειν καὶ τὰς
ἀμπέλους καὶ τὴν ληνὸν καὶ τοὺς πίθους καὶ ἀλη-
θῶς Δρύαντα πίνοντα.

37. Τρίτος δὴ γέρων οὗτος εὐδοκιμήσας ἐπ᾽
ὀρχήσει, φιλεῖ Χλόην καὶ Δάφνιν. οἱ δὲ μάλα
ταχέως ἀναστάντες ὠρχήσαντο τὸν μῦθον τοῦ
Λάμωνος. ὁ Δάφνις Πᾶνα ἐμιμεῖτο, τὴν Σύριγγα
Χλόη. ὁ μὲν ἱκέτευε πείθων, ἡ δὲ ἀμελοῦσα
ἐμειδία. ὁ μὲν ἐδίωκε καὶ ἐπ᾽ ἄκρων τῶν ὀνύχων
ἔτρεχε τὰς χηλὰς μιμούμενος, ἡ δὲ ἐνέφαινε τὴν
κάμνουσαν ἐν τῇ φυγῇ. ἔπειτα Χλόη μὲν εἰς τὴν
ὕλην ὡς εἰς ἕλος κρύπτεται· Δάφνις δὲ λαβὼν
τὴν Φιλητᾶ σύριγγα τὴν μεγάλην, ἐσύρισε γοερὸν
ὡς ἐρῶν, ἐρωτικὸν ὡς πείθων, ἀνακλητικὸν ὡς
ἐπιζητῶν· ὥστε ὁ Φιλητᾶς θαυμάσας φιλεῖ τε
ἀναπηδήσας καὶ τὴν σύριγγα χαρίζεται φιλήσας,
καὶ εὔχεται καὶ Δάφνιν καταλιπεῖν αὐτὴν ὁμοίῳ
διαδόχῳ. ὁ δὲ τὴν ἰδίαν ἀναθεὶς τῷ Πανὶ τὴν
σμικρὰν καὶ φιλήσας ὡς ἐκ φυγῆς ἀληθινῆς
εὑρεθεῖσαν τὴν Χλόην, ἀπήλαυνε τὴν ἀγέλην
συρίττων, νυκτὸς ἤδη γενομένης. 38. ἀπήλαυνε

press. And now he acted to the life the cutting and gathering of the grapes, now the carrying of the baskets, then the treading of the grapes in the press, then presently the tunning of the wine into the butts, and then again their joyful and hearty carousing the must. All these things he represented so aptly and clearly in his dancing, that they all thought they verily saw before their face the vines, the grapes, the press, the butts, and that Dryas did drink indeed.

37. This third old man when he had pleased them so well with his dance, embraced and kissed Daphnis and Chloe. Therefore they two, rising quickly, fell to dancing Lamo's tale. Daphnis played Pan, and Chloe Syrinx. He woos and prays to persuade and win her; she shews her disdain, laughs at his love, and flies him. Daphnis follows as to force her, and running on his tiptoes, imitates the hooves of Pan. Chloe on the other side, acts Syrinx wearied with her flight, and throws herself into the wood as she had done into the fen. But Daphnis, catching up that great pipe of Philetas, plays at first something that was doleful and bewailing, as a lover, then something that made love and was persuasive to relenting, then a recall from the wood, as from one that dearly sought her. Insomuch that Philetas, struck with admiration and joy, could not hold from leaping up and kissing Daphnis. Then he gave him that pipe of his and commanded him to leave it to a successor like himself. Daphnis hanged up his own small one to Pan, and when he had kissed his Chloe, as returning from a true unfeigned flight, he began to drive home his flocks (for night was fallen), piping all the way. 38. Chloe too by the same

<δὲ> καὶ ἡ Χλόη τὴν ποίμνην τῷ μέλει τῆς σύριγ-
γος συνάγουσα. καὶ αἵ τε αἶγες πλησίον τῶν προ-
βάτων ᾔεσαν ὅ τε Δάφνις ἐβάδιζεν ἐγγὺς τῆς
Χλόης· ὥστε ἐνέπλησαν ἕως νυκτὸς ἀλλήλους καὶ
συνέθεντο θᾶττον τὰς ἀγέλας τῆς ἐπιούσης κατε-
λάσαι.

Καὶ οὕτως ἐποίησαν. ἄρτι γοῦν ἀρχομένης
ἡμέρας ἦλθον εἰς τὴν νομήν. καὶ τὰς Νύμφας
προτέρας, εἶτα τὸν Πᾶνα προσαγορεύσαντες, τὸ
ἐντεῦθεν ὑπὸ τῇ δρυΐ καθεσθέντες ἐσύριττον, εἶτα
ἀλλήλους ἐφίλουν, περιέβαλλον, κατεκλίνοντο·
καὶ οὐδὲν δράσαντες πλέον ἀνίσταντο. ἐμέλησεν
αὐτοῖς καὶ τροφῆς, καὶ ἔπιον οἶνον μίξαντες γάλα.
39. καὶ τούτοις ἅπασι θερμότεροι γενόμενοι καὶ
θρασύτεροι, πρὸς ἀλλήλους ἤριζον ἔριν ἐρωτικήν,
καὶ κατ' ὀλίγον εἰς ὅρκων πίστιν προῆλθον. ὁ μὲν
δὴ Δάφνις τὸν Πᾶνα ὤμοσεν ἐλθὼν ἐπὶ τὴν πίτυν,
μὴ ζήσεσθαι μόνος ἄνευ Χλόης, μηδὲ μιᾶς χρόνον
ἡμέρας· ἡ δὲ Χλόη Δάφνιδι τὰς Νύμφας εἰσελ-
θοῦσα εἰς τὸ ἄντρον τὸν αὐτὸν στέρξειν[1] καὶ
θάνατον καὶ βίον.

Τοσοῦτον δὲ ἄρα τῇ Χλόῃ τὸ ἀφελὲς προσῆν[2]
ὡς κόρῃ, ὥστε ἐξιοῦσα τοῦ ἄντρου καὶ δεύτερον
ἠξίου λαβεῖν ὅρκον παρ' αὐτοῦ, "Ὦ Δάφνι,"
λέγουσα, "θεὸς ὁ Πᾶν ἐρωτικός ἐστι καὶ ἄπιστος.
ἠράσθη μὲν Πίτυος, ἠράσθη δὲ Σύριγγος, παύεται
δὲ οὐδέποτε Δρυάσιν ἐνοχλῶν καὶ Ἐπιμηλίσι
Νύμφαις παρέχων πράγματα. οὗτος[3] μὲν οὖν,
ἀμεληθεὶς ἐν τοῖς ὅρκοις ἀμελήσει σε κολάσαι, κἂν

<δὲ> Herch.   [1] Uiii ἕξειν   [2] pq ἦν   [3] pq ὁ

music gathered together her flocks and drove them home, the goats stritting along with the sheep, and Daphnis walking close by Chloe. Thus till it was night they filled themselves the one with the other, and agreed to drive out their flocks sooner the next morning.

And so they did. For as soon as it was day they went out to pasture, and when they had first saluted the Nymphs and then Pan, afterwards sitting down under the oak they had the music of the pipe. After that, they kissed, embraced, and hugged one another, and lay down together on the ground; and so rose up again. Nor were they incurious of their meat, and for their drink they drank wine mingled with milk. 39. With all which incentives being more heated and made more lively and forward, they practised between them an amorous controversy about their love to one another, and by little and little came to bind themselves by the faith of oaths. For Daphnis coming up to the pine, swore by Pan that he would not live alone in this world without Chloe so much as the space of one day. And Chloe swore in the cave of the Nymphs that she would have the same death and life with Daphnis.

Yet such was the simplicity of Chloe, as being but a girl, that when she came out of the cave she demanded another oath of Daphnis. "Daphnis," quoth she, " Pan is a wanton, faithless God; for he loved Pitys, he loved Syrinx too. Besides, he never ceases to trouble and vex the Dryads and to solicit the Nymphs the president Goddesses of our flocks. Therefore he, if by thy faithlessness shouldst neglect him, would not take care to punish thee, although

DAPHNIS AND CHLOE

ἐπὶ πλείονας ἔλθῃς γυναῖκας τῶν ἐν τῇ σύριγγι
καλάμων. σὺ δέ μοι τὸ αἰπόλιον τοῦτο ὄμοσον
καὶ τὴν αἶγα ἐκείνην ἥ σε ἀνέθρεψε, μὴ καταλιπεῖν
Χλόην ἔστ' ἂν πιστή σοι μένῃ· ἄδικον δὲ εἰς σὲ
καὶ τὰς Νύμφας γενομένην καὶ φεῦγε καὶ μίσει
καὶ ἀπόκτεινον ὥσπερ λύκον." ἥδετο ὁ Δάφνις
ἀπιστούμενος, καὶ στὰς εἰς μέσον τὸ αἰπόλιον καὶ
τῇ μὲν τῶν χειρῶν αἰγός, τῇ δὲ τράγου λαβόμενος,
ὤμνυε Χλόην φιλῆσαι φιλοῦσαν· κἂν ἕτερον δὲ
προκρίνῃ Δάφνιδος, ἀντ' ἐκείνης αὐτὸν ἀποκτενεῖν.[1]
ἡ δὲ ἔχαιρε καὶ ἐπίστευεν, ὡς κόρη καὶ νέμουσα,
καὶ νομίζουσα τὰς αἶγας καὶ τὰ πρόβατα ποιμένων
καὶ αἰπόλων ἰδίους[2] θεούς.

---

[1] so Moll: pq -κτείνειν: Α ἀπέκτενε   [2] A omits

thou shouldst go to more maids then there are quills
in that pipe. But do thou swear to me by this flock
of goats, and by that goat which was thy nurse, that
thou wilt never forsake Chloe so long as she is
faithful to thee; and when she is false and injurious
to thee and the Nymphs, then fly her, then hate her,
and kill her like a wolf." Daphnis was pleased with
this pretty jealousy, and standing in the midst of
his flocks, with one hand laying hold on a she-goat
and the other on a he, swore that he would love
Chloe that loved him, and that if she preferred any
other to Daphnis, then he would slay, not her, but
him that she preferred. Of this Chloe was glad,
and believed him as a poor and harmless maid, one
that was bred a shepherdess and thought that flocks
of sheep and goats were proper deities of the
shepherds.

THE END OF THE SECOND BOOK

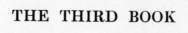

THE THIRD BOOK

A SUMMARY OF THE THIRD BOOK

THE *Mytilenaeans, upon that incursion, send Hippasus their general with land-forces against Methymna. But the quarrel is taken up. Daphnis and Chloe take it heavily that they are parted by the winter. Daphnis, to see her, goes a fowling before Dryas his cottage, and looks as if he minded not her. Dryas brings him in to the feast of Dionysus. The spring returning, they return to their pastorals. Daphnis complains of his ignorance in love. Lycaenium cozens him. Daphnis, as the mariners sail by, tells Chloe the Tale of Echo. Many and rich suitors are now about Chloe, and Dryas almost gives his consent. Daphnis is sad as being poor, but by direction of the Nymphs he finds a purse full of silver. He gives it Dryas, and Chloe is contracted to him; only Lamo, because he was a servant to Dionysophanes, says his lord is to be expected that he may ratify the business. Daphnis gives Chloe a rare apple.*

ΛΟΓΟΣ ΤΡΙΤΟΣ

1. Μυτιληναῖοι δέ, ὡς ᾔσθοντο τὸν ἐπίπλουν[1] τῶν δέκα νεῶν, καί τινες ἐμήνυσαν αὐτοῖς τὴν ἁρπαγὴν ἐλθόντες ἐκ τῶν ἀγρῶν, οὐκ ἀνασχετὸν νομίσαντες ταῦτα ἐκ Μηθυμναίων παθεῖν ἔγνωσαν καὶ αὐτοὶ τὴν ταχίστην ἐπ᾽ αὐτοὺς τὰ ὅπλα κινεῖν· καὶ καταλέξαντες ἀσπίδα τρισχιλίαν καὶ ἵππον πεντακοσίαν[2] ἐξέπεμψαν κατὰ γῆν τὸν στρατηγὸν Ἵππασον, ὀκνοῦντες ἐν ὥρᾳ χειμῶνος τὴν θάλατταν.

2. Ὁ δὲ ἐξορμηθεὶς ἀγροὺς μὲν οὐκ ἐληλάτει τῶν Μηθυμναίων οὐδὲ ἀγέλας καὶ κτήματα ἥρπαζε γεωργῶν καὶ ποιμένων, λῃστοῦ νομίζων ταῦτα ἔργα μᾶλλον[3] ἢ στρατηγοῦ· ταχὺ δ᾽ ᾔει[4] ἐπὶ τὴν πόλιν αὐτήν, ὡς ἐπεισπεσούμενος ἀφρουρήτοις ταῖς πύλαις. καὶ αὐτῷ σταδίους ὅσον ἑκατὸν ἀπέχοντι κῆρυξ ἀπαντᾷ σπονδὰς κομίζων. οἱ γὰρ Μηθυμναῖοι μαθόντες παρὰ τῶν ἑαλωκότων ὡς οὐδὲν ἴσασι Μυτιληναῖοι τῶν γεγενημένων, ἀλλὰ γεωργοὶ καὶ ποιμένες ὑβρίζοντας[5] τοὺς νεανίσκους ταῦτα ἔδρασαν, μετεγίνωσκον μὲν

---

[1] q κατα- E : mss δὲ [2] A ἵππον μὲν πεντ. [3] A omits [4] δ᾽ ᾔει [5] mss nom.

128

THE THIRD BOOK

1. But the Mytilenaeans, when they heard of the expedition of those ten ships, and some of the countrymen coming up from the farms had told them what a plundering and rapine there had bin, thought it too disgraceful to be borne, and therefore decreed to raise arms against Methymna with all speed. And having chosen out three thousand targeteers and five hundred horse, they sent away their general Hippasus by land, not daring to trust the sea in winter.

2. He did not as he marched depopulate[1] the fields of Methymna, nor did he rob the farms of the husbandmen or the pastures of the shepherds, counting such actions as those to suit better with a larron[2] then the grand captain of an army; but hasted up to the town itself to surprise it. But while he was yet an hundred furlongs off from the town an herald met him with articles. For after that the Methymnaeans were informed by the captives that the Mytilenaeans knew nothing of those things that had happened, and that ploughmen and shepherds provoked by the young gentlemen were they that were the causes of it all, it repented them of that

---

[1] lay waste. [2] freebooter.

ὀξύτερα τολμήσαντες εἰς γείτονα πόλιν ἢ σω-
φρονέστερα· σπουδὴν [1] δὲ εἶχον ἀποδόντες πᾶσαν
τὴν ἁρπαγὴν ἀδεῶς ἐπιμίγνυσθαι καὶ κατὰ γῆν
καὶ κατὰ θάλατταν.

Τὸν μὲν οὖν κήρυκα τοῖς Μυτιληναίοις ὁ Ἵπ-
πασος ἀποστέλλει, καίτοιγε αὐτοκράτωρ στρα-
τηγὸς κεχειροτονημένος, αὐτὸς δὲ τῆς Μηθύμνης
ὅσον ἀπὸ δέκα σταδίων στρατόπεδον βαλόμενος
τὰς ἐκ τῆς πόλεως ἐντολὰς ἀνέμενε. καὶ δύο
διαγενομένων ἡμερῶν ἐλθὼν ὁ ἄγγελος τήν τε
ἁρπαγὴν ἐκέλευσε κομίσασθαι καὶ ἀδικήσαντα
μηδὲν ἀναχωρεῖν οἴκαδε· πολέμου γὰρ καὶ εἰρήνης
ἐν αἱρέσει γενόμενοι τὴν εἰρήνην εὑρίσκειν [2] κερδα-
λεωτέραν. 3. ὁ μὲν δὴ Μηθυμναίων καὶ Μυτι-
ληναίων πόλεμος ἀδόκητον λαβὼν ἀρχὴν καὶ
τέλος οὕτω διελύθη.

Γίνεται δὲ χειμὼν Δάφνιδι καὶ Χλόῃ τοῦ πο-
λέμου πικρότερος· ἐξαίφνης γὰρ περιπεσοῦσα [3]
πολλὴ χιὼν πάσας μὲν ἀπέκλεισε τὰς ὁδούς,
πάντας δὲ κατέκλεισε τοὺς γεωργούς. λάβροι
μὲν οἱ χείμαρροι κατέρρεον, ἐπεπήγει δὲ κρύ-
σταλλος· τὰ δένδρα ἐῴκει κατακλωμένοις· ἡ γῆ
πᾶσα ἀφανὴς ἦν, ὅτι μὴ περὶ πηγάς που καὶ
ῥεύματα. οὔτ᾽ οὖν ἀγέλην τις εἰς νομὴν ἦγεν
οὔτε αὐτὸς προῄει τῶν θυρῶν, ἀλλὰ πῦρ καύ-
σαντες μέγα περὶ ᾠδὰς ἀλεκτρυόνων οἱ μὲν λίνον

---

[1] prob. old var : ApB σπονδὴν   [2] so *E* : mss εὕρισκον
[3] Parr πεσοῦσα

expedition of Bryaxis against a neighbouring city, as of an action more precipitant then moderate and wise; and they were eager to return all the prey and spoil that was taken and carried away, and to have commerce and trade securely with them by land and by sea.

Therefore Hippasus dispatches away that herald to Mytilene, although he had bin created the general of the war and so had power to sign as he listed;[1] and pitching his camp about ten furlongs from Methymna, there he attended mandates from the city. Two days after, the messenger returned, and brought a command that they should receive the plundered goods and all the captives, and march home without doing the least harm, because Methymna, when war or peace were offered to be chosen, found peace to be more profitable. 3. And this quarrel betwixt Methymna and Mytilene, which was of an unexpected beginning and end, was thus taken up and composed.

And now winter was come on, a winter more bitter then war to Daphnis and Chloe. For on a sudden there fell a great snow, which blinded all the paths, stopped up all the ways, and shut up all the shepherds and husbandmen. The torrents rushed down in flood, and the lakes were frozen and glazed with crystal. The hedges and trees looked as if they had bin breaking down. All the ground was hoodwinked up but that which lay upon the fountains and the rills. And therefore no man drove out his flocks to pasture or did so much as come out of the door, but about the cock's crowing made their fires nose-high, and some spun flax, some wove tarpaulin for the

[1] The Greek is "general with full powers."

ἔστρεφον, οἱ δὲ αἰγῶν τρίχας ἔπλεκον, οἱ δὲ πάγας
ὀρνίθων ἐσοφίζοντο. τότε βοῶν ἐπὶ φάτναις
φροντὶς ἦν ἄχυρον ἐσθιόντων, αἰγῶν καὶ προ-
βάτων[1] ἐν τοῖς σηκοῖς φυλλάδας, ὑῶν ἐν τοῖς
συφεοῖς ἄκυλον καὶ βαλάνους.

4. Ἀναγκαίας οὖν οἰκουρίας ἐπεχούσης ἅπαν-
τας, οἱ μὲν ἄλλοι γεωργοὶ καὶ νομεῖς ἔχαιρον
πόνων τε ἀπηλλαγμένοι πρὸς ὀλίγον καὶ τροφὰς
ἑωθινὰς ἐσθίοντες καὶ καθεύδοντες μακρὸν ὕπνον·
ὥστε αὐτοῖς τὸν χειμῶνα δοκεῖν καὶ θέρους καὶ
μετοπώρου καὶ ἦρος αὐτοῦ γλυκύτερον. Χλόη δὲ
καὶ Δάφνις ἐν μνήμῃ γενόμενοι τῶν καταλειφθέν-
των τερπνῶν, ὡς ἐφίλουν, ὡς περιέβαλλον, ὡς
ἅμα τὴν τροφὴν προσεφέροντο, νύκτας τε ἀγρύ-
πνους διῆγον καὶ λυπηρὰς <ἡμέρας>, καὶ τὴν
ἠρινὴν[2] ὥραν ἀνέμενον ἐκ θανάτου παλιγγενεσίαν.

Ἐλύπει δὲ αὐτοὺς ἢ πήρα τις ἐλθοῦσα εἰς
χεῖρας, ἐξ ἧς συνήσθιον,[3] ἢ γαυλὸς ὀφθείς, ἐξ οὗ
συνέπιον, ἢ σύριγξ ἀμελῶς ἐρριμμένη, δῶρον
ἐρωτικὸν γεγενημένη. εὔχοντο δὴ ταῖς Νύμφαις
καὶ τῷ Πανὶ καὶ τούτων αὐτοὺς ἐκλύσασθαι τῶν

---

[1] A προβ. τῶν   <ἡμέρας> E   [2] so Valck : p εἰρίνην
(Uii perh. εἰαρίνης) : q εἰρήνης : A τὴν ὥραν τῆς εἰρήνης
[3] so Hirsch : mss ἦσθ.

132

sea,[1] others with all their sophistry[2] made gins and
nets and traps for birds. At that time their care
was employed about the oxen and cows that were
foddered with chaff in the stalls, about the goats and
about the sheep which fed on green leaves in the
sheepcotes and the folds, or else about fatting their
hogs in the sties with acorns and other mast.

4. When all was thus taken up perforce with their
domestic affairs, the other husbandmen and shepherds
were very jovial and merry, as being for a while
discharged of their labours and able to have their
breakfast in the morning after sleeping long winter
nights; so that the winter was to them more
pleasant then the summer, the autumn, or the very
spring. But Chloe and Daphnis, when they re-
membered what a sweet conversation they had held
before, how they had kissed, how they had embraced
and hugged one another, how they had lived at a
common scrip, all which were now as pleasures lost,
now they had long and sleepless nights, now they
had sad and pensive days, and desired nothing so
much as a quick return of the spring, to become
their regeneration and return from death.

Besides this, it was their grief and complaint if
but a scrip came to their hands out of which they
had eaten together, or a sillibub-piggin out of which
they had used both to drink, or if they chanced to
see a pipe laid aside and neglected such as had bin
not long before a lover's gift from one to the other.
And therefore they prayed severally to Pan and the
Nymphs that they would deliver them from these as

---

[1] the translator had in view Vergil *Geor.* 3. 312 where we
are told that goats'-hair cloth (the Greek phrase here) was
used by soldiers and sailors.   [2] cunning.

κακῶν καὶ δεῖξαί ποτε αὐτοῖς καὶ ταῖς ἀγέλαις
ἥλιον· καὶ ἅμα εὐχόμενοι τέχνην ἐζήτουν, δι' ἧς
ἀλλήλους θεάσονται. ἡ μὲν δὴ Χλόη δεινῶς
ἄπορος ἦν καὶ ἀμήχανος, ἀεὶ γὰρ αὐτῇ συνῆν ἡ
δοκοῦσα μήτηρ ἔριά τε ξαίνειν διδάσκουσα καὶ
ἀτράκτους στρέφειν καὶ γάμου μνημονεύουσα· ὁ
δὲ Δάφνις, οἷα σχολὴν ἄγων καὶ συνετώτερος
κόρης, τοιόνδε σόφισμα εὗρεν ἐς θέαν τῆς Χλόης·

5. πρὸ τῆς αὐλῆς τοῦ Δρύαντος, ὑπ' [1] αὐτῇ τῇ
αὐλῇ μυρρίναι μεγάλαι δύο καὶ κιττὸς ἐπεφύκει,
αἱ μυρρίναι πλησίον ἀλλήλων, ὁ κιττὸς ἀμφο-
τέρων μέσος· ὥστε ἐφ' ἑκατέραν διαθεὶς τοὺς
ἀκρέμονας ὡς ἄμπελος ἄντρου σχῆμα διὰ τῶν
φύλλων ἐπαλλαττόντων ἐποίει, καθ' οὗ [2] κόρυμβος
πολὺς καὶ μέγας [3] ὡς βότρυς κλημάτων ἐξεκρέ-
ματο.   ἦν οὖν πολὺ πλῆθος περὶ αὐτὸν τῶν
χειμερινῶν ὀρνίθων ἀπορίᾳ τῆς ἔξω τροφῆς, πολὺς
μὲν κόψιχος, πολλὴ δὲ κίχλη, καὶ φάτται καὶ
ψᾶρες καὶ ὅσον ἄλλο κιττοφάγον πτερόν.

Τούτων τῶν ὀρνίθων ἐπὶ προφάσει θήρας, ἐξώρ-
μησεν ὁ Δάφνις, ἐμπλήσας μὲν τὴν πήραν
ὀψημάτων μεμελιτωμένων, κομίζων δὲ ἐς πίστιν
ἰξὸν καὶ βρόχους. τὸ μὲν οὖν μεταξὺ σταδίων
ἦν οὐ πλέον δέκα· οὔπω δὲ [4] ἡ χιὼν λελυμένη

---

[1] A ἐπ'   [2] so E, cf. 4. 14 κατὰ τῶν ὤμων ἐξηρτημένος :
mss καὶ ὁ   [3] Uiii μέσος   ὡς E : mss ὅσος a misunder-
standing correction of μέγας ὡς   [4] οὔπω δὲ ; A οὐ πολλὴ

from the other evils and miseries, and shew to them and their flocks the Sun again. And while they prayed, they laboured too and cast about to find a way by which they might come to see one another. Poor Chloe was void of all counsel and had no device nor plot. For the old woman her reputed mother was by her continually, and taught her to card the fine wool and twirl the spindle, or else was still a clocking for her, and ever and anon casting in words and twattling to her about her marriage. But Daphnis, who was now at leisure enough and was of a more projecting wit then a maid, devised this sophism[1] to see her:

5. Before Dryas his cottage, and indeed under the very cottage itself, there grew two tall myrtles and an ivy-bush. The myrtles stood not far off from one another, and between them the ivy ran, and so that it made a kind of arbour by clasping the arms[2] about them both and by the order, the thickness, and interweaving of its branches and leaves, many and great clusters of berries hanging from it like those of the vines from the palmits. And therefore it was, that great store of winter birds haunted the bush, for want, it seems, of food abroad, many blackbirds, many thrushes, stock-doves and starlings, with other birds that feed on berries.

Under pretext of birding there, Daphnis came out, his scrip furnished indeed with sweet country dainties, but bringing with him, to persuade and affirm his meaning, snares and lime-twigs for the purpose. The place lay off but ten furlongs, and yet the snow that lay unmelted found him somewhat

---

[1] cunning plan.   [2] Thornley avoids "its."

πολὺν αὐτῷ κάματον παρέσχεν. ἔρωτι δὲ ἄρα
πάντα βάσιμα, καὶ πῦρ καὶ ὕδωρ καὶ Σκυθικὴ
χιών. 6. πόνῳ[1] οὖν πρὸς τὴν αὐλὴν ἔρχεται,
καὶ ἀποσεισάμενος τῶν σκελῶν τὴν χιόνα τούς τε
βρόχους ἔστησε καὶ τὸν ἰξὸν ῥάβδοις μακραῖς
ἐπήλειψε, καὶ ἐκαθέζετο[2] τὸ ἐντεῦθεν ὄρνιθας καὶ
τὴν Χλόην περιμενῶν.[3]

Ἀλλ᾽ ὄρνιθες μὲν καὶ ἧκον πολλοὶ καὶ ἐλή-
φθησαν ἱκανοί, ὥστε πράγματα μυρία ἔσχε
συλλέγων αὐτοὺς καὶ ἀποκτιννὺς καὶ ἀποδύων
τὰ πτερά· τῆς δὲ αὐλῆς προῆλθεν οὐδείς, οὐκ
ἀνήρ, οὐ γύναιον, οὐ κατοικίδιος ὄρνις, ἀλλὰ
πάντες τῷ πυρὶ παραμένοντες ἔνδον κατεκέκλειντο·
ὥστε πάνυ ἠπορεῖτο ὁ Δάφνις, ὡς οὐκ αἰσίοις[4]
ὄρνισιν ἐλθών. καὶ ἐτόλμα πρόφασιν σκηψάμενος
ὤσασθαι διὰ θυρῶν καὶ ἐζήτει πρὸς αὐτὸν ὅ τι
λεχθῆναι πιθανώτατον·[5] "Πῦρ ἐναυσόμενος[6]
ἦλθον. Μὴ γὰρ οὐκ ἦσαν ἀπὸ σταδίου[7] γείτονες;
Ἄρτους αἰτησόμενος ἧκον. Ἀλλ᾽ ἡ πήρα μεστὴ
ἦν[8] τροφῆς. Οἴνου ἐδεόμην.[9] Καὶ μὴν χθὲς καὶ
πρῴην ἐτρύγησας. Λύκος με ἐδίωκε. Καὶ ποῦ
τὰ ἴχνη τοῦ λύκου; Θηράσων ἀφικόμην τοὺς
ὄρνιθας. Τί οὖν θηράσας οὐκ ἄπει; Χλόην θεάσα-
σθαι βούλομαι. Πατρὶ δὲ τίς καὶ μητρὶ παρθένου[10]
τοῦτο ὁμολογεῖς; πταίων δὴ πανταχοῦ σιωπῇ.

---

[1] so E: mss δρόμῳ   [2] A κάθηται   [3] so Cour: mss
μεριμνῶν   [4] so Moll: mss αἴσιον   [5] mss -τερον   [6] A
ἀναψόμενος   [7] perh. δέκα σταδίων, cf. 5   [8] A accidentally
transposes ἦν and ἡ   [9] so E: mss pres.   [10] παρθ. . . .
θηραθέντα: (ὁμολογεῖς E: pq -εῖ) A παρθένος. καὶ τοῦτο
ὡμολόγει. πταίων δὴ πανταχοῦ σιωπῇ τὰ θηραθέντα, taking
οὐδὲν τούτων πάντων ἀνύποπτον as a comment on the state

to do to pass through it. But all things are pervious to love, even fire, water, and Scythian snows. 6. Therefore plodding through, he came up to the cottage, and when he had shook off the snow from his thighs, he set his snares and pricked his lime-twigs. Then he sate down and waited for Chloe and the birds.

There flew to the bushes many birds, and a sufficient number was taken to busy[1] Daphnis a thousand ways, in running up and down, in gathering, killing, and depluming[2] his game. But nobody stirred out of the cottage, not a man or woman to be seen, not so much as a hen at the door, but all were shut up in the warm house; so that poor Daphnis knew not what in the world to do, but was at a stand as if his luck had bin less fair than fowl.[3] And assuredly he would have ventured to intrude himself, if he could but have found out some specious cause and plausible enough; and so deliberated with himself what was the likeliest[4] to be said : "I'll say I came to fetch fire; And was there no neighbour, they will say, within a furlong, let alone ten? I came to borrow bread; But thy scrip is stuffed with cakes. I wanted wine; Thy vintage was but tother day. A wolf pursued me; Where are the tracings of a wolf? I came hither to catch birds; And when thou hast caught them why gettest thou not thyself home? I have a mind to see Chloe; But who art thou to confess such a thing as that to the father and mother of a maid?—and then, on every side vanquished,

of the text, and supposing σιωπὴ to show that the continuation of the speech is interpolated   πταίων : q παιδων

-[1] make busy.   [2] plucking.   [3] there is a play upon ὄρνιθες "birds" and ὄρνιθες "omens,"   [4] best.

ἀλλ' οὐδὲν τούτων ἁπάντων ἀνύποπτον. ἄμεινον
ἄρα σιγᾶν· Χλόην δὲ ἦρος ὄψομαι, ἐπεὶ μὴ εἵ-
μαρτο, ὡς ἔοικε, χειμῶνός με ταύτην ἰδεῖν."

Τοιαῦτα δή τινα διανοηθεὶς καὶ τὰ θηραθέντα
συλλαβὼν ὥρμητο ἀπιέναι, καί, ὥσπερ αὐτὸν
οἰκτείραντος τοῦ Ἔρωτος, τάδε γίνεται· 7. περὶ
τράπεζαν [1] εἶχον οἱ ἀμφὶ τὸν Δρύαντα· κρέα διη-
ρεῖτο, ἄρτοι παρετίθεντο, κρατὴρ ἐκιρνᾶτο. εἷς
δὴ κύων τῶν προβατευτικῶν ἀμέλειαν φυλάξας,
κρέας ἁρπάσας, ἔφυγε διὰ θυρῶν. ἀλγήσας ὁ
Δρύας (καὶ γὰρ ἦν ἐκείνου μοῖρα) ξύλον ἁρπασά-
μενος ἐδίωκε κατ' ἴχνος ὥσπερ κύων. διώκων δὲ
καὶ κατὰ τὸν κιττὸν γενόμενος ὁρᾷ τὸν Δάφνιν
ἀνατεθειμένον ἐπὶ τοὺς ὤμους τὴν ἄγραν καὶ ἀπο-
σοβεῖν ἐγνωκότα. κρέως μὲν οὖν καὶ κυνὸς αὐτίκα
ἐπελάθετο, μέγα δὲ βοήσας, "Χαῖρε, ὦ παῖ,"
περιεπλέκετο καὶ κατεφίλει καὶ ἦγεν [2] ἔσω λα-
βόμενος.

Μικροῦ μὲν οὖν ἰδόντες ἀλλήλους εἰς τὴν γῆν
κατερρύησαν, μεῖναι δὲ καρτερήσαντες ὀρθοὶ
προσηγόρευσάν τε καὶ κατεφίλησαν, καὶ τοῦτο
οἱονεὶ ἔρεισμα αὐτοῖς τοῦ μὴ πεσεῖν ἐγένετο.
8. τυχὼν δὲ [3] ὁ Δάφνις παρ' ἐλπίδας καὶ φιλή-
ματος καὶ Χλόης, τοῦ τε πυρὸς ἐκαθέσθη πλησίον,

---

[1] A περιτράπεζον: pq τράπεζαν   [2] pq περιῆγεν cf. last
note   [3] τυχ. δὲ: A τὰ οὖν

I shall stand mum. But enough; there is not one
of all these things that carries not suspicion with it.
Therefore it's better to go presently away in silence;
and I shall see Chloe at the first peeping of the
spring, since, as it seems, the Fates prohibit it in
winter."

These thoughts cast up and down in his anxious
mind and his prey taken up, he was thinking to be
gone and was making away, when, as if Love him-
self had pitied his cause, it happened thus: 7. Dryas
and his family were at table, the meat was taken up
and divided to messes, the bread was laid out, the
wine-bowl set and trimmed.[1] But one of the flock-
dogs took his time while they were busy, and ran out
adoors with a shoulder of mutton. Dryas was vexed
(for that belonged to his mess), and snatching up a
club, followed at his heels as if it had bin another
dog. This pursuit brought him up to the ivy, where
he espied the young Daphnis with his birds on his
back, and about to pack away. With that, forgetting
the dog and the flesh, he cries out amain, " Hail,
boy! hail, boy!" and fell on his neck to kiss him,
and catching him by the hand, led him along into
the house.

And then it wanted but a little that Daphnis and
Chloe fell not both to the ground when at first they
saw one another. Yet while they strove with them-
selves to stand upright, there passed salutations and
kisses between them, and those to them were as
pillars and sustentations to hold them from toppling
into swoons. 8. Daphnis having now got, beyond all
hope, not only a kiss but Chloe herself too, sate

---

[1] the Greek has "mixed."

καὶ ἐπὶ τὴν τράπεζαν ἀπὸ τῶν ὤμων τὰς φάττας
ἀπεφορτίσατο καὶ τοὺς κοψίχους, καὶ διηγεῖτο
πῶς ἀσχάλλων πρὸς τὴν οἰκουρίαν ὥρμησε πρὸς
ἄγραν, καὶ ὅπως τὰ μὲν βρόχοις αὐτῶν, τὰ δὲ
ἰξῷ λάβοι τῶν μύρτων καὶ τοῦ κιττοῦ γλιχόμενα.

Οἱ δὲ ἐπήνουν τὸ ἐνεργὸν[1] καὶ ἐκέλευον
ἐσθίειν ὧν[2] ὁ κύων κατέλιπεν. ἐκέλευον δὲ τῇ
Χλόῃ πιεῖν ἐγχέαι. καὶ ἣ[3] χαίρουσα τοῖς τε
ἄλλοις ὥρεξε καὶ Δάφνιδι μετὰ τοὺς ἄλλους·
ἐσκήπτετο γὰρ ὀργίζεσθαι, διότι ἐλθὼν ἔμελλεν
ἀποτρέχειν οὐκ ἰδών. ὅμως μέντοι πρὶν προσε-
νεγκεῖν ἀπέπιεν, εἶθ' οὕτως ἔδωκεν. ὁ δὲ καίτοι
διψῶν βραδέως ἔπινε, παρέχων ἑαυτῷ διὰ τῆς
βραδύτητος μακροτέραν ἡδονήν.

9. Ἡ μὲν δὴ τράπεζα ταχέως ἐγένετο κενὴ
ἄρτων καὶ κρεῶν. καθήμενοι δὲ περὶ τῆς Μυρτά-
λης καὶ τοῦ Λάμωνος ἐπυνθάνοντο, καὶ εὐδαιμό-
νιζον αὐτοὺς τοιοῦτον γηροτρόφον εὐτυχήσαντας.
καὶ τοῖς ἐπαίνοις μὲν ἥδετο Χλόης ἀκρωμένης,
ὅτε δὲ κατεῖχον αὐτὸν ὡς θύσοντες Διονύσῳ τῆς
ἐπιούσης ἡμέρας, μικροῦ δεῖν ὑφ' ἡδονῆς ἐκείνους
ἀντὶ τοῦ Διονύσου προσεκύνησεν. αὐτίκα οὖν
ἐκ τῆς πήρας προυκόμιζε μελιτώματα πολλὰ

[1] Uiii ἑκάεργοι [2] A & [3] Uiii ἥδε

down by the fire and laid upon the table his black-birds and stock-doves; and fell to tell them how tedious the business of the house and keeping within had bin to him, and that therefore he was come to recreate himself and, as they saw, to catch birds; how he had taken some with lime-twigs, some with snares, as they were feeding greedily upon the ivy and the myrtle-berries.

They, on the other side, fell to commend and praise Daphnis his diligence, and bade him eat of that which the dog had left; and commanded Chloe to wait on them and fill their wine. She with a merry countenance filled to the rest, and after them to Daphnis; for she feigned a pretty anger because that when he was there he would offer to go away in such a manner and not see her. Yet before she gave it to him she kissed the cup and sipped a little, and so gave it. Daphnis, although he was almost choked for want of drink, drank slowly, tickling himself, by that delay, with longer pleasure.

9. Dinner was quickly done and the table voided of bread and meat, and when they were sate down everybody began to ask how Lamo and Myrtale had done a great while, and so went on to pronounce them happy folks who had got such a stay and cherisher of their old age. And it was no small pleasure to Daphnis to be praised so in the hearing of Chloe. And when, besides, they said that he must and should tarry with them the next day because it was their sacrifice to Bacchus, it wanted but a little that for very pleasure the ravished lover had worshipped them instead of Bacchus himself; and therefore presently he drew out of his scrip

DAPHNIS AND CHLOE

καὶ τοὺς θηραθέντας δὲ τῶν ὀρνίθων· καὶ τούτους
ἐς τράπεζαν νυκτερινὴν ηὐτρέπιζον.

Δεύτερος κρατὴρ ἵστατο καὶ δεύτερον πῦρ
ἀνεκάετο. καὶ ταχὺ μάλα νυκτὸς γενομένης
δευτέρας τραπέζης ἐνεφοροῦντο· μεθ᾽ ἣν τὰ μὲν
μυθολογήσαντες, τὰ δὲ ᾄσαντες εἰς ὕπνον ἐχώρουν,
Χλόη μετὰ τῆς μητρός, Δρύας ἅμα Δάφνιδι.
Χλόῃ μὲν οὖν οὐδὲν χρηστὸν ἦν, ὅτι μὴ τῆς
ἐπιούσης ἡμέρας ὀφθησόμενος ὁ Δάφνις. Δάφνις
δὲ κενὴν τέρψιν ἐτέρπετο· τερπνὸν γὰρ ἐνόμιζε
καὶ πατρὶ συγκοιμηθῆναι Χλόης· ὥστε περιέ-
βαλλεν αὐτὸν καὶ κατεφίλει πολλάκις, ταῦτα
πάντα ποιεῖν Χλόην ὀνειροπολούμενος.

10. Ὡς δὲ ἐγένετο ἡμέρα, κρύος μὲν ἦν ἐξαίσιον
καὶ αὔρα βόρειος ἀπέκαε πάντα. οἱ δὲ ἀναστάντες
θύουσι τῷ Διονύσῳ κριὸν ἐνιαύσιον, καὶ πῦρ
ἀνακαύσαντες μέγα παρεσκευάζοντο τροφήν. τῆς
οὖν Νάπης ἀρτοποιούσης καὶ τοῦ Δρύαντος τὸν
κριὸν ἕψοντος, σχολῆς ὁ Δάφνις καὶ ἡ Χλόη
λαβόμενοι προῆλθον τῆς αὐλῆς ἵνα ὁ κιττός· καὶ
πάλιν βρόχους στήσαντες καὶ ἰξὸν ἐπαλείψαντες
ἐθήρων πλῆθος οὐκ ὀλίγον ὀρνίθων. ἦν δὲ αὐτοῖς
καὶ φιλημάτων ἀπόλαυσις συνεχὴς καὶ λόγων
ὁμιλία τερπνή· "Διὰ σὲ ἦλθον, Χλόη." "Οἶδα,
Δάφνι." "Διὰ σὲ ἀπολλύω τοὺς ἀθλίους κοψί-
χους." "Τίς¹ οὖν σοι γένωμαι;" "Μέμνησό μου."
"Μνημονεύω, νὴ τὰς Νύμφας, ἃς ὤμοσά ποτε
εἰς ἐκεῖνο τὸ ἄντρον, εἰς ὃ ἥξομεν εὐθέως,² ἂν ἡ

¹ Α τί, but cf. τίς ἐκεῖνος θεασάμενος ἔσται; 4. 8   pq γένο-
μαι   ² pq εὐθύς

142

good store of sweet-cakes and the birds he had caught, and these were ordered to be made ready for supper.

A fresh bowl of wine was set, a new fire kindled up, and night soon coming on they fell to eat again. When supper was done and part of their time was spent in telling of old tales, part in singing some of the ditties of the fields, they went to bed, Chloe with her mother, Daphnis with Dryas. But then nothing was sweet and pleasing to poor Chloe but that the next morning she should see her Daphnis again ; and Daphnis entertained the night himself with a fantastic, empty pleasure ; for it was sweet to his imagination to lie but with the father of Chloe, and he often embraced and kissed him, dreaming to himself that it was she.

10. In the morning it was a sharp frost and the north wind was very nipping, when they all rose and prepared to celebrate. A young ram was sacrificed to Bacchus and a huge fire built up to cook the meat. While Nape was making the bread and Dryas boiling the ram, Daphnis and Chloe had time to go forth as far as the ivy-bush ; and when he had set his snares again and pricked his lime-twigs, they not only catched good store of birds, but had a sweet collation of kisses without intermission, and a dear conversation in the language of love : " Chloe, I came for thy sake." " I know it, Daphnis." " 'Tis long of thee that I destroy the poor birds." " What wilt thou with me ? " [1] " Remember me." " I remember thee, by the Nymphs by whom heretofore I have sworn in yonder cave, whither we will go as

[1] or, less likely (cf. 4. 35), " What wilt thou shall become of me ? "

χιὼν τακῇ.'' '''Αλλὰ πολλή ἐστι, Χλόη, καὶ
δέδοικα μὴ ἐγὼ πρὸ ταύτης τακῶ'' ''Θάρρει,
Δάφνι· θερμός ἐστιν ὁ ἥλιος.'' ''Ει γὰρ οὕτως
γένοιτο, Χλόη, θερμός, ὡς τὸ κᾶον πῦρ τὴν
καρδίαν τὴν ἐμήν.'' ''Παίζεις ἀπατῶν με.'' ''Οὐ
μὰ τὰς αἶγας, ἃς σύ με ἐκέλευες ὀμνύειν.''

11. Τοιαῦτα ἀντιφωνήσασα πρὸς τὸν Δάφνιν
ἡ Χλόη καθάπερ Ἠχώ, καλούντων αὐτοὺς τῶν
περὶ τὴν Νάπην, εἰσέδραμον πολὺ περιττοτέραν
τῆς χθιζῆς θήραν κομίζοντες. καὶ ἀπαρξάμενοι
τῷ Διονύσῳ κρατῆρος ἤσθιον κιττῷ τὰς κεφαλὰς
ἐστεφανωμένοι. καὶ ἐπεὶ καιρὸς ἦν, ἰακχάσαντες [1]
καὶ εὐάσαντες προύπεμπον τὸν Δάφνιν πλήσαντες
αὐτοῦ τὴν πήραν κρεῶν καὶ ἄρτων. ἔδωκαν δὲ
καὶ τὰς φάττας καὶ τὰς κίχλας Λάμωνι καὶ
Μυρτάλῃ κομίζειν, ὡς αὐτοὶ θηράσοντες [2] ἄλλας,
ἔστ' ἂν ὁ χειμὼν μένῃ καὶ ὁ κιττὸς μὴ λείπῃ. ὁ
δὲ ἀπῄει φιλήσας αὐτοὺς προτέρους Χλόης, ἵνα
τὸ ἐκείνης καθαρὸν μείνῃ φίλημα. καὶ ἄλλας
δὲ πολλὰς ἦλθεν ὁδοὺς ἐπ' ἄλλαις τέχναις· ὥστε
μὴ παντάπασιν αὐτοῖς γενέσθαι τὸν χειμῶνα
ἀνέραστον.

12. Ἤδη δὲ ἦρος ἀρχομένου καὶ τῆς μὲν χιόνος
λυομένης, τῆς δὲ γῆς γυμνουμένης καὶ τῆς πόας
ὑπανθούσης, οἵ τε ἄλλοι νομεῖς ἦγον τὰς ἀγέλας
εἰς νομήν, καὶ πρὸ τῶν ἄλλων Χλόη καὶ Δάφνις,
οἷα μείζονι δουλεύοντες ποιμένι. εὐθὺς οὖν δρόμος
ἦν ἐπὶ τὰς Νύμφας καὶ τὸ ἄντρον, ἐντεῦθεν ἐπὶ
τὸν Πᾶνα καὶ τὴν πίτυν, εἶτα ἐπὶ τὴν δρῦν· ὑφ' [3]
ἣν καθίζοντες καὶ τὰς ἀγέλας ἔνεμον [4] καὶ ἀλλή-

---

[1] Uiii ἰακχεύσ.   [2] A aor.   before ἄλλας Par i ἄλλοτε,
ii ἄλλα, iii ἄλλο   [3] A ἐς τὴν δρῦν ἐφ'   [4] A νέμοντες

soon as ever the snow melts." "But it lies very deep, Chloe, and I fear I shall melt before the snow." "Courage, man; the Sun burns hot." "I would it burnt like that fire which now burns my very heart." "You do but gibe and cozen me!" "I do not, by the goats by which thou didst once bid me to swear to thee."

11. While Chloe, like another Echo, was holding her antiphona to Daphnis, Nape called and in they ran, with even more birds then had bin taken the day before. Now when they had made a libation from the bowl to Dionysus, they fell to their meat, with ivy crowns upon their heads. And when it was time, having cried the Jacchus and Euoe, they sent away Daphnis, his scrip first crammed with flesh and bread. They gave him too the stock-doves and thrushes to carry Lamo and Myrtale, as being like to catch themselves more while the frost and ivy lasted. And so Daphnis went his way when he had kissed the rest first and then Chloe, that he might carry along with him her kiss untouched and entire. And now by that device and now by this he came often thither, insomuch that the winter escaped not away wholly without some fruition of the sweets of love.

12. It was now the beginning of spring, the snow melting, the earth uncovering herself, and the grass growing green, when the other shepherds drove out their flocks to pasture, and Chloe and Daphnis before the rest, as being servants to a greater shepherd. And forthwith they took their course up to the Nymphs and that cave, and thence to Pan and his pine; afterwards to their own oak, where they sate

λους κατεφίλουν. ἀνεζήτησάν τε καὶ ἄνθη, στεφα-
νῶσαι θέλοντες τοὺς θεούς· τὰ δὲ ἄρτι ὁ ζέφυρος
τρέφων καὶ ὁ ἥλιος θερμαίνων ἐξῆγεν, ὅμως δὲ
εὑρέθη καὶ ἴα καὶ νάρκισσος καὶ ἀναγαλλὶς καὶ
ὅσα ἦρος πρωτοφορήματα. καὶ τούτοις[1] στεφα-
νοῦντες τὰ ἀγάλματα κατέσπεισαν ἡ μὲν Χλόη
ἀπ᾽ οἴων τινῶν ὁ δὲ Δάφνις ἀπὸ αἰγῶν γάλα νέον.
ἀπήρξαντο καὶ σύριγγος, καθάπερ τὰς ἀηδόνας
ἐς τὴν μουσικὴν ἐρεθίζοντες· αἱ δὲ ὑπεφθέγγοντο
ἐν ταῖς λόχμαις καὶ τὸν Ἴτυν κατ᾽ ὀλίγον ἠκρί-
βουν, ὥσπερ ἀναμιμνησκόμεναι τῆς ᾠδῆς ἐκ
μακρᾶς σιωπῆς.

13. Ἐβλήχασατό που καὶ ποίμνια,[2] ἐσκίρτησάν
που καὶ ἄρνες, καὶ ταῖς μητράσιν ὑποκλάσαντες
αὑτοὺς τὴν θηλὴν ἔσπασαν. τὰς δὲ μήπω
τετοκυίας οἱ κριοὶ κατεδίωκόν τε[3] καὶ κάτω[4]
στήσαντες ἔβαινον ἄλλος ἄλλην. ἐγίνοντο καὶ
τράγων διώγματα καὶ ἐς τὰς αἶγας ἐρωτικώτερα
πηδήματα, καὶ ἐμάχοντο περὶ τῶν αἰγῶν, καὶ
ἕκαστος εἶχεν ἰδίας καὶ ἐφύλαττε μή τις αὐτὰς
μοιχεύσῃ λαθών. κἂν[5] γέροντας ὁρῶντας ἐξώρ-
μησεν[6] εἰς Ἀφροδίτην τὰ τοιαῦτα θεάματα· οἱ
δὲ καὶ[7] νέοι καὶ[8] σφριγῶντες καὶ πολὺν ἤδη
χρόνον ἔρωτα ζητοῦντες, ἐξεκάοντο πρὸς τὰ
ἀκούσματα καὶ ἐτήκοντο πρὸς τὰ θεάματα, καὶ
ἐζήτουν καὶ αὐτοὶ περιττότερόν τι φιλήματος καὶ
περιβολῆς, μάλιστα δὲ ὁ Δάφνις. οἷα γοῦν

---

[1] mss τοῦτο : hence down to νέον mss invert two 44-letter
lines with emendations thus ἡ μὲν Χ. καὶ ἀπὸ αἰγῶν καὶ ἀπὸ
οἴων τινῶν γάλα νέον καὶ τοῦτο στεφ. τὰ ἀγάλμ. κατέσπ. (A
omits 2nd καὶ ἀπὸ : q marg. forte Δάφνις)   [2] so E : mss -ον
[3] A κατεδιώκοντες : pq καταδιώκοντες   [4] q καμάτῳ   [5] so
Brunck : mss καὶ   [6] A -σαν   [7] p omits   [8] A omits

down to look to their flocks and kiss each other. They sought about for flowers too to crown the statues of the Gods. The soft breath of Zephyrus, and the warm Sun, had but now brought them forth ; but there were then to be found the violet, the daffodil, the anagall, with the other primes and dawnings of the spring. And when they had crowned the statues of the Gods with them, they made a libation with new milk, Chloe from the sheep and Daphnis from the goats. They paid too the first-fruits of the pipe, as it were to provoke and challenge the nightingales with their music and song. The nightingales answered softly from the groves, and as if they remembered their long intermitted song, began by little and little to jug and warble their Tereus and Itys again.[1]

13. Here and there the blating of the flocks was heard, and the lambs came skipping and inclined themselves obliquely under the dams to wriggle and nussle at their dugs. But those which had not yet teemed, the rams pursued, and had their will of them. There were seen too the more ardent chases of the he-goats, which sometimes had battles for the she's, and everyone had his own wives and kept them solicitously. Even old men, seeing such sights as these, had bin pricked to love, but the young and lusty were wholly inflamed with what they heard and melted away with what they saw, and amongst them was Daphnis chief. For he, as having spent

---

[1] Thornley has added Tereus ; the nightingale's song was the lament of a metamorphosed woman for the child Itys (*see index*).

DAPHNIS AND CHLOE

ἐνηβήσας τῇ κατὰ τὸν χειμῶνα οἰκουρίᾳ καὶ
ἀσχαλίᾳ,[1] πρός τε τὰ φιλήματα ὤργα καὶ πρὸς[2]
τὰς περιβολὰς ἐσκιτάλιζε, καὶ ἦν ἐς πᾶν ἔργον
περιεργότερος καὶ θρασύτερος.

14. Ἥιτει δὲ τὴν Χλόην χαρίσασθαί οἱ πᾶν
ὅσον βούλεται καὶ γυμνὴν γυμνῷ συγκατακλιθῆναι
μακρότερον ἢ πρόσθεν εἴωθεσαν (τοῦτο γὰρ
δὴ λείπειν τοῖς Φιλητᾶ παιδεύμασιν), ἵνα δὴ
γένηται τὸ μόνον ἔρωτα παῦον φάρμακον. τῆς δὲ
πυνθανομένης τί πλέον ἐστὶ φιλήματος καὶ
περιβολῆς καὶ αὐτῆς κατακλίσεως, καὶ τί ἔγνωκε[3]
δρᾶσαι γυμνὸς γυμνῇ συγκατακλιθείς,[4] "Τοῦτο,"
εἶπεν, "ὃ οἱ κριοὶ ποιοῦσι τὰς οἶς καὶ οἱ τράγοι
τὰς αἶγας. ὁρᾷς ὡς μετὰ τοῦτο τὸ ἔργον
οὔτε ἐκεῖναι φεύγουσιν ἔτι αὐτοὺς οὔτε ἐκεῖνοι
κάμνουσι διώκοντες, ἀλλ᾽ ὥσπερ κοινῆς λοιπὸν
ἀπολαύσαντες ἡδονῆς συννέμονται; γλυκύ τι,
ὡς ἔοικεν, ἐστὶ τὸ ἔργον καὶ νικᾷ τὸ ἔρωτος
πικρόν." "Εἶτα οὐχ ὁρᾷς, ὦ Δάφνι, τὰς αἶγας
καὶ τοὺς τράγους καὶ τοὺς κριοὺς καὶ τὰς οἶς, ὡς
ὀρθοὶ μὲν ἐκεῖνοι δρῶσιν, ὀρθαὶ δὲ ἐκεῖναι
πάσχουσιν, οἱ μὲν πηδήσαντες, αἱ δὲ κατανωτι-
σάμεναι; σὺ δέ με ἀξιοῖς συγκατακλιθῆναι, καὶ
ταῦτα γυμνήν. καίτοιγε ἐκεῖναι πόσον ἐνδεδυμένης
ἐμοῦ λασιώτεραι;" πείθει δὲ[5] Δάφνις, καὶ συγκατα-
κλιθεὶς αὐτῇ πολὺν χρόνον ἔκειτο, καὶ οὐδὲν ὧν
ἕνεκα ὤργα ποιεῖν ἐπιστάμενος, ἀνίστησιν αὐτὴν
καὶ κατόπιν περιεφύετο μιμούμενος τοὺς τράγους.

---

[1] so Cob. cf. 8 : mss ἀσχολίᾳ   [2] ὤργα καὶ πρὸς : A καὶ
[3] A ἔγνω καὶ : pq ἔγνω   [4] mss -κλινείς (and below)   [5] so
E : mss πείθεται

his time in keeping tediously at home all the winter, was carried furiously to kissing and embracing, and in what he did was now more vehement then ever before.

14. He therefore asked Chloe to do exactly what he wanted and lie down naked with him longer than they had done before (this alone of Philetas's instructions remaining to be carried out) in order to effect the only remedy to ease the pain of love. When Chloe asked what more there was than kissing and embracing and lying down, and what he proposed to do when they were lying down together naked, he said: "What rams do to ewes, and billies to she-goats. Don't you see that after it the females cease fleeing the males, who are relieved of the trouble of pursuit, and then they both graze together as if having gained some mutual pleasure? What they do is evidently something enjoyable, which overcomes the bitterness of love." "But don't you see, Daphnis, that the she-goats and the billies and the rams and the ewes remain upright, the males jumping on to the females, and these receiving them upon their backs? Yet you ask me to lie down with you, and naked as well. And look how much more thickly clothed they are with their hair than I am even fully dressed!" Nevertheless Daphnis had his way, and lying down with her he remained there for a long time; then not knowing how to accomplish his desire he made her get up and tried clinging to her from behind in imitation of the billies. But he became more frustrated than ever, and sitting down he burst

DAPHNIS AND CHLOE

πολὺ δὲ μᾶλλον ἀπορηθείς, καθίσας ἔκλαεν εἰ καὶ κριῶν ἀμαθέστερος εἰς τὰ ἔρωτος ἔργα.

15. Ἦν δέ τις αὐτῷ γείτων, γεωργὸς γῆς ἰδίας, Χρόμις[1] τὸ ὄνομα, παρηβῶν ἤδη τὸ σῶμα. τούτῳ γύναιον ἦν ἐπακτὸν ἐξ ἄστεος, νέον καὶ ὡραῖον καὶ ἀγροικίας ἁβρότερον. τούτῳ Λυκαίνιον ὄνομα ἦν. αὕτη ἡ Λυκαίνιον ὁρῶσα τὸν Δάφνιν καθ᾽ ἑκάστην ἡμέραν παρελαύνοντα τὰς αἶγας ἕωθεν εἰς νομήν, νύκτωρ ἐκ νομῆς, ἐπεθύμησεν ἐραστὴν κτήσασθαι δώροις δελεάσασα. καὶ δή ποτε λοχήσασα μόνον, καὶ σύριγγα δῶρον ἔδωκε καὶ μέλι ἐν κηρίῳ καὶ πήραν ἐλαφείου.[2] εἰπεῖν δέ τι ὤκνει, τὸν Χλόης ἔρωτα καταμαντευομένη· πάντα[3] γὰρ ἑώρα προσκείμενον αὐτὸν τῇ κόρῃ.

Πρότερον μὲν οὖν ἐκ νευμάτων καὶ γέλωτος συνεβάλετο τοῦτο, τότε δὲ ἐξ ἑωθινοῦ σκηψαμένη πρὸς Χρόμιν ὡς παρὰ τίκτουσαν ἄπεισι γείτονα, κατόπιν τε αὐτοῖς παρηκολούθησε[4] καὶ εἴς τινα λόχμην ἐγκρύψασα ἑαυτήν, ὡς μὴ βλέποιτο, πάντα ἤκουσεν ὅσα εἶπον, πάντα εἶδεν ὅσα ἔπραξαν· οὐκ ἔλαθεν αὐτὴν οὐδὲ κλαύσας ὁ Δάφνις. συναλγήσασα δὴ τοῖς ἀθλίοις καὶ καιρὸν ἥκειν νομίσασα διττόν, τὸν μὲν εἰς τὴν ἐκείνων σωτηρίαν τὸν δὲ εἰς τὴν ἑαυτῆς ἐπιθυμίαν, ἐπιτεχνᾶταί τι τοιόνδε·

16. τῆς ἐπιούσης ὡς παρὰ τὴν γυναῖκα λαβὴν[5]

---

[1] so E, cf. Theocr. i. 24 : A Χρέμης (but Χρόμιν below and Χρόμης 4. 38 :) pq Χρῶμις   [2] pq ἐλάφου   [3] pq πάνυ

into tears for being less skilled than rams in ways of love.

15. But there was a certain neighbour of his, a landed man, Chromis his name, and was now by his age somewhat declining. He married out of the city a young, fair, and buxom girl, one that was too fine and delicate for the country and a clown. Her name was Lycaenium, and she, observing Daphnis as every day early in the morning he drove his goats by to the fields and home again at the first twilight, had a great mind to beguile the youth by gifts to become her sweetheart. And therefore once when she had skulked for her opportunity and catched him alone, she had given him a curious fine pipe, some precious honeycombs, and a new scrip of stag-skin, but durst not break her mind to him because she could easily conjecture at that dear love he bore to Chloe; for she saw him wholly addicted to the girl.

So much then she had perceived before by the winking, nodding, laughing, and tittering that was between them. But that morning she had made Chromis believe that she was to go to a woman's labour, and had followed softly behind them two at some distance, and then slipped away into a thicket and hid herself; and so had heard all that they said and seen too all that they did, and even the tears of the untaught Daphnis had bin perfectly within her sight. Wherefore she began to condole the condition of the wretched lovers, and finding that she had light upon a double opportunity, she projected to accomplish both her desires by this device:

16. The next day, making as if she went to that

---

⁴ A τε αὐτῆς παρηκ.: pq αὐτοῖς κατηκ.   ⁵ "as a pretext": A λαβεῖν: mss add gloss τὴν τίκτουσαν

ἀπιοῦσα, φανερῶς ἐπὶ τὴν δρῦν ἐν[1] ᾗ ἐκάθηντο[2]
Δάφνις καὶ Χλόη παραγίνεται, καὶ ἀκριβῶς
μιμησαμένη τὴν τεταραγμένην "Σῶσόν με," εἶπε,
"Δάφνι, τὴν ἀθλίαν. ἔκ[3] μοι τῶν χηνῶν τῶν
εἴκοσιν ἕνα τὸν κάλλιστον ἀετὸς ἥρπασε, καὶ οἷα
μέγα φορτίον ἀράμενος οὐκ ἐδυνήθη μετέωρος ἐπὶ
τὴν συνήθη τὴν ὑψηλὴν κομίσαι ἐκείνην πέτραν,
ἀλλ' εἰς τήνδε τὴν ὕλην τὴν ταπεινὴν ἔχων κατέ-
πεσε. σὺ τοίνυν πρὸς τῶν Νυμφῶν καὶ τοῦ Πανὸς
ἐκείνου, συνεισελθὼν[4] εἰς τὴν ὕλην (μόνη γὰρ
δέδοικα) σῶσόν μοι τὸν χῆνα, μηδὲ περιΐδῃς ἀτελῆ
μου τὸν ἀριθμὸν γενόμενον. τάχα δὲ καὶ αὐτὸν τὸν
ἀετὸν ἀποκτενεῖς καὶ οὐκέτι πολλοὺς ὑμῶν ἄρνας
καὶ ἐρίφους ἁρπάσει. τὴν δὲ ἀγέλην τέως φρουρή-
σει Χλόη· πάντως αὐτὴν ἴσασιν αἱ αἶγες ἀεί σοι
συννέμουσαν."

17. Οὐδὲν οὖν τῶν μελλόντων ὑποπτεύσας, ὁ
Δάφνις εὐθὺς ἀνίσταται,[5] καὶ ἀράμενος τὴν
καλαύροπα κατόπιν ἠκολούθει τῇ Λυκαινίῳ. ἡ δὲ
ἡγεῖτο ὡς μακροτάτω τῆς Χλόης, καὶ ἐπειδὴ κατὰ
τὸ πυκνότατον ἐγένοντο, πηγῆς πλησίον καθίσαι
κελεύσασα αὐτόν, "Ἐρᾷς,"[6] εἶπε, "Δάφνι, Χλόης.
καὶ τοῦτο ἔμαθον ἐγὼ νύκτωρ παρὰ τῶν Νυμφῶν
δι' ὀνείρατος, καὶ[7] τὰ χθιζά σου διηγήσαντο
δάκρυα καὶ ἐκέλευσάν σε σῶσαι διδαξαμένην τὰ
ἔρωτος ἔργα. τὰ δέ ἐστιν οὐ φιλήματα καὶ περι-
βολὴ καὶ οἷα δρῶσι κριοὶ καὶ τράγοι, ‹ἀλλ'› ἄλλα
ταῦτα πηδήματα καὶ τῶν ἐκεῖ γλυκύτερα·
πρόσεστι γὰρ αὐτοῖς χρόνος μακρότερος[8] ἡδονῆς.

---

[1] "at"   [2] so Cob: A ἐκάθητο: pq ἐκαθέζετο   [3] with
ἥρπασε, cf. i. 4 : pq ἐκ γάρ μοι   [4] so Hirsch. : mss εἰσελθ.
[5] A ἐγείρεται   [6] Par iii ἔρως : then Uiii omits Δάφνι . . .

woman again, she came up openly to the oak where
Daphnis and Chloe were sitting together, and skil-
fully counterfeiting that she was scared, " Help,
Daphnis, help me," quoth she ; " an eagle has carried
clean away from me the goodliest goose of twenty in
a flock, which yet by reason of the great weight she
was not able to carry to the top of that her wonted
high crag, but is fallen down with her into yonder
copse. For the Nymphs' sake and this Pan's, do
thou, Daphnis, come in the wood with me and
rescue my goose. For I dare not go in myself alone.
Let me not thus lose the tale of my geese. And it
may be thou mayst kill the eagle too, and then she
will scarce come hither any more to prey upon the
kids and lambs. Chloe for so long will look to the
flock ; the goats know her as thy perpetual com-
panion in the fields."

17. Now Daphnis, suspecting nothing of that that
was to come, gets up quickly, and taking his staff,
followed Lycaenium, who led him as far from Chloe
as possibly she could. And when they were come
into the thickest part of the wood and she had bid
him sit down by a fountain, " Daphnis," quoth she,
" thou dost love Chloe, and that I learnt last night
of the Nymphs. Those tears which yesterday thou
didst pour down were shewn to me in a dream by
them, and they commanded me that I should save
thee by teaching thee the way to make love. And
this involves not just kissing and embracing and
doing what rams and billies do, but also a frolicking
that is different from theirs and much more delicious,
since the pleasure it brings lasts longer.

Νυμφῶν and adds αἱ Νύμφαι before διηγήσαντο   [7] pB omit
    <ἀλλ'> E   [8] so E: mss -αs

εἰ δή σοι φίλον ἀπηλλάχθαι κακῶν καὶ ἐν πείρᾳ
γενέσθαι <τῶν> ζητουμένων τερπνῶν, ἴθι, παρα-
δίδου μοι τερπνὸν σεαυτὸν μαθητήν· ἐγὼ δὲ
χαριζομένη ταῖς Νύμφαις ἐκεῖνα διδάξω."

18. Οὐκ ἐκαρτέρησεν ὁ Δάφνις ὑφ' ἡδονῆς,
ἀλλ' ἅτε ἄγροικος καὶ αἰπόλος καὶ [1] ἐρῶν καὶ νέος,
πρὸ τῶν ποδῶν καταπεσὼν τὴν Λυκαίνιον ἱκέτευεν [2]
ὅτι τάχιστα διδάξαι τὴν τέχνην, δι' ἧς ὃ βούλεται
δράσει Χλόην. καὶ ὥσπερ τι μέγα καὶ θεόπεμπ-
τον ἀληθῶς μέλλων διδάσκεσθαι, καὶ ἔριφον
αὐτῇ [3] δώσειν ἀπηγγείλατο καὶ τυροὺς ἁπαλοὺς
πρωτορρύτου [4] γάλακτος καὶ τὴν αἶγα αὐτήν.
εὑροῦσα δὴ ἡ Λυκαίνιον αἰπολικὴν ἀφέλειαν [5] οἵαν
οὐ προσεδόκησεν, ἤρχετο παιδεύειν τὸν Δάφνιν
τοῦτον τὸν τρόπον· ἐκέλευσεν αὐτὸν καθίσαι
πλησίον αὐτῆς ὡς ἔχει καὶ φιλήματα φιλεῖν οἷα
εἰώθει καὶ ὅσα, καὶ φιλοῦντα ἅμα περιβάλλειν καὶ
κατακλίνεσθαι χαμαί. ὡς δὲ ἐκαθέσθη καὶ
ἐφίλησε καὶ κατεκλίθη, μαθοῦσα ἐνεργόν τε [6] καὶ
σφριγῶντα, ἀπὸ μὲν τῆς ἐπὶ πλευρὰν κατακλίσεως
ἀνίστησιν, αὐτὴν δὲ ὑποστορέσασα ἐντέχνως ἐς
τὴν τέως ζητουμένην ὁδὸν ἦγε. τὸ δὲ ἐντεῦθεν
οὐδὲν περιειργάζετο [7] ξένον· αὐτὴ γὰρ ἡ φύσις
λοιπὸν ἐπαίδευσε τὸ πρακτέον.

19. Τελεσθείσης δὲ τῆς ἐρωτικῆς παιδαγωγίας,
ὁ μὲν Δάφνις ἔτι ποιμενικὴν γνώμην ἔχων ὥρμητο [8]
τρέχειν ἐπὶ τὴν Χλόην καὶ ὅσα ἐπεπαίδευτο δρᾶν
αὐτίκα, καθάπερ δεδοικὼς μὴ βραδύνας ἐπιλάθοιτο.
ἡ δὲ Λυκαίνιον κατασχοῦσα αὐτὸν ἔλεξεν ὧδε·

<τῶν> Herch   [1] p omits   [2] q -ει   [3] A αὐτῇ
σηκίτην, but such kids have lost their mothers (see below)
[4] Uiii πρωτοτύρου   [5] so Huetius : mss ἀφθονίαν   Ap οἷα

If then thou wouldst be rid of thy misery, come on,
deliver thyself to me a sweet scholar, and I, to
gratify the Nymphs, will be thy mistress."

18. At this, Daphnis, as being a rustic goatherd
and a sanguine youth, could not contain himself for
mere pleasure, but throws himself at the foot of
Lycaenium and begs her that she would teach him
that lesson quickly; and as if he were about to
accept some rare and brave thing sent from the
Gods, for her kindness he promised he would give
her too a young kid, some of the finest beastings,
nay, besides, he promised her the dam herself.
Wherefore Lycaenium, now she had found a rustic
simplicity beyond her expectation, gave the lad all
his instruction. She bade him sit down close beside
her and kiss her as often and intensely as he kissed
Chloe; while kissing her he was to embrace her and
recline on the ground. So he sat down and kissed her
and reclined. When Lycaenium found him res-
ponsive and his body fully roused, she lifted him up
from his sideways posture and, nimbly sliding under
him, guided him along the path he had sought so
long. Thereafter she made no special effort, for
Nature herself taught Daphnis the remainder of the
lesson.

19. On the completion of this instruction in love-
making Daphnis, as simple-minded as ever, wanted
to run back to Chloe and put into instant practice
the art he had just been taught, as though fearing
that, if he tarried, he might forget it. But Lycaen-

⁶ so *E* : A εὐεργεῖν τε : pq ἐνεργεῖν δυνάμενον   ⁷ Uiii
περιηγάγετο   ⁸ pq ὥρμησε

"Ἔτι καὶ ταῦτά σε δεῖ μαθεῖν, Δάφνι. ἐγὼ γυνὴ
τυγχάνουσα πέπονθα νῦν οὐδέν. πάλαι γάρ με
ταῦτα ἀνὴρ ἄλλος ἐπαίδευσε μισθὸν τὴν παρθενίαν
λαβών. Χλόη δὲ συμπαλαίουσά σοι ταύτην τὴν
πάλην, καὶ [1] οἰμώξει καὶ κλαύσεται κἂν [2] αἵματι
κείσεται πολλῷ καθάπερ πεφονευμένη. ἀλλὰ σὺ
τὸ αἷμα μὴ φοβήθῃς, ἀλλ᾿ ἡνίκα ἂν πείσῃς αὐτήν
σοι παρασχεῖν, ἄγαγε αὐτὴν εἰς τοῦτο τὸ χωρίον,
ἵνα κἂν βοήσῃ [3] μηδεὶς ἀκούσῃ, κἂν δακρύσῃ [4]
μηδεὶς ἴδῃ, κἂν αἱμάχθῃ λούσηται τῇ πηγῇ. καὶ
μέμνησο, ὅτι σε ἐγὼ ἄνδρα πρὸ Χλόης πεποίηκα."

20. Ἡ μὲν οὖν Λυκαίνιον τοσαῦτα ὑποθεμένη,
κατ᾿ ἄλλο μέρος τῆς ὕλης ἀπῆλθεν ὡς ἔτι ζη-
τοῦσα τὸν χῆνα. ὁ δὲ Δάφνις εἰς λογισμὸν ἄγων
τὰ εἰρημένα τῆς μὲν προτέρας ὁρμῆς ἀπήλλακτο,
διοχλεῖν δὲ τῇ Χλόῃ περιττότερον ὤκνει φιλή-
ματος καὶ περιβολῆς, μήτε βοῆσαι θέλων αὐτὴν
ὡς πρὸς πολέμιον, μήτε δακρῦσαι ὡς ἀλγοῦσαν,
μήτε αἱμαχθῆναι καθάπερ πεφονευμένην. ἀρτι-
μαθὴς γὰρ ὢν ἐδεδοίκει τὸ αἷμα καὶ ἐνόμιζεν ὅτι
ἄρα ἐκ μόνου τραύματος αἷμα γίνεται.

Γνοὺς δὲ τὰ συνήθη τέρπεσθαι μετ᾿ αὐτῆς
ἐξέβη τῆς ὕλης· καὶ ἐλθὼν ἵν᾿ ἐκάθητο στεφα-
νίσκον ἴων πλέκουσα, τόν τε χῆνα τοῦ ἀετοῦ τῶν
ὀνύχων ἐψεύσατο ἐξαρπάσαι καὶ περιφὺς [5] ἐφί-
λησεν, οἷον ἐν τῇ τέρψει Λυκαίνιον· τοῦτο γὰρ
ἐξῆν ὡς ἀκίνδυνον. ἡ δὲ τὸν στέφανον ἐφήρμοσεν
αὐτοῦ τῇ κεφαλῇ καὶ τὴν κόμην ἐφίλησεν ὡς τῶν
ἴων κρείττονα. κἀκ [6] τῆς πήρας προκομίσασα [7]

---

[1] Uiii omits　　[2] so Schaef: mss καὶ　　[3] A βοᾷ　　[4] A
δακρύῃ　　[5] pq -θεὶς　　[6] so Schaef: mss καὶ　　[7] προκομίσασα
παλάθης: p προσκομ. παλ.: Uiii πρὸς: A omits τὸ φαγεῖν

ium held him back and said: "Daphnis, there is still something for you to learn. Since I happen to be an initiated woman, I didn't suffer at all just now; a long while ago another man taught me this lesson and took my virginity as payment. But when Chloe first engages with you in this form of wrestling, she will cry out and weep and bleed a good deal as if she had been stabbed. Still, don't let the thought of her bleeding deter you, but when you have prevailed on her to yield, bring her to this spot: then if she cries, no one will hear; if she weeps, no one will see; and if she bleeds, she can wash herself in the spring. And don't forget that I made a man of you before Chloe did."

20. After giving this advice Lycaenium went off to another part of the wood, still seemingly looking for her goose. But on pondering her words Daphnis found his initial enthusiasm gone; he hesitated to bother Chloe for more than kisses and embraces, for he did not want her to cry out as if assaulted or weep as if in pain or bleed as if stabbed. As a novice he was scared at the thought of her bleeding, under the impression that blood only flows when an injury has been inflicted.

Deciding therefore to enjoy himself with her in the usual way he left the wood and came to the place where Chloe sat platting a garland of violets, and told her a yarn that he had rescued the goose from the claws of the eagle; then, flinging his arms about her and clasping her to him, he kissed her as he had kissed Lycaenium, for that he thought he could safely do. But Chloe fitted the chaplet to his head, and then kissed his locks as being fairer and sweeter than the violets; and out of her scrip she gave him

παλάθης μοῖραν καὶ ἄρτους τινὰς ἔδωκε φαγεῖν,
καὶ ἐσθίοντος ἀπὸ τοῦ στόματος ἥρπαζε καὶ
οὕτως ἤσθιεν ὥσπερ νεοττὸς ὄρνιθος.

21. Ἐσθιόντων δὲ αὐτῶν καὶ περιττότερα φι-
λούντων ὧν ἤσθιον, ναῦς ἁλιέων ὤφθη παρα-
πλέουσα. ἄνεμος μὲν οὐκ ἦν, γαλήνη δὲ ἦν, καὶ
ἐρέττειν ἐδόκει. καὶ ἤρεττον ἐρρωμένως· ἠπεί-
γοντο γὰρ νεαλεῖς ἰχθῦς[1] εἰς τὴν πόλιν δια-
σώσασθαι τῶν τινι[2] πλουσίων. οἷον οὖν εἰώ-
θασι ναῦται δρᾶν εἰς καμάτων ἀμέλειαν, τοῦτο
κἀκεῖνοι δρῶντες τὰς κώπας ἀνέφερον. εἷς μὲν
αὐτοῖς κελευστὴς ναυτικὰς ᾖδεν ᾠδάς, οἱ δὲ
λοιποὶ καθάπερ χορὸς ὁμοφώνως κατὰ καιρὸν
τῆς ἐκείνου φωνῆς ἐβόων. ἡνίκα μὲν οὖν ἐν[3]
ἀναπεπταμένῃ τῇ θαλάττῃ ταῦτα ἔπραττον,
ἠφανίζετο ἡ βοή, χεομένης τῆς φωνῆς εἰς πολὺν
ἀέρα· ἐπεὶ δὲ ἄκρᾳ τινὶ ὑποδραμόντες εἰς κόλπον
μηνοειδῆ καὶ κοῖλον εἰσήλασαν, μείζων μὲν
ἠκούετο <ἡ> βοή, σαφῆ δὲ ἐξέπιπτεν εἰς τὴν γῆν
τὰ κελεύσματα.[4] κοῖλος γὰρ αὐλὼν[5] ὑποκεί-
μενος καὶ τὸν ἦχον εἰς αὐτὸν ὡς ὄργανον δεχό-
μενος, πάντων τῶν <ποιουμένων καὶ> λεγομένων
μιμητὴν φωνὴν ἀπεδίδου, ἰδίᾳ μὲν τῶν κωπῶν τὸν
ἦχον, ἰδίᾳ δὲ τὴν βοὴν[6] τῶν ναυτῶν. καὶ ἐγίνετο
ἄκουσμα τερπνόν· φθανούσης γὰρ τῆς ἀπὸ τῆς
θαλάττης φωνῆς, ἡ ἐκ τῆς γῆς φωνὴ τοσοῦτον
ἐπαύετο βράδιον[7] ὅσον ἤρξατο.

---

[1] A ἰχθύος τῶν πετραίων (from 2. 12)   [2] so Hemsterhusius,
cf. 2. 13: mss τινῶν   [3] pq omit   <ἡ> E   [4] so E:
mss τὰ τῶν κελευσμάτων ᾄσματα with incorp. gloss   [5] so E:

of her cakes and simnels to eat, and snatched it by
stealth from his mouth again as he was eating, and
fed like a young bird in a nest.

21. While thus they eat and take more kisses
then bits, they saw a fisherman's boat come by.
The wind was down, the sea was smooth, and there
was a great calm. Wherefore when they saw there
was need of rowing, they fell to ply the oars stoutly.
For they made haste to bring in some fish fresh from
the sea to fit the palate of one of the richer citizens of
Mytilene. That therefore which other mariners use
to elude the tediousness of labour, these began, and
held on as they rowed along. There was one
amongst them that was the boatswain, and he had
certain sea-songs. The rest, like a chorus all together,
strained their throats to a loud holla, and catched his
voice at certain intervals. While they did thus in
the open sea, their voices vanished, as being diffused
in the vast air. But when they came under a pro-
montore into a flexuous, horned, hollow bay, there,
as the voices of the rowers were heard stronger,
so the songs of the boatswain to the answering
mariners fell clearer to the land. For a hollow valley
below received into itself that shrill sound as into
an organ, and by an imitating voice rendered from
itself all that was said, all that was done, and every-
thing distinctly by itself; by itself the clattering of
the oars, by itself the whooping of the seamen; and
certainly it was a most pleasant hearing. The sound
coming first from the sea, the sound from the land
ended so much the later by how much it was slower
to begin.

mss τὸ πεδίον αὐλῶν (p αὐλῶν) a gloss   B ὑπερκείμενος
<ποιουμ. καὶ> E   6 so E: mss φωνὴν from above
7 "later," cf. i. 28

22. Ὁ μὲν οὖν Δάφνις εἰδὼς τὸ πραττόμενον
μόνῃ τῇ θαλάττῃ προσεῖχε, καὶ ἐτέρπετο τῇ νηὶ
παρατρεχούσῃ τὸ πεδίον θᾶττον πτεροῦ, καὶ
ἐπειρᾶτό τινα διασώσασθαι τῶν κελευσμάτων,[1]
ὡς γένοιτο τῆς σύριγγος μέλη. ἡ δὲ Χλόη τότε
πρῶτον πειρωμένη τῆς καλουμένης ἠχοῦς ποτὲ
μὲν εἰς τὴν θάλατταν ἀπέβλεπε τῶν ναυτῶν
κελευόντων, ποτὲ δὲ εἰς τὴν ὕλην ὑπέστρεφε
ζητοῦσα τοὺς ἀντιφωνοῦντας. καὶ ἐπεὶ παραπλευ-
σάντων[2] ἦν κἂν τῷ αὐλῶνι σιγή, ἐπυνθάνετο τοῦ
Δάφνιδος, εἰ καὶ ὀπίσω τῆς ἄκρας ἐστὶ θάλαττα
καὶ ναῦς ἄλλη παραπλεῖ καὶ ἄλλοι ναῦται τὰ
αὐτὰ ᾖδον καὶ ἅμα πάντες σιωπῶσι. γελάσας
οὖν ὁ Δάφνις ἡδὺ καὶ φιλήσας ἥδιον φίλημα καὶ
τὸν τῶν ἴων στέφανον ἐκείνῃ περιθείς, ἤρξατο
αὐτῇ μυθολογεῖν τὸν μῦθον τῆς Ἠχοῦς, αἰτήσας,
εἰ διδάξειε, μισθὸν παρ' αὐτῆς ἄλλα φιλήματα
δέκα·

23. "Νυμφῶν, ὦ κόρη, πολὺ <τὸ> γένος,
Μελίαι[3] καὶ Δρυάδες καὶ Ἔλειοι, πᾶσαι καλαί,
πᾶσαι μουσικαί.[4] καὶ μιᾶς τούτων θυγάτηρ
Ἠχὼ γίνεται, θνητὴ μὲν ἐκ πατρὸς θνητοῦ, καλὴ
δὲ ἐκ μητρὸς καλῆς. τρέφεται μὲν ὑπὸ Νυμφῶν,
παιδεύεται δὲ ὑπὸ Μουσῶν συρίττειν, αὐλεῖν, τὰ
πρὸς λύραν, τὰ πρὸς κιθάραν, πᾶσαν ᾠδήν. ὥστε

---

[1] so E : pq τῶν ᾀσμάτων : A τὰ τῶν λευκασμάτων   [2] p
παρακελευσ.   <τὸ> E   [3] so Jung : mss Μελικαὶ   pq
omit καὶ   [4] Parr omit πᾶσ. κ. πᾶσ. μ.

22. Daphnis, therefore, knowing what it was, attended wholly to the sea, and was sweetly affected with the pinnace gliding by like a bird in the air, endeavouring the while to preserve to himself some of those tones [1] to play afterwards upon his pipe. But Chloe, having then her first experience of that which is called echo, now cast her eyes towards the sea, minding the loud songs of the mariners, now to the woods, seeking for those who answered from thence with such a clamour. And when because the pinnace was passed away there was in the valley too a deep silence, she asked of Daphnis whether there were sea beyond the promontore and another ship did pass by there, and whether there were other mariners that had sung the same songs and all now were whist [2] and kept silence together. At this, Daphnis laughed a sweet laugh, and giving her a sweeter kiss, put the violet chaplet upon her head, and began to tell her the tale of Echo, requiring first that when he had taught her that, he should have of her for his wages ten kisses more:

23. "There are of the Nymphs, my dear girl, more kinds then one. There are the Meliae of the Ash, there are the Dryades of the Oak, there are the Heleae of the Fen. All are beautiful, all are musical. To one of these Echo was daughter, and she mortal because she came of a mortal father, but a rare beauty, deriving from a beauteous mother. She was educated by the Nymphs, and taught by the Muses to play on the hautboy and the pipe, to strike the lyre, to touch the lute, and in sum, all music. And therefore when she was grown up and in the flower

---

[1] perhaps Thornley intended "tunes."   [2] silent.

καὶ παρθενίας εἰς ἄνθος ἀκμάσασα ταῖς Νύμφαις·
συνεχόρευε, ταῖς Μούσαις συνῇδει· ἄρρενας δὲ
ἔφευγε πάντας καὶ ἀνθρώπους καὶ θεούς, φιλοῦσα
τὴν παρθενίαν. ὁ Πὰν ὀργίζεται τῇ κόρῃ, τῆς μου-
σικῆς φθονῶν, τοῦ κάλλους μὴ τυχών, καὶ μανίαν
ἐμβάλλει τοῖς ποιμέσι καὶ τοῖς αἰπόλοις. οἱ δὲ
ὥσπερ κύνες ἢ λύκοι διασπῶσιν αὐτὴν καὶ ῥίπ-
τουσιν εἰς πᾶσαν γῆν ἔτι ᾄδοντα[1] τὰ μέλη. καὶ τὰ
μέλη <ἡ> Γῆ χαριζομένη Νύμφαις[2] ἔκρυψε
πάντα καὶ ἐτήρησε τὴν μουσικήν· καὶ <ἃ> γνώμῃ
Μουσῶν ἀφίησι φωνὴν καὶ μιμεῖται πάντα, κα-
θάπερ τότε ἡ κόρη, θεούς, ἀνθρώπους, ὄργανα,
θηρία. μιμεῖται καὶ αὐτὸν συρίττοντα τὸν Πάνα·
ὁ δὲ ἀκούσας ἀναπηδᾷ καὶ διώκει κατὰ τῶν ὀρῶν,
οὐκ ἐρῶν τυχεῖν ἀλλ' ἢ τοῦ μαθεῖν, τίς ἐστιν ὁ
λανθάνων μιμητής."[3] ταῦτα μυθολογήσαντα τὸν
Δάφνιν οὐ δέκα μόνον ἄλλα[4] φιλήματα, ἀλλὰ
πάνυ πολλὰ κατεφίλησεν ἡ Χλόη· μικροῦ γὰρ
καὶ τὰ αὐτὰ εἶπεν ἡ Ἠχώ, καθάπερ μαρτυροῦσα
ὅτι μηδὲν ἐψεύσατο.

24. Θερμοτέρου δὲ καθ' ἑκάστην ἡμέραν γινο-
μένου τοῦ ἡλίου, οἷα τοῦ μὲν ἦρος παυομένου τοῦ
δὲ θέρους ἀρχομένου, πάλιν αὐτοῖς ἐγίνοντο καιναὶ
τέρψεις καὶ θέρειοι. ὁ μὲν γὰρ ἐνήχετο ἐν τοῖς
ποταμοῖς, ἡ δὲ ἐν ταῖς πηγαῖς ἐλούετο· ὁ μὲν
ἐσύριττεν ἁμιλλώμενος πρὸς τὰς πίτυς, ἡ δὲ ᾖδε
ταῖς ἀηδόσιν ἐρίζουσα. ἐθήρων ἀκρίδας λάλους,

---

[1] p ᾄδουσαν   <ἡ> Hirsch.   [2] A καὶ Νύμ.   <ἃ> E,
"they"   [3] so Richards: mss μαθητής   [4] so E, cf. 22 fin:
A ἀλλὰ: pq omit

of her virgin beauty, she danced together with the
Nymphs and sung in consort with the Muses; but
fled from all males, whether men or Gods, because
she loved virginity.   Pan sees that, and takes
occasion to be angry at the maid, and to envy her
music because he could not come at her beauty.
Therefore he sends a madness among the shepherds
and goatherds, and they in a desperate fury, like so
many dogs and wolves, tore her all to pieces and
flung about them all over the earth her yet singing
limbs.[1]   The Earth in observance of the Nymphs
buried them all, preserving to them still their music
property, and they by an everlasting sentence and
decree of the Muses breathe out a voice.   And they
imitate all things now as the maid did before, the
Gods, men, organs, beasts.   Pan himself they imitate
too when he plays on the pipe; which when he hears
he bounces out and begins to post over the mountains,
not so much to catch and hold as to know what
clandestine imitator that is that he has got."   When
Daphnis thus had told his tale, Chloe gave him not
only ten more kisses but innumerable.   For Echo
said almost the same, as if to bear him witness that
he did not lie.

24. But now, when the Sun grew every day more
burning, the spring going out and summer coming
in, they were invited to new and summer pleasure.
Daphnis he swom in the rivers, Chloe she bathed in
the springs; he with his pipe contended with the
pines, she with her voice strove with the nightin-
gales.   Sometimes they hunted the prattling locusts,
sometimes they catched the chirping grasshoppers.

[1] there is a pun in the Greek on μέλη "limbs" and μέλη
"songs."

ἐλάμβανον τέττιγας ἠχοῦντας· ἄνθη συνέλεγον,
δένδρα συνέσειον, ὀπώρας συνήσθιον.[1] ἤδη ποτὲ
καὶ γυμνοὶ συγκατεκλίθησαν καὶ ἓν δέρμα αἰγὸς
ἐπεσύραντο. καὶ ἐγένετο ἂν γυνὴ Χλόη ῥᾳδίως,
εἰ μὴ Δάφνιν ἐτάραξε τὸ αἷμα. ἀμέλει καὶ δεδοι-
κὼς μὴ νικηθῇ τὸν λογισμόν ποτε, πολλὰ γυμνοῦ-
σθαι τὴν Χλόην οὐκ ἐπέτρεπεν· ὥστε ἐθαύμαζε
μὲν ἡ Χλόη, τὴν δὲ αἰτίαν ᾐδεῖτο πυνθάνεσθαι.[2]

25. Ἐν τῷ θέρει τῷδε καὶ μνηστήρων πλῆθος
ἦν περὶ τὴν Χλόην καὶ πολλοὶ πολλαχόθεν ἐφοί-
των παρὰ τὸν Δρύαντα πολλὰ[3] πρὸς γάμον
αἰτοῦντες αὐτήν. καὶ οἱ μέν τι δῶρον ἔφερον, οἱ
δὲ ἐπηγγέλλοντο μεγάλα. ἡ μὲν οὖν Νάπη ταῖς
ἐλπίσιν ἐπαιρομένη συνεβούλευεν ἐκδιδόναι τὴν
Χλόην, μηδὲ κατέχειν οἴκοι πρὸς πλέον τηλικαύ-
την κόρην, ἣ τάχα μικρὸν ὕστερον νέμουσα
ἄνδρα ποιήσεταί τινα τῶν ποιμένων ἐπὶ μήλοις ἢ
ῥόδοις, ἀλλ' ἐκείνην τε ποιῆσαι δέσποιναν οἰκίας,
καὶ αὐτοὺς πολλὰ λαβόντας ἰδίῳ φυλάττειν αὐτὰ
καὶ γνησίῳ παιδίῳ· ἐγεγόνει δὲ αὐτοῖς ἄρρεν
παιδίον οὐ πρὸ πολλοῦ τινος.

Ὁ δὲ Δρύας ποτὲ μὲν ἐθέλγετο τοῖς λεγομένοις
(μείζονα γὰρ ἢ κατὰ ποιμαίνουσαν κόρην δῶρα
ὠνομάζετο παρ' ἑκάστου), ποτὲ δὲ <ἐννοήσας> ὡς
κρείττων ἐστὶν ἡ παρθένος μνηστήρων γεωργῶν,
καὶ ὡς, εἴ ποτε τοὺς ἀληθινοὺς γονέας εὕροι,
μεγάλως αὐτοὺς εὐδαίμονας[4] θήσει, ἀνεβάλλετο
τὴν ἀπόκρισιν καὶ εἷλκε[5] χρόνον ἐκ χρόνου, καὶ
ἐν τῷ τέως ἀπεκέρδαινεν οὐκ ὀλίγα δῶρα.

---

[1] so E: mss ἔσειον and ἦσθιον   [2] pq πυθέσθαι   [3] pq
omit <ἐννοήσ.> Hirsch.   [4] A αὐτὴν εὐδαίμονα   [5] q ἤνεγκε

Side by side they would pick flowers, shake the trees, and eat the fruit. Afterwards they would lie naked side by side with just a goatskin to cover them. At such times it would have been very easy for Daphnis to make a woman of her, only he was afraid at the thought of her bleeding. Indeed he was so scared that his resolution might sometime give way that he often forbade Chloe to take off her clothes. Chloe was surprised at this, but was too shy to ask the reason.

25. That summer Chloe had many suitors, and many came from many places, and came often, to Dryas, to get his goodwill to have her. Some brought their gifts along with them, others promised great matters if they should get her. Nape was tempted by her hope, and began to persuade him that the girl should be bestowed, and to urge that a maid of her age should not longer be kept at home; for who knows whether one time or other she may not for an apple or a rose, as she keeps the field, make some unworthy shepherd a man; and therefore it was better she should now be made the dame of a house, and that they getting much by her, it should be laid up for their own son, for of late they had born a jolly boy.

But Dryas was variously affected with what was said. Sometimes he was ready to give way; for greater gifts were named to him by everyone then suited with a rural girl, a shepherdess. Sometimes again he thought the maid deserved better then to be married to a clown, and that if ever she should find her true parents she might make him and his family happy. Then he defers his answer to the wooers and puts them off from day to day, and in the interim has many presents.

DAPHNIS AND CHLOE

Ἡ μὲν δὴ μαθοῦσα λυπηρῶς πάνυ διῆγε, καὶ τὸν Δάφνιν ἐλάνθανεν ἐπὶ πολὺ λυπεῖν οὐ θέλουσα· ὡς δὲ ἐλιπάρει καὶ ἐνέκειτο πυνθανόμενος καὶ ἐλυπεῖτο μᾶλλον μὴ μανθάνων ἢ ἔμελλε μαθών, πάντα αὐτῷ διηγεῖται, τοὺς μνηστευομένους ὡς πολλοὶ καὶ πλούσιοι, τοὺς λόγους οὓς ἡ Νάπη σπεύδουσα πρὸς τὸν γάμον ἔλεγεν, ὡς οὐκ ἀπείπατο Δρύας, ἀλλ᾽ ὡς εἰς τὸν τρυγητὸν ἀναβέβληται. 26. ἔκφρων ἐπὶ τούτοις ὁ Δάφνις γίνεται καὶ ἐδάκρυσε καθήμενος, ἀποθανεῖσθαι μηκέτι νεμούσης[1] Χλόης λέγων, καὶ οὐκ αὐτὸς μόνος, ἀλλὰ καὶ τὰ πρόβατα μετὰ τοιοῦτον ποιμένα.

Εἶτα ἀνενεγκὼν ἐθάρρει, καὶ πείσειν ἐνόει τὸν πατέρα, καὶ ἕνα τῶν μνωμένων αὐτὸν ἠρίθμει, καὶ πολὺ κρατήσειν ἤλπιζε τῶν ἄλλων. ἓν αὐτὸν ἐτάραττεν· οὐκ ἦν Λάμων πλούσιος·[2] τοῦτο μόνον αὐτοῦ τὴν ἐλπίδα λεπτὴν εἰργάζετο. ὅμως δὲ ἐδόκει μνᾶσθαι, καὶ τῇ Χλόῃ συνεδόκει. τῷ Λάμωνι μὲν οὖν οὐδὲν ἐτόλμησεν εἰπεῖν, τῇ Μυρτάλῃ δὲ θαρρήσας καὶ τὸν ἔρωτα ἐμήνυσε καὶ περὶ τοῦ γάμου λόγους προσήνεγκεν. ἡ δὲ τῷ Λάμωνι νύκτωρ ἐκοινώσατο. σκληρῶς δὲ ἐκείνου τὴν ἔντευξιν ἐνεγκόντος, καὶ λοιδορήσαντος εἰ

[1] p μενούσης   [2] A adds ἀλλ᾽ οὐδὲ ἐλεύθερος εἰ καὶ πλούσιος
(prob. gloss from 31)   μόνον here Herch : mss after ἐλπ.

When Chloe came to the knowledge of this, she
was very sad, and hid it long from Daphnis because
she would not give him a cause of grief.   But when
he was importunate and urged her to tell him what
the matter was, and seemed to be more troubled
when he knew it not, than he should be when he
knew it, then, poor girl, she told him all, as well of
the wooers that were so many and so rich, as of the
words by which Nape incited Dryas to marry her
speedily, and how Dryas had not denied it but only
had put it off to the vintage. 26. Daphnis with this is
at his wit's end, and sitting down he wept bitterly,
and said that if Chloe were no longer to tend sheep
with him he would die, and not only he, but all the
flocks that lost so sweet a shepherdess.

After this passion Daphnis came to himself again
and took courage, thinking he should persuade Dryas
in his own behalf, and resolved to put himself among
the wooers with hope that his desert would say for
him, " Room for your betters."   There was one thing
troubled him worst of all, and that was, his father
Lamo was not rich.   That disheartened him, that
allayed his hope much.   Nevertheless it seemed best
that he should come in for a suitor, and that was
Chloe's sentence [1] too. To Lamo he durst not venture
to speak, but put on a good face and spoke to
Myrtale, and did not only shew her his love, but
talked to her of marrying the girl.   And in the
night, when they were in bed, she acquainted Lamo
with it.   But Lamo entertaining what she said in
that case very harshly, and chiding her that she
should offer to make a match between a shepherd's

---

[1] verdict.

παιδὶ θυγάτριον ποιμένων προξενεῖ μεγάλην ἐν
τοῖς γνωρίσμασιν ἐπαγγελλομένῳ τύχην, ὃς αὐτοὺς
εὑρὼν τοὺς οἰκείους καὶ ἐλευθέρους θήσει καὶ
δεσπότας ἀγρῶν μειζόνων, ἡ Μυρτάλη διὰ τὸν
ἔρωτα φοβουμένη, μὴ τελέως ἀπελπίσας ὁ Δάφνις
τὸν γάμον τολμήσει τι θανατῶδες, ἄλλας αὐτῷ
τῆς ἀντιρρήσεως αἰτίας ἀπήγγελλε·

"Πένητές ἐσμεν, ὦ παῖ, καὶ δεόμεθα νύμφης
φερούσης τι μᾶλλον <ἢ αἰτούσης>, οἱ δὲ πλούσιοι
καὶ πλουσίων νυμφίων δεόμενοι. ἴθι δή, πεῖσον
Χλόην, ἡ δὲ τὸν πατέρα μηδὲν αἰτεῖν μέγα καὶ
γαμεῖν. πάντως δέ που κἀκείνη φιλεῖ σε καὶ
βούλεται συγκαθεύδειν πένητι καλῷ μᾶλλον ἢ
πιθήκῳ πλουσίῳ." 27. Μυρτάλη μέν, οὔποτε
ἐλπίσασα Δρύαντα τούτοις συνθήσεσθαι μνη-
στῆρας ἔχοντα πλουσιωτέρους[1], εὐπρεπῶς ᾤετο
παρῃτῆσθαι[2] τὸν γάμον.

Δάφνις δὲ οὐκ εἶχε μέμφεσθαι τὰ λελεγμένα,
λειπόμενος δὲ πολὺ τῶν αἰτουμένων τὸ σύνηθες
ἐρασταῖς πενομένοις ἔπραττεν, ἐδάκρυε καὶ τὰς
Νύμφας αὖθις ἐκάλει βοηθούς. αἱ δὲ αὐτῷ καθεύ-
δοντι νύκτωρ ἐν τοῖς αὐτοῖς ἐφίστανται σχήμασιν
ἐν οἷς καὶ πρότερον. ἔλεγε δὲ ἡ πρεσβυτάτη
πάλιν· "Γάμου μὲν μέλει τῆς Χλόης ἄλλῳ θεῷ,
δῶρα δέ σοι δώσομεν ἡμεῖς, ἃ θέλξει Δρύαντα. ἡ
ναῦς, ἡ τῶν Μηθυμναίων νεανίσκων, ἧς τὴν λύγον

<ἢ αἰτούσ.> E (Amyot by emi.)   [1] A -τάτους   [2] A pres.

daughter and such a youth as he, whose tokens did declare him a great fortune and of high extraction, and one that if his true parents were found would not only make them free but possessors of larger lands, Myrtale, considering the power of love, and therefore fearing, if he should altogether despair of the marriage, lest he should attempt something upon his life, returned him other causes then Lamo had, to contradict:

" My son, we are but poor, and have more need to take a bride that does bring us something then one that will have much from us. They, on the other side, are rich and such as look for rich husbands. Go thou and persuade Chloe, and let her persuade her father, that he shall ask no great matter, and give you his consent to marry. For, on my life, she loves thee dearly, and had rather a thousand times lie with a poor and handsome man then a rich monkey." 27. And now Myrtale, who expected that Dryas would never consent to these things because there were rich wooers, thought she had finely excused to him their refusing of the marriage.

Daphnis knew not what to say against this, and so finding himself far enough off from what he desired, that which is usual with lovers who are beggars, that he did. With tears he lamented his condition, and again implored the help of the Nymphs. They appeared to him in the night in his sleep, in the same form and habit as before, and she that was eldest spoke again : " Some other of the Gods takes the care about the marrying of Chloe, but we shall furnish thee with gifts which will easily make [1] her father Dryas. That ship of the Methymnaeans,

[1] bring over, persuade.

αἱ σαί ποτε αἶγες κατέφαγον, ἡμέρᾳ μὲν ἐκείνῃ
μακρὰν τῆς γῆς ὑπηνέχθη πνεύματι· νυκτὸς δέ,
πελαγίου ταράξαντος ἀνέμου τὴν θάλατταν, εἰς
τὴν γῆν εἰς τὰς τῆς ἄκρας πέτρας ἐξεβράσθη.
αὕτη μὲν οὖν διεφθάρη καὶ πολλὰ τῶν ἐν αὐτῇ·
βαλάντιον δὲ τρισχιλίων δραχμῶν ὑπὸ τοῦ κύμα-
τος ἀπεπτύσθη, καὶ κεῖται φυκίοις κεκαλυμμένον
πλησίον δελφῖνος νεκροῦ, δι᾽ ὃν [1] οὐδεὶς οὐδὲ
προσῆλθεν ὁδοιπόρος, τὸ δυσῶδες τῆς σηπεδόνος
παρατρέχων. ἀλλὰ σὺ πρόσελθε καὶ προσελθὼν
ἀνελοῦ καὶ ἀνελόμενος δός. ἱκανόν σοι νῦν δόξαι [2]
μὴ πένητι· χρόνῳ δὲ ὕστερον ἔσῃ καὶ πλούσιος."
28. αἱ μὲν ταῦτα εἰποῦσαι τῇ νυκτὶ συναπῆλθον.

Γενομένης δὲ ἡμέρας ἀναπηδήσας ὁ Δάφνις
περιχαρὴς ἤλαυνε ῥοίζῳ πολλῷ τὰς αἶγας εἰς τὴν
νομήν, καὶ τὴν Χλόην φιλήσας καὶ τὰς Νύμφας
προσκυνήσας κατῆλθεν ἐπὶ θάλατταν, ὡς περι-
ράνασθαι θέλων, καὶ ἐπὶ τῆς ψάμμου, πλησίον
τῆς κυματωγῆς [3] ἐβάδιζε ζητῶν τὰς τρισχιλίας.
ἔμελλε δὲ ἄρα οὐ πολὺν κάματον ἕξειν· ὁ γὰρ
δελφὶς οὐκ ἀγαθὸν ὀδωδὼς αὐτῷ προσέπιπτεν ἐρ-
ριμμένος καὶ μυδῶν, οὗ τῇ σηπεδόνι καθάπερ
ἡγεμόνι χρώμενος ὁδοῦ προσῆλθέ τε εὐθὺς καὶ τὰ
φυκία ἀφελὼν εὑρίσκει τὸ βαλάντιον ἀργυρίου
μεστόν. τοῦτο ἀνελόμενος καὶ εἰς τὴν πήραν
ἐνθέμενος, οὐ πρόσθεν ἀπῆλθε, πρὶν τὰς Νύμφας

---

[1] A omits δι᾽ ὃν and has οὖν for οὐδὲ   [2] Amyot apparently
σε δεῖξαι   [3] q κυματώδους γῆς

when thy goats had eaten her cable, that very day was carried off by the winds far from the shore. But that night there arose a tempestuous sea-wind that blew to the land and dashed her against the rocks of the promontore ; there she perished with much of that which was in her. But the waves cast up a purse in which there are three thousand drachmas, and that thou shalt find covered with ouse [1] hard by a dead dolphin, near which no passenger comes, but turns another way as fast as he can, detesting the stench of the rotting fish. But do thou make haste thither, take it, and give it to Dryas. And let it suffice that now thou art not poor, ard hereafter in time thou shalt be rich." 28. This spoken, they passed away together with the night.

It was now day, and Daphnis leapt out of bed as full of joy as his heart could hold, and hurried his goats, with much whistling, to the field ; and after he had kissed Chloe and adored the Nymphs, to the sea he goes, making as if that morning he had a mind to bedew himself with sea-water. And walking there upon the gravel, near the line of the excursion and breaking of the waves, he looked for his three thousand drachmas. But soon he found he should not be put to much labour. For the stench of the dolphin had reached him as he lay cast up and was rotting upon the slabby sand. When he had got that scent for his guide, he came up presently to the place, and removing the ouse, found the purse full of silver. He took it up and put it into his scrip ; yet went not away till with joyful devotion he had blest

---

[1] sea-weed.

εὐφημῆσαι καὶ αὐτὴν τὴν θάλατταν· καίπερ γὰρ
αἰπόλος ὤν, ἤδη καὶ τὴν θάλατταν ἐνόμιζε τῆς γῆς
γλυκυτέραν, ὡς εἰς τὸν γάμον αὐτῷ τὸν Χλόης
συλλαμβάνουσαν.

29. Εἰλημμένος δὲ τῶν τρισχιλίων οὐκέτ᾽
ἔμελλεν, ἀλλ᾽, ὡς πάντων ἀνθρώπων πλουσιώ-
τατος,[1] οὐ μόνον τῶν ἐκεῖ γεωργῶν, αὐτίκα ἐλθὼν
παρὰ τὴν Χλόην διηγεῖται αὐτῇ τὸ ὄναρ, δείκνυσι
τὸ βαλάντιον, κελεύει τὰς ἀγέλας φυλάττειν ἔστ᾽
ἂν ἐπανέλθῃ, καὶ συντείνας σοβεῖ παρὰ τὸν
Δρύαντα. καὶ εὑρὼν πυρούς τινας ἁλωνοτρι-
βοῦντα μετὰ τῆς Νάπης, πάνυ θρασὺν ἐμβάλλει
λόγον περὶ γάμου· "Ἐμοὶ δὸς Χλόην γυναῖκα.
ἐγὼ καὶ συρίττειν οἶδα καλῶς καὶ κλᾶν ἄμπελον
καὶ φυτὰ κατορύττειν.[2] οἶδα καὶ γῆν ἀροῦν καὶ
λικμῆσαι πρὸς ἄνεμον. ἀγέλην δὲ ὅπως νέμω
μάρτυς Χλόη· πεντήκοντα αἶγας παραλαβὼν
διπλασίονας πεποίηκα· ἔθρεψα καὶ τράγους
μεγάλους καὶ καλούς· πρότερον δὲ ἀλλοτρίοις
τὰς αἶγας ὑπεβάλλομεν. ἀλλὰ καὶ νέος εἰμὶ
καὶ γείτων ὑμῖν ἄμεμπτος· καί με ἔθρεψεν αἴξ,
ὡς Χλόην οἶς. τοσοῦτον δὲ τῶν ἄλλων κρατῶν
οὐδὲ δώροις ἡττηθήσομαι· ἐκεῖνοι δώσουσιν αἶγας
καὶ πρόβατα καὶ ζεῦγος ψωραλέων βοῶν καὶ
σῖτον μηδὲ ἀλεκτορίδας θρέψαι δυνάμενον, παρ᾽

---

[1] A -τερος   [2] A κορύσσειν

the Nymphs and the very sea; for though he was a keeper of goats, yet he was now obliged to the sea, and had a sweeter sense of that then the land, because it had promoted him to marry Chloe.

29. Thus having got his three thousand drachmas, he made no longer stay, but as if now he were not only richer then any of the clowns that dwelt there but then any man that trod on the ground, he hastens to Chloe, tells her his dream, shews her the purse, and bids her look to his flocks till he comes again. Then stretching and stritting along, he bustles in like a lord upon Dryas, whom he then found with Nape at the threshing-floor, and on a sudden talked very boldly about the marrying of Chloe: "Give me Chloe to my wife. For I can play finely on the pipe, I can cut the vines, and I can plant them. Nor am I ignorant how and when the ground is to be ploughed, or how the corn is to be winnowed and fanned by the wind. But how I keep and govern flocks, Chloe can tell. Fifty she-goats I had of my father Lamo; I have made them as many more and doubled the number. Besides, I have brought up goodly, proper he-goats; whereas before, we went for leaps to other men's. Moreover, I am a young man, your neighbour too, and one that you cannot twit in the teeth with anything. And, further, I had a goat to my nurse as your Chloe had a sheep. Since in these I have got the start and outgone others, neither in gifts shall I be any whit behind them. They may give you the scrag-end of a small flock of sheep and goats, a rascal pair of oxen, and so much corn as scant will serve to keep the hens. But from me, look you here, three

ἐμοῦ δὲ αἵδε[1] ὑμῖν τρισχίλιαι. μόνον ἴστω τοῦτο
μηδείς, μὴ Λάμων αὐτὸς οὑμὸς πατήρ." ἅμα τε
ἐδίδου καὶ περιβαλὼν κατεφίλει.

30. Οἱ δὲ παρ' ἐλπίδα ἰδόντες τοσοῦτον
ἀργύριον, αὐτίκα τε δώσειν ἐπηγγέλλοντο τὴν
Χλόην καὶ πείσειν ὑπισχνοῦντο τὸν Λάμωνα.
ἡ μὲν δὴ Νάπη μετὰ τοῦ Δάφνιδος αὐτοῦ μένουσα
περιήλαυνε τὰς βοῦς καὶ τοῖς τριβείοις[2] κατειργά-
ζετο τὸν στάχυν· ὁ δὲ Δρύας θησαυρίσας τὸ
βαλάντιον ἔνθα ἀπέκειτο τὰ γνωρίσματα, ταχὺς
τὴν πρὸς[3] Λάμωνα καὶ τὴν Μυρτάλην ἐφέρετο
μέλλων παρ' αὐτῶν, τὸ καινότατον, μνᾶσθαι
νυμφίον. εὑρὼν δὲ κἀκείνους κριθία[4] μετροῦντας
οὐ πρὸ πολλοῦ λελικμημένα, ἀθύμως τε ἔχοντας
ὅτι μικροῦ δεῖν ὀλιγώτερα ἦν τῶν καταβλη-
θέντων σπερμάτων, ἐπ' ἐκείνοις μὲν παρεμυθή-
σατο κοινὴν ὁμολογήσας αἰτίαν[5] γεγονέναι παντα-
χοῦ, τὸν δὲ Δάφνιν ᾔτεῖτο Χλόῃ, καὶ ἔλεγεν ὅτι
πολλὰ ἄλλων διδόντων οὐδὲν παρ' αὐτῶν λήψεται,
μᾶλλον δέ τι[6] οἴκοθεν αὐτοῖς ἐπιδώσει· συντετρά-
φθαι[7] γὰρ ἀλλήλοις, κἂν τῷ νέμειν συνῆφθαι
φιλίᾳ[8] ῥᾳδίως λυθῆναι μὴ δυναμένῃ· ἤδη δὲ καὶ
ἡλικίαν ἔχειν ὡς καθεύδειν μετ' ἀλλήλων. ὁ μὲν
ταῦτα καὶ ἔτι πλείω ἔλεγεν, οἷα τοῦ πεῖσαι λέγων
ἆθλον ἔχων τὰς[9] τρισχιλίας.

---

[1] A omits   p omits ὑμῖν   [2] so E: mss τριβίοις: Jung.
τριβόλοις   [3] τὴν πρὸς E (sc. ὁδὸν): A τὸν πρὸς: pq παρὰ τὸν
[4] only here: Vill. κριθίδια   [5] A ἔτι, but κοινὴ αἰτία is

thousand drachmas. Only let nobody know of this, no, not so much as my father Lamo." With that, he gave it into his hand, embraced Dryas, and kissed him.

30. They, when they saw such an unexpected sum of money, without delay promised him Chloe and to procure Lamo's consent. Nape therefore stayed there with Daphnis and drove her oxen about the floor to break the ears very small and slip out the grain, with her hurdle set with sharp stones. But Dryas, having carefully laid up the purse of silver in that place where the tokens of Chloe were kept, makes away presently to Lamo and Myrtale on a strange errand, to woo them for a bridegroom. Them he found a measuring barley newly fanned, and much dejected because that year the ground had scarcely restored them their seed. Dryas put in to comfort them concerning that, affirming it was a common cause,[1] and that everywhere he met with the same cry; and then asks their good will that Daphnis should marry Chloe, and told them withal that although others did offer him great matters, yet of them he would take nothing, nay, rather he would give them somewhat for him : "For," quoth he, "they have bin bred up together, and by keeping their flocks together in the fields are grown to so dear a love as is not easy to be dissolved, and now they are of such an age as says they may go to bed together." This said Dryas and much more, because for the fee of his oratory to the marriage he had at home three thousand drachmas.

prob. a proverb   [6] pq τοι   [7] mss συντέθραπται and συνῆπται   [8] Uiii φιλία and δυναμένη   [9] A omits

---

[1] case.

DAPHNIS AND CHLOE

Ὁ δὲ Λάμων μήτε πενίαν ἔτι προβάλλεσθαι δυνάμενος (αὐτοὶ γὰρ οὐχ ὑπερηφάνουν), μήτε ἡλικίαν Δάφνιδος (ἤδη γὰρ μειράκιον ἦν), τὸ μὲν ἀληθὲς οὐδ᾽ ὡς [1] ἐξηγόρευσεν, ὅτι κρείττων ἐστὶ τοιούτου γάμου· χρόνον δὲ σιωπήσας ὀλίγον οὕτως ἀπεκρίνατο· 31. "Δίκαια ποιεῖτε τοὺς γείτονας προτιμῶντες τῶν ξένων καὶ πενίας ἀγαθῆς πλοῦτον μὴ νομίζοντες κρείττονα. ὁ Πὰν ὑμᾶς καὶ αἱ Νύμφαι ἀντὶ τῶνδε φιλήσειαν.[2] ἐγὼ δὲ σπεύδω μὲν καὶ αὐτὸς τὸν γάμον τοῦτον. καὶ γὰρ ἂν μαινοίμην εἰ μὴ γέρων τε [3] ὢν ἤδη καὶ χειρὸς εἰς τὰ ἔργα περιττοτέρας δεόμενος, ᾤμην [4] καὶ τὸν ὑμέτερον οἶκον φίλον προσλαβεῖν ἀγαθόν τι μέγα· περισπούδαστος δὲ καὶ Χλόη, καλὴ καὶ ὡραία κόρη καὶ πάντα ἀγαθή. δοῦλος δὲ ὢν οὐδενός εἰμι τῶν ἐμῶν κύριος, ἀλλὰ δεῖ τὸν δεσπότην μανθάνοντα ταῦτα συγχωρεῖν. φέρε οὖν, ἀναβαλώμεθα τὸν γάμον εἰς τὸ μετόπωρον. ἀφίξεσθαι τότε λέγουσιν αὐτὸν οἱ παραγινόμενοι πρὸς ἡμᾶς ἐξ ἄστεος. τότε ἔσονται ἀνὴρ καὶ γυνή· νῦν δὲ φιλείτωσαν [5] ἀλλήλους ὡς ἀδελφοί. ἴσθι μόνον, ὦ Δρύα, τοσοῦτον· σπεύδεις περὶ μειράκιον κρεῖττον ἡμῶν." ὁ μὲν ταῦτα εἰπὼν ἐφίλησέ τε αὐτὸν καὶ ὤρεξε ποτόν, ἤδη μεσημβρίας ἀκμαζούσης, καὶ προὔπεμψε μέχρι τινὸς φιλοφρονούμενος πάντα.

[1] p ὅλως   [2] Amyot perh. ὠφελήσειαν   [3] so Cour. (Amyot by em.): ApB εἰ μὴ γέροντες : Uiii ἡμιγέρων τε   [4] so Cour. (Am. by em.): mss ὡς μὴ   [5] A φιλησάτωσαν

And now Lamo could no longer obtend poverty (for Chloe's parents themselves did not disdain his lowness), nor yet Daphnis his age (for he was come to his flowery youth). That indeed which troubled him, and yet he would not say so, was this, namely that Daphnis was of higher merit then such a match could suit withal. But after a short silence, he returned him this answer : 31. "You do well to prefer your neighbours to strangers, and not to esteem riches better then honest poverty. Pan and the Nymphs be good to you for this. And I for my part do not at all hinder this marriage. It were madness in me who am now ancient and want many hands to my daily work, if I should not think it a great and desirable good to join to me the friendship and alliance of your family. Besides, Chloe is sought after by very many, a fair maid and altogether of honest manners and behaviour. But because I am only a servant, and not the lord of anything I have, it is necessary my lord and master should be acquainted with this, that he may give his consent to it. Go to, then, let us agree to put off the wedding till the next autumn. Those that use to come from the city to us, tell us that he will then be here. Then they shall be man and wife, and in the mean time let them love like sister and brother. Yet know this, Dryas ; the young man thou art in such haste and earnest about is far better then us." And Lamo having thus spoke embraced Dryas and kissed him, and made him sit and drink with him when now it was hot at high noon, and going along with him part of his way treated him altogether kindly.

32. Ὁ [1] δὲ Δρύας, οὐ παρέργως ἀκούσας τὸν ὕστερον λόγον τοῦ Λάμωνος, ἐφρόντιζε βαδίζων καθ' αὑτὸν ὅστις ὁ Δάφνις· "Ἐτράφη μὲν ὑπὸ αἰγός, ὡς κηδομένων θεῶν, ἔστι δὲ καλὸς καὶ οὐδὲν ἐοικὼς σιμῷ γέροντι καὶ μαδώσῃ γυναικί, εὐπόρησε δὲ καὶ τρισχιλίων, ὅσον [2] οὐδὲ ἀχράδων εἰκὸς ἔχειν αἰπόλον. ἆρα καὶ τοῦτον ἐξέθηκέ τις ὡς Χλόην; ἆρα καὶ τοῦτον εὗρε Λάμων, ὡς ἐκείνην ἐγώ; ἆρα καὶ γνωρίσματα ὅμοια παρέκειτο τοῖς εὑρεθεῖσιν ὑπ' ἐμοῦ; ἐὰν ταῦτα οὕτως, ὦ δέσποτα Πὰν καὶ Νύμφαι φίλαι, τάχα οὗτος τοὺς ἰδίους εὑρὼν εὑρήσει τι καὶ τῶν Χλόης ἀπορρήτων."

Τοιαῦτα μὲν πρὸς αὑτὸν ἐφρόντιζε καὶ ὠνειροπόλει μέχρι τῆς ἄλω, ἐλθὼν δὲ ἐκεῖ καὶ τὸν Δάφνιν μετέωρον πρὸς τὴν ἀκοὴν καταλαβών, ἀνέρρωσέ τε γαμβρὸν προσαγορεύσας, καὶ τῷ μετοπώρῳ τοὺς γάμους θύσειν [3] ἐπαγγέλλεται, δεξιάν τε ἔδωκεν, ὡς οὐδενὸς ἐσομένης, ὅτι μὴ Δάφνιδος, Χλόης.

33. Θᾶττον οὖν νοήματος μηδὲν πιὼν μηδὲ φαγὼν παρὰ τὴν Χλόην κατέδραμε, καὶ εὑρὼν αὐτὴν ἀμέλγουσαν καὶ τυροποιοῦσαν, τόν τε γάμον εὐηγγελίζετο καὶ ὡς γυναῖκα λοιπὸν μὴ λανθάνων κατεφίλει καὶ ἐκοινώνει τοῦ πόνου. ἤμελγε μὲν εἰς γαυλοὺς τὸ γάλα, ἐνεπήγνυ δὲ ταρσοῖς

---

[1] A having lost a page is not available till 4. 5   [2] so Jung : mss ὅσων   [3] so Elsner : mss θήσειν

32. But Dryas had not heard the last words of Lamo only as a chat; and therefore as he walked along he anxiously enquired of himself who Daphnis should be: "He was suckled indeed and nursed up by a goat, as if the providence of the Gods had appointed it so. But he's of a sweet and beautiful aspect, and no whit like either that flat-nosed old fellow or the baldpate old woman. He has besides three thousand drachmas, and one would scarcely believe that a goatherd should have so many pears in his possession. And has somebody exposed him too as well as Chloe? and was it Lamo's fortune to find him as it was mine to find her? And was he trimmed up with such like tokens as were found by me? If this be so, O mighty Pan, O ye beloved Nymphs, it may be that he having found his own parents may find out something of Chloe's secret too!"

These moping thoughts he had in his mind, and was in a dream up to the floor. When he came there, he found Daphnis expecting and pricking up his ears for Lamo's answer. "Hail, son," quoth he, "Chloe's husband," and promised him they should be married in the autumn; then giving him his right hand, assured him on his faith that Chloe should be wife to nobody but Daphnis.

33. Therefore without eating or drinking, swifter then thought he flies to Chloe, finds her at her milking and her cheese-making, and full of joy brings her the annunciation of the marriage, and presently began to kiss her, not as before by stealth in a corner of the twilight, but as his wife thenceforward, and took upon him part of her labour. He helped her about the milking-pail, he put her cheeses into the

τοὺς τυρούς, προσέβαλλε ταῖς μητράσι τοὺς
ἄρνας καὶ τοὺς ἐρίφους. καλῶς δὲ ἐχόντων τού-
των, ἀπελούσαντο, ἐνέφαγον, ἐνέπιον,[1] περιῇεσαν
ζητοῦντες ὀπώραν ἀκμάζουσαν.

Ἦν δὲ ἀφθονία πολλὴ διὰ τὸ τῆς ὥρας πάμ-
φορον, πολλαὶ μὲν ἀχράδες, πολλαὶ δὲ ὄχναι,
πολλὰ δὲ μῆλα, τὰ μὲν ἤδη πεπτωκότα κάτω, τὰ
δὲ ἔτι ἐπὶ τῶν φυτῶν, τὰ ἐπὶ τῆς γῆς εὐωδέ-
στερα, τὰ ἐπὶ τῶν κλάδων εὐανθέστερα, τὰ μὲν
οἷον οἶνος ἀπῶζε, τὰ δὲ οἷον χρυσὸς ἀπέλαμπε.
μία μηλέα τετρύγητο καὶ οὔτε καρπὸν εἶχεν οὔτε
φύλλον· γυμνοὶ πάντες ἦσαν οἱ κλάδοι. καὶ ἓν
μῆλον ἐπέτετο, ἐν αὐτοῖς <τοῖς> ἄκροις ἀκρότατον,
μέγα καὶ καλὸν καὶ τῶν πολλῶν τὴν εὐωδίαν
ἐνίκα μόνον. ἔδεισεν ὁ τρυγῶν ἀνελθεῖν ἢ[2]
ἠμέλησε καθελεῖν· τάχα δὲ καὶ ἐφυλάττετο <τὸ>
καλὸν μῆλον ἐρωτικῷ ποιμένι.

34. Τοῦτο τὸ μῆλον ὡς εἶδεν ὁ Δάφνις, ὥρμα
τρυγᾶν ἀνελθών, καὶ Χλόης κωλυούσης[3] ἠμέ-
λησεν. ἡ μὲν ἀμεληθεῖσα, ὀργισθεῖσα[4] πρὸς τὰς
ἀγέλας ἀπῄει·[5] Δάφνις δὲ ἀναδραμὼν ἐξίκετο·
<καὶ> τρυγήσας καὶ κομίσας[6] δῶρον Χλόῃ
λόγον τοιόνδε εἶπεν ὠργισμένῃ· "Ὦ παρθένε,
τοῦτο τὸ μῆλον ἔφυσαν ὧραι καλαί, καὶ φυτὸν
καλὸν ἔθρεψε πεπαίνοντος ἡλίου καὶ ἐτήρησε

[1] so E: mss ἔπιον   <τοῖς> E   [2] so Cour: p omits:
B καὶ   <τὸ> Seil.   [3] p καμούσης   [4] so Schaef: mss
180

press, suckled the lambkins and the kids. And
when all was done they washed themselves, eat and
drank their fill, and went to look for mellow fruits.

And at that time there was huge plenty because it
was the season for almost all. There were abundance
of pears, abundance of apples. Some were now
fallen to the ground, some were hanging on the
trees. Those on the ground had a sweeter scent,
those on the boughs a sweeter blush. Those had
the fragrancy of wine, these had the flagrancy of
gold. There stood one apple-tree that had all its
apples pulled; all the boughs were now bare, and
they had neither fruit nor leaves, but only there was
one apple that swung upon the very top of the spire
of the tree; a great one it was and very beautiful,
and such as by its rare and rich smell would alone
outdo many together. It should seem that he that
gathered the rest was afraid to climb so high, or
cared not to come by it. And peradventure that
excellent apple was reserved for a shepherd that was
in love.

34. When Daphnis saw it, he mantled to be at it,
and was even wild to climb the tree, nor would he
hear Chloe forbidding him. But she, perceiving her
interdictions neglected, made in anger towards the
flocks. Daphnis got up into the tree, and came to
the place, and pulling it brought it to Chloe. To
whom, as she shewed her anger against that
adventure, he thus spoke: "Sweet maid, fair seasons
begot this apple, and a goodly tree brought it up;
it was ripened by the beams of the Sun and pre-
served by the care and kindness of Fortune. Nor

ὁρμηθεῖσα   ⁵ so *E*: mss ἀπῆλθε   ⁶ so *E*: mss ἐξίκετο
τρυγῆσαι κ. κομίσαι and καί after Χλόῃ

τύχῃ. καὶ οὐκ ἔμελλον αὐτὸ καταλιπεῖν ὀφθαλ-
μοὺς ἔχων, ἵνα πέσῃ χαμαὶ καὶ ἢ ποίμνιον αὐτὸ
πατήσῃ νεμόμενον, ἢ ἑρπετὸν φαρμάξῃ συρόμενον,
ἢ χρόνος δαπανήσῃ ἐκεῖ μένον,[1] βλεπόμενον, ἐπαι-
νούμενον. τοῦτο Ἀφροδίτη κάλλους ἔλαβεν
ἆθλον, τοῦτο ἐγὼ σοὶ δίδωμι νικητήριον. ὁμοίως[2]
ἔχομεν <καὶ ὁ ἐκείνης καὶ> ὁ σὸς μάρτυρες·[3]
ἐκεῖνος ἦν ποιμήν, αἰπόλος ἐγώ." ταῦτα εἰπὼν
ἐντίθησι τοῖς κόλποις, ἡ δὲ ἐγγὺς γενόμενον κατε-
φίλησεν. ὥστε ὁ Δάφνις οὐ μετέγνω τολμήσας
ἀνελθεῖν εἰς τοσοῦτον ὕψος· ἔλαβε γὰρ κρεῖττον
καὶ χρυσοῦ μήλου φίλημα.

---

[1] ἐκεῖ μένον so E : mss κείμενον, but time destroys it on the
tree   [2] q ὁμοίους and ὁμοίως   [3] so E (Amyot by em.):
mss τοὺς σοὺς μάρτυρας by em. following loss of καὶ ὁ ἐκείνης
by haplogr.

might I let it alone so long as I had these eyes, lest either it should fall to the ground and some of the cattle as they feed should tread upon it or some creeping thing poison it, or else it should stay aloft for time to spoil while we only look at and praise it. Venus, for the victory of her beauty, carried away no other prize ; I give thee this the palmary [1] of thine. For we are alike, I that witness thy beauty and he that witnessed hers. Paris was but a shepherd upon Ida, and I am a goatherd in the happy fields of Mytilene." With that, he put it into her bosom, and Chloe pulling him to her kissed him. And so Daphnis repented him not of the boldness to climb so high a tree. For he received a kiss from her more precious then a golden apple.

[1] prize.

THE END OF THE THIRD BOOK

THE FOURTH BOOK

A SUMMARY OF THE FOURTH BOOK

A FELLOW-SERVANT *of Lamo's brings word that their lord would be there speedily. A pleasant garden is pleasantly described. Lamo, Daphnis, and Chloe make all things fine. Lampis the herdsman spoils the garden to provoke the lord against Lamo, who had denied Chloe in marriage. Lamo laments it the next day. Eudromus teaches him how he may escape the anger. Astylus, their young master, comes first, with Gnatho, his parasite. Astylus promises to excuse them for the garden and procure their pardon from his father. Gnatho is taken with Daphnis. Dionysophanes the lord, with his wife Clearista, comes down. Amongst other things sees the goats, where he hears Daphnis his music, and all admire his art of piping. Gnatho begs of Astylus that he may carry Daphnis along with him to the city, and obtains it. Eudromus hears it, and tells Daphnis. Lamo, thinking it was now time, tells Dionysophanes the whole story, how Daphnis was found, how brought up. He and Clearista considering the thing carefully, they find that Daphnis is their son. Therefore they receive him with great joy, and Dionysophanes tells*

186

A SUMMARY OF THE FOURTH BOOK

the reason why he exposed him. The country fellows come in to gratulate. Chloe in the interim complains that Daphnis has forgot her. She's stolen and carried away by Lampis. Daphnis laments by himself. Gnatho hears him, rescues Chloe, and is received to favour. Dryas then tells Chloe's story. Her they take to the city too. There at a banquet Megacles of Mytilene owns her for his daughter. And the wedding is kept in the country.

ΛΟΓΟΣ ΤΕΤΑΡΤΟΣ

1. Ἥκων δέ τις ἐκ τῆς Μυτιλήνης ὁμόδουλος τοῦ Λάμωνος ἤγγειλεν, ὅτι ὀλίγον πρὸ τοῦ τρυγητοῦ ὁ δεσπότης ἀφίξεται μαθησόμενος μή τι τοὺς ἀγροὺς ὁ τῶν Μηθυμναίων εἴσπλους ἐλυμήνατο. ἤδη οὖν τοῦ θέρους ἀπιόντος καὶ τοῦ μετοπώρου προσιόντος, παρεσκεύαζεν αὐτῷ τὴν καταγωγὴν ὁ Λάμων εἰς πᾶσαν θέας ἡδονήν· πηγὰς ἐξεκάθαιρεν ὡς τὸ ὕδωρ καθαρὸν ἔχοιεν, τὴν κόπρον ἐξεφόρει τῆς αὐλῆς ὡς ἀπόζουσα μὴ διοχλοίη, τὸν παράδεισον ἐθεράπευεν ὡς ὀφθείη καλός.

2. Ἦν δὲ ὁ παράδεισος πάγκαλόν τι χρῆμα καὶ κατὰ τοὺς βασιλικούς. ἐκτέτατο μὲν εἰς σταδίου μῆκος, ἐπέκειτο δὲ ἐν χώρῳ μετεώρῳ, τὸ εὖρος ἔχων πλέθρων τεττάρων· εἴκασεν ἄν τις αὐτὸν πεδίῳ μακρῷ. εἶχε δὲ πάντα δένδρα, μηλέας, μυρρίνας, ὄχνας καὶ ῥοιὰς καὶ συκῆν[1] καὶ ἐλαίας. ἑτέρωθι ἄμπελος ὑψηλὴ ἐπέκειτο[2] ταῖς μηλέαις καὶ ταῖς ὄχναις περκάζουσα, καθάπερ περὶ τοῦ

---

[1] for sing. cf. ὑάκινθος 2. 3, but perh. ἦν originated in ἦν a gloss on ὑψηλὴ below   [2] so E : mss ἄμπελον ὑψηλήν. καὶ ἐπ.

THE FOURTH BOOK

1. AND now one of Lamo's fellow-servants brought word from Mytilene that their lord would come towards the vintage, to see whether that irruption of the Methymnaeans had made any waste in those fields. When therefore the summer was now parting away and the autumn approaching, Lamo bestirred himself that his lord's sojourn should present him with pleasure everywhere. He scoured the fountains, that the water might be clear and transparent. He mucked the yard, lest the dung should offend him with the smell. The garden he trimmed with great care and diligence, that all might be pleasant, fresh, and fair.

2. And that garden indeed was a most beautiful and goodly thing, and such as might become a prince. For it lay extended in length a whole furlong. It was situate on a high ground, and had to its breadth four acres. To a spacious field one would easily have likened it. Trees it had of all kinds, the apple, the pear, the myrtle, the pomegranate, the fig, and the olive ; and to these on the one side there grew a rare and taller sort of vines, that bended over and reclined their ripening bunches of grapes among the apples and pomegranates, as if they would vie and contend for beauty

καρποῦ αὐταῖς προσερίζουσα. τοσαῦτα ἥμερα.
ἦσαν δὲ καὶ κυπάριττοι καὶ δάφναι καὶ πλάτανοι
καὶ πίτυς· ταύταις πάσαις ἀντὶ τῆς ἀμπέλου
κιττὸς ἐπέκειτο, καὶ ὁ κόρυμβος αὐτοῦ μέγας ὢν
καὶ μελαινόμενος βότρυν ἐμιμεῖτο.

Ἔνδον ἦν τὰ καρποφόρα φυτά, καθάπερ φρου-
ρούμενα, ἔξωθεν περιειστήκει τὰ ἄκαρπα, καθάπερ
θριγκὸς χειροποίητος· καὶ ταῦτα μέντοι λεπτῆς
αἱμασιᾶς περιέθει περίβολος. τέτμητο καὶ δια-
κέκριτο πάντα, καὶ στέλεχος στελέχους ἀφει-
στήκει. ἐν μετεώρῳ δὲ οἱ κλάδοι συνέπιπτον
ἀλλήλοις καὶ ἐπήλλαττον τὰς κόμας· ἐδόκει
μέντοι καὶ ἡ τούτων φύσις εἶναι τέχνης. ἦσαν
καὶ ἀνθῶν πρασιαί, ὧν τὰ μὲν ἔφερεν ἡ γῆ, τὰ δὲ
ἐποίει τέχνη· ῥοδωνιὰ καὶ ὑάκινθοι [1] καὶ κρίνα
χειρὸς ἔργα, ἰωνιὰς καὶ ναρκίσσους καὶ ἀναγαλ-
λίδας ἔφερεν ἡ γῆ. σκιά τε ἦν θέρους καὶ ἦρος
ἄνθη καὶ μετοπώρου ὀπώρα, καὶ κατὰ πᾶσαν
ὥραν τρυφή. 3. ἐντεῦθεν εὔοπτον μὲν ἦν τὸ [2]
πεδίον καὶ ἦν ὁρᾶν τοὺς νέμοντας, εὔοπτος δὲ ἡ
θάλαττα καὶ ἑωρῶντο οἱ παραπλέοντες· ὥστε

---

[1] Uiii sing. cf. 2. 3   [2] p omits

and worth of fruits with them. So many kinds there
were of satives, or of such as are planted, grafted, or
set. To these were not wanting the cypress, the
laurel, the platan, and the pine. And towards them,
instead of the vine, the ivy leaned, and with the
errantry of her boughs and her scattered black-
berries did imitate the vines and shadowed beauty of
the ripening grapes.

Within were kept, as in a garrison, trees of lower
growth that bore fruit. Without stood the barren
trees, enfolding all, much like a fort or some strong
wall that had bin built by the hand of art; and
these were encompassed with a spruce, thin hedge.
By alleys and glades there was everywhere a
just distermination of things from things, an orderly
discretion of tree from tree; but on the tops the
boughs met to interweave their limbs and leaves
with one another's, and a man would have thought
that all this had not bin, as indeed it was, the wild
of nature, but rather the work of curious art. Nor
were there wanting to these, borders and banks of
various flowers, some the earth's own volunteers,
some the structure of the artist's hand. The roses,
hyacinths, and lilies were set and planted by the
hand; the violet, the daffodil, and anagall the earth
gave up of her own good will. In the summer there
was shade, in the spring the beauty and fragrancy of
flowers, in the autumn the pleasantness of the fruits;
and at every season amusement and delight. 3. Be-
sides, from the high ground there was a fair and
pleasing prospect to the fields, the herdsmen, the
shepherds, and the cattle feeding; the same too
looked to the sea and saw all the boats and pinnaces

καὶ ταῦτα μέρος ἐγίνετο τῆς ἐν τῷ[1] παραδείσῳ
τρυφῆς.

Ἵνα τοῦ παραδείσου τὸ μεσαίτατον ἐπὶ μῆκος
καὶ εὖρος ἦν, νεὼς Διονύσου καὶ βωμὸς ἦν·
περιεῖχε τὸν μὲν βωμὸν κιττός, τὸν νεὼν δὲ κλή-
ματα. εἶχε δὲ καὶ ἔνδοθεν ὁ νεὼς Διονυσιακὰς
γραφάς, Σεμέλην τίκτουσαν, Ἀριάδνην καθεύ-
δουσαν, Λυκοῦργον δεδεμένον, Πενθέα διαιρούμενον·
ἦσαν καὶ Ἰνδοὶ νικώμενοι καὶ Τυρρηνοὶ μεταμορ-
φούμενοι· πανταχοῦ Σάτυροι <πατοῦντες>, παν-
ταχοῦ Βάκχαι χορεύουσαι. οὐδὲ ὁ Πὰν ἠμέλητο,
ἐκαθέζετο δὲ καὶ αὐτὸς συρίττων ἐπὶ πέτρας,
ὅμοιος[2] ἐνδιδόντι κοινὸν μέλος καὶ τοῖς πατοῦσι
καὶ ταῖς χορευούσαις.

4. Τοιοῦτον ὄντα τὸν παράδεισον ὁ Λάμων
ἐθεράπευε, τὰ ξηρὰ ἀποτέμνων, τὰ κλήματα ἀνα-
λαμβάνων· τὸν Διόνυσον ἐστεφάνωσε· τοῖς ἄν-
θεσιν ὕδωρ ἐπωχέτευσε. πηγή τις ἦν, ἣν[3] εὗρεν
ἐς τὰ ἄνθη Δάφνις. ἐσχόλαζε μὲν τοῖς ἄνθεσιν ἡ
πηγή, Δάφνιδος δὲ ὅμως ἐκαλεῖτο πηγή.

[1] pUiii omit (Christian emendation?)   <πατοῦντες>
Schaef. see below   [2] so Hirsch : mss -ον   [3] ἣν ἣν : pUiii
ἣν : B ἣν and in marg. ἣν

a sailing by; insomuch that that was no small addition to the pleasure of this most sweet and florid place.

In the midst of this paradise, to the positure of the length and breadth of the ground, stood a fane and an altar sacred to Bacchus. About the altar grew the wandering, encircling, clinging ivy; about the fane the palmits of the vines did spread themselves. And in the more inward part of the fane were certain pictures that told the story of Bacchus and his miracles; Semele bringing forth her babe, the fair Ariadne laid fast asleep, Lycurgus bound in chains, wretched Pentheus torn limb from limb, the Indians conquered, the Tyrrhenian mariners transformed, Satyrs treading the grapes and Bacchae dancing all about. Nor was Pan neglected in this place of pleasure; for he was set up upon the top of a crag, playing upon his pipes and striking up a common jig to those Satyrs that trod the grapes in the press and the Bacchae that danced about it.

4. Therefore in such a garden as this that all might be fine, Lamo now was very busy, cutting and pruning what was withered and dry, and checking and putting back the too forward palmits. Bacchus he had crowned with flowery chaplets, and then brought down with curious art rills of water from the fountains, amongst the borders and the knots. There was a spring, one that Daphnis first discovered, and that, although it was set apart for this purpose of watering the flowers, was nevertheless, in favour to him, always called Daphnis his fountain.[1]

---

[1] the watering is by irrigation; no water was ever drawn there, but nevertheless it was called by a dignified name.

Παρεκελεύετο δὲ καὶ τῷ Δάφνιδι ὁ Λάμων
πιαίνειν τὰς αἶγας ὡς δυνατὸν μάλιστά που,
πάντως κἀκείνας λέγων ὄψεσθαι τὸν δεσπότην
ἀφικόμενον διὰ μακροῦ. ὁ δὲ ἐθάρρει μέν, ὡς
ἐπαινεθησόμενος ἐπ᾽ αὐταῖς· διπλασίονάς τε γὰρ
ὧν ἔλαβεν ἐποίησε, καὶ λύκος οὐδὲ μίαν ἥρπασε,
καὶ ἦσαν πιότεραι τῶν οἰῶν· βουλόμενος δὲ
προθυμότερον αὐτὸν γενέσθαι πρὸς τὸν γάμον,
πᾶσαν θεραπείαν καὶ προθυμίαν προσέφερεν,
ἄγων τε αὐτὰς πάνυ ἕωθεν καὶ ἀπάγων τὸ
δειλινόν· δὶς ἡγεῖτο ἐπὶ ποτόν, ἀνεζήτει τὰ
εὐνομώτατα τῶν χωρίων· ἐμέλησεν αὐτῷ καὶ σκα-
φίδων καινῶν καὶ γαυλῶν πλειόνων[1] καὶ ταρσῶν
μειζόνων· τοσαύτη δὲ ἦν κηδεμονία, ὥστε καὶ τὰ
κέρατα ἤλειφε καὶ τὰς τρίχας ἐθεράπευε· Πανὸς
ἄν τις ἱερὰν ἀγέλην ἔδοξεν ὁρᾶν. ἐκοινώνει δὲ
παντὸς εἰς αὐτὰς καμάτου καὶ ἡ Χλόη, καὶ τῆς
ποίμνης παραμελοῦσα τὸ πλέον ἐκείναις ἐσχό-
λαζεν, ὥστε ἐνόμιζεν ὁ Δάφνις δι᾽ ἐκείνην αὐτὰς
φαίνεσθαι καλάς.

5. Ἐν[2] τούτοις οὖσιν αὐτοῖς, δεύτερος ἄγγελος
ἐλθὼν ἐξ ἄστεος ἐκέλευεν ἀποτρυγᾶν τὰς ἀμπέ-
λους ὅτι τάχιστα, καὶ αὐτὸς ἔφη παραμενεῖν[3]

[1] so E: mss πολλῶν   [2] near the end of this § (Seil. does
not say where) Λ recommences   [3] so Cob: mss pres.

194

But Lamo besides commanded Daphnis to use his best skill to have his goats as fat as might be ; for their lord would be sure to see them too, who now would come into the country after he had bin so long away. Now Daphnis indeed was very confident, because he thought he should be looked upon and praised for them. For he had doubled the number he had received of Lamo, nor had a wolf ravened away so much as one, and they were all more twadding fat then the very sheep. But because he would win upon the lord to be more forward to approve and confirm the match, he did his business with great diligence and great alacrity. He drove out his goats betimes in the morning, and late in the evening brought them home. Twice a day he watered them, and culled out for them the best pasture ground. He took care too to have the dairy-vessels new, better store of milking-pails and piggins, and greater crates[1] for the cheese. He was so far from being negligent in anything, that he tried to make their horns to shine with vernich,[2] and combed their very shag to make them sleek, insomuch that if you had seen this you had said it was Pan's own sacred flock. Chloe herself too would take her share in this labour, and leaving her sheep would devote herself for the most part to the goats ; and Daphnis thought 'twas Chloe's hand and Chloe's eyes that made his flocks appear so fair.

5. While both of them are thus busied, there came another messenger from the city, and brought a command that the grapes should be gathered with all speed ; and told them withal he was to tarry with

---

[1] larger pieces of straw or reed matting, out of which to cut "platters" for the cheeses.   [2] varnish.

DAPHNIS AND CHLOE

ἔστ' ἂν τοὺς βότρυς ποιήσωσι γλεῦκος, εἶτα
οὕτως κατελθὼν εἰς τὴν πόλιν ἄξειν τὸν δεσπό-
την, ἤδη μετεώρου οὔσης τῆς ¹ τρύγης. τοῦτόν
τε οὖν τὸν Εὔδρομον (οὕτω γὰρ ἐκαλεῖτο, ὅτι
ἦν αὐτῷ ἔργον τρέχειν) ἐδεξιοῦντο πᾶσαν δεξίω-
σιν, καὶ ἅμα τὰς ἀμπέλους ἀπετρύγων, τοὺς
βότρυς ἐς τὰς ληνοὺς κομίζοντες, τὸ γλεῦκος
εἰς τοὺς πίθους φέροντες, τῶν βοτρύων τοὺς
ἡβῶντας ἐπὶ κλημάτων ἀφαιροῦντες, ὡς εἴη
καὶ τοῖς ἐκ τῆς πόλεως ἐλθοῦσιν ἐν εἰκόνι καὶ
ἡδονῇ γενέσθαι τρυγητοῦ.

6. Μέλλοντος δὲ ἤδη σοβεῖν ἐς ἄστυ τοῦ
Εὐδρόμου, καὶ ἄλλα μὲν οὐκ ὀλίγα αὐτῷ Δάφνις
ἔδωκεν, ἔδωκε δὲ καὶ ὅσα ἀπὸ αἰπολίου ² δῶρα,
τυροὺς εὐπαγεῖς, ἔριφον ὀψίγονον, δέρμα αἰγὸς
λευκὸν καὶ λάσιον, ὡς ἔχοι χειμῶνος ἐπιβάλ-
λεσθαι τρέχων. ὁ δὲ ἤδετο, καὶ ἐφίλει τὸν
Δάφνιν, καὶ ἀγαθόν τι ἐρεῖν περὶ αὐτοῦ πρὸς
τὸν δεσπότην ἐπηγγέλλετο.

Καὶ ὁ μὲν ἀπῄει φίλα φρονῶν· ὁ δὲ Δάφνις
ἀγωνιῶν τῇ Χλόῃ συνένεμεν.³ εἶχε δὲ κἀκείνην ⁴
πολὺ δέος· μειράκιον εἰωθὸς ⁵ αἶγας βλέπειν
καὶ ὄρος καὶ γεωργοὺς καὶ Χλόην, πρῶτον
ἔμελλεν ὄψεσθαι δεσπότην οὗ πρότερον ⁶ μόνον
ἤκουε τὸ ὄνομα. ὑπέρ τε οὖν τοῦ Δάφνιδος
ἐφρόντιζεν, ὅπως ἐντεύξεται τῷ δεσπότῃ καὶ

---

¹ μετ. οὔσ. τῆς: so *E*, met. from ships reaching the open
sea : mss τῆς μετοπωρινῆς (A omits τῆς and obelizes) from
μετεωρούσης (haplogr.) ² q αἰπόλου ³ Uiii συνέμενεν

them there till the must was made, and then return
to the town to wait upon his lord thither, the vintage
being then at the height. This Eudromus [1] (for that
was his name, because he was a foot-page) they all
received and entertained with great kindness; and
presently began the vintage. The grapes were
gathered, cast into the press; the must made, and
tunned into the vessels. Some of the fairest bunches
of the grapes, together with their branches, were
cut, that to those who came from the city a shew of
the vintage-work and some of the pleasure of it
might still remain.

6. And now Eudromus made haste to be gone and
return to the town, and Daphnis gave him great
variety of pretty gifts, but especially whatever could
be had from a flock of goats; cheeses that were close
pressed, a kid of the late fall, with a goatskin white
and thick-shagged to fling about him when he ran in
the winter. With this, Eudromus was very pleasantly
affected, and kissed Daphnis, and told him that he
would speak a good word for him to his master; and
so went away with a benevolent mind to them.

But Daphnis went to feed his flock beside Chloe
full of anxious thought; and Chloe, too, was not free
from fear, namely, that a lad that had bin used to see
nothing but goats, mountains, ploughmen, and Chloe,
should then first be brought into the presence of his
lord, of whom before he had heard nothing but only his
name. For Daphnis, therefore, she was very solicitous,
how he would come before his master, how he would
behave himself, how the bashful youth would salute

⁴ so Vill: mss nom.   ⁵ q μειρ. γὰρ εἰωθ.   ⁶ so Schaef:
mss πρῶτον from above

---

[1] the runner.

περὶ τοῦ γάμου τὴν ψυχὴν ἐταράττετο, μὴ
μάτην ὀνειροπολοῦσιν αὐτόν. συνεχῆ μὲν οὖν τὰ
φιλήματα καὶ ὥσπερ συμπεφυκότων αἱ περι-
βολαί· καὶ τὰ φιλήματα δειλὰ ἦν καὶ αἱ
περιβολαὶ σκυθρωπαί, καθάπερ ἤδη παρόντα
τὸν δεσπότην φοβουμένων ἢ λανθανόντων.

Προσγίνεται δέ τις αὐτοῖς καὶ τοιόσδε τάραχος·
7. Λάμπις τις ἦν ἀγέρωχος βουκόλος. οὗτος καὶ
αὐτὸς ἐμνᾶτο τὴν Χλόην παρὰ τοῦ Δρύαντος,
καὶ δῶρα ἤδη πολλὰ ἐδεδώκει σπεύδων τὸν
γάμον. αἰσθόμενος οὖν ὡς, εἰ[1] συγχωρηθείη
παρὰ τοῦ δεσπότου, Δάφνις αὐτὴν ἄξεται,
τέχνην ἐζήτει δι' ἧς τὸν δεσπότην αὐτοῖς ποιήσει[2]
πικρόν· καὶ εἰδὼς πάνυ αὐτὸν τῷ παραδείσῳ
τερπόμενον, ἔγνω τοῦτον, ὅσον οἷός τέ ἐστι,
διαφθεῖραι καὶ ἀποκοσμῆσαι. δένδρα μὲν οὖν
τέμνων ἔμελλεν ἁλώσεσθαι διὰ τὸν κτύπον,
ἐπεῖχε δὲ τοῖς ἄνθεσιν, ὥστε διαφθεῖραι αὐτά.
νύκτα δὴ φυλάξας καὶ ὑπερβὰς τὴν αἱμασιάν,
τὰ μὲν ἀνώρυξε, τὰ δὲ κατέκλασε, τὰ δὲ κατεπά-
τησεν ὥσπερ σῦς.

Καὶ ὁ μὲν λαθὼν ἀπεληλύθει· Λάμων δὲ
τῆς ἐπιούσης παρελθὼν εἰς τὸν κῆπον ἔμελλεν
ὕδωρ αὐτοῖς ἐκ τῆς πηγῆς ἐπάξειν. ἰδὼν δὲ πᾶν
τὸ χωρίον δεδῃωμένον καὶ ἔργον οἷον <ἂν>

---

[1] p omits   [2] so Seil : mss *-σειε*   <ἂν> Herch

him. About the marriage, too, she was much troubled, fearing lest they might but only dream of a mere chance, or nothing at all. Therefore kisses passed between them without number, and such embracings of one another as if both of them were grown into one piece; but those kisses were full of fear, those embraces very pensive, as of them that feared their lord as then there, or kissed and clipped in hugger-mugger to him.[1]

Moreover, then there arose to them such a distraction as this: 7. There was one Lampis, an untoward, blustering, fierce herdsman; and he amongst the rest had wooed Dryas for Chloe, and given him many gifts, too, to bring on and dispatch the marriage. Therefore, perceiving that if their lord did not dislike it, Daphnis was to have the girl, he sets himself to find and practise a cunning trick to enrage and alienate their lord. And knowing that he was wonderfully pleased and delighted with that garden, he thought it best to spoil that as much as he could and devest it of all its beauty. To cut the trees he durst not attempt, for he would then be taken by the noise. Wherefore he thinks to ruin the flowers[2]; and when 'twas night, gets over the hedge, and some he pulled up by the roots, of some he grasped and tore the stems, the rest he trod down like a boar; and so escaped unheard, unseen.

Lamo the next morning went into the garden to water the flowers from the spring.[3] But when he saw all the place now made a waste, and that it was like the work of a mischievous enemy rather

---

[1] on the sly.   [2] the Greek is "he stopped short at destroying the flowers," i.e. went no further than that.

[3] i.e. by opening the sluice.

DAPHNIS AND CHLOE

ἐχθρὸς οὐ [1] λῃστὴς ἐργάσαιτο, κατερρήξατο μὲν
εὐθὺς τὸν χιτωνίσκον, βοῇ δὲ μεγάλῃ θεοὺς
ἀνεκάλει· ὥστε καὶ ἡ Μυρτάλη τὰ ἐν χερσὶ
καταλιποῦσα ἐξέδραμε καὶ ὁ Δάφνις ἐάσας [2] τὰς
αἶγας ἀνέδραμε· καὶ ἰδόντες ἐβόων καὶ βοῶντες
ἐδάκρυον. 8. καὶ ἦν μὲν κενὸν [3] πένθος ἀνθῶν,
ἀλλ᾽ οἱ μὲν πτοούμενοι [4] τὸν δεσπότην ἔκλαον·
ἔκλαυσε δ᾽ ἄν τις καὶ ξένος ἐπιστάς.[5] ἀποκεκό-
σμητο γὰρ ὁ τόπος καὶ ἦν λοιπὸν πᾶσα ἡ [6]
γῆ πηλώδης. τῶν δὲ εἴ τι διέφυγε τὴν ὕβριν,
ὑπήνθει καὶ ἔλαμπε καὶ ἦν ἔτι καλὸν καὶ
κείμενον.[7] ἐπέκειντο δὲ καὶ μέλιτται αὐτοῖς,
συνεχὲς καὶ ἄπαυστον βομβοῦσαι καὶ θρηνούσαις
ὅμοιον.

Ὁ μὲν οὖν [8] Λάμων ὑπ᾽ ἐκπλήξεως κἀκεῖνα
ἔλεγε· "φεῦ τῆς ῥοδωνιᾶς ὡς κατακέκλασται,
φεῦ τῆς ἰωνιᾶς ὡς πεπάτηται, φεῦ τῶν ὑακίνθων
καὶ τῶν ναρκίσσων οὓς ἀνώρυξέ τις πονηρὸς
ἄνθρωπος. ἀφίξεται τὸ ἦρ, τὰ δὲ οὐκ ἀνθήσει,
ἔσται τὸ θέρος, τὰ δὲ οὐκ ἀκμάσει, μετόπωρον,
ἀλλὰ τάδε οὐδένα στεφανώσει. οὐδὲ σύ, δέσποτα
Διόνυσε, τὰ ἄθλια ταῦτα ἠλέησας ἄνθη, οἷς
παρῴκεις καὶ ἔβλεπες, ἀφ᾽ ὧν ἐστεφάνωσά σε
πολλάκις καὶ ἐτερπόμην; [9] πῶς, πῶς δείξω νῦν
τὸν παράδεισον τῷ δεσπότῃ; τίς ἐκεῖνος [10] θεασά-

[1] Ap omit [2] so Cob: mss ἐλάσας [3] A omits
ᾗ καινὸν (Amyot οὐ καιν.) Parr i ii omit πένθ. ἀνθ. [4] p
αἰδούμενοι: B lac. (2nd hand σποδούμενοι) [5] A ἐπὶ τούτοις

then a thief or robber, he rent his clothes, and called
so long upon the Gods, that Myrtale left all and
ran out thither, and Daphnis, too, let his goats
go where they would and ran back again. When
they saw it, they cried out, lamented, and wept.
8. To grieve for the flowers it was in vain, but
alas! their lord they feared. And indeed a mere
stranger, had he come there, might very well
have wept with them. For all the glory of the
place was gone, and nothing now remained but a
lutulent soil. If any flower had escaped the outrage,
it had yet, as it was then, a half-hid floridness and
its glance, and still was fair although 'twas laid.
And still the bees did sit upon them, and all along,
in a mourning murmur, sang the funeral of the
flowers.

And so Lamo out of his great consternation broke
forth into these words: "Alas, alas, the rosaries,
how are they broken down and torn! Woe is me,
the violaries, how are they spurned and trodden
down! Ah me, the hyacinths and daffodils which
some villain has pulled up, the wickedest of all
mortals! The spring will come, but those will not
grow green again; it will be summer and these will
not blow; the autumn will come, but these will give
no chaplets for our heads. And didst not thou,
Bacchus, lord of the garden, pity the suffering of
these flowers, among which thou dwelledst, upon
which thou lookedst, and with which I have crowned
thee so often in joy and gladness? How shall
I now shew this garden to my lord? In what mind

---

[6] A omits πᾶσα ἡ   [7] Cf. Sappho 94   [8] so Hirsch: A
ὁ μὲν: pq ὁ μὲν γὰρ   [9] pq omit καὶ ἐτερπ. but for syntax
cf. ἔβλεπες with οἷς above   [10] A -ον

μενος ἔσται; κρεμᾷ γέροντα ἄνθρωπον ἐκ μιᾶς[1]
πίτυος ὡς Μαρσύαν, τάχα δὲ καὶ Δάφνιν, ὡς
τῶν αἰγῶν ταῦτα εἰργασμένων." 9. δάκρυα ἦν
ἐπὶ τούτοις θερμότερα, καὶ ἐθρήνουν οὐ τὰ ἄνθη
λοιπόν, ἀλλὰ τὰ αὑτῶν σώματα. ἐθρήνει καὶ
Χλόη Δάφνιν[2] εἰ κρεμήσεται, καὶ ηὔχετο μηκέτι
ἐλθεῖν τὸν δεσπότην αὐτῶν, καὶ ἡμέρας διήντλει
μοχθηράς, ὡς ἤδη Δάφνιν βλέπουσα μαστιγού-
μενον.

Καὶ ἤδη νυκτὸς ἀρχομένης ὁ Εὔδρομος αὐτοῖς
ἀπήγγελλεν, ὅτι ὁ μὲν πρεσβύτερος δεσπότης
μεθ᾽ ἡμέρας ἀφίξεται τρεῖς, ὁ δὲ παῖς αὐτοῦ
τῆς ἐπιούσης[3] πρόεισι. σκέψις οὖν ἦν περὶ[4]
τῶν συμβεβηκότων, καὶ κοινωνὸν[5] εἰς τὴν γνώμην
τὸν Εὔδρομον παρελάμβανον. ὁ δὲ εὔνους ὢν
τῷ Δάφνιδι παρῄνει τὸ συμβὰν ὁμολογῆσαι
πρότερον τῷ νέῳ δεσπότῃ, καὶ αὐτὸς συμπράξειν
ἐπηγγέλλετο τιμώμενος ὡς ὁμογάλακτος· καὶ
ἡμέρας γενομένης οὕτως ἐποίησαν.

10. Ἧκε μὲν ὁ Ἀστύλος ἐπὶ ἵππου καὶ παρά-
σιτος αὐτοῦ, καὶ οὗτος ἐπὶ[6] ἵππου, ὁ μὲν ἀρτι-
γένειος,[7] ὁ δὲ Γνάθων (τουτὶ γὰρ ἐκαλεῖτο), τὸν
πώγωνα ξυρώμενος πάλαι. ὁ δὲ Λάμων ἅμα[8] τῇ
Μυρτάλῃ καὶ τῷ Δάφνιδι πρὸ τῶν ποδῶν αὐτοῦ
καταπεσών, ἱκέτευεν οἰκτεῖραι γέροντα ἀτυχῆ καὶ
πατρῴας ὀργῆς ἐξαρπάσαι τὸν οὐδὲν ἀδικήσαντα,
ἅμα τε αὐτῷ καταλέγει πάντα. οἰκτείρει τὴν

---

[1] = τινος   [2] A omits Δάφ. . . . ἤδη   [3] A αὐτῇ τῇ ἐπιούσῃ
[4] pq ὑπὲρ   [5] A κοινὸν   [6] A omits οὗτος ἐπὶ   [7] A
-γέννης   [8] A omits ἅμα . . . ποδῶν

will he look upon it? How will he take it? He
will hang me up for an old rogue, like Marsyas upon
a pine, and perchance poor Daphnis too, thinking
his goats have done the deed." [1] 9. With these
there fell more scalding tears; for now they wept
not for the flowers, but themselves. And Chloe be-
wailed poor Daphnis his case if he should be hanged
up and scourged, and wished their lord might never
come, spending her days in misery, as if even then
she looked upon her sweet Daphnis under the whip.

But towards night Eudromus came and brought
them word that their lord would come within three
days, and that their young master would be there
to-morrow. Therefore about what had befallen them
they fell to deliberate, and took in good Eudromus
into their council. This Eudromus was altogether
Daphnis his friend, and he advised they should first
open the chance to their young lord, and promised
himself an assistant too, as one of some account [2] with
him; for Astylus was nursed with his milk, and he
looked upon him as a foster-brother. And so they
did the next day.

10. Astylus came on horseback, a parasite of his
with him, and he on horseback too. Astylus was
now of the first down,[3] but his Gnatho (that was his
name) had long tried the barber's tools. But Lamo,
taking Myrtale and Daphnis with him, and flinging
himself at the feet of Astylus, humbly beseeched
him to have mercy on an unfortunate old man, and
save him from his father's anger, one that was not in
fault, one that had done nothing amiss; and then
told him what had befallen them. Astylus had pity

---

[1] Thornley has "goats has done." [2] Thornley has "accompt."
    [3] *i.e.* the first down was upon his cheek.

ἱκεσίαν ὁ Ἀστύλος καὶ ἐπὶ τὸν παράδεισον ἐλθὼν
καὶ τὴν ἀπώλειαν τῶν ἀνθῶν ἰδών, αὐτὸς ἔφη
παραιτήσεσθαι τὸν πατέρα καὶ κατηγορήσειν τῶν
ἵππων,[1] ὡς ἐκεῖ δεθέντες ἐξύβρισαν καὶ τὰ μὲν
κατέκλασαν, τὰ, δὲ κατεπάτησαν, τὰ δὲ ἀνώρυξαν
λυθέντες.

Ἐπὶ τούτοις εὔχονται[2] μὲν αὐτῷ πάντα τὰ
ἀγαθὰ <ὁ> Λάμων καὶ ἡ Μυρτάλη· Δάφνις δὲ
δῶρα προσεκόμισεν ἐρίφους, τυρούς, ὄρνιθας καὶ
τὰ ἔκγονα αὐτῶν, βότρυς ἐπὶ κλημάτων, μῆλα[3]
ἐπὶ κλάδων· ἦν ἐν τοῖς δώροις καὶ ἀνθοσμίας
οἶνος Λέσβιος,[4] ποθῆναι κάλλιστος οἶνος. 11. ὁ
μὲν δὴ Ἀστύλος ἐπῄνει ταῦτα καὶ περὶ θήραν
εἶχε λαγῶν, οἷα πλούσιος νεανίσκος καὶ τρυφῶν
ἀεὶ καὶ ἀφιγμένος εἰς τὸν ἀγρὸν εἰς ἀπόλαυσιν
ξένης ἡδονῆς.

Ὁ δὲ Γνάθων, οἷα μαθὼν ἐσθίειν ἄνθρωπος καὶ
πίνειν εἰς μέθην καὶ λαγνεύειν[5] μετὰ τὴν μέθην
καὶ οὐδὲν ἄλλο ὢν ἢ γνάθος καὶ γαστὴρ καὶ τὰ
ὑπὸ γαστέρα, οὐ παρέργως εἶδε τὸν Δάφνιν τὰ
δῶρα κομίσαντα, ἀλλὰ καὶ φύσει παιδεραστὴς
ὢν καὶ κάλλος οἷον οὐδὲ ἐπὶ τῆς πόλεως εὑρών,
ἐπιθέσθαι διέγνω[6] τῷ Δάφνιδι καὶ πείσειν ᾤετο
ῥᾳδίως ὡς αἰπόλον.

Γνοὺς δὲ ταῦτα, θήρας μὲν οὐκ ἐκοινώνει τῷ

---

[1] A τὸν ἵππον : q τῶν ἱππείων (B -είων)   [2] pq imperf.
[3] pq μῆλα δὲ   [4] A Λέσβ. δὲ   [5] pq omit λαγν. . . .
οὐδὲν   [6] cf. Xen. Eph. 3. 2.

on the wretched suppliant, and went with him to the garden; and having seen the destruction of it as to flowers, he promised to procure them his father's pardon and lay the fault on the fiery horses, that were tied thereabouts, boggled o'er something,[1] and broke their bridles, and so it happened that almost all the flowers everywhere were trodden down, broken, and torn, and flundered up.

At this, Lamo and Myrtale prayed the Gods would prosper him in everything; and young Daphnis soon after presented him with things made ready to that purpose; young kids, cream-cheeses, a numerous brood of hen-and-chickens, bunches of grapes hanging still upon their palmits, and apples on the boughs, and amongst them a bottle of the Lesbian wine, fragrant wine and the most excellent of drinks. 11. Astylus commended their oblation and entertainment, and went a hunting the hare; for he was rich, and given to pleasure, and therefore came to take it abroad in the country.

But Gnatho, a man that had learnt only to guttle, and drink till he was drunk, and afterwards play the lecher, a man that minded nothing but his belly[2] and his lasciviousness under that, he had taken a more curious view of Daphnis then others had, when he presented the gifts. Not only was he by nature fond of boys but in Daphnis he discerned such beauty as was not to be found in the whole city; and so he determined to make advances to him, expecting that success would be easy with a goatherd like him.

When he had now thus deliberated with himself, he went not along with Astylus a hunting, but

---

[1] Thornley misprints "or something."   [2] the Greek has a pun on γνάθος "jaw," and "Gnatho."

Ἀστύλῳ, κατιὼν δὲ ἵνα ἔνεμεν ὁ Δάφνις λόγῳ μὲν
τῶν αἰγῶν τὸ δὲ ἀληθὲς Δάφνιδος ἐγίνετο θεατής.
μαλθάσσων δὲ αὐτὸν τάς τε αἶγας ἐπῄνει καὶ
συρίσαι τι[1] αἰπολικὸν ἠξίωσε· καὶ ἔφη ταχέως
ἐλεύθερον θήσειν τὸ πᾶν δυνάμενος. 12. ὡς δὲ
εἶχε χειροήθη, νύκτωρ λοχήσας ἐκ τῆς νομῆς
ἐλαύνοντα τὰς αἶγας, πρῶτον μὲν ἐφίλησε προσ-
δραμών. εἶτα <ἔδειτο>, ὄπισθεν παρασχεῖν τοι-
οῦτον οἷον αἱ αἶγες τοῖς τράγοις. τοῦ δὲ βραδέως
νοήσαντος καὶ λέγοντος ὡς αἶγας μὲν βαίνειν
τράγους καλόν, τράγον δὲ οὐπώποτε εἶδέ τις
βαίνοντα τράγον, οὐδὲ κριὸν ἀντὶ τῶν οἰῶν κριόν,
οὐδὲ ἀλεκτρυόνας ἀντὶ τῶν ἀλεκτορίδων ἀλεκ-
τρυόνας, οἷος[2] ἦν ὁ Γνάθων βιάζεσθαι[3] τὰς χεῖρας
προσφέρων. ὁ δὲ μεθύοντα ἄνθρωπον ἑστῶτα
μόλις παρωσάμενος ἔσφηλεν εἰς τὴν γῆν, καὶ
ὥσπερ σκύλαξ ἀποδραμών, κείμενον κατέλιπεν,
ἀνδρὸς οὐ παιδὸς εἰς[4] χειραγωγίαν δεόμενον. καὶ
οὐκέτι προσίετο ὅλως, ἀλλὰ ἄλλοτε ἄλλῃ τὰς
αἶγας ἔνεμεν, ἐκεῖνον μὲν φεύγων, Χλόην δὲ τηρῶν.

Οὐδὲ ὁ Γνάθων ἔτι περιειργάζετο καταμαθὼν
ὡς οὐ μόνον καλός, ἀλλὰ καὶ ἰσχυρός ἐστιν. ἐπε-
τήρει δὲ καιρὸν διαλεχθῆναι περὶ αὐτοῦ τῷ Ἀσ-
τύλῳ καὶ ἤλπιζε δῶρον αὐτὸν ἕξειν παρὰ τοῦ
νεανίσκου πολλὰ καὶ μεγάλα χαρίζεσθαι θέλοντος.
13. τότε μὲν οὖν οὐκ ἠδυνήθη· προσῄει γὰρ ὁ
Διονυσοφάνης ἅμα τῇ Κλεαρίστῃ, καὶ ἦν θόρυβος

---

[1] so Brunck (Amyot): mss τὸ   <ἔδειτο> E   [2] so
Cob: mss οἷός τε as in Parth. 7 and Ach. Tat. 4. 9   [3] A
βιάζεται   [4] q πρὸς

going down into the field where Daphnis kept, he said he came to see the goats, but came indeed spectator of the youth. He began to palp him with soft words, praised his goats, called fondly on him for a pastoral tune, and said withal he would speedily impetrate his liberty for him, as being able to do what he would with his lord. 12. When Gnatho had won the other's confidence, he lay in wait for him one night as he drove his flocks home from pasture, and ran up to him and kissed him, then asked him to suffer himself to be mounted from behind as she-goats are by billies. Daphnis was slow to realise what he was up to, but then said that whilst it was proper for billies to cover she-goats, no one had ever seen a billy covering a billy or a ram another ram instead of a ewe or a cock a cock instead of a hen. At this Gnatho tried to lay hands on him and take him by violence. But Daphnis flung off this drunken sot, who scarce could stand upon his legs, and laid him on the ground, and then whipped away and left him. Nor would Daphnis endure it he should near him ever after, and therefore still removed his flocks, avoiding him and keeping Chloe carefully.

And indeed Gnatho did not proceed to trouble him further; for he had found him already not only a fair but a stout boy. But he waited an occasion to speak concerning him to Astylus, hoping to beg him of the gallant, as one that would bestow upon him many and better gifts then that. 13. But it was not a time to talk of it now; for Dionysophanes was come with his wife Clearista, and all about was a busy noise, tumultuous pudder of carriages,[1] and a

_____
[1] pack animals.

πολὺς κτηνῶν, οἰκετῶν, ἀνδρῶν, γυναικῶν. μετὰ
δὲ τοῦτο συνέταττε λόγον καὶ ἐρωτικὸν καὶ
μακρόν.

Ἦν δὲ ὁ Διοννσοφάνης μεσαιπόλιος μὲν ἤδη,
μέγας δὲ καὶ καλὸς καὶ μειρακίοις ἁμιλλᾶσθαι
δυνάμενος, ἀλλὰ καὶ πλούσιος ἐν ὀλίγοις καὶ
χρηστὸς ὡς οὐδεὶς ἕτερος. οὗτος ἐλθὼν τῇ πρώτῃ
μὲν ἡμέρᾳ θεοῖς ἔθυσεν ὅσοι προεστᾶσιν ἀγροικίας,
Δήμητρι καὶ Διονύσῳ καὶ Πανὶ καὶ Νύμφαις, καὶ
κοινὸν πᾶσι τοῖς παροῦσιν ἔστησε κρατῆρα, ταῖς δὲ
ἄλλαις ἡμέραις ἐπεσκόπει τὰ τοῦ Λάμωνος ἔργα.
καὶ ὁρῶν τὰ μὲν πεδία ἐν αὔλακι, τὰς δὲ ἀμπέλους
ἐν κλήματι, τὸν δὲ παράδεισον ἐν κάλλει (περὶ
γὰρ τῶν ἀνθῶν Ἀστύλος τὴν αἰτίαν ἀνελάμβανεν),
ἤδετο περιττῶς, καὶ τὸν Λάμωνα ἐπήνει καὶ ἐλεύ-
θερον ἀφήσειν ἐπηγγέλλετο.

Κατῆλθε μετὰ ταῦτα καὶ εἰς τὸ αἰπόλιον
τάς τε αἶγας ὀψόμενος καὶ τὸν νέμοντα. 14. Χλόη
μὲν οὖν εἰς τὴν ὕλην ἔφυγεν ὄχλον τοσοῦτον
αἰδεσθεῖσα καὶ φοβηθεῖσα, ὁ δὲ Δάφνις εἱστήκει
δέρμα λάσιον αἰγὸς ἐζωσμένος, πήραν νεορραφῆ
κατὰ τῶν ὤμων ἐξηρτημένος, κρειῶν ἀμφοτέραις,[1]
τῇ μὲν ἀρτιπαγεῖς τυρούς, τῇ δὲ ἐρίφους [2] γαλα-
θηνούς· εἴ ποτε Ἀπόλλων Λαομέδοντι θητεύων
ἐβουκόλησε, τοιόσδε ἦν οἷος τότε ὤφθη Δάφνις.
αὐτὸς μὲν οὖν εἶπεν οὐδέν, ἀλλὰ ἐρυθήματος
πλησθεὶς ἔνευσε κάτω προτείνας τὰ δῶρα· ὁ
δὲ Λάμων, "Οὗτος," εἶπε, "σοί, δέσποτα, τῶν
αἰγῶν αἰπόλος. σὺ μὲν ἐμοὶ πεντήκοντα νέμειν

[1] so E: mss ταῖς χερσὶν ἀμ.   [2] q omits (not Amyot)

208

long retinue of menservants and maids. But he thought with himself to make afterwards a speech concerning Daphnis, sufficient for love, sufficient for length.

Dionysophanes was now half gray, but very tall and well-limbed, and able at any exercise to grapple in the younger list. For his riches few came near him ; for honest life, justice, and excellent manners, scant such another to be found. He, when he was come, offered the first day to the president Gods of rural business, to Ceres, Bacchus, Pan, and the Nymphs, and set up a common bowl for all that were present. The other days he walked abroad to take a view of Lamo's works ; and seeing how the ground was ploughed, how swelled with palmits and how trim the vineyard was, how fair and flourishing the viridary (for as for the flowers, Astylus took the fault upon himself), he was wonderfully pleased and delighted with all ; and when he had praised Lamo much, he promised besides to make him free.

Afterwards he went into the other fields to see the goats and him that kept them. 14. Now Chloe fled into the wood ; for she could not bear so strong a presence and was afraid of so great a company. But Daphnis stood girt with a skin from a thick-shagged goat, a new scrip about his shoulders, in one hand holding green cheeses, with the other leading suckling kids. If ever Apollo would be hired to serve Laomedon and tend on herds, just so he looked as Daphnis then. He spoke not a word, but all on a blush, casting his eyes upon the ground, presented the rural gifts to his lord. But Lamo spoke : " Sir," quoth he, " this is the keeper of those goats. To me you

δέδωκας καὶ δύο τράγους, οὗτος δέ σοι πεποίηκεν
ἑκατὸν καὶ δέκα τράγους. ὁρᾷς ὡς λιπαραὶ καὶ
τὰς τρίχας λάσιαι καὶ τὰ κέρατα ἄθραυστοι;
πεποίηκε δ᾽ αὐτὰς καὶ μουσικάς· σύριγγος γοῦν
ἀκούουσαι ποιοῦσι πάντα."

15. Παροῦσα δὲ τοῖς λεγομένοις ἡ Κλεαρίστη
πεῖραν ἐπεθύμησε τοῦ λεχθέντος λαβεῖν, καὶ
κελεύει τὸν Δάφνιν ταῖς αἰξὶν οἷον εἴωθε συρίσαι,
καὶ ἐπαγγέλλεται συρίσαντι χαριεῖσθαι χιτῶνα
καὶ χλαῖναν καὶ ὑποδήματα. ὁ δὲ καθίσας
αὐτοὺς ὥσπερ θέατρον, στὰς ὑπὸ τῇ φηγῷ
καὶ ἐκ τῆς πήρας τὴν σύριγγα προκομίσας, πρῶτα
μὲν ὀλίγον ἐνέπνευσε· καὶ αἱ αἶγες ἔστησαν τὰς
κεφαλὰς ἀράμεναι. εἶτα[1] ἐνέπνευσε τὸ νόμιον·
καὶ αἱ αἶγες ἐνέμοντο νεύσασαι κάτω. αὖθις
λιγυρὸν ἐνέδωκε· καὶ ἀθρόαι κατεκλίθησαν. ἐσύ-
ρισέ τι καὶ ὀξὺ μέλος· αἱ δέ, ὥσπερ[2] λύκου
προσιόντος, εἰς τὴν ὕλην κατέφυγον. μετ᾽ ὀλίγον
ἀνακλητικὸν ἐφθέγξατο· καὶ ἐξελθοῦσαι τῆς ὕλης
πλησίον αὐτοῦ τῶν ποδῶν συνέδραμον. οὐδὲ
ἀνθρώπους οἰκέτας εἶδεν ἄν τις οὕτω πειθομένους
προστάγματι δεσπότου. οἵ τε οὖν ἄλλοι πάντες
ἐθαύμαζον καὶ πρὸ πάντων ἡ Κλεαρίστη, καὶ
τὰ δῶρα ἀποδώσειν ὤμοσε καλῷ τε ὄντι αἰπόλῳ
καὶ μουσικῷ.

Καὶ ἀνελθόντες εἰς τὴν ἔπαυλιν ἀμφὶ ἄριστον

---

[1] A omits εἶτα . . . κάτω   [2] A ὡς

committed fifty she's and two he's. Of them he
has made you an hundred now and ten he-goats.
Do you see how plump and fat they are, how shaggy
and rough their hair is, how entire and unshattered
their horns? Besides he has made them musical.
For if they do but hear his pipe, they are ready to
do whatsoever he will."

15. Clearista heard him what he said, and being
struck with a longing to have it presently tried
whether it were so indeed or not, she bids Daphnis
to play to his goats as he wonted to do, promising
to give him for his piping a coat, a mantle, and new
shoes. Daphnis, when all the company was sate as
a theatre, went to his oak, and standing under it
drew his pipe out of his scrip. And first he blowed
something that was low and smart, and presently
the goats rose up and held their heads bolt upright.
Then he played the pastoral or grazing tune, and
the goats cast their heads downwards to graze.
Then again he breathed a note was soft and sweet,
and all lay down together to rest. Anon he struck
up a sharp, violent, tumultuous sound, and they all
rushed into the wood as if a wolf had come upon
them. After a while he piped aloud the recall, and
they wheeled out of the wood again and came up
to his very feet. Never was there any master of a
house that had his servants so obsequious to his
commands. All the spectators admired his art, but
especially Clearista, insomuch that she could not
but swear she would give him the things she
promised, who was so fair a goatherd and skilled in
music even to wonder.

From this pleasure they returned to the cottage

εἶχον καὶ τῷ Δάφνιδι ἀφ' ὧν ἤσθιον ἔπεμψαν.
16. ὁ δὲ μετὰ τῆς Χλόης ἤσθιε καὶ ἤδετο
γενόμενος ἀστικῆς ὀψαρτυσίας, καὶ εὔελπις ἦν
τεύξεσθαι τοῦ γάμου πείσας τοὺς δεσπότας.
ὁ δὲ Γνάθων προσεκκαυθεὶς τοῖς κατὰ τὸ
αἰπόλιον γεγενημένοις καὶ ἀβίωτον νομίζων τὸν
βίον εἰ μὴ τεύξεται Δάφνιδος, περιπατοῦντα
τὸν Ἀστύλον ἐν τῷ παραδείσῳ φυλάξας, καὶ
ἀναγαγὼν εἰς τὸν τοῦ Διονύσου νεών, πόδας
καὶ χεῖρας κατεφίλει. τοῦ δὲ πυνθανομένου,
τίνος ἕνεκα ταῦτα δρᾷ, καὶ λέγειν κελεύοντος καὶ
ὑπουργήσειν ὀμνύοντος, " Οἴχεταί σοι Γνάθων,"
ἔφη, " δέσποτα· ὁ μέχρι νῦν μόνης τραπέζης
τῆς σῆς ἐρῶν, ὁ πρότερον ὀμνὺς ὅτι μηδέν ἐστιν
ὡραιότερον οἴνου γέροντος, ὁ κρείττους τῶν ἐφήβων
τῶν ἐν Μυτιλήνῃ τοὺς σοὺς ὀψαρτυτὰς λέγων,
μόνον λοιπὸν καλὸν εἶναι Δάφνιν νομίζω. καὶ
τροφῆς μὲν τῆς πολυτελοῦς οὐ γεύομαι καίτοι
τοσούτων παρασκευαζομένων ἑκάστης ἡμέρας,
κρεῶν, ἰχθύων, μελιτωμάτων, ἡδέως δ' ἂν αἲξ
γενόμενος πόαν ἐσθίοιμι καὶ φύλλα τῆς Δάφνιδος
ἀκούων σύριγγος καὶ ὑπ' ἐκείνου [1] νεμόμενος. σὺ
δὲ σῶσον Γνάθωνα τὸν σὸν καὶ τὸν ἀήττητον
ἔρωτα νίκησον. εἰ δὲ μή, σὲ [2] ἐπόμνυμι τὸν ἐμὸν
θεόν, ξιφίδιον λαβὼν καὶ ἐμπλήσας τὴν γαστέρα
τροφῆς ἐμαυτὸν ἀποκτενῶ πρὸ τῶν Δάφνιδος
θυρῶν· σὺ δὲ οὐκέτι καλέσεις Γναθωνάριον,
ὥσπερ εἰώθεις παίζων ἀεί."

[1] so Hirsch : A -ων: pq -φ   [2] so Vill : mss σοὶ

to dine, and sent Daphnis some of their choicer fare to the fields ; 16. where he feasted himself with Chloe, and was sweetly affected by those delicates and confections from the city, and hoped he had pleased his lord and lady so, that now he should not miss the maid. But Gnatho now was more inflamed with those things about the goats ; and counting his life no life at all unless he had Daphnis at his will, he catched Astylus walking in the garden, and leading him with him into Bacchus his fane, he fell to kiss his hands and his feet. But he inquiring why he did so and bidding him tell what was the matter with him, and swearing withal to hear and help him in anything, "Master, thy Gnatho is undone," quoth he ; "for I who heretofore was in love with nothing but thy plenteous table, and swore nothing was more desirable, nothing of a more precious tang, then good old wine, I that have often affirmed that thy confectioners and cooks were the sweetest things in Mytilene, I shall now here-after for ever think that nothing is fair and sweet but Daphnis ; and giving over to feed high, although thou art furnished every day with flesh, with fish, with banqueting, nothing could be more pleasant to me then to be turned into a goat, to eat grass and green leaves, hear Daphnis his pipe and be fed at his hand. But do thou preserve thy Gnatho, and be to him the victor of victorious love. Unless it be done, I swear by thee that art my God, that when I have filled my paunch with meat, I'll take this dagger and kill myself at Daphnis his door. And then you may go look your little pretty Gnatho, as thou usest daily to call me."

DAPHNIS AND CHLOE

17. Οὐκ ἀντέσχε κλάοντι καὶ αὖθις τοὺς πόδας καταφιλοῦντι νεανίσκος μεγαλόφρων καὶ οὐκ ἄπειρος ἐρωτικῆς λύπης, ἀλλ' αἰτήσειν αὐτὸν παρὰ τοῦ πατρὸς ἐπηγγείλατο κομίζειν [1] εἰς τὴν πόλιν αὐτῷ μὲν δοῦλον ἐκείνῳ δὲ ἐρώμενον. εἰς εὐθυμίαν [2] δὲ καὶ αὐτὸν ἐκεῖνον θέλων προαγαγεῖν, ἐπυνθάνετο μειδιῶν εἰ οὐκ αἰσχύνεται Λάμωνος υἱὸν φιλῶν ἀλλὰ καὶ σπουδάζει συγκατακλιθῆναι νέμοντι αἶγας μειρακίῳ, καὶ ἅμα ὑπεκρίνετο τὴν τραγικὴν δυσωδίαν μυσάττεσθαι.

Ὁ δέ, οἷα πᾶσαν ἐρωτικὴν μυθολογίαν ἐν τοῖς τῶν ἀσώτων [3] συμποσίοις πεπαιδευμένος, οὐκ ἀπὸ σκοποῦ καὶ ὑπὲρ αὐτοῦ καὶ ὑπὲρ τοῦ Δάφνιδος ἔλεγεν· "Οὐδεὶς ταῦτα, δέσποτα, ἐραστὴς πολυπραγμονεῖ, ἀλλ' ἐν οἵῳ ποτὲ ἂν σώματι εὕρῃ τὸ κάλλος, ἑάλωκε. διὰ τοῦτο καὶ φυτοῦ τις ἠράσθη καὶ ποταμοῦ καὶ θηρίου. καίτοι τίς οὐκ ἂν ἐραστὴν ἠλέησεν ὃν ἔδει φοβεῖσθαι τὸν ἐρώμενον; ἐγὼ δὲ σώματος μὲν ἐρῶ δούλου, κάλλους δὲ ἐλευθέρου. ὁρᾷς ὡς ὑακίνθῳ μὲν τὴν κόμην ὁμοίαν ἔχει, λάμπουσι δὲ ὑπὸ ταῖς ὀφρύσιν οἱ ὀφθαλμοὶ καθάπερ ἐν χρυσῇ σφενδόνῃ ψηφίς; καὶ τὸ μὲν πρόσωπον ἐρυθήματος μεστόν, τὸ δὲ στόμα λευκῶν ὀδόντων ὥσπερ ἐλέφαντος; τίς ἐκεῖθεν οὐκ ἂν εὔξαιτο λαβεῖν ἐραστὴς γλυκέα [3] φιλήματα; εἰ δὲ νέμοντος ἠράσθην, θεοὺς ἐμιμησάμην. βουκόλος ἦν Ἀγχίσης καὶ

[1] so E : mss καὶ κομ.   [2] Α ἐπι- : Β ἐν-   [3] τῶν ἀσώτ. :
Α τῆς ἀσωμάτοις from σώματι below   [3] so Vill : mss λευκὰ
from above

17. Astylus, a generous youth and one that was not to learn that love was a tormentous fire, could not endure to see him weep in such a manner and kiss his feet again and again; but promised him to beg Daphnis of his father to wait upon him at Mytilene. And to hearten up Gnatho, as he before had bin heartened up himself, he smiled upon him and asked him whether he were not ashamed to be in love with a son of Lamo's, nay, with a boy that kept goats. And while he said that, he made as if to show how abominable to him was the strong perfume of goats.

Gnatho on the other side, like one that had learnt the wanton discourse among good fellows in the drinking schools, was ready to answer him pat concerning himself and Daphnis thus: "We lovers, Sir, are never curious about such things as those. But wheresoever we meet with beauty, there undoubtedly we are catched. And hence it is that some have fallen in love with a tree, some with a river, some with a beast. And who would not pity that miserable lover whom we know fatally bound to live in fear of that that's loved? But I, as I love the body of a servant, so in that the beauty of the most ingenuous.[1] Do you not see his locks are like the hyacinths? and his eyes under the brows like diamonds burning in their golden sockets? how sweetly ruddy are his cheeks, and his mouth rowed with elephant-pearl? And what lover would not be fond to take from thence the sweetest kisses? But if I love a keeper of flocks, in that I imitate the Gods. Anchises was a herds-

---

[1] high-born.

ἔσχεν αὐτὸν Ἀφροδίτη· αἶγας ἔνεμε Βράγχος [1]
καὶ Ἀπόλλων αὐτὸν ἐφίλησε· ποιμὴν ἦν Γανυμή-
δης καὶ αὐτὸν ὁ τῶν ὅλων βασιλεὺς [2] ἥρπασε.
μὴ καταφρονῶμεν παιδὸς ᾧ καὶ αἶγας, ὡς ἐρώσας,
πειθομένας εἴδομεν, ἀλλ᾽ εἰ καὶ [3] ἔτι μένειν ἐπὶ
γῆς ἐπιτρέπουσι τοιοῦτον κάλλος χάριν ἔχωμεν
τοῖς Διὸς ἀετοῖς.”

18. Ἡδὺ γελάσας ὁ Ἀστύλος ἐπὶ τούτῳ
μάλιστα τῷ λεχθέντι, καὶ ὡς μεγάλους ὁ Ἔρως
ποιεῖ σοφιστὰς εἰπὼν ἐπετήρει καιρόν, ἐν ᾧ τῷ
πατρὶ περὶ Δάφνιδος διαλέξεται.

Ἀκούσας δὲ τὰ λεχθέντα κρύφα πάντα ὁ
Εὔδρομος, καὶ τὰ μὲν τὸν Δάφνιν φιλῶν ὡς
ἀγαθὸν νεανίσκον, τὰ δὲ ἀχθόμενος εἰ Γνάθωνος
ἐμπαροίνημα γενήσεται τοιοῦτον κάλλος, αὐτίκα
καταλέγει πάντα ἐκείνῳ [4] καὶ Λάμωνι. ὁ μὲν
οὖν Δάφνις ἐκπλαγεὶς ἐγίνωσκεν ἅμα τῇ Χλόῃ
τολμῆσαι φυγεῖν ἢ ἀποθανεῖν, κοινωνὸν κἀκείνην
λαβών. ὁ δὲ Λάμων προσκαλεσάμενος ἔξω
τῆς αὐλῆς τὴν Μυρτάλην, “Οἰχόμεθα,” εἶπεν,
“ὦ γύναι. ἥκει καιρὸς ἐκκαλύπτειν τὰ κρυπτά.[5]
ἔρρει μοι [6] καὶ τὸ αἰπόλιον καὶ τὰ λοιπὰ πάντα.
ἀλλ᾽ οὐ μὰ τὸν Πᾶνα καὶ τὰς Νύμφας, οὐδ᾽ εἰ
μέλλω βοῦς, φασίν, ἐν αὐλίῳ καταλείπεσθαι,
τὴν Δάφνιδος τύχην ἥτις ἐστὶν οὐ σιωπήσομαι,
ἀλλὰ καὶ ὅτι εὗρον ἐκκείμενον ἐρῶ, καὶ ὅπως
τρεφόμενον μηνύσω καὶ ὅσα εὗρον συνεκκείμενα
δείξω. μαθέτω Γνάθων ὁ μιαρὸς οἷος ὢν οἵων
ἐρᾷ. παρασκεύαζέ μοι μόνον εὐτρεπῆ τὰ γνωρί-
σματα.”

[1] q Βράγχιος (not Amyot)   [2] τῶν ὅλ. βασ. : pq Ζεὺς
[3] pq omit   A omits ἔτι   [4] pq κἀκείνῳ from below

216

man, and Venus had him ; Branchus was a goat-
herd, and Apollo loved him ; Ganymedes was but a
shepherd, and yet he was the rape of the king of
all. We ought not then to contemn a youth to
whom we see even the goats, for very love of one
so fair, every way obedient. Nay rather, that they
let such a beauty as that continue here upon the
earth, we owe our thanks to Jupiter's eagles."

18. At that word Astylus had a sweet laugh, and
saying, " O what mighty sophisters this Love can
make," began to cast about him for a fit time to
speak to his father about Daphnis.

Eudromus hearkened in secret what was said,
and because he both loved Daphnis as an honest
youth and detested in himself that such a flower of
beauty should be put into the hands of a filthy sot,
he presently told both Daphnis and Lamo all that
happened. Daphnis was struck to the heart with
this, and soon resolved either to run away with
Chloe or to die with her. But Lamo, getting
Myrtale out of doors, " What shall we do ? " quoth
he ; " we are all undone. Now or never is our
time to open all that hitherto has bin concealed.
Gone is my herd of goats, and gone all else too.
But by Pan and all the Nymphs, though I should
be left alone to myself like an ox forgotten in a
stall, I will not longer hide his story, but declare I
found him an exposed child, make it known how he
was nursed, and shew the significations found
exposed together with him. And let that rotten
rascal Gnatho know himself, and what it is he dares
to love. Only make ready the tokens for me."

<hr />

⁵ p κρύφα   ⁶ so Cob. : mss ἔρημοι   καὶ τὸ αἰπ. so *E* :
mss δὲ αἱ αἶγες a correction following the corruption

19. Οἱ μὲν ταῦτα συνθέμενοι ἀπῆλθον εἴσω πάλιν· ὁ δὲ Ἀστύλος σχολὴν ἄγοντι τῷ πατρὶ προσρυείς, αἰτεῖ τὸν Δάφνιν εἰς τὴν πόλιν κατ- αγαγεῖν, ὡς καλόν τε ὄντα καὶ ἀγροικίας κρείττονα καὶ ταχέως ὑπὸ Γνάθωνος καὶ τὰ ἀστικὰ διδα- χθῆναι δυνάμενον. χαίρων ὁ πατὴρ δίδωσι, καὶ μεταπεμψάμενος τὸν Λάμωνα καὶ τὴν Μυρτάλην εὐηγγελίζετο μὲν αὐτοῖς, ὅτι Ἀστύλον θεραπεύσει λοιπὸν ἀντὶ αἰγῶν καὶ τράγων Δάφνις, ἐπηγγέλ- λετο δὲ δύο ἀντ' ἐκείνου δώσειν αὐτοῖς αἰπόλους.

Ἐνταῦθα ὁ Λάμων, πάντων ἤδη συνερρυηκότων καὶ ὅτι καλὸν ὁμόδουλον ἕξουσιν ἡδομένων, αἰ- τήσας λόγον ἤρξατο λέγειν· "Ἄκουσον, ὦ δέ- σποτα, παρὰ ἀνδρὸς γέροντος ἀληθῆ λόγον· ἐπ- όμνυμι δὲ τὸν Πᾶνα καὶ τὰς Νύμφας, ὡς οὐδὲν ψεύσομαι. οὐκ εἰμὶ Δάφνιδος πατήρ, οὐδ' εὐτύ- χησέ ποτε Μυρτάλη μήτηρ γενέσθαι. ἄλλοι[1] πατέρες ἐξέθηκαν τοῦτον, παιδίων[2] πρεσβυτέρων ἅλις ἔχοντες· ἐγὼ δὲ εὗρον ἐκκείμενον καὶ ὑπὸ αἰγὸς ἐμῆς τρεφόμενον· ἣν καὶ ἀποθανοῦσαν ἔθαψα ἐν τῷ περικήπῳ, φιλῶν ὅτι ἐποίησε μητρὸς ἔργα. εὗρον αὐτῷ καὶ γνωρίσματα συνεκκείμενα· ὁμολογῶ, δέσποτα, καὶ φυλάττω· τύχης γάρ ἐστι μείζονος ἢ καθ' ἡμᾶς σύμβολα. Ἀστύλου μὲν οὖν εἶναι δοῦλον αὐτὸν οὐχ ὑπερηφανῶ, καλὸν οἰκέτην καλοῦ καὶ ἀγαθοῦ δεσπότου· παροίνημα

---

[1] A ἀλλ' οἱ   [2] so E : A τοῦτον πεδίῳ ἴσως παιδίων : q τοῦτον παιδίῳ ἴσως παιδίων : p τοῦτο τὸ παιδίον ἴσως παιδίων (ἴσως, and παιδίων rather than παίδων, betray the gloss)

218

19. This agreed, they went again into the house. But Astylus, his father being at leisure, went quickly to him and asked his leave to take Daphnis from the country to serve him at Mytilene; for he was a fine boy, far above the clownish life, and one that Gnatho soon could teach the city garb.[1] His father grants it willingly, and presently sending for Lamo and Myrtale, lets them know the joyful news that Daphnis should hereafter wait upon Astylus in the city, and leave his keeping goats; and instead of him he promised to give them two goatherds.

And now, when Lamo saw the servants running together and hug one another for joy they were to have so sweet a fellow-servant in the house, he asked leave to speak to his lord, and thus began: "Hear me, Sir, a true story that an old man is about to tell you. And I swear by Pan and the Nymphs that I will not lie a jot. I am not the father of Daphnis, nor was Myrtale so happy as to be the mother of so sweet a youth. Other parents exposed that child, having enow before. And I found him where he was laid and suckled by a goat of mine; which goat, when she died, I buried in yonder skirt of the garden, to use her kindly because she had played the part of a mother. Together with him I found habiliments exposed and signs, methought, of what he was. I confess them to you, Sir, and have kept them to this day. For they make him of higher fortune then we have any claim to. Wherefore, although I think not much he should become the servant of the noble Astylus, a good servant of a good and honest lord, yet I

---

[1] ways.

δὲ Γνάθωνος οὐ δύναμαι περιϊδεῖν γενόμενον, ὃς
εἰς Μυτιλήνην αὐτὸν ἄγειν ἐπὶ γυναικῶν ἔργα
σπουδάζει."

20. Ὁ μὲν Λάμων ταῦτα εἰπὼν ἐσιώπησε καὶ
πολλὰ ἀφῆκε δάκρυα. τοῦ δὲ Γνάθωνος θρασυ-
νομένου καὶ πληγὰς ἀπειλοῦντος, ὁ Διονυσοφάνης
τοῖς εἰρημένοις ἐκπλαγεὶς τὸν μὲν Γνάθωνα σιω-
πᾶν ἐκέλευσε σφόδρα τὴν ὀφρὺν εἰς αὐτὸν τοξο-
ποιήσας, τὸν δὲ Λάμωνα πάλιν ἀνέκρινε καὶ παρε-
κελεύετο τἀληθῆ λέγειν, μηδὲ ὅμοια πλάττειν
μύθοις ἐπὶ τῷ κατέχειν ὡς υἱόν. ὡς δὲ ἀτενὴς
ἦν καὶ κατὰ πάντων ὤμνυε θεῶν καὶ ἐδίδου βα-
σανίζειν αὐτόν,' εἰ διαψεύδεται, καθημένης τῆς
Κλεαρίστης ἤλεγχε[1] τὰ λελεγμένα· "Τί δ᾽ ἂν
ἐψεύδετο Λάμων μέλλων ἀνθ᾽ ἑνὸς δύο λαμβάνειν
αἰπόλους; πῶς δ᾽ ἂν καὶ ταῦτα ἔπλασσεν ἄ-
γροικος; οὐ γὰρ εὐθὺς ἦν ἄπιστον, ἐκ τοιούτου
γέροντος καὶ μήτρας[2] εὐτελοῦς υἱὸν καλὸν οὕτω
γενέσθαι;"

21. Ἐδόκει μὴ μαντεύεσθαι ἐπὶ πλέον, ἀλλὰ
ἤδη τὰ γνωρίσματα σκοπεῖν, εἰ λαμπρᾶς[3] καὶ
ἐνδοξοτέρας τύχης. ἀπῄει μὲν Μυρτάλη κομί-
σουσα πάντα, φυλαττόμενα ἐν πήρᾳ παλαιᾷ.
κομισθέντα δὲ πρῶτος Διονυσοφάνης ἐπέβλεπε,
καὶ ἰδὼν χλανίδιον[4] ἁλουργές, πόρπην χρυσή-
λατον, ξιφίδιον ἐλεφαντόκωπον, μέγα βοήσας
"Ὦ Ζεῦ δέσποτα," καλεῖ τὴν γυναῖκα θεασομένην.
ἡ δὲ ἰδοῦσα μέγα καὶ αὐτὴ βοᾷ· "Φίλαι Μοῖραι·

---

[1] so E, cf. 4. 23: mss ἐβασάνιζε (emendation following
corruption through haplogr.)   Α λεγόμενα   [2] Α μήτρως

cannot endure to have him now exposed to the drunken glutton Gnatho, and as it were be made a slave to such a drivel."

20. Lamo, when he had thus said, held his peace and wept amain. But Gnatho beginning to bluster and threatening to cudgel Lamo, Dionysophanes was wholly amazed at what was said, and commanded him silence, bending his brows and looking stern and grim upon him ; then again questioned Lamo, charging him to speak the truth and tell him no such tales as those to keep Daphnis his son. But when he stood to what he said and swore to it by all the Gods, and would submit it to torture if he did deceive him, he examined every passage over again, Clearista sitting judge to him :[1] "What cause is there that Lamo should lie, when for one he is to have two goatherds ? And how should a simple country-fellow feign and forge such things as these ? No, sure ; it had been straightway incredible that of such an old churl and such an urchin as his wife there should come a child so fair."

21. And now it seemed best to insist no longer upon conjectures, but to view the tokens and try if they reported anything of a more noble and splendid fortune. Myrtale therefore went and brought them all to them, laid up safe in an old scrip. Dionysophanes looked first, and seeing there the purple mantle, the gold brooch, the dagger with the ivory heft, he cried out loud "Great Jupiter the governor !" and called his wife that she might see. She too, when she saw them, cried out amain, "O

---

[3] perh. λαμπροτέρας   [4] so Cob : A χλαμίδ. : pq χλαμύδ. : cf. i. 2

---

[1] cf. 2. 15.

οὐ ταῦτα ἡμεῖς συνεξεθήκαμεν ἰδίῳ παιδί;[1] οὐκ
εἰς τούτους τοὺς ἀγροὺς κομίσουσαν Σωφρόνην[2]
ἀπεστείλαμεν; οὐκ ἄλλα μὲν οὖν, ἀλλ᾽ αὐτὰ
ταῦτα,[3] φίλε ἄνερ. ἡμέτερόν ἐστι τὸ παιδίον, σὸς
υἱός ἐστι Δάφνις, καὶ πατρῴας ἔνεμεν αἶγας."

22. Ἔτι λεγούσης αὐτῆς καὶ τοῦ Διονυσο-
φάνους τὰ γνωρίσματα φιλοῦντος καὶ ὑπὸ περιτ-
τῆς ἡδονῆς δακρύοντος, ὁ Ἀστύλος συνεὶς ὡς
ἀδελφός ἐστι, ῥίψας θοἰμάτιον ἔθει κατὰ τοῦ
παραδείσου, πρῶτος τὸν Δάφνιν φιλῆσαι θέλων.
ἰδὼν δὲ αὐτὸν ὁ Δάφνις θέοντα[4] μετὰ πολλῶν καὶ
βοῶντα " Δάφνι," νομίσας ὅτι συλλαβεῖν αὐτὸν
βουλόμενος τρέχει, ῥίψας τὴν πήραν καὶ τὴν
σύριγγα πρὸς τὴν θάλατταν ἐφέρετο ῥίψων
ἑαυτὸν ἀπὸ τῆς μεγάλης πέτρας. καὶ ἴσως
ἄν, τὸ καινότατον, εὑρεθεὶς ἀπολώλει, εἰ μὴ
συνεὶς ὁ Ἀστύλος ἐβόα πάλιν· "Στῆθι, Δάφνι,
μηδὲν φοβηθῇς· ἀδελφός εἰμί σου καὶ γονεῖς
οἱ μέχρι νῦν δεσπόται. νῦν ἡμῖν Λάμων τὴν
αἶγα εἶπε καὶ τὰ γνωρίσματα ἔδειξεν· ὅρα
δὲ ἐπιστραφείς, πῶς ἴασι φαιδροὶ καὶ γε-
λῶντες. ἀλλ᾽ ἐμὲ πρῶτον φίλησον· ὄμνυμι δὲ
τὰς Νύμφας, ὡς οὐ ψεύδομαι." 23. μόλις οὖν
μετὰ τοὺς ὅρκους[5] ἔστη καὶ τὸν Ἀστύλον τρέ-
χοντα[6] περιέμεινε καὶ προσελθόντα κατεφίλησεν.

Ἐν ᾧ δὲ ἐκεῖνον ἐφίλει, πλῆθος τὸ λοιπὸν
ἐπιρρεῖ θεραπόντων, θεραπαινῶν, αὐτὸς ὁ πατήρ,
ἡ μήτηρ μετ᾽ αὐτοῦ. οὗτοι πάντες περιέβαλλον,

---

[1] A παιδίῳ   οὐκ: p (Amyot) καὶ   [2] so Cour: mss
Σωφροσύνην: cf. Men. Epit.   [3] αὐτὰ ταῦτα: so Cour: A
αὐτὰ: pq ταῦτα   [4] pq omit ὁ Δ. θέ.   [5] pq sing.   [6] Uiii
στρέφοντα

dear, dear Fates! are not these those very things we exposed with a son of our own? Did we not send Sophrone to lay him here in these fields? They are no other, but the same, my dear! This is our child without doubt. Daphnis is thy son, and he kept his father's goats."

22. While Clearista was yet speaking, and Dionysophanes was kissing those sweet revelations of his child and weeping over them for joy, Astylus hearing it was his brother, flings off his cloak, and o'er the green away he flies in an earnest desire to be the first to entertain him with a kiss. Daphnis, seeing him make towards him so fast with such a company, and hearing his own name in the noise, thinking he came to apprehend him, flung away his scrip and his pipe, and in the scare set a running towards the sea to cast himself from the high crag. And peradventure the new-found Daphnis, strange to tell, had then bin lost, but that Astylus perceiving it cried out to him more clearly, "Stay, Daphnis; be not afraid; I am thy brother, and they thy parents that were hitherto thy lords. Now Lamo has told us all concerning the goat, and shewed the tokens thou hadst about thee. Turn thee and see with what a rejoicing, cheerful face they come along. But do thou kiss me first of all. By the Nymphs I do not lie." 23. After that oath he ventured to stand, and stayed till Astylus came at him, and then offered him a kiss.

While they were kissing and embracing, the rest of the company came in, the men-servants, the maids, the father, and with him the mother. Everyone kissed him and hugged him in their arms,

κατεφίλουν, χαίροντες, κλάοντες. ὁ δὲ τὸν πατέρα
καὶ τὴν μητέρα πρὸ τῶν ἄλλων ἐφιλοφρονεῖτο·
καὶ ὡς πάλαι εἰδὼς προσεστερνίζετο καὶ ἐξελθεῖν
τῶν περιβόλων οὐκ ἤθελεν· οὕτω φύσις ταχέως
πιστεύεται. ἐξελάθετο καὶ Χλόης πρὸς [1] ὀλίγον.

24. Καὶ ἐλθὼν εἰς τὴν ἔπαυλιν ἐσθῆτά τε
ἔλαβε πολυτελῆ, καὶ παρὰ τὸν πατέρα τὸν
ἴδιον καθεσθεὶς ἤκουεν [2] αὐτοῦ λέγοντος οὕτως·
"Ἔγημα, ὦ παῖδες, κομιδῇ νέος. καὶ χρόνου διελ-
θόντος ὀλίγου, πατήρ, ὡς ᾤμην, εὐτυχὴς ἐγεγόνειν·
ἐγένετο [3] γάρ μοι πρῶτος υἱὸς καὶ δευτέρα θυ-
γάτηρ καὶ τρίτος Ἄστυλος. ᾤμην ἱκανὸν εἶναι
τὸ γένος, καὶ γενόμενον ἐπὶ πᾶσι τοῦτο τὸ παιδίον
ἐξέθηκα οὐ γνωρίσματα ταῦτα συνεκθείς, ἀλλὰ
ἐντάφια. τὰ δὲ τῆς Τύχης ἄλλα βουλεύματα.
ὁ μὲν γὰρ πρεσβύτερος παῖς καὶ ἡ θυγάτηρ ὁμοίᾳ
νόσῳ μιᾶς ἡμέρας ἀπώλοντο· σὺ δέ μοι προνοίᾳ
θεῶν ἐσώθης, ἵνα πλείους ἔχωμεν χειραγωγούς.
μήτε οὖν σύ μοι μνησικακήσῃς ποτὲ τῆς ἐκθέσεως
(ἑκὼν γὰρ οὐκ ἐβουλευσάμην), μήτε σὺ λυπηθῇς,
Ἄστυλε, μέρος ληψόμενος ἀντὶ πάσης τῆς οὐσίας
(κρεῖττον γὰρ τοῖς εὖ φρονοῦσιν ἀδελφοῦ κτῆμα
οὐδέν)· ἀλλὰ φιλεῖτε ἀλλήλους, καὶ χρημάτων
ἕνεκα καὶ βασιλεῦσιν ἐρίζετε. πολλὴν μὲν γὰρ
ἐγὼ ὑμῖν καταλείψω γῆν, πολλοὺς δὲ οἰκέτας

---

[1] ρq παρ'   [2] A aor.   [3] so Hirsch: mss ἐγίν.

rejoicing and weeping. But Daphnis embraced his father and his mother the most familiarly of all the rest, and clinged to them as if he had known them long before, and would not part out of their arms. So quickly comes belief to join with nature. And he forgot even Chloe for a little while.

24. And when they got back to the cottage, they turned him out of his old clothes and put him in a gallant habit; and then seated near his own father he heard him speak to this purpose: "I married a wife, my dear sons, when I was yet very young, and after a while it was my happiness (so I thought it) to be a father. For first I had a son born, the second a daughter, and then Astylus the third. I thought there was enow of the breed; and therefore I exposed this boy, who was born after the rest, and set him out with those toys, not for the tokens of his stock but for sepulchral ornaments. But Fortune had other thoughts and counsels about him. For so it was that my eldest son and my daughter died on the same disease upon one and the same day. But thou, by the providence of the Gods, art kept alive and saved for us, in design to make us happy by more helps and manductors to our age. So do not thou, when it comes in thy mind that thou wast exposed, take it unkindly or think evil of me; for it was not with a willing mind. Neither do thou, good Astylus, take it ill that now thou art to have but a part for the whole inheritance; for to any man that's wise there is no possession more precious then a brother is. Therefore esteem and love one another, and for your riches compare and vie yourselves with kings. For I shall leave you

δεξιούς, χρυσόν, ἄργυρον, ὅσα ἄλλα εὐδαιμόνων
κτήματα. μόνον ἐξαίρετον τοῦτο Δάφνιδι τὸ
χωρίον δίδωμι καὶ Λάμωνα καὶ Μυρτάλην καὶ
τὰς αἶγας ἃς αὐτὸς ἔνεμεν."

25. Ἔτι αὐτοῦ λέγοντος, Δάφνις ἀναπηδήσας
" Καλῶς με," εἶπε, " πάτερ, ἀνέμνησας. ἄπειμι
τὰς αἶγας ἀπάξων ἐπὶ ποτόν, αἵ που νῦν διψῶσαι
περιμένουσι¹ τὴν σύριγγα τὴν ἐμήν, ἐγὼ δὲ
ἐνταυθὶ² καθέζομαι." ἡδὺ πάντες ἐξεγέλασαν,
ὅτι δεσπότης γεγενημένος ἔτι θέλει εἶναι³ αἰ-
πόλος.

Κἀκείνας μὲν θεραπεύσων ἐπέμφθη τις ἄλλος·
οἱ δὲ θύσαντες Διὶ Σωτῆρι συμπόσιον συνε-
κρότουν. εἰς τοῦτο τὸ συμπόσιον μόνος οὐχ ἧκε
Γνάθων, ἀλλὰ φοβούμενος ἐν τῷ νεῷ τοῦ Διονύσου
καὶ τὴν ἡμέραν ἔμεινε καὶ τὴν νύκτα, ὥσπερ
ἱκέτης. ταχείας δὲ φήμης εἰς πάντας ἐλθούσης,
ὅτι Διονυσοφάνης εὗρεν υἱὸν καὶ ὅτι Δάφνις ὁ
αἰπόλος δεσπότης τῶν ἀγρῶν⁴ εὑρέθη, ἅμα ἕῳ
συνέτρεχον ἄλλος ἀλλαχόθεν τῷ μὲν μειρακίῳ
συνηδόμενοι, τῷ δὲ πατρὶ αὐτοῦ δῶρα κομίζοντες·
ἐν οἷς καὶ ὁ Δρύας πρῶτος ὁ τρέφων τὴν Χλόην.

26. Ὁ δὲ Διονυσοφάνης κατεῖχε πάντας κοινω-
νοὺς μετὰ τὴν εὐφροσύνην καὶ τῆς ἑορτῆς ἐσο-
μένους.⁵ παρεσκεύαστο δὲ πολὺς μὲν οἶνος, πολλὰ
δὲ ἄλευρα, ὄρνιθες ἕλειοι, χοῖροι γαλαθηνοί,
μελιτώματα ποικίλα· καὶ ἱερεῖα δὲ πολλὰ τοῖς

¹ pq παρα   ² so Hirsch : A ἐνταῦθα : pq -θοῖ   ³ θέλ.
εἶν. : q ἦν   ⁴ p (Amyot) αἰγῶν   ⁵ so Jung : mss -ης

large lands, servants industrious and true, gold and
silver, all the fortunate possess. Only in special I
give to Daphnis this manor, with Lamo and Myrtale,
and the goats that he has kept."

25. While he was still going on in speech, Daphnis
starting, " 'Tis well remembered, father," quoth he ;
" 'tis time to go and lead my goats to watering.
They are now dry and now expecting my pipe, and
I am loitering and lolling here." They all laughed
sweetly at this, to see him that was now a lord
turning into a goatherd again ; and so another was
sent away to rid his mind of that care.

And now, when they had sacrificed to Jupiter
Soter, the saviour of the exposed child, they made
ready a jovial, rejoicing feast. And only Gnatho
was not there ; for he was in a mighty fear, and
took sanctuary in Bacchus his fane, and there he
was a sneaking suppliant night and day. But
the fame flying abroad that Dionysophanes had
found a son, and that Daphnis the goatherd proved
the lord both of the goats and the fields they fed
in, the rurals came in with the early day, some from
one place, some another, there to congratulate the
youth and bring their presents to his father. And
amongst these Dryas was first, Dryas to whom Chloe
was nursling.

26. And Dionysophanes made them all stay as
partakers of his joy and exultation, and to celebrate
also the great feast of the Invention [1] of Daphnis.
Therefore great store of wine and bread was fur-
nished out, water-fowl of all sorts, sucking-pigs,
various curiosities of sweet cakes, wafers, simnels,
and pies. And many victims that day were slain

[1] finding.

ἐπιχωρίοις θεοῖς ἐθύετο. ἐνταῦθα ὁ Δάφνις
συναθροίσας πάντα τὰ ποιμενικὰ κτήματα διένει-
μεν ἀναθήματα τοῖς θεοῖς. τῷ Διονύσῳ μὲν ἀνέ-
θηκε τὴν πήραν καὶ τὸ δέρμα, τῷ Πανὶ τὴν
σύριγγα καὶ τὸν πλάγιον αὐλόν, τὴν καλαύροπα
ταῖς Νύμφαις καὶ τοὺς γαυλοὺς οὓς αὐτὸς ἐτεκτή-
νατο. οὕτως δὲ ἄρα τὸ σύνηθες ξενιζούσης εὐδαι-
μονίας τερπνότερόν ἐστιν, ὥστε ἐδάκρυεν ἐφ᾽
ἑκάστῳ τούτων ἀπαλλαττόμενος· καὶ οὔτε τοὺς
γαυλοὺς ἀνέθηκε πρὶν ἀμέλξαι, οὔτε τὸ δέρμα πρὶν
ἐνδύσασθαι, οὔτε τὴν σύριγγα πρὶν συρίσαι· ἀλλὰ
καὶ ἐφίλησεν αὐτὰ πάντα, καὶ τὰς αἶγας προσεῖπε
καὶ τοὺς τράγους ἐκάλεσεν ὀνομαστί· τῆς μὲν γὰρ
πηγῆς καὶ ἔπιεν, ὅτι <καὶ ἔπιε> πολλάκις καὶ
μετὰ Χλόης. οὔπω δὲ ὡμολόγει τὸν ἔρωτα, καιρὸν
παραφυλάττων.[1]

27. Ἐν ᾧ δὲ Δάφνις ἐν θυσίαις ἦν, τάδε γίνεται
περὶ τὴν Χλόην. ἐκάθητο κλάουσα, τὰ πρόβατα
νέμουσα, λέγουσα οἷα εἰκὸς ἦν· '' Ἐξελάθετό μου
Δάφνις· ὀνειροπολεῖ γάμους πλουσίους. τί γὰρ
αὐτὸν ὀμνύειν ἀντὶ τῶν Νυμφῶν τὰς αἶγας ἐκέ-
λευον; κατέλιπε ταύτας ὡς καὶ Χλόην. οὐδὲ
θύων ταῖς Νύμφαις καὶ τῷ Πανὶ ἐπεθύμησεν
ἰδεῖν Χλόην.[2] εὗρεν ἴσως παρὰ τῇ μητρὶ θερα-

<καὶ ἔπιε> *E* : A πηγ. ὅτι καὶ ἔπιε πολλ. : pq πηγ. καὶ ἔπιεν
πολλ.   [1] A φυλάττων   [2] A omits

228

and offered to the Gods of Lesbos. Daphnis then,
having got all his pastoral furniture about him, cast
it into several offerings, his thankful donaries to the
Gods. To Bacchus he dedicates his scrip and
mantle, to Pan his whistle and his oblique pipe, his
goat-hook to the holy Nymphs, and milking-pails
that he himself had made. But so it is, that those
things we have long bin acquainted withal and used
ourselves to, are more acceptable and pleasing to us
then a new and insolent [1] felicity ; and therefore tears
fell from his eyes at every valediction to this and
that, nor did he offer the pails to the Nymphs till he
had milked into them first, nor his mantle till he had
lapped himself in it, nor his pipe till he had piped a
tune or two ; but he looked wistly upon all the
things and would not let them go without a kiss.
Then he spoke to the she-goats, and called the
he-goats by their names. Out of the fountain too
he needs must drink before he goes, because he had
drank there many a time, and with his sweetest,
dearest Chloe. But as yet he did not openly profess
to his love, because he waited a season to it.

27. And therefore in the mean time, while he was
keeping holy-day, it was thus with poor Chloe : By
the flocks she sate and wept, and complained to
herself and them, as it was like, in this manner :
"Daphnis has forgot me. Now he dreams of a great
marriage. To what purpose is it now, that instead
of the Nymphs I would make him swear to me by
the goats ? He has forsaken them and me. And
when he sacrificed to Pan and to the Nymphs, he
would not so much as see Chloe. Perchance he has
found a prettier wench then I amongst his mother's

---

[1] unaccustomed.

παίνας ἐμοῦ κρείττονας. χαιρέτω· ἐγὼ δὲ οὐ
ζήσομαι."

28. Τοιαῦτα λέγουσαν, τοιαῦτα ἐννοοῦσαν, ὁ
Λάμπις ὁ βουκόλος μετὰ χειρὸς γεωργικῆς ἐπιστὰς
ἥρπασεν αὐτήν, ὡς οὔτε Δάφνιδος ἔτι γαμή-
σοντος καὶ Δρύαντος ἐκεῖνον ἀγαπήσοντος. ἡ
μὲν οὖν ἐκομίζετο βοῶσα ἐλεεινόν· τῶν δέ τις
ἰδόντων [1] ἐμήνυσε τῇ Νάπῃ, κἀκείνη τῷ Δρύαντι
καὶ ὁ Δρύας τῷ Δάφνιδι. ὁ δὲ ἔξω τῶν φρενῶν
γενόμενος, οὔτε εἰπεῖν πρὸς τὸν πατέρα ἐτόλμα,
καὶ καρτερεῖν μὴ δυνάμενος εἰς τὸν περίκηπον
εἰσελθὼν ὠδύρετο "῏Ω πικρᾶς ἀνευρέσεως"
λέγων· "πόσον ἦν μοι κρεῖττον νέμειν· πόσον
ἤμην μακαριώτερος, δοῦλος ὤν· τότε ἔβλεπον
Χλόην, τότ' <ἐφίλουν>, νῦν δὲ τὴν μὲν Λάμπις
ἁρπάσας οἴχεται, νυκτὸς δὲ γενομένης συγκοι-
μήσεται.[2] ἐγὼ δὲ πίνω καὶ τρυφῶ, καὶ μάτην τὸν
Πᾶνα καὶ τὰς αἶγας[3] ὤμοσα."

29. Ταῦτα τοῦ Δάφνιδος λέγοντος ἤκουσεν[4] ὁ
Γνάθων ἐν τῷ παραδείσῳ λανθάνων· καὶ καιρὸν
ἥκειν διαλλαγῶν πρὸς αὐτὸν νομίζων, τινὰς τῶν
τοῦ Ἀστύλου νεανίσκων προσλαβών, μεταδιώκει
τὸν Δρύαντα. καὶ ἡγεῖσθαι κελεύσας ἐπὶ τὴν τοῦ
Λάμπιδος ἔπαυλιν, συνέτεινε δρόμον· καὶ καταλα-
βὼν ἄρτι εἰσάγοντα τὴν Χλόην, ἐκείνην τε
ἀφαιρεῖται καὶ <τοὺς> ἀνθρώπους συνηλόησε

[1] cf. 2. 13   <ἐφίλουν> E: mss τότ' and lac.   [2] so
Valck. (Amyot): mss κοιμ.   [3] after αἶγ. mss have καὶ τὰς

maids. Fare him well! But I must die, and will not live."

28. While thus she was maundering and afflicting herself, Lampis the herdsman, coming upon her with a band of rustics, ravished her away, presuming Daphnis had cast off all thoughts of Chloe and Dryas too would be content to let him have her. And so she was carried away, crying out most piteously. But one that saw it told it Nape, she Dryas, and Dryas Daphnis. This put Daphnis almost quite out of his wits, and to his father he durst not speak, nor was he able to endure in that condition; and therefore slinking away into the circuit-walks of the garden, broke forth into lamentations: "O the bitter invention of Daphnis! How much better was it for me to keep a flock! And how much happier was I when I was a servant! Then I fed my eyes with the sight of Chloe and my lips with her kisses; but now she is the rape of Lampis, and with him she lies to-night. And I stay here and melt myself away in wine and soft delights, and so in vain have sworn to her by Pan and by the goats."

29. These heavy complaints of Daphnis it was Gnatho's fortune to hear as he was skulking in the garden. And presently apprehending the happy hour to appease Daphnis and make him propitious, he takes some of Astylus his servants, makes after Dryas, bids them shew him to Lampis his cottage, and plucks up his heels to get thither. And lighting on him in the nick as he was hauling Chloe in, he took her from him and banged his band of clowns. And

Νύμφας, but cf. 2. 39 (Cour. keeps and reads ὠμόσαμεν)
[4] A impf. <τοὺς> ἀνθ. *E*: mss add γεωργοὺς (gloss)

πληγαῖς. ἐσπούδαζε δὲ καὶ τὸν Λάμπιν δήσας
ἄγειν ὡς αἰχμάλωτον ἐκ πολέμου τινός, εἰ μὴ
φθάσας ἀπέδρα. κατορθώσας δὲ τηλικοῦτον ἔργον
νυκτὸς ἀρχομένης ἐπανέρχεται. καὶ τὸν μὲν
Διονυσοφάνην εὑρίσκει καθεύδοντα, τὸν δὲ Δάφνιν
ἀγρυπνοῦντα καὶ ἔτι ἐν τῷ περικήπῳ δακρύοντα.
προσάγει δὴ τὴν Χλόην αὐτῷ καὶ διδοὺς διηγεῖται
πάντα· καὶ δεῖται μηδὲν ἔτι μνησικακοῦντα
δοῦλον ἔχειν οὐκ ἄχρηστον, μηδὲ ἀφελέσθαι
τραπέζης, μεθ᾿ ὃ¹ τεθνήξεται λιμῷ. ὁ δὲ ἰδὼν
Χλόην καὶ ἔχων ἐν ταῖς χερσὶ Χλόην,² τῷ μὲν ὡς
εὐεργέτῃ διηλλάττετο, τῇ δὲ ὑπὲρ τῆς ἀμελείας
ἀπελογεῖτο.

30. Βουλευομένοις δὲ αὐτοῖς ἐδόκει τὸν γάμον
κρύπτειν, ἔχειν δὲ κρύφα τὴν Χλόην πρὸς μόνην
ὁμολογήσαντα τὸν ἔρωτα τὴν μητέρα. ἀλλ᾿ οὐ
συνεχώρει Δρύας, ἠξίου δὲ τῷ πατρὶ λέγειν καὶ
πείσειν αὐτὸς ἐπηγγέλλετο. καὶ γενομένης ἡμέρας
ἔχων ἐν τῇ πήρᾳ τὰ γνωρίσματα πρόσεισι τῷ
Διονυσοφάνει καὶ τῇ Κλεαρίστῃ καθημένοις ἐν
τῷ παραδείσῳ (παρῆν δὲ καὶ ὁ Ἀστύλος καὶ
αὐτὸς ὁ Δάφνις), καὶ σιωπῆς γενομένης ἤρξατο
λέγειν· "Ὁμοία με ἀνάγκη Λάμωνι τὰ μέχρι νῦν
ἄρρητα ἐκέλευσε λέγειν. Χλόην ταύτην οὔτε
ἐγέννησα οὔτε ἀνέθρεψα· ἀλλὰ ἐγέννησαν μὲν
ἄλλοι, κειμένην δὲ ἐν ἄντρῳ Νυμφῶν ἀνέτρεφεν
οἷς. εἶδον τοῦτο αὐτὸς καὶ ἰδὼν ἐθαύμασα,

¹ so E: mss ἦν   ² p (Amyot) omits

Lampis himself he endeavoured to take and bring him bound as a captive from some war; but he prevented that by flight. This undertaking happily performed, he returned with the night, and found Dionysophanes at his rest, but Daphnis' yet watching, weeping, and waiting in the walks. There he presents his Chloe to him, gives her into his hands, and tells the story of the action; then beseeches him to bear him no grudge, but take him as a servant not altogether unuseful, and not interdict him the table to make him die for want. Daphnis, seeing Chloe and having her now in his own hands, was reconciled by that service, and received him into favour; then excused himself to Chloe for his seeming to neglect her.

30. And now advising together about their intended wedding, it was, they thought, the best way still to conceal it, and to hide Chloe in some hole or other, then to acquaint his mother only with their love. But Dryas was not of that opinion. He would have the father know the whole business as it was, and himself undertakes to bring him on. In the morning betimes, with Chloe's tokens in his scrip, he goes to Dionysophanes and Clearista who were sitting in the garden. And Astylus was there present, and Daphnis himself. And silence made, the old goatherd thus begun: "Such a necessity as Lamo had, compels me now to speak those things that hitherto have bin concealed. This Chloe I neither begot nor had anything to do in her nursing up. But some others were her parents, and a sheep gave her suck in the Nymphaeum where she lay. I myself saw it done and wondered at it; wondering

θαυμάσας ἔθρεψα. μαρτυρεῖ μὲν καὶ τὸ κάλλος
(ἔοικε γὰρ οὐδὲν ἡμῖν), μαρτυρεῖ δὲ καὶ τὰ
γνωρίσματα (πλουσιώτερα γὰρ ἢ κατὰ ποιμένα).
ἴδετε ταῦτα καὶ τοὺς προσήκοντας τῇ κόρῃ
ζητήσατε, ἂν ἀξία ποτὲ Δάφνιδος φανῇ."

31. Τοῦτο οὔτε Δρύας ἀσκόπως ἔρριψεν οιτε
Διονυσοφάνης ἀμελῶς ἤκουσεν, ἀλλὰ ἰδὼν εἰς τὸν
Δάφνιν καὶ ὁρῶν αὐτὸν χλωριῶντα καὶ κρύφα
δακρύοντα ταχέως ἐφώρασε τὸν ἔρωτα· καὶ ὡς
ὑπὲρ παιδὸς ἰδίου μᾶλλον ἢ κόρης ἀλλοτρίας
δεδοικώς, διὰ πάσης ἀκριβείας ἤλεγχε τοὺς λόγους
τοῦ Δρύαντος. ἐπεὶ δὲ καὶ τὰ γνωρίσματα εἶδε
κομισθέντα, ‹τὰ› ὑποδήματα ‹τὰ› κατάχρυσα,
τὰς περισκελίδας, τὴν μίτραν, προσκαλεσάμενος
τὴν Χλόην παρεκελεύετο θαρρεῖν, ὡς ἄνδρα μὲν
ἔχουσαν ἤδη, ταχέως δὲ εὑρήσουσαν καὶ τὸν
πατέρα καὶ τὴν μητέρα. καὶ τὴν μὲν ἄρ' ἡ
Κλεαρίστη παραλαβοῦσα[1] ἐκόσμει λοιπὸν ὡς
υἱοῦ γυναῖκα, τὸν δὲ Δάφνιν ὁ Διονυσοφάνης
ἀναστήσας μόνον, ἀνέκρινεν εἰ παρθένος ἐστί·
τοῦ δὲ ὀμόσαντος μηδὲν γεγονέναι φιλήματος καὶ
ὅρκων πλεῖον, ἡσθεὶς ἐπὶ τῷ συνωμοσίῳ κατέ-
κλινεν αὐτούς.

32. Ἦν οὖν μαθεῖν οἷόν ἐστι τὸ κάλλος, ὅταν
κόσμον προσλάβῃ·[2] ἐνδυθεῖσα γὰρ ἡ Χλόη καὶ

‹τὰ› . . . ‹τὰ› Hirsch   [1] Α μὲν ηρα Κ. λαβ. : ρη μὲν
ἡ Κ. παραλαβ.   [2] ρη προσλάβηται   Uiii ἐνδῦσα

at it, took her home and brought her up. And
the excessive sweetness of her face bears me witness
to what I say; for she is nothing like to us. The
fine accoutrements she had about her make it more
apparent too; for they are richer then becomes a
shepherd's coat. Here they are; view them well,
seek out her kin, and so try whether at length she
may not be found not unworthy to marry Daphnis.''

31. These words, as they were not unadvisedly
cast in by Dryas, so neither were they heard by
Dionysophanes without regard. But casting his
eyes upon Daphnis, and seeing him look pale upon
it and his tears stealing down his face, presently
deprehended it was love. Then, as one that was
solicitous rather about his own son then another
man's daughter, he falls with all accurateness to
reprehend[1] what Dryas had said. But when he
saw the monitory ornaments, her girdle, her ankle-
bands, and her gilded shoes, he called her to him,
bid her be of good cheer, as one that now had a
husband and ere long should find her father and her
mother. So Clearista took her to her care, and
tricked her up and made her fine, as from that time
her son's wife. And Dionysophanes, taking Daphnis
aside, asked him if Chloe were a maid; and he
swearing that nothing had passed betwixt them but
only kissing, embracing, and oaths, his father was
much delighted to hear of that pretty conjuration
by which they had bound themselves to one another,
and made them sit down together to a banquet
brought in.

32. And then one might presently see what
beauty was when it had got its proper dress. For

---

[1] examine.

ἀναπλεξαμένη τὴν κόμην καὶ ἀπολούσασα τὸ
πρόσωπον, εὐμορφοτέρα τοσοῦτον ἐφάνη πᾶσιν,
ὥστε καὶ Δάφνις αὐτὴν μόλις ἐγνώρισεν· ὤμοσεν
ἄν τις καὶ ἄνευ τῶν γνωρισμάτων, ὅτι τοιαύτης
κόρης Δρύας οὐκ ἦν πατήρ. ὅμως μέντοι παρῆν
καὶ αὐτός, καὶ συνειστιᾶτο μετὰ τῆς Νάπης
συμπότας ἔχων ἐπὶ κλίνης ἰδίας[1] τὸν Λάμωνα καὶ
τὴν Μυρτάλην.

Πάλιν οὖν ταῖς ἑξῆς ἡμέραις ἐθύετο ἱερεῖα καὶ
κρατῆρες ἵσταντο· καὶ ἀνετίθει καὶ Χλόη τὰ
ἑαυτῆς, τὴν σύριγγα, τὴν πήραν, τὸ δέρμα, τοὺς
γαυλούς· ἐκέρασε δὲ καὶ τὴν πηγὴν οἴνῳ, τὴν
ἐν τῷ ἄντρῳ, ὅτι καὶ ἐτράφη παρ' αὐτῇ καὶ
ἐλούσατο πολλάκις ἐν αὐτῇ. ἐστεφάνωσε καὶ τὸν
τάφον τῆς οἰός, δείξαντος Δρύαντος. καὶ ἐσύρισέ
τι καὶ αὐτὴ τῇ ποίμνῃ· καὶ ταῖς θεαῖς συρίσασα
ηὔξατο τοὺς ἐκθέντας εὑρεῖν ἀξίους τῶν Δάφνιδος
γάμων.

33. Ἐπεὶ δὲ ἅλις ἦν τῶν κατ' ἀγρὸν[2] ἑορτῶν,
ἔδοξε βαδίζειν εἰς τὴν πόλιν, καὶ τούς τε τῆς
Χλόης πατέρας ἀναζητεῖν καὶ περὶ τὸν γάμον[3]
αὐτῶν μηκέτι βραδύνειν. ἕωθεν οὖν ἐνσκευασάμενοι
τῷ Δρύαντι μὲν ἔδωκαν ἄλλας τρισχιλίας, τῷ
Λάμωνι δὲ τὴν ἡμίσειαν μοῖραν τῶν ἀγρῶν
θερίζειν καὶ τρυγᾶν, καὶ τὰς αἶγας ἅμα τοῖς
αἰπόλοις, καὶ ζεύγη βοῶν τέτταρα, καὶ ἐσθῆτας
χειμερινάς, καὶ ἐλευθέραν[4] τὴν γυναῖκα. καὶ
μετὰ τοῦτο ἤλαυνον ἐπὶ Μυτιλήνην ἵπποις καὶ
ζεύγεσι καὶ τρυφῇ πολλῇ.

Τότε μὲν οὖν ἔλαθον τοὺς πολίτας νυκτὸς

---

[1] so Cour: mss -ᾳ   [2] so Valck: mss -ῶν   [3] Ap τῶν
γάμων prob. old var.   [4] Amyot apparently read ἐλευθερίαν

Chloe being so clothed, washed, and dressed in her hair, did so outshine to every eye her former beauty, that her own Daphnis now could scarce know her. And any man, without the faith of tokens, might now have sworn that Dryas was not the father of so fair a maid. But he was there, and Nape, and Lamo and Myrtale, feasting at a private table.

And again for some days after, upon this invention of Chloe, were immolations to the Gods, and the settings up of bowls of wine. And Chloe consecrated her trinkets, that skin she used to wear, her scrip, her pipe, her milking-pails. She mingled wine, too, with that fountain in the cave, because close by it she was nursed, and had often washed in it. The grave of her nurse, shown to her by Dryas, she adorned with many garlands; and to her flock, as Daphnis had done, played a little on her pipe. Then she prays to the Goddesses that she might find them, that exposed her, to be such as would not misbecome her marriage with Daphnis.

33. And now they had enough of feasting and holy-days in the fields, and would return to Mytilene, look out Chloe's parents there, and speedily have a wedding on't. In the morning betime when they were ready to go, to Dryas they gave other three thousand drachmas; to Lamo half of that land, to sow and mow and find him wine, and the goats together with the goatherds, four pair of oxen for the plough, winter clothes, and made his wife free. Then anon with a great pomp and a brave shew of horses and waggons, on they moved towards Mytilene.

And because it was night before they could come

DAPHNIS AND CHLOE

κατελθόντες· τῆς δὲ ἐπιούσης ὄχλος ἠθροίσθη
περὶ τὰς θύρας, ἀνδρῶν, γυναικῶν. οἱ μὲν τῷ
Διονυσοφάνει συνήδοντο παῖδα εὑρόντι, καὶ μᾶλλον
ὁρῶντες τὸ κάλλος τοῦ Δάφνιδος· αἱ δὲ τῇ Κλεα-
ρίστῃ συνέχαιρον ἅμα κομιζούσῃ καὶ παῖδα καὶ
νύμφην. ἐξέπληττε γὰρ κἀκείνας ἡ Χλόη, κάλλος
ἐκφέρουσα[1] παρευδοκιμηθῆναι μὴ δυνάμενον. ὅλη
γὰρ ἐκίττα[2] ἡ πόλις ἐπὶ τῷ μειρακίῳ καὶ τῇ
παρθένῳ, καὶ εὐδαιμόνιζον μὲν ἤδη τὸν γάμον·
ηὔχοντο δὲ καὶ τὸ γένος ἄξιον τῆς μορφῆς εὑρεθῆ-
ναι τῆς κόρης· καὶ γυναῖκες πολλαὶ τῶν μέγα[3]
πλουσίων ἠράσαντο θεοῖς αὐταὶ πιστευθῆναι
μητέρες[4] θυγατρὸς οὕτω καλῆς.

34. Ὄναρ δὲ Διονυσοφάνει μετὰ φροντίδα
πολλὴν εἰς βαθὺν ὕπνον κατενεχθέντι τοιόνδε γίνε-
ται· ἐδόκει τὰς Νύμφας δεῖσθαι τοῦ Ἔρωτος ἤδη[5]
ποτὲ αὐτοῖς κατανεῦσαι τὸν γάμον· τὸν δὲ ἐκλύ-
σαντα τὸ τοξάριον καὶ ἀποθέμενον τὴν[6] φαρέτραν
κελεῦσαι τῷ Διονυσοφάνει, πάντας τοὺς ἀρίστους
Μυτιληναίων θέμενον συμπότας, ἡνίκα ἂν τὸν
ὕστατον πλήσῃ κρατῆρα, τότε δεικνύειν ἑκάστῳ
τὰ γνωρίσματα· τὸ δὲ ἐντεῦθεν ᾄδειν τὸν ὑμέναιον.
ταῦτα ἰδὼν καὶ ἀκούσας ἕωθεν ἀνίσταται, καὶ
κελεύσας λαμπρὰν ἑστίασιν παρασκευασθῆναι τῶν
ἀπὸ γῆς, τῶν ἀπὸ θαλάττης, καὶ εἴ τι ἐν λίμναις
καὶ εἴ τι ἐν ποταμοῖς, πάντας τοὺς ἀρίστους
Μυτιληναίων ποιεῖται συμπότας.

Ὡς δὲ ἤδη νὺξ ἦν καὶ πέπληστο <ὁ> κρατὴρ

---

[1] 'displaying'   [2] pq ἐκινεῖτο   [3] A μάλα : Uiii omits
[4] pq αὐτὰς and μητέρας   [5] so Cour : mss εἰ δὴ   [6] A
omits : pq παρὰ τὴν   <ὁ> Schaef.

in, they escaped the citizens' gaping upon them. But the next day there was a throng of men and women at the door, these to give joys and rejoice with Dionysophanes who had found a son (and their joy was much augmented when they saw the excessive sweetness of the youth), those to exult with Clearista who had brought home not only a son but a bride too. For Chloe's beauty had struck the eyes of them, a beauty for its lustre beyond estimation, beyond excess by any other. In fine, the whole city was with child to see the young man and the maid, and now with loud ingeminations cried "A happy marriage, a blessed marriage." They prayed, too, the maid might find her birth as great as she was fair, and many of the richer ladies prayed the Gods they might be taken for mothers of so sweet a girl.

34. Now Dionysophanes, after many solicitous thoughts, fell into a deep sleep, and in that had this vision : He thought he saw the Nymphs petition Cupid to grant them at length a licence for the wedding ; then that Love himself, his bow unbent and his quiver laid by, commanded him to invite the whole nobility of Mytilene to a feast, and when he had set the last bowl, there to show the tokens to everyone ; and from that point commence and sing the Hymenaeus. When he had seen and heard this, up he gets as soon as day, and gave order that a splendid supper should be provided of all varieties, from the land, from the sea, from the marshes, from the rivers ; and had to his guests all the best of the Mytilenaeans.

And when night was fallen and the last bowl

ἐξ οὗ σπένδουσιν Ἑρμῇ, εἰσκομίζει τις ἐπὶ σκεύους
ἀργυροῦ [1] θεράπων τὰ γνωρίσματα καὶ περιφέρων
ἐνδέξια [2] πᾶσιν ἐδείκνυε. 35. τῶν μὲν οὖν ἄλλων
ἐγνώρισεν [3] οὐδείς· Μεγακλῆς δέ τις διὰ γῆρας
ὕστατος [4] κατακείμενος, ὡς εἶδε, γνωρίσας πάνυ
μέγα καὶ νεανικὸν ἐκβοᾷ· [5] "Τίνα ὁρῶ ταῦτα; τί
γέγονάς μοι, θυγάτριον; ἆρα καὶ σὺ ζῇς; ἢ ταῦτά
τις ἐβάστασε μόνα [6] ποιμὴν ἐντυχών; δέομαι,
Διονυσόφανες, εἰπέ μοι, πόθεν ἔχεις ἐμοῦ παιδίου
γνωρίσματα; μὴ φθονήσῃς μετὰ Δάφνιν εὑρεῖν τι
κἀμέ."

Κελεύσαντος δὲ τοῦ Διονυσοφάνους πρότερον
ἐκεῖνον λέγειν τὴν ἔκθεσιν, ὁ Μεγακλῆς οὐδὲν
ὑφελὼν τοῦ τόνου τῆς φωνῆς ἔφη· "Ἦν ὀλίγος μοι
βίος τὸ πρότερον· [7] ὃν γὰρ εἶχον, εἰς τριηραρχίας [8]
καὶ χορηγίας ἐξεδαπάνησα. ὅτε ταῦτα ἦν,
γίνεταί μοι θυγάτριον. τοῦτο τρέφειν ὀκνήσας
ἐν πενίᾳ, τούτοις τοῖς γνωρίσμασι κοσμήσας
ἐξέθηκα, εἰδὼς ὅτι πολλοὶ καὶ οὕτω σπουδάζουσι
πατέρας γενέσθαι. καὶ τὸ μὲν ἐξέκειτο ἐν ἄντρῳ
Νυμφῶν πιστευθὲν ταῖς θεαῖς· ἐμοὶ δὲ πλοῦτος
ἐπέρρει καθ' ἑκάστην ἡμέραν κληρονόμον οὐκ
ἔχοντι. οὐκέτι γοῦν οὐδὲ [9] θυγατρίου γενέσθαι

---

[1] so Hirsch : mss acc.   [2] so Brunck : perh. ἐπὶ δ. E :
mss ἐν δεξιᾷ   [3] A impf.   [4] The most honourable place
was known as πρῶτος and the least as ἔσχατος ; the former is
called ὕστατος here because the servant reaches it last ; the
ἔσχατος τόπος is for a similar reason called ὕστατος by Plato,
Symp. 177 e   [5] pq ἐβόα   [6] so Schaef : A μὲν ἃ : pq μὲν

was filled, out of which a libation is wont to be
poured to Mercury, one of the servants came in
with Chloe's trinkets upon a silver plate, and carry-
ing them about towards the right hand,[1] presented
them to every eye. 35. Of the others there was
none that knew them. Only one Megacles, who for
his age sate last,[2] when he saw them, knowing
presently what they were, cried out amain with a
youthful strong voice : " Bless me ! what is this that
I see ? What is become of thee, my little daughter ?
Art thou yet indeed alive ? or did some shepherd
find thee and carry these home without thee ? Tell
me for God's sake, Dionysophanes, how came you by
the monuments of my child ? Envy not me the
finding something after Daphnis."

But Dionysophanes bidding him first relate the
exposing of the child, he remitted nothing of his
former tone, but thus went on: "Some years ago I
had but a scanty livelihood. For I spent what I had
on the providing of plays and shews and the fur-
nishing out the public galleys. In this condition I
had a daughter born. And despairing, because of
my want, of an honourable education for her, I
exposed her with these monumental toys, knowing
that even by that way many are glad to be made
fathers. In a Nymphaeum she was laid, and left to
the trust of the resident Goddesses. After that, I
began to be rich, and grew richer every day, yet
had no heir ; nor was I afterwards so fortunate as to

[7] ρϙ τὸν πρότ. χρόνον   [8] Uiii -ίαν καὶ -ίαν   [9] ρϙ οὔτε : A
omits γοῦν οὐδὲ

---

[1] *i.e.* of the guests, the reverse of the modern custom.

[2] he sat in the most honourable place, but was reached
last.

πατὴρ ηὐτύχησα· ἀλλ' οἱ θεοὶ ὥσπερ[1] γέλωτά με
ποιούμενοι νύκτωρ ὀνείρους μοι ἐπιπέμπουσι,
δηλοῦντες ὅτι με πατέρα ποιήσει ποίμνιον."

36. Ἀνεβόησεν ὁ Διονυσοφάνης μεῖζον τοῦ
Μεγακλέους, καὶ ἀναπηδήσας εἰσάγει Χλόην πάνυ
καλῶς κεκοσμημένην, καὶ λέγει· "Τοῦτο τὸ παιδίον
ἐξέθηκας. ταύτην σοι τὴν παρθένον οἷς προνοίᾳ
θεῶν[2] ἐξέθρεψεν, ὡς αἲξ Δάφνιν ἐμοί. λαβὲ τὰ
γνωρίσματα καὶ τὴν θυγατέρα· λαβὼν δὲ ἀπόδος
Δάφνιδι νύμφην. ἀμφοτέρους ἐξεθήκαμεν, ἀμφο-
τέρους εὑρήκαμεν· ἀμφοτέρων ἐμέλησε Πανὶ καὶ
Νύμφαις καὶ Ἔρωτι." ἐπῄνει τὰ λεγόμενα ὁ
Μεγακλῆς, καὶ τὴν γυναῖκα Ῥόδην μετεπέμπετο
καὶ τὴν Χλόην ἐν τοῖς κόλποις εἶχε. καὶ ὕπνον
αὐτοῦ μένοντες εἵλοντο· Δάφνις γὰρ οὐδενὶ
διώμνυτο προήσεσθαι τὴν Χλόην, οὐδὲ αὐτῷ τῷ
πατρί.

37. Ἡμέρας δὲ γενομένης συνθέμενοι πάλιν εἰς
τὸν ἀγρὸν ἤλαυνον· ἐδεήθησαν γὰρ τοῦτο Δάφνις
καὶ Χλόη μὴ φέροντες τὴν ἐν ἄστει διατριβήν.
ἐδόκει δὲ κἀκείνοις ποιμενικούς τινας αὐτοῖς
ποιῆσαι τοὺς γάμους. ἐλθόντες οὖν παρὰ τὸν
Λάμωνα, τόν τε Δρύαντα τῷ Μεγακλεῖ προσή-
γαγον καὶ τὴν Νάπην τῇ Ῥόδῃ συνέστησαν, καὶ
τὰ πρὸς τὴν ἑορτὴν παρεσκευάζοντο λαμπρῶς.
παρέδωκε μὲν οὖν ἐπὶ[3] ταῖς Νύμφαις τὴν Χλόην
ὁ πατήρ, καὶ μετ' ἄλλων πολλῶν ἐποίησεν

---

[1] so Hirsch. (Amyot): mss ὥσπερ οἱ θεοὶ   [2] Α νυμφῶν,
but in view of νύμφην below, this is prob. a gloss   [3] Αρ
(Amyot) ἔτι prob. old var. : Uiii ἐστι

be father but to a daughter. But the Gods, as if they mocked me for what I had done, sent me a dream which signified that a sheep should make me a father."

36. Dionysophanes upon that burst out louder then Megacles, and sprung away into a near withdrawing-room, and brought in Chloe finely dressed as curiosity could do it. And in haste to Megacles "This," quoth he, "is that same daughter of thine that thou didst expose. This girl a sheep by a divine providence did nurse for thee, as a goat did my Daphnis. Take her tokens, take thy daughter; then by all means give her to Daphnis for a bride. We exposed both of them, and have now found them both. Pan, the Nymphs, and Love himself took care of both." Megacles highly approved the motion, and commanded his wife Rhode should be sent for thither, and took his sweet girl to his bosom. And that night they lay where they were; for Daphnis had sworn by all the Gods he would not let Chloe go, no, not to her own father.

37. When it was day, 'twas agreed to turn again into the fields. For Daphnis and Chloe had impetrated that, by reason of the strangeness of city conversation [1] to them. Besides, to the others too it seemed the best to make it a kind of pastoral wedding. Therefore coming to Lamo's house, to Megacles they brought Dryas, Nape to Rhode, and all things were finely disposed and furnished to the rural celebration. Then before the statues of the Nymphs her father gave Chloe to Daphnis, and with other more precious things suspended her tokens for

[1] way of life.

ἀναθήματα τὰ γνωρίσματα, καὶ Δρύαντι τὰς
λειπούσας εἰς τὰς μυρίας ἐπλήρωσεν.

38. Ὁ δὲ Διονυσοφάνης, εὐημερίας οὔσης,
αὐτοῦ πρὸ τοῦ ἄντρου στιβάδας ὑπεστόρεσεν ἐκ
χλωρᾶς φυλλάδος, καὶ πάντας τοὺς κωμήτας
κατακλίνας εἱστία πολυτελῶς. παρῆσαν δὲ
Λάμων καὶ Μυρτάλη, Δρύας καὶ Νάπη, οἱ
Δόρκωνι προσήκοντες, <Φιλητᾶς>, οἱ Φιλητᾶ
παῖδες, Χρόμις[1] καὶ Λυκαίνιον· οὐκ ἀπῆν οὐδὲ
Λάμπις, συγγνώμης ἀξιωθείς.

Ἦν οὖν, ὡς ἐν τοιοῖσδε συμπόταις, πάντα γεωρ-
γικὰ καὶ ἄγροικα· ὁ μὲν ᾖδεν οἷα ᾄδουσι θερί-
ζοντες, ὁ δὲ ἔσκωπτε τὰ ἐπὶ ληνοῖς σκώμματα.
Φιλητᾶς ἐσύρισε· Λάμπις ηὔλησε· Δρύας καὶ
Λάμων ὠρχήσαντο· Χλόη καὶ Δάφνις ἀλλήλους
κατεφίλουν. ἐνέμοντο δὲ καὶ αἱ αἶγες πλησίον,
ὥσπερ καὶ αὐταὶ κοινωνοῦσαι τῆς ἑορτῆς. τοῦτο
τοῖς μὲν ἀστικοῖς οὐ πάνυ τερπνὸν ἦν· ὁ δὲ Δάφνις
καὶ ἐκάλεσέ τινας αὐτῶν ὀνομαστὶ καὶ φυλλάδα
χλωρὰν ἔδωκε καὶ κρατήσας ἐκ τῶν κεράτων
κατεφίλησε.

39. Καὶ ταῦτα οὐ τότε μόνον, ἀλλ' ἔστε ἔζων,
τὸν πλεῖστον χρόνον ποιμενικὸν εἶχον, θεοὺς σέ-
βοντες Νύμφας καὶ Πᾶνα καὶ Ἔρωτα, ἀγέλας
δὲ προβάτων καὶ αἰγῶν πλείστας κτησάμενοι,
ἡδίστην δὲ τροφὴν νομίζοντες ὀπώραν[2] καὶ
γάλα. ἀλλὰ καὶ ἄρρεν τε[3] παιδίον <αἰγὶ>

<Φιλητᾶς> Coraes   [1] cf. 3. 15   [2] pq plur.   [3] so E:
A omits : pq μὲν   <αἰγὶ> Schaef. (Amyot)

offerings in the cave. Then in recognition of Dryas his care, they made up his number ten thousand drachmas.

38. And Dionysophanes for his share, the day being serene, open, and fair, commanded there should be beds of green leaves made up before the very cave, and there disposed the villagers to their high feasting jollity. Lamo was there and Myrtale, Dryas and Nape, Dorco's kindred and friends, Philetas and his lads, Chromis and his Lycaenium. Nor was even Lampis absent; for he was pardoned by that beauty that he had loved.

Therefore then, as usually when rural revellers are met together at a feast, nothing but georgics,‘ nothing but what was rustical was there. Here one sang like the reapers, there another prattled it and flung flirts and scoffs as in the autumn from the press. Philetas played upon his pipes, Lampis upon the hautboy. Dryas and Lamo danced to them. Daphnis and Chloe clipped and kissed. The goats too were feeding by, as themselves part of that celebrity; and that was not beyond measure pleasing to those from the city, but Daphnis calls up some of the goats by their names, and gives them boughs to browze upon from his hand, and catching them fast by the horns, took kisses thence.

39. And thus they did not only then for that day; but for the most part of their time held on still the pastoral mode, serving as their Gods the Nymphs, Cupid, and Pan, possessed of sheep and goats innumerable, and nothing for food more pleasant to them then apples and milk. Besides, they laid a son down under a goat, to take the

ὑπέθηκαν, καὶ θυγάτριον γενόμενον δεύτερον οἱὸς
ἐλκύσαι θηλὴν ἐποίησαν· καὶ ἐκάλεσαν τὸν μὲν
Φιλοποίμενα, τὴν δὲ Ἀγελαίαν.[1] οὕτως αὐτοῖς
καὶ ταῦτα συνεγήρασεν. καὶ[2] τὸ ἄντρον ἐκό-
σμησαν καὶ εἰκόνας ἀνέθεσαν, καὶ βωμὸν εἵσαντο
Ποιμένος Ἔρωτος· καὶ τῷ Πανὶ δὲ ἔδοσαν ἀντὶ
τῆς πίτυος οἰκεῖν νεών,[3] Πᾶνα Στρατιώτην ὀνο-
μάσαντες.

40. Ἀλλὰ ταῦτα μὲν ὕστερον καὶ ὠνόμασαν
καὶ ἔπραξαν. τότε δὲ νυκτὸς γενομένης πάντες
αὐτοὺς παρέπεμπον εἰς τὸν θάλαμον, οἱ μὲν συ-
ρίττοντες, οἱ δὲ αὐλοῦντες, οἱ δὲ δᾷδας μεγάλας
ἀνίσχοντες. καὶ ἐπεὶ πλησίον ἦσαν τῶν θυρῶν,
ᾖδον σκληρᾷ καὶ ἀπηνεῖ τῇ φωνῇ, καθάπερ τρι-
αίναις γῆν ἀναρρηγνύντες, οὐχ ὑμέναιον ᾄδοντες.
Δάφνις δὲ καὶ Χλόη γυμνοὶ συγκατακλιθέντες
περιέβαλλον ἀλλήλους καὶ κατεφίλουν, ἀγρυπνή-
σαντες τῆς νυκτὸς ὅσον οὐδὲ γλαῦκες. καὶ ἔδρασέ
τι Δάφνις ὧν αὐτὸν ἐπαίδευσε Λυκαίνιον, καὶ τότε
Χλόη πρῶτον ἔμαθεν ὅτι τὰ ἐπὶ τῆς ὕλης γενό-
μενα ἦν παιδίων[4] παίγνια.

ΤΕΛΟΣ ΛΟΓΓΟΥ ΠΟΙΜΕΝΙΚΩΝ ΤΩΝ ΠΕΡΙ ΔΑΦΝΙΝ
ΚΑΙ ΧΛΟΗΝ ΛΕΣΒΙΑΚΩΝ ΛΟΓΟΙ ΤΕΣΣΑΡΕΣ.

[1] so E following Amyot's emendation "Agelée" (not
Agelé) "qui signifie prenant plaisir aux troupeaux:" mss
Ἀγέλην   [2] so E: mss οὗτοι καὶ (οὗτ. added in the belief
that ταῦτα meant the children)   [3] A omits οἰκ. νεών
[4] so E, perh. an old var.: mss ποιμένων (perh. from colophon)
which Amyot either omitted or read as παιδίων   colophon:
so A, but Λόγου and λόγοι τέσσαρες

dug, and a daughter that was born after him under a sheep. Him they called Philopoemen, her they named the fair Agelaea. And so the pastoral mode grew old with them. The cave they adorned with curious work, set up statues, built an altar of Cupid the Shepherd, and to Pan a fane to dwell instead of a pine, and called him Pan Stratiotes, Pan the Soldier.

40. But this adorning of the cave, building an altar and a fane, and giving them their names, was afterwards at their opportunity. Then, when it was night, they all lead the bride and bridegroom to their chamber, some playing upon whistles and hautboys, some upon the oblique pipes, some holding great torches. And when they came near to the door, they fell to sing, and sang, with the grating harsh voices of rustics, nothing like the Hymenaeus, but as if they had bin singing at their labour with mattock and hoe. But Daphnis and Chloe lying together began to clip and kiss, sleeping no more then the birds of the night. And Daphnis now profited by Lycaenium's lesson ; and Chloe then first knew that those things that were done in the wood were only the sweet sports of children.

FINIS

PARTHENIUS
LOVE ROMANCES
POETICAL FRAGMENTS

THE ALEXANDRIAN EROTIC FRAGMENT
THE NINUS ROMANCE

EDITED AND FOR THE FIRST TIME TRANSLATED
INTO ENGLISH BY

STEPHEN GASELEE, M.A.
FELLOW AND LIBRARIAN OF MAGDALENE COLLEGE, CAMBRIDGE

INTRODUCTION

I

THE most important piece of evidence for the life
of Parthenius is the notice of him in Suidas'[1]
Lexicon: " Parthenius, the son of Heraclides and
Eudora (Hermippus[2] gives his mother's name as
Tētha) was a native of Nicaea[3] or Myrlĕa[4] : he was
an elegiac poet and also composed in other metres.
He was taken as a captive by Cinna,[5] when the

---

[1] Suidas, living in the tenth century, composed something
between a dictionary and an encyclopaedia, using many
ancient and valuable materials which have long since dis-
appeared. Justus Lipsius described him, so far as his value
to Greek scholars goes, in a happy epigram: *Pecus est
Suidas, sed pecus aurei velleris.*

[2] Of Berytus, about the third century A.D., the author of
a work περὶ τῶν ἐν παιδείᾳ διαλαμψάντων (an account of those
distinguished in education).

[3] In Bithynia, on the southern bank of the river Ascania,
famous for the Council held there which condemned
Arianism. Stephanus of Byzantium (475₂) definitely states
that Parthenius was a native of Nicaea.

[4] Originally a colony of Colophon in Hellespontine Phrygia,
afterwards annexed to Bithynia, on the southern shore of the
sinus Cianus : later called Apamea.

[5] If the name of Cinna is correct, it refers, not to any
general in the war, but to the master (perhaps the father of
the poet C. Helvius Cinna) whose slave Parthenius became.
Hillscher suggested that for Κίννα we should read Κόττα, one
of the Roman generals of the third Mithridatic war.

INTRODUCTION

Romans defeated Mithridates ; but he was spared because of his value as a teacher, and lived until the reign of Tiberius.[1] He wrote in elegiacs a poem called *Aphrodite*,[2] a *Dirge on Arete*[3] his wife, an *Encomium upon Arete* in three books, and many other works." In addition to this brief biography we have very little mention of Parthenius in Greek or Latin literature ; by far the most interesting is that quoted from Macrobius in frg. 30 below, to the effect that he was Virgil's tutor in Greek. He knew Cornelius Gallus well, as is clear from the dedicatory letter of the *Love Romances,* and Gallus was on terms of the closest intimacy with Virgil, so that there is no particular reason to doubt the statement of Macrobius, as some have done. We have a colourless allusion to him, as a writer who dealt in strange and out of the way stories and legends, in the book of Artemidorus on the interpretation of dreams ; and a rather slighting mention in Lucian,[4] who contrasts Homer's

---

[1] This reckoning gives him a suspiciously long life. Tiberius, whether he knew him personally or not, admired his writings : "he made (Suetonius *Tib.* 70) likewise Greek poems in imitation of Euphorion, Rhianus, and Parthenius : in which poets being much delighted, their writings and images he dedicated in the public libraries among the ancient and principal authors." Suetonius reflects on the bad taste of Tiberius in reckoning these Alexandrine writers as the equals of the classics.

[2] *cf. frg.* 3.

[3] *cf. frg.* 1. All three vowels are long in this name.

[4] *Quomodo historia sit conscribenda*, § 57.

directness of allusion with the elaborate and lengthy descriptions of Parthenius, Euphorion, and Callimachus.[1]

II

Parthenius, then, was known to the literary world of the ancients as one of the regular Alexandrine school of poets; rather pedantic and obscure, and treating of out-of-the-way stories and the less well known legends of mythology; and of these works of his we have fragments fairly numerous but tantalizingly small. With us, however, his claim to fame —if fame it can be called—rests not on his poetical remains, but on a single short work in prose, his *Love Romances*. This is a collection of skeleton stories, mostly belonging to fiction or mythology, some with an apocryphal claim to be historical, which were brought together to be used by Cornelius Gallus as themes for poems: they are just of the kind he would himself have employed, and in one case (No. xi = Frg. 29) he had already done so. The book has a double interest; for the study of Greek mythology—though most of the stories are so far off the beaten track that they are with

---

[1] Some have thought that the epigram of Erycius (*Anth. Pal.* vii. 377) written against Parthenius τὸν Φωκαέα, τὸν εἰς τὸν Ὅμηρον παροινήσαντα should in reality be referred to Parthenius of Nicaea: but this theory does not yet appear to me to be proved. *cf. frg.* 7, p. 352.

INTRODUCTION

difficulty brought into line with the regular mytho-
logical writers—and for the development of the love-
story (mostly love unfortunate) in Greek Romance.

III

The Love Romances exist only in one manuscript,
the famous Palatinus 398 ; a facsimile of a page of
it is given at the end of Martini's edition ; in his
critical notes will be found all the necessary records
of manuscript error and perversity, and the best of
the conjectures of learned men to remedy the same.
The text of the present edition does not profess to
follow closely the opinion of any one editor ; but I
have been to some extent persuaded by the argu-
ments of Mayer-G'Schrey [1] that we must not expect
from Parthenius the observance of the rigid standards
of classical Greek, and some grammatical usages
will be found left in the text which would horrify a
schoolmaster looking over a boy's Greek Prose. In
the fragments I have followed the numeration of
Martini, whose collection is the fullest and most
satisfactory. [2]

[1] *Parthenii Nicaeensis quale in fabulis amatoriis dicendi
genus sit*, Heidelberg, 1898.
[2] I have taken no account of the indication of Vossius and
Joseph Scaliger that Parthenius wrote a Μυττωτός or Μυσωτός
which was the Greek original of Virgil's *Moretum*. Evidence
is lacking—and we must remember Virgil's nickname of
Parthenias.

INTRODUCTION

IV

Editio princeps : Basle, Froben, 1531, ed. by Janus Cornarius, a physician of Zwiccau.

Among later editions of importance, mention should be made of those of Thomas Gale (*Historiae poeticae scriptores antiqui*), Paris, 1675 : Legrand and Heyne, Göttingen, 1798 : Passow (*Corpus scriptorum eroticorum Graecorum*), Leipzig, 1824 : Meineke (*Analecta Alexandrina*), Berlin, 1843 (of great importance for the fragments) : Hirschig (*Erotici scriptores*), Paris, Didot, 1856 (still in some ways the most convenient edition) : Hercher (*Erotici Scriptores Graeci*), Leipzig, 1858 : and Martini, Leipzig, Teubner, 1902. The last-named is the standard and best edition : anyone wishing to work on the legends will find full clues to the places where parallels may be found, and references to the work of various scholars on the subjects of them. There have been translations of Parthenius into French and German, but not previously into English.

ΠΑΡΘΕΝΙΟΥ ΠΕΡΙ ΕΡΩΤΙΚΩΝ
ΠΑΘΗΜΑΤΩΝ

ΠΑΡΘΕΝΙΟΣ ΚΟΡΝΗΛΙΩ ΓΑΛΛΩ ΧΑΙΡΕΙΝ

1. Μάλιστά σοι δοκῶν ἁρμόττειν, Κορνήλιε
Γάλλε, τὴν ἄθροισιν τῶν ἐρωτικῶν παθημάτων,
ἀναλεξάμενος ὡς ὅτι μάλιστα ἐν βραχυτάτοις
ἀπέσταλκα. τὰ γὰρ παρά τισι τῶν ποιητῶν
κείμενα τούτων, μὴ αὐτοτελῶς λελεγμένα,[1] κατα-
νοήσεις ἐκ τῶνδε τὰ πλεῖστα· 2. αὐτῷ τέ σοι
παρέσται εἰς ἔπη καὶ ἐλεγείας ἀνάγειν τὰ μάλιστα
ἐξ αὐτῶν ἁρμόδια. μηδὲ[2] διὰ τὸ μὴ παρεῖναι
τὸ περιττὸν αὐτοῖς, ὃ δὴ σὺ μετέρχῃ, χεῖρον περὶ
αὐτῶν ἐννοηθῇς· οἱονεὶ γὰρ ὑπομνηματίων τρόπον
αὐτὰ συνελεξάμεθα, καί σοι νυνὶ τὴν χρῆσιν
ὁμοίαν, ὡς ἔοικε, παρέξεται.

---

[1] MS. λελεγμένων : corrected by Lehrs.
[2] μηδέ is not in the MS., but was inserted by Lehrs.

THE LOVE ROMANCES OF
PARTHENIUS

(*Preface*)

Parthenius to Cornelius Gallus, Greeting

1. I THOUGHT, my dear Cornelius Gallus, that
to you above all men there would be something
particularly agreeable in this collection of romances
of love, and I have put them together and set
them out in the shortest possible form. The
stories, as they are found in the poets who treat
this class of subject, are not usually related with
sufficient simplicity ; I hope that, in the way I
have treated them, you will have the summary of
each : (2) and you will thus have at hand a storehouse
from which to draw material, as may seem best to
you, for either epic or elegiac verse. I am sure
that you will not think the worse of them because they
have not that polish of which you are yourself such
a master : I have only put them together as aids
to memory, and that is the sole purpose for which
they are meant to be of service to you.

THE LOVE ROMANCES OF PARTHENIUS

Α΄

ΠΕΡΙ ΛΥΡΚΟΥ

Ἡ ἱστορία παρὰ Νικαινέτῳ ἐν τῷ Λύρκῳ καὶ Ἀπολλωνίῳ Ῥοδίῳ Καύνῳ

1. Ἀρπασθείσης Ἰοῦς τῆς Ἀργείας ὑπὸ λῃστῶν, ὁ πατὴρ αὐτῆς Ἴναχος μαστῆράς τε καὶ ἐρευνητὰς ἄλλους καθῆκεν, ἐν δὲ αὐτοῖς Λύρκον τὸν Φορωνέως, ὃς μάλα πολλὴν γῆν ἐπιδραμὼν καὶ πολλὴν θάλασσαν περαιωθείς, τέλος, ὡς οὐχ εὕρισκεν, ἀπεῖπε τῷ καμάτῳ· καὶ εἰς μὲν Ἄργος, δεδοικὼς τὸν Ἴναχον, οὐ μάλα τι κατῄει, ἀφικόμενος δὲ εἰς Καῦνον πρὸς Αἰγιαλὸν γαμεῖ αὐτοῦ τὴν θυγατέρα Εἰλεβίην· 2. φασὶ[1] γὰρ τὴν κόρην ἰδοῦσαν τὸν Λύρκον εἰς ἔρωτα ἐλθεῖν καὶ πολλὰ τοῦ πατρὸς δεηθῆναι κατασχεῖν αὐτόν· ὁ δὲ τῆς τε βασιλείας μοῖραν οὐκ ἐλαχίστην ἀποδασάμενος καὶ τῶν λοιπῶν ὑπαργμάτων γαμβρὸν εἶχε. χρόνου δὲ πολλοῦ προϊόντος, ὡς τῷ Λύρκῳ παῖδες οὐκ ἐγίγνοντο, ἦλθεν εἰς Διδυμέως, χρησόμενος περὶ γονῆς τέκνων· καὶ αὐτῷ θεσπίζει ὁ θεὸς παῖδας φύσειν, ᾗ ἂν ἐκ τοῦ ναοῦ χωρισθεὶς πρώτῃ

---

[1] MS. ἔφασαν. Rohde saw that a present was necessary.

[1] A little-known Alexandrine poet, whose works are not now extant.

[2] No longer extant. In addition to the *Argonautica*, which we possess, Apollonius Rhodius wrote several epics

THE STORY OF LYRCUS

I

THE STORY OF LYRCUS

From the Lyrcus *of Nicaenetus* [1] *and the* Caunus [2] *of*
Apollonius Rhodius

1. WHEN Io, daughter of the King of Argos, had
been captured by brigands, her father Inachus sent
several men to search for her and attempt to find
her. One of these was Lyrcus the son of Phoroneus,
who covered a vast deal of land and sea without
finding the girl, and finally renounced the toilsome
quest : but he was too much afraid of Inachus to
return to Argos, and went instead to Caunus, where
he married Hilebia, daughter of King Aegialus, (2)
who, as the story goes, had fallen in love with Lyrcus
as soon as she saw him, and by her instant prayers
had persuaded her father to betroth her to him ;
he gave him as dowry a good share of the realm
and of the rest of the regal attributes, and accepted
him as his son-in-law. So a considerable period
of time passed, but Lyrcus and his wife had no
children : and accordingly he made a journey to
the oracle at Didyma,[3] to ask how he might
obtain offspring ; and the answer was, that he
would beget a child upon the first woman with
whom he should have to do after leaving the

describing the history of various towns and countries in
which he lived at different times. The same work is
called the Καύνου κτίσις in the title of No. XI.
   [3] Lit. " to the temple of Apollo at Didyma," an old town
south of Miletus, famous for its oracle.

συγγένηται· 3. ὁ δὲ μάλα γεγηθὼς ἠπείγετο
πρὸς τὴν γυναῖκα πειθόμενος κατὰ νοῦν αὐτῷ
χωρήσειν τὸ μαντεῖον. ἐπεὶ δὲ πλέων ἀφίκετο ἐς
Βύβαστον πρὸς Στάφυλον τὸν Διονύσου, μάλα
φιλοφρόνως ἐκεῖνος αὐτὸν ὑποδεχόμενος εἰς πολὺν
οἶνον προετρέψατο, καὶ ἐπειδὴ πολλῇ μέθῃ παρ-
εῖτο, συγκατέκλινεν αὐτῷ Ἡμιθέαν τὴν θυγατέρα.
4. ταῦτα δὲ ἐποίει προπεπυσμένος τὸ τοῦ χρη-
στηρίου καὶ βουλόμενος ἐκ ταύτης αὐτῷ παῖδας
γενέσθαι. δι' ἔριδος μέντοι ἐγένοντο Ῥοιώ τε καὶ
Ἡμιθέα αἱ τοῦ Σταφύλου, τίς αὐτῶν μιχθείη
τῷ ξένῳ· τοσοῦτος ἀμφοτέρας κατέσχε πόθος.
5. Λύρκος δὲ ἐπιγνοὺς τῇ ὑστεραίᾳ οἷα ἐδεδράκει,
τὴν Ἡμιθέαν ὁρῶν συγκατακεκλιμένην, ἐδυσφόρει
τε καὶ πολλὰ κατεμέμφετο τὸν Στάφυλον, ὡς
ἀπατεῶνα γενόμενος αὐτοῦ· ὕστερον δὲ μηδὲν
ἔχων ὅ τι ποιῇ, περιελόμενος τὴν ζώνην δίδωσι τῇ
κόρῃ κελεύων ἡβήσαντι τῷ παιδὶ φυλάττειν, ὅπως
ἔχῃ γνώρισμα, ὁπότ' ἂν ἀφίκοιτο πρὸς τὸν πατέρα
αὐτοῦ εἰς Καῦνον, καὶ ἐξέπλευσεν. 6. Αἰγιαλὸς
δὲ ὡς ᾔσθετο τά τε κατὰ τὸ χρηστήριον καὶ τὴν
Ἡμιθέαν, ἤλαυνε τῆς γῆς αὐτόν. ἔνθα δὴ μάχη
συνεχὴς ἦν τοῖς τε τὰ Λύρκου προσιεμένοις καὶ
τοῖς τὰ Αἰγιαλοῦ φρονοῦσι· μάλιστα δὲ συνεργὸς
ἐγίνετο Εἰλεβίη, οὐ γὰρ ἀπεῖπεν τὸν Λύρκον.
μετὰ δὲ ταῦτα ἀνδρωθεὶς ὁ ἐξ Ἡμιθέας καὶ Λύρκου,

shrine.   3. At this he was mightily pleased, and
began to hasten on his homeward journey back to
his wife, sure that the prediction was going to be
fulfilled according to his wish; but on his voyage,
when he arrived at Bybastus,[1] he was entertained
by Staphylus, the son of Dionysus, who received him
in the most friendly manner and enticed him to much
drinking of wine, and then, when his senses were
dulled by drunkenness, united him with his own
daughter Hemithea, having had previous intimation of
what the sentence of the oracle had been, and desiring
to have descendants born of her: but actually a bitter
strife arose between Rhoeo and Hemithea, the two
daughters of Staphylus, as to which should have
the guest, for a great desire for him had arisen in
the breasts of both of them.   5. On the next
morning Lyrcus discovered the trap that his host
had laid for him, when he saw Hemithea by his side:
he was exceedingly angry, and upbraided Staphylus
violently for his treacherous conduct; but finally,
seeing that there was nothing to be done, he took
off his belt and gave it to the girl, bidding her to
keep it until their future offspring had come to man's
estate, so that he might possess a token by which he
might be recognised, if he should ever come to his
father at Caunus: and so he sailed away home.
6. Aegialus, however, when he heard the whole story
about the oracle and about Hemithea, banished him
from his country; and there was then a war of
great length between the partisans of Lyrcus and
those of Aegialus: Hilebia was on the side of the
former, for she refused to repudiate her husband.
In after years the son of Lyrcus and Hemithea,

---

[1] Also called Bubasus, an old town in Caria.

Βασίλος αὐτῷ ὄνομα, ἦλθεν εἰς τὴν Καυνίαν, καὶ
αὐτὸν γνωρίσας ὁ Λύρκος ἤδη γηραιὸς ὢν ἡγεμόνα
καθίστησι τῶν σφετέρων λαῶν.

Β'

ΠΕΡΙ ΠΟΛΥΜΗΛΗΣ

Ἱστορεῖ Φιλητᾶς Ἑρμῇ

1. Ὀδυσσεὺς ἀλώμενος περὶ Σικελίαν καὶ τὴν
Τυρρηνῶν καὶ τὴν Σικελῶν θάλασσαν, ἀφίκετο
πρὸς Αἴολον εἰς Μελιγουνίδα νῆσον, ὃς αὐτὸν
κατὰ κλέος σοφίας τεθηπὼς ἐν πολλῇ φροντίδι
εἶχε· τὰ περὶ Τροίας ἅλωσιν καὶ ὃν τρόπον
αὐτοῖς ἐσκεδάσθησαν αἱ νῆες κομιζομένοις ἀπὸ
τῆς Ἰλίου διεπυνθάνετο, ξενίζων τε αὐτὸν πολὺν
χρόνον διῆγε. 2. τῷ δὲ ἄρα καὶ αὐτῷ ἦν ἡ μονὴ
ἡδομένῳ·[1] Πολυμήλη γὰρ τῶν Αἰολιδῶν τις
ἐρασθεῖσα αὐτοῦ κρύφα συνῆν. ὡς δὲ τοὺς ἀνέ-
μους ἐγκεκλεισμένους παραλαβὼν ἀπέπλευσεν, ἡ
κόρη φωρᾶταί τινα τῶν Τρωικῶν λαφύρων ἔχουσα
καὶ τούτοις μετὰ πολλῶν δακρύων ἀλινδουμένη.
3. ἔνθα ὁ Αἴολος τὸν μὲν Ὀδυσσέα καίπερ οὐ
παρόντα ἐκάκισεν, τὴν δὲ Πολυμήλην ἐν νῷ
ἔσχε τίσασθαι. ἔτυχε δὲ αὐτῆς ἠρασμένος ὁ
ἀδελφὸς Διώρης, ὃς αὐτὴν παραιτεῖταί τε καὶ
πείθει τὸν πατέρα αὐτῷ συνοικίσαι.

---

[1] MS. ἡδομένη : corrected by Leopardus.

whose name was Basilus, came, when he was a grown man, to the Caunian land; and Lyrcus, now an old man, recognized him as his son, and made him ruler over his peoples.

II

THE STORY OF POLYMELA

From the Hermes *of Philetas.*[1]

1. WHILE Ulysses was on his wanderings round about Sicily, in the Etruscan and Sicilian seas, he arrived at the island of Meligunis, where King Aeolus made much of him because of the great admiration he had for him by reason of his famous wisdom: he inquired of him about the capture of Troy and how the ships of the returning heroes were scattered, and he entertained him well and kept him with him for a long time. 2. Now, as it fell out, this stay was most agreeable to Ulysses, for he had fallen in love with Polymela, one of Aeolus's daughters, and was engaged in a secret intrigue with her. But after Ulysses had gone off with the winds shut up in a bag, the girl was found jealously guarding some stuffs from among the Trojan spoils which he had given her, and rolling among them with bitter tears. Aeolus reviled Ulysses bitterly although he was away, and had the intention of exacting vengeance upon Polymela; however, her brother Diores was in love with her, and both begged her off her punishment and persuaded his father to give her to him as his wife.[2]

---

[1] An elegiac poet of Cos, a little later than Callimachus. We do not now possess his works.

See *Odyssey* x. 7. Aeolus had six sons and six daughters, all of whom he married to each other.

Iᵛ

ΠΕΡΙ ΕΥΙΠΠΗΣ

Ἱστορεῖ Σοφοκλῆς Εὐρυάλῳ

1. Οὐ μόνον δὲ Ὀδυσσεὺς περὶ Αἴολον ἐξή-
μαρτεν, ἀλλὰ καὶ μετὰ τὴν ἄλην, ὡς τοὺς μνηστῆ-
ρας ἐφόνευσεν, εἰς Ἤπειρον ἐλθὼν χρηστηρίων
τινῶν ἕνεκα, τὴν Τυρίμμα θυγατέρα ἔφθειρεν
Εὐίππην, ὃς αὐτὸν οἰκείως τε ὑπεδέξατο καὶ
μετὰ πάσης προθυμίας ἐξένιζε· παῖς δὲ αὐτῷ
γίνεται ἐκ ταύτης Εὐρύαλος. 2. τοῦτον ἡ μήτηρ,
ἐπεὶ εἰς ἥβην ἦλθεν, ἀποπέμπεται εἰς Ἰθάκην,
συμβόλαιά τινα δοῦσα ἐν δέλτῳ κατεσφραγισμένα.
τοῦ δὲ Ὀδυσσέως κατὰ τύχην τότε μὴ παρόντος,
Πηνελόπη καταμαθοῦσα ταῦτα καὶ ἄλλως δὲ
προπεπυσμένη τὸν τῆς Εὐίππης ἔρωτα, πείθει
τὸν Ὀδυσσέα παραγενόμενον, πρὶν ἢ γνῶναί τι
τούτων ὡς ἔχει, κατακτεῖναι τὸν Εὐρύαλον ὡς
ἐπιβουλεύοντα αὐτῷ. 3. καὶ Ὀδυσσεὺς μὲν διὰ
τὸ μὴ ἐγκρατὴς φῦναι μηδὲ ἄλλως ἐπιεικής,
αὐτόχειρ τοῦ παιδὸς ἐγένετο. καὶ οὐ μετὰ πολὺν
χρόνον ἢ τόδε ἀπειργάσθαι πρὸς τῆς αὐτὸς αὐτοῦ
γενεᾶς τρωθεὶς ἀκάνθῃ θαλασσίας τρυγόνος ἐτε-
λεύτησεν.

THE STORY OF EVIPPE

III

THE STORY OF EVIPPE

From the Euryalus [1] *of Sophocles*

1. AEOLUS was not the only one of his hosts to whom Ulysses did wrong : but even after his wanderings were over and he had slain Penelope's wooers, he went to Epirus to consult an oracle,[2] and there seduced Evippe, the daughter of Tyrimmas, who had received him kindly and was entertaining him with great cordiality ; the fruit of this union was Euryalus. 2. When he came to man's estate, his mother sent him to Ithaca, first giving him certain tokens, by which his father would recognise him, sealed up in a tablet. Ulysses happened to be from home, and Penelope, having learned the whole story (she had previously been aware of his love for Evippe), persuaded him, before he knew the facts of the case, to kill Euryalus, on the pretence that he was engaged in a plot against him. 3. So Ulysses, as a punishment for his incontinence and general lack of moderation, became the murderer of his own son ; and not very long after this met his end after being wounded by his own offspring [3] with a sea-fish's [4] prickle.

---

[1] No longer extant.
[2] Just possibly " by the command of an oracle."
[3] Telegonus.
[4] According to the dictionaries, a kind of roach with a spike in its tail.

THE LOVE ROMANCES OF PARTHENIUS

Δ΄

ΠΕΡΙ ΟΙΝΩΝΗΣ

Ἱστορεῖ Νίκανδρος ἐν τῷ περὶ ποιητῶν καὶ Κεφάλων ὁ
Γεργίθιος ἐν Τρωϊκοῖς

1. Ἀλέξανδρος ὁ Πριάμου βουκολῶν κατὰ τὴν
Ἴδην ἠράσθη τῆς Κεβρῆνος θυγατρὸς Οἰνώνης·
λέγεται δὲ ταύτην ἔκ του θεῶν κατεχομένην
θεσπίζειν περὶ τῶν μελλόντων, καὶ ἄλλως δὲ
ἐπὶ συνέσει φρενῶν ἐπὶ μέγα διαβεβοῆσθαι.   2.
ὁ οὖν Ἀλέξανδρος αὐτὴν ἀγαγόμενος παρὰ τοῦ
πατρὸς εἰς τὴν Ἴδην, ὅπου αὐτῷ οἱ σταθμοὶ ἦσαν,
εἶχε γυναῖκα, καὶ αὐτῇ φιλοφρονούμενος ὤμνυε[1]
μηδαμὰ προλείψειν, ἐν περισσοτέρᾳ τε τιμῇ ἄξειν·
3. ἡ δὲ συνιέναι μὲν ἔφασκεν εἰς τὸ παρὸν ὡς
δὴ πάνυ αὐτῆς ἐρῷη· χρόνον μέντοι τινὰ γενή-
σεσθαι, ἐν ᾧ ἀπαλλάξας αὐτὴν εἰς τὴν Εὐρώπην
περαιωθήσεται, κἀκεῖ πτοηθεὶς ἐπὶ γυναικὶ ξένῃ
πόλεμον ἐπάξεται τοῖς οἰκείοις· 4. ἐξηγεῖτο δέ,
ὡς δεῖ αὐτὸν ἐν τῷ πολέμῳ τρωθῆναι, καὶ ὅτι
οὐδεὶς αὐτὸν οἷός τε ἔσται ὑγιῆ ποιῆσαι ἢ αὐτή·
ἑκάστοτε δὲ ἐπιλεγομένης αὐτῆς, ἐκεῖνος οὐκ εἴα
μεμνῆσθαι.

Χρόνου δὲ προϊόντος, ἐπειδὴ Ἑλένην ἔγημεν,
ἡ μὲν Οἰνώνη μεμφομένη τῶν πραχθέντων τὸν
Ἀλέξανδρον εἰς Κεβρῆνα, ὅθενπερ ἦν γένος,

[1] A word has clearly dropped out of the text.   I insert
ὤμνυε, suggested by Zangoiannes after Cobet.

[1] A poet of Colophon in the second century B.C.
[2] Also called Cephalion (Athenaeus 393 D) of Gergitha or

THE STORY OF OENONE

IV

THE STORY OF OENONE

From the Book *of Poets of Nicander* [1] *and the* Trojan
History *of Cephalon* [2] *of Gergitha*

1. WHEN Alexander,[3] Priam's son, was tending his
flocks on Mount Ida, he fell in love with Oenone the
daughter of Cebren [4] : and the story is that she was
possessed by some divinity and foretold the future, and
generally obtained great renown for her understanding
and wisdom.   2. Alexander took her away from her
father to Ida, where his pasturage was, and lived with
her there as his wife, and he was so much in love with
her that he would swear to her that he would never
desert her, but would rather advance her to the
greatest honour.   3. She however said that she
could tell that for the moment indeed he was wholly
in love with her, but that the time would come when
he would cross over to Europe, and would there, by
his infatuation for a foreign woman, bring the horrors
of war upon his kindred.   4. She also foretold that
he must be wounded in the war, and that there
would be nobody else, except herself, who would be
able to cure him : but he used always to stop her,
every time that she made mention of these matters.

Time went on, and Alexander took Helen to wife :
Oenone took his conduct exceedingly ill, and re-
turned to Cebren, the author of her days : then,

Gergis. For further particulars see Pauly-Wissowa, *s.v.*
Hegesianax. Neither of these works is now extant.
    [3] More usually called Paris.
    [4] A river-god of the Troad.

267

THE LOVE ROMANCES OF PARTHENIUS

ἀπεχώρησεν· ὁ δέ, παρήκοντος ἤδη τοῦ πολέμου,
διατοξευόμενος Φιλοκτήτῃ τιτρώσκεται.   5. ἐν
νῷ δὲ λαβὼν τὸ τῆς Οἰνώνης ἔπος, ὅτε ἔφατο
αὐτὸν πρὸς αὑτῆς μόνης οἷόν τε εἶναι ἰαθῆναι,
κήρυκα πέμπει δεησόμενον, ὅπως ἐπειχθεῖσα
ἀκέσηταί τε αὐτὸν καὶ τῶν παροιχομένων λήθην
ποιήσηται, ἅτε δὴ κατὰ θεῶν βούλησίν γε
ἀφικομένων·[1] 6. ἡ δὲ αὐθαδέστερον ἀπεκρίνατο
ὡς χρὴ παρ' Ἑλένην αὐτὸν ἰέναι, κἀκείνης δεῖ-
σθαι· αὐτὴ δὲ μάλιστα ἠπείγετο ἔνθα δὴ ἐπέ-
πυστο κεῖσθαι αὐτόν. τοῦ δὲ κήρυκος τὰ λεχ-
θέντα παρὰ τῆς Οἰνώνης θᾶττον ἀπαγγείλαντος,
ἀθυμήσας ὁ Ἀλέξανδρος ἐξέπνευσεν· 7. Οἰνώνη
δέ, ἐπεὶ νέκυν ἤδη κατὰ γῆς κείμενον ἐλθοῦσα
εἶδεν, ἀνῴμωξέ τε καὶ πολλὰ κατολοφυραμένη
διεχρήσατο ἑαυτήν.

Ε΄

ΠΕΡΙ ΛΕΥΚΙΠΠΟΥ

Ἱστορεῖ Ἑρμησιάναξ Λεοντίῳ

1. Λεύκιππος δέ, Ξανθίου παῖς, γένος τῶν ἀπὸ
Βελλεροφόντου, διαφέρων ἰσχύϊ μάλιστα τῶν
καθ' ἑαυτὸν ἤσκει τὰ πολεμικά. διὸ πολὺς ἦν
λόγος περὶ αὐτοῦ παρά τε Λυκίοις καὶ τοῖς
προσεχέσι τούτοις, ἅτε δὴ ἀγομένοις καὶ πᾶν
ὁτιοῦν δυσχερὲς πάσχουσιν. 2. οὗτος κατὰ
μῆνιν Ἀφροδίτης εἰς ἔρωτα ἀφικόμενος τῆς

[1] So Legrand, for the MS. ἀφικόμενον.

[1] For what may be regarded as a continuation of this story
see No. XXXIV.

when the war came on, Alexander was badly wounded
by an arrow from the bow of Philoctetes. 5. He then
remembered Oenone's words, how he could be cured
by her alone, and he sent a messenger to her to ask
her to hasten to him and heal him, and to forget all
the past, on the ground that it had all happened
through the will of the gods. 6. She returned him
a haughty answer, telling him he had better go to
Helen and ask *her*; but all the same she started off
as fast as she might to the place where she had been
told he was lying sick. However, the messenger
reached Alexander first, and told him Oenone's
reply, and upon this he gave up all hope and
breathed his last : (7) and Oenone, when she arrived
and found him lying on the ground already dead,
raised a great cry and, after long and bitter mourning,
put an end to herself.[1]

V

THE STORY OF LEUCIPPUS

From the Leontium *of* Hermesianax [2]

1. Now Leucippus the son of Xanthius, a de-
scendant of Bellerophon, far outshone his contem-
poraries in strength and warlike valour. Conse-
quently he was only too well known among the
Lycians and their neighbours, who were con-
stantly being plundered and suffering all kinds
of ill treatment at his hands. 2. Through the
wrath of Aphrodite he fell in love with his own

---

[2] An elegiac poet of Colophon, a younger contemporary of
Philetas. We possess little of his works except a single long
extract given by Athenaeus 597–599.

THE LOVE ROMANCES OF PARTHENIUS

ἀδελφῆς, τέως μὲν ἐκαρτέρει, οἰόμενος ῥᾶστα
ἀπαλλάξασθαι τῆς νόσου· ἐπεὶ μέντοι χρόνου
διαγενομένου οὐδὲ ἐπ' ὀλίγον ἐλώφα τὸ πάθος,
ἀνακοινοῦται τῇ μητρὶ καὶ πολλὰ καθικέτευε,
μὴ περιιδεῖν αὐτὸν ἀπολλύμενον· εἰ γὰρ αὐτῷ
μὴ συνεργήσειεν, ἀποσφάξειν αὐτὸν ἠπείλει. τῆς
δὲ παραχρῆμα τὴν ἐπιθυμίαν φαμένης τελευτή-
σειν,[1] ῥᾴων ἤδη γέγονεν· 3. ἀνακαλεσαμένη δὲ
τὴν κόρην συγκατακλίνει τἀδελφῷ, κἀκ τούτου
συνῆσαν οὐ μάλα τινὰ δεδοικότες, ἕως τις ἐξαγ-
γέλλει τῷ κατηγγυημένῳ τὴν κόρην μνηστῆρι. ὁ
δὲ τόν τε αὑτοῦ πατέρα παραλαβὼν καί τινας τῶν
προσηκόντων, πρόσεισι τῷ Ξανθίῳ καὶ τὴν
πρᾶξιν καταμηνύει, μὴ δηλῶν τοὔνομα τοῦ Λευ-
κίππου. 4. Ξάνθιος δὲ δυσφορῶν ἐπὶ τοῖς προσηγ-
γελμένοις πολλὴν σπουδὴν ἐτίθετο φωρᾶσαι τὸν
φθορέα, καὶ διεκελεύσατο τῷ μηνύτῃ, ὁπότε ἴδοι
συνόντας, αὐτῷ δηλῶσαι· τοῦ δὲ ἑτοίμως ὑπακού-
σαντος καὶ αὐτίκα τὸν πρεσβύτην ἐπαγομένου τῷ
θαλάμῳ, ἡ παῖς, αἰφνιδίου ψόφου γενηθέντος,
ἵετο διὰ θυρῶν, οἰομένη λήσεσθαι τὸν ἐπιόντα·
καὶ αὐτὴν ὁ πατὴρ ὑπολαβὼν εἶναι τὸν φθορέα
πατάξας μαχαίρᾳ καταβάλλει. 5. τῆς δὲ περιω-
δύνου γενομένης καὶ ἀνακραγούσης, ὁ Λεύκιππος
ἐπαμύνων αὐτῇ καὶ διὰ τὸ ἐκπεπλῆχθαι μὴ προϊ-
δόμενος ὅστις ἦν, κατακτείνει τὸν πατέρα. δι' ἣν
αἰτίαν ἀπολιπὼν τὴν οἰκίαν Θετταλοῖς τοῖς[2]
συμβεβηκόσιν εἰς Κρήτην ἡγήσατο, κἀκεῖθεν

[1] The MS. has τελεύτειν, and Martini's correction τελευτή-
σειν seems the simplest : Legrand suggested τελέσειν.
[2] MS. ἐπὶ τοῖς : the omission was suggested by Rohde.
A copyist might have supposed that the dative after ἡγέομαι
needed a preposition, which then fell into the wrong place.

sister : at first he held out, thinking that he would easily be rid of his trouble ; but when time went on and his passion did not abate at all, he told his mother of it, and implored her earnestly not to stand by and see him perish ; for he threatened that, if she would not help him, he would kill himself. She promised immediately that she would help him to the fulfilment of his desires, and he was at once much relieved : (3) she summoned the maiden to her presence and united her to her brother, and they consorted thenceforward without fear of anybody, until someone informed the girl's intended spouse, who was indeed already betrothed to her. But he, taking with him his father and certain of his kinsfolk, went to Xanthius and informed him of the matter, concealing the name of Leucippus. 4. Xanthius was greatly troubled at the news, and exerted all his powers to catch his daughter's seducer, and straitly charged the informer to let him know directly he saw the guilty pair together. The informer gladly obeyed these instructions, and had actually led the father to her chamber, when the girl jumped up at the sudden noise they made, and tried to escape by the door, hoping so to avoid being caught by whoever was coming : her father, thinking that she was the seducer, struck her with his dagger and brought her to the ground. 5. She cried out, being in great pain ; Leucippus ran to her rescue, and, in the confusion of the moment not recognising his adversary, gave his father his death-blow. For this crime he had to leave his home : he put himself at the head of a party of Thessalians who had united to invade Crete, and after being driven

ἐξελαθεὶς ὑπὸ τῶν προσοίκων εἰς τὴν Ἐφεσίαν
ἀφίκετο, ἔνθα χωρίον ᾤκησε τὸ Κρητιναῖον
ἐπικληθέν.   6. τοῦ δὲ Λευκίππου τούτου λέγεται
τὴν Μανδρολύτου θυγατέρα Λευκοφρύην ἐρασθεῖ-
σαν προδοῦναι τὴν πόλιν τοῖς πολεμίοις, ὧν
ἐτύγχανεν ἡγούμενος ὁ Λεύκιππος, ἑλομένων αὐτὸν
κατὰ θεοπρόπιον τῶν δεκατευθέντων ἐκ Φερῶν ὑπ'
Ἀδμήτου.[1]

ϛ′

ΠΕΡΙ ΠΑΛΛΗΝΗΣ

Ἱστορεῖ Θεαγένης[2] καὶ Ἡγήσιππος ἐν Παλληνιακοῖς

1. Λέγεται καὶ Σίθωνα, τὸν Ὀδομάντων βασι-
λέα, γεννῆσαι θυγατέρα Παλλήνην, καλήν τε
καὶ ἐπίχαριν, καὶ διὰ τοῦτο ἐπὶ πλεῖστον χωρῆ-
σαι κλέος αὐτῆς, φοιτᾶν τε μνηστῆρας οὐ μόνον
ἀπ' αὐτῆς Θρᾴκης, ἀλλὰ καὶ ἔτι πρόσωθέν τινας,
ἀπό τε Ἰλλυρίδος καὶ[3] τῶν ἐπὶ Τανάϊδος
ποταμοῦ κατῳκημένων·   2. τὸν δὲ Σίθωνα πρῶτον
μὲν κελεύειν τοὺς ἀφικνουμένους μνηστῆρας πρὸς
μάχην ἰέναι τὴν κόρην ἔχοντα, εἰ δὲ ἥττων φανείη,
τεθνάναι, τούτῳ τε τῷ τρόπῳ πάνυ συχνοὺς
ἀνῃρήκει.   3. μετὰ δέ, ὡς αὐτόν τε ἡ πλείων

---

[1] The events of the last part of this story are referred to
in two inscriptions published by O. Kern, *Die Gründungs-
geschichte von Magnesia am Maiandros*, p. 7 *sqq.* They are
too long to set out here, but are reprinted in the preface to
Sakolowski's edition of Parthenius.

[2] MS. Διογένης. The correction is made from Stephanus
of Byzantium.

[3] καί is not in the MS., but was supplied by Cornarius.

thence by the inhabitants of the island, repaired to the country near Ephesus, where he colonised a tract of land which gained the name of Cretinaeum. 6. It is further told of Leucippus that, by the advice of an oracle, he was chosen as leader by a colony of one in ten [1] sent out from Pherae by Admetus,[2] and that, when he was besieging a city, Leucophrye the daughter of Mandrolytus fell in love with him, and betrayed the town to her father's enemies.

VI

The Story of Pallene

From Theagenes [3] and the Palleniaca *of Hegesippus* [4]

1. THE story is told that Pallene was the daughter of Sithon, king of the Odomanti,[5] and was so beautiful and charming that the fame of her went far abroad, and she was sought in marriage by wooers not only from Thrace, but from still more distant parts, such as from Illyria and those who lived on the banks of the river Tanais. 2. At first Sithon challenged all who came to woo her to fight with him for the girl, with the penalty of death in case of defeat, and in this manner caused the destruction of a considerable number. 3. But later on, when his vigour began to

---

[1] A remedy for over-population. One man in ten was sent out to found a colony elsewhere.

[2] The husband of the famous Alcestis.

[3] An early logographer and grammarian. This story may well come from the Μακεδονικά we know him to have written.

[4] Of Mecyberna, probably in the third century B.C. For a full discussion of his work and date see Pauly-Wissowa, *s.v.*

[5] A people living on the lower Strymon in north-eastern Macedonia.

THE LOVE ROMANCES OF PARTHENIUS

ἰσχὺς ἐπιλελοίπει, ἔγνωστό τε αὐτῷ τὴν κόρην
ἁρμόσασθαι, δύο μνηστῆρας ἀφιγμένους, Δρύαντά
τε καὶ Κλεῖτον, ἐκέλευεν, ἄθλου προκειμένου τῆς
κόρης, ἀλλήλοις διαμάχεσθαι· καὶ τὸν μὲν
τεθνάναι, τὸν δὲ περιγενόμενον τήν τε βασιλείαν
καὶ τὴν παῖδα ἔχειν. 4. τῆς δὲ ἀφωρισμένης
ἡμέρας παρούσης, ἡ Παλλήνη (ἔτυχε γὰρ ἐρῶσα
τοῦ Κλείτου) πάνυ ὀρρώδει περὶ αὐτοῦ· καὶ
σημῆναι μὲν οὐκ ἐτόλμα τινὶ τῶν ἀμφ' αὑτήν,
δάκρυα δὲ πολλὰ κατεχεῖτο τῶν παρειῶν αὐτῆς,
ἕως ὅτε τροφεὺς αὐτῆς πρεσβύτης ἀναπυνθανό-
μενος καὶ ἐπιγνοὺς τὸ πάθος, τῇ μὲν θαρρεῖν
παρεκελεύσατο, ὡς ᾗ βούλεται, ταύτῃ τοῦ πράγ-
ματος χωρήσοντος. αὐτὸς δὲ κρύφα ὑπέρχεται
τὸν ἡνίοχον τοῦ Δρύαντος, καὶ αὐτῷ χρυσὸν
πολὺν ὁμολογήσας πείθει διὰ τῶν ἁρματηγῶν
τροχῶν μὴ διεῖναι τὰς περόνας. 5. ἔνθα δὴ ὡς ἐς
μάχην ἐξῄεσαν καὶ ἤλαυνεν ὁ Δρύας ἐπὶ τὸν
Κλεῖτον, καὶ οἱ τροχοὶ περιερρύησαν αὐτῷ τῶν
ἁρμάτων, καὶ οὕτως πεσόντα αὐτὸν ἐπιδραμὼν ὁ
Κλεῖτος ἀναιρεῖ. 6. αἰσθόμενος δὲ ὁ Σίθων τόν
τε ἔρωτα καὶ τὴν ἐπιβουλὴν τῆς θυγατρός, μάλα
μεγάλην πυρὰν νήσας καὶ ἐπιθεὶς τὸν Δρύαντα,
οἷός τε ἦν[1] ἐπισφάξειν καὶ τὴν Παλλήνην.
φαντάσματος δὲ θείου γενομένου καὶ ἐξαπιναίως
ὕδατος ἐξ οὐρανοῦ πολλοῦ καταρραγέντος,
μετέγνω τε καὶ γάμοις ἀρεσάμενος τὸν παρόντα
Θρᾳκῶν ὅμιλον, ἐφίησι τῷ Κλείτῳ τὴν κόρην
ἄγεσθαι.

[1] The first hand of the MS. has something like οἰστεοσιν
ἐπισφάξειν. The reading given, which is due to Martini,
seems the simplest correction, but there have been several
other proposals for emending the text.

fail him, he realised that he must find her a husband, and when two suitors came, Dryas and Clitus, he arranged that they should fight one another with the girl as the prize of victory ; the vanquished was to be killed, while the survivor was to have both her and the kingship. 4. When the day appointed for the battle arrived, Pallene (who had fallen deeply in love with Clitus) was terribly afraid for him : she dared not tell what she felt to any of her companions, but tears coursed down and down over her cheeks until her old tutor [1] realised the state of affairs, and, after he had become aware of her passion, encouraged her to be of good cheer, as all would come about according to her desires : and he went off and suborned the chariot-driver of Dryas, inducing him, by the promise of a heavy bribe, to leave undone the pins of his chariot-wheels. 5. In due course the combatants came out to fight : Dryas charged Clitus, but the wheels of his chariot came off, and Clitus ran upon him as he fell and put an end to him. 6. Sithon came to know of his daughter's love and of the stratagem that had been employed ; and he constructed a huge pyre, and, setting the body of Dryas upon it, proposed to slay Pallene at the same time [2] ; but a heaven-sent prodigy occurred, a tremendous shower bursting suddenly from the sky, so that he altered his intention and, deciding to give pleasure by the celebration of a marriage to the great concourse of Thracians who were there, allowed Clitus to take the girl to wife.

---

[1] Literally, a male nurse. *cf.* Weigall's *Cleopatra* (1914), p. 104. We have no exact equivalent in English.

[2] Presumably as an offering to the shade of Dryas, for whose death Pallene had been responsible.

THE LOVE ROMANCES OF PARTHENIUS

Ζ΄

ΠΕΡΙ ΙΠΠΑΡΙΝΟΥ

Ἱστορεῖ Φανίας ὁ Ἐρέσιος

1. Ἐν δὲ τῇ Ἰταλῇ Ἡρακλείᾳ παιδὸς διαφόρου τὴν ὄψιν (Ἱππαρῖνος ἦν αὐτῷ ὄνομα) τῶν πάνυ δοκίμων, Ἀντιλέων ἠράσθη· ὃς πολλὰ μηχανώμενος οὐδαμῇ δυνατὸς ἦν αὐτὸν ἁρμόσασθαι, περὶ δὲ γυμνάσια διατρίβοντι πολλὰ τῷ παιδὶ προσρυεὶς ἔφη τοσοῦτον αὐτοῦ πόθον ἔχειν, ὥστε πάντα πόνον ἂν τλῆναι,[1] καὶ ὅ τι ἂν κελεύοι μηδενὸς αὐτὸν ἁμαρτήσεσθαι. 2. ὁ δὲ ἄρα κατειρωνευόμενος προσέταξεν αὐτῷ, ἀπό τινος ἐρυμνοῦ χωρίου, ὃ μάλιστα ἐφρουρεῖτο ὑπὸ τοῦ τῶν Ἡρακλεωτῶν τυράννου, τὸν κώδωνα κατακομίσαι, πειθόμενος μὴ ἄν ποτε τελέσειν αὐτὸν τόνδε τὸν ἆθλον. Ἀντιλέων δὲ κρύφα τὸ φρούριον ὑπελθὼν καὶ λοχήσας τὸν φύλακα τοῦ κώδωνος κατακαίνει· καὶ ἐπειδὴ ἀφίκετο πρὸς τὸ μειράκιον ἐπιτελέσας τὴν ὑπόσχεσιν, ἐν πολλῇ αὐτῷ εὐνοίᾳ ἐγένετο, καὶ ἐκ τοῦδε μάλιστα ἀλλήλους ἐφίλουν. 3. ἐπεὶ δὲ ὁ τύραννος τῆς ὥρας ἐγλίχετο τοῦ παιδὸς καὶ οἷός τε ἦν αὐτὸν βίᾳ ἄγεσθαι, δυσανασχετήσας ὁ Ἀντιλέων ἐκείνῳ μὲν παρεκελεύσατο μὴ ἀντιλέγοντα κινδυνεύειν, αὐτὸς δὲ οἴκοθεν

---

[1] Meineke's correction for the MS. ἀνατλῆναι.

THE STORY OF HIPPARINUS

VII

THE STORY OF HIPPARINUS

From Phanias [1] of Eresus [2]

1. IN the Italian city of Heraclea there lived a boy
of surpassing beauty—Hipparinus was his name—and
of noble parentage. Hipparinus was greatly beloved
by one Antileon, who tried every means but could
never get him to look kindly upon him. He was
always by the lad's side in the wrestling-schools, and
he said that he loved him so dearly that he would
undertake any labour for him, and if he cared to
give him any command, he should not come short
of its fulfilment in the slightest degree. 2. Hipparinus,
not intending his words to be taken seriously, bade
him bring away the bell from a strong-room over
which a very close guard was kept by the tyrant of
Heraclea, imagining that Antileon would never be able
to perform this task. But Antileon privily entered
the castle, surprised and killed the warder, and then
returned to the boy after fulfilling his behest. This
raised him greatly in his affections, and from that
time forward they lived in the closest bonds of
mutual love. 3. Later on the tyrant himself was
greatly struck by the boy's beauty, and seemed likely
to take him by force. At this Antileon was greatly
enraged; he urged Hipparinus not to endanger his
life by a refusal, and then, watching for the moment
when the tyrant was leaving his palace, sprang upon

[1] A Peripatetic philosopher, perhaps a pupil of Aristotle.
Athenaeus tells us that he wrote a book on "how tyrants
met their ends," from which this story is doubtless taken.

[2] In Lesbos.

ἐξιόντα τὸν τύραννον προσδραμὼν ἀνεῖλεν· 4. καὶ
τοῦτο δράσας δρόμῳ ἵετο καὶ διέφυγεν ἄν, εἰ μὴ
προβάτοις συνδεδεμένοις ἀμφιπεσὼν ἐχειρώθη.
διὸ τῆς πόλεως εἰς τἀρχαῖον ἀποκαταστάσης,
ἀμφοτέροις παρὰ τοῖς Ἡρακλεώταις ἐτέθησαν
εἰκόνες χαλκαῖ, καὶ νόμος ἐγράφη, μηδένα ἐλαύ-
νειν τοῦ λοιποῦ πρόβατα συνδεδεμένα.

Η΄

ΠΕΡΙ ΗΡΙΠΠΗΣ

Ἱστορεῖ Ἀριστόδημος ὁ Νυσαεὺς ἐν α΄ Ἱστοριῶν περὶ τού-
των, πλὴν ὅτι τὰ ὀνόματα ὑπαλλάττει, ἀντὶ Ἡρίππης
καλῶν Εὐθυμίαν, τὸν δὲ βάρβαρον Καυάραν

1. Ὅτε δὲ οἱ Γαλάται κατέδραμον τὴν Ἰωνίαν
καὶ τὰς πόλεις ἐπόρθουν, ἐν Μιλήτῳ Θεσμο-
φορίων ὄντων καὶ συνηθροισμένων γυναικῶν ἐν τῷ
ἱερῷ ὃ βραχὺ τῆς πόλεως ἀπέχει, ἀποσπασθέν τι
μέρος τοῦ βαρβαρικοῦ διῆλθεν εἰς τὴν Μιλησίαν
καὶ ἐξαπιναίως ἐπιδραμὸν ἀνεῖλεν τὰς γυναῖκας.
2. ἔνθα δὴ τὰς μὲν ἐρρύσαντο, πολὺ ἀργύριόν τε

---

[1] The whole story is a close parallel to that of the end of
Pisistratid rule in Athens brought about by Harmodius and
Aristogiton.

[2] A grammarian and rhetorician, who paid a visit of some
length to Rome, and died about 50-40 B.C. The title given
to his work by Parthenius (ἱστορίαι περὶ τούτων) is ambiguous :

him and killed him.   4. As soon as he had done the
deed, he fled, running ; and he would have made
good his escape if he had not fallen into the midst of
a flock of sheep tied together, and so been caught and
killed.   When the city regained its ancient constitu-
tion, the people of Heraclea set up bronze statues to
both of them,[1] and a law was passed that in future
no one should drive sheep tied together.

VIII

The Story of Herippe

From the first book of the Stories of Aristodemus[2] *of
Nysa : but he there alters the names, calling the
woman Euthymia instead of Herippe, and giving the
barbarian the name of Cavaras*[3]

1. During the invasion of Ionia by the Gauls[4] and
the devastation by them of the Ionian cities, it
happened that on one occasion at Miletus, the feast
of the Thesmophoria[5] was taking place, and the
women of the city were congregated in the temple a
little way outside the town.   At that time a part of
the barbarian army had become separated from the
main body and had entered the territory of Miletus ;
and there, by a sudden raid, it carried off the women.
2. Some of them were ransomed for large sums of

but it appears that he must have collected a series of love-
stories not unlike those of Parthenius' own.

[3] This may be a gentile name.   The Cavares were a people
of Gallia Narbonensis.   [4] About b.c. 275.

[5] A festival, celebrated oy women, in honour of Demeter
and Proserpine.

καὶ χρυσίον ἀντιδόντες, τινὲς δέ, τῶν βαρβάρων
αὐταῖς οἰκειωθέντων, ἀπήχθησαν, ἐν δὲ αὐταῖς
καὶ Ἡρίππη, γυνὴ ἡ Ξάνθου, ἀνδρὸς ἐν Μιλήτῳ
πάνυ δοκίμου γένους τε τοῦ πρώτου, παιδίον
ἀπολιποῦσα διετές.

3. Ταύτης πολὺν πόθον ἔχων ὁ Ξάνθος ἐξηργυρί-
σατο μέρος τῶν ὑπαργμάτων, καὶ κατασκευασά-
μενος χρυσοῦς δισχιλίους[1] τὸ μὲν πρῶτον εἰς
Ἰταλίαν ἐπεραιώθη· ἐντεῦθεν δὲ ὑπὸ ἰδιοξένων
τινῶν κομιζόμενος εἰς Μασσαλίαν ἀφικνεῖται
κἀκεῖθεν εἰς τὴν Κελτικήν· 4. καὶ προσελθὼν τῇ
οἰκίᾳ, ἔνθα αὐτοῦ συνῆν ἡ γυνὴ ἀνδρὶ τῶν μάλιστα
παρὰ Κελτοῖς δοξαζομένων, ὑποδοχῆς ἐδεῖτο
τυχεῖν. τῶν δὲ διὰ φιλοξενίαν ἑτοίμως αὐτὸν
ὑποδεξαμένων, εἰσελθὼν ὁρᾷ τὴν γυναῖκα, καὶ
αὐτὸν ἐκείνη τὼ χεῖρε ἀμφιβαλοῦσα μάλα
φιλοφρόνως προσηγάγετο. 5. παραχρῆμα δὲ τοῦ
Κελτοῦ παραγενομένου, διεξῆλθεν αὐτῷ τήν τε
ἄλλην τἀνδρὸς ἡ Ἡρίππη, καὶ ὡς αὐτῆς ἕνεκα[2]
ἥκοι λύτρα καταθησόμενος· ὁ δὲ ἠγάσθη τῆς
ψυχῆς τὸν Ξάνθον, καὶ αὐτίκα συνουσίαν ποιη-
σάμενος τῶν μάλιστα προσηκόντων, ἐξένιζεν
αὐτόν· παρατείνοντος δὲ τοῦ πότου, τὴν γυναῖκα
συγκατακλίνει αὐτῷ καὶ δι᾿ ἑρμηνέως ἐπυνθάνετο,
πηλίκην οὐσίαν εἴη κεκτημένος τὴν σύμπασαν·
τοῦ δὲ εἰς ἀριθμὸν χιλίων χρυσῶν φήσαντος, ὁ
βάρβαρος εἰς τέσσαρα μέρη κατανέμειν αὐτὸν
ἐκέλευε, καὶ τὰ μὲν τρία ὑπεξαιρεῖσθαι αὐτῷ,
γυναικί, παιδίῳ, τὸ δὲ τέταρτον ἀπολείπειν
ἄποινα τῆς γυναικός.

---

[1] A correction by Passow from the MS. χιλίους.
[2] The MS. has καὶ ἥκοι. The omission was proposed by Bast.

silver and gold, but there were others to whom the barbarians became closely attached, and these were carried away : among these latter was one Herippe, the wife of Xanthus, a man of high repute and of noble birth among the men of Miletus, and she left behind her a child two years old.

3. Xanthus felt her loss so deeply that he turned a part of his best possessions into money and, furnished with two thousand pieces of gold, first crossed to Italy : he was there furthered by private friends and went on to Marseilles, and thence into the country of the Celts ; (4) and finally, reaching the house where Herippe lived as the wife of one of the chief men of that nation, he asked to be taken in. The Celts received him with the utmost hospitality : on entering the house he saw his wife, and she, flinging her arms about his neck, welcomed him with all the marks of affection. 5. Immediately the Celt appeared, Herippe related to him her husband's journeyings, and how he had come to pay a ransom for her. He was delighted at the devotion of Xanthus, and, calling together his nearest relations to a banquet, entertained him warmly ; and when they had drunk deep, placed his wife by his side, and asked him through an interpreter how great was his whole fortune. " It amounts to a thousand pieces of gold," said Xanthus ; and the barbarian then bade him divide it into four parts—one each for himself, his wife, and his child, and the fourth to be left for the woman's ransom.

THE LOVE ROMANCES OF PARTHENIUS

6. Ὡς δὲ ἐς κοῖτον τότε ἀπετράπετο, πολλὰ
κατεμέμφετο τὸν Ξάνθον ἡ γυνὴ διὰ τὸ μὴ ἔχοντα
τοσοῦτο χρυσίον ὑποσχέσθαι τῷ βαρβάρῳ, κινδυ-
νεύσειν τε αὐτόν, εἰ μὴ ἐμπεδώσειε τὴν ἐπαγγελίαν·
7. τοῦ δὲ φήσαντος ἐν ταῖς κρηπῖσι τῶν παίδων
καὶ ἄλλους τινὰς χιλίους χρυσοῦς κεκρύφθαι διὰ
τὸ μὴ ἐλπίζειν ἐπιεικῆ τινα βάρβαρον καταλή-
ψεσθαι, δεήσειν δὲ πολλῶν λύτρων, ἡ γυνὴ τῇ
ὑστεραίᾳ τῷ Κελτῷ καταμηνύει τὸ πλῆθος τοῦ
χρυσοῦ καὶ παρεκελεύετο κτεῖναι τὸν Ξάνθον,
φάσκουσα πολὺ μᾶλλον αἱρεῖσθαι αὐτὸν τῆς τε
πατρίδος καὶ τοῦ παιδίου, τὸν μὲν γὰρ Ξάνθον
παντάπασιν ἀποστυγεῖν. 8. τῷ δὲ ἄρα οὐ πρὸς
ἡδονῆς ἦν τὰ λεχθέντα· ἐν νῷ δὲ εἶχεν αὐτὴν
τίσασθαι. ἐπειδὴ δὲ ὁ Ξάνθος ἐσπούδαζεν
ἀπιέναι, μάλα φιλοφρόνως προὔπεμπεν ὁ Κελτὸς
ἐπαγόμενος καὶ τὴν Ἡρίππην· ὡς δὲ ἐπὶ τοὺς
ὅρους τῆς Κελτῶν χώρας ἀφίκοντο, θυσίαν ὁ
βάρβαρος ἔφη τελέσαι βούλεσθαι πρὶν αὐτοὺς ἀπ'
ἀλλήλων χωρισθῆναι· 9. καὶ κομισθέντος ἱερείου,
τὴν Ἡρίππην ἐκέλευεν ἀντιλαβέσθαι· τῆς δὲ
κατασχούσης, ὡς καὶ ἄλλοτε σύνηθες αὐτῇ,
ἐπανατεινάμενος τὸ ξίφος καθικνεῖται καὶ τὴν
κεφαλὴν αὐτῆς ἀφαιρεῖ, τῷ τε Ξάνθῳ παρεκε-
λεύετο μὴ δυσφορεῖν, ἐξαγγείλας τὴν ἐπιβουλὴν
αὐτῆς, ἐπέτρεπέ τε τὸ χρυσίον ἅπαν κομίζειν
αὐτῷ.

THE STORY OF HERIPPE

6. After he had retired to his chamber, Herippe upbraided Xanthus vehemently for promising the barbarian this great sum of money which he did not possess, and told him that he would be in a position of extreme jeopardy if he did not fulfil his promise: (7) to which Xanthus replied that he even had another thousand gold pieces which had been hidden in the soles of his servants' boots, seeing that he could scarcely have hoped to find so reasonable a barbarian, and would have been likely to need an enormous ransom for her. The next day she went to the Celt and informed him of the amount of money which Xanthus had in his possession, advising him to put him to death: she added that she preferred him, the Celt, far above both her native country and her child, and, as for Xanthus, that she utterly abhorred him. 8. Her tale was far from pleasing to the Celt, and he decided to punish her: and so, when Xanthus was anxious to be going, he most amiably accompanied him for the first part of his journey, taking Herippe with them; and when they arrived at the limit of the Celts' territory, he announced that he wished to perform a sacrifice before they separated from one another. 9. The victim was brought up, and he bade Herippe hold it: she did so, as she had been accustomed to do on previous occasions, and he then drew his sword, struck with it, and cut off her head. He then explained her treachery to Xanthus, telling him not to take in bad part what he had done, and gave him all the money to take away with him.

Θ'

ΠΕΡΙ ΠΟΛΥΚΡΙΤΗΣ

Ἡ ἱστορία αὕτη ἐλήφθη ἐκ τῆς α' Ἀνδρίσκου Ναξιακῶν·
γράφει περὶ αὐτῆς καὶ Θεόφραστος ἐν τῷ δ' τῶν [1]
Πρὸς τοὺς καιρούς

1. Καθ' ὃν δὲ χρόνον ἐπὶ Ναξίους Μιλήσιοι
συνέβησαν σὺν ἐπικούροις καὶ τεῖχος πρὸ τῆς
πόλεως ἐνοικοδομησάμενοι τήν τε χώραν ἔτεμνον
καὶ καθείρξαντες τοὺς Ναξίους ἐφρούρουν, τότε
παρθένος ἀπολειφθεῖσα κατά τινα δαίμονα ἐν
Δηλίῳ ἱερῷ, ὃ πλησίον τῆς πόλεως κεῖται, (Πολυ-
κρίτη ὄνομα αὐτῇ) τὸν τῶν Ἐρυθραίων ἡγεμόνα
Διόγνητον εἷλεν, ὃς οἰκείαν δύναμιν ἔχων συν-
εμάχει τοῖς Μιλησίοις. 2. πολλῷ δὲ συνεχόμενος
πόθῳ διεπέμπετο πρὸς αὐτήν· οὐ γὰρ δή γε
θεμιτὸν ἦν ἱκέτιν οὖσαν ἐν τῷ ἱερῷ βιάζεσθαι· ἡ
δὲ ἕως μέν τινος οὐ προσίετο τοὺς παραγινο-
μένους· ἐπεὶ μέντοι πολὺς ἐνέκειτο, οὐκ ἔφη
πεισθήσεσθαι αὐτῷ, εἰ μὴ ὀμόσειεν ὑπηρετήσειν
αὐτῇ ὅ τι ἂν βουληθῇ. 3. ὁ δὲ Διόγνητος, οὐδὲν
ὑποτοπήσας τοιόνδε, μάλα προθύμως ὤμοσεν
Ἄρτεμιν χαριεῖσθαι αὐτῇ ὅ τι ἂν προαιρῆται·

---

[1] This τῶν is not in the MS., but was supplied by
Legrand.

---

[1] The story is somewhat differently told by Plutarch in
No. 17 of his treatise *On the Virtues of Women*: he makes
Polycrite a captive in the hands of Diognetus, and she de-
ceives him, instead of persuading him to treachery, by the
stratagem of the loaves. Plutarch also makes Diognetus
taken prisoner by the Naxians, and his life is saved by Poly-
crite's prayers. It is clear from his text that there were

THE STORY OF POLYCRITE

IX

The Story of Polycrite [1]

From the first book of the Naxiaca *of* Andriscus [2] *; and the story is also related by Theophrastus* [3] *in the fourth book of his* Political History

1. ONCE the men of Miletus made an expedition against the Naxians with strong allies ; they built a wall round their city, ravaged their country, and blockaded them fast. By the providence of some god, a maiden named Polycrite had been left in the temple of the Delian goddess [4] near the city : and she captured by her beauty the love of Diognetus, the leader of the Erythraeans, who was fighting on the side of the Milesians at the head of his own forces. 2. Constrained by the strength of his desire, he kept sending messages to her (for it would have been impiety to ravish her by force in the very shrine) ; at first she would not listen to his envoys, but when she saw his persistence she said that she would never consent unless he swore to accomplish whatever wish she might express. 3. Diognetus had no suspicion of what she was going to exact, and eagerly swore by Artemis that he would

several versions of the story, one of which he ascribes to Aristotle.

[2] Little is known of Andriscus beyond this reference. He was probably a Peripatetic philosopher and historian of the third or second century B.C.

[3] The famous pupil and successor of Aristotle. This work, of which the full title was πολιτικὰ πρὸς τοὺς καιρούς, was a survey of politics as seen in historical events.

[4] I am a little doubtful as to this translation. As Polycrite made Diognetus swear by Artemis, it is at least possible that she was in a temple of Artemis.

285

κατομοσαμένου δὲ ἐκείνου, λαβομένη [1] τῆς χειρὸς
αὐτοῦ ἡ Πολυκρίτη μιμνήσκεται περὶ προδοσίας
τοῦ χωρίου, καὶ πολλὰ καθικετεύει αὐτήν τε
οἰκτείρειν καὶ τὰς συμφορὰς τῆς πόλεως. 4. ὁ
Διόγνητος ἀκούσας τοῦ λόγου ἐκτός τε ἐγένετο
αὑτοῦ καὶ σπασάμενος τὴν μάχαιραν ὥρμησε
διεργάσασθαι τὴν κόρην. ἐν νῷ μέντοι λαβὼν
τὸ εὔγνωμον αὐτῆς καὶ ἅμα ὑπ᾽ ἔρωτος κρατού-
μενος, ἔδει γάρ, ὡς ἔοικε, καὶ Ναξίοις μεταβολὴν
γενέσθαι τῶν παρόντων κακῶν, τότε μὲν οὐδὲν
ἀπεκρίνατο, βουλευόμενος τί ποιητέον εἴη· τῇ δὲ
ὑστεραίᾳ καθωμολογήσατο προδώσειν.

5. Καὶ ἐν τῷ δὴ τοῖς Μιλησίοις ἑορτὴ μετὰ τρίτην
ἡμέραν Θαργήλια ἐπῄει, ἐν ᾗ πολύν τε ἄκρατον εἰσ-
φοροῦνται καὶ τὰ πλείστου ἄξια καταναλίσκουσι·
τότε παρεσκευάζετο προδιδόναι τὸ χωρίον. καὶ
εὐθέως διὰ τῆς Πολυκρίτης ἐνθέμενος εἰς ἄρτον
μολυβδίνην ἐπιστολὴν ἐπιστέλλει [2] τοῖς ἀδελφοῖς
αὐτῆς (ἐτύγχανον δὲ ἄρα τῆς πόλεως ἡγεμόνες οὗτοι)
ὅπως εἰς ἐκείνην τὴν νύκτα παρασκευασάμενοι
ἥκωσιν· σημεῖον δὲ αὐτοῖς ἀνασχήσειν αὐτὸς ἔφη
λαμπτῆρα. 6. καὶ ἡ Πολυκρίτη δὲ τῷ κομίζοντι
τὸν ἄρτον φράζειν ἐκέλευε τοῖς ἀδελφοῖς μὴ
ἐνδοιασθῆναι,[3] ὡς τῆς πράξεως ἐπὶ τέλος ἀχθησο-
μένης, εἰ μὴ ἐκεῖνοι ἐνδοιασθεῖεν. τοῦ δὲ ἀγγέλου
ταχέως εἰς τὴν πόλιν ἐλθόντος, Πολυκλῆς, ὁ τῆς
Πολυκρίτης ἀδελφός, ἐν πολλῇ φροντίδι ἐγίνετο,

[1] The MS. has καὶ λαβομένη, which can hardly stand. It
is a pity that καταλαβομένη, the obvious correction, does not
seem to be used in this sense.

[2] Some verb is needed, and Legrand's ἐπιστέλλει is palæo-
graphically not improbable.

[3] Passow's correction for ἐνδοιᾶσθαι.

perform her every behest : and after he had taken
the oath, Polycrite seized his hand and claimed that
he should betray the blockade, beseeching him
vehemently to take pity upon her and the sorrows of
her country. 4. When Diognetus heard her request,
he became quite beside himself, and, drawing his
sword, was near putting an end to her. But when,
however, he came to ponder upon her patriotism,
being at the same time mastered by his passion,—
for it was appointed, it seems, that the Naxians should
be relieved of the troubles that beset them—for the
moment he returned no answer, taking time to
consider his course of action, and on the morrow
consented to the betrayal.

5. Meanwhile, three days later, came the Mile-
sians' celebration of the Thargelia [1]—a time when
they indulge in a deal of strong wine and make
merry with very little regard to the cost; and
he decided to take advantage of this for the
occasion of his treachery. He then and there
enclosed a letter, written on a tablet of lead, in
a loaf of bread, and sent it to Polycrite's brothers,
who chanced to be the citizens' generals, in which
he bade them get ready and join him that very
night ; and he said that he would give them the
necessary direction by holding up a light : (6) and
Polycrite instructed the bearer of the loaf to tell her
brothers not to hesitate ; for if they acted without hesi-
tation the business would be brought to a successful
end. When the messenger had arrived in the city,
Polycles, Polycrite's brother, was in the deepest

---

[1] A festival of Apollo and Artemis, held at Athens in the
early summer.

εἴτε πεισθείη τοῖς ἐπεσταλμένοις, εἴτε μή·
7. τέλος δέ, ὡς ἐδόκει πᾶσι πείθεσθαι καὶ νὺξ
ἐπῆλθεν ἐν ᾗ προσετέτακτο πᾶσι παραγίνεσθαι,
πολλὰ κατευξάμενοι τοῖς θεοῖς, δεχομένων
αὐτοὺς τῶν ἀμφὶ Διόγνητον, ἐσπίπτουσιν εἰς τὸ
τεῖχος τῶν Μιλησίων, οἱ μέν τινες κατὰ τὴν
ἀνεῳγμένην πυλίδα, οἱ δὲ καὶ τὸ τεῖχος ὑπερελ-
θόντες, ἀθρόοι τε ἐντὸς γενόμενοι κατέκαινον τοὺς
Μιλησίους· 8. ἔνθα δὴ κατ᾽ ἄγνοιαν ἀποθνήσκει
καὶ Διόγνητος. τῇ δὲ ἐπιούσῃ οἱ Νάξιοι πάντες
πολὺν πόθον εἶχον ἱλάσασθαι[1] τὴν κόρην· καὶ οἱ
μέν τινες αὐτὴν μίτραις ἀνέδουν, οἱ δὲ ζώναις, αἷς
βαρηθεῖσα ἡ παῖς διὰ πλῆθος τῶν ἐπιρριπτου-
μένων ἀπεπνίγη. καὶ αὐτὴν δημοσίᾳ θάπτουσιν
ἐν τῷ πεδίῳ, πρόβατα[2] ἑκατὸν ἐναγίσαντες
αὐτῇ. φασὶ δέ τινες καὶ Διόγνητον ἐν τῷ αὐτῷ
καῆναι ἐν ᾧ καὶ ἡ παῖς, σπουδασάντων τῶν
Ναξίων.

I

ΠΕΡΙ ΛΕΥΚΩΝΗΣ

1. Ἐν δὲ Θεσσαλίᾳ Κυάνιππος, υἱὸς Φάρακος,
μάλα καλῆς παιδὸς εἰς ἐπιθυμίαν Λευκώνης

---

[1] The MS. has βιάσασθαι—surely the strangest of readings.
It is difficult to say with certainty what the original word
was, but ἱλάσασθαι, which was proposed independently by
Meineke and Rossbach, gives a satisfactory sense.

[2] Rohde's suggestion for the MS. πάντα.

---

[1] If Martini records the MS. tradition aright, the word οὐ
occurs beneath the title of this story, which may perhaps
mean that, if the indications of sources were not supplied by
Parthenius himself, as is possible, the scholar who added
them could not find this tale in any earlier historical or mytho-
logical writer. Some support might be lent to this view by

anxiety as to whether he should obey the message or no : (7) finally universal opinion was on the side of action and the night-time came on, when they were bidden to make the sally in force. So, after much prayer to the gods, they joined Diognetus' company and then made an attack on the Milesians' blockading wall, some through a gate left open for them and others by scaling the wall ; and then, when once through, joined together again and inflicted a terrible slaughter upon the Milesians, (8) and in the fray Diognetus was accidentally killed. On the following day all the Naxians were most desirous of doing honour to the girl : but they pressed on her such a quantity of head-dresses and girdles that she was overcome by the weight and quantity of the offerings, and so was suffocated. They gave her a public funeral in the open country, sacrificing a hundred sheep to her shade : and some say that, at the Naxians' particular desire, the body of Diognetus was burnt upon the same pyre as that of the maiden.

X

THE STORY OF LEUCONE [1]

1. IN Thessaly there was one Cyanippus, the son of Pharax, who fell in love with a very beautiful girl

a passage in the *Parallela Minora* ascribed to Plutarch, No. 21 ; the same tale is given in rather a shorter form, ending with the words ὡς Παρθένιος ὁ ποιητής, which might either mean that it was taken from this work (Parthenius being better known as a poet than as a writer of prose), or that Parthenius had made it a subject of one of his own poems. "Ascribed to Plutarch" I say of the *Parallela Minora* : for "*In the margin of an old manuscript copie, these words were found written in Greek*: This booke was never of PLUTARCHS making, who was an excellent and most learned Author ; but penned by some odde vulgar writer, altogether ignorant both of Poetrie (*or, Learning*), and also of Grammar."

THE LOVE ROMANCES OF PARTHENIUS

ἐλθών, παρὰ τῶν πατέρων αἰτησάμενος αὐτὴν
ἠγάγετο γυναῖκα. ἦν δὲ φιλοκύνηγος· μεθ'
ἡμέραν μὲν ἐπί τε λέοντας καὶ κάπρους ἐφέρετο,
νύκτωρ δὲ κατῄει πάνυ κεκμηκὼς πρὸς τὴν κόρην,
ὥστε μηδὲ διὰ λόγων ἔσθ' ὅτε γινόμενον αὐτῇ
ἐς βαθὺν ὕπνον καταφέρεσθαι. 2. ἡ δὲ ἄρα ὑπό
τε ἀνίας καὶ ἀλγηδόνων συνεχομένη, ἐν πολλῇ
ἀμηχανίᾳ ἦν σπουδήν τε ἐποιεῖτο κατοπτεῦσαι
τὸν Κυάνιππον, ὅ τι ποιῶν ἥδοιτο τῇ κατ' ὄρος
διαίτῃ· αὐτίκα δὲ εἰς γόνυ ζωσαμένη κρύφα τῶν
θεραπαινίδων εἰς τὴν ὕλην καταδύνει. 3. αἱ δὲ
τοῦ Κυανίππου κύνες ἐδίωκον μὲν ἔλαφον· οὖσαι
δὲ οὐ πάνυ κτίλοι, ἅτε δὴ ἐκ πολλοῦ ἠγριωμέναι,
ὡς ὠσφράσαντο τῆς κόρης, ἐπηνέχθησαν αὐτῇ
καὶ μηδενὸς παρόντος πᾶσαν διεσπάραξαν· καὶ
ἡ μὲν διὰ πόθον ἀνδρὸς κουριδίου ταύτῃ τέλος
ἔσχεν. 4. Κυάνιππος δέ, ὡς ἐπελθὼν κατελάβετο
λελωβημένην τὴν Λευκώνην, μεγάλῳ τε ἄχει
ἐπληρώθη, καὶ ἀνακαλεσάμενος τοὺς ἀμφ' αὑτόν,
ἐκείνην μὲν πυρὰν νήσας ἐπέθετο, αὐτὸς δὲ
πρῶτον μὲν τὰς κύνας ἐπικατέσφαξε τῇ πυρᾷ,
ἔπειτα δὲ πολλὰ ἀποδυρόμενος τὴν παῖδα διεχρή-
σατο ἑαυτόν.

named Leucone : he begged her hand from her parents, and married her. Now he was a mighty hunter ; all day he would chase lions and wild boars, and when night came he used to reach the damsel utterly tired out, so that sometimes he was not even able to talk to her before he fell into a deep sleep.[1] 2. At this she was afflicted by grief and care ; and, not knowing how things stood, determined to take all pains to spy upon Cyanippus, to find out what was the occupation which gave him such delight during his long periods of staying out on the mountains. So she girded up her skirts above the knee,[2] and, taking care not to be seen by her maid-servants, slipped into the woods. 3. Cyanippus' hounds were far from tame ; they had indeed become extremely savage from their long experience of hunting : and when they scented the damsel, they rushed upon her, and, in the huntsman's absence, tore her to pieces ; and that was the end of her, all for the love she bore to her young husband. 4. When Cyanippus came up and found her all torn by the dogs, he called together his companions and made a great pyre, and set her upon it ; first he slew his hounds on the pyre, and then, with much weeping and wailing for his wife, put an end to himself as well.

[1] "These, however, were the only seasons when Mr. Western saw his wife ; for when he repaired to her bed he was generally so drunk that he could not see ; and in the sporting season he always rose from her before it was light."—*Tom Jones*, Bk. vii, ch. 4.

[2] Like the statues of Artemis as huntress.

ΙΔ΄

ΠΕΡΙ ΒΥΒΛΙΔΟΣ [1]

Ἱστορεῖ Ἀριστόκριτος περὶ Μιλήτου καὶ Ἀπολλώνιος ὁ
Ῥόδιος Καύνου κτίσει

1. Περὶ δὲ Καύνου καὶ Βυβλίδος, τῶν Μιλήτου
παίδων, διαφόρως ἱστορεῖται. Νικαίνετος μὲν
γάρ φησι τὸν Καῦνον ἐρασθέντα τῆς ἀδελφῆς, ὡς
οὐκ ἔληγε τοῦ πάθους, ἀπολιπεῖν τὴν οἰκίαν καὶ
ὁδεύσαντα πόρρω τῆς οἰκείας χώρας, πόλιν τε
κτίσαι καὶ τοὺς ἀπεσκεδασμένους τότε Ἴωνας
ἐνοικίσαι· 2. λέγει δὲ ἔπεσι τοῖσδε·

αὐτὰρ ὅ γε προτέρωσε κιὼν Οἰκούσιον ἄστυ
κτίσσατο, Τραγασίῃ δὲ Κελαινέος [2] εἴχετο παιδί,
ἥ οἱ Καῦνον ἔτικτεν ἀεὶ φιλέοντα θέμιστας·
γείνατο δὲ ῥαδαλῆς ἐναλίγκιον ἀρκεύθοισι
Βυβλίδα, τῆς ἤτοι ἀέκων ἠράσσατο Καῦνος·   5
βῆ δὲ πέρην Δίας,[3] φεύγων ὀφιώδεα Κύπρον
καὶ Κάπρος ὑλιγενὲς καὶ Κάρια ἱρὰ λοετρά·
ἔνθ᾽ ἤτοι πτολίεθρον ἐδείματο πρῶτος Ἰώνων.

---

[1] The MS. inclines to the spelling Βιβλίς throughout: but
from other versions of the story Βυβλίς seems certain.
[2] So Passow and Ellis for the MS. κελαινέες. The whole of
this little poem is very corrupt.
[3] So Passow for the MS. βῆ δὲ φερενδιος. Κύπρον and Κάπρος
are both probably wrong.

XI

THE STORY OF BYBLIS

From Aristocritus' [1] *History of Miletus and the Foundation of Caunus* [2] *by Apollonius of Rhodes*

1. THERE are various forms of the story about Caunus and Byblis, the children of Miletus. Nicaenetus [3] says that Caunus fell in love with his sister, and, being unable to rid himself of his passion, left his home and travelled far from his native land : he there founded a city to be inhabited by the scattered Ionian people. 2. Nicaenetus speaks of him thus in his epic :—

> Further he [4] fared and there the Oecusian town
> Founded, and took to wife Tragasia,
> Celaeneus' daughter, who twain children bare :
> First Caunus, lover of right and law, and then
> Fair Byblis, whom men likened to the tall junipers.
> Caunus was smitten, all against his will,
> With love for Byblis ; straightway left his home,
> And fled beyond Dia : Cyprus did he shun,
> The land of snakes, and wooded Capros too,
> And Caria's holy streams ; and then, his goal
> Once reached, he built a township, first of all
> The Ionians.   But his sister far away,

---

[1] A mythological historian of Miletus ; he may be considered as a prose follower of the Alexandrine poets.

[2] See note on the title of No. I.

[3] An Alexandrine poet, author of a γυναικῶν κατάλογος (from which these lines may perhaps be taken) on the model of the *Eoiai* of Hesiod.

[4] Miletus, the founder of the city of the same name.

THE LOVE ROMANCES OF PARTHENIUS

αὐτοκασιγνήτη δ᾽,[1] ὀλολυγόνος οἶτον ἔχουσα,
Βυβλὶς ἀποπρὸ πυλῶν Καύνου ὠδύρατο νόστον.[2] 10

3. Οἱ δὲ πλείους τὴν Βυβλίδα φασὶν ἐρα-
σθεῖσαν τοῦ Καύνου λόγους αὐτῷ προσφέρειν καὶ
δεῖσθαι μὴ περιιδεῖν αὐτὴν εἰς πᾶν κακὸν προελ-
θοῦσαν· ἀποστυγήσαντα δὲ οὕτως τὸν Καῦνον
περαιωθῆναι εἰς τὴν τότε ὑπὸ Λελέγων κατεχο-
μένην γῆν, ἔνθα κρήνη Ἐχενηΐς, πόλιν τε κτίσαι
τὴν ἀπ᾽ αὐτοῦ κληθεῖσαν Καῦνον· τὴν δὲ ἄρα,
ὑπὸ τοῦ πάθους μὴ ἀνιεμένην, πρὸς δὲ καὶ
δοκοῦσαν αἰτίαν γεγονέναι Καύνῳ τῆς ἀπαλλαγῆς,
ἀναψαμένην ἀπό τινος δρυὸς τὴν μίτραν, ἐνθεῖναι
τὸν τράχηλον· 4. λέγεται δὲ καὶ παρ᾽ ἡμῖν
οὕτως·

ἡ δ᾽ ὅτε δή[3] ῥ᾽ ὀλοοῖο κασιγνήτου νόον ἔγνω,
κλαῖεν ἀηδονίδων[4] θαμινώτερον, αἵ τ᾽ ἐνὶ βήσσῃς
Σιθονίῳ κούρῳ πέρι μυρίον αἰάζουσιν·
καί ῥα κατὰ στυφελοῖο σαρωνίδος αὐτίκα μίτρην
ἁψαμένη δειρὴν ἐνεθήκατο, ταὶ δ᾽ ἐπ᾽ ἐκείνῃ   5
βεύδεα παρθενικαὶ Μιλησίδες ἐρρήξαντο.

Φασὶ δέ τινες καὶ ἀπὸ τῶν δακρύων κρήνην
ῥυῆναι ἰδίᾳ[5] τὴν καλουμένην Βυβλίδα.

---

[1] Legrand's correction for αὐτὴ δὲ γνωτή.

[2] These lines appear to be a good deal compressed. It is likely that after l. 5 the flight of Caunus was described, and after l. 7 his arrival at the place where he founded the city called after him.

[3] Rightly inserted for metrical reasons by Legrand.

[4] The MS. has Ἀδονίδων. The correction is due to Daniel Heinsius.

[5] Zangoiannes suggests ἀΐδιον, "continual, everlasting," which is quite possibly right.

THE STORY OF BYBLIS

Poor Byblis, to an owl divinely changed,
Still sat without Miletus' gates, and wailed
For Caunus to return, which might not be.

3. However, most authors say that Byblis fell in
love with Caunus, and made proposals to him,
begging him not to stand by and see the sight of her
utter misery. He was horrified at what she said, and
crossed over to the country then inhabited by the
Leleges, where the spring Écheneïs rises, and there
founded the city called Caunus after himself. She,
as her passion did not abate, and also because she
blamed herself for Caunus' exile, tied the fillets of
her head-dress [1] to an oak, and so made a noose for
her neck. 4. The following are my own lines on the
subject :—

She, when she knew her brother's cruel heart,
Plained louder than the nightingales in the groves
Who weep for ever the Sithonian [2] lad ;
Then to a rough oak tied her snood, and made
A strangling noose, and laid therein her neck :
For her Milesian virgins rent their robes.

Some also say that from her tears sprang a stream
called after her name, Byblis.

---

[1] A head-dress with long bands (" *habent redimicula
mitrae* "), which she could therefore use as a rope with
which to hang herself. In an epigram by Aristodicus (*Anth.
Pal.* vii. 473) two women, Demo and Methymna, hearing of
the death of a friend or lover—

ζωὰν ἀρνήσαντο, τανυπλέκτων δ' ἀπὸ μιτρᾶν
χερσὶ δεραιούχους ἐκρεμάσαντο βρόχους.

[2] Itys, for whom Philomel weeps in the well-known story.

THE LOVE ROMANCES OF PARTHENIUS

IB´

ΠΕΡΙ ΚΑΛΧΟΥ

1. Λέγεται δὲ καὶ Κίρκης, πρὸς ἣν Ὀδυσσεὺς
ἦλθε, Δαυνιόν τινα Κάλχον ἐρασθέντα, τήν τε
βασιλείαν ἐπιτρέπειν τὴν Δαυνίων αὐτῇ καὶ ἄλλα
πολλὰ μειλίγματα παρέχεσθαι· τὴν δὲ ὑποκαιο-
μένην Ὀδυσσέως, τότε γὰρ ἐτύγχανε παρών,
ἀποστυγεῖν τε αὐτὸν καὶ κωλύειν ἐπιβαίνειν τῆς
νήσου. 2. ἐπεὶ μέντοι οὐκ ἀνίει φοιτῶν καὶ διὰ
στόμα ἔχων τὴν Κίρκην, μάλα ἀχθεσθεῖσα
ὑπέρχεται αὐτόν, καὶ αὐτίκα εἰσκαλεσαμένη,
τράπεζαν αὐτῷ παντοδαπῆς θοίνης πλήσασα
παρατίθησιν· ἦν δὲ ἄρα φαρμάκων ἀνάπλεω τὰ
ἐδέσματα, φαγών τε ὁ Κάλχος εὐθέως παραπλὴξ
ἵεται, καὶ αὐτὸν ἤλασεν ἐς συφεούς. 3. ἐπεὶ
μέντοι μετὰ χρόνον Δαύνιος στρατὸς ἐπῄει τῇ
νήσῳ ζήτησιν ποιούμενος τοῦ Κάλχου, μεθίησιν
αὐτόν, πρότερον ὁρκίοις καταδησαμένη μὴ
ἀφίξεσθαί ποτε εἰς τὴν νῆσον, μήτε μνηστείας
μήτε ἄλλου του χάριν.

IΓ´

ΠΕΡΙ ΑΡΠΑΛΥΚΗΣ

Ἱστορεῖ Εὐφορίων Θρᾳκὶ καὶ Δεκτάδας

1. Κλύμενος δὲ ὁ Τελέως ἐν Ἄργει γήμας
Ἐπικάστην γεννᾷ παῖδας, ἄρρενας μὲν Ἴδαν καὶ

---

[1] I imagine that this implies that Circe's victims were not
actually changed into swine, but that, like Nebuchadnezzar,
became animals in their minds and habits.

[2] One of the most typical of the Alexandrine poets, who
served as a model almost more than all the others to the poets

296

THE STORY OF HARPALYCE

XII

THE STORY OF CALCHUS

1. THE story is that Calchus the Daunian was greatly in love with Circe, the same to whom Ulysses came. He handed over to her his kingship over the Daunians, and employed all possible bland-ishments to gain her love; but she felt a passion for Ulysses, who was then with her, and loathed Calchus and forbade him to land on her island. 2. However, he would not stop coming, and could talk of nothing but Circe, and she, being extremely angry with him, laid a snare for him and had no sooner invited him into her palace but she set before him a table covered with all manner of dainties. But the meats were full of magical drugs, and as soon as Calchus had eaten of them, he was stricken mad,[1] and she drove him into the pig-styes. 3. After a certain time, however, the Daunians' army landed on the island to look for Calchus; and she then released him from the enchantment, first binding him by oath that he would never set foot on the island again, either to woo her or for any other purpose.

XIII

THE STORY OF HARPALYCE

From the Thrax *of Euphorion* [2] *and from Dectadas.*[3]

1. CLYMENUS the son of Teleus at Argos married Epicasta and had two sons, who were called Idas and

of Rome; he was of particular interest to Cornelius Gallus, because some of his works were translated into Latin by him.

[3] Otherwise unknown. Various attempts have been made, without any very satisfactory result, to emend the name into Aretadas, Dosiadas, Dieuchidas, Dinias, Athanadas, etc.

Θήραγρον, θυγατέρα δὲ Ἁρπαλύκην, πολύ τι
τῶν ἡλίκων θηλειῶν κάλλει διαφέρουσαν. ταύτης
εἰς ἔρωτα ἐλθὼν χρόνον μέν τινα ἐκαρτέρει
καὶ περιῆν τοῦ παθήματος· ὡς δὲ πολὺ μᾶλλον
αὐτὸν ὑπέρρει τὸ νόσημα, τότε διὰ τῆς τροφοῦ
κατεργασάμενος τὴν κόρην, λαθραίως αὐτῇ συν-
ῆλθεν. 2. ἐπεὶ μέντοι γάμου καιρὸς ἦν καὶ
παρῆν Ἀλάστωρ, εἷς τῶν Νηλειδῶν, ἀξόμενος
αὐτήν, ᾧ καθωμολόγητο, παραχρῆμα μὲν ἐνεχεί-
ρισε, πάνυ λαμπροὺς γάμους δαίσας· 3. μετα-
γνοὺς δὲ οὐ πολὺ ὕστερον διὰ τὸ ἔκφρων εἶναι
μεταθεῖ τὸν Ἀλάστορα, καὶ περὶ μέσην ὁδὸν
αὐτῶν ἤδη ὄντων, ἀφαιρεῖται τὴν κόρην, ἀγαγό-
μενός τε εἰς Ἄργος ἀναφανδὸν αὐτῇ ἐμίσγετο. ἡ
δὲ δεινὰ καὶ ἔκνομα πρὸς τοῦ πατρὸς ἀξιοῦσα
πεπονθέναι, τὸν νεώτερον ἀδελφὸν κατακόπτει,
καί τινος ἑορτῆς καὶ θυσίας παρ᾽ Ἀργείοις
τελουμένης, ἐν ᾗ δημοσίᾳ πάντες εὐωχοῦνται,
τότε[1] σκευάσασα τὰ κρέα τοῦ παιδὸς παρατίθησι
τῷ πατρί. 4. καὶ ταῦτα δράσασα αὐτὴ μὲν
εὐξαμένη θεοῖς ἐξ ἀνθρώπων ἀπαλλαγῆναι, μετα-
βάλλει τὴν ὄψιν εἰς χαλκίδα[2] ὄρνιν· Κλύμενος
δέ, ὡς ἔννοιαν ἔλαβε τῶν συμφορῶν, διαχρῆται
ἑαυτόν.

---

[1] MS. καὶ τότε. The omission is due to Legrand.
[2] MS. καλχίδα. It is a bird, apparently of the hawk tribe, inhabiting mountainous countries. Gods call it Chalcis, men Cymindis. Homer, *Iliad* xiv. 291.

THE STORY OF HARPALYCE

Therager, and a daughter, Harpalyce, who was far the most beautiful woman of her time. Clymenus was seized with love for her. For a time he held out and had the mastery of his passion; but it came over him again with increased force, and he then acquainted the girl of his feelings through her nurse, and consorted with her secretly. 2. However, the time arrived when she was ripe for marriage, and Alastor, one of the race of Neleus, to whom she had previously been betrothed, had come to wed her. Clymenus handed her over to him without hesitation, and celebrated the marriage in magnificent style. 3. But after no long period his madness induced him to change his mind; he hurried after Alastor, caught the pair of them when they were half-way on their journey, seized the girl, took her back to Argos, and there lived with her openly as his wife. Feeling that she had received cruel and flagitious treatment at her father's hands, she killed and cut in pieces her younger brother, and when there was a festival and sacrifice being celebrated among the people of Argos at which they all feast at a public banquet, she cooked the boy's flesh and set it as meat before her father. 4. This done, she prayed Heaven that she might be translated away from among mankind, and she was transformed into the bird called the Chalcis. Clymenus when he began to reflect on all these disasters that had happened to his family, took his own life.

ΙΔ΄

ΠΕΡΙ ΑΝΘΕΩΣ

Ἱστορεῖ Ἀριστοτέλης καὶ οἱ τὰ Μιλησιακά

1. Ἐκ δὲ Ἁλικαρνασσοῦ παῖς Ἀνθεὺς ἐκ βασιλείου γένους ὡμήρευσε παρὰ Φοβίῳ, ἑνὶ τῶν Νηλειδῶν, τότε κρατοῦντι Μιλησίων. τούτου Κλεόβοια, ἥν τινες Φιλαίχμην ἐκάλεσαν, τοῦ Φοβίου γυνή, ἐρασθεῖσα πολλὰ ἐμηχανᾶτο εἰς τὸ προσαγαγέσθαι τὸν παῖδα. 2. ὡς δὲ ἐκεῖνος ἀπεωθεῖτο, ποτὲ μὲν φάσκων ὀρρωδεῖν μὴ κατάδηλος γένοιτο, ποτὲ δὲ Δία Ξένιον καὶ κοινὴν τράπεζαν προϊσχόμενος, ἡ Κλεόβοια κακῶς φερομένη ἐν νῷ εἶχε τίσασθαι αὐτόν, ἀνηλεῆ τε καὶ ὑπέραυχον ἀποκαλουμένη. 3. ἔνθα δὴ χρόνου προϊόντος, τοῦ μὲν ἔρωτος ἀπηλλάχθαι προσεποιήθη· πέρδικα δὲ τιθασσὸν εἰς βαθὺ φρέαρ κατασοβήσασα, ἐδεῖτο τοῦ Ἀνθέως ὅπως κατελθὼν ἀνέλοιτο αὐτόν· 4. τοῦ δὲ ἑτοίμως ὑπακούσαντος διὰ τὸ μηδὲν ὑφορᾶσθαι, ἡ Κλεόβοια ἐπισείει στιβαρὸν αὐτῷ πέτρον· καὶ ὁ μὲν παραχρῆμα ἐτεθνήκει· ἡ δὲ ἄρα ἐννοηθεῖσα ὡς δεινὸν ἔργον δεδράκοι, καὶ ἄλλως δὲ καιομένη σφοδρῷ ἔρωτι τοῦ παιδός, ἀναρτᾷ ἑαυτήν. 5. Φοβίος μέντοι διὰ ταύτην τὴν αἰτίαν ὡς ἐναγὴς παρεχώρησε Φρυγίῳ τῆς ἀρχῆς. ἔφασαν δέ τινες, οὐ πέρδικα, σκεῦος δὲ χρυσοῦν εἰς τὸ φρέαρ

---

[1] Some scholars, such as Mueller, have doubted whether this story can really come from any of Aristotle's works, and have proposed to read some other name, such as Aristodicus. But the philosophers often employed mythological tales in

XIV

The Story of Antheus

From Aristotle[1] *and the writers of* Milesian History

1. A YOUTH named Antheus, of royal blood, had been sent as a hostage from Halicarnassus to the court of Phobius, one of the race of Neleus, who was at that time ruler of Miletus. Cleoboea, the wife of Phobius (other authorities call her Philaechme), fell in love with him, and employed all possible means to gain his affections. 2. He, however, repelled her advances : sometimes he declared that he trembled at the thought of discovery, while at others he appealed to Zeus as god of hospitality and the obligations imposed on him by the King's table at which they both sat. Cleoboea's passion took an evil turn ; she called him void of pity and proud, and determined to wreak vengeance on him : (3) and so, as time went on, she pretended that she was rid of her love, and one day she chased a tame partridge down a deep well, and asked Antheus to go down and fetch it out. 4. He readily consented, suspecting nothing ill ; but when he had descended, she pushed down an enormous stone upon him, and he instantly expired. Then she realised the terrible crime she had committed and, being also still fired with an exceeding passion for the lad, hanged herself : (5) but Phobius considered himself as under a curse because of these events, and handed over his kingship to Phrygius. Other authorities say that it was not a partridge, but

their more serious works, as Phanias in No. VII., and this may possibly belong to a description of the form of government at Miletus.

βεβλῆσθαι, ὡς καὶ Ἀλέξανδρος ὁ Αἰτωλὸς μέμνη-
ται ἐν τοῖσδε ἐν Ἀπόλλωνι·

Παῖς Ἱπποκλῆος Φοβίος Νηληϊάδαο
ἔσται ἰθαιγενέων γνήσιος ἐκ πατέρων·
τῷ δ' ἄλοχος μνηστὴ δόμον ἵξεται, ἧς ἔτι νύμφης
ἠλάκατ' ἐν θαλάμοις καλὸν ἑλισσομένης,
Ἀσσησοῦ βασιλῆος ἐλεύσεται ἔκγονος Ἀνθεύς,   5
ὅρκι' ὁμηρείης πίστ' ἐπιβωσάμενος,
πρωθήβης, ἔαρος θαλερώτερος· οὐδὲ Μελίσσῳ
Πειρήνης τοιόνδ' ἀλφεσίβοιον ὕδωρ
θηλήσει τέρεν¹ υἱόν, ἀφ' οὗ μέγα χάρμα Κορίνθῳ
ἔσται καὶ βριαροῖς ἄλγεα Βακχιάδαις·   10
Ἀνθεὺς Ἑρμείῃ ταχινῷ φίλος, ᾧ ἔπι νύμφη
μαινὰς ἄφαρ σχήσει τὸν λιθόλευστον ἔρων·
καί ἑ καθαψαμένη γούνων ἀτέλεστα κομίσσαι
πείσει· ὁ δὲ Ζῆνα Ξείνιον αἰδόμενος,
σπονδάς τ' ἐν Φοβίου καὶ ἄλα ξυνεῶνα θα-
λάσσης,   15
κρήναις καὶ ποταμοῖς νίψετ' ἀεικὲς ἔπος·

---

¹ The MS. reads μέγαν, which is intrinsically most un-
likely, and probably derived from μέγα further on in the
same line. The correction in the text is due to HAUPT, and
is as likely as any other.

---

¹ Of Pleuron in Aetolia, a contemporary of Aratus and
Philetas. This extract apparently comes from a poem in
which Apollo is predicting the fates of various victims of
unhappy love affairs.
² Lit. " while she was still a young bride and was turning
the wool on her distaff in the inner chambers of the
palace."
³ Assesus was a city in the territory of Miletus. The
word may be here either the name of the city or of its
eponymous founder.

THE STORY OF ANTHEUS

a cup of gold, that was thrown down into the well.
This is the story given by Alexander Aetolus[1] in his
Apollo :—

> Next is the tale of Phobius begun,
> Of Neleus' noble line the true-born son.
> This child of Hippocles a spouse shall win,
> Young, and content to sit at home and spin :[2]
> But lo, Assesus[3] sends a royal boy,
> Antheus, as hostage,[4] than the spring's first joy
> A stripling lovelier—not he[5] so fair
> Whom to Melissus did Pirene bear
> (That fruitful fount), who joyful Corinth freed,
> To the bold Bacchiads a bane indeed.
> Antheus is dear to Mercury above,
> But the young wife for him feels guilty[6] love :
> Clasping his knees, she prays him to consent ;[7]
> But he refuses, fearing punishment,
> If Jove, the god of hospitality,
> And the host's bread and salt[8] outragèd be :
> He will not so dishonour Phobius' trust,
> But casts to sea and stream the thought of lust.[9]

[4] Lit. "invoking the sure oaths of hostage-ship."

[5] Actaeon, whose death was the cause of the expulsion of
the clan who had tyrannized over Corinth. The full story
may be found in Plutarch, *Narrationes Amatoriae* 2.

[6] Lit. "deserving of being stoned."

[7] The meaning is a little doubtful, and some have proposed
ἀθέμιστα τελέσσαι. But I think that ἀτέλεστα can mean
"that which *ought* not to come to pass."

[8] A mysterious expression. If ἅλα ξυνεῶνα really means
"the salt of hospitality," θαλάσσης must be changed, though
the conjectures (θαλείης, τραπέζης) are most unsatisfactory.
I doubt if it is really any more than a conventional expres-
sion, "salt, the comrade of the sea."

[9] Lit. "will wash away in springs and rivers the unseemly
word."

303

ἡ δ' ὅταν ἀρνῆται μελεὸν γάμον ἀγλαὸς Ἀνθεύς,
  δὴ τότε οἱ τεύξει μητιόεντα δόλον,
μύθοις ἐξαπαφοῦσα· λόγος δέ οἱ ἔσσεται οὗτος·
  Γαυλός μοι χρύσεος φρείατος ἐκ μυχάτου   20
νῦν ὅτ' [1] ἀνελκόμενος διὰ μὲν καλὸν ἤρικεν οὖσον,
  αὐτὸς δ' ἐς Νύμφας ᾤχετ' ἐφυδριάδας·
πρὸς σὲ θεῶν, ἀλλ' εἴ μοι, ἐπεὶ καὶ πᾶσιν ἀκούω
  ῥηϊδίην οἶμον τοῦδ' ἔμεναι στομίου,
ἰθύσας ἀνέλοιο, τότ' ἂν μέγα φίλτατος εἴης.   25
  ὧδε μὲν ἡ Φοβίου Νηλιάδαο δάμαρ
φθέγξεθ'· ὁ δ' οὐ φρασθεὶς ἀπὸ μὲν Λελεγήϊον εἷμα
  μητρὸς ἑῆς ἔργον θήσεται Ἑλλαμενῆς·
αὐτὸς δὲ σπεύδων κοῖλον καταβήσεται ἄγκος
  φρείατος· ἡ δ' ἐπί οἱ λιρὰ νοεῦσα γυνὴ   30
ἀμφοτέραις χείρεσσι μυλακρίδα λᾶαν ἐνήσει·
  καὶ τόθ' ὁ μὲν ξείνων πολλὸν ἀποτμότατος
ἠρίον ὀγκώσει τὸ μεμορμένον· ἡ δ' ὑπὸ δειρὴν
  ἁψαμένη σὺν τῷ βήσεται εἰς Ἀΐδην.

ΙΕ'

ΠΕΡΙ ΔΑΦΝΗΣ

Ἡ ἱστορία παρὰ Διοδώρῳ τῷ Ἐλαΐτῃ ἐν ἐλεγείαις καὶ
Φυλάρχῳ ἐν ιε'

1. Περὶ δὲ τῆς Ἀμύκλα θυγατρὸς τάδε λέγεται
Δάφνης· αὕτη τὸ μὲν ἅπαν εἰς πόλιν οὐ κατῄει,
οὐδ' ἀνεμίσγετο ταῖς λοιπαῖς παρθένοις· παρε-
σκευασμένη δὲ πολλοὺς [2] κύνας ἐθήρευεν καὶ ἐν

---

[1] MS. ὀγ (ὅ γ). The correction is due to Meineke.

[2] For πολλοὺς κύνας the MS. has πυκνάς. Zangoiannnes ingeniously suggested that the π was a misread contraction for πολλούς, while υκνας is merely the letters of κύνας in another order.

Antheus refusing, she will then devise
A baneful stratagem.   These are her lies:—
" Drawing my golden cup from out the well
Just now, the cord broke through, and down it
   fell :
Wilt thou descend and – easy 'tis, they say—
Save what were else the water-maidens' prey ?
Thus wilt thou gain my thanks."   So speaks the
   queen :
He, guileless, doffs his tunic (which had been
His mother's handiwork, her son to please,
Hellamene, among the Leleges),
And down he climbs : the wicked woman straight
A mighty mill-stone rolls upon his pate.
Can guest or hostage sadder end e'er have ?
The well will be his fate-appointed grave :
While she must straightway knit her neck a noose,
And death and shades of Hell with him must
   choose.

XV

THE STORY OF DAPHNE

From the elegiac poems of Diodorus[1] *of Elaea and the twenty-fifth book of Phylarchus*[2]

1. THIS is how the story of Daphne, the daughter of Amyclas, is related.   She used never to come down into the town, nor consort with the other maidens ; but she got together a large pack of hounds and used to hunt, either in Laconia, or

---

[1] Otherwise unknown.

[2] A historian, variously described as being of Athens or Egypt.   Besides his historical works, he wrote a μυθικὴ ἐπιτομή, from which this story may be taken.

τῇ Λακωνικῇ καὶ ἔστιν ὅτε ἐπιφοιτῶσα εἰς τὰ
λοιπὰ τῆς Πελοποννήσου ὄρη· δι’ ἣν αἰτίαν μάλα
καταθύμιος ἦν Ἀρτέμιδι, καὶ αὐτὴν εὔστοχα
βάλλειν ἐποίει.   2. ταύτης περὶ τὴν Ἠλιδίαν
ἀλωμένης Λεύκιππος Οἰνομάου παῖς εἰς ἐπιθυ-
μίαν ἦλθε, καὶ τὸ μὲν ἄλλως πως αὐτῆς πειρᾶ-
σθαι ἀπέγνω, ἀμφιεσάμενος δὲ γυναικείαις ἀμ-
πεχόναις καὶ ὁμοιωθεὶς κόρῃ συνεθήρα αὐτῇ.
ἔτυχε δέ πως αὐτῇ κατὰ νοῦν γενόμενος, οὐ
μεθίει τε αὐτὸν ἀμφιπεσοῦσά τε καὶ ἐξηρτημένη
πᾶσαν ὥραν.   3. Ἀπόλλων δὲ καὶ αὐτὸς τῆς
παιδὸς πόθῳ καιόμενος, ὀργῇ τε καὶ φθόνῳ εἴχετο
τοῦ Λευκίππου συνόντος, καὶ ἐπὶ νοῦν αὐτῇ
βάλλει σὺν ταῖς λοιπαῖς παρθένοις ἐπὶ κρήνην
ἐλθούσαις λούεσθαι.   ἔνθα δὴ ὡς ἀφικόμεναι
ἀπεδιδύσκοντο καὶ ἑώρων τὸν Λεύκιππον μὴ
βουλόμενον, περιέρρηξαν αὐτόν· μαθοῦσαι δὲ τὴν
ἀπάτην καὶ ὡς ἐπεβούλευεν αὐταῖς, πᾶσαι μεθίε-
σαν εἰς αὐτὸν τὰς αἰχμάς.   4. καὶ ὁ μὲν δὴ κατὰ
θεῶν βούλησιν ἀφανὴς γίγνεται· Ἀπόλλωνα δὲ
Δάφνη ἐπ’ αὐτὴν ἰόντα προϊδομένη, μάλα ἐρρω-
μένως ἔφευγεν· ὡς δὲ συνεδιώκετο, παρὰ Διὸς
αἰτεῖται ἐξ ἀνθρώπων ἀπαλλαγῆναι· καὶ αὐτήν
φασι γενέσθαι τὸ δένδρον τὸ ἐπικληθὲν ἀπ’
ἐκείνης δάφνην.

sometimes going into the further mountains of the Peloponnese. For this reason she was very dear to Artemis, who gave her the gift of shooting straight. 2. On one occasion she was traversing the country of Elis, and there Leucippus, the son of Oenomaus, fell in love with her; he resolved not to woo her in any common way, but assumed women's clothes, and, in the guise of a maiden, joined her hunt. And it so happened that she very soon became extremely fond of him, nor would she let him quit her side, embracing him and clinging to him at all times. 3. But Apollo was also fired with love for the girl, and it was with feelings of anger and jealousy that he saw Leucippus always with her; he therefore put it into her mind to visit a stream with her attendant maidens, and there to bathe. On their arrival there, they all began to strip; and when they saw that Leucippus was unwilling to follow their example, they tore his clothes from him: but when they thus became aware of the deceit he had practised and the plot he had devised against them, they all plunged their spears into his body. 4. He, by the will of the gods, disappeared; but Daphne, seeing Apollo advancing upon her, took vigorously to flight; then, as he pursued her, she implored Zeus that she might be translated away from mortal sight, and she is supposed to have become the bay-tree which is called *daphne* after her.

THE LOVE ROMANCES OF PARTHENIUS

IϚ

ΠΕΡΙ ΛΑΟΔΙΚΗΣ

Ἱστορεῖ Ἡγήσιππος Παλληνιακῶν [1] αʹ

1. Ἐλέχθη δὲ καὶ περὶ Λαοδίκης ὅδε λόγος,
ὡς ἄρα παραγενομένων ἐπὶ Ἑλένης ἀπαίτησιν
Διομήδους καὶ Ἀκάμαντος, πολλὴν ἐπιθυμίαν
ἔχειν μιγῆναι παντάπασι νέῳ ὄντι Ἀκάμαντι·
καὶ μέχρι μέν τινος ὑπ᾽ αἰδοῦς κατέχεσθαι,
ὕστερον δὲ νικωμένην ὑπὸ τοῦ πάθους ἀνακοινώ-
σασθαι Περσέως γυναικί (Φιλοβίη αὐτῇ ὄνομα)
παρακαλεῖν τε αὐτὴν ὅσον οὐκ ἤδη διοιχομένη
ἀρήγειν αὐτῇ. 2. κατοικτείρουσα δὲ τὴν συμ-
φορὰν τῆς κόρης δεῖται τοῦ Περσέως ὅπως
συνεργὸς αὐτῇ γένηται, ἐκέλευέ τε ξενίαν καὶ
φιλότητα τίθεσθαι πρὸς τὸν Ἀκάμαντα. Περσεὺς
δὲ τὸ μὲν καὶ τῇ γυναικὶ βουλόμενος ἁρμόδιος
εἶναι, τὸ δὲ καὶ τὴν Λαοδίκην οἰκτείρων, πάσῃ
μηχανῇ [2] τὸν Ἀκάμαντα εἰς Δάρδανον ἀφικέσθαι
πείθει· καθίστατο γὰρ ὕπαρχος τοῦ χωρίου.
3. ἦλθε καὶ Λαοδίκη ὡς εἰς ἑορτήν τινα σὺν
ἄλλαις τῶν Τρῳάδων ἔτι παρθένος οὖσα. ἔνθα
δὴ παντοδαπὴν θοίνην ἑτοιμασάμενος συγκατα-
κλίνει καὶ τὴν Λαοδίκην αὐτῷ, φάμενος μίαν
εἶναι τῶν τοῦ βασιλέως παλλακίδων. 4. καὶ
Λαοδίκη μὲν οὕτως ἐξέπλησε τὴν ἐπιθυμίαν,

---

[1] The MS. has Μιλησιακῶν, which is a mistake introduced
from some of the other titles (e.g. No. XIV.). We know
from No. VI. that Hegesippus wrote Παλληνιακά.

[2] μηχανῇ is followed in the MS. by ἐπί or ἐπεί. Jacobs'

THE STORY OF LAODICE

XVI

THE STORY OF LAODICE

From the first book of the Palleniaca *of* Hegesippus [1]

1. IT was told of Laodice that, when Diomede and
Acamas came to ask for the restoration of Helen,
she was seized with the strongest desire to have to
do with the latter, who was still in his first youth.
For a time shame and modesty kept her back ; but
afterwards, overcome by the violence of her passion,
she acquainted Philobia, the wife of Perseus, with
the state of her affections, and implored her to come
to her rescue before she perished utterly for love.
2. Philobia was sorry for the girl's plight, and asked
Perseus to do what he could to help, suggesting
that he should come to terms of hospitality and
friendship with Acamas. He, both because he
desired to be agreeable to his wife and because he
pitied Laodice, spared no pains to induce Acamas to
come to Dardanus, where he was governor : (3) and
Laodice, still a virgin, also came, together with other
Trojan women, as if to a festival. Perseus there made
ready a most sumptuous banquet, and, when it was
over, he put Laodice to sleep by the side of Acamas,
telling him that she was one of the royal concubines.
4. Thus Laodice accomplished her desire ; and in

---

[1] See title of No. VI.

ἐπείγων is the most attractive conjecture if any word is
really represented there : but it seems more likely that it is
simply a mistaken introduction, as in V. 5.

χρόνου δὲ προϊόντος γίνεται τῷ Ἀκάμαντι υἱὸς
Μούνιτος ὃν ὑπ᾽ Αἴθρας τραφέντα μετὰ Τροίας
ἅλωσιν διεκόμισεν ἐπ᾽ οἴκου· καὶ αὐτὸν θηρεύοντα
ἐν Ὀλύνθῳ τῆς Θρᾴκης ὄφις ἀνεῖλεν.

IZ´

ΠΕΡΙ ΤΗΣ ΠΕΡΙΑΝΔΡΟΥ ΜΗΤΡΟΣ

1. Λέγεται δὲ καὶ Περίανδρον τὸν Κορίνθιον
τὴν μὲν ἀρχὴν ἐπιεικῆ τε καὶ πρᾶον εἶναι, ὕστερον
δὲ φονικώτερον γενέσθαι δι᾽ αἰτίαν τήνδε. ἡ
μήτηρ αὐτοῦ κομιδῇ νέου πολλῷ πόθῳ[1] κατεί-
χετο, καὶ τέως ἀνεπίμπλατο τῆς ἐπιθυμίας περι-
πλεκομένη τῷ παιδί. 2. προϊόντος δὲ τοῦ χρόνου
τὸ πάθος ἐπὶ μεῖζον ηὔξετο, καὶ κατέχειν τὴν νόσον
οὐκ ἔτι οἵα τε ἦν, ἕως ἀποτολμήσασα προσφέρει
λόγους τῷ παιδί, ὡς αὐτοῦ γυνή τις ἐρῴη τῶν
πάνυ καλῶν, παρεκάλει τε αὐτὸν μὴ περιορᾶν
αὐτὴν περαιτέρω καταξαινομένην. 3. ὁ δὲ τὸ μὲν
πρῶτον οὐκ ἔφη φθερεῖν ἐζευγμένην γυναῖκα ὑπό
τε νόμων καὶ ἐθῶν· λιπαρῶς δὲ προσκειμένης τῆς
μητρὸς συγκατατίθεται. καὶ ἐπειδὴ νὺξ ἐπῆλθεν
εἰς ἣν ἐτέτακτο τῷ παιδί, προεδήλωσεν αὐτῷ
μήτε λύχνα φαίνειν ἐν τῷ θαλάμῳ μήτε ἀνάγκην
αὐτῇ ἐπάγειν πρὸς τὸ διαλεχθῆναί τι· ἐπιπροσ-
δεῖσθαι[2] γὰρ αὐτὴν ὑπ᾽ αἰδοῦς. 4. καθομολογη-

---

[1] This word is not in the MS., but was inserted by Gale.
[2] The MS. ἐπιπροσθεῖσθαι is meaningless. Robinson Ellis
suggested ἐπιπροσκεῖσθαι, translating "for the woman herself
seconded her urgent appeal from a feeling of shame."

due course of time a son, called Munitus, was born
to Acamas by her. He was brought up by Aethra,[1]
and after the capture of Troy Acamas took him
home with him; later, he was killed by the bite of a
snake while hunting in Olynthus in Thrace..

XVII

The Story of Periander and his Mother

1. It is said that Periander of Corinth began by
being reasonable and mild, but afterwards became a
bloody tyrant: and this is the reason of the change.
When he was quite young, his mother [2] was seized
with a great passion of love for him, and for a time
she satisfied her feelings by constantly embracing
the lad; (2) but as time went on her passion in-
creased and she could no longer control it, so that
she took a reckless resolve and went to the lad
with a story that she made up, to the effect that
a lady of great beauty was in love with him; and
she exhorted him not to allow the poor woman to
waste away any more for unrequited love. 3. At
first Periander said he would not betray a woman
who was bound to her husband by all the sanctions
of law and custom, but, at the urgent insistence
of his mother, he yielded at last. Then, when
the pre-arranged night was at hand, she told him
that there must be no light in the chamber, nor
must he compel his partner to address any word
to him, for she made this additional request by
reason of shame. 4. Periander promised to carry

---

[1] The boy's great-grandmother (Aethra–Theseus–Acamas–
Munitus), who had accompanied Helen to Troy.

[2] Her name is said to have been Cratea.

σαμένου δὲ τοῦ Περιάνδρου πάντα ποιήσειν κατὰ
τὴν ὑφήγησιν τῆς μητρός, ὡς ὅτι κράτιστα αὐτὴν
ἀσκήσασα εἰσέρχεται παρὰ τὸν παῖδα, καὶ πρὶν ἢ
ὑποφαίνειν ἕω λαθραίως ἔξεισιν. τῇ δὲ ὑστεραίᾳ
ἀναπυνθανομένης αὐτῆς εἰ κατὰ νοῦν αὐτῷ
γένοιτο, καὶ εἰ αὖτις λέγοι αὐτὴν παρ' αὐτὸν
ἀφικέσθαι, ὁ Περίανδρος σπουδάζειν τε ἔφη καὶ
ἡσθῆναι οὐ μετρίως. 5. ὡς δὲ ἐκ¹ τούτου οὐκ
ἀνίει φοιτῶσα πρὸς τὸν παῖδα καί τις ἔρως ἐπῄει
τὸν Περίανδρον, ἤδη σπουδὴν ἐτίθετο γνωρίσαι
τὴν ἄνθρωπον ἥτις ἦν. καὶ ἕως μέν τινος ἐδεῖτο
τῆς μητρὸς ἐξικετεῦσαι ἐκείνην, ὅπως τε εἰς
λόγους αὐτῷ ἀφίκοιτο, καὶ ἐπειδὴ εἰς πολὺν
πόθον ἐπαγάγοιτο αὐτόν, δῆλη τότε γε γένηται·
νυνὶ δὲ παντάπασι πρᾶγμα ἄγνωμον πάσχειν διὰ
τὸ μὴ ἐφίεσθαι αὐτῷ καθορᾶν τὴν ἐκ πολλοῦ
χρόνου συνοῦσαν αὐτῷ. 6. ἐπεὶ δὲ ἡ μήτηρ
ἀπείργεν, αἰτιωμένη τὴν αἰσχύνην τῆς γυναικός,
κελεύει τινὰ τῶν ἀμφ' αὐτὸν οἰκετῶν λύχνα
κατακρύψαι· τῆς δὲ κατὰ τὸ σύνηθες ἀφικομένης
καὶ μελλούσης κατακλίνεσθαι, ἀναδραμὼν ὁ Περί-
ανδρος ἀναιρεῖ τὸ φῶς, καὶ κατιδὼν τὴν μητέρα
ὥρμησεν ἐπὶ τὸ διεργάσασθαι αὐτήν. 7. κατα-
σχεθεὶς δὲ ὑπό τινος δαιμονίου φαντάσματος
ἀπετράπετο, κἀκ τούτου παραπλὴξ ἦν νοῦ τε καὶ
φρενῶν, κατέσκηψέ τε εἰς ὠμότητα καὶ πολλοὺς
ἀπέσφαξε τῶν πολιτῶν· ἡ δὲ μήτηρ πολλὰ
κατολοφυραμένη τὸν ἑαυτῆς δαίμονα ἀνεῖλεν
ἑαυτήν.

¹ ἐκ is not in the MS., but must be inserted.

out all his mother's instructions; she then prepared herself with all care and went in to the youth, slipping out secretly before the first gleam of dawn. The next day she asked him if all had gone to his taste, and if he would like the woman to come again; to which Periander answered that he would like it particularly, and that he had derived no little pleasure from the experience. 5. From that time onward she thus visited the lad constantly. But he began to feel real love for his visitant, and became desirous of knowing who she really was. For a time then he kept asking his mother to implore the woman to consent to speak to him, and that, since she had now enmeshed him in a strong passion, she should at last reveal herself: for as things stood, he found it extremely distasteful that he was never allowed to see the woman who had been consorting with him for so long a time. 6. But when his mother refused, alleging the shame felt by the woman, he bade one of his body-servants conceal a light in the chamber; and when she came as usual, and was about to lay herself down, Periander jumped up and revealed the light: and when he saw that it was his mother, he made as if to kill her. 7. However, he was restrained by a heaven-sent apparition, and desisted from his purpose, but from that time on he was a madman, afflicted in brain and heart; he fell into habits of savagery, and slaughtered many of the citizens of Corinth. His mother, after long and bitterly bewailing her evil fate, made away with herself.

THE LOVE ROMANCES OF PARTHENIUS

ΙΗ΄

ΠΕΡΙ ΝΕΑΙΡΑΣ

Ἱστορεῖ Θεόφραστος ἐν α΄ τῶν Πρὸς τοὺς καιρούς

1. Ὑψικρέων δὲ Μιλήσιος καὶ Προμέδων
Νάξιος μάλιστα φίλω ἤστην. ἀφικομένου οὖν
ποτε Προμέδοντος εἰς Μίλητον, θατέρου λέγεται
τὴν γυναῖκα Νέαιραν ἐρασθῆναι αὐτοῦ· καὶ
παρόντος μὲν τοῦ Ὑψικρέοντος μὴ τολμᾶν αὐτὴν
διαλέγεσθαι τῷ ξένῳ· μετὰ δὲ χρόνον, ὡς ὁ μὲν
Ὑψικρέων ἐτύγχανεν ἀποδημῶν, ὁ δὲ αὖτις ἀφί-
κετο, νύκτωρ αὐτοῦ κοιμωμένου ἐπεισέρχεται ἡ
Νέαιρα· 2. καὶ πρῶτα¹ μὲν οἷά τε ἦν πείθειν αὐτόν·
ἐπειδὴ δὲ ἐκεῖνος οὐκ ἐνεδίδου,² Δία τε Ἑταιρήιον
καὶ Ξένιον αἰδούμενος, προσέταξεν ἡ Νέαιρα ταῖς
θεραπαίναις ἀποκλεῖσαι τὸν θάλαμον· καὶ οὕτως,
πολλὰ ἐπαγωγὰ ποιούσης, ἠναγκάσθη μιγῆναι
αὐτῇ. 3. τῇ μέντοι ὑστεραίᾳ, δεινὸν ἡγησάμενος
εἶναι τὸ πραχθέν, ᾤχετο πλέων ἐπὶ τῆς Νάξου·
ἔνθα καὶ ἡ Νέαιρα, δείσασα τὸν Ὑψικρέοντα,
διέπλευσεν εἰς τὴν Νάξον· καὶ ἐπειδὴ αὐτὴν
ἐξῄτει ὁ Ὑψικρέων, ἱκέτις προσκαθίζετο ἐπὶ τῆς
ἑστίας τῆς ἐν τῷ πρυτανείῳ. 4. οἱ δὲ Νάξιοι
λιπαροῦντι τῷ Ὑψικρέοντι ἐκδώσειν μὲν οὐκ
ἔφασαν· ἐκέλευον μέντοι πείσαντα αὐτὴν ἄγεσθαι·
δόξας δὲ ὁ Ὑψικρέων ἀσεβεῖσθαι, πείθει Μιλη-
σίους πολεμεῖν τοῖς Ναξίοις.

¹ MS. πρώτη. I prefer Palairet's correction of πρῶτα
to the more ordinary πρῶτον.
² Herz's suggestion for the MS. ἐδίδου, which can hardly
be construed.

THE STORY OF NEAERA

XVIII

The Story of Neaera

From the first book of Theophrastus' [1] Political History

1. HYPSICREON of Miletus and Promedon of Naxos were two very great friends. The story is that when on one occasion Promedon was on a visit to Miletus, his friend's wife fell in love with him. While Hypsicreon was there, she did not venture to disclose the state of her affections to her guest; but later, when Hypsicreon happened to be abroad and Promedon was again there, she went in to him at night when he was asleep. 2. To begin with she tried to persuade him to consent; when he would not give in, fearing Zeus the god of Comradeship and Hospitality, she bade her serving-maids lock the doors of the chamber upon them; and so at last, overcome by the multitude of her blandishments, he was forced to content her. 3. On the morrow, however, feeling that he had committed an odious crime, he left her and sailed away for Naxos; and then Neaera, in fear of Hypsicreon, also journeyed to Naxos; and, when her husband came to fetch her, took up a suppliant's position at the altar-hearth of the Prytaneum. [2] 4. When Hypsicreon asked the Naxians to give her up, they refused, rather advising him to do what he could to get her away by persuasion; but he, thinking that this treatment of him was against all the canons of right, induced Miletus to declare war upon Naxos.

---

[1] See the title of No. IX.
[2] The town-hall, the centre of the civic life of the state.

ΙΘ´

ΠΕΡΙ ΠΑΓΚΡΑΤΟΥΣ

Ἱστορεῖ Ἀνδρίσκος ἐν Ναξιακῶν β´

Σκέλλις δὲ καὶ Ἀγασσαμενός, οἱ Ἑκήτορος ἐκ
Θρᾴκης,¹ ὁρμήσαντες ἀπὸ νήσου τῆς πρότερον μὲν
Στρογγύλης, ὕστερον δὲ Νάξου κληθείσης, ἐληΐ-
ζοντο μὲν τήν τε Πελοπόννησον καὶ τὰς πέριξ
νήσους· προσσχόντες δὲ Θεσσαλίᾳ πολλάς τε
ἄλλας γυναῖκας κατέσυραν, ἐν δὲ καὶ τὴν Ἀλωέως
γυναῖκα Ἰφιμέδην καὶ θυγατέρα αὐτῆς Παγκρατώ·
ἧς ἀμφότεροι εἰς ἔρωτα ἀφικόμενοι ἀλλήλους
κατέκτειναν.

Κ´

ΠΕΡΙ ΑΕΡΟΥΣ²

1. Λέγεται δὲ καὶ Οἰνοπίωνος καὶ νύμφης
Ἑλίκης Ἀερὼ κόρην γενέσθαι· ταύτης δὲ Ὠρίωνα
τὸν Ὑριέως ἐρασθέντα παρ' αὐτοῦ παραιτεῖσθαι
τὴν κόρην, καὶ διὰ ταύτην τήν τε νῆσον ἐξημερῶσαι
τότε θηρίων ἀνάπλεων οὖσαν, λείαν τε πολλὴν
περιελαύνοντα τῶν προσχώρων ἕδνα διδόναι·
2. τοῦ μέντοι Οἰνοπίωνος ἑκάστοτε ὑπερτιθεμένου
τὸν γάμον διὰ τὸ ἀποστυγεῖν αὐτῷ γαμβρὸν
τοιοῦτον γενέσθαι, ὑπὸ μέθης ἔκφρονα γενόμενον

---

¹ The MS. is here gravely corrupt, giving Σ. τε καὶ Κασσα-
μενὸς κήτορος οἱ Θ. The text as printed is the suggestion of
Knaacke, who used the parallel account given by Diodorus
in his *Bibliotheca* (v. 50).

² The MS. gives the name as Haero, for which Hero,

XIX

The Story of Pancrato

From the second book of the Naxiaca *of Andriscus*[1]

SCELLIS and Agassamenus, the sons of Hecetor, who came from Thrace, started from the island originally called Strongyle but afterwards Naxos, and plundered the Peloponnese and the islands about it: then reaching Thessaly they carried a great number of women into captivity; among them Iphimede the wife of Haloeus and her daughter Pancrato. With this maiden they both of them fell in love, and fought for her and killed each other.

XX

The Story of Aëro

1. AËRO, so the story runs, was the daughter of Oenopion and the nymph Helice. Orion, the son of Hyrieus, fell in love with her, and asked her father for her hand; for her sake he rendered the island[2] where they lived habitable (it was formerly full of wild beasts), and he also gathered together much booty from the folk who lived there and brought it as a bridal-gift for her. 2. Oenopion however constantly kept putting off the time of the wedding, for he hated the idea of having such a man as his daughter's husband. Then Orion, maddened

---

[1] See the title of No. IX.   [2] Chios.

Maero, Mero, and Pero have been variously conjectured. The restoration Aëro is due to Knaacke.

THE LOVE ROMANCES OF PARTHENIUS

τὸν Ὠρίωνα κατᾶξαι τὸν θάλαμον, ἔνθα[1] ἡ παῖς
ἐκοιμᾶτο, καὶ βιαζόμενον ἐκκαῆναι τοὺς ὀφθαλ-
μοὺς ὑπὸ τοῦ Οἰνοπίωνος.

ΚΔ΄

ΠΕΡΙ ΠΕΙΣΙΔΙΚΗΣ

1. Λέγεται δὲ καὶ ὅτε Ἀχιλλεὺς πλέων τὰς
προσεχεῖς τῇ ἠπείρῳ νήσους ἐπόρθει, προσσχεῖν
αὐτὸν Λέσβῳ· ἔνθα δὴ καθ' ἑκάστην τῶν πόλεων
αὐτὸν ἐπιόντα κεραΐζειν. 2. ὡς δὲ οἱ Μήθυμναν
οἰκοῦντες μάλα καρτερῶς ἀντεῖχον, καὶ ἐν πολλῇ
ἀμηχανίᾳ ἦν διὰ τὸ μὴ δύνασθαι ἑλεῖν τὴν πόλιν,
Πεισιδίκην τινὰ Μηθυμναίαν, τοῦ βασιλέως θυγα-
τέρα, θεασαμένην ἀπὸ τοῦ τείχους τὸν Ἀχιλλέα,
ἐρασθῆναι αὐτοῦ, καὶ οὕτως, τὴν τροφὸν διαπεμ-
ψαμένην, ὑπισχνεῖσθαι ἐγχειριεῖν αὐτῷ τὴν πόλιν,
εἴ γε μέλλοι αὐτὴν γυναῖκα ἕξειν. 3. ὁ δὲ τὸ μὲν
παραυτίκα καθωμολογήσατο· ἐπεὶ μέντοι ἐγ-
κρατὴς τῆς[2] πόλεως ἐγένετο, νεμεσήσας ἐπὶ τῷ
δρασθέντι, προὐτρέψατο τοὺς στρατιώτας κατα-
λεῦσαι τὴν κόρην. μέμνηται τοῦ πάθους τοῦδε
καὶ ὁ τὴν Λέσβου κτίσιν ποιήσας ἐν τοῖσδε·

Ἔνθα δὲ Πηλείδης κατὰ μὲν κτάνε Λάμπετον ἥρω,
ἐκ δ' Ἱκετάονα πέφνεν, ἰθαιγενέος Λεπετύμνου
υἱέα Μηθύμνης τε, καὶ ἀλκήεστατον ἄλλων
αὐτοκασίγνητον Ἑλικάονος, ἔνδοθι πάτρης

[1] The MS. has καὶ ἔνθα. Heyne saw that the καί must be
omitted.
[2] τῆς, which had fallen out of the MS. by haplography,
was supplied by Schneider.

318

by strong drink, broke in the doors of the chamber
where the girl was lying asleep, and as he was
offering violence to her Oenopion attacked him and
put out his eyes with a burning brand.

XXI

THE STORY OF PISIDICE

1. THERE is a story that Achilles, when he was
sailing along and laying waste the islands close to
the mainland, arrived at Lesbos, and there attacked
each of its cities in turn and plundered it. 2. But
the inhabitants of Methymna held out against him
very valiantly, and he was in great straits because
he was unable to take the city, when a girl of
Methymna named Pisidice, a daughter of the king,
saw him from the walls and fell in love with him.
Accordingly she sent him her nurse, and promised to
put the town into his possession if he would take her
to wife. 3. At the moment, indeed, he consented
to her terms; but when the town was in his power
he felt the utmost loathing for what she had done,
and bade his soldiers stone her. The poet[1] of the
founding of Lesbos relates this tragedy in these
words :—

Achilles slew the hero Lampetus
And Hicetaon (of Methymna son
And Lepetymnus, born of noble sires)
And Helicaon's brother, bold like him,

---

[1] Probably, though not quite certainly, Apollonius of
Rhodes.

τηλίκον ¹ Ὑψίπυλον· θαλερὴ δέ μιν ἄασε Κύ-
   πρις.   5
ἡ γὰρ ἐπ' Αἰακίδῃ κούρῃ φρένας ἐπτοίησε
Πεισιδίκη, ὅτε τόν γε μετὰ προμάχοισιν Ἀχαιῶν
χάρμῃ ἀγαλλόμενον θηέσκετο,² πολλὰ δ' ἐς ὑγρὴν
ἠέρα χεῖρας ἔτεινεν ἐελδομένη φιλότητος.

4. εἶτα μικρὸν ὑποβάς·

Δέκτο μὲν αὐτίκα λαὸν Ἀχαϊκὸν ἔνδοθι πάτρης   10
παρθενική, κληῖδας ὑποχλίσσασα πυλάων,
ἔτλη δ' οἷσιν ἰδέσθαι ἐν ὀφθαλμοῖσι τοκῆας
χαλκῷ ἐληλαμένους καὶ δούλια δεσμὰ γυναικῶν
ἑλκομένων ἐπὶ νῆας ὑποσχεσίης Ἀχιλῆος,
ὄφρα νυὸς γλαυκῆς Θέτιδος πέλοι, ὄφρα οἱ εἶεν   15
πενθεροὶ Αἰακίδαι, Φθίῃ δ' ἐνὶ δώματα ναίοι
ἀνδρὸς ἀριστῆος πινυτὴ δάμαρ· οὐ δ' ὅ γ' ἔμελλε
τὰ ῥέξειν, ὀλοῷ δ' ἐπαγάσσατο πατρίδος οἴτῳ·
ἔνθ' ἥ γ' αἰνότατον γάμον εἴσιδε Πηλείδαο
Ἀργείων ὑπὸ χερσὶ δυσάμμορος, οἵ μιν ἔπεφνον   20
πανσυδίῃ θαμινῇσιν ἀράσσοντες λιθάδεσσιν.

ΚΒ'
ΠΕΡΙ ΝΑΝΙΔΟΣ

Ἡ ἱστορία παρὰ Λικυμνίῳ τῷ Χίῳ μελοποιῷ καὶ Ἑρμησιά-
νακτι

1. Ἔφασαν δέ τινες καὶ τὴν Σαρδίων ἀκρό-
πολιν ὑπὸ Κύρου τοῦ Περσῶν βασιλέως ἁλῶναι,

---

¹ Almost certainly corrupt : but no satisfactory remedy
has been found.
² The MS. has θυέσκετο. The correction is due to Gale.

THE STORY OF NANIS

Hypsipylus, the strongest man alive.
But lady Venus laid great wait for him :
For she set poor Pisidice's young heart
A-fluttering with love for him, whenas
She saw him revelling in battle's lust
Amid the Achaean champions ; and full oft
Into the buxom air her arms she flung
In craving for his love.

4. Then, a little further down, he goes on :—

Within the city straight the maiden brought
The whole Achaean hosts, the city gates
Unbarring stealthily ; yea, she endured
With her own eyes to see her aged sires
Put to the sword, the chains of slavery
About the women whom Achilles dragged
—So had he sworn—down to his ships : and all
That she might sea-born Thetis' daughter be,
The sons of Aeacus her kin, and dwell
At Phthia, royal husband's goodly spouse.
But it was not to be : he but rejoiced
To see her city's doom, while her befell
A sorry marriage with great Peleus' son,
Poor wretch, at Argive hands ; for her they slew,
Casting great stones upon her, one and all.

XXII

THE STORY OF NANIS

From the lyrics of Licymnius [1] *of Chios and from
Hermesianax* [2]

1. THE story has been told that the citadel of
Sardis was captured by Cyrus, the king of the

---

[1] A dithyrambic poet of the third century B.C.
[2] See title of No. V.

THE LOVE ROMANCES OF PARTHENIUS

προδούσης τῆς Κροίσου θυγατρὸς Νανίδος. ἐπειδὴ
γὰρ ἐπολιόρκει Σάρδεις Κῦρος καὶ οὐδὲν αὐτῷ
εἰς ἅλωσιν τῆς πόλεως προῦβαινεν, ἐν πολλῷ
τε δέει ἦν, μὴ ἀθροισθὲν τὸ συμμαχικὸν αὐτῖς[1]
τῷ Κροίσῳ διαλύσειεν αὐτῷ τὴν στρατιάν,
(2) τότε τὴν παρθένον ταύτην εἶχε λόγος περὶ
προδοσίας συνθεμένην τῷ Κύρῳ, εἰ κατὰ νόμους
Περσῶν ἕξει γυναῖκα αὐτήν, κατὰ τὴν ἄκραν,
μηδενὸς φυλάσσοντος δι' ὀχυρότητα τοῦ χωρίου,
εἰσδέχεσθαι τοὺς πολεμίους, συνεργῶν αὐτῇ καὶ
ἄλλων τινῶν γενομένων· τὸν μέντοι Κῦρον μὴ
ἐμπεδῶσαι αὐτῇ τὴν ὑπόσχεσιν.

ΚΓ΄

ΠΕΡΙ ΧΕΙΛΩΝΙΔΟΣ

1. Κλεώνυμος ὁ Λακεδαιμόνιος, βασιλείου γένους
ὢν καὶ πολλὰ κατορθωσάμενος Λακεδαιμονίοις,
ἔγημε Χειλωνίδα προσήκουσαν αὐτῷ κατὰ γένος.
ταύτῃ σφοδρῶς ἐπιτεταμένου τοῦ Κλεωνύμου καὶ
τὸν ἔρωτα οὐκ ἠρέμα φέροντος, τοῦ μὲν κατηλόγει,
πᾶσα δὲ ἐνέκειτο Ἀκροτάτῳ, τῷ τοῦ βασιλέως
υἱεῖ.   2. καὶ γὰρ ὁ μειρακίσκος αὐτῆς ἀναφανδὸν
ὑπεκαίετο, ὥστε πάντας ἀνὰ στόμα ἔχειν τὴν
ὁμιλίαν αὐτῶν. δι' ἣν αἰτίαν δυσανασχετήσας
ὁ Κλεώνυμος καὶ ἄλλως δὲ οὐκ ἀρεσκόμενος
τοῖς Λακεδαιμονίοις ἤθεσιν, ἐπεραιώθη πρὸς Πύρ-
ρον εἰς Ἤπειρον καὶ αὐτὸν ἀναπείθει πειρᾶσθαι

[1] The MS. has αὐτῆς, and Cobet's αὐτις must be considered
as little more than a makeshift.

Persians, through its betrayal by Nanis, the daughter of Croesus. Cyrus was besieging Sardis, and none of the devices he employed resulted in the capture of the city : he was indeed in great fear that Croesus would get together again an army of allies and would come and destroy his blockading force. 2. Then (so the story went) this girl, Nanis, made an agreement to betray the place to Cyrus if he would take her to wife according to the customs of the Persians ; she got together some helpers and let in the enemy by the extreme summit of the citadel, a place where no guards were posted owing to its natural strength. Cyrus, however, refused to perform the promise which he had made to her.

XXIII

THE STORY OF CHILONIS

1. CLEONYMUS of Sparta, who was of royal stock and had done great things for the Lacedaemonians, took to wife his kinswoman Chilonis. He loved her with a great love—his was no gentle passion—but she despised him, and gave her whole heart to Acrotatus, the son of the king. 2. Indeed the stripling let the fire of his love shew openly, so that all men were talking of their intrigue ; wherefore Cleonymus, being sorely vexed, and having besides no liking for the Lacedaemonians and their ways, crossed over to Pyrrhus in Epirus and advised him to attack the

τῆς Πελοποννήσου, ὡς εἰ καὶ ἐντόνως ἅψαιντο
τοῦ πολέμου, ῥαδίως ἐκπολιορκήσοντες τὰς ἐν
αὐτοῖς πόλεις· ἔφη δὲ καὶ αὐτῷ τι ἤδη προδιειρ-
γάσθαι, ὥστε καὶ στάσιν ἐγγενέσθαι τισὶ τῶν
πόλεων.

ΚΔ´

ΠΕΡΙ ΙΠΠΑΡΙΝΟΥ

1. Ἱππαρῖνος δὲ Συρακοσίων τύραννος εἰς
ἐπιθυμίαν ἀφίκετο πάνυ καλοῦ παιδός, Ἀχαιὸς
αὐτῷ ὄνομα· τοῦτον ἐξαλλάγμασι πολλοῖς ὑπαγό-
μενος πείθει τὴν οἰκίαν ἀπολιπόντα σὺν αὐτῷ
μένειν· χρόνου δὲ προϊόντος, ὡς πολεμίων τις
ἔφοδος προσηγγέλθη πρός τι τῶν ὑπ᾽ ἐκείνου
κατεχομένων χωρίων καὶ ἔδει κατὰ τάχος βοη-
θεῖν, ἐξορμῶν ὁ Ἱππαρῖνος παρεκελεύσατο τῷ
παιδί, εἴ τις ἐντὸς τῆς αὐλῆς βιάζοιτο, κατα-
καίνειν αὐτὸν τῇ σπάθῃ ἣν ἐτύγχανεν αὐτῷ
κεχαρισμένος. 2. καὶ ἐπειδὴ συμβαλὼν τοῖς
πολεμίοις κατὰ κράτος αὐτοὺς εἷλεν, ἐπὶ πολὺν
οἶνον ἐτράπετο καὶ συνουσίαν· ἐκκαιόμενος δὲ
ὑπὸ μέθης καὶ πόθου τοῦ παιδός, ἀφίππευσεν
εἰς τὰς Συρακούσας καὶ παραγενόμενος ἐπὶ τὴν
οἰκίαν ἔνθα τῷ παιδὶ παρεκελεύσατο μένειν, ὃς

---

[1] The latter part of the story is missing. It appears from
the account given by Plutarch (in the *Life of Pyrrhus*) that
during the siege of Sparta by Pyrrhus, Chilonis made ready
a halter, in order never to fall into Cleonymus' hands alive,
but that the siege was raised first by the personal valour of

Peloponnese; if they prosecuted the war vigorously, he said, they would without difficulty storm the Lacedaemonian cities; and he added that he had already prepared the ground, so that in many of the cities there would be a revolt in his favour.[1]

XXIV

THE STORY OF HIPPARINUS

1. HIPPARINUS, tyrant of Syracuse, felt a great affection for a very fair boy named Achaeus, and, by means of presents[2] of varying kinds, persuaded him to leave his home and stay with him in his palace. Some little time after, the news was brought to him of a hostile incursion into one of the territories belonging to him, and he had to go with all speed to help his subjects. When he was starting, he told the boy that if anyone of the courtiers offered violence to him, he was to stab him with the dagger which he had given him as a present. 2. Hipparinus met his enemies and inflicted on them an utter defeat, and celebrated his victory by deep potations of wine and by banqueting: then, heated with the wine and by desire to see the lad, he rode off at full gallop to Syracuse. Arriving at the house where he had bidden the boy to stay, he did not tell him who

Acrotatus, and then by the arrival of his father, King Areus, from Crete with reinforcements.

[2] The meaning of ἐξαλλάγμασι is a little doubtful. It may either be "entertainments," or "changes, variation of gifts."

μὲν ἦν οὐκ ἐδήλου, Θετταλίζων δὲ τῇ φωνῇ, τὸν
Ἱππαρῖνον ἔφησεν ἀπεκτονηκέναι· ὁ δὲ παῖς
διαγανακτήσας σκότους ὄντος παίει καιρίαν τὸν
Ἱππαρῖνον· ὁ δὲ τρεῖς ἡμέρας ἐπιβιούς, καὶ τοῦ
φόνου τὸν Ἀχαιὸν ἀπολύσας, ἐτελεύτησεν.

ΚΕ′

ΠΕΡΙ ΦΑΥΛΛΟΥ

Ἱστορεῖ Φύλαρχος

1. Φάϋλλος δὲ τύραννος ἠράσθη τῆς Ἀρίστωνος
γυναικός, ὃς Οἰταίων προστάτης ἦν· οὗτος δια-
πεμπόμενος πρὸς αὐτήν, χρυσόν τε πολὺν καὶ
ἄργυρον ἐπηγγέλλετο δώσειν, εἴ τέ τινος ἄλλου
δέοιτο, φράζειν ἐκέλευεν ὡς οὐχ ἁμαρτησομένην.
2. τὴν δὲ ἄρα πολὺς εἶχε πόθος ὅρμου τοῦ
τότε κειμένου ἐν τῷ τῆς Προνοίας Ἀθηνᾶς ἱερῷ,
ὃν εἶχε λόγος Ἐριφύλης γεγονέναι, ἠξίου τε
ταύτης τῆς δωρεᾶς τυχεῖν. Φάϋλλος δὲ τά τε
ἄλλα κατασύρων ἐκ Δελφῶν ἀναθήματα, ἀναιρεῖ-
ται καὶ τὸν ὅρμον. 3. ἐπεὶ δὲ διεκομίσθη εἰς
οἶκον τὸν Ἀρίστωνος, χρόνον μέν τινα ἐφόρει
αὐτὸν ἡ γυνὴ μάλα περίπυστος οὖσα, μετὰ δὲ
ταῦτα παραπλήσιον αὐτῇ πάθος συνέβη τῶν
περὶ τὴν Ἐριφύλην γενομένων· ὁ γὰρ νεώτερος

---

[1] Parthenius has not mentioned the nationality of the
enemy, and it seems doubtful whether Thessalians would be
likely to come into conflict with a Sicilian monarch.
Meineke proposed ψελλίζων, "stammering, lisping."
[2] See title of No. XV.　　[3] Of Phocis.
[4] προστάτης might also mean that he was the protector or

he was, but, putting on a Thessalian [1] accent, cried out that he had killed Hipparinus: it was dark, and the boy, in his anger and grief, struck him and gave him a mortal wound. He lived for three days, acquitted Achaeus of the guilt of his death, and then breathed his last.

XXV

THE STORY OF PHAYLLUS

From Phylarchus [2]

1. THE tyrant Phayllus [3] fell in love with the wife of Ariston, chief [4] of the Oetaeans: he sent envoys to her, with promises of much silver and gold, and told them to add that if there were anything else which she wanted, she should not fail of her desire. 2. Now she had a great longing for a necklace that was at that time hanging in the temple [5] of Athene the goddess of Forethought: it was said formerly to have belonged to Eriphyle; and this was the present for which she asked. Phayllus took a great booty of the offerings at Delphi, the necklace among the rest: (3) it was sent to the house of Ariston, and for some considerable time the woman wore it, and was greatly famed for so doing. But later she suffered a fate very similar to that of Eriphyle [6]:

consul of the Oetaeans at Phocis. But Oeta is a wild mountain-range, the inhabitants of which would hardly be so highly organized as to have a representative in foreign cities.   [5] At Delphi.

[6] The expedition of the Seven against Thebes could not be successful without the company of Amphiaraus, whom his wife Eriphyle, bribed by a necklace, persuaded to go. He there met his end, and was avenged by his son Alcmaeon, who killed his mother.

τῶν υἱῶν αὐτῆς μανεὶς τὴν οἰκίαν ὑφῆψε, καὶ
τήν τε μητέρα καὶ τὰ πολλὰ τῶν κτημάτων
κατέφλεξεν.

ΚϚ´

ΠΕΡΙ ΑΠΡΙΑΤΗΣ

Ἱστορεῖ Εὐφορίων Θρᾳκί

1. Ἐν Λέσβῳ παιδὸς Ἀπριάτης Τράμβηλος ὁ
Τελαμῶνος ἐρασθεὶς πολλὰ ἐποιεῖτο εἰς τὸ
προσαγαγέσθαι τὴν κόρην· ὡς δὲ ἐκείνη οὐ πάνυ
ἐνεδίδου, ἐνενοεῖτο δόλῳ καὶ ἀπάτῃ περιγενέσθαι
αὐτῆς. 2. πορευομένην οὖν ποτε σὺν θεραπαινι-
δίοις ἐπί τι τῶν πατρῴων χωρίων, ὃ πλησίον τῆς
θαλάσσης ἔκειτο, λοχήσας εἷλεν. ὡς δὲ ἐκείνη
πολὺ μᾶλλον ἀπεμάχετο περὶ τῆς παρθενίας,
ὀργισθεὶς Τράμβηλος ἔρριψεν αὐτὴν εἰς τὴν
θάλασσαν· ἐτύγχανε δὲ ἀγχιβαθὴς οὖσα. καὶ ἡ
μὲν ἄρα οὕτως ἀπολώλει· τινὲς [1] μέντοι ἔφασαν
διωκομένην ἑαυτὴν ῥῖψαι. 3. Τράμβηλον δὲ οὐ
πολὺ μετέπειτα τίσις ἐλάμβανεν ἐκ θεῶν· ἐπειδὴ
γὰρ Ἀχιλλεὺς ἐκ τῆς Λέσβου πολλὴν λείαν
ἀποτεμόμενος ἤγαγεν, οὗτος, ἐπαγομένων αὐτὸν
τῶν ἐγχωρίων βοηθόν, συνίσταται αὐτῷ. 4. ἔνθα
δὴ πληγεὶς εἰς τὰ στέρνα παραχρῆμα πίπτει·
ἀγάμενος δὲ τῆς ἀλκῆς αὐτὸν Ἀχιλλεὺς ἔτι

---

[1] There is here a marginal note in the MS., which may be
considered as a continuation of the information in the title—
γρ. Ἀριστόκριτος ἐν τοῖς περὶ Μιλήτου.

her youngest son went mad and set fire to their house, and in the course of the conflagration both she and a great part of their possessions were consumed.

XXVI

The Story of Apriate

From the Thrax of Euphorion [1]

1. TRAMBELUS the son of Telamon fell in love with a girl named Apriate in Lesbos. He used every effort to gain her : but, as she shewed no signs at all of relenting, he determined to win her by strategy and guile. 2. She was walking one day with her attendant handmaids to one of her father's domains which was by the seashore, and there he laid an ambush for her and made her captive ; but she struggled with the greatest violence to protect her virginity, and at last Trambelus in fury threw her into the sea, which happened at that point to be deep inshore. Thus did she perish ; the story has, however, been related by others [2] in the sense that she threw herself in while fleeing from his pursuit. 3. It was not long before divine vengeance fell upon Trambelus : Achilles was ravaging Lesbos [3] and carrying away great quantities of booty, and Trambelus got together a company of the inhabitants of the island, and went out to meet him in battle. 4. In the course of it he received a wound in the breast and instantly fell to the ground ; while he was still breathing, Achilles, who had

[1] See title of No. XIII.
[2] *i.e.* by Aristocritus, writer on the early history of Miletus. See title of No. XI.   [3] See No. XXI., 1.

THE LOVE ROMANCES OF PARTHENIUS

ἔμπνουν ἀνέκρινεν ὅστις τε ἦν καὶ ὁπόθεν· ἐπεὶ
δὲ ἔγνω παῖδα Τελαμῶνος ὄντα, πολλὰ κατοδυρό-
μενος ἐπὶ τῆς ἠϊόνος μέγα χῶμα ἔχωσε· τοῦτο ἔτι
νῦν ἡρῷον Τραμβήλου καλεῖται.

ΚΖ΄

ΠΕΡΙ ΑΛΚΙΝΟΗΣ

Ἱστορεῖ Μοιρὼ ἐν ταῖς Ἀραῖς

1. Ἔχει δὲ λόγος καὶ Ἀλκινόην, τὴν Πολύβου
μὲν τοῦ Κορινθίου θυγατέρα, γυναῖκα δὲ Ἀμφι-
λόχου τοῦ Δρύαντος, κατὰ μῆνιν Ἀθηνᾶς
ἐπιμανῆναι ξένῳ Σαμίῳ· Ξάνθος αὐτῷ ὄνομα.
ἐπὶ μισθῷ γὰρ αὐτὴν ἀγαγομένην χερνῆτιν
γυναῖκα Νικάνδρην καὶ ἐργασαμένην ἐνιαυτὸν
ὕστερον ἐκ τῶν οἰκίων ἐλάσαι, μὴ ἐντελῆ τὸν
μισθὸν ἀποδοῦσαν· τὴν δὲ ἀράσασθαι πολλὰ
Ἀθηνᾷ τίσασθαι αὐτὴν ἀντ᾽ ἀδίκου στερήσεως.
2. ὅθεν εἰς τοσοῦτον [1] ἐλθεῖν, ὥστε ἀπολιπεῖν
οἶκόν τε καὶ παῖδας ἤδη γεγονότας, συνεκπλεῦσαί
τε τῷ Ξάνθῳ· γενομένην δὲ κατὰ μέσον πόρον
ἔννοιαν λαβεῖν τῶν εἰργασμένων, καὶ αὐτίκα
πολλά τε δάκρυα προΐεσθαι καὶ ἀνακαλεῖν ὁτὲ
μὲν ἄνδρα κουρίδιον, ὁτὲ δὲ τοὺς παῖδας· τέλος δέ,

---

[1] The MS. has τοσοῦτόν τε. The omission of τε was
rightly proposed by Peerlkamp.

---

[1] The brother of his own father Peleus.

[2] Or Myro, of Byzantium, a poetess of about 250 B.C.,
daughter of the tragedian Homerus. She wrote epigrams
(we have two in the *Palatine Anthology*), and epic and lyric
poetry. Such poems as the *Dirae* were not uncommon in

admired his valour, inquired of his name and origin. When he was told that he was the son of Telamon,[1] he bewailed him long and deeply, and piled up a great barrow for him on the beach : it is still called " the hero Trambelus' mound."

XXVII

THE STORY OF ALCINOE

From the Curses of Moero [2]

1. ALCINOE, so the story goes, was the daughter of Polybus of Corinth and the wife of Amphilochus the son of Dryas ; by the wrath of Athene she became infatuated with a stranger from Samos, named Xanthus. This was the reason of her visitation : she had hired a woman named Nicandra to come and spin for her, but after she had worked for her for a year, she turned her out of her house without paying her the full wages she had promised, and Nicandra had earnestly prayed Athene to avenge her for the unjust withholding of her due.[3] 2. Thus afflicted, Alcinoe reached such a state that she left her home and the little children she had borne to Amphilochus, and sailed away with Xanthus ; but in the middle of the voyage she came to realise what she had done. She straightway shed many tears, calling often, now upon her young husband

the Alexandrine period—invective against an enemy illustrated by numerous mythological instances. We have an example surviving in Ovid's *Ibis*.

[3] Deuteronomy xxiv. 14 : "Thou shalt not oppress an hired servant that is poor and needy, . . . at his day thou shalt give him his hire, neither shall the sun go down upon it ; for he is poor, and setteth his heart upon it : lest he cry against thee unto the Lord, and it be sin unto thee."

πολλὰ τοῦ Ξάνθου παρηγοροῦντος καὶ φαμένου γυναῖκα ἕξειν, μὴ πειθομένην ῥῖψαι ἑαυτὴν εἰς θάλασσαν.

ΚΗ΄

ΠΕΡΙ ΚΛΕΙΤΗΣ

Ἱστορεῖ Εὐφορίων Ἀπολλοδώρῳ, τὰ ἑξῆς Ἀπολλώνιος
Ἀργοναυτικῶν α΄

1. Διαφόρως δὲ ἱστορεῖται περὶ Κυζίκου τοῦ Αἰνέου·[1] οἱ μὲν γὰρ αὐτὸν ἔφασαν ἁρμοσάμενον Λάρισαν[2] τὴν Πιάσου, ᾗ ὁ πατὴρ ἐμίγη πρὸ γάμου, μαχόμενον ἀποθανεῖν· τινὲς δὲ προσφάτως γήμαντα Κλείτην συμβαλεῖν δι᾽ ἄγνοιαν τοῖς μετὰ Ἰάσονος ἐπὶ τῆς Ἀργοῦς πλέουσι, καὶ οὕτως πεσόντα πᾶσι μεγάλως ἀλγεινὸν πόθον ἐμβαλεῖν, ἐξόχως δὲ τῇ Κλείτῃ· 2. ἰδοῦσα γὰρ αὐτὸν ἐρριμμένον, περιεχύθη καὶ πολλὰ κατωδύρατο, νύκτωρ δὲ λαθοῦσα τὰς θεραπαινίδας ἀπό τινος δένδρου ἀνήρτησεν ἑαυτήν.[3]

ΚΘ΄

ΠΕΡΙ ΔΑΦΝΙΔΟΣ

Ἱστορεῖ Τίμαιος Σικελικοῖς

1. Ἐν Σικελίᾳ δὲ Δάφνις Ἑρμοῦ παῖς ἐγένετο, σύριγγι δή τι δεξιὸς[4] χρῆσθαι καὶ τὴν ἰδέαν

---

[1] Probably corrupt. Αἰνέως and Αἴνου have been suggested.

[2] It is better to keep the spelling with one σ, as in the MS.

[3] ἑαυτήν is not in the MS., but is wanted after the active verb (Goens).

[4] The MS. has δή τε δεξιῶς: the corrections are due to Jacobs and Gale.

and now upon her children, and though Xanthus did his best to comfort her, saying that he would make her his wife, she would not listen to him, but threw herself into the sea.

XXVIII

THE STORY OF CLITE

From the Apollodorus *of Euphorion*[1]: *the latter part from the first book of the* Argonautica[2] *of Apollonius.*

1. THERE are various forms of the story of Cyzicus the son of Aeneus.[3] Some have told how he married Larisa the daughter of Piasus, with whom her father had to do before she was married, and afterwards died in battle; others, how when he had but recently married Clite, he met in battle (not knowing who his adversaries were) the heroes who were sailing with Jason in the Argo; and that his fall in this combat caused the liveliest regret to all, but to Clite beyond all measure. 2. Seeing him lying dead, she flung her arms round him and bewailed him sorely, and then at night she avoided the watch of her serving-maids and hung herself from a tree.

XXIX

THE STORY OF DAPHNIS

From the Sicelica *of Timaeus*[4]

1. IN Sicily was born Daphnis the son of Hermes, who was skilled in playing on the pipes and also

---

[1] See title of No. XIII.   [2] Ll. 936–1076.
[3] See note on the Greek text.
[4] Of Tauromenium or Taormina, the historian of early Sicily, about B.C. 300.

THE LOVE ROMANCES OF PARTHENIUS

ἐκπρεπής. οὗτος εἰς μὲν τὸν πολὺν ὅμιλον ἀνδρῶν
οὐ κατῄει, βουκολῶν δὲ κατὰ τὴν Αἴτνην χείματός
τε καὶ θέρους ἠγραύλει. τούτου λέγουσιν
Ἐχεναΐδα νύμφην ἐρασθεῖσαν παρακελεύσασθαι
αὐτῷ γυναικὶ μὴ πλησιάζειν· μὴ πειθομένου γὰρ
αὐτοῦ, συμβήσεσθαι¹ τὰς ὄψεις ἀποβαλεῖν. 2. ὁ
δὲ χρόνον μέν τινα καρτερῶς ἀντεῖχε, καίπερ
οὐκ ὀλίγων ἐπιμαινομένων αὐτῷ· ὕστερον δὲ μία
τῶν κατὰ τὴν Σικελίαν βασιλίδων οἴνῳ πολλῷ
δηλησαμένη αὐτὸν ἤγαγεν εἰς ἐπιθυμίαν αὐτῇ
μιγῆναι. καὶ οὗτος ἐκ τοῦδε, ὁμοίως Θαμύρᾳ τῷ
Θρᾳκί, δι᾽ ἀφροσύνην ἐπεπήρωτο.

Λ'

ΠΕΡΙ ΚΕΛΤΙΝΗΣ

1. Λέγεται δὲ καὶ Ἡρακλέα, ὅτε ἀπ᾽ Ἐρυθείας
τὰς Γηρυόνου βοῦς ἤγαγεν, ἀλώμενον διὰ τῆς
Κελτῶν χώρας ἀφικέσθαι παρὰ Βρεταννόν· τῷ δὲ
ἄρα ὑπάρχειν θυγατέρα Κελτίνην ὄνομα· ταύτην
δὲ ἐρασθεῖσαν τοῦ Ἡρακλέους κατακρύψαι τὰς
βοῦς, μὴ θέλειν τε ἀποδοῦναι εἰ μὴ πρότερον αὐτῇ
μιχθῆναι. 2. τὸν δὲ Ἡρακλέα τὸ μέν τι καὶ τὰς
βοῦς ἐπειγόμενον ἀνασώσασθαι, πολὺ μᾶλλον
μέντοι τὸ κάλλος ἐκπλαγέντα τῆς κόρης, συγ-
γενέσθαι αὐτῇ· καὶ αὐτοῖς, χρόνου περιήκοντος,
γενέσθαι παῖδα Κελτόν, ἀφ᾽ οὗ δὴ Κελτοὶ
προσηγορεύθησαν.

¹ The MS. has συμβήσεται : but the infinitive (restored by
Legrand) is necessary in the Oratio Obliqua.

exceedingly beautiful. He would never frequent the places where men come together, but spent his life in the open, both winter and summer, keeping his herds on the slopes of Etna. The nymph Echenais, so the story runs, fell in love with him, and bade him never have to do with mortal woman; if he disobeyed, his fate would be to lose his eyes. 2. For some considerable time he stood out strongly against all temptation, although not a few women were madly in love with him; but at last one of the Sicilian princesses worked his ruin by plying him with much wine, and so brought him to the desire to consort with her. Thus he, too, like Thamyras[1] the Thracian, was thenceforward blind through his own folly.

XXX

THE STORY OF CELTINE

1. HERCULES, it is told, after he had taken the kine of Geryones[2] from Erythea, was wandering through the country of the Celts and came to the house of Bretannus, who had a daughter called Celtine. Celtine fell in love with Hercules and hid away the kine, refusing to give them back to him unless he would first content her. 2. Hercules was indeed very anxious to bring the kine safe home, but he was far more struck with the girl's exceeding beauty, and consented to her wishes; and then, when the time had come round, a son called Celtus was born to them, from whom the Celtic race derived their name.

[1] Or Thamyris, a mythical poet, who entered into a contest with the Muses, and was blinded on his defeat.

[2] Or Geryon, who was supposed to have lived in Spain. This was one of the twelve labours of Hercules.

THE LOVE ROMANCES OF PARTHENIUS

ΛΑ'

ΠΕΡΙ ΔΙΜΟΙΤΟΥ [1]

Ἱστορεῖ Φύλαρχος

1. Λέγεται δὲ καὶ Διμοίτην ἁρμόσασθαι μὲν Τροιζῆνος τἀδελφοῦ θυγατέρα Εὐῶπιν· αἰσθανό-μενον [2] δὲ συνοῦσαν αὐτὴν διὰ σφοδρὸν ἔρωτα τἀδελφῷ, δηλῶσαι τῷ Τροιζῆνι· τὴν δὲ διά τε [3] δέος καὶ αἰσχύνην ἀναρτῆσαι αὑτήν, πολλὰ πρότερον λυπηρὰ καταρασαμένην τῷ αἰτίῳ τῆς συμφορᾶς. 2. ἔνθα δὴ τὸν Διμοίτην μετ' οὐ πολὺν χρόνον ἐπιτυχεῖν γυναικὶ μάλα καλῇ τὴν ὄψιν ὑπὸ τῶν κυμάτων ἐκβεβλημένῃ καὶ αὐτῆς εἰς ἐπιθυμίαν ἐλθόντα συνεῖναι· ὡς δὲ ἤδη ἐνεδίδου τὸ σῶμα διὰ μῆκος χρόνου, χῶσαι αὐτῇ μέγαν τάφον, καὶ οὕτως μὴ ἀνιέμενον τοῦ πάθους, ἐπι-κατασφάξαι αὑτόν.

ΛΒ'

ΠΕΡΙ ΑΝΘΙΠΠΗΣ

1. Παρὰ δὲ Χάοσι μειρακίσκος τις τῶν πάνυ δοκίμων Ἀνθίππης ἠράσθη. ταύτην ὑπελθὼν

[1] It is quite possible that, as Maass contends (*Gött. gel. Anz.* 1889, pp. 826 sqq.), this hero's name should be Θυμοίτης : but I have not felt that his arguments are quite strong enough to justify making the change in the text.

[2] The accusative (due to Heyne) is necessary, though the MS. has αἰσθανόμενος.

[3] MS. τό. The correction is due to Rohde.

THE STORY OF ANTHIPPE

XXXI

THE STORY OF DIMOETES

From Phylarchus [1]

1. DIMOETES is said to have married his brother Troezen's daughter, Evopis, and afterwards, seeing that she was afflicted with a great love for her own brother, and was consorting with him, he informed Troezen; the girl hung herself for fear and shame, first calling down every manner of curse on him who was the cause of her fate. 2. It was not long before Dimoetes came upon the body of a most beautiful woman thrown up by the sea, and he conceived the most passionate desire for her company; but soon the body, owing to the period of time since her death, began to see corruption, and he piled up a huge barrow for her; and then, as even so his passion was in no wise relieved, he killed himself at her tomb.

XXXII

THE STORY OF ANTHIPPE

1. AMONG the Chaonians [2] a certain youth of most noble birth fell in love with a girl named Anthippe; he addressed her with every art to attempt

---

[1] See title of No. XV.
[2] A people in the north-west of Epirus, supposed to be descended from Chaon, the son of Priam.

πάσῃ μηχανῇ πείθει αὑτῷ συμμιγῆναι· ἡ δὲ
ἄρα καὶ αὐτὴ οὐκ ἐκτὸς ἦν τοῦ πρὸς τὸν παῖδα
πόθου· καὶ ἐκ τοῦδε λανθάνοντες τοὺς αὑτῶν
γονεῖς ἐξεπίμπλασαν τὴν ἐπιθυμίαν. 2. ἑορτῆς
δέ ποτε τοῖς Χάοσι δημοτελοῦς ἀγομένης καὶ
πάντων εὐωχουμένων, ἀποσκεδασθέντες εἴς τινα
δρυμὸν κατειλήθησαν. ἔτυχε δὲ ἄρα ὁ τοῦ
βασιλέως υἱὸς Κίχυρος πάρδαλιν διώκων, ἧς
συνελασθείσης εἰς ἐκεῖνον τὸν δρυμόν, ἀφίησιν
ἐπ' αὐτὴν τὸν ἄκοντα· καὶ τῆς μὲν ἁμαρτάνει,
τυγχάνει δὲ τῆς παιδός. 3. ὑπολαβὼν δὲ τὸ
θηρίον καταβεβληκέναι ἐγγυτέρω τὸν ἵππον
προσελαύνει· καὶ καταμαθὼν τὸ μειράκιον ἐπὶ
τοῦ τραύματος τῆς παιδὸς ἔχον τὼ χεῖρε, ἐκτός
τε φρενῶν ἐγένετο καὶ περιδινηθεὶς ἀπολισθάνει
τοῦ ἵππου εἰς χωρίον ἀπόκρημνον καὶ πετρῶδες.
ἔνθα δὴ ὁ μὲν ἐτεθνήκει, οἱ δὲ Χάονες, τιμῶντες
τὸν βασιλέα, κατὰ τὸν αὐτὸν τόπον τείχη περιε-
βάλοντο καὶ τὴν πόλιν ἐκάλεσαν Κίχυρον.
4. φασὶ δέ τινες τὸν δρυμὸν ἐκεῖνον εἶναι τῆς
Ἐχίονος θυγατρὸς Ἠπείρου, ἣν μεταναστᾶσαν ἐκ
Βοιωτίας βαδίζειν μεθ' Ἁρμονίας καὶ Κάδμου,
φερομένην τὰ Πενθέως λείψανα, ἀποθανοῦσαν δὲ
περὶ τὸν δρυμὸν τόνδε ταφῆναι· διὸ καὶ τὴν γῆν
Ἤπειρον ἀπὸ ταύτης ὀνομασθῆναι.

THE STORY OF ANTHIPPE

her virtue, and indeed she too was not untouched by love for the lad, and soon they were taking their fill of their desires unknown to their parents. 2. Now on one occasion a public festival was being celebrated by the Chaonians, and while all the people were feasting, the young pair slipped away and crept in under a certain bush. But it so happened that the king's son, Cichyrus, was hunting a leopard; the beast was driven into the same thicket, and he hurled his javelin at it; he missed it, but hit the girl. 3. Thinking that he had hit his leopard, he rode up; but when he saw the lad trying to staunch the girl's wound with his hands, he lost his senses, flung away, and finally fell off his horse down a precipitous and stony ravine. There he perished; but the Chaonians, to honour their king, put a wall round the place and gave the name of Cichyrus to the city so founded. 4. The story is also found in some authorities that the thicket in question was sacred to Epirus, the daughter of Echion; she had left Boeotia and was journeying with Harmonia and Cadmus,[1] bearing the remains of Pentheus; dying there, she was buried in this thicket. That is the reason that country was named Epirus, after her.

[1]
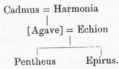

Agave with the rest of the Bacchants had torn Pentheus in pieces as a punishment for his blasphemy against the worship of Dionysus.

THE LOVE ROMANCES OF PARTHENIUS

ΛΓ´

ΠΕΡΙ ΑΣΣΑΟΝΟΣ

Ἱστορεῖ Ξάνθος Λυδιακοῖς καὶ Νεάνθης[1] β´ καὶ Σιμμίας
ὁ Ῥόδιος

1. Διαφόρως δὲ καὶ τοῖς πολλοῖς ἱστορεῖται
καὶ τὰ Νιόβης· οὐ γὰρ Ταντάλου φασὶν αὐτὴν
γενέσθαι, ἀλλ᾽ Ἀσσάονος μὲν θυγατέρα, Φιλότ-
του δὲ γυναῖκα· εἰς ἔριν δὲ ἀφικομένην Λητοῖ
περὶ καλλιτεκνίας ὑποσχεῖν τίσιν τοιάνδε. 2. τὸν
μὲν Φίλοττον ἐν κυνηγίᾳ διαφθαρῆναι, τὸν δὲ
Ἀσσάονα τῆς θυγατρὸς πόθῳ σχόμενον αὐτὴν
αὑτῷ γήμασθαι βούλεσθαι·[2] μὴ ἐνδιδούσης δὲ
τῆς Νιόβης, τοὺς παῖδας αὐτῆς εἰς εὐωχίαν
καλέσαντα καταπρῆσαι. 3. καὶ τὴν μὲν διὰ
ταύτην τὴν συμφορὰν ἀπὸ πέτρας ὑψηλοτάτης
αὐτὴν ῥῖψαι, ἔννοιαν δὲ λαβόντα τῶν σφετέ-
ρων ἁμαρτημάτων διαχρήσασθαι τὸν Ἀσσάονα
ἑαυτόν.

ΛΔ´

ΠΕΡΙ ΚΟΡΥΘΟΥ

Ἱστορεῖ Ἑλλάνικος Τρωικῶν β´[3] καὶ Κεφάλων ὁ Γερ-
γίθιος

1. Ἐκ δὲ Οἰνώνης καὶ Ἀλεξάνδρου παῖς
ἐγένετο Κόρυθος· οὗτος ἐπίκουρος ἀφικόμενος

---

[1] The MS. calls him Νέανθος, but Νεάνθης is certain.

[2] This word was inserted by Zangoiannes. The *homoeo-
teleuton* would account for it dropping out.

[3] The number of the book has dropped out. Heyne's
restoration of β´ is probably correct : Meursius thought there
never was a number, and that Τρωικῶν is a mistake for
Τρωικοῖς.

THE STORY OF CORYTHUS

XXXIII

THE STORY OF ASSAON

From the Lydiaca *of Xanthus,*[1] *the second book of Neanthes,*[2] *and Simmias*[3] *of Rhodes.*

1. THE story of Niobe is differently told by various authorities; some, for instance, say that she was not the daughter of Tantalus, but of Assaon, and the wife of Philottus; and for having had her dispute with Leto about the beauty of their children, her punishment was as follows: 2. Philottus perished while hunting; Assaon, consumed with love for his own daughter, desired to take her to wife; on Niobe refusing to accede to his desires, he asked her children to a banquet, and there burned them all to death. 3. As a result of this calamity, she flung herself from a high rock; Assaon, when he came to ponder upon these his sins, made away with himself.

XXXIV

THE STORY OF CORYTHUS

From the second book of Hellanicus'[4] Troica, *and from Cephalon*[5] *of Gergitha*

1. OF the union of Oenone and Alexander[6] was born a boy named Corythus. He came to Troy to

---

[1] The historian of Lydia, fifth century B.C.   [2] Of Cyzicus.
[3] An early Alexandrine poet. We possess various *technopaegnia* by him in the *Palatine Anthology*—poems written in the shape of a hatchet, an egg, an altar, wings, panpipes, etc.
[4] Of Mytilene, an historian contemporary with Herodotus and Thucydides.   [5] See title of No. IV.
[6] This story is thus a continuation of No. IV. Another version of the legend is that Oenone, to revenge herself on Paris, sent Corythus to guide the Greeks to Troy.

THE LOVE ROMANCES OF PARTHENIUS

εἰς Ἴλιον Ἑλένης ἠράσθη, καὶ αὐτὸν ἐκείνη
μάλα φιλοφρόνως ὑπεδέχετο· ἦν δὲ τὴν ἰδέαν
κράτιστος· φωράσας δὲ αὐτὸν ὁ πατὴρ ἀνεῖλεν.
2. Νίκανδρος μέντοι τὸν Κόρυθον οὐκ Οἰνώνης,
ἀλλὰ Ἑλένης καὶ Ἀλεξάνδρου φησὶ γενέσθαι,
λέγων ἐν τούτοις·

Ἠρία τ᾽ εἰν Ἀΐδαο κατοιχομένου Κορύθοιο,
ὅν τε καὶ ἁρπακτοῖσιν ὑποδμηθεῖσ᾽ ὑμεναίοις
Τυνδαρίς, αἶν᾽ ἀχέουσα, κακὸν γόνον ἤρατο
βούτεω.

ΛΕ΄

ΠΕΡΙ ΕΥΛΙΜΕΝΗΣ [1]

1. Ἐν δὲ Κρήτῃ ἠράσθη Λύκαστος τῆς Κύ-
δωνος θυγατρὸς Εὐλιμένης, ἣν ὁ πατὴρ Ἀπτέρῳ
καθωμολόγητο πρωτεύοντι τότε Κρητῶν· ταύτῃ
κρύφα συνὼν ἐλελήθει. 2. ὡς δὲ τῶν Κρητικῶν
τινὲς πόλεων ἐπισυνέστησαν Κύδωνι καὶ πολὺ
περιῆσαν, πέμπει τοὺς πευσομένους εἰς θεοῦ, ὅ
τι ἂν ποιῶν κρατήσειε τῶν πολεμίων· καὶ αὐτῷ
θεσπίζεται τοῖς ἐγχωρίοις ἥρωσι σφαγιάσαι παρ-
θένον. 3. ἀκούσας δὲ τοῦ χρηστηρίου Κύδων
διεκλήρου τὰς παρθένους πάσας, καὶ κατὰ δαί-
μονα ἡ θυγάτηρ λαγχάνει.[2] Λύκαστος δὲ δείσας
περὶ αὐτῆς μηνύει τὴν φθορὰν καὶ ὡς ἐκ πολλοῦ
χρόνου συνείη αὐτῇ· ὁ δὲ πολὺς ὅμιλος πολὺ

---

[1] See note on title of No. XXXVI.
[2] Heyne's correction for the MS. τυγχάνει.

help the Trojans, and there fell in love with Helen.
She indeed received him with the greatest warmth—
he was of extreme beauty—but his father discovered
his aims and killed him. 2. Nicander [1] however
says that he was the son, not of Oenone, but of
Helen and Alexander, speaking of him as follows :—

> There was the tomb of fallen Corythus,
> Whom Helen bare, the fruit of marriage-rape,
> In bitter woe, the Herdsman's [2] evil brood.

XXXV

THE STORY OF EULIMENE

1. IN Crete Lycastus fell in love with Eulimene,
the daughter of Cydon, though her father had
already betrothed her to Apterus, who was at that
time the most famous man among the Cretans ; and
he used to consort with her without the knowledge
of her father and her intended spouse. 2. But when
some of the Cretan cities revolted against Cydon,
and easily withstood his attacks, he sent ambassadors
to inquire of the oracle by what course of action he
could get the better of his enemies, and the answer
was given him that he must sacrifice a virgin to the
heroes worshipped in the country. 3. Cydon, on hear-
ing the oracle's reply, cast lots upon all the virgins
of his people, and, as the gods would have it, the fatal
lot fell upon his own daughter. Then Lycastus,
in fear for her life, confessed that he had corrupted
her and had indeed been her lover for a long time ;

---

[1] See title of No. IV.   [2] Paris.

THE LOVE ROMANCES OF PARTHENIUS

μᾶλλον ἐδικαίου αὐτὴν τεθνάναι. 4. ἐπειδὴ δὲ
ἐσφαγιάσθη, ὁ Κύδων τὸν ἱερέα κελεύει αὐτῆς
διατεμεῖν τὸ ἐπομφάλιον, καὶ οὕτως εὑρέθη
ἔγκυος. Ἄπτερος δὲ δόξας ὑπὸ Λυκάστου δεινὰ
πεπονθέναι λοχήσας αὐτὸν ἀνεῖλε, καὶ διὰ
ταύτην τὴν αἰτίαν ἔφυγε πρὸς Ξάνθον εἰς
Τέρμερα.

ΛϚ′

ΠΕΡΙ ΑΡΓΑΝΘΩΝΗΣ [1]

Ἱστορεῖ Ἀσκληπιάδης ὁ Μυρλεανὸς Βιθυνιακῶν α′

1. Λέγεται δὲ καὶ Ῥῆσον, πρὶν ἐς Τροίαν
ἐπίκουρον ἐλθεῖν, ἐπὶ πολλὴν γῆν ἰέναι προσαγό-
μενόν τε καὶ δασμὸν ἐπιτιθέντα· ἔνθα δὴ καὶ
εἰς Κίον ἀφικέσθαι κατὰ κλέος γυναικὸς καλῆς·
Ἀργανθώνη αὐτῇ ὄνομα. 2. αὕτη τὴν μὲν κατ’
οἶκον δίαιταν καὶ μονὴν ἀπέστυγεν, ἀθροισαμένη
δὲ κύνας πολλοὺς ἐθήρευεν οὐ μάλα τινὰ προσιε-
μένη. ἐλθὼν οὖν ὁ Ῥῆσος εἰς τόνδε τὸν χῶρον,
βίᾳ μὲν αὐτὴν οὐκ ἦγεν· ἔφη δὲ θέλειν αὐτῇ
συγκυνηγεῖν, καὶ αὐτὸς γὰρ ὁμοίως ἐκείνῃ τὴν
πρὸς ἀνθρώπους ὁμιλίαν ἐχθαίρειν· ἡ δὲ ταῦτα
λέξαντος ἐκείνου κατῄνεσε πειθομένη αὐτὸν ἀληθῆ
λέγειν. 3. χρόνου δὲ [2] πολλοῦ διαγενομένου, εἰς

---

[1] In the MS. the source of No. XXXVI wrongly appears as
the source of No. XXXV. The correction is due to
Sakolowski.

[2] For this δέ Jacobs would write δ’ οὐ. From the context
it is really impossible to say whether she fell in love soon or
late.

but the assembly only voted all the more inflexibly [1]
that she must die. 4. After she had been sacrificed,
Cydon told the priest to cut through her belly by
the navel, and this done she was found to be with
child. Apterus considering himself mortally injured
by Lycastus, laid an ambush and murdered him :
and for that crime was obliged to go into exile and
flee to the court of Xanthus at Termera.[2]

XXXVI

The Story of Arganthone

From the first book of the Bithyniaca *of Asclepiades* [3]
of Myrlea

1. Rhesus, so the story goes, before he went to
help Troy, travelled over many countries, subduing
them and imposing contributions ; and in the course
of his career he came to Cius,[4] attracted by the fame
of a beautiful woman called Arganthone. 2. She
had no taste for indoor life and staying at home,
but she got together a great pack of hounds and
used to hunt, never admitting anybody to her com-
pany. When Rhesus came to this place, he made
no attempt to take her by force ; he professed to
desire to hunt with her, saying that he, like her,
hated the company of men ; and she was delighted
at what he said, believing that he was speaking the
truth. 3. After some considerable time had passed,

---

[1] Not, I think, as a punishment for her unchastity : they
thought that Lycastus was trying to save her life by a
trumped-up story.   [2] In Lycia.
[3] A grammarian, who probably lived at Pergamus in the
first century B.C.   [4] A town in Bithynia.

πολὺν ἔρωτα παραγίνεται τοῦ Ῥήσου· καὶ τὸ μὲν
πρῶτον ἡσυχάζει αἰδοῖ κατεχομένη· ἐπειδὴ δὲ
σφοδρότερον ἐγίνετο τὸ πάθος, ἀπετόλμησεν εἰς
λόγους ἐλθεῖν αὐτῷ, καὶ οὕτως ἐθέλων ἐθέλουσαν [1]
αὐτὴν ἐκεῖνος ἡγάγετο γυναῖκα. 4. ὕστερον δὲ
πολέμου γενομένου τοῖς Τρωσί, μετῆεσαν αὐτὸν
οἱ βασιλεῖς ἐπίκουρον· ἡ δὲ Ἀργανθώνη, εἴτε καὶ
δι' ἔρωτα ὃς πολὺς ὑπῆν αὐτῇ, εἴτε καὶ ἄλλως
καταμαντευομένη τὸ μέλλον, βαδίζειν αὐτὸν
οὐκ εἴα. Ῥῆσος δὲ μαλακιζόμενος τῇ [2] ἐπιμονῇ
οὐκ ἠνέσχετο, ἀλλὰ ἦλθεν εἰς Τροίαν καὶ μαχό-
μενος ἐπὶ ποταμῷ, τῷ νῦν ἀπ' ἐκείνου Ῥήσῳ
καλουμένῳ, πληγεὶς ὑπὸ Διομήδους ἀποθνήσκει.
5. ἡ δὲ ὡς ᾔσθετο τεθνηκότος αὐτοῦ, αὖτις ἀπε-
χώρησεν εἰς τὸν τόπον ἔνθα ἐμίγη πρῶτον αὐτῷ,
καὶ περὶ αὐτὸν ἀλωμένη θαμὰ ἐβόα τοὔνομα τοῦ
Ῥήσου· τέλος δὲ σῖτα καὶ ποτὰ μὴ [3] προσιεμένη
διὰ λύπην ἐξ ἀνθρώπων ἀπηλλάγη.

ΠΑΡΘΕΝΙΟΤ ΝΙΚΑΕΩΣ

ΠΕΡΙ ΕΡΩΤΙΚΩΝ ΠΑΘΗΜΑΤΩΝ

[1] ἐθέλουσαν (not in the MS.) was rightly supplied by
Passow.
[2] τῇ is not in the MS. Rohde first showed how this
passage was to be taken : the older editors used to change
μαλακιζόμενος into μάλα κακιζόμενος.
[3] A palmary emendation by Rohde. The MS. has εἶτα
καὶ ποταμῷ, from which no sense can be extracted.

she fell deeply in love with him : at first, restrained by shame, she would not confess her affection; but then, her passion growing stronger, she took courage to tell him, and so by mutual consent he took her to wife. 4. Later on, when the Trojan war broke out, the princes on the Trojan side sent to fetch him as an ally [1]; but Arganthone, either because of her very great love for him, or because she somehow knew the future, would not let him go. But Rhesus could not bear the thought of becoming soft and unwarlike by staying at home. He went to Troy, and there, fighting at the river now called Rhesus after him, was wounded by Diomed and died. 5. Arganthone, when she heard of his death, went once more to the place where they had first come together, and wandering about there called unceasingly " Rhesus, Rhesus "; and at last, refusing all meat and drink for the greatness of her grief, passed away from among mankind.

THE END

OF

THE LOVE ROMANCES

OF

PARTHENIUS OF NICAEA

[1] If he could once have got his horses into Troy, the town would have been impregnable : but he was surprised and killed on the first night of his arrival.

FRAGMENTS

FRAGMENTS

1. *Schol.* Pind. *Isthm.* ii. 68.   Παρθένιος ἐν τῇ
’Αρήτῃ[1] τὸ ἄννεμε[2] ἀντὶ τοῦ ἀνάγνωθι.

2. Hephaest. *Enchir.*, p. 6₉.   Παρθένιος ἐπική-
δειον εἰς ’Αρχελαΐδα γράφων ἐλεγειακόν, τὸν
τελευταῖον μόνον στίχον ἀντὶ ἐλεγείου ἰαμβικὸν
ἐποίησεν, ἐν ᾧ τὸ ὄνομα ἐρεῖν ἔμελλεν· ’Αμυσχ-
ρὸν οὔνομ’ ἔσσετ’ ’Αρχελαΐδος.

3. Steph. Byz., p. 56₁₀.   Παρθένιος ἐν ’Αφροδίτῃ
Ακαμαντίδα[3] αὐτήν φησιν.

4. Choerobosc. *Schol. in Theodos. canon.*, p. 252₂₄·
ὅτι [*sc.* τὸ ἵλαος] ἐκτείνει τὸ α, ἐδήλωσε Παρθένιος

---

[1] It is not possible to decide whether this is the *Dirge on
Arete* or the *Encomium of Arete* mentioned by Suidas (see
Introduction) as among Parthenius' works.   In the *Corpus
Inscriptionum Graecarum*, iv. 6857 is an inscription (printed by
Martini on p. 6 of his edition of Parthenius) which was found
near Rome (perhaps at Hadrian's Villa at Tibur), but un-
fortunately greatly damaged and incomplete.   This describes
how the tomb on which it was placed originally bore a poem
in which Parthenius lamented the death of his wife Arete.
The Anio had risen, damaging the tomb and defacing the
poem, and it was restored by Hadrian and a new inscription
placed upon it.   [2] MSS. ἄννειμε, corrected by Valckenaer.
[3] Stephanus appears to refer this epithet to the town of
Acamantium in Phrygia. but it is doubtless really derived
from a promontory in Cyprus named Acamas, which is
mentioned by the Elder Pliny in his *Natural History*, v. 129,
and by Ptolemy and Strabo.

FRAGMENTS

1. *The Scholiast on Pindar's Isthmians* ii. 68. Parthenius in his *Arete* uses ἄννεμε for ἀνάγνωθι "*read*."

2. *Hephaestion,*[1] *Enchiridion, p.* 6₉. Parthenius wrote a dirge on Archelais in elegiacs, but made the last line, in which he had to introduce the name of his subject, an iambic instead of a pentameter: *Holy and undefiled shall the name of Archelais be.*

3. *Stephanus*[2] *of Byzantium, p.* 56₁₀. Parthenius in his *Aphrodite*[3] calls her[4] *Acamantis.*

4. *Choeroboscus,*[5] *Scholia on the Canons of Theodosius, p.* 252₂₄. Parthenius in his poem on Bias shows that

---

[1] Of Alexandria, a writer on metre in the age of the Antonines.

[2] A geographical writer of the late fifth or early sixth century A.D.

[3] Also mentioned by Suidas as among the elegiac poems of Parthenius.   [4] *i.e.* Aphrodite.

[5] George Choeroboscus, a professor at the University of Constantinople, of doubtful date: Krumbacher remarks that "he lived nearer to the sixth than the tenth century." The "Canons of Theodosius" are a collection of commentaries on the school grammar of Dionysius Thrax—they can hardly be ascribed to Theodosius of Alexandria himself, who lived not long after 400 A.D. To them we owe the non-existent forms (*e.g.* ἔτυπον) of the paradigms of our youth.

PARTHENIUS

ἐν τῷ εἰς Βίαντα εἰπών· "Ιλαος ταύτην
δέχνυσο[1] πυρκαϊήν. ἔστι δὲ ἐλεγεῖον τὸ
μέτρον.

5. Schol. Townl. ad *Hom. Il.* 9₄₄₆· γῆρας ἀποξύ-
σας. ἀττική[2] ἐστιν ἡ ἔκτασις. Παρθένιος γοῦν
ἐν Βίαντι συνέστειλεν· "Οστις ἐπ' ἀνθρώπους
ἔξυσεν αἰγανέας.

6. Steph. Byz., *p.* 213₁₀· λέγεται καὶ Γρύ-
νειος Ἀπόλλων, ὡς Παρθένιος Δήλῳ.

7. Steph. Byz., *p.* 705₁₄· Παρθένιος ὁ Νικαεὺς[3]
Δήλῳ· Σὺν τῇ ἐγὼ Τηθύν[4] τε καὶ ὠγενίης[5]
Στυγὸς ὕδωρ.

8. Steph. Byz., *p.* 161₁₈· Παρθένιος ἐν Δήλῳ·
Οὐδ' ἀπὸ τηλίτων[6] [τῶν πόρρω][7] ἄκρα
Βεληδονίων.

9. Etymol. genuin., *s.v.* "Αρπυς· ὁ "Ερως· ἡ
χρῆσις παρὰ Παρθενίῳ ἐν Κριναγόρᾳ· Ἀμφοτέ-

---

[1] MSS. δὲ χρυσο etc., corrected by Bekker.
[2] Meineke thought it absurd to explain an Homeric
quantity by Attic usage, and proposed ἰακή.
[3] MSS. Φωκαεύς: corrected by Meineke.
[4] MSS. τηθα : corrected by Salmasius.
[5] Supposed to equal Ὠκεανός. Hesychius glosses ὠγένιον
as παλαιόν. Some other goddess had presumably been men-
tioned in the previous line. The whole is clearly an oath—
possibly taken by Leto.
[6] Various suggestions have been made for the correction
of these two words—ἀπὸ τηλίστων, ἐπὶ τηλίστων, ἀποτηλίτων,
ἀποτηλίστων.
[7] Salmasius saw that this was a gloss on the preceding
words.

the α in ἵλαος is long, when he says: *Do thou graciously accept the funeral pyre.* The metre is elegiac.

5. *The Townley Scholiast on Homer's Iliad* 9₄₄₆. " Stripping off old age " : the lengthening [of the υ of ἀποξύσας] is Attic [*Ionic*, Meineke]. At any rate in his *Bias* Parthenius wrote: " *Who sharpened spears against men,*" [with the υ in ἔξυσεν short.]

6. *Stephanus of Byzantium, p.* 213₁₀. The expression *Apollo of Gryni*[1] is also found, as in the *Delos* of Parthenius.

7. *Stephanus of Byzantium, p.* 705₁₄. Parthenius of Nicaea in his *Delos*: *With whom* [*I swear also by*] *Tethys*[2] *and the water of ancient*[3] *Styx.*

8. *Stephanus of Byzantium, p.* 161₁₈. Parthenius in his *Delos*: *Nor the distant lands*[4] *of the far-off Beledonii.*[5]

9. *Etymologicum genuinum,*[6] *s.v.* Ἄρπυς: Love. So used by Parthenius in his *Crinagoras*[7]: *Love, the*

---

[1] Stephanus describes this as a little city belonging to the people of Myrina (in Mysia, on the Eleatic gulf). Virgil (*Aen.* iv. 345) also uses the expression *Grynaeus Apollo.*

[2] A sea-goddess, wife of Oceanus.

[3] Stephanus explains Ogenus as an ancient deity. The word is also supposed to be a form of ὠκεανός.

[4] Or perhaps " the mountain-tops."

[5] Explained by Stephanus as an ἔθνος παρ᾽ ὠκεανῷ. Ihm identifies them with the Belendi, a people of Aquitaine, mentioned by the Elder Pliny in his *Natural History* iv. 108.

[6] The smaller original of our *Etymologicum magnum.*

[7] Perhaps addressed to the elegiac poet Crinagoras of Mitylene, who "lived at Rome as a sort of court poet during the latter part of the reign of Augustus." (MACKAIL.)

ροις ἐπιβὰς "Αρπυς ἐλητίσατο. εἴρηται δὲ
παρὰ τὸ ἁρπάζειν [1] τὰς φρένας.

10. Steph. Byz., p. 324₁₉. Παρθένιος ἐν Λευ-
καδίαις· [2] Ἰβηρίτῃ πλεύσει ἐν αἰγιαλῷ.

11. Steph. Byz., p. 381₁₆. Κρανίδες. συνοι-
κία πρὸς τῷ Πόντῳ. Παρθένιος ἐν Ἀνθίππῃ.

12. Steph. Byz., p. 409₁₅. Λάμπεια· [3] ὄρος
Ἀρκαδίας. Παρθένιος Ἀνθίππῃ.

13. Steph. Byz., p. 197₁₉. Γαλλήσιον· πόλις [4]
Ἐφέσου. Παρθένιος ἐν ἐπικηδείῳ τῷ εἰς
Αὐξίθεμιν.

14. Apollon. De pronom., p. 92₂₀. αἱ πληθυν-
τικαὶ καὶ κοινολεκτοῦνται κατ' εὐθεῖαν πρός τε
Ἰώνων καὶ Ἀττικῶν, ἡμεῖς, ὑμεῖς, σφεῖς. ἔστι
πιστώσασθαι καὶ τὸ ἀδιαίρετον τῆς εὐθείας παρ'
Ἴωσιν ἐκ τῶν περὶ Δημόκριτον, Φερεκύδην,
Ἑκαταῖον. τὸ γὰρ ἐν Εἰδωλοφανεῖ Ὑμέες
Αἰόλιον περιχεύετε παρὰ Παρθενίῳ ὑπὸ

[1] Hesychius "Αρπυν· Ἔρωτα. An improbable derivation
has also been given to the effect that ἅρπυς is an Aeolic form
for ἅρπυς, union, and so love.

[2] Meineke would have preferred to write Λευκαδία, and
one of the MSS. reads Λευκαδίας. But there is nothing to
make the form certain.

[3] Two of the MSS. of Stephanus read Λάμεια, and in
another a later hand has erased the π.

[4] Meineke suggested ὄρος, Martin ὄρος πλησίον

354

Spoiler, leaped upon both and plundered them. So
called from his *spoiling* the understanding.

10. *Stephanus of Byzantium, p.* 324₁₉. Parthenius
in his *Leucadiae*[1] : *He shall sail along the Iberian
shore.*

11. *Stephanus of Byzantium, p.* 381₁₆. *The Cranides:*
a settlement in Pontus. So used by Parthenius in
his *Anthippe.*[2]

12. *Stephanus of Byzantium, p.* 409₁₅. *Lampeia :*
a mountain in Arcadia. So used by Parthenius in
his *Anthippe.*

13. *Stephanus of Byzantium, p.* 197₁₉. Gallesium :
a town (*al.* a mountain) near Ephesus. So used by
Parthenius in his *Dirge on Auxithemis.*

14. *Apollonius*[3] *on Pronouns, p.* 92₂₀. The plurals
too are ordinarily used in the nominative in Ionic
and Attic in the forms ἡμεῖς, ὑμεῖς, σφεῖς : but the
uncontracted form of the nominative is also estab-
lished in the Ionic writers of the school of Demo-
critus, Pherecydes, Hecataeus. The expression *Do
all of you* (ὑμέες) *bathe Aeolius*[4] in the *Idolophanes* of
Parthenius must only be ascribed to poetic licence,

---

[1] Leucadia is an island, formerly a peninsula, in the
Ionian Sea, opposite Acarnania. The plural form of the title
is doubtful.

[2] Parthenius may possibly have treated in his *Anthippe*
the story he has related in ch. xxxii. of his *Romances.* But
another Anthippe is also known (Apollodorus, *Bibliotheca*
ii. 16²).

[3] Apollonius Dyscolus of Alexandria, a famous grammarian
of the time of Marcus Aurelius.

[4] It is not even certain whether this is a proper name.
There was an Aeolius among the wooers of Hippodamia.

PARTHENIUS

ποιητικῆς ἀδείας παραληφθὲν οὐ καταψεύσεται
διαλέκτου πιστουμένης ἐλλογίμοις συγγραφεῦσιν.

15. Steph. Byz., p. 339₁₄. ἔστι καὶ θηλυκὸν
Ἰσσὰς¹ ἐπὶ τῆς Λέσβου παρὰ Παρθενίῳ ἐν
Ἡρακλεῖ.

16. Steph. Byz., p. 486₁₃. Οἰνώνη· νῆσος τῶν
Κυκλάδων.² οἱ οἰκήτορες Οἰνωναῖοι, ὡς Παρθέ-
νιος Ἡρακλεῖ.

17. Etym. genuin., s.v. αὐροσχάς· ἡ ἄμπελος·
μέμνηται Παρθένιος ἐν Ἡρακλεῖ· Αὐροσχάδα
βότρυν³ Ἰκαριωνείης.

18. Etym. magnum, s.v. ἐρίσχηλος. Παρθένιος
ἐν Ἡρακλεῖ· Ἐρισχήλοις κορυνήταις.

19. Steph. Byz., p. 109₂₁. Παρθένιος ἐν Ἰφίκλῳ·
Καὶ εἰναλίην Ἀράφειαν.⁴

20. Schol. Dionys. Perieg. v. 420. ὡς Παρθέ-
νιος ἐν ταῖς Μεταμορφώσεσι λέγει, ἐπειδὴ Μίνως
λαβὼν τὰ Μέγαρα διὰ Σκύλλης⁵ τῆς Νίσου

¹ Two MSS. have Ἰσσεύς, and Salmasius proposed Ἰσσηΐς.
² MSS. Αἰακίδων : Κυκλάδων was restored by Meineke, who
would also have preferred to insert μία before τῶν.
³ Martini would omit βότρυν : the compiler of the *Etym.
genuin.* goes on Ἐρατοσθένης δὲ ἐν Ἐπιθαλαμίῳ τὸ κατὰ βότρυν
κλῆμα, and he suggests that the βότρυν in the Parthenius
quotation is derived from that in the succeeding sentence.
In that case the words from Parthenius, instead of forming
the end of an hexameter and the beginning of another line,
must be reversed, and will then form the beginning of an
hexameter.
⁴ An island, as Stephanus explains, off the Carian coast.
⁵ This word is not in the scholion as it has come down to
us with the text of Dionysius ; but Eustathius (12th century)

and cannot be considered as belying the rule of the language established by the classical writers.

15. *Stephanus of Byzantium, p.* 339₁₄. The feminine adjective *Issas* is used by Parthenius in his *Hercules* as an epithet of Lesbos.[1]

16. *Stephanus of Byzantium, p.* 486₁₃. Oenone : an island in the Cyclades. Those who live there are called *Oenonaeans*, as found in the *Hercules* of Parthenius.

17. *Etymologicum genuinum, s.v.* αὐροσχάς : the vine : used by Parthenius in his *Hercules : The vine-cluster of the daughter of Icarius.*[2]

18. *Etymologicum magnum, s.v.* ἐρίσχηλος : Parthenius in his *Hercules* speaks of *The railing bearers of clubs.*[3]

19. *Stephanus of Byzantium, p.* 109₂₁. Parthenius in his *Iphiclus*[4] : *And sea-girt Araphea.*

20. *The Scholiast on Dionysius Periegetes,*[5] *l.* 420. As Parthenius says in his *Metamorphoses : Minos took Megara by the help of Scylla the daughter of*

---

[1] Stephanus explains that Issa was a town in Lesbos called successively Himera, Pelasgia, and Issa.

[2] Erigone. For her connexion with Bacchus and wine see Hyginus, *Fab.* 130.

[3] See κορυνήτης and κορυνηφόρος in Liddell and Scott's *Lexicon.*

[4] More than one Iphiclus was known to Greek mythology. The most celebrated was one of the Argonauts.

[5] A geographer who wrote in verse in the second century A.D. The scholia probably date from the fourth or fifth century.

---

produced a commentary on him which includes the text of the scholia in a better form. He gives Σκύλλης.

PARTHENIUS

θυγατρός, ἐρασθείσης αὐτοῦ καὶ ἀποτε-
μούσης τῆς κεφαλῆς τοῦ πατρὸς τὸν
μόρσιμον πλόκαμον καὶ οὕτως αὐτὸν
προδούσης, ἐννοηθεὶς ὡς ἡ πατέρα προ-
δοῦσα οὐδενὸς ἄν ποτε ῥαδίως[1] φείσαιτο,
προσδήσας αὐτὴν πηδαλίῳ νεὼς ἀφῆκεν[2]
ἐπισύρεσθαι τῇ θαλάσσῃ,[3] ἔστ᾽[4] εἰς ὄρνεον
ἡ κόρη μετεβλήθη.

21. Steph. Byz., p. 401₁₈. Κώρυκος·[5] πόλις
Κιλικίας· Παρθένιος Προπεμπτικῷ.

22. Steph. Byz. ap. Eustath. ad Hom. Il. 2₇₁₂.
κώμη Κιλικίας ἐστὶ Γλαφύραι καλουμένη, ἀπέ-
χουσα Ταρσοῦ τριάκοντα σταδίους πρὸς δύσιν, ἐν
ᾗ πηγὴ ἀπὸ ῥωγάδος καταρρέουσα καὶ συνιοῦσα
τῷ εἰς Ταρσὸν εἰσβάλλοντι ποταμῷ; περὶ ἧς
Παρθένιος γράφων ἄλλα τε λέγει καὶ ὅτι

παρθένος ἡ Κιλίκων εἶχεν ἀνακτορίην.[6]
ἀγχίγαμος δ᾽ ἔπελεν, καθαρῷ δ᾽ ἐπεμαί-
νετο Κύδνῳ

---

[1] So Eustathius : the MSS. of the scholia, ῥᾷστα.
[2] The words πηδαλίῳ νεὼς ἀφῆκεν are found in Eustathius,
not in the MSS. of the scholia.
[3] At this point followed the words ὅθεν Σαρωνικὸς οὗτος ὁ
πόντος ἐκλήθη, which must have crept in from elsewhere.
Immediately before the quotation from Parthenius the
Scholiast had been describing the Isthmus of Corinth, and,
after naming the two seas on either side of it, explains the
name "Saronic" of one of them as being derived from a
certain hunter Saron who was drowned there.
[4] So Martini for the MSS. ὅτι.   [5] cf. frg. 24.
[6] In the text παρθένος Κιλίκων ἀνακτορίην ἔχουσα, omitting

FRAGMENTS

Nisus ; she fell in love with him and cut off her father's fateful lock [1] *of hair and thus betrayed him ; but Minos thought that one who had betrayed her father would certainly have no pity upon anybody else, so he tied her to the rudder of his ship and let her drag after him through the sea, until the maiden was changed into a bird.* [2]

21. *Stephanus of Byzantium, p.* 401[18]. Corycus : a city in Cilicia, mentioned by Parthenius in his *Propempticon.* [3]

22. *Stephanus of Byzantium quoted by Eustathius on Homer's Iliad* 2[712]. There is a village in Cilicia called Glaphyrae, thirty furlongs to the west of Tarsus, where there is a spring that rises from a cleft rock and joins the river [4] that flows towards Tarsus. Among what Parthenius writes about it are the following lines : . . . *A maiden* [5] *who held the lordship among the Cilicians : and she was nigh to the time of wedlock, and she doted upon pure* [6] *Cydnus,*

---

[1] A purple lock : as long as it was intact on his head, no enemy could prevail against him.

[2] For a slightly different version of the story, in which Scylla becomes the sea-monster so well known to us in epic poetry, see Hyginus *Fab.* 198.

[3] Properly, a poem written to accompany or escort a person, or to wish him good cheer on his way, like Horace *Odes* i. 3, *Sic te diva potens Cypri.*   [4] The Cydnus.

[5] Her name appears to have been Comaetho.

[6] Because of his cold, clear waters.

δέ in the next line. The metrical form was restored by Hermann.

PARTHENIUS

Κύπριδος ἐξ ἀδύτων πυρσὸν ἀναψαμένη,
εἰσόκε μιν Κύπρις πηγὴν θέτο, μῖξε δ'
    ἔρωτι
Κύδνου καὶ νύμφης ὑδατόεντα γάμον.

23. Etym. genuin., s.v. ᾿Αῶος· ποταμὸς τῆς
Κύπρου . . . . καὶ ὄρος τι ὠνομάσθη ᾿Αώϊον,
ἐξ οὗ β' ποταμῶν φερομένων, Σετράχου[1] καὶ
᾿Απλιέως, τὸν ἕνα τούτων ὁ Παρθένιος ᾿Αῶον
κέκληκεν.

24. Ibid. ἢ διὰ τὸ πρὸς τὴν ἠῶ τετραμμένην
ἔχειν τὴν ῥύσιν, καθά φησιν ὁ Παρθένιος·
Κωρυκίων σεύμενος ἐξ ὀρέων ἀνατολικῶν
ὄντων.

25. Etym. genuin., s.v. δρύψελον·[2] τὸ λέμμα,
ὁ φλοιός. Παρθένιος οἷον Οὐδὲ πόροι ῥίζης
δρύψελα Ποντιάδος. παρὰ τὸ δρύψαι, ὅ
ἐστι λεπίσαι· δρύψελον γὰρ ὁ ἀποδρυπτόμενος
φλοιός.

26. Ibid. καταχρηστικῶς δὲ καὶ φύλλον
δρύψελον ἐπὶ τοῦ σελίνου ὁ Παρθένιος.

---

[1] MSS. Σεράχου, corrected by Martini.
[2] Here and below the MSS. wrongly give δρύψελλον.

---

[1] Some have suspected that this fragment comes from
Parthenius' *Metamorphoses* (*cf.* frg. 20): but this is quite
doubtful, and it is likely that the *Metamorphoses* were
written in hexameters.
[2] The Setrachus. This fragment has something to do with

*fanning within her a spark from the innermost altar of
Cypris' fane, until Cypris turned her into a spring, and
made in love a watery match betwixt Cydnus and the
maid.*[1]

23. *Etymologicum genuinum, s.v.* Ἀῶος : A river in
Cyprus. . . . There was a mountain called Aoïan,
from which flowed two rivers, the Setrachus and
the Aplieus, and one[2] of them Parthenius called the
Aous.

24. *Ibid.* Or, because its[3] flow was towards the
East (ἠῶς), as Parthenius says of it : *Hurrying from
the Corycian*[4] *hills*, which were in the East.

25. *Etymologicum genuinum, s.v.* δρύψελον : peel,
husk. Parthenius uses it in such an expression as
Nor would she (?) furnish peelings of Pontic[5] *root.*
The derivation is from δρύπτω, to scrape, which is
the same as to peel : δρύψελον is the scraped-off
husk.

26. *Ibid.* Parthenius also uses δρύψελον, *a scrap-
ing*, as a term of contempt for the leaf of the
parsley.

Adonis (*cf.* frg. 37), of whom Aous was another name :
the Setrachus was the scene of the loves of Venus and
Adonis.
[3] This is rather confusing, because Parthenius is now
speaking not of the Aous in Cyprus, but of another river of
the same name in Cilicia.
[4] *cf.* frg. 21.
[5] The famous poisons of Colchis.

PARTHENIUS

27. *Anth. Pal.* xi. 130 (Pollianus) :

τοὺς κυκλίους τούτους, τοὺς αὐτὰρ ἔπειτα λέγοντας
  μισῶ, λωποδύτας ἀλλοτρίων ἐπέων,
καὶ διὰ τοῦτ' ἐλέγοις ἐπέχω πλέον· οὐδὲν ἔχω
  γάρ
Παρθενίου κλέπτειν ἢ πάλι Καλλιμάχου.
θηρὶ μὲν οὐατόεντι γενοίμην, εἴ ποτε γράψω,
  εἴκελος, Ἐκ ποταμῶν χλωρὰ χελιδόνια.[1]
οἱ δ' οὕτως τὸν Ὅμηρον ἀναιδῶς λωποδυτοῦσιν,
  ὥστε γράφειν ἤδη μῆνιν ἄειδε θεά.

28. Etym. genuin., *s.v.* Ἑρκύνιος δρυμός· ὁ τῆς
Ἰταλίας ἐνδοτάτω· Ἀπολλώνιος ἐν δ' Ἀργοναυτι-
κῶν· καὶ Παρθένιος· Ἀλλ' ὅτ' ἀφ' ἑσπερίης
Ἑρκυνίδος ὤρετο γαίης.

29. Parthenius *Narr. amat.* xi. 4, *q.v.*

30. Aulus Gellius *Noct. Att.* xiii. 27 (*al.* 26). De
versibus quos Vergilius sectatus videtur Homeri
ac Parthenii. Parthenii poetae versus est : Γλαύκῳ

---

[1] MS. χελιδόνεα ; the correct form was restored by H.
Stephanus. We know from Eustathius on Homer's *Iliad* 11,
p. 817, and 23, p. 1412, that Callimachus used the descrip-
tion θὴρ οὐατόεις of a donkey, so that we can be sure that the
other expression quoted from the elegy belongs to Parthenius.

[1] Perhaps a grammarian, and of about the time of Hadrian.
But nothing is certainly known of him.
[2] Strictly, the cyclic poets were the continuers of Homer
and the poets of the " cycle " of Troy. But here all the
modern epic writers are doubtless included, as in the famous
poem (*Anth. Pal.* xii. 42) in which Callimachus is believed to

FRAGMENTS

27. *Pollianus* [1] in the *Palatine Anthology* xi. 130 :
I hate the cyclic [2] poets, who begin every sentence
with " But then in very deed," plunderers of others'
epics ; and that is why I give more time to elegists,
for there is nothing that I could wish to steal from
Parthenius, or again from Callimachus.[3] May I
become like " a beast with long, long ears " if I ever
write of " *green swallow-wort from out the river-beds* " :
but the epic writers pillage Homer so shamelessly
that they do not scruple to put down " Sing, Muse,
Achilles' wrath."

28. *Etymologicum genuinum, s.v.* Ἑρκύνιος δρυμός.
The Hercynian [4] forest : that inside Italy. So
Apollonius in the fourth book [5] of his *Argonautica* and
Parthenius : *But when he set forth from that western
Hercynian land.*

29. *Parthenius, Love Romances* xi. 4.   See p. 295.

30. *Aulus Gellius,*[6] *Noctes Atticae* xiii. 27 (*al.* 26).
Of the lines of Homer and Parthenius which Virgil
seems to have imitated.   The line *To Glaucus and*

have attacked Apollonius of Rhodes, Ἐχθαίρω τὸ ποίημα τὸ
κυκλικόν.

[3] Lucian also couples Callimachus with our author.   See
Introduction.

[4] The Hercynian forest known to history was in Germany,
between the Black Forest and the Hartz.   But it appears
that in early days all the wooded mountains of central
Europe were called *Hercynian* by the ancients, and that the
use of the word was afterwards narrowed down.

[5] l. 640.

[6] A dilettante scholar of the middle and end of the second
century A.D., interested in many points of Latin literary
criticism.

PARTHENIUS

καὶ Νηρῆι[1] καὶ εἰναλίῳ Μελικέρτῃ. Eum
versum Vergilius aemulatus est, itaque fecit duobus
vocabulis venuste immutatis parem : Glauco et
Panopeae et Inoo Melicertae.[2]

Macrobius *Sat.* v. 18. Versus est Parthenii, quo
grammatico in Graecis Vergilius usus est : Γλαύκῳ
καὶ Νηρῆι καὶ Ἰνώῳ Μελικέρτῃ.[3]

31. *Schol.* Dionys. Perieg. *v.* 456. ἐνταῦθά
εἰσιν αἱ στῆλαι τοῦ Ἡρακλέους· ὁ δὲ Παρθένιος
Βριάρεω τὰς στήλας φησὶν εἶναι·

Μάρτυρα δ' ἄμμιν τῆς[4] ἐπὶ Γαδείρῃ λίπεθ'
    οἴμου,[5]
ἀρχαίου Βριαρεῶος ἀπ' οὔνομα τὸ πρὶν ἀράξας.

32. Choerobosc. *Schol. in Theodos. canon., p.*
252₂₁. τὸ ἵλαος συνεσταλμένον ἔχον τὸ α, οἷον
ὡς παρὰ Παρθενίῳ· Ἵλαος, ὦ Ὑμέναιε.

33. Etym. Gud., *s.v.* ἀργεϊφόντης· ὁ Ἑρμῆς
παρ' Ὁμήρῳ καὶ παρὰ πολλοῖς· παρὰ δὲ Σοφο-

---

[1] Both here and in the citation from Macrobius the form
Νηρεῖ is found, which was corrected by Joseph Scaliger.

[2] *Georg.* i. 437.

[3] In *Anth. Pal.* vi. 164 there is an epigram by Lucillius
(who lived in the time of Nero), or by Lucian, in which the
line is quoted in the form Γλαύκῳ καὶ Νηρῆι καὶ Ἰνοῖ καὶ
Μελικέρτῃ. This is perhaps a direct reminiscence of Virgil—
the subject is the same as in the passage of the Georgics,
shipwrecked mariners' votive offerings for their saved lives.

[4] MSS. τήν.

[5] MSS. λίπε θυμόν. There are various ways of reconstituting
this line, for which see Martini's edition. Some have made it
into a pentameter : some into the parts of two hexameters.

FRAGMENTS

Nereus and the sea-god Melicertes is from the poet
Parthenius: this line Virgil copied, and produced a
translation, changing two words with the most
exquisite taste: "To Glaucus and Nereus and Meli-
certes, Ino's son."

    Macrobius,[1] *Saturnalia* v. 18. The following verse
is by Parthenius, who was Virgil's tutor in Greek:
To Glaucus and Nereus and Melicertes, Ino's son.

    31. *The Scholiast on Dionysius Periegetes, l.* 456.
There[2] are the columns of Hercules; but Parthenius
calls them the columns of Briareus[3]; *And he left us
a witness of his journey to Gades, taking away from
them their ancient name of old-time Briareus.*[4]

    32. *Choeroboscus, Scholia on the Canons of Theodosius,
p.* 252₂₁, Ἴλαος with the α short, as in Parthenius:
Be favourable (ἵλᾰος),[5] *O Hymenaeus.*

    33. *Etymologicum Gudianum, s.v.* ἀργεϊφόντης:[6] an
epithet applied to Hermes in Homer and many other

---

    [1] Macrobius lived at the end of the fourth and beginning
of the fifth centuries, and often (as in this instance) founded
his work on that of Aulus Gellius. He has altered the line
of Parthenius into closer conformity with the Virgilian
imitation, so belying Gellius' evidence, who tells us that *two*
words were changed.

    [2] At Cadiz.

    [3] The famous Titan with an hundred arms.

    [4] As the quotation is about Hercules, some have wished to
refer it to the poem from which frgg. 15–18 are taken.

    [5] *cf.* frg. 4. The words in the present passage would
probably come from an Epithalamium.

    [6] An epithet which used to be translated "slayer of Argus,"
but now supposed to mean "bright-appearing."

κλεῖ καὶ ἐπὶ τοῦ Ἀπόλλωνος, καὶ παρὰ Παρθενίῳ καὶ ἐπὶ τοῦ Τηλέφου.

34. Apoll. *De adverb.*, p. 127₅. τὸ πλῆρες τῆς φωνῆς ἀκούουσιν ὦ ἐμοί, ὡς ἔχει καὶ παρὰ Παρθενίῳ· Ὦ ἐμὲ[1] τὴν τὰ περισσά.

35. Steph. Byz., p. 643₂₂. Τυφρηστός· πόλις τῆς Τραχῖνος ὀνομασθεῖσα ἀπὸ τῆς τέφρας Ἡρακλέους ἢ ἀπὸ Τυφρηστοῦ υἱοῦ Σπερχειοῦ. τὸ ἐθνικὸν Τυφρήστιος. καὶ τὸ οὐδέτερον Παρθένιος· Τυφρήστιον αἶπος.[2]

36. Etym. genuin., *s.v.* δείκελον· λέγεται δὲ καὶ δείκηλον. σημαίνει δὲ ἄγαλμα ἢ ὁμοίωμα ... εὕρηται[3] γὰρ διὰ τοῦ η, εὕρηται δὲ καὶ δείκελον παρὰ Παρθενίῳ· Δείκελον Ἰφιγόνης.[4]

37. Steph. Byz., p. 176₁₉. ἀπὸ γὰρ τῆς εἰς ος εὐθείας ἡ διὰ τοῦ ιτης παραγωγὴ πλεονάζει μιᾷ συλλαβῇ, ὡς τόπος τοπίτης, Κανωπίτης ὁ Ἄδωνις παρὰ Παρθενίῳ.

38. Steph. Byz., p. 202₇. Γενέα· κώμη Κορίνθου, ὁ οἰκήτωρ Γενεάτης .... τινὲς τὰς ἀπὸ ταύτης

---

[1] It will be observed that the grammarian is explaining ὦ ἐμοί, but cites an instance of the use of ὦ ἐμέ.

[2] MSS. ἔπος ; corrected by Salmasius.

[3] The MSS. are here rather corrupt : this reading, a combination of that presented by the two best, gives the required sense, though it is hardly probable that it exactly represents the original.

[4] MSS. Ἰφιγένης. Meineke restored Ἰφιγόνης, which is found in Euripides.

FRAGMENTS

writers: in Sophocles to Apollo as well, and in Parthenius to *Telephus*.[1]

34. *Apollonius Dyscolus on Adverbs, p.* 127₅. The full phrase[2] is ὦ ἐμοί, just as we find in Parthenius: *Woe is me* (ὦ ἐμέ) [*that am suffering*] *all too much.*

35. *Stephanus of Byzantium, p.* 643₂₂. Typhrestus, a city in Trachis,[3] so called either from the ashes (τέφρα) of Hercules or from Typhrestus the son of Spercheius. The gentile adjective is Typhrestius, which Parthenius uses in the neuter: *The Typhrestian height.*

36. *Etymologicum genuinum, s.v.* δείκελον: also δείκηλον, meaning an image or likeness. It is found with an η, and also as δείκελον in Parthenius: *The image of Iphigenia.*

37. *Stephanus of Byzantium, p.* 176₁₉. When words ending in -ites are derived from words ending in -os, they are one syllable longer than their originals, as τοπίτης from τόπος, and Adonis[4] is called *Canopites* (of Canopus) by Parthenius.

38. *Stephanus of Byzantium, p.* 202₇. Genea: a village in the territory of Corinth; a man who lives there is called Geneates .... Some call the women

---

[1] Son of Hercules and king of Mysia. He was wounded before Troy by the spear of Achilles, and afterwards healed by means of the rust of the same weapon.

[2] Of which ὤμοι or οἴμοι is the shortened form.

[3] In central Greece, on the borders of Doris and Locris: it contained Mount Oeta, where Hercules ascended his pyre. It is thus just possible that this fragment, like 15–18, also comes from the *Hercules* of Parthenius.

[4] *cf.* frg. 23, which also seems to refer to Adonis.

367

καλοῦσι Γενειάδας, ὡς Παρθένιος. τινὲς δὲ
Τενέα γράφουσιν.

39. Steph. Byz., p. 266₁₃· . . . ¹ Παρθένιος δὲ
Ἐλεφαντίδα αὐτήν φησιν.

40. Steph. Byz., p. 273₃· Ἐπίδαμνος· πόλις
Ἰλλυρίας . . . . τὸ ἐθνικὸν Ἐπιδάμνιος. εὕρηται
παρὰ Παρθενίῳ καὶ διὰ διφθόγγου.²

41. Steph. Byz., p. 424₁₉· Μαγνησία· πόλις
παρὰ τῷ Μαιάνδρῳ καὶ χώρα . . . . ὁ πολίτης
Μάγνης . . . . τὸ θηλυκὸν Μάγνησσα παρὰ
Καλλιμάχῳ καὶ Μαγνησὶς ³ παρὰ Παρθενίῳ καὶ
Μαγνῆτις παρὰ Σοφοκλεῖ.

42. Steph. Byz., p. 463₁₄· Μύρκινος· τόπος καὶ
πόλις κτισθεῖσα παρὰ τῷ Στρυμόνι ποταμῷ. τὸ
ἐθνικὸν Μυρκίνιος καὶ Μυρκινία· Παρθένιος δὲ
Μυρκιννίαν αὐτήν φησιν.

43. Steph. Byz., p. 465₇· οἱ δὲ ἀπὸ Μύτωνος
τοῦ Ποσειδῶνος καὶ Μυτιλήνης· ὅθεν Μυτωνίδα
καλεῖ τὴν Λέσβον Καλλίμαχος ἐν τῷ τετάρτῳ,
Παρθένιος δε Μυτωνίδας τὰς Λεσβικάς ⁴ φησιν.

44. Etym. genuin., s.v. δροίτη· ἡ πύελος· ὁ δὲ
Αἰτωλός φησι τὴν σκάφην ἐν ᾗ τιθηνεῖται τὰ
βρέφη· Παρθένιος δὲ τὴν σορόν, καὶ Αἰσχύλος.

¹ The description of the place is lost. Isaac Vossius
suggested Ἐλεφαντίνη· πόλις Αἰγύπτου. ² i.e. Ἐπιδάμνειος.
³ Some editors would prefer to write Μαγνησσίς, the form
found in Nonnus (*Dionys.* x. 322).
⁴ We should perhaps read Λεσβίας or Λεσβίδας.

of it *Geneiades,* as does Parthenius. Some write the name of the village with a T, Tenea.

39. *Stephanus of Byzantium, p.* 266₁₃. [Elephantine¹: a city of Egypt;] but Parthenius calls it *Elephantis.*

40. *Stephanus of Byzantium, p.* 273₈. Epidamnus : a city of Illyria .... The gentile derivative is Epidamnius, but it is also found in Parthenius with a diphthong, *Epidamneius.*

41. *Stephanus of Byzantium, p.* 424₁₉. Magnesia ; a city on the Maeander, and the surrounding country .... The citizen of it is called Magnes .... the feminine Magnessa in Callimachus, *Magnesis* in Parthenius, and Magnetis in Sophocles.

42. *Stephanus of Byzantium, p.* 463₁₄. Myrcinus : a place and the city founded on the river Strymon. The gentile derivatives are Myrcinius and Myrcinia, the latter called *Myrcinnia* by Parthenius.

43. *Stephanus of Byzantium, p.* 465₇. Some [say that Mytilene was so named] from Myton the son of Posidon and Mytilene. Whence Callimachus in his fourth book calls Lesbos Mytonis and Parthenius calls the women of Lesbos *Mytonides.*

44. *Etymologicum genuinum, s.v.* δροίτη. A bathing-tub. The Aetolian poet² so calls a cradle in which nurses put children : Parthenius and Aeschylus³ use it for a bier.

---

¹ The town on the island just north of Syene or Assouan.
² Alexander Aetolus : see *Love Romances* xiv. p. 302.
³ *Agamemnon* 1540.

45. Choerob. *de Orthogr.* (Crameri *Anecd. Oxon.* ii. 266₁₀). Ταύχειρα· ει, ἐπειδὴ καὶ εὕρηται καὶ χωρὶς τοῦ ι παρὰ Παρθενίῳ· ἐκεῖνος γὰρ εἶπεν Ταυχέριος τὸ ἐθνικον.

Cyrill. *Lex.* (Crameri *Anecd. Paris.* iv. 191₃₁). Ταύχειρα· πόλις Λιβύης· [1] Ταυχερίων γοῦν· ὁ Παρθένιος.

46. Etym. genuin., *s.v.* ἠλαίνω· τὸ μωραίνω, καὶ ἠλαίνουσα παρὰ Παρθενίῳ.

47. Steph. Byz., *p.* 472₄. Νέμαυσος· πόλις Γαλλίας [2] ἀπὸ Νεμαύσου Ἡρακλείδου, ὡς Παρθένιος.

[48. Ps.-Apul. *de Orthogr.* § 64. At Phaedra indignata filium patri incusavit quod se appellasset ; [3] qui diras in filium iactavit, quae ratae fuerunt, a suis enim equis in rabiem versis discerptus est. Sic illam de se et sorore ultionem scripsit Lupus Anilius ; idem scribit in Helene tragoedia : Parthenius aliter.]

---

[1] It is clear that something is here lost, and Martini would insert (from Steph. Byz. p. 609) ὁ πολίτης Ταυχείριος καὶ Ταυχέριος, "the inhabitant of it is called both Taucheirius and Taucherius."

[2] MSS. Ἰταλίας. But it is impossible to describe Nîmes as being in Italy, and it was rightly emended to Γαλλίας by Xylander.

[3] Meineke suggests *attentasset*.

FRAGMENTS

45. *Choeroboscus on Orthography* (*Cramer's Anecdota Oxoniensia*, ii. 266₁₀). Taucheira, spelt with an *ei* though it is also found without the *i* in Parthenius, who uses *Taucherius* as the gentile derivative.

Cyril's [1] *Lexicon* (*Cramer's Anecdota Parisiensia* iv. 191₈₁). Taucheira: a city of Libya .... Parthenius at any rate uses the form *Taucherius* [in the genitive plural].

46. *Etymologicum genuinum, s.v.* ἡλαίνω.[2] To be mad. The expression ἡλαίνουσα, *wandering,* is found in Parthenius.

47. *Stephanus of Byzantium, p.* 472₄. *Nemausus,* a city of Gaul, so-called from Nemausus, one of the Heraclidae, as Parthenius [3] tells us.

[48. *Lucius Caecilius Minutianus Apuleius on Orthography,*[4] §. 64. But Phaedra in anger accused Hippolytus to his father of having made an attempt upon her virtue. He cursed his son, and the curses were fulfilled; he was torn to pieces by his own horses which had gone mad. This is the description of the vengeance that overtook him and his sister given by Lupus Anilius. The same description is given (?) in the tragedy called *Helen*: Parthenius relates it differently.]

---

[1] A Lexicon ascribed to St. Cyril, Patriarch of Alexandria.
[2] To wander, and so, to be wandering in mind.
[3] Meineke thought that this might perhaps refer to the other Parthenius, of Phocaea.
[4] This work is a forgery by Caelius Rhodiginus, Professor at Ferrara 1508–1512, so that we need not consider the points raised by the quotation.

THE ALEXANDRIAN EROTIC
FRAGMENT

THE ALEXANDRIAN EROTIC
FRAGMENT

I

THIS was first published by Bernard P. Grenfell
in a volume entitled *An Alexandrian Erotic Fragment
and other Greek Papyri, chiefly Ptolemaic*, Oxford,
1896, and may now most conveniently be found in
the miscellaneous pieces at the end of the fourth edi-
tion of O. Crusius' *editio minor* of Herodas, Teubner,
1905. The most important critical articles upon it
were those of Otto Crusius (*Philologus* 55 (1896),
p. 353), Ulrich von Wilamowitz-Moellendorf (*Nach-
richten von der Königl. Gesellschaft der Wissenschaften
zu Göttingen*, 1896, *Phil.-hist. Klasse*, p. 209), Weil
(*Revue des études grecques*, ix. p. 169), Blass (*Jahrb.
f. class. Phil.* 1896, p. 147), and A. Mancini (*Rivista
di Storia Antica*, ii. 3. [Messina, 15 June, 1897], p. 1).

II

The text is found on the back of a contract
dated B.C. 173 ; palaeographical considerations forbid
it to be regarded as written later than the end of the
second century B.C.

Its first editor described it as " a kind of declamation
in character, the lament of some Ariadne for her
Theseus, written in half poetical, half rhetorical
prose, remarkable for the somewhat harsh elisions
and frequent asyndeta." We have several examples

in Greek literature of the παρακλαυσίθυρον, or melancholy serenade of a lover at his mistress's closed door : this is of the same kind with the sexes reversed. Blass regarded it as more like a μελέτη or exercise on some such theme as τίνας ἂν εἴποι λόγους κόρη ἀπολειφθεῖσα ὑπὸ τοῦ ἐραστοῦ : but its real passion and very poetical form seem to make it something better than a rhetorical exercise.

Crusius and v. Wilamowitz-Moellendorf both regard it as something more than poetical prose : as verse, loosely-constructed it is true, but still verse. The best "scheme" is that written out at length by the latter of the two scholars in his article cited above : but I am not satisfied that, even with the violences to which he occasionally subjects it and with the metrical liberties which he allows, he has been able to prove his point. I should prefer to compare it with the rhyming prose into which the ordinary narration in Arabic literature sometimes drops : and to say that it has a strong poetical and metrical [1] element, rather than that it is itself verse.

It is more than doubtful whether it can be regarded as in the direct line of descent of the Greek Romance. It is possible, however, to find many parallels to its language and sentiments in the frequent rhetorical love-appeals found throughout the Novelists, and its influence on the Romance, though collateral and subsidiary, is not negligible. Its comparatively early date makes it of especial value to us.

[1] The foot which occurs throughout is the dochmiac ˘ ‒ ‒ ˘ ‒ or its equivalents and developments. The second half of the second paragraph and the whole of the third are written almost entirely in this measure.

THE ALEXANDRIAN EROTIC
FRAGMENT

(Col. 1.) Ἐξ ἀμφοτέρων γέγον' αἵρεσις· ἐζευ-
γίσμεθα· τῆς φιλίας Κύπρις ἐστ' ἀνάδοχος.
ὀδύνη μ' ἔχει ὅταν ἀναμνησθῶ ὥς με κατεφίλει
ἐπιβούλως μέλλων με καταλιμπάν[ει]ν, ἀκατα-
στασίης εὑρετής· καὶ ὁ τὴν φιλίαν ἐκτικὼς
ἔλαβέ μ' ἔρως. οὐκ ἀπαναίναμαι αὐτὸν ἔχουσ'
ἐν τῇ διανοίᾳ.

Ἄστρα φίλα καὶ συνερῶσα πότνια νύξ μοι
παράπεμψον ἔτι με νῦν πρὸς ὃν ἡ Κύπρις ἔγδοτον[1]
ἄγει μ[ε] καὶ ὁ πολὺς ἔρως παραλαβών· συνο-
δηγὸν ἔχω τὸ πολὺ πῦρ τὸ ἐν τῇ ψυχῇ μου
καιόμενον· ταῦτά μ' ἀδικεῖ, ταῦτά μ' ὀδυνᾷ. ὁ
φρεναπάτης ὁ πρὸ τοῦ μέγα φρονῶν, καὶ ὁ τὴν
Κύπριν οὐ φάμενος εἶναι τοῦ ἐρᾶν μοι[2] αἰτίαν, οὐκ
ἤνεγκε λίαν τὴν τυχοῦσαν ἀδικίαν.

Μέλλω μαίνεσθαι, ζῆλος γάρ μ' ἔχει καὶ κατα-
κάομαι καταλελειμμένη. αὐτὸ δὲ τοῦτό μοι τοὺς
στεφάνους βάλε οἷς μεμονωμένη χρωτισθήσομαι.
κύριε, μή μ' ἀφῇς, ἀποκεκλει(κλει)μένην δέξαι μ'·
εὐδοκῶ ζήλῳ δουλεύειν, ἐπιμανοῦσ' ὁρᾶν. μέγαν
ἔχει πόνον, ζηλοτυπεῖν γὰρ δεῖ, στέγειν, καρτερεῖν·

---

[1] We should write ἔκδοτον.
[2] This passage is extremely uncertain and difficult. For
μοι αἰτίαν Grenfell says that μεταιτίαν is possible, and Hunt
has suggested ποιήτριαν. The following οὐκ might possibly
be ἀν-, and λίαν τήν might also be read as πάντων.

THE ALEXANDRIAN EROTIC
FRAGMENT

(Col. I.) From both of us was the choice:
we were united: Cypris is the surety of our love.
Grief holds me fast when I remember how he
traitorously kissed me, meaning to desert me all the
while, the contriver of inconstancy. Love, the
stablisher of friendship, overcame me; I do not
deny that I have him ever within my soul.

Ye dear stars, and thou, lady night, partner of my
love, bring me even now to him to whom Cypris
leads me as slave and the great love that has taken
hold upon me: to light me on my way I have the
great fire that burns in my soul: this is my hurt,
this is my grief. He, the deceiver of hearts, he
that was aforetime so proud and claimed that Cypris
had nought to do[1] with our love, hath brought
upon me (?) . . . this wrong that is done me.

I shall surely go mad, for jealousy possesses me,
and I am all afire in my deserted state. Throw me
the garlands—this at least I must have—for me
to lie and hug them close, since I am all alone.
My lover and lord, drive me not forth, take me
in, the maid locked out: I have good will to serve
thee zealously, all mad to see thee.[2] Thy case
hath great pain: thou must be jealous, keep

[1] Reading μεταιτίαν. The following words are quite
uncertain; Crusius thinks ἀνήνεγκε more probable than οὐκ
ἤνεγκε, and doubts λίαν: Blass reads ἤνεγκ᾽ ἐμήν.

[2] The alternative is to put a stop after δουλεύειν, and then
to read ἐπιμανεῖς ὁρᾶν closely with the following words.

377

THE ALEXANDRIAN EROTIC FRAGMENT

ἐὰν δ' ἑνὶ προσκάθει[1] μόνον, ἄφρων ἔσει· ὁ γὰρ
μονιὸς ἔρως μαίνεσθαι ποιεῖ.

Γίνωσχ' ὅτι θυμὸν ἀνίκητον ἔχω ὅταν ἔρις
λάβῃ με· μαίνομ' ὅταν ἀναμ[νη]σθῶ εἰ μονοκοι-
τήσω, σὺ δὲ χρωτίζεσθ' ἀποτρέχεις. νῦν ἀν-
οργισθῶμεν. εὐθὺ δεῖ καὶ διαλύεσθαι· οὐχὶ διὰ
τοῦτο φίλους ἔχομεν, οἳ κρινοῦσι τίς ἀδικεῖ;

Col. 2 is very fragmentary.

```
        νυν ον μη επι[
        ερω κυριε τον [
        νυν μεν ουθε[
        πλυτης ο[
        δυνησομαι: [                                    5
        κοιτασον ης εχ[
        ικανως σου ει[
        κυριε πως μα[
        πρωτος με πειρ[
        κυρι αν ατυχ[η]ς ου[                           10
        οπυασθωμεθα εμων[..]εδε[....επι
        τηδειως αισθεσθω μ[..]ταν[
        εγω δε μελλω ζηλουν τω[
        δουλ[....] ταν διαφορου η[
        ανθρ[ωπου]ς ακριτως θαυμαζεις            15
        με[.......]φ[ο]ρη προσικου δω
        θαυ[μα.....]χριαν κατειδεν ο
        σχω[..........]τω τοιυται ετυ[
        κου[.........ε]νοσησα νηπια συ δε κυριε
        και [..........]μμεν [                          20
        λελαλ[ηκ.......πε]ρι εμην[
```

¹ We must write προσκαθῇ.

thine own counsel, endure: if thou [1] fix thy heart on one alone, thou must lose thy senses ; a love of one, and one alone, makes mad.

Know that I have a heart unconquerable when hate takes hold upon me. Mad am I when I think that here I lie alone, while thou dost fly off to harlotry. But come, let us cease from this fury : yes, we must quickly be reconciled ; why else have we common friends, but to judge who is in the wrong?

(Col. II. The words are too fragmentary to make any attempt at translation possible. On the whole, it appears as if the reconciliation hinted at were taking place. κοίτασον. . . , ὁπυὰς θώμεθα . . . " let us put the seal on it by a fresh union," and she will again be his faithful slave.)

---

[1] With considerable hesitation I have regarded the whole of this passage as an address by the girl to herself. In the next paragraph she turns to the lover.

THE NINUS ROMANCE

THE NINUS ROMANCE

THE FIRST FRAGMENT

The first column is so incomplete that it is necessary to print it line by line, showing the probable number of letters absent in each case. A dot beneath a letter means that the reading of it is uncertain.

A I

. . . .] πλουσε [. .] νον

. . . .] αρεστι π[. . .

. . . .]ο σφόδρα ἐρῶν

. . . .]όμενον [. . . .] α

. . . .] ὑπολαμβ[άν]ων   5

. . . . κίν]δυνον ἐν ᾧ

. . . .]ν τῆς εὐχ[ῆ]ς ἀ-

. . . .] ἐλπίδα [. . .] α

. . . .] πολὺ καὶ ηϵνη

. . . .]ξιν αἰδὼς ἀ[π]ε   10

1 π ? η. ϵ ? ο.
4 Probably κ or χ before α. 9 ϵ ? σι.
10 (? γυναιξίν). Faint traces of the [π].

THE NINUS ROMANCE

I

THE papyrus was first published by Ulrich Wilcken in *Hermes* 28 (1893), p. 161. Help towards establishing the text may be found in Schubart, *Pap. Gr. Berol.* 18 (a facsimile), and in articles by Enea Piccolomini (*Rendiconti della R. Accademia dei Lincei* V. ii. (1893), p. 313), Lionello Levi (*Rivista di Filologia* 23 (1895), p. 1), and Girolamo Vitelli (*Studi Italiani di Filologia classica* 2, p. 297). Piccolomini has written on the literary value of the fragment in the *Nuova Antologia* 46 (130), p. 490 : and perhaps the best estimate of its position in the history of Greek fiction is to be found in the work of Otmar Schissel von Fleschenberg, *Entwickelungsgeschichte des griechischen Romanes im Altertum* (Halle, 1913), p. 14.

II

The papyrus comes from Egypt—we do not know with certainty from what part of the country. On the back of it are written some accounts of the year A.D. 101 : the writing of the Romance is careful and calligraphic, and experts have considered that it may be dated between B.C. 100 and A.D. 50. It consists

THE NINUS ROMANCE

          ....]ν θάρσος. ὁ δὲ
          ....]ειν ἐβούλ[ετ]ο
          ......ε]ις καὶ ταῦτα
          ....]κησαν τῶν α[...
          ......τ]ῶν γονέων ἀ[...   15
          ....]ω πλανή[σ]εσθαι
          ....] χρόνους ἐν οἷς
          ....]ορον καὶ ἀπει
          ....]ης φυλάξειν
          ....]οκει· ἀποθα-   20
          ......τῆ]ς φυλακῆ[ς] τῶν
          ....] γενήσεσθαι
          ......πρ]ὸς τ[ὴ]ν ἀναβο-
λὴν τῶν γάμων] ἀλλὰ δέξ[ε]σ-
θαι........]αμεν δουλῳ   25
          ....] λέγοντα κ[α]ὶ
          ....] μεν οὐδὲ τὸ
          ....]η ὑπέμειναν
          ....] αὐτὸ βουλομε-
          ....] τὴν πεῖραν   30
          ....]ς ἀνένεγκεν

13 Faint traces of the ε.
20 Before οκει an α or a λ, not a δ.
25 A γ or τ before αμεν.
27 The line should possibly be ended with a [ν.

of two unconnected fragments, and I have printed
the texts in the order of their original publication by
Wilcken: there are the remains of five
columns on the first, and three on the second. It
is quite doubtful whether this order is correct: in
the first (A) the hero, Ninus, and the heroine
(unnamed), deeply in love with one another,
approach each the other's mother and set forth
their love, asking for a speedy marriage; in the
second (B) the young couple seem to be together at
the beginning, but almost immediately Ninus is
found leading an army of his Assyrians, with Greek
and Carian allies, against the Armenian enemy. If
this is the right order of the fragments there is
comparatively little missing: but it seems to me on
the whole rather more probable that the order
should be reversed, in which case it is more likely that
there is a large gap between them, and B may be
near the beginning of the story, while A will come
almost at the end, shortly before their final and
happy union. Ninus is doubtless the mythical
founder of Nineveh, and his beloved may perhaps be
the famous Semiramis, who is represented as younger
and more innocent than the Oriental queen of
mythology. Early as the Romance is, compared
with our extant Greek novels, there are resemblances
with them in language and in the situations, and it
may be regarded as in the direct line of descent of
them all. It would take too long here to attempt to
estimate its exact place in Greek fiction; the
arguments will be found in the articles mentioned
above. Much of the papyrus is so fragmentary that
restoration and translation are highly conjectural.

οὔτε ὁ Νίνος οὔτ]ε ἡ παῖς ἐτόλ-
μα, προειλο]ντο δὲ τοὺς
συγγενεῖς, ἐ]θάρρουν γὰρ ἀμ-
φότεροι πρὸς τ]ὰς τηθίδας μᾶλ-   35
λον ἢ πρὸς τὰς ἑαυτῶν μ]ητέρας. ὁ
δὲ Νῖνος ἤδη π]ρὸς τὴν Δερ-
κείαν διαλεγόμε]νος· "Ὦ μῆτερ,"
[A II.] εἶπεν, " εὐορκήσας ἀφῖγμαι καὶ εἰς τὴν σὴν
ὄψιν καὶ εἰς τὰς περιβολὰς τῆς ἐμοὶ τερπνοτάτης
ἀνεψιᾶς· καὶ τοῦτο ἴστωσαν μὲν οἱ θεοὶ πρῶτον,
ὥσπερ δὴ καὶ ἴσασιν· τεκμηριώσομαι δὲ κἀγὼ
τάχα καὶ τῷ νῦν λόγῳ· διελθὼν γὰρ τοσαύτην
γῆν καὶ τοσούτων δεσπόσας ἐθνῶν ἢ δορικτήτων
ἢ π[α]τρῴῳ κράτει θεραπευόντων με καὶ προσ-
κυνούντων ἐδυνάμην εἰς κόρον ἐκπλῆσαι πᾶσαν
ἀπόλαυσιν· ἦν τε ἄν μοι τοῦτο ποιήσαντι δι'
ἐλάττονος¹ ἴσως ἡ ἀνεψιὰ πόθου· νῦν δὲ ἀδιά-
φθορος ἐληλυθὼς [ὑπὸ] τοῦ θεοῦ νικῶμαι καὶ ὑπὸ
τῆς ἡλικίας· ἑπτακαιδέκατον ἔτος ἄγω καθάπερ
οἶσθας καὶ ἐνεκρίθην μὲν εἰς ἄνδρας ἤδη πρὸ
ἐνιαυτοῦ. παῖς δὲ ἄχρι νῦν εἰμὶ νήπιος. καὶ εἰ
μὲν οὐκ ᾐσθανόμην Ἀφροδίτης, μακάριος ἂν ἦν
τῆς στερρότητος. νῦν δὲ [τ]ῆς ὑμετέρας θυγατρὸς
οὐκ [.]ισχρω² ἀλλὰ ὑμῶν ἐθελησάντ[ων αἰ]χ-
μάλωτος ἄχρι τίνος ἑαλωκὼς ἀρνήσομαι;

32 A correction, perhaps ᾽τ, before the first ε.

37, 38 Levi: Νίνος δάκρυσι π]ρὸς τὴν Δερ[κείαν τραπό-
με]νος . . . . Vitelli: μὲν οὖν Νίνος π]ρὸς τὴν Δερ[κείαν
ἀφικόμε]νος. . .

¹ Between ἐλάττονος and ἴσως an ο, marked for omission by
two dots above it.

² Only the top half of these letters remains. There seems
to be no trace of writing after the ω. The word is presumably
αἰσχρῶς.

THE FIRST FRAGMENT

(A I.) Ninus and the maiden were both equally anxious for an immediate marriage. Neither of them dared to approach their own mothers—Thambe and Derceia, two sisters, the former Ninus' mother, the latter the mother of the girl—but preferred each to address themselves to the mother of the other: for each felt (l. 34) more confidence towards their aunts than towards their own parents. So Ninus spoke to Derceia: "Mother," (A II.) said he, "with my oath kept true do I come into thy sight and to the embrace of my most sweet cousin. This let the gods know first of all—yes, they do know it, and I will prove it to you now as I speak. I have travelled over so many lands and been lord over so many nations, both those subdued by my own spear and those who, as the result of my father's might, serve and worship me, that I might have tasted of every enjoyment to satiety—and, had I done so, perhaps my passion for my cousin would have been less violent: but now that I have come back uncorrupted I am worsted by the god of love and by my age; I am, as thou knowest, in my seventeenth year, and already a year ago have I been accounted as having come to man's estate. Up to now I have been nought but a boy, a child: and if I had had no experience of the power of Aphrodite, I should have been happy in my firm strength. But now that I have been taken prisoner—thy daughter's prisoner, in no shameful wise, but agreeably to the desires both of thee and her, how long must I bear refusal?

THE NINUS ROMANCE

"Καὶ ὅτι μὲν οἱ ταύτης τῆς ἡλικίας ἄνδρες ἱκανοὶ
γαμεῖν, δῆλον· πόσοι γὰρ ἄχρι πεντεκαιδεκ[α] ἐφυ-
λάχθησαν ἐτῶν ἀδιάφθοροι; νόμος δὲ βλάπτει με
οὐ γεγραμμένος, ἄλλως δὲ ἔθει φλυάρῳ πλ[η]ρού-
μενος, ἐπειδὴ [A III.] παρ' ἡμῖν πεντεκαίδεκα ὡς
ἐπὶ τὸ πλεῖστον ἐτῶν γαμοῦνται παρθένοι· ὅτι
δὲ ἡ φύσις τῶν τοιούτων συνόδων κάλλιστος
ἐστι νόμος, τίς ἂν εὖ φρονῶν ἀντείποι; τετρα-
καίδεκα ἐτῶν κυοφοροῦσιν γυναῖκες καί τινες
ν[ὴ] Δία καὶ τίκτουσιν· ἡ δὲ σὴ θυγάτηρ οὐδὲ
γαμήσεται; δύ' ἔτη περιμείνωμεν, εἴποις ἄν;
ἐκδεχώμεθα, μῆτερ, εἰ καὶ ἡ τύχη περιμενεῖ·
θνητὸ[ς δ]ὲ ἀνὴρ θνητὴν ἡρμοσάμην παρθένον·
καὶ οὐδὲ τοῖς κοινοῖς τούτοις ὑπεύ[θυ]νός εἰμι
μόνον, νόσοις λέ[γω] καὶ τύχῃ πολλάκις καὶ τοὺς
[ἐπ]ὶ τῆς οἰκείας ἑστίας ἠρεμοῦντας ἀν[α]ιροῦσῃ·
ἀλλὰ ναυτιλίαι μ' ἐκδέχονται καὶ ἐκ πολέμων
πόλεμοι καὶ οὐδὲ ἄτολμος ἐγὼ καὶ βοηθὸν ἀσφα-
λείας δειλίαν προκαλυπτόμενος, ἀλλ' οἷον [ο]ἶσθας,
ἵνα μὴ φορτικὸς ὦ λ[έ]γων· σπ[ε]υσάτω δὴ ἡ
βασιλεία, σπευσάτω ἡ ἐπιθυμία, σπευσάτω τὸ
ἀστάθμητον καὶ ἀτέκμαρτον τῶν ἐκδ[ε]χομένων
με χρόνων, προλαβ[έ]τω τι καὶ φθήτω καὶ τὸ
μονογενὲ[ς] ἡμῶν ἀμφοτέρων, ἵνα κἂν ἄλλως ἡ
τύχη κακ[όν] τι βουλεύηται περὶ ἡμῶν, κατα-
λείπωμεν ὑμῖν ἐνέχυρα. ἀναιδὴ¹ τάχα με ἐρεῖς
περὶ τού[τ]ων διαλεγόμενον· ἐγὼ δὲ ἀναιδὴς ἂν
ἤμην λάθρᾳ [A IV.] πειρῶν καὶ κλεπτομένην
ἀπόλαυσιν ἁρπάζων καὶ νυκτὶ καὶ μέθῃ καὶ
θερ[ά]ποντι καὶ τιθηνῷ κοινούμενος τὸ πάθος·

¹ Wilcken had originally read ἀλλὰ δή, but Kaibel's
ἀναιδῆ is clearly far superior.

THE FIRST FRAGMENT

" That men of this age of mine are ripe for mar-
riage, is clear enough : how many have kept them-
selves unspotted until their fifteenth year ? But I am
injured by a law, not a written law, but one sanctified
by foolish custom, that [A III.] among our people
virgins generally marry at fifteen years. Yet what
sane man could deny that nature is the best law for
unions such as this ? Why, women of fourteen years
can conceive, and some, I vow, even bear children
at that age. Then is not thy daughter to be wed ?
' Let us wait for two years,' you will say : let us be
patient, mother, but will Fate wait ? I am a mortal
man and betrothed to a mortal maid : and I am
subject not merely to the common fortunes of all
men—diseases, I mean, and that Fate which often
carries off those who stay quietly at home by their
own fire-sides ; but sea-voyages are waiting for me,
and wars after wars, and I am not the one to shew
any lack of daring and to employ cowardice to afford
me safety, but I am what you know I am, to avoid
vulgar boasting. Let the fact that I am a king, my
strong desire, the unstable and incalculable future
that awaits me, let all these hasten our union, let
the fact that we are each of us only children be
provided for and anticipated, so that if Fate wills
us anything amiss, we may at least leave you some
pledge of our affection. Perhaps you will call me
shameless for speaking to you of this : but I should
indeed have been shameless if I had privily (A IV.)
approached the maiden, trying to snatch a secret
enjoyment, and satisfying our common passion by the
intermediaries of night or wine, or servants, or tutors[1] :

---

[1] A male nurse or foster-father, like τροφεύς in Parthenius
vi. 4.

ο[ὐ]κ ἀναιδὴς δὲ μητρὶ περὶ γάμων θυγατρὸς
εὐκταίων διαλεγόμενος καὶ ἀπαιτῶν ἃ ἔδωκας καὶ
δεόμενος τὰς κοινὰς τῆς [ο]ἰκίας καὶ τῆς βασι-
λείας ἁπάσης εὐχὰς μὴ εἰς τοῦτον ἀναβάλλεσθαι
τὸν καιρόν."

Ταῦτα πρὸς βουλομένην ἔλεγε τὴν Δερκείαν
καὶ τάχ[α] ἐβιάσατο τοὺς περὶ τούτων ποιή-
σασθαι λόγους· ἀκκισαμένη δ' οὖν βραχέα συνη-
γορήσε[ι]ν ὑπισχνεῖτο. τῇ κόρῃ δ' ἐν ὁμοίοις
πάθεσιν οὐχ ὁμοία παρρησία τῶν λόγων ἦν πρὸς
τὴν Θάμβην. ἡ γὰρ παρθέ[νος ἐντὸς τ]ῆς γυναι-
κωνίτιδ[ος ζῶσα ο]ὐκ εὐπρεπεῖς ἐπο[ίει τοὺς
λό]γους αὐτῆς· αἰτ[ουμένη δ]ὲ καιρὸν ἐδάκρυσ[ε
καὶ ἐβο]ύλετό τι λέγειν, [ἐν τῷ δ' ἄρξ]ασθαι
ἀπεπαύετο· [τάχα δὲ μ]έλλησιν αὐτόμ[ατ]ον
[σημ]ήνασα λόγου τὰ χείλη μὲν ἂν διῆρε καὶ
ἀνέβλεψεν ὥ[σπερ τ]ι λέξουσα. ἐφθέγγετο δ[ὲ
τελε]ίως οὐδέν· κατερρήγνυ[το δὲ] αὐτῆς δάκρυα,
καὶ ἠρυ[θαίνο]ντο μὲν αἱ παρειαὶ πρὸ[ς τὴν] α[ἰ]δῶ
τῶν λόγων· ἐξ ὑ[πογύου] δὲ πάλιν ἀρχομέν[η]ς
[βούλε]σθαι[1] λέγειν ὠχραίνο[ντο, καὶ]
[Α V.][2] τὸ δέος μεταξὺ [ἦν φόβου
καὶ ἐπιθυμίας, καὶ [ὀκνούσης μὲν
αἰδοῦς, θρασυνομέ[νου δὲ καὶ
τοῦ πάθους, ἀποδε[ούσης δὲ
τῆς γνώμης, ἐκύ[μαινε σφόδρα   5
καὶ με[τὰ π]ολλοῦ κ[λόνου· ἡ δὲ Θάμ-
βη τὰ [δάκρ]υα ταῖς χ[ερσὶν ἀπο]μάττο[υσα

---

[1] Piccolomini suggests πειρᾶ]σθαι.

[2] The first six lines of this column are very incomplete. I
have printed in the text Diels' restoration (quoted by Picco-
lomini), but it must be regarded as far from certain. Levi

but there is nothing shameful in me speaking to thee, a mother, about thy daughter's marriage that has been so long the object of thy vows, and asking for what thou hast promised, and beseeching that the prayers both of our house and of the whole kingdom may not lack fulfilment beyond the present time."

So did he speak to the willing Derceia, and easily compelled her to come to terms on the matter : and when she had for a while dissembled, she promised to act as his advocate. Meanwhile although the maiden's passion was equally great, yet her speech with Thambe was not equally ready and free ; she had ever lived within the women's apartments, and could not so well speak for herself in a fair shew of words : she asked for an audience—wept, and desired to speak, but ceased as soon as she had begun. As soon as she had shewn that she was desirous of pleading, she would open her lips and look up as if about to speak, but could finally utter nothing : she heaved with broken sobs, her cheeks reddened in shame at what she must say, and then as she tried to improvise a beginning, grew pale again : and (A V.) her fear was something between alarm and desire and shame as she shrank from the avowal ; and then, as her affections got the mastery of her and her purpose failed, she kept swaying with inward disturbance between her varying emotions. But Thambe wiped away her tears with

proposes a slightly different arrangement : διά for καί at the end of A IV., with a colon after δέος (A V., l. 1) : then μεταξὺ [γὰρ ἦν ὁμοῦ] καὶ ἐπιθυμίας καὶ [παρθενίας] αἰδοῦς, θρασυνομέ[νου μὲν οὖν]τοῦ. . . .

π]ροσέτ[αττε θαρ]ρεῖν κα[ὶ ὅ]τι βούλοιτ[ο δια-
λέ]γεσθαι· ὡς δὲ οὐδὲν [ἤνυσεν], ἀλλὰ ὁμοίοις ἡ
παρθέ[νος κατεί]χετο κακοῖς, " Ἅπαν[τος τουτό]
μοι λόγου κάλλιον," ἡ [Θάμβη] διαλέγεται, " μή
τι μέ[μψῃ τὸν] ἐμὸν υἱ[όν· οὐδὲν μὲ[ν γὰρ]
τετόλμηκεν οὐδὲ θ[ρασυς ἡ]μῖν ἀπὸ τῶν κατορθω-
[ματων] καὶ τροπαίων ἐπανε[λθὼν] οἷ[α πο]λε-
μιστὴς πεπ[αρῴνη]κεν [1] εἰς σέ· τάχα δὲ κ[οὐδὲ
τὰς][2] ὠπὰς τοιούτου γενομ[ένου εἶδες]. βραδὺς
ὁ νόμος τ[οῖς μακα]ρίοις γάμων ; σπεύδει δ[ὴ
γαμεῖν][3] ὁ ἐμὸς υίός· οὐδὲ διὰ τ[ουτο] κλαίεις
βιασθῆναί σε δ[εῖν];" ἅμα μιδιῶσα[4] περιέ-
βα[λλεν] αὐτὴν καὶ ἠσπάζετο· [διὰ δέος δὲ][5]
φθέγξασθαι μέν τι οὐ[δὲ τό]τε ἐτόλμησεν ἡ κόρη,
[παλ]λομένην δὲ τὴν καρδί[αν τοῖς] στέρνοις
αὐτῆς προσθε[ῖσα] καὶ λιπαρέστερον κατα-
[φιλοῦ]σα τοῖς τε πρότερον δάκ[ρυσι κ]αὶ τῇ τότε
χαρᾷ μόνο[ν οὐχ]ὶ καὶ λάλος ἔδοξεν ε[ἶ]να[ι ὧν]
ἐβούλετο. συνῆλθον οὖ[ν αἱ ἀ]δελφαὶ καὶ προτέρα
μὲν [ἡ Δερκ]εία, " Περὶ σπουδαίων," ἔφ[η . . .

---

[1] So Diels. Wilcken had proposed πεπ[είρα]κεν.

[2] Vitelli : τάχα δὲ κ[οὐκ ἄν ἐσι]ώπας τοιούτου γενο[μένου. ἀλλὰ] βραδύς. . . .

[3] Levi thinks that there is hardly room for γαμεῖν in the papyrus, and that the sense does not require it.

[4] So written for μειδιῶσα.

[5] Vitelli : [διὰ χάραν δέ] or [χαρᾷ δέ].

her hands and bade her boldly speak out what-
ever she wished to say. But when she could not
succeed, and the maiden was still held back by
her sorrow, "This," cried Thambe, "I like better
than any words thou couldst utter. Blame not my
son at all: he has made no over-bold advance, and
he has not come back from his successes and his
victories like a warrior with any mad and insolent
intention against thee: I trust that thou hast not
seen any such intention in his eyes. Is the law
about the time of marriage too tardy for such a happy
pair? Truly my son is in all haste to wed: nor
needest thou weep for this that any will try to force
thee at all": and at the same time with a smile she
embraced and kissed her. Yet not even then could
the maiden venture to speak, so great was her fear
(*or*, her joy), but she rested her beating heart against
the other's bosom, and kissing her more closely still
seemed almost ready to speak freely of her desires
through her former tears and her present joy. The
two sisters therefore met together, and Derceia
spoke first. "As to the actual (marriage ?)," said
she . . . .

THE NINUS ROMANCE

THE SECOND FRAGMENT[1]

B I

.........] οὐ γὰρ ἀπελείφθη
...... τ]ῆς μητρὸς ἐν το-
.... ἀλλ' ἠκο]λούθησεν ἀκα-
τάσχετος] καὶ περιερρηγμέ-
νος καὶ οὐδ]αμῶς ἱεροπρεπὴς   5
... ἔκλαι]ε δακρύων καὶ κο-
.... ἐ]κ τοῦ σχήματος
........]ειρχθεὶς ἅτε με-
..... ἀνα]πηδήσασαν δὲ αὐ-
τὴν ἐκ κλί]νης καὶ βουλομέ-   10
νην ......]αι ταῦτα πιέσας
.... ταῖς χ]ερσὶν ὁ Νίνος
ἔλεγε· "Ὅστι]ς εἰπών σοι με
........]θενων ἔστω καὶ
.... τ]ῆς μητρὸς καὶ η   15
.........] οὕτως ἀγομε-
.... κ]αὶ τάχα που κἀγὼ

[1] Perhaps an interview between Ninus and the maiden.
He asks for a rapid accomplishment of his desires, and when
she jumps up from the couch on which she is sitting and
would leave him, he restrains her, pointing out that he has
no designs to overcome her virtue, but only desires an
honourable marriage. The young couple spend all their
days together.

8 The scribe seems to have divided up the words ....
ειρχθεῖσα τεμε. The attempts which have been made to com-

394

THE SECOND FRAGMENT

.........]ς· οὐ δὴ βούλομαι
.........]ων μᾶλλον ἢ πρό-
τερον .....]νεύεσθαι· οὐδ' αὐ-   20
.........] σαμ[. .] ὑπονοη-
.........]στις ἔστω· του
.........] ὀμοσθέντα το
.........]κου πεπιστευ-
.......οἱ] δὲ πανήμε-   25
ροι συνῆσαν] ἀλλήλοις ὅσα μὴ
ὑπο τῶν στρατιωτ]ικῶν ἀφείλ-
κετο, οὐδ' ἐλ]λιπῶς ὁ ἔρως ἀνερ
ἐθίζων ....] κόρῳ μὲν τὸ
.......] δι' αἰτήσεως ἀμ   30
φοτερ.....]εδεις τὰς ἐπι
......χ]ερσὶ διαζεύξε-
ως.....]μενος· οὔπω
δὲ τοῦ ἦρος ἀκ]μάζοντος
.........]γος Ἀρμενι-   35
.............]νοση

(*Two lines missing.*)

plete this column by Piccolomini, and, to a less extent, by
Levi and Diels, seem to me too hazardous to be recorded.

11 *sq.* Perhaps βουλομέ[νην ἀπέρχεσθ]αι, ταῦτα, πιέσας
[ταις αὐτοῦ χ]ερσίν. . . .

23 The letters -ομο- might also be read -αλ-.

25 The traces of letters visible before δέ might well form
part of οἱ.

29 Possibly an ι before κόρῳ.

31 Before -εδεις perhaps a τ or a π.

THE NINUS ROMANCE

B II

ἀνόπλου[1] συγκροτεῖν τῶν ἐπιχωρίων. δοκοῦν
δὴ καὶ τῷ πατρὶ τὸ Ἑλληνικὸν καὶ Καρικὸν ἅπαν
σύνταγμα καὶ μυριάδας Ἀσσυρίων ἐπιλέκτους
ἑπτὰ πεζὰς καὶ τρεῖς ἱππέων ἀναλαβὼν ὁ Νίνος
ἐλέφαντάς τε πεντήκοντα πρὸς τοῖς ἑκατὸν
ἤλαυνε· καὶ φόβος μὲν ἦν κρυμῶν καὶ χιόνων
περὶ τὰς ὀρείους ὑπερβολάς. παραλογώτατα δὲ
θῆλυς καὶ πολὺ θερειότερος τῆς ὥρας ἐπιπεσὼν
νότος λῦσαί τε ἐδυνήθη τὰς χιόνα[ς κ]αὶ τ[οῖς
ὁδεύ]ουσιν ἐπεικῆ[2] πέ[ρ]ᾳ πά[σης ἐλ]πίδος τὸν
ἀέρα παρασχεῖν. ἐμόχθησαν δὴ [τα]ῖς διαβάσεσιν[3]
τῶν ποταμῶν μᾶλλον ἢ ταῖς διὰ τῶν ἀκρωρειῶν
πορείαις· καὶ ὀλίγος μέν τις ὑποζυγίων φθόρος
καὶ τῆς θεραπείας ἐγένετο· ἀπαθὴς δὲ ἡ στρατιὰ
καὶ ἀπ᾽ αὐτῶν ὧν ἐκινδύνευσε θρασυτέρα κατὰ
τῶν πολεμίων διεσέσωστο. νενικηκυῖα γὰρ ὁδῶν
ἀπορίας καὶ μεγέθη ποταμῶν ὑπερβάλλοντα
βραχὺν εἶναι πόνον ὑπελάμβανε μεμηνότας ἑλεῖν
Ἀρμενίους. εἰς δὲ τὴν ποταμίαν ἐμβαλὼν ὁ
Νίνος καὶ λείαν ἐλασάμενος πολλὴν ἐρυμνὸν
περιβάλλεται στρατόπεδον ἔν τινι πεδίῳ· δέκα
τε ἡμέρας ἀναλαβὼν μάλιστα τοὺς ἐλέφαντας ἐν
ταῖς πορείαις ἀποτε-[B III.]-τρυμένους ὡς ἐκ-
[είνους ὁρᾷ] μετὰ πολλῶν ὁ[ρμῶντας μυρι]άδων
ἐξαγαγὼ[ν τὴν δύνα]μιν παρατάττε[ι· κατέστησε]
δὲ τὴν μὲν ἵππο[ν ἐπὶ τῶν] κεράτων, ψειλοὺ[ς[4]

---

[1] There seems hardly room for a π at the beginning of this
word.   [2] We should write ἐπεικῆ.
[3] A dot over the ν, possibly to signify that it should be
omitted.
[4] ψειλούς—we should ordinarily write ψιλούς. cf. μιδιῶσα
supra.

396

THE SECOND FRAGMENT

(Ninus has gone to the wars, and is making his dispositions against the Armenian enemy.)

B II. . . . . According to the instructions of his father, Ninus took the whole body of the Greek and Carian allies, seventy thousand chosen Assyrian foot and thirty thousand horse, and a hundred and fifty elephants, and advanced. What he most had to fear were the frosts and snows over the mountain passes : but most unexpectedly a gentle south wind, much more summer-like than the season would warrant, sprang up, both melting the snow and making the air temperate to the travellers beyond all that they could dare to hope. They had more trouble over crossing the rivers than in traversing the high passes : they did have some losses of animals and of their servants, but the army regarded it not, and from its very dangers came through all the more bold to contend against the enemy ; having overcome the impassability of roads and the enormous breadth of rivers, it thought that it would be but a slight labour to capture a host of mad Armenians. Ninus invaded the river-country, taking much booty, and built a fortified camp on a piece of flat ground : and there for ten days he halted his army, especially the elephants, who were very tired (B III.) from the journey : then, seeing the enemy advancing in great numbers against him, led out his troops and disposed them thus. On the wings he put his cavalry, and the light-armed troops

δὲ καὶ γυ]μνήτας τό τε ἄγ[ημα τὸ ξενι]κὸν ἅπαν
ἐπὶ τῶ[ν κεράτων]¹ τῶν ἱππέων· μέ[ση δ' ἡ πεζῶν
φά]λαγξ παρέτεινεν· [πρόσθεν δὲ] οἱ ἐλέφαντες
ἱκα[νὸν ἀπ' ἀλ]λήλων μεταίχμ[ιον διαστάν]τες
πυργηδὸν ὡ[πλισμένοι] προεβέβληντο τῇ²[ς
φάλαγγος], καθ' ἕκαστον δὲ α[ὐτῶν ἦν] χώρα
διεστηκότ[ων τῶν λό]χων ὡς εἴ τί που τα[ραχθείη
θηρίον ἔχ[ο]ι διελθ[εῖν τὴν] κατόπιν. οὕτως [δὲ
διεκεκό]σμητο ἡ κατ' ἐκ[εῖνα . . . . .]ρος³ τῶν
λόχων ὥ[στε ταχέως] ἐπιμῦσαί τε ὁπότ[ε βουλη-
θεί]η⁴ δύνασθαι καὶ πά[λιν διεκ]στῆναι τὸ μὲν εἰς
[τὴν ὑπο]δοχὴν τῶν θηρίω[ν, τὸ δὲ εἰς] κώλυσιν
τῆς εἰσδρο[μῆς τῶν] πολεμίων· τοῦτο[ν οὖν
τὸν] τρόπον ὁ Νίνος τὴ[ν ὅλην δια]τάξας δύ-
ναμιν ἱππέ[ας λαβὼν ἐ]λαύνει· καὶ καθάπερ
[. . . . .]⁵αν προτείνων τὰς [χεῖρας], "Τὸ
θεμέλιον," ἔφη, "τ[ά τε κρί]σιμα τῶν ἐμῶν
ἐλπ[ίδων τάδε ἐ]στίν· ἀπὸ τῆσδε τῆς [ἡμέρας] ἢ
ἄρξομαί τινος μεί[ζονος], ἢ πεπαύσομαι καὶ τῇ[ς
νῦν ἀρχῆς]. τῶν γὰρ ἐπ' Αἰγυπτίο[υς . . . . . .]
τὰ τῆς ἄλλης πολεμ[. . . . . .

---

¹ Piccolomini would prefer πλευρῶν.
² This letter may be an ι, not an η.
³ The ρ might perhaps be a φ. Piccolomini proposes
ἀντίπλευ]ρος (sc. μερίς). Diels εὔπορος (sc. ὁδός).
⁴ Piccolomini ὁπότ[ε χρεὼν εἴ]η: Levi ὁπότ[ε κελευσθεί]η.
⁵ Piccolomini's ingenious suggestion for filling this bracket
is οἴσων θυσί]αν: Diels had informed him that the next letter
after καθάπερ was either an ο or a σ or a φ.

and scouts outside them again; in the centre the solid phalanx of infantry was deployed; in[1] front of the phalanx, between the two opposing armies, were the elephants, some considerable distance from one another and each armed with a turret upon its back; and behind each there was a space left between the different companies of the phalanx, so that if the beast were frightened, it would have sufficient room to retire between the ranks. These intervals were so arranged that they could be quickly filled up[2] if necessary, and again opened—the latter to receive the retiring elephants, the former to stop a charge of the enemy.

Thus Ninus arranged his whole force, and began the advance at the head of his cavalry: and stretching out his hands as if (offering sacrifice?), "This," he cried, "is the foundation and crisis of my hopes: from this day I shall begin some greater career, or I shall fall from the power I now possess. For the wars against the Egyptians and the others (through which I have passed were nothing in comparison to this. . . .)"

---

[1] The text of the next few lines is not very certain, and the translation only attempts to give the sense.

[2] Presumably by other troops from the rear.

APPENDIX
ON THE GREEK NOVEL

BY

S. GASELEE

APPENDIX ON THE GREEK NOVEL

THE works of fiction that have come down to us in Greek are not in favour at the present day. The scholar finds their language decadent, artificial, and imitative: the reader of novels turns away from their tortuous plots, their false sentiment, their exaggerated and sensational episodes. We are inclined to be surprised at the esteem in which they were held when they became widely known in the later Renaissance; that at least three of them were thought worthy of translation in Elizabethan times, and that Shakespeare's casual reference to "the Egyptian thief" who "at point of death Killed what he loved" should indicate that a knowledge of the *Aethiopica* was common property of the ordinary well-read man among his hearers: rather should we sympathize with Pantagruel on his voyage to the Oracle of the Holy Bottle, who was found "taking a nap, slumbering and nodding on the quarter-deck, with an Heliodorus in his hand." But novels were few in the sixteenth century, and literary appetites unjaded; the Greek romances were widely read, and left their mark upon the literature of the time; and they would therefore deserve our attention as sources, even if they were intrinsically worthless.

But they surely have a further interest for us, in a light which they throw upon a somewhat obscure side

of Greek culture. Although Greek civilisation pro-
foundly affected the intellectual history of the world,
it was itself hardly affected *by* the world. It was,
generally speaking, self-contained and self-sufficient :
the educated Greek very seldom knew any language
but his own, and cared little for the institutions,
manners, or learning of any foreign country. Political
changes might bring him for a time into contact with
Persia or under the empire of Rome : but he would
never confess that he had anything to learn from
East or West, and persisted in that wonderful process
of self-cultivation with its results that still move the
intellectual world of to-day. In this little corner of
Greek literature now under consideration we find one
of the very few instances of the Greek mind under
an external influence—it might almost be said,
Oriental ideas expressing themselves in Greek lan-
guage and terms of thought.

The most significant feature of the Greek novels
is their un-Greek character. We can always point
to Oriental elements in their substance, and almost
always to Oriental blood in their writers. Sometimes
it would almost seem that the accident that they
were written in Greek has preserved them to us in
their present form, rather than in some some such
shape as that of the *Thousand and one Nights*, but it
would be a narrow Hellenism that would count them
for that reason deserving the less attention or
commanding a fainter interest. The student of the
intellectual history of humanity will rather investigate
more closely the evidence which exists of one of
these rare points of contact between Hellenic and
other thought.

Fortunately no general enquiry into the origin of

fiction is necessary for the consideration of these works. In the early history of every race, Eastern and Western, stories of a kind are to be found: "Tell me a story," the child's constant cry, was the expression of a need, and a need satisfied in various ways, of the childhood of the world. But as the world grew up, it put away its childish things and forgot its stories: and it was only, generally speaking, when a more adult culture, one capable of preserving a permanent form, was superimposed upon a less advanced civilisation (ordinarily a story-telling civilisation) that a result was produced which could give a lasting expression to what was a naturally ephemeral condition, a result that could endure the wear and tear of ages. Of this nature was the stereotyping of Oriental matter by Greek form in the Greek novel.

Poetic fiction may be left almost entirely out of account. It is perhaps easier to feel than to define the difference between epic or tragic poetry and a romance, but the two can never really be confused. Some of the Byzantine imitators of the Greek novels cast their tales into more or less accentual iambics, but romances they remain in spite of their versified form: on the other hand the *Odyssey*, though it contains material for thirty ancient novels, or three hundred modern ones, is eminently, and almost only, a poem. We may indeed be content to accept the definition of the learned Bishop of Avranches, the first modern scholar to turn his attention to the origins of this branch of classical literature, when he described the objects of his study as *des fictions d'aventures écrites en prose avec art et imagination pour le plaisir et l'instruction du lecteur.*

APPENDIX ON THE GREEK NOVEL

The first appearance in Greek of relations that can be called prose fiction is in Herodotus, and we at once notice the nationality and origin of the stories that he tells. Nothing could be more Oriental than the description of the means by which Gyges rose to power, the foolish pride of Candaules in the charms of his wife; and indeed the whole Croesus legend seems little more than a romance. Among the Egyptian λόγοι the story of the treasure-house of Rhampsinitus immediately meets our definition: and of this Maspero justly remarks that "if it was not invented in Egypt, it had been Egyptianised long before Herodotus wrote it down." Again of an Eastern complexion is the story of the too fortunate Polycrates; only of all of these it might be said that the atmosphere of romantic love, so necessary for the later novels, was lacking; and this may be found better developed in a single episode in a writer but little later—that of Abradatas and Panthea in Xenophon. It forms part of the *Cyropaedia*, itself a work, as Cicero remarked, composed with less regard to historical truth than to Xenophon's ideal of what a king and his kingdom should be. The opening of the story is really not unlike the beginning of one of the long novels of later times. On the capture by Cyrus of the Assyrian camp, the beautiful Panthea is given into the custody of Cyrus' bosom friend Araspes, her husband being absent on a mission to the king of Bactria. We find Araspes holding a long conversation with Cyrus, in which he begins by mentioning her beauty and goes on to the subject of love in general, while he boasts that he has self-control enough not to allow himself to be affected by his charming captive. But he has overestimated his strength of will : and Cyrus, seeing his imminent danger, packs him off as a spy among the enemy. Panthea is greatly delighted, and sends a message to her husband telling him what has happened; and he, as a recompense for the delicacy with which she has been treated, joins Cyrus with all his troops, and fights on his side for the future. Soon there comes a touching farewell scene between wife and husband when he is leaving for battle : she melts down her jewellery and makes golden armour for him, saying that nevertheless in him she has " kept her greatest ornament." She goes on to praise the moderation and justice of Cyrus : and Abradatas lifts his eyes to heaven and prays : " O supreme Jove, grant me to prove myself a husband worthy of Panthea and a friend worthy of Cyrus, who has done us so much honour," and then leaves her in an affecting and emotional scene. The end of the story is obvious enough : Abradatas, in turning the fortunes of the battle, meets a hero's death; Cyrus does his best to console the widow, and offers to do any service for her; she asks for a few moments alone with the dead, and stabs herself over the corpse; and a splendid funeral pyre consumes both bodies together. So like is the whole to the later romantic novels that it would hardly be rash to conjecture that it was a current story in Persia and was told to Xenophon there, and that similar tales from the unchanging East formed the foundation for many of the late romances.

We need not stay much longer over classical Greek. The philosophers employed a kind of fiction for illustrative purposes, but it is rather of the nature of the myth than of the novel : and for the romantic element of which we are in search, we must look to the cycle that began to grow up later around Alexander; the story of Timoclea related by Aristobulus, again the fate of a captive woman in the conqueror's army, will remind us vividly of the older romance of which Cyrus was the hero. We note occasionally that the historians whom Parthenius quotes as his authorities when describing the early, semi-mythical history of a country or city, did not hesitate to relate fabulous and romantic stories of the adventures of the founders. But popular taste seems to have turned, at any rate for a time, to another species of fiction—to the short story or anecdote rather than to the continuous novel. The great cities along the coast of Asia Minor seem to have had collections of such stories—originally floating, no doubt, and handed down by word of mouth—which were finally reduced to literary form by some local antiquarian or man of leisure. The most important in their effect on the history of literature were those composed at Miletus and written down by Aristides under the name of Μιλησιακά. Very little trace of the original stories remains to us: but we know of what kind they were by several references, and their influence was greater upon the Latin novel than upon the specimens of the Greek novel that we now possess. The *Milesian Tales* appear to have been short stories, little longer than anecdotes, dealing ordinarily with love affairs, and descending often to ribaldry. But they were used to good effect by Petronius and Apuleius: the latter indeed describes his long novel as " many stories strung together into the form of a Milesian tale:" some we meet again—and so they have not failed to exercise an effect on the literature, of the modern world—in the *Decameron* of Boccaccio.

But we fortunately have one piece of evidence to shew that the taste for the long novel had not entirely been driven out by the short story—the fragments of the Ninus romance discovered in Egypt a quarter of a century ago, which we must date at about the beginning of our era. Its incompleteness is more a source of regret to the classical scholar than to the reader of novels; for, judging by what we have, little praise can be given to the work. It appears to have been crowded with tasteless rhetoric and wildly sensational adventures: the nobility and restraint of classical Greek seem to have disappeared, and it prepares us well for the coming of the long novels we shall meet three centuries later: its value to us is that of a link—a link long missing—between the earlier works to which allusion has been made and those which have come down to us comprised in the general category of " the Greek novels."

Nearly of the same date—perhaps half a century earlier—is the collection of Parthenius' *Love Romances*. These are not in the same line of developement as the story of Ninus: rather do they represent a parallel line of descent in the history of fiction, and the two were afterwards to combine to produce the Greek novel that we know. Mythology had become in Alexandrine and Hellenistic times the vehicle for the expression of art: it was almost a conventional literary form. The mythological tales which Parthenius has given us in his collection have little interest in the way of folk-lore or religion;

the mythology is above all made the groundwork for the development of emotion. Cornelius Gallus, or any writer with an artistic sense who determined to found his work on the summaries given him in these skeleton *Love Romances*, would find that the characteristics lending themselves best to elaboration would not be their religious or historical elements, but rather those of emotion; jealousy, hatred, ambition, and above all unhappy and passionate love. Take away the strictly mythological element (substitute, that is, the names of unknown persons for the semi-historical characters of whom the stories are related), and almost all might serve as the plots for novels, or rather parts of novels, of the kind under consideration.

Of the actual genesis of the long novels remaining to us there are several theories, but little certainty. Rohde would have us believe that they were begotten of a union of accounts of fabulous travels on the one side with love stories on the other, or at any rate that a love interest was added to tales of travel and war. But such speculations are still in the region of hypothesis, and we shall do better to examine the works as they are than to hazard rash conjectures as to their origin.

One of the Byzantine imitators of the Greek novels prefixed to his romance a little preface or argument :—

" Here read Drusilla's fate and Charicles'—
Flight, wandering, captures, rescues, roaring seas,
Robbers and prisons, pirates, hunger's grip ;
Dungeons so deep that never sun could dip

CHARACTERISTICS

His rays at noon-day to their dark recess,
Chained hands and feet; and, greater heaviness,
Pitiful partings. Last the story tells
Marriage, though late, and ends with wedding-
    bells."

Nicetas Eugenianus' very moderate verses might
really have served as the description of almost any
one of the series, changing the names alone of the
hero and heroine. A romantic love story is the
thread on which is hung a succession of sentimental
and sensational episodes; the two main characters
either fall in love with one another soon after
the opening of the story, or in some cases are
actually married and immediately separated; they
are sundered time and again by the most improbable
misfortunes, they face death in every form; subsidiary
couples are sometimes introduced, the course of
whose true love runs very little smoother; both the
hero and heroine inspire a wicked and hopeless
love in the breasts of others, who become hostile
influences, seeming at times likely to accomplish
their final separation, but never with complete
success; occasionlly the narrative stops for the
description of a place, a scene, or some natural
object, usually redolent of the common-place book,
only to be resumed at once with the painful ad-
ventures of the loving couple; and on the last
page all is cleared up, the complicated threads
of the story fall apart with detailed and lengthy
explanations, and the happy pair is united for ever
with the prospect of a long and prosperous life before
them.

No attempt can here be made to give the plots of
the novels individually: the English reader may

APPENDIX ON THE GREEK NOVEL

perhaps best judge of their length and complication in Dunlop's *History of Fiction*. The work of more recent scholars has however rather changed the chronological sequence from that in which they were formerly believed to occur : and the following list gives a rough idea of current opinion on the subject. The papyrus finds in Egypt of the last thirty years have unsettled earlier theories, and our conclusions may well be disturbed again by further discoveries.

Chariton of Aphrodisias (in Caria).	Chaereas and Callirrhoe.
Xenophon of Ephesus.	*Ephesiaca*, Habrocomes and Anthea.
(Author unknown.)	Apollonius of Tyre.[1]
Iamblichus (a Syrian).	*Babyloniaca*,[2] Rhodanes and Sinonis.
Antonius Diogenes.	*The wonderful things beyond Thule.*[3]
Heliodorus of Emesa.	*Aethiopica*, Theagenes and Chariclea.
Longus.	*Pastorals*, Daphnis and Chloe.
Achilles Tatius of Alexandria.	Clitophon and Leucippe.

Eustathius.[4]	Hysmine and Hysminias.
Nicetas Eugenianus.	Charicles and Drusilla.
Theodorus Prodromus.	Dosicles and Rhodanthe.
Constantine Manasses.	Aristander and Callithea.

---

[1] The Greek original is lost, and the novel is known to us only in a Latin translation.

[2] Now existent only in an abstract in the *Bibliotheca* of Photius.

[3] Also known through Photius. This is a combination of a love-story with a travel-book of marvellous adventures, of the kind satirized in Lucian's *Vera Historia*. It is thus the starting-point of Rohde's theory of the origin of the Greek novel mentioned above.

[4] His name was also formerly written Eumathius, but Eustathius is now believed to be correct.

THE NOVELISTS

The series from Chariton to Achilles Tatius may be considered to cover from the early second century A.D. to the late third: the last four names are those of Byzantine imitators of a far later time, dating probably from the twelfth century. The imitation of Eustathius is comparatively close: he follows the footsteps of Heliodorus and even tries to reproduce his style. Nicetas Eugenianus and Theodorus Prodromus wrote in semi-accentual iambics; Constantine Manasses, of whom we have but fragments, in the accentual "political" verse which is characteristic of modern Greek poetry.

"It is chiefly in the fictions of an age," says Dunlop, though he is wise enough to introduce his sentiment by the saving clause, *it has been remarked,* "that we can discover the modes of living, dress, and manners of the period." But it is to be feared that little could be predicated of the manners or thoughts of the authors of the works under consideration, or of their contemporaries, from internal evidence alone. The contents of a page of a note-book are sometimes introduced, not always very appropriately; but in general the action seems to be taking place in a curious timeless world—the Graecised East, where civilisation changed very little for a thousand years. Egypt, Persia, Babylonia, wherever the action is laid, are but names: the surroundings and people are the same whatever the country is called. Of psychology there is scarcely a trace, except perhaps in the scenes of love's awakening in the *Daphnis and Chloe*: any attempt indeed at character-drawing is faint and rough. Then what, it may be asked, is the resultant value to us of this class of literature? And the answer must be that it is much less in these works themselves than in their successors and the descendants they have had in modern days. Our forefathers of the later Renaissance read Heliodorus with pleasure, as we know, where we soon tire: but our feeling is only one of satiety—brought up on good novels, we are bored with their rude predecessors of antiquity. The value of these surely lies not only in the fact that they are a product, however imperfect, of Greek thought and taste, but that they are the result of the working of Oriental ideas on European minds—a happy conjunction of body and spirit which begat that whole class of literature which is, while not our serious study, at least one of the greatest sources of our pleasure. Fiction is one of the very few of the inventions of man that have improved in the course of the ages: and the keen-sighted may amuse themselves by espying the germ of "Treasure Island" in the *Aethiopica,* and the *Daphnis and Chloe* may fairly be considered the spiritual forbear of "The Forest Lovers."

It has been necessary to consider a very large subject in a very few pages: and it will be found that the following books will repay study for those who wish to go into the subject in any detail. The texts of the works themselves will soon be available, it is to be hoped, in the LOEB Series: they may at present be found in the Teubner classical texts, edited by Hercher (Leipzig, 1858, out of print), and in the Firmin-Didot classics (Paris, 1856, etc., still obtainable), edited by Hirschig. Apart from separate editions of the various novelists, this latter is perhaps the most convenient form in which they may be read: they are contained in a single volume, with a Latin translation side by side with the text. For the

BIBLIOGRAPHY

general consideration of the subject, the following books are recommended :—

Huet, P. D. *Traité de l'origine des Romans.* 1671, etc.
> The first investigation of a modern scholar. Chiefly of historical interest, but containing many acute remarks on sources, which are of permanent value.

Dunlop, J. *The History of Fiction.* Edinburgh, 1816.
> Still in print in the Bohn Libraries. The best general work on the subject—a credit to English literary scholarship.

Chassang, A. *Histoire du roman . . . dans l'antiquité grecque et latine.* Paris, 1862.
> A very wide survey of the whole of ancient fiction : it contains much that cannot be found elsewhere.

Rohde, E. *Der griechische Roman.* Leipzig, 1876, 1900, 1914.
> Profound, if speculative. The latest edition contains a *resumé* of the most modern discoveries and theories by W. Schmid.

Schmid, W. *Der griechische Roman*, in *Neue Jahrbücher für des Klassische Altertum*, p. 465. Leipzig, 1904.
> A review of the position taken up by modern scholarship on the Greek novel.

Wolff, S. L. *The Greek Romances in Elizabethan Prose Fiction.* New York, Columbia University Press, 1912.
> Careful analyses of Heliodorus, Longus, and Achilles Tatius : and their influence on English sixteenth and seventeenth century literature.

Phillimore, J. S. *The Greek Romances*, in *English Literature and the Classics*, p. 87. Oxford, 1912.
> An essay, at once original and conveniently summarising ascertained results, which is perhaps the best approach to the subject for the general reader.

Schüssel von Fleschenberg, O. *Entwickelungsgeschichte des griechischen Romanes in Altertum.* Halle, 1913.
> Speculative, but not unsound. The author carries on Rohde's tradition, but looks at the Greek novel almost entirely from the point of view of literary form.

APPENDIX ON THE GREEK NOVEL

Calderini, A. *Le avventure di Cherea e Calliroe.* Turin, 1913.

A translation of Chariton's work with a very full introduction on the Greek novel at large. The book, which is too little known to English scholars, contains perhaps the widest investigation of the novels left to us: the author is steeped in his subject, and is particularly successful in shewing the interdependence of the novelists and in pointing out their borrowings from each other.

INDEX TO DAPHNIS AND CHLOE

AGELAEA: IV. 39

Amaryllis: II. 5, 8

Anchises: IV. 17; a princely cowherd of Mt. Ida in the Troad; he was the father by Aphrodite of Aeneas

Aphrodite (Venus): III. 34; IV. 17

Apollo: IV. 14

Ariadne: IV. 3; daughter of Minos king of Crete; having saved Theseus from the Minotaur, she left Crete with him, only to be abandoned by him in the island of Naxos when asleep. Dionysus found her there and made her his wife

Astylus: IV. 10–13, 16, 18, 19, 22–24, 29

Baccha: II. 2; a female Bacchanal, priestess or votary of Bacchus

Bacchus: see Dionysus

Bosphorus (Bosporus): I. 30; the name of several straits, most commonly applied to the Channel of Constantinople

Branchus: IV. 17; a youth beloved by Apollo; his descendants, the Branchidae, were the ministers of the temple and oracle of Apollo Didymeus near Miletus

Bryaxis: II. 28

Caria: I. 28; a district of S.W. Asia Minor

Ceres (Demeter): IV. 13

Chloe: I. 6, etc.

Chromis: III. 15; IV. 38

Clearista: IV. 13, 15, 20, 30, 31, 33

Cupid: see Love

Daphnis: I. 3, etc.

Demeter: see Ceres

Dionysophanes: IV. 13, 20–22, 25 26, 29–31, 33–36, 38

Dionysus (Bacchus): I. 16; II. 2, 36; III. 9–11; IV. 3, 4, 8, 13, 16, 25, 26

Dorco: I. 15–21, 28, 30–32; IV. 38

Dryads: II. 39; III. 23; tree-nymphs

Dryas: I. 4, 7, 19, 28; II. 14, 36; III. 5, 7, 9, 10, 25, 27, 29–32; IV. 7, 25, 28, 31–33, 37, 38

Earth: III. 23

Echo: II. 7; III. 23

Epimelian Nymphs: II. 39; nymphs who presided over the flocks

Eudromus: IV. 5, 6, 9, 18

Fates: IV. 21

Fortune: III. 34; IV. 24

Ganymēdes (Ganymed): IV. 17; a beautiful youth carried off by eagles to be the cupbearer of Zeus

Gnatho: IV. 10–12, 16, 18–20, 29

Heleän Nymphs: III. 23; fen-nymphs

Hermes: see Mercury

Hippāsus: III. 1, 2

Indians: IV. 3; one of the stories of Dionysus was that he made an expedition against the Indians and triumphed over them

Jove: I. 16; II. 7; IV. 17, 21, 25

Lamo: I. 2, 7, 12; II. 14, 23, 24, 30, 33, 35; III. 9, 11, 26, 30, 32; IV. 1, 4, 7, 8, 10, 13, 14, 17–20, 22, 24, 30, 32, 33, 37, 38

Lampis: IV. 7, 28, 29, 38

Laomedon: IV. 14; king of Troy and father of Priam; having displeased Zeus, Poseidon and

417

INDEX TO DAPHNIS AND CHLOE

Apollo were made to serve Laomedon for wages; Poseidon built the walls of Troy, and Apollo tended the king's flocks

Lesbos : Proem 1; I. 1; II. 1; a large island of the E. Aegean

Love (Cupid) : Proem 2; I. 11, 32; II. 6–8, 23, 27; IV. 18, 34, 36. 39

Lycaenium : III. 15, 17–20 ; IV. 38 40

Lycurgus : IV. 3; Dionysus, expelled from the territory of the Edones of Thrace by their king Lycurgus, visited him with madness and made the vines of the country barren ; in obedience to an oracle the Edones bound him and entombed him in a rock

Marsyas : IV. 8; a Phrygian, who with his flute challenged Apollo with his lyre to a musical contest ; Apollo, having won the day, bound him to a tree and flayed him alive

Megacles : IV. 35–37

Melian Nymphs : III. 23; Nymphs of the ash-tree

Mercury (Hermes) : IV. 34

Methymna : the second city of Lesbos : II. 12–20, 23, 25, 27, 29; III. 2, 27, ; IV. 1

Muses : III. 23

Myrtalè : I. 3, 12; II. 23; III. 9, 11, 26, 27, 30; IV. 7, 10, 18, 19, 21, 24, 32, 38

Mytilenè : the chief city of Lesbos; I. 1; II. 12, 19, 20; III. 1–3; IV. 1, 33, 34

Napè : I. 6; III. 10, 11, 25, 29, 30; IV. 28, 32, 37, 38

Nymphs : Proem 1, 2; I. 4, 6–9, 24, 32; II. 2, 8, 17, 18, 20–24, 27, 30, 31, 34, 38, 39; III. 4, 12, 16, 17, 23, 27, 28, 31, 32; IV. 13, 18, 19, 22, 26–28, 30, 34–37, 39

Pan : Proem 2; I. 16, 27; II. 7, 8, 17, 23, 24, 26, 27, 29, 30, 32, 34, 35, 37–39; III. 4, 12, 16, 23, 31, 32; IV. 3, 4, 13, 18, 19, 26–28, 36, 39

Pentheus : IV. 3 ; son of Agavè and grandson of Cadmus, mythical king of Thebes; he was killed by his mother in a Bacchic frenzy for resisting the introduction of the worship of Dionysus

Philetas : II. 3, 7, 8, 15, 17, 32, 33, 35, 37; III. 14; IV. 38

Philopoemen : IV. 39

Pitys : I. 27; II. 7, 39; a maiden beloved both by Pan and by Boreas; when she preferred Pan, Boreas struck her to the ground, whereupon she became a pine-tree

Rhodè : IV. 36, 37

Saturn (Cronus) : II. 5; father of the Olympian Gods

Satyrs : I. 16; II. 2; IV. 3; the half-bestial attendants of Dionysus

Scythia : III. 5; the S. part of what is now Russia

Seasons : III. 34

Semelè : IV. 3; daughter of Cadmus king of Thebes, and mother by Zeus of Dionysus

Shepherd, Love the : IV. 39

Sicily : II. 33

Soldier, Pan the : IV. 39

Sophrônè : IV. 21

Soter (the Saviour) : IV. 25

Syrinx : II. 34, 37, 39

Tityrus : II. 32, 33, 35

Tyrians : I. 28

Tyrrhenians : IV. 3; in order to sail to Naxos Dionysus once chartered a ship which belonged to some Tyrrhenian (or Etruscan) pirates; upon their steering for Asia instead, in the hope of selling him as a slave, he avenged himself by turning the crew into dolphins

Zeus : see Jove

INDEX TO PARTHENIUS, THE ALEXANDRIAN EROTIC FRAGMENT, THE NINUS ROMANCE, AND APPENDIX ON THE GREEK NOVEL

Abradatas, 406
Acamantis, 351
Acamas, 309
Achaeans, 321
Achaeus, 324
Achilles, 319, 329, 363, 367
Achilles Tatius, 412, 413
Acrotatus, 323
Actaeon, 303
Admetus, 273
Adonis, 361, 367
Aeacus, 321
Aegialus, 259
Aeneus, 333
Aeolus, 263
Aëro, 317
Aeschylus, 369
Aethiopica, 403, 412, 414
Aethra, 311
Agassamenus, 317
Agave, 339
Alastor, 299
Alcinoe, 331
Alcmaeon, 327
Alexander, *or* Paris, 267, 341
Alexander Aetolus, poet, 303, 369
Alexander the Great, 408
Alexandria, 412
Amphiaraus, 327
Amphilochus, 331
Amyclas, father of Daphne, 305
Andriscus, philosopher, 285, 317
Anthea, 412
Antheus, 301
Anthippe, 337, 355
Antileon, 277
Antonius Diogenes, 412
Aous, river and mountain, 361

Aphrodisias, 412
Aphrodite, 269, 321, 351, 387
Aplieus, river, 361
Apollo, 307, 353, 367
Apollonius Rhodius, poet, 259, 293, 319, 333, 363
Apollonius of Tyre, 412
Apriate, 329
Apterus, 343
Apuleius, 408
Arabian Nights, 404
Araphea, 357
Araspes, 406
Archelais, 351
Arete, wife of Parthenius, 252, 351
Arganthone, 345
Argives, 321
Argo, The, 333
Argos, 259, 299
Aristander, 412
Aristides, 408
Aristobulus, 408
Aristocritus, historian, 293, 329
Aristodemus of Nysa, grammarian, 279
Ariston, 327
Aristotle, 301
Armenians, 397
Artemidorus, writer on dreams, 252
Artemis, 285, 291, 307
Asclepiades of Myrlea, grammarian, 345
Assaon, 341
Assesus, 303
Assyrians, 397, 406
Athena, 327, 331
Aulus Gellius, *see* Gellius
Auxithemis, 355

419

INDEX TO PARTHENIUS, ETC.

Babyloniaca, 412
Bacchantes, 339
Bacchiadae, 303
Bactria, 406
Basilus, 263
Beledonii, 353
Bellerophon, 269
Bias, 351
Boccaccio, 409
Boeotia, 339
Bretannus, 335
Briareus, 365
Bubasus, *see* Bybastus
Bybastus in Caria, 261
Byblis, 293
Byzantine novelists, 405, 413

Cadmus, 339
Calchus, 297
Callimachus, poet, 253, 363, 369
Callithea, 412
Candaules, 406
Canopus, 367
Capros, 293
Caria, 261, 293, 412
Carians, 397
Caunus, 259, 293
Cavaras, 279
Cebren, father of Oenone, 267
Celaeneus, 293
Celtine, 335
Celts, 281, 335
Celtus, 335
Cephalon of Gergitha, 267, 341
Chaonians, 337
Chariclea, 412
Charicles, 410, 412
Chariton, novelist, 412, 413, 416
Chilonis, 323
Chios, 317
Chloe, 412, 413
Cichyrus, 337
Cilicia, 359
Cinna, 251
Circe, 297
Cius, 345
Cleoboea, 301
Cleonymus, 323
Clite, 333
Clitophon, 412
Clitus, 275
Clymenus, 297
Comaetho, 359
Constantine Manasses, novelist, 412
Corinth, 303, 311, 331, 358, 367

Cornelius Gallus, *see* Gallus
Corycian hills, 631
Corycus, 359
Corythus, 341
Cotta, 251
Cranides, 355
Cratea, 311
Crete, 271, 343
Cretinaeum, 273
Crinagoras, 353
Croesus, 323, 406
Cyanippus, 289
Cyclic poets, 362
Cydnus, river, 359
Cydon, 343
Cyprus, 293, 361
Cyrus, 321, 406
Cyzicus, 333

Daphne, 305
Daphnis, 333
Daphnis and Chloe, 412, 413
Dardanus, 309
Daunians, 297
Dectadas, 297
Delian goddess, 285
Delos, 353
Delphi, 327
Derceia, 387
Dia, 293
Didyma, 259
Dimoetes, 337
Diognetus, 285
Diodorus of Elaea, 305
Diogenes, *see* Antonius
Diomede, 309, 347
Dionysus, 261, 339
Diores, son of Aeolus, 263
Dochmiac, metrical foot, 375
Drusilla, 410, 412
Dryas, suitor for Pallene, 275
Dryas, father of Amphilochus, 331

Echenais, nymph, 335
Echeneis, spring, 295
Echion, 339
Egypt, 369
Egyptian fiction, 406
Egyptians, 399
Elephantine, 369
Elis, 307
Emesa, 412
Ephesiaca, 412
Ephesus, 273, 412
Epicasta, 297

Epidamnus, 369
Epirus, 265, 323
Epirus, daughter of Echion, 339
Eresus, 277
Erigone, 357
Eriphyle, 327
Erythea, 335
Erythraeans, 285
Etna, mountain, 335
Eudora, mother of Parthenius, 251
Eugenianus, see Nicetas Eugenianus
Eumathius, see Eustathius
Euphorion, poet, 253, 297, 329, 333
Euryalus, 265
Eustathius, novelist, 412
Euthymia, 279
Evippe, 265
Evopis, 337

Forethought, Goddess of, 327

Gades, 367
Gallesium, 355
Gallus, Cornelius, 252, 253, 257, 297, 410
Gaul, 371
Gauls invade Ionia, 279
Gellius, Aulus, 363
Genea, 367
Geryones, 335
Glaucus, 363
Greek allies of Assyrians, 397
Greek culture and the external world, 404, 414
Gryni, 353
Gyges, 406

Habrocomes, 412
Halicarnassus, 301
Haloeus, 317
Harmonia, 339
Harpalyce, 299
Hecetor, 317
Hegesippus of Mecyberna, 273, 309
Helen, 267, 311, 343
Helicaon, 319
Helice, nymph, 317
Heliodorus, novelist, 403, 412, 413, 414
Hellamene, 305
Hellanicus, historian, 341
Hemithea, 261
Heraclea, 277
Heraclidae, 371

Heraclides, father of Parthenius, 251
Hercules, 335, 357, 365, 367
Hercynian forest, 363
Herippe, 281
Hermes, 303, 333, 365
Hermesianax, poet, 269, 321
Hermippus, grammarian, 251
Herodotus, historian, 406
Hicetaon, 319
Hilebia, 259
Hipparinus, of Heraclea, 277
Hipparinus, tyrant of Syracuse, 325
Hippocles father of Phobius, 303
Hippolytus, 371
Homer, 252, 363, 365, 405
Huet, P. D., 405, 415
Hymenaeus, 365
Hypsicreon, 315
Hypsipylus, 321
Hyrieus, 317
Hysmine and Hysminias, 412

Iamblichus, 412
Iberia, 355
Icarius, 357
Ida, mountain, 267
Idas, 297
Idolophanes, 355
Illyria, 273, 369
Inachus, 259
Ino, 365
Io, 259
Ionia invaded by Gauls, 279
Ionians, 293
Iphiclus, 357
Iphigenia, 367
Iphimede, 317
Issa, 357
Italy, 277, 281
Ithaca, 265
Itys, 295

Jason, 333

Lacedaemonians, 323
Laconia, 305
Laodice, 309
Lampeia, 355
Lampetus, 319
Larisa, 333
Leleges, 295, 305
Lepetymnus, 319
Lesbos, 319, 329, 357
Leto, 341

Leucadiae. 355
Leucippe, 412
Leucippus, son of Oenomaus, 307
Leucippus, son of Xanthius, 269
Leucone, 291
Leucophrye, 273
Licymnius of Chios, poet, 321
Longus, 412. 413
Lucian, 252
Lycastus, 343
Lycians, 269
Lyrcus, 259

Macrobius, grammarian, 252, 365
Magnesia, 369
Manasses, *see* Constantine Manasses
Mandrolytus, 273
Marseilles, 281
Megara, 357
Melicertes, 365
Meligunis, island, 263
Melissus, 303
Metamorphoses, 357
Methymna, 319
Milesian tales, 408
Miletus, 279, 285, 293, 301, 315, 329, 408
Minos, 357
Mithridatic war, 251
Moero, poetess, 331
Munitus, 311
Myrcinus, 369
Myrlea, 251, 345
Mytilene, 369
Myton, 369

Nanis, 323
Naxians, 285, 315
Naxos, 315, 317
Neaera, 315
Neanthes, 341
Neleus, 299, 301
Nemausus, 371
Nereus, 365
Nicaea, 251
Nicaenetus, poet, 259, 293
Nicander, poet, 267, 343
Nicandra, 331
Nicetas Eugenianus, novelist, 411, 412, 413
Ninus, 385, 409
Niobe, 341
Nisus, 359
Nysa, 279

Odomanti, 273
Oecusa, 293
Oenomaus, 307
Oenone, 267, 341
Oenone, island, 357
Oenopion, 317
Oetaeans, 327
Olynthus, 311
Oriental elements in Greek fiction, 404, 405, 414
Orion, 317

Pallene, 273
Pancrato, 317
Pantagruel, 403
Panthea, 406
Paris, *see* Alexander
Parthenius, 251, 408, 409
Pastoralia, 412
Peleus, 321
Peloponnese, 307, 317, 323
Penelope, 265
Pentheus, 339
Periander of Corinth, 311
Perseus, husband of Philobia, 309
Persian fiction, 407
Persians, 323
Petronius, 408
Phaedra, 371
Phanias of Eresus, philosopher, 277
Pharax, 289
Phayllus, 327
Pherae, 273
Philaechme, 301
Philetas of Cos, poet, 263
Philobia, 309
Philoctetes, 269
Philomel, 295
Philottus, 341
Phobius, 301
Phocis, 326
Phoroneus, father of Lyrcus, 259
Photius, grammarian, 412
Phrygius, 301
Phthia, 321
Phylarchus, 305, 327, 337
Piasus, 333
Pirene, spring, 303
Pisidice, 319
Plutarch, 284, 289, 303, 324
Pollianus, poet, 363
Polybus, 331
Polycles, brother of Polycrite, 287
Polycrite, 285
Polymela, 263

INDEX TO PARTHENIUS, ETC.

Pontic (*i.e.*, Colchian), poisons, 361
Posidon, 369
Priam, 267
Prodromus, *see* Theodorus Prodromus
Promedon, 315
Propempticon, 359
Prytaneum at Lesbos, 315
Pyrrhus, 323

Rhesus, 345
Rhodanes, 412
Rhoeo, 261

Samos, 331
Sardis, 321
Scellis, 317
Scylla, 357
Semiramis, 385
Setrachus, river, 361
Shakespeare, 403
Sicily, 333
Simmias of Rhodes, 341
Sinonis, 412
Sithon, king of the Odomanti, 273
Sithonian lad (Itys), 295
Sophocles, poet, 265, 367
Sparta, 323
Spercheius, 367
Staphylus, 261
Strongyle, old name of Naxos, 317
Strymon, river, 369
Styx, 353
Suidas, grammarian, 251
Syracuse, 325

Tanais, river, 273
Tantalus, 341
Tarsus, 359
Tatius, *see* Achilles Tatius
Taucheira, 371
Telamon, 329
Telegonus, 265
Telephus, 367
Teleus, father of Clymenus, 297
Tenea, 369
Termera, 345

Tetha, variant name of mother of Parthenius, 251
Tethys, 353
Thambe, 387
Thamyras, 335
Thargelia, 287
Theagenes and Chariclea, 412
Theagenes, logographer, 273
Theodorus Prodromus, novelist, 412
Theophrastus, 285, 315
Therager, 299
Theseus, 311
Thesmophoria, 279
Thessalians, 271, 327
Thessaly, 289
Thetis, 321
Thrace, 273, 311, 317, 335
Thule, 412
Thymoetes, *see* Dimoetes
Tiberius, 252
Timaeus, historian, 333
Timoclea, 408
Trachis, 367
Tragasia, 293
Trambelus, 329
Troezen, 337
Trojans, 309, 343, 347
Troy, 263, 341, 345
Typhrestus, 367
Tyre, 412
Tyrimmas, 265

Ulysses, 263, 265, 297

Virgil, 252, 363

Xanthius, father of Leucippus, 269
Xanthus, historian, 341
Xanthus, husband of Herippe, 281
Xanthus, of Samos, 331
Xanthus, of Termera, 345
Xenophon, historian, 406
Xenophon, novelist, 412

Zeus, 307, 407
Zeus, god of hospitality, 301, 303, 315

THE LOEB CLASSICAL LIBRARY

VOLUMES ALREADY PUBLISHED

Latin Authors

AMMIANUS MARCELLINUS. J. C. Rolfe. 3 Vols.

APULEIUS: THE GOLDEN ASS (METAMORPHOSES). W. Adlington (1566). Revised by S. Gaselee.

ST. AUGUSTINE: CITY OF GOD. 7 Vols. Vol. I. G. E. McCracken. Vols. II and VII. W. M. Green. Vol. III. D. Wiesen. Vol. IV. P. Levine. Vol. V. E. M. Sanford and W. M. Green. Vol. VI. W. C. Greene.

ST. AUGUSTINE, CONFESSIONS. W. Watts (1631). 2 Vols.

ST. AUGUSTINE, SELECT LETTERS. J. H. Baxter.

AUSONIUS. H. G. Evelyn White. 2 Vols.

BEDE. J. E. King. 2 Vols.

BOETHIUS: TRACTS and DE CONSOLATIONE PHILOSOPHIAE. Rev. H. F. Stewart and E. K. Rand. Revised by S. J. Tester.

CAESAR: ALEXANDRIAN, AFRICAN and SPANISH WARS. A. G. Way.

CAESAR: CIVIL WARS. A. G. Peskett.

CAESAR: GALLIC WAR. H. J. Edwards.

CATO: DE RE RUSTICA. VARRO: DE RE RUSTICA. H. B. Ash and W. D. Hooper.

CATULLUS. F. W. Cornish. TIBULLUS. J. B. Postgate. PERVIGILIUM VENERIS. J. W. Mackail. Revised by G. P. Goold.

CELSUS: DE MEDICINA. W. G. Spencer. 3 Vols.

CICERO: BRUTUS and ORATOR. G. L. Hendrickson and H. M. Hubbell.

[CICERO]: AD HERENNIUM. H. Caplan.

CICERO: DE ORATORE, etc. 2 Vols. Vol. I. DE ORATORE, Books I and II. E. W. Sutton and H. Rackham. Vol. II. DE ORATORE, Book III. DE FATO; PARADOXA STOICORUM; DE PARTITIONE ORATORIA. H. Rackham.

CICERO: DE FINIBUS. H. Rackham.

CICERO: DE INVENTIONE, etc. H. M. Hubbell.

CICERO: DE NATURA DEORUM and ACADEMICA. H. Rackham.

CICERO: DE OFFICIIS. Walter Miller.

CICERO: DE RE PUBLICA and DE LEGIBUS. Clinton W. Keyes.

CICERO: DE SENECTUTE, DE AMICITIA, DE DIVINATIONE. W. A. Falconer.

CICERO: IN CATILINAM, PRO FLACCO, PRO MURENA, PRO SULLA. New version by C. Macdonald.

CICERO: LETTERS TO ATTICUS. E. O. Winstedt. 3 Vols.

CICERO: LETTERS TO HIS FRIENDS. W. Glynn Williams, M. Cary, M. Henderson. 4 Vols.

CICERO: PHILIPPICS. W. C. A. Ker.

CICERO: PRO ARCHIA, POST REDITUM, DE DOMO, DE HARUSPICUM RESPONSIS, PRO PLANCIO. N. H. Watts.

CICERO: PRO CAECINA, PRO LEGE MANILIA, PRO CLUENTIO, PRO RABIRIO. H. Grose Hodge.

CICERO: PRO CAELIO, DE PROVINCIIS CONSULARIBUS, PRO BALBO. R. Gardner.

CICERO: PRO MILONE, IN PISONEM, PRO SCAURO, PRO FONTEIO, PRO RABIRIO POSTUMO, PRO MARCELLO, PRO LIGARIO, PRO REGE DEIOTARO. N. H. Watts.

CICERO: PRO QUINCTIO, PRO ROSCIO AMERINO, PRO ROSCIO COMOEDO, CONTRA RULLUM. J. H. Freese.

CICERO: PRO SESTIO, IN VATINIUM. R. Gardner.

CICERO: TUSCULAN DISPUTATIONS. J. E. King.

CICERO: VERRINE ORATIONS. L. H. G. Greenwood. 2 Vols.

CLAUDIAN. M. Platnauer. 2 Vols.

COLUMELLA: DE RE RUSTICA. DE ARBORIBUS. H. B. Ash, E. S. Forster and E. Heffner. 3 Vols.

CURTIUS, Q.: HISTORY OF ALEXANDER. J. C. Rolfe. 2 Vols.

FLORUS. E. S. Forster.

FRONTINUS: STRATAGEMS and AQUEDUCTS. C. E. Bennett and M. B. McElwain.

FRONTO: CORRESPONDENCE. C. R. Haines. 2 Vols.

GELLIUS. J. C. Rolfe. 3 Vols.

HORACE: ODES and EPODES. C. E. Bennett.

HORACE: SATIRES, EPISTLES, ARS POETICA. H. R. Fairclough.

JEROME: SELECTED LETTERS. F. A. Wright.

JUVENAL and PERSIUS. G. G. Ramsay.

LIVY. B. O. Foster, F. G. Moore, Evan T. Sage, and A. C. Schlesinger and R. M. Geer (General Index). 14 Vols.

LUCAN. J. D. Duff.

LUCRETIUS. W. H. D. Rouse. Revised by M. F. Smith.

MANILIUS. G. P. Goold.

MARTIAL. W. C. A. Ker. 2 Vols. Revised by E. H. Warmington

MINOR LATIN POETS: from PUBLILIUS SYRUS to RUTILIUS NAMATIANUS, including GRATTIUS, CALPURNIUS SICULUS, NEMESIANUS, AVIANUS and others, with "Aetna" and the "Phoenix." J. Wight Duff and Arnold M. Duff. 2 Vols.

MINUCIUS FELIX. Cf. TERTULLIAN.

2

NEPOS, CORNELIUS. J. C. Rolfe.

OVID: THE ART OF LOVE and OTHER POEMS. J. H. Mozley. Revised by G. P. Goold.

OVID: FASTI. Sir James G. Frazer. Revised by G. P. Goold.

OVID: HEROIDES and AMORES. Grant Showerman. Revised by G. P. Goold.

OVID: METAMORPHOSES. F. J. Miller. 2 Vols. Revised by G. P. Goold.

OVID: TRISTIA and EX PONTO. A. L. Wheeler. Revised by G. P. Goold.

PERSIUS. Cf. JUVENAL.

PERVIGILIUM VENERIS. Cf. CATULLUS.

PETRONIUS. M. Heseltine. SENECA: APOCOLOCYNTOSIS. W. H. D. Rouse. Revised by E. H. Warmington.

PHAEDRUS and BABRIUS (Greek). B. E. Perry.

PLAUTUS. Paul Nixon. 5 Vols.

PLINY: LETTERS, PANEGYRICUS. Betty Radice. 2 Vols.

PLINY: NATURAL HISTORY. 10 Vols. Vols. I.–V. and IX. H. Rackham. VI.–VIII. W. H. S. Jones. X. D. E. Eichholz.

PROPERTIUS. H. E. Butler.

PRUDENTIUS. H. J. Thomson. 2 Vols.

QUINTILIAN. H. E. Butler. 4 Vols.

REMAINS OF OLD LATIN. E. H. Warmington. 4 Vols. Vol. I. (ENNIUS AND CAECILIUS) Vol. II. (LIVIUS, NAEVIUS PACUVIUS, ACCIUS) Vol. III. (LUCILIUS and LAWS OF XII TABLES) Vol. IV. (ARCHAIC INSCRIPTIONS).

RES GESTAE DIVI AUGUSTI. Cf. VELLEIUS PATERCULUS.

SALLUST. J. C. Rolfe.

SCRIPTORES HISTORIAE AUGUSTAE. D. Magie. 3 Vols.

SENECA, THE ELDER: CONTROVERSIAE, SUASORIAE. M. Winterbottom. 2 Vols.

SENECA: APOCOLOCYNTOSIS. Cf. PETRONIUS.

SENECA: EPISTULAE MORALES. R. M. Gummere. 3 Vols.

SENECA: MORAL ESSAYS. J. W. Basore. 3 Vols.

SENECA: TRAGEDIES. F. J. Miller. 2 Vols.

SENECA: NATURALES QUAESTIONES. T. H. CORCORAN. 2 VOLS.

SIDONIUS: POEMS and LETTERS. W. B. Anderson. 2 Vols.

SILIUS ITALICUS. J. D. Duff. 2 Vols.

STATIUS. J. H. Mozley. 2 Vols.

SUETONIUS. J. C. Rolfe. 2 Vols.

TACITUS: DIALOGUS. Sir Wm. Peterson. AGRICOLA and GERMANIA. Maurice Hutton. Revised by M. Winterbottom, R. M. Ogilvie, E. H. Warmington.

TACITUS: HISTORIES and ANNALS. C. H. Moore and J. Jackson. 4 Vols.

TERENCE. John Sargeaunt. 2 Vols.

TERTULLIAN: APOLOGIA and DE SPECTACULIS. T. R. Glover. MINUCIUS FELIX. G. H. Rendall.

Tibullus. Cf. Catullus.
Valerius Flaccus. J. H. Mozley.
Varro: De Lingua Latina. R. G. Kent. 2 Vols.
Velleius Paterculus and Res Gestae Divi Augusti. F. W. Shipley.
Virgil. H. R. Fairclough. 2 Vols.
Vitruvius: De Architectura. F. Granger. 2 Vols.

Greek Authors

Achilles Tatius. S. Gaselee.
Aelian: On the Nature of Animals. A. F. Scholfield. 3 Vols.
Aeneas Tacticus. Asclepiodotus and Onasander. The Illinois Greek Club.
Aeschines. C. D. Adams.
Aeschylus. H. Weir Smyth. 2 Vols.
Alciphron, Aelian, Philostratus: Letters. A. R. Benner and F. H. Fobes.
Andocides, Antiphon. Cf. Minor Attic Orators Vol. I.
Apollodorus. Sir James G. Frazer. 2 Vols.
Apollonius Rhodius. R. C. Seaton.
Apostolic Fathers. Kirsopp Lake. 2 Vols.
Appian: Roman History. Horace White. 4 Vols.
Aratus. Cf. Callimachus.
Aristides: Orations. C. A. Behr.
Aristophanes. Benjamin Bickley Rogers. 3 Vols. Verse trans.
Aristotle: Art of Rhetoric. J. H. Freese.
Aristotle: Athenian Constitution, Eudemian Ethics, Vices and Virtues. H. Rackham.
Aristotle: Generation of Animals. A. L. Peck.
Aristotle: Historia Animalium. A. L. Peck. Vols. I.–II.
Aristotle: Metaphysics. H. Tredennick. 2 Vols.
Aristotle: Meteorologica. H. D. P. Lee.
Aristotle: Minor Works. W. S. Hett. On Colours, On Things Heard, On Physiognomies, On Plants, On Marvellous Things Heard, Mechanical Problems, On Indivisible Lines, On Situations and Names of Winds, On Melissus, Xenophanes, and Gorgias.
Aristotle: Nicomachean Ethics. H. Rackham.
Aristotle: Oeconomica and Magna Moralia. G. C. Armstrong (with Metaphysics, Vol. II).
Aristotle: On the Heavens. W. K. C. Guthrie.
Aristotle: On the Soul, Parva Naturalia, On Breath. W. S. Hett.
Aristotle: Categories, On Interpretation, Prior Analytics. H. P. Cooke and H. Tredennick.

4

ARISTOTLE: POSTERIOR ANALYTICS, TOPICS. H. Tredennick and E. S. Forster.

ARISTOTLE: ON SOPHISTICAL REFUTATIONS.
On Coming-to-be and Passing-Away, On the Cosmos. E. S. Forster and D. J. Furley.

ARISTOTLE: PARTS OF ANIMALS. A. L. Peck; MOTION AND PROGRESSION OF ANIMALS. E. S. Forster.

ARISTOTLE: PHYSICS. Rev. P. Wicksteed and F. M. Cornford. 2 Vols.

ARISTOTLE: POETICS and LONGINUS. W. Hamilton Fyfe; DEMETRIUS ON STYLE. W. Rhys Roberts.

ARISTOTLE: POLITICS. H. Rackham.

ARISTOTLE: PROBLEMS. W. S. Hett. 2 Vols.

ARISTOTLE: RHETORICA AD ALEXANDRUM (with PROBLEMS. Vol. II). H. Rackham.

ARRIAN: HISTORY OF ALEXANDER and INDICA. Rev. E. Iliffe Robson. 2 Vols. New version P. Brunt.

ATHENAEUS: DEIPNOSOPHISTAE. C. B. Gulick. 7 Vols.

BABRIUS and PHAEDRUS (Latin). B. E. Perry.

ST. BASIL: LETTERS. R. J. Deferrari. 4 Vols.

CALLIMACHUS: FRAGMENTS. C. A. Trypanis. MUSAEUS: HERO AND LEANDER. T. Gelzer and C. Whitman.

CALLIMACHUS, Hymns and Epigrams and LYCOPHRON. A. W. Mair; ARATUS. G. R. Mair.

CLEMENT OF ALEXANDRIA. Rev. G. W. Butterworth.

COLLUTHUS. Cf. OPPIAN.

DAPHNIS AND CHLOE. Thornley's translation revised by J. M. Edmonds: and PARTHENIUS. S. Gaselee.

DEMOSTHENES I.: OLYNTHIACS, PHILIPPICS and MINOR ORATIONS I.–XVII. and XX. J. H. Vince.

DEMOSTHENES II.: DE CORONA and DE FALSA LEGATIONE. C. A. Vince and J. H. Vince.

DEMOSTHENES III.: MEIDIAS, ANDROTION, ARISTOCRATES, TIMOCRATES and ARISTOGEITON I. and II. J. H. Vince.

DEMOSTHENES IV.–VI.: PRIVATE ORATIONS and IN NEAERAM. A. T. Murray.

DEMOSTHENES VII.: FUNERAL SPEECH, EROTIC ESSAY, EXORDIA and LETTERS. N. W. and N. J. DeWitt.

DIO CASSIUS: ROMAN HISTORY. E. Cary. 9 Vols.

DIO CHRYSOSTOM. J. W. Cohoon and H. Lamar Crosby. 5 Vols.

DIODORUS SICULUS. 12 Vols. Vols. I.–VI. C. H. Oldfather. Vol. VII. C. L. Sherman. Vol. VIII. C. B. Welles. Vols. IX. and X. R. M. Geer. Vol. XI. F. Walton. Vol. XII. F. Walton. General Index. R. M. Geer.

DIOGENES LAERTIUS. R. D. Hicks. 2 Vols. New Introduction by H. S. Long.

DIONYSIUS OF HALICARNASSUS: ROMAN ANTIQUITIES. Spelman's translation revised by E. Cary. 7 Vols.

DIONYSIUS OF HALICARNASSUS: CRITICAL ESSAYS. S. Usher. 2 Vols.
EPICTETUS. W. A. Oldfather. 2 Vols.
EURIPIDES. A. S. Way. 4 Vols. Verse trans.
EUSEBIUS: ECCLESIASTICAL HISTORY. Kirsopp Lake and J. E. L. Oulton. 2 Vols.
GALEN: ON THE NATURAL FACULTIES. A. J. Brock.
GREEK ANTHOLOGY. W. R. Paton. 5 Vols.
GREEK BUCOLIC POETS (THEOCRITUS, BION, MOSCHUS). J. M. Edmonds.
GREEK ELEGY AND IAMBUS with the ANACREONTEA. J. M. Edmonds. 2 Vols.
GREEK LYRIC. D. A. Campbell. 4 Vols. Vols. I. and II.
GREEK MATHEMATICAL WORKS. Ivor Thomas. 2 Vols.
HERODAS. Cf. THEOPHRASTUS: CHARACTERS.
HERODIAN. C. R. Whittaker. 2 Vols.
HERODOTUS. A. D. Godley. 4 Vols.
HESIOD AND THE HOMERIC HYMNS. H. G. Evelyn White.
HIPPOCRATES and the FRAGMENTS OF HERACLEITUS. W. H. S. Jones and E. T. Withington. 7 Vols. Vols. I.–VI.
HOMER: ILIAD. A. T. Murray. 2 Vols.
HOMER: ODYSSEY. A. T. Murray. 2 Vols.
ISAEUS. E. W. Forster.
ISOCRATES. George Norlin and LaRue Van Hook. 3 Vols.
[ST. JOHN DAMASCENE]: BARLAAM AND IOASAPH. Rev. G. R. Woodward, Harold Mattingly and D. M. Lang.
JOSEPHUS. 10 Vols. Vols. I.–IV. H. Thackeray. Vol. V. H. Thackeray and R. Marcus. Vols. VI.–VII. R. Marcus. Vol. VIII. R. Marcus and Allen Wikgren. Vols. IX.–X. L. H. Feldman.
JULIAN. Wilmer Cave Wright. 3 Vols.
LIBANIUS. A. F. Norman. 2 Vols..
LUCIAN. 8 Vols. Vols. I.–V. A. M. Harmon. Vol. VI. K. Kilburn. Vols. VII.–VIII. M. D. Macleod.
LYCOPHRON. Cf. CALLIMACHUS.
LYRA GRAECA, III. J. M. Edmonds. (Vols. I.and II. have been replaced by GREEK LYRIC I. and II.)
LYSIAS. W. R. M. Lamb.
MANETHO. W. G. Waddell.
MARCUS AURELIUS. C. R. Haines.
MENANDER. W. G. Arnott. 3 Vols. Vol. I.
MINOR ATTIC ORATORS (ANTIPHON, ANDOCIDES, LYCURGUS, DEMADES, DINARCHUS, HYPERIDES). K. J. Maidment and J. O. Burtt. 2 Vols.
MUSAEUS: HERO AND LEANDER. Cf. CALLIMACHUS.
NONNOS: DIONYSIACA. W. H. D. Rouse. 3 Vols.
OPPIAN, COLLUTHUS, TRYPHIODORUS. A. W. Mair.
PAPYRI. NON-LITERARY SELECTIONS. A. S. Hunt and C. C. Edgar. 2 Vols. LITERARY SELECTIONS (Poetry). D. L. Page.

PARTHENIUS. Cf. DAPHNIS AND CHLOE.

PAUSANIAS: DESCRIPTION OF GREECE. W. H. S. Jones. 4 Vols. and Companion Vol. arranged by R. E. Wycherley.

PHILO. 10 Vols. Vols. I.–V. F. H. Colson and Rev. G. H. Whitaker. Vols. VI.–IX. F. H. Colson. Vol. X. F. H. Colson and the Rev. J. W. Earp.

PHILO: two supplementary Vols. (*Translation only.*) Ralph Marcus.

PHILOSTRATUS: THE LIFE OF APOLLONIUS OF TYANA. F. C. Conybeare. 2 Vols.

PHILOSTRATUS: IMAGINES; CALLISTRATUS: DESCRIPTIONS. A. Fairbanks.

PHILOSTRATUS and EUNAPIUS: LIVES OF THE SOPHISTS. Wilmer Cave Wright.

PINDAR. Sir J. E. Sandys.

PLATO: CHARMIDES, ALCIBIADES, HIPPARCHUS, THE LOVERS, THEAGES, MINOS and EPINOMIS. W. R. M. Lamb.

PLATO: CRATYLUS, PARMENIDES, GREATER HIPPIAS, LESSER HIPPIAS. H. N. Fowler.

PLATO: EUTHYPHRO, APOLOGY, CRITO, PHAEDO, PHAEDRUS. H. N. Fowler.

PLATO: LACHES, PROTAGORAS, MENO, EUTHYDEMUS. W. R. M. Lamb.

PLATO: LAWS. Rev. R. G. Bury. 2 Vols.

PLATO: LYSIS, SYMPOSIUM, GORGIAS. W. R. M. Lamb.

PLATO: REPUBLIC. Paul Shorey. 2 Vols.

PLATO: STATESMAN, PHILEBUS. H. N. Fowler; ION. W. R. M. Lamb.

PLATO: THEAETETUS and SOPHIST. H. N. Fowler.

PLATO: TIMAEUS, CRITIAS, CLEITOPHON, MENEXENUS, EPISTULAE. Rev. R. G. Bury.

PLOTINUS: A. H. Armstrong. 7 Vols.

PLUTARCH: MORALIA. 16 Vols. Vols. I.–V. F. C. Babbitt. Vol. VI. W. C. Helmbold. Vols. VII. and XIV. P. H. De Lacy and B. Einarson. Vol. VIII. P. A. Clement and H. B. Hoffleit. Vol. IX. E. L. Minar, Jr., F. H. Sandbach, W. C. Helmbold. Vol. X. H. N. Fowler. Vol. XI. L. Pearson and F. H. Sandbach. Vol. XII. H. Cherniss and W. C. Helmbold. Vol. XIII. 1–2. H. Cherniss. Vol. XV. F. H. Sandbach.

PLUTARCH: THE PARALLEL LIVES. B. Perrin. 11 Vols.

POLYBIUS. W. R. Paton. 6 Vols.

PROCOPIUS. H. B. Dewing. 7 Vols.

PTOLEMY: TETRABIBLOS. F. E. Robbins.

QUINTUS SMYRNAEUS. A. S. Way. Verse trans.

SEXTUS EMPIRICUS. Rev. R. G. Bury. 4 Vols.

SOPHOCLES. F. Storr. 2 Vols. Verse trans.

STRABO: GEOGRAPHY. Horace L. Jones. 8 Vols.

THEOCRITUS. Cf. GREEK BUCOLIC POETS.

THEOPHRASTUS: CHARACTERS. J. M. Edmonds. HERODAS, etc. A. D. Knox.

THEOPHRASTUS: ENQUIRY INTO PLANTS. Sir Arthur Hort, Bart. 2 Vols.

THEOPHRASTUS: DE CAUSIS PLANTARUM. G. K. K. Link and B. Einarson. 3 Vols. Vol. I.

THUCYDIDES. C. F. Smith. 4 Vols.

TRYPHIODORUS. Cf. OPPIAN.

XENOPHON: CYROPAEDIA. Walter Miller. 2 Vols.

XENOPHON: HELLENICA. C. L. Brownson. 2 Vols.

XENOPHON: ANABASIS. C. L. Brownson.

XENOPHON: MEMORABILIA and OECONOMICUS. E. C. Marchant. SYMPOSIUM and APOLOGY. O. J. Todd.

XENOPHON: SCRIPTA MINORA. E. C. Marchant. CONSTITUTION OF THE ATHENIANS. G. W. Bowersock.

8